PENGUIN ENGLISH LIBRARY

LE MORTE D'ARTHUR
VOLUME II

SIR THOMAS MALORY

John Lawlor is Professor of English Language and Literature at the University of Keele, and has held visiting appointments at the Folger Shakespeare Library, Brandeis University and the Universities of California, British Columbia, and New Mexico. He is author of *The Tragic Sense in Shakespeare, Piers Plowman: an Essay in Criticism* and *Chaucer*.

Janet Cowen is a lecturer in English at King's College, University of London.

D0441923

SIR THOMAS MALORY

Le Morte D'Arthur

IN TWO VOLUMES

VOLUME II

EDITED BY JANET COWEN
King's College, University of London

WITH AN INTRODUCTION BY JOHN LAWLOR
Professor of English, University of Keele

PENGUIN BOOKS

Penguin Books Ltd, Harmondsworth, Middlesex, England
Penguin Books Inc., 7110 Ambassador Road, Baltimore, Maryland 21207, U.S.A.
Penguin Books Australia Ltd, Ringwood, Victoria, Australia
Penguin Books Canada Ltd, 41 Steelcase Road West, Markham, Ontario, Canada
Penguin Books (N.Z.) Ltd, 182–190 Wairau Road, Auckland 10, New Zealand

—

Published in Penguin Books 1969
Reprinted 1973, 1975, 1976

—

Introduction copyright © John Lawlor, 1969
Notes and Glossary copyright © Janet Cowen, 1969

—

Made and printed in Great Britain
by Hazell Watson & Viney Ltd
Aylesbury, Bucks
Set in Linotype Juliana

This book is sold subject to the condition
that it shall not, by way of trade or otherwise
be lent, re-sold, hired out, or otherwise circulated
without the publisher's prior consent in any form of
binding or cover other than that in which it is
published and without a similar condition
including this condition being imposed
on the subsequent purchaser

CONTENTS

Le Morte D'Arthur

Book X

CHAPTER 1: *How Sir Tristram jousted, and smote down King Arthur, because he told him not the cause why he bare that shield*

'And if so be ye can descrive what ye bear, ye are worthy to bear the arms.'

'As for that,' said Sir Tristram, 'I will answer you: this shield was given me, not desired, of Queen Morgan le Fay; and as for me, I can not descrive these arms, for it is no point of my charge, and yet I trust to God to bear them with worship.'

'Truly,' said King Arthur, 'ye ought not to bear none arms but if ye wist what ye bear; but I pray you tell me your name.'

'To what intent?' said Sir Tristram.

'For I would wit,' said Arthur.

'Sir, ye shall not wit as at this time.'

'Then shall ye and I do battle together,' said King Arthur.

'Why,' said Sir Tristram, 'will ye do battle with me but if I tell you my name? And that little needeth you and ye were a man of worship, for ye have seen me this day have had great travail, and therefore ye are a villainous knight to ask battle of me, considering my great travail; howbeit I will not fail you, and have ye no doubt that I fear not you, though ye think ye have me at a great advantage yet shall I right well endure you.'

And therewithal King Arthur dressed his shield and his spear, and Sir Tristram against him, and they came so eagerly together. And there King Arthur brake his spear all to pieces upon Sir Tristram's shield. But Sir Tristram hit

descrive: explain.

Arthur again, that horse and man fell to the earth. And there was King Arthur wounded on the left side, a great wound and a perilous.

Then when Sir Uwain saw his lord Arthur lie on the ground sore wounded, he was passing heavy. And then he dressed his shield and his spear, and cried aloud unto Sir Tristram and said, 'Knight, defend thee !'

So they came together as thunder, and Sir Uwain bruised his spear all to pieces upon Sir Tristram's shield, and Sir Tristram smote him harder and sorer, with such a might that he bare him clean out of his saddle to the earth.

With that Sir Tristram turned about and said, 'Fair knights, I had no need to joust with you, for I have had enough to do this day.'

Then arose Arthur and went to Sir Uwain, and said to Sir Tristram, 'We have as we have deserved, for through our orgulity we demanded battle of you, and yet we knew not your name.'

'Nevertheless, by Saint Cross,' said Sir Uwain, 'he is a strong knight at mine advice as any is now living.'

Then Sir Tristram departed, and in every place he asked and demanded after Sir Launcelot, but in no place he could not hear of him whether he were dead or alive; wherefore Sir Tristram made great dole and sorrow.

So Sir Tristram rode by a forest, and then was he ware of a fair tower by a marsh on that one side, and on that other side a fair meadow. And there he saw ten knights fighting together. And ever the nearer he came he saw how there was but one knight did battle against nine knights, and that one did so marvellously that Sir Tristram had great wonder that ever one knight might do so great deeds of arms. And then within a little while he had slain half their horses and unhorsed them, and their horses ran in the fields and forest.

Then Sir Tristram had so great pity of that one knight that endured so great pain, and ever he thought it should be Sir

orgulity: pride.

Palomides, by his shield. And so he rode unto the knights and cried unto them, and bad them cease of their battle, for they did themself great shame so many knights to fight with one.

Then answered the master of those knights, his name was called Breunis Saunce Pité, that was at that time the most mischievoust knight living, and said thus: 'Sir knight, what have ye ado with us to meddle? And therefore, and ye be wise, depart on your way as ye came, for this knight shall not escape us.'

'That were pity,' said Sir Tristram, 'that so good a knight as he is should be slain so cowardly; and therefore I warn you I will succour him with all my puissance.'

CHAPTER 2: *How Sir Tristram saved Sir Palomides' life, and how they promised to fight together within a fortnight*

So Sir Tristram alit off his horse because they were on foot, that they should not slay his horse, and then dressed his shield, with his sword in his hand, and he smote on the right hand and on the left hand passing sore, that well-nigh at every stroke he struck down a knight. And when they espied his strokes they fled all with Breunis Saunce Pité unto the tower, and Sir Tristram followed fast after with his sword in his hand, but they escaped into the tower, and shut Sir Tristram without the gate. And when Sir Tristram saw this he returned aback unto Sir Palomides, and found him sitting under a tree sore wounded.

'Ah, fair knight,' said Sir Tristram, 'well be ye found.'

'Gramercy,' said Sir Palomides, 'of your great goodness, for ye have rescued me of my life and saved me from my death.'

'What is your name?' said Sir Tristram.

He said, 'My name is Sir Palomides.'

'O Jesu,' said Sir Tristram, 'thou hast a fair grace of me this day that I should rescue thee, and thou art the man in the world that I most hate; but now make thee ready, for I will do battle with thee.'

'What is your name?' said Sir Palomides.

'My name is Sir Tristram, your mortal enemy.'

'It may be so,' said Sir Palomides; 'but ye have done over much for me this day that I should fight with you; for inasmuch as ye have saved my life it will be no worship for you to have ado with me, for ye are fresh and I am wounded sore, and therefore, and ye will needs have ado with me, assign me a day and then I shall meet with you without fail.'

'Ye say well,' said Sir Tristram, 'now I assign you to meet me in the meadow by the river of Camelot, where Merlin set the peron.'

So they were agreed. Then Sir Tristram asked Sir Palomides why the ten knights did battle with him.

'For this cause,' said Sir Palomides: 'as I rode up mine adventures in a forest here beside I espied where lay a dead knight, and a lady weeping beside him. And when I saw her making such dole, I asked her who slew her lord. "Sir," she said, "the falsest knight of the world now living, and he is the most villain that ever man heard speak of, and his name is Sir Breunis Saunce Pité." Then for pity I made the damosel to leap on her palfrey, and I promised her to be her warrant, and to help her to inter her lord. And so, suddenly, as I came riding by this tower, there came out Sir Breunis Saunce Pité, and suddenly he struck me from my horse. And then or I might recover my horse this Sir Breunis slew the damosel. And so I took my horse again, and I was sore ashamed, and so began the medley betwixt us; and this is the cause wherefore we did this battle.'

'Well,' said Sir Tristram, 'now I understand the manner of your battle, but in any wise have remembrance of your promise that ye have made with me to do battle with me this day fortnight.'

'I shall not fail you,' said Sir Palomides.

peron: large block of stone.

'Well,' said Sir Tristram, 'as at this time I will not fail you till that ye be out of the danger of your enemies.'

So they mounted upon their horses, and rode together unto that forest, and there they found a fair well, with clear water burbling.

'Fair sir,' said Sir Tristram, 'to drink of that water have I courage;' and then they alit off their horses.

And then were they ware by them where stood a great horse tied to a tree, and ever he neighed. And then were they ware of a fair knight armed, under a tree, lacking no piece of harness, save his helm lay under his head.

'By the good lord,' said Sir Tristram, 'yonder lieth a well-faring knight. What is best to do?'

'Awake him,' said Sir Palomides.

So Sir Tristram awaked him with the butt of his spear. And so the knight arose up hastily and put his helm upon his head, and gat a great spear in his hand; and without any more words he hurled unto Sir Tristram, and smote him clean from his saddle to the earth, and hurt him on the left side, that Sir Tristram lay in great peril. Then he walloped farther, and fetched his course, and came hurling upon Sir Palomides, and there he struck him a part through the body, that he fell from his horse to the earth. And then this strange knight left them there, and took his way through the forest. With this Sir Palomides and Sir Tristram were on foot, and gat their horses again, and either asked counsel of other, what was best to do.

'By my head,' said Sir Tristram, 'I will follow this strong knight that thus hath shamed us.'

'Well,' said Sir Palomides, 'and I will repose me hereby with a friend of mine.'

'Beware,' said Sir Tristram unto Palomides, 'that ye fail not that day that ye have set with me to do battle, for, as I deem, ye will not hold your day, for I am much bigger than ye.'

'As for that,' said Sir Palomides, 'be it as it be may, for I fear you not, for and I be not sick nor prisoner, I will not fail

courage : desire.

5

you; but I have cause to have more doubt of you that ye will not meet with me, for ye ride after yonder strong knight. And if ye meet with him it is an hard adventure and ever ye escape his hands.'

Right so Sir Tristram and Sir Palomides departed, and either took their ways diverse.

CHAPTER 3: *How Sir Tristram sought a strong knight that had smitten him down, and many other knights of the Round Table*

And so Sir Tristram rode long after this strong knight. And at the last he saw where lay a lady overthwart a dead knight.

'Fair lady,' said Sir Tristram, 'who hath slain your lord?'

'Sir,' she said, 'here came a knight riding, as my lord and I rested us here, and asked him of whence he was, and my lord said of Arthur's court. "Therefore," said the strong knight, "I will joust with thee, for I hate all these that be of Arthur's court." And my lord that lieth here dead amounted upon his horse, and the strong knight and my lord encountered together, and there he smote my lord throughout with his spear, and thus he hath brought me in great woe and damage.'

'That me repenteth,' said Sir Tristram, 'of your great anger. And it please you tell me your husband's name.'

'Sir,' said she, 'his name was Galardoun, that would have proved a good knight.'

So departed Sir Tristram from that dolorous lady, and had much evil lodging. Then on the third day Sir Tristram met with Sir Gawain and with Sir Bleoberis in a forest at a lodge, and either were sore wounded. Then Sir Tristram asked Sir Gawain and Sir Bleoberis if they met with such a knight, with such a cognisance, with a covered shield.

'Fair sir,' said these knights, 'such a knight met with us to our great damage.'

'And first he smote down my fellow, Sir Bleoberis, and sore

6

wounded him because he bad me I should not have ado with him, for why he was overstrong for me. That strong knight took his words at scorn, and said he said it for mockery. And then they rode together, and so he hurt my fellow. And when he had done so I might not for shame but I must joust with him. And at the first course he smote me down and my horse to the earth. And there he had almost slain me, and from us he took his horse and departed, and in an evil time we met with him.'

'Fair knights,' said Sir Tristram, 'so he met with me, and with another knight that hight Palomides, and he smote us both down with one spear, and hurt us right sore.'

'By my faith,' said Sir Gawain, 'by my counsel ye shall let him pass and seek him no further: for at the next feast of the Round Table, upon pain of my head ye shall find him there.'

'By my faith,' said Sir Tristram, 'I shall never rest till that I find him.'

And then Sir Gawain asked him his name.

Then he said, 'My name is Sir Tristram.'

And so either told other their names, and then departed Sir Tristram and rode his way. And by fortune in a meadow Sir Tristram met with Sir Kay, the Seneschal, and Sir Dinadan.

'What tidings with you,' said Sir Tristram, 'with you knights?'

'Not good,' said these knights.

'Why so?' said Sir Tristram; 'I pray you tell me, for I ride to seek a knight.'

'What cognisance beareth he?' said Sir Kay.

'He beareth,' said Sir Tristram, 'a covered shield close with a cloth.'

'By my head,' said Sir Kay, 'that is the same knight that met with us, for this night we were lodged within a widow's house, and there was that knight lodged; and when he wist we were of Arthur's court he spake great villainy by the king, and specially by the Queen Guenever, and then on the morn was waged battle with him for that cause. And at the first recounter,' said Sir Kay, 'he smote me down from my horse and hurt me passing sore; and when my fellow, Sir Dinadan, saw me smitten down and hurt he would not revenge me, but fled from me; and thus is he departed.'

And then Sir Tristram asked them their names, and so either told other their names.

And so Sir Tristram departed from Sir Kay, and from Sir Dinadan, and so he passed through a great forest into a plain, till he was ware of a priory, and there he reposed him with a good man six days.

CHAPTER 4: *How Sir Tristram smote down Sir Sagramore le Desirous and Sir Dodinas le Savage*

And then he sent his man that hight Gouvernail, and commanded him to go to a city thereby to fetch him new harness; for it was long time afore that that Sir Tristram had been refreshed, his harness was bruised and broken. And when Gouvernail, his servant, was come with his apparel, he took his leave at the widow, and mounted upon his horse, and rode his way early on the morn.

And by sudden adventure Sir Tristram met with Sir Sagramore le Desirous, and with Sir Dodinas le Savage. And these two knights met with Sir Tristram and questioned with him, and asked him if he would joust with them.

'Fair knights,' said Sir Tristram, 'with a good will I would joust with you, but I have promised at a day set, near hand, to do battle with a strong knight; and therefore I am loth to have ado with you, for and it misfortuned me here to be hurt I should not be able to do my battle which I promised.'

'As for that,' said Sagramore, 'maugre your head, ye shall joust with us or ye pass from us.'

'Well,' said Sir Tristram, 'if ye enforce me thereto I must do what I may.'

And then they dressed their shields, and came running

widow: widower.

8

together with great ire. But through Sir Tristram's great force
he struck Sir Sagramore from his horse.

Then he hurled his horse farther, and said to Sir Dodinas,
'Knight, make thee ready!'

And so through fine force Sir Tristram struck Dodinas
from his horse. And when he saw them lie on the earth he
took his bridle, and rode forth on his way, and his man
Gouvernail with him.

Anon as Sir Tristram was passed, Sir Sagramore and Sir
Dodinas gat again their horses, and mounted up lightly and
followed after Sir Tristram. And when Sir Tristram saw them
come so fast after him he returned with his horse to them,
and asked them what they would.

'It is not long ago sithen I smote you to the earth at your
own request and desire. I would have ridden by you, but ye
would not suffer me, and now meseemeth ye would do more
battle with me.'

'That is truth,' said Sir Sagramore and Sir Dodinas, 'for we
will be revenged of the despite ye have done to us.'

'Fair knights,' said Sir Tristram, 'that shall little need you,
for all that I did to you ye caused it; wherefore I require you
of your knighthood leave me as at this time, for I am sure and
I do battle with you I shall not escape without great hurts,
and as I suppose ye shall not escape all lotless. And this is
the cause why I am so loth to have ado with you: for I must
fight within these three days with a good knight, and as
valiant as any is now living, and if I be hurt I shall not be able
to do battle with him.'

'What knight is that,' said Sir Sagramore, 'that ye shall
fight withal?'

'Sirs,' said he, 'it is a good knight called Sir Palomides.'

'By my head,' said Sir Sagramore and Sir Dodinas, 'ye have
cause to dread him, for ye shall find him a passing good
knight, and a valiant. And because ye shall have ado with
him we will forbear you as at this time, and else ye should
not escape us lightly.'

lotless: without harm.

9

'But, fair knight,' said Sir Sagramore, 'tell us your name.'

'Sir,' said he, 'my name is Sir Tristram de Liones.'

'Ah,' said Sagramore and Sir Dodinas, 'well be ye found, for much worship have we heard of you.'

And then either took leave of other, and departed on their way.

CHAPTER 5: *How Sir Tristram met at the peron with Sir Launcelot, and how they fought together unknown*

Then departed Sir Tristram and rode straight unto Camelot, to the peron that Merlin had made tofore, where Sir Lanceor, that was the King's son of Ireland, was slain by the hands of Balin. And in that same place was the fair lady Colombe slain, that was love unto Sir Lanceor; for after he was dead she took his sword and thrust it through her body. And by the craft of Merlin he made to inter this knight, Lanceor, and his lady, Colombe, under one stone. And at that time Merlin prophesied that in that same place should fight two the best knights that ever were in Arthur's days, and the best lovers.

So when Sir Tristram came to the tomb where Lanceor and his lady were buried he looked about him after Sir Palomides. Then was he ware of a seemly knight came riding against him all in white, with a covered shield.

When he came nigh Sir Tristram he said on high, 'Ye be welcome, sir knight, and well and truly have ye hold your promise.'

And then they dressed their shields and spears, and came together with all their mights of their horses; and they met so fiercely that both their horses and knights fell to the earth, and, as fast as they might, avoided their horses, and put their shields afore them; and they struck together with bright swords, as men that were of might, and either wounded other wonderly sore, that the blood ran out upon the grass. And thus they fought the space of four hours, that never one

would speak to other one word, and of their harness they
had hewn off many pieces.

'O Lord Jesu,' said Gouvernail, 'I marvel greatly of the
strokes my master hath given to your master.'

'By my head,' said Sir Launcelot's servant, 'your master
hath not given so many but your master hath received as
many or more.'

'O Jesu,' said Gouvernail, 'it is too much for Sir Palomides to suffer or Sir Launcelot, and yet pity it were that
either of these good knights should destroy other's blood.'

So they stood and wept both, and made great dole when
they saw the bright swords over-covered with blood of their
bodies.

Then at the last spake Sir Launcelot and said, 'Knight, thou
fightest wonderly well as ever I saw knight, therefore, and
it please you, tell me your name.'

'Sir,' said Sir Tristram, 'that is me loth to tell any man my
name.'

'Truly,' said Sir Launcelot, 'and I were required, I was never
loth to tell my name.'

'It is well said,' said Sir Tristram. 'Then I require you to
tell me your name.'

'Fair knight,' he said, 'my name is Sir Launcelot du Lake.'

'Alas,' said Sir Tristram, 'what have I done? For ye are the
man in the world that I love best.'

'Fair knight,' said Sir Launcelot, 'tell me your name.'

'Truly,' said he, 'my name is Sir Tristram de Liones.'

'O Jesu,' said Sir Launcelot, 'what adventure is befall me !'

And therewith Sir Launcelot kneeled down and yielded
him up his sword. And therewithal Sir Tristram kneeled
adown, and yielded him up his sword. And so either gave
other the degree. And then they both forthwithal went to
the stone, and set them down upon it, and took off their
helms to cool them, and either kissed other an hundred times.

And then anon after they took off their helms[1] and rode
to Camelot. And there they met with Sir Gawain and with
Sir Gaheris that had made promise to Arthur never to come

again to the court till they had brought Sir Tristram with them.

CHAPTER 6: *How Sir Launcelot brought Sir Tristram to the court, and of the great joy that the king and other made for the coming of Sir Tristram*

'Return again,' said Sir Launcelot, 'for your quest is done, for I have met with Sir Tristram: lo, here is his own person!'

Then was Sir Gawain glad, and said to Sir Tristram, 'Ye are welcome, for now have ye eased me greatly of my labour. For what cause,' said Sir Gawain, 'came ye into this court?'

'Fair sir,' said Sir Tristram, 'I came into this country because of Sir Palomides; for he and I had assigned at this day to have done battle together at the peron, and I marvel I hear not of him. And thus by adventure my lord, Sir Launcelot, and I met together.'

With this came King Arthur, and when he wist that there was Sir Tristram, then he ran unto him and took him by the hand and said, 'Sir Tristram, ye are as welcome as any knight that ever came to this court.'

And when the king had heard how Sir Launcelot and he had foughten, and either had wounded other wonderly sore, then the king made great dole. Then Sir Tristram told the king how he came thither for to have had ado with Sir Palomides. And then he told the king how he had rescued him from the nine knights and Breunis Saunce Pité; and how he found a knight lying by a well, 'and that knight smote down Sir Palomides and me, but his shield was covered with a cloth. So Sir Palomides left me, and I followed after that knight; and in many places I found where he had slain knights, and forjousted many.'

'By my head,' said Sir Gawain, 'that same knight smote me down and Sir Bleoberis, and hurt us sore both, he with the covered shield.'

'Ah,' said Sir Kay, 'that knight smote me adown and hurt

me passing sore, and fain would I have known him, but I might not.'

'Jesu, mercy,' said Arthur 'what knight was that with the covered shield?'

'I know not,' said Sir Tristram; and so said they all.

'Now,' said King Arthur, 'then wot I, for it is Sir Launcelot.'

Then they all looked upon Sir Launcelot and said, 'Ye have beguiled us with your covered shield.'

'It is not the first time,' said Arthur, 'he hath done so.'

'My lord,' said Sir Launcelot, 'truly wit ye well I was the same knight that bare the covered shield; and because I would not be known that I was of your court I said no worship of your house.'

'That is truth,' said Sir Gawain, Sir Kay, and Sir Bleoberis.

Then King Arthur took Sir Tristram by the hand and went to the Table Round.

Then came Queen Guenever and many ladies with her, and all those ladies saiden at one voice, 'Welcome, Sir Tristram !'

'Welcome,' said the damosels.

'Welcome,' said knights.

'Welcome,' said Arthur, 'for one of the best knights, and the gentlest of the world, and the man of most worship; for of all manner of hunting thou bearest the prize, and of all measures of blowing thou art the beginning and of all the terms of hunting and hawking ye are the beginner, of all instruments of music ye are the best; therefore, gentle knight,' said Arthur, 'ye are welcome to this court. And also, I pray you,' said Arthur, 'grant me a boon.'

'It shall be at your commandment,' said Tristram.

'Well,' said Arthur, 'I will desire of you that ye will abide in my court.'

'Sir,' said Sir Tristram, 'thereto is me loth, for I have ado in many countries.'

'Not so,' said Arthur, 'ye have promised it me, ye may not say nay.'

'Sir,' said Sir Tristram, 'I will as ye will.'

Then went Arthur unto the sieges about the Round Table, and looked in every siege the which were void that lacked knights. And then the king saw in the siege of Marhaus letters that saiden: THIS IS THE SIEGE OF THE NOBLE KNIGHT, SIR TRISTRAM. And then Arthur made Sir Tristram knight of the Table Round, with great nobley and great feast as might be thought.

For Sir Marhaus was slain afore by the hands of Sir Tristram in an island; and that was well known at that time in the court of Arthur, for this Marhaus was a worthy knight. And for evil deeds that he did unto the country of Cornwall Sir Tristram and he fought. And they fought so long, tracing and traversing, till they fell bleeding to the earth; for they were so sore wounded that they might not stand for bleeding. And Sir Tristram by fortune recovered, and Sir Marhaus died through the stroke on the head.

So leave we of Sir Tristram and speak we of King Mark.

CHAPTER 7: *How for the despite of Sir Tristram King Mark came with two knights into England, and how he slew one of the knights*

Then King Mark had great despite of the renown of Sir Tristram, and then he chased him out of Cornwall. Yet was he nephew unto King Mark, but he had great suspicion unto Sir Tristram because of his queen, La Beale Isoud; for him seemed that there was too much love between them both. So when Sir Tristram departed out of Cornwall into England King Mark heard of the great prowess that Sir Tristram did there, the which grieved him sore.

So he sent on his part men to espy what deeds he did. And the queen sent privily on her part spies to know what deeds he had done, for great love was between them twain. So when the messengers were come home they told the truth as they had heard, that he passed all other knights but if it were Sir

14

Launcelot. Then King Mark was right heavy of these tidings, and as glad was La Beale Isoud.

Then in great despite he took with him two good knights and two squires, and disguised himself, and took his way into England, to the intent for to slay Sir Tristram. And one of these two knights hight Bersules, and the other knight was called Amant. So as they rode King Mark asked a knight that he met, where he should find King Arthur.

He said, 'At Camelot.' Also he asked that knight after Sir Tristram, whether he heard of him in the court of King Arthur.

'Wit you well,' said the knight, 'ye shall find Sir Tristram there for a man of as great worship as is now living; for through his prowess he won the tournament of the Castle of Maidens that standeth by the Hard Rock. And sithen he hath won with his own hand thirty knights that were men of great honour. And the last battle that ever he did he fought with Sir Launcelot; and that was a marvellous battle. And not by force Sir Launcelot brought Sir Tristram to the court, and of him King Arthur made passing great joy, and so made him knight of the Table Round; and his seat was where the good knight's, Sir Marhaus', seat was.'

Then was King Mark passing sorry when he heard of the honour of Sir Tristram; and so they departed. Then said King Mark unto his two knights,

'Now will I tell you my counsel: ye are the men that I trust most to alive, and I will that ye wit my coming hither is to this intent, for to destroy Sir Tristram by wiles or by treason; and it shall be hard if ever he escape our hands.'

'Alas,' said Sir Bersules, 'what mean you? For ye be set in such a way ye are disposed shamefully; for Sir Tristram is the knight of most worship that we know living, and therefore I warn you plainly I will never consent to do him to the death; and therefore I will yield my service, and forsake you.'

When King Mark heard him say so, suddenly he drew his sword and said, 'Ah, traitor!' and smote Sir Bersules on the head, that the sword went to his teeth.

When Amant, the knight, saw him do that villainous deed, and his squires, they said it was foul done, and mischievously: 'Wherefore we will do thee no more service, and wit ye well, we will appeach thee of treason afore Arthur.'

Then was King Mark wonderly wroth and would have slain Amant; but he and the two squires held them together, and set nought by his malice. When King Mark saw he might not be revenged on them, he said thus unto the knight, Amant,

'Wit thou well, and thou appeach me of treason I shall thereof defend me afore King Arthur; but I require thee that thou tell not my name, that I am King Mark, whatsomever come of me.'

'As for that,' said Sir Amant, 'I will not discover your name.'

And so they departed, and Amant and his fellows took the body of Bersules and buried it.

CHAPTER 8: *How King Mark came to a fountain where he found Sir Lamorak complaining for the love of King Lot's wife*

Then King Mark rode till he came to a fountain, and there he rested him, and stood in a doubt whether he would ride to Arthur's court or none, or return again to his country. And as he thus rested him by that fountain there came by him a knight well armed on horseback; and he alit, and tied his horse until a tree, and set him down by the brink of the fountain; and there he made great languor and dole, and made the dolefullest complaint of love that ever man heard; and all this while was he not ware of King Mark. And this was a great part of his complaint: he cried and wept, saying,

'O fair Queen of Orkney, King Lot's wife, and mother of Sir Gawain, and to Sir Gaheris, and mother to many other, for thy love I am in great pains.'

appeach: accuse.

16

Then King Mark arose and went near him and said, 'Fair knight, ye have made a piteous complaint.'

'Truly,' said the knight, 'it is an hundred part more ruefuller than my heart can utter.'

'I require you,' said King Mark, 'tell me your name.'

'Sir,' said he, 'as for my name I will not hide it from no knight that beareth a shield, and my name is Sir Lamorak de Gales.'

But when Sir Lamorak heard King Mark speak, then wist he well by his speech that he was a Cornish knight. 'Sir,' said Sir Lamorak, 'I understand by your tongue ye be of Cornwall, wherein there dwelleth the shamefullest king that is now living, for he is a great enemy to all good knights; and that proveth well, for he hath chased out of that country Sir Tristram, that is the worshipfullest knight that now is living, and all knights speaken of him worship; and for jealousness of his queen he hath chased him out of his country. It is pity,' said Sir Lamorak, 'that ever any such false knight coward as King Mark is should be matched with such a fair lady and good as La Beale Isoud is, for all the world of him speaketh shame, and of her worship that any queen may have.'

'I have not ado in this matter,' said King Mark, 'neither nought will I speak thereof.'

'Well said,' said Sir Lamorak.

'Sir, can ye tell me any tidings?'

'I can tell you,' said Sir Lamorak, 'that there shall be a great tournament in haste beside Camelot, at the Castle of Jagent, and the King with the Hundred Knights and the King of Ireland, as I suppose, make that tournament.'

Then there came a knight that was called Sir Dinadan, and saluted them both. And when he wist that King Mark was a knight of Cornwall he reproved him for the love of King Mark a thousand fold more than did Sir Lamorak. Then he proffered to joust with King Mark. And he was full loth thereto, but Sir Dinadan egged him so, that he jousted with Sir Lamorak. And Sir Lamorak smote King Mark so sore that he bare him on his spear end over his horse's tail.

And then King Mark arose again, and followed after Sir Lamorak. But Sir Dinadan would not joust with Sir Lamorak, but he told King Mark that Sir Lamorak was Sir Kay, the Seneschal.

'That is not so,' said King Mark, 'for he is much bigger than Sir Kay;' and so he followed and overtook him, and bad him abide.

'What will ye do?' said Sir Lamorak.

'Sir,' he said, 'I will fight with a sword, for ye have shamed me with a spear;' and therewith they dashed together with swords, and Sir Lamorak suffered him and forbare him.

And King Mark was passing hasty, and smote thick strokes. Sir Lamorak saw he would not stint, and waxed some-what wroth, and doubled his strokes, for he was one of the noblest knights of the world; and he beat him so on the helm that his head hung nigh on the saddle bow.

When Sir Lamorak saw him fare so, he said, 'Sir knight, what cheer? Meseemeth ye have nigh your fill of fighting; it were pity to do you any more harm, for ye are but a mean knight, therefore I give you leave to go where ye list.'

'Gramercy,' said King Mark, 'for ye and I be not matches.'

Then Sir Dinadan mocked King Mark and said, 'Ye are not able to match a good knight.'

'As for that,' said King Mark, 'at the first time that I jousted with this knight ye refused him.'

'Think ye that it is a shame to me?' said Sir Dinadan. 'Nay, sir, it is ever worship to a knight to refuse that thing that he may not attain, therefore your worship had been much more to have refused him as I did; for I warn you plainly he is able to beat such five as ye and I be; for ye knights of Cornwall are no men of worship as other knights are. And because ye are no men of worship ye hate all men of worship, for never was bred in your country such a knight as is Sir Tristram.'

CHAPTER 9: *How King Mark, Sir Lamorak, and Sir Dinadan came to a castle, and how King Mark was known there*

Then they rode forth all together, King Mark, Sir Lamorak, and Sir Dinadan, till that they came to a bridge, and at the end thereof stood a fair tower. Then saw they a knight on horseback well armed, brandishing a spear, crying and proffering himself to joust.

'Now,' said Sir Dinadan unto King Mark, 'yonder are two brethren, that one hight Alein, and the other hight Trian, that will joust with any that passeth this passage. Now proffer yourself,' said Dinadan to King Mark, 'for ever ye be laid to the earth.'

Then King Mark was ashamed, and therewith he fewtered his spear, and hurtled to Sir Trian, and either brake their spears all to pieces, and passed through anon. Then Sir Trian sent King Mark another spear to joust more; but in no wise he would not joust no more.

Then they came to the castle all three knights, and prayed the lord of the castle of harbour.

'Ye are right welcome,' said the knights of the castle, 'for the love of the lord of this castle, the which hight Sir Tor le Fise Aries.'

And then they came into a fair court well repaired, and they had passing good cheer, till the lieutenant of this castle, that hight Berluse, espied King Mark of Cornwall. Then said Berluse,

'Sir knight, I know you better than ye ween, for ye are King Mark that slew my father afore mine own eyen; and me had ye slain had I not escaped into a wood; but wit ye well, for the love of my lord of this castle I will neither hurt you ne harm you, nor none of your fellowship. But wit ye well, when ye are past this lodging I shall hurt you and I may, for ye slew my father traitorly. But first for the love of my lord, Sir Tor, and for the love of Sir Lamorak, the honourable knight that here is lodged, ye shall have none ill lodging; for it is pity that ever ye should be in the company of good knights; for ye are the most villainous knight or king that is now known alive, for ye are a destroyer of good knights, and all that ye do is but treason.'

CHAPTER 10: *How Sir Berluse met with King Mark, and how Sir Dinadan took his part*

Then was King Mark sore ashamed, and said but little again. But when Sir Lamorak and Sir Dinadan wist that he was King Mark they were sorry of his fellowship. So after supper they went to lodging.

So on the morn they arose early, and King Mark and Sir Dinadan rode together; and three mile from their lodging there met with them three knights, and Sir Berluse was one, and that other his two cousins.

Sir Berluse saw King Mark, and then he cried on high, 'Traitor, keep thee from me, for wit thou well that I am Berluse.'

'Sir knight,' said Sir Dinadan, 'I counsel you to leave off at this time, for he is riding to King Arthur; and because I have promised to conduct him to my lord King Arthur, needs must I take a part with him, howbeit I love not his condition, and fain I would be from him.'

'Well, Dinadan,' said Sir Berluse, 'me repenteth that ye will take part with him, but now do your best.'

And then he hurtled to King Mark, and smote him sore upon the shield, that he bare him clean out of his saddle to the earth.

That saw Sir Dinadan, and he fewtered his spear, and ran to one of Berluse's fellows, and smote him down off his saddle. Then Dinadan turned his horse, and smote the third knight in the same wise to the earth, for Sir Dinadan was a good knight on horseback; and there began a great battle, for Berluse and his fellows held them together strongly on foot. And so through the great force of Sir Dinadan King

Mark had Berluse to the earth, and his two fellows fled; and had not been Sir Dinadan, King Mark would have slain him. And so Sir Dinadan rescued him of his life, for King Mark was but a murderer.

And then they took their horses and departed, and left Sir Berluse there sore wounded. Then King Mark and Sir Dinadan rode forth a four leagues English, till that they came to a bridge where hoved a knight on horseback, armed and ready to joust.

'Lo,' said Sir Dinadan unto King Mark, 'yonder hoveth a knight that will joust, for there shall none pass this bridge but he must joust with that knight.'

'It is well,' said King Mark, 'for this jousts falleth with thee.'

Sir Dinadan knew the knight well that he was a noble knight, and fain he would have jousted, but he had had lever King Mark had jousted with him, but by no mean King Mark would not joust. Then Sir Dinadan might not refuse him in no manner.

And then either dressed their spears and their shields, and smote together, so that through fine force Sir Dinadan was smitten to the earth; and lightly he arose up and gat his horse, and required that knight to do battle with swords. And he answered and said,

'Fair knight, as at this time I may not have ado with you no more, for the custom of this passage is such.'

Then was Sir Dinadan passing wroth that he might not be revenged of that knight; and so he departed, and in no wise would that knight tell his name. But ever Sir Dinadan thought he should know him by his shield that it should be Sir Tor.

CHAPTER 11 : *How King Mark mocked Sir Dinadan, and how they met with six knights of the Round Table*

So as they rode by the way King Mark then began to mock Sir Dinadan, and said, 'I weened you knights of the Table Round might not in no wise find their matches.'

'Ye say well,' said Sir Dinadan. 'As for you, on my life I call you none of the best knights; but sith ye have such a despite at me I require you to joust with me to prove my strength.'

'Not so,' said King Mark, 'for I will not have ado with you in no manner; but I require you of one thing, that when ye come to Arthur's court discover not my name, for I am there so hated.'

'It is shame to you,' said Sir Dinadan, 'that ye govern you so shamefully; for I see by you ye are full of cowardice, and ye are a murderer, and that is the greatest shame that a knight may have; for never a knight being a murderer hath worship, nor never shall have; for I saw but late through my force ye would have slain Sir Berluse, a better knight than ye, or ever shall be, and more of prowess.'

Thus they rode forth talking till they came to a fair place, where stood a knight, and prayed them to take their lodging with him. So at the request of that knight they reposed them there, and made them well at ease, and had great cheer. For all errant knights were welcome to him, and specially all those of Arthur's court.

Then Sir Dinadan demanded his host what was the knight's name that kept the bridge.

'For what cause ask you it?' said his host.

'For it is not long ago,' said Sir Dinadan, 'sithen he gave me a fall.'

'Ah, fair knight,' said his host, 'thereof have ye no marvel, for he is a passing good knight, and his name is Sir Tor, the son of Aries le Vaysher.'

'Ah,' said Sir Dinadan, 'was that Sir Tor? For truly so ever me thought.'

Right as they stood thus talking together they saw come riding to them over a plain six knights of the court of King Arthur, well armed at all points. And there by their shields Sir Dinadan knew them well. The first was the good knight Sir Uwain, the son of King Uriens, the second was the noble knight Sir Brandiles, the third was Ozana le Cure Hardy, the fourth was Uwain les Avoutres, the fifth was Sir Agravain, the sixth Sir Mordred, brother to Sir Gawain.

When Sir Dinadan had seen these six knights he thought in himself he would bring King Mark by some wile to joust with one of them. And anon they took their horses and ran after these knights well a three mile English.

Then was King Mark ware where they sat all six about a well, and ate and drank such meats as they had, and their horses walking and some tied, and their shields hung in divers places about them.

'Lo.' said Sir Dinadan, 'yonder are knights errant that will joust with us.'

'God forbid,' said King Mark, 'for they be six and we but two.'

'As for that,' said Sir Dinadan, 'let us not spare, for I will assay the foremost;' and therewith he made him ready.

When King Mark saw him do so, as fast as Sir Dinadan rode toward them, King Mark rode froward them with all his menial meyne.

So when Sir Dinadan saw King Mark was gone, he set the spear out of the rest, and threw his shield upon his back, and came riding to the fellowship of the Table Round. And anon Sir Uwain knew Sir Dinadan, and welcomed him, and so did all his fellowship.

CHAPTER 12: *How the six knights sent Sir Dagonet to joust with King Mark, and how King Mark refused him*

And then they asked him of his adventures, and whether he had seen Sir Tristram or Sir Launcelot.

'So God me help,' said Sir Dinadan, 'I saw none of them sithen I departed from Camelot.'

'What knight is that,' said Sir Brandiles, 'that so suddenly departed from you, and rode over yonder field?'

'Sir,' said he, 'it was a knight of Cornwall, and the most horrible coward that ever bestrode horse.'

'What is his name?' said all these knights.

'I wot not,' said Sir Dinadan.

So when they had reposed them, and spoken together, they took their horses and rode to a castle where dwelt an old knight that made all knights errant good cheer. Then in the meanwhile that they were talking came into the castle Sir Griflet le Fise de Dieu, and there was he welcome; and they all asked him whether he had seen Sir Launcelot or Sir Tristram.

'Sirs,' he answered, 'I saw him not sithen he departed from Camelot.'

So as Sir Dinadan walked and beheld the castle, thereby in a chamber he espied King Mark, and then he rebuked him, and asked him why he departed so.

'Sir,' said he, 'for I durst not abide because they were so many. But how escaped ye?' said King Mark.

'Sir,' said Sir Dinadan, 'they were better friends than I weened they had been.'

'Who is captain of that fellowship?' said the king.

Then for to fear him Sir Dinadan said that it was Sir Launcelot.

'O Jesu,' said the king, 'might I know Sir Launcelot by his shield?'

'Yea,' said Dinadan, 'for he beareth a shield of silver and black bends.' All this he said to fear the king, for Sir Launcelot was not in his fellowship.

'Now I pray you,' said King Mark, 'that ye will ride in my fellowship.'

'That is me loth to do,' said Sir Dinadan, 'because ye forsook my fellowship.'

Right so Sir Dinadan went from King Mark, and went to his own fellowship; and so they mounted upon their horses, and rode on their ways, and talked of the Cornish knight, for Dinadan told them that he was in the castle where they were lodged.

'It is well said,' said Sir Griflet, 'for here have I brought Sir Dagonet, King Arthur's fool, that is the best fellow and the merriest in the world.'

'Will ye do well?' said Sir Dinadan. 'I have told the Cornish knight that here is Sir Launcelot, and the Cornish knight asked me what shield he bare. Truly, I told him that he bare the same shield that Sir Mordred beareth.'

'Will ye do well?' said Sir Mordred. 'I am hurt and may not well bear my shield nor harness, and therefore put my shield and my harness upon Sir Dagonet, and let him set upon the Cornish knight.'

'That shall be done,' said Sir Dagonet, 'by my faith.'

Then anon was Dagonet armed him in Mordred's harness and his shield, and he was set on a great horse, and a spear in his hand.

'Now,' said Dagonet, 'show me the knight, and I trow I shall bear him down.'

So all these knights rode to a woodside, and abode till King Mark came by the way. Then they put forth Sir Dagonet, and he came on all the while his horse might run, straight upon King Mark.

And when he came nigh King Mark, he cried as he were wood, and said, 'Keep thee, knight of Cornwall, for I will slay thee!'

Anon, as King Mark beheld his shield, he said to himself, 'Yonder is Sir Launcelot; alas, now am I destroyed;' and therewithal he made his horse to run as fast as it might through thick and thin. And ever Sir Dagonet followed after King

Mark, crying and rating him as a wood man, through a great forest.

When Sir Uwain and Sir Brandiles saw Dagonet so chase King Mark, they laughed all as they were wood. And then they took their horses, and rode after to see how Sir Dagonet sped, for they would not for no good that Sir Dagonet were shent, for King Arthur loved him passing well, and made him knight his own hands. And at every tournament he began to make King Arthur to laugh. Then the knights rode here and there, crying and chasing after King Mark, that all the forest rang of the noise.

CHAPTER 13 : *How Sir Palomides by adventure met King Mark fleeing, and how he overthrew Dagonet and other knights*

So King Mark rode by fortune by a well, in the way where stood a knight errant on horseback, armed at all points, with a great spear in his hand. And when he saw King Mark coming fleeing he said,

'Knight, return again for shame and stand with me, and I shall be thy warrant.'

'Ah, fair knight,' said King Mark, 'let me pass, for yonder cometh after me the best knight of the world, with the black bended shield.'

'Fie, for shame,' said the knight, 'he is none of the worthy knights, and if he were Sir Launcelot or Sir Tristram I should not doubt to meet the better of them both.'

When King Mark heard him say that word, he turned his horse and abode by him. And then that strong knight bare a spear to Dagonet, and smote him so sore that he bare him over his horse's tail, and nigh he had broken his neck.

And anon after him came Sir Brandiles, and when he saw Dagonet have that fall he was passing wroth, and cried, 'Keep thee, knight!' and so they hurtled together wonder

26

sore. But the knight smote Sir Brandiles so sore that he went to the earth, horse and man.

Sir Uwain came after and saw all this.

'Jesu,' said he, 'yonder is a strong knight.'

And then they fewtered their spears, and this knight came so eagerly that he smote down Sir Uwain. Then came Ozana with the hardy heart, and he was smitten down.

'Now,' said Sir Griflet, 'by my counsel let us send to yonder errant knight, and wit whether he be of Arthur's court, for as I deem it is Sir Lamorak de Gales.'

So they sent unto him, and prayed the strange knight to tell his name, and whether he were of Arthur's court or not.

'As for my name they shall not wit, but tell them I am a knight errant as they are, and let them wit that I am no knight of King Arthur's court.' And so the squire rode again unto them and told them his answer of him.

'By my head,' said Sir Agravain, 'he is one of the strongest knights that ever I saw, for he hath overthrown three noble knights, and needs we must encounter with him for shame.'

So Sir Agravain fewtered his spear, and that other was ready, and smote him down over his horse to the earth. And in the same wise he smote Sir Uwain les Avoutres and also Sir Griflet. Then had he served them all but Sir Dinadan, for he was behind, and Sir Mordred was unarmed, and Dagonet had his harness.

So when this was done, this strong knight rode on his way a soft pace, and King Mark rode after him, praising him mickle; but he would answer no words, but sighed wonderly sore, hanging down his head, taking no heed to his words.

Thus they rode well a three mile English, and then this knight called to him a varlet, and bad him, 'Ride until yonder fair manor, and recommend me to the lady of that castle and place, and pray her to send me refreshing of good meats and drinks. And if she ask thee what I am, tell her that I am the knight that followeth the Glatisant Beast.' (That is in English to say the Questing Beast; for that beast wheresomever he yede he quested in the belly with such a noise as it had been a thirty couple of hounds.)

Then the varlet went his way and came to the manor, and saluted the lady, and told her from whence he came. And when she understood that he came from the knight that followed the Questing Beast, 'O sweet Lord Jesu,' she said, 'when shall I see that noble knight, my dear son Palomides? Alas, will he not abide with me?' and therewith she swooned and wept, and made passing great dole.

And then also soon as she might she gave the varlet all that he asked. And the varlet returned unto Sir Palomides, for he was a varlet of King Mark. And as soon as he came, he told the knight's name was Sir Palomides.

'I am well pleased,' said King Mark, 'but hold thee still and say nothing.'

Then they alit and set them down and reposed them a while. Anon withal King Mark fell asleep. When Sir Palomides saw him sound asleep he took his horse and rode his way, and said to them, 'I will not be in the company of a sleeping knight.' And so he rode forth a great pace.

CHAPTER 14: *How King Mark and Sir Dinadan heard Sir Palomides making great sorrow and mourning for La Beale Isoud*

Now turn we unto Sir Dinadan, that found these seven knights passing heavy. And when he wist how they sped, as heavy was he.

'My lord Uwain,' said Dinadan, 'I dare lay my head it is Sir Lamorak de Gales. I promise you all I shall find him and he may be found in this country.'

And so Sir Dinadan rode after this knight; and so did King Mark, that sought him through the forest. So as King Mark rode after Sir Palomides he heard a noise of a man that made great dole. Then King Mark rode as nigh that noise as he might and as he durst. Then was he ware of a knight that was descended off his horse, and had put off his helm, and there he made a piteous complaint and a dolorous, of love.

Now leave we that, and talk we of Sir Dinadan, that rode to seek Sir Palomides. And as he came within a forest he met with a knight, a chaser of a deer.

'Sir,' said Sir Dinadan, 'met ye with a knight with a shield of silver and lions' heads?'

'Yea, fair knight,' said the other, 'with such a knight met I with but a while agone, and straight yonder way he yede.'

'Gramercy,' said Sir Dinadan, 'for might I find the track of his horse I should not fail to find that knight.'

Right so as Sir Dinadan rode in the even late he heard a doleful noise as it were of a man. Then Sir Dinadan rode toward that noise; and when he came nigh that noise he alit off his horse, and went near him on foot. Then was he ware of a knight that stood under a tree, and his horse tied by him, and the helm off his head; and ever that knight made a doleful complaint as ever made knight. And always he made his complaint of La Beale Isoud, the Queen of Cornwall, and said,

'Ah, fair lady, why love I thee? For thou art fairest of all other, and yet showest thou never love to me, nor bounty. Alas, yet must I love thee. And I may not blame thee, fair lady, for mine eyen be cause of this sorrow. And yet to love thee I am but a fool, for the best knight of the world loveth thee, and ye him again, that is Sir Tristram de Liones. And the falsest king and knight is your husband, and the most coward and full of treason, is your lord, King Mark. Alas, that ever so fair a lady and peerless of all other should be matched with the most villainous knight of the world.'

All this language heard King Mark, what Sir Palomides said by him; wherefore he was adread when he saw Sir Dinadan, lest, and he espied him, that he would tell Sir Palomides that he was King Mark; and therefore he withdrew him, and took his horse and rode to his men, where he commanded them to abide.

And so he rode as fast as he might unto Camelot; and the

same day he found there Amant, the knight, ready, that afore Arthur had appelled him of treason; and so, lightly the king commanded them to do battle. And by misadventure King Mark smote Amant through the body. And yet was Amant in the righteous quarrel. And right so he took his horse and departed from the court for dread of Sir Dinadan, that he would tell Sir Tristram and Sir Palomides what he was.

Then were there maidens that La Beale Isoud had sent to Sir Tristram, that knew Sir Amant well.

CHAPTER 15: *How King Mark had slain Sir Amant wrongfully tofore King Arthur, and Sir Launcelot fetched King Mark to King Arthur*

Then by the licence of King Arthur they went to him and spake with him; for while the truncheon of the spear stuck in his body he spake:

'Ah, fair damosels,' said Amant, 'recommend me unto La Beale Isoud, and tell her that I am slain for the love of her and of Sir Tristram.' And there he told the damosels how cowardly King Mark had slain him, and Sir Bersules, his fellow. 'And for that deed I appelled him of treason, and here am I slain in a righteous quarrel; and all was because of Sir Bersules and I would not consent by treason to slay the noble knight, Sir Tristram.'

Then the two maidens cried aloud that all the court might hear it, and said, 'O sweet Lord Jesu, that knowest all hid things, why sufferest Thou so false a traitor to vanquish and slay a true knight that fought in a righteous quarrel?'

Then anon it was sprung to the king, and the queen, and to all the lords, that it was King Mark that had slain Sir Amant, and Sir Bersules aforehand; wherefore they did their battle.

Then was King Arthur wroth out of measure, and so were all the other knights. But when Sir Tristram knew all the matter he made great dole and sorrow out of measure, and wept for sorrow for the loss of the noble knights, Sir Bersules and of Sir Amant.

When Sir Launcelot espied Sir Tristram weep he went hastily to King Arthur, and said, 'Sir, I pray you give me leave to return again to yonder false king and knight.'

'I pray you,' said King Arthur, 'fetch him again, but I would not that ye slew him, for my worship.'

Then Sir Launcelot armed him in all haste, and mounted upon a great horse, and took a spear in his hand and rode after King Mark. And from thence a three mile English Sir Launcelot overtook him, and bad him: 'Turn recreant king and knight, for whether thou wilt or not thou shalt go with me to King Arthur's court.'

King Mark returned and looked upon Sir Launcelot, and said, 'Fair sir, what is your name?'

'Wit thou well,' said he, 'my name is Sir Launcelot, and therefore defend thee.'

And when King Mark wist that it was Sir Launcelot, and came so fast upon him with a spear, he cried then aloud, 'I yield me to thee, Sir Launcelot, honourable knight.'

But Sir Launcelot would not hear him, but came fast upon him. King Mark saw that, and made no defence, but tumbled adown out of his saddle to the earth as a sack, and there he lay still, and cried Sir Launcelot mercy.

'Arise, recreant knight and king!'

'I will not fight,' said King Mark, 'but whither that ye will I will go with you.'

'Alas, alas,' said Sir Launcelot, 'that I may not give thee one buffet for the love of Sir Tristram and of La Beale Isoud, and for the two knights that thou hast slain traitorly.'

And so he mounted upon his horse and brought him to King Arthur; and there King Mark alit in that same place, and threw his helm from him upon the earth, and his sword, and fell flat to the earth of King Arthur's feet, and put him in his grace and mercy.

'So God me help,' said Arthur, 'ye are welcome in a manner, and in a manner ye are not welcome. In this manner ye are welcome, that ye come hither maugre thy head, as I suppose.'

'That is truth,' said King Mark, 'and else I had not been here, for my lord, Sir Launcelot, brought me hither through his fine force, and to him am I yielden to as recreant.'

'Well,' said Arthur, 'ye understand ye ought to do me service, homage, and fealty. And never would ye do me none, but ever ye have been against me, and a destroyer of my knights; now how will ye acquit you?'

'Sir,' said King Mark, 'right as your lordship will require me, unto my power, I will make a large amends.' For he was a fair speaker, and false thereunder.

Then for great pleasure of Sir Tristram, to make them twain accorded, the king withheld King Mark as at that time, and made a broken love day between them.

CHAPTER 16: *How Sir Dinadan told Sir Palomides of the battle between Sir Launcelot and Sir Tristram*

Now turn we again unto Sir Palomides, how Sir Dinadan comforted him in all that he might, from his great sorrow.

'What knight are ye?' said Sir Palomides.

'Sir, I am a knight errant as ye be, that hath sought you long by your shield.'

'Here is my shield,' said Sir Palomides, 'wit ye well, and ye will ought, therewith I will defend it.'

'Nay,' said Sir Dinadan, 'I will not have ado with you but in good manner.'

'And if ye will, ye shall find me soon ready.'

'Sir,' said Sir Dinadan, 'whitherward ride you this way?'

'By my head,' said Sir Palomides, 'I wot not, but as fortune leadeth me.'

'Heard ye or saw ye ought of Sir Tristram?'

'So God me help, of Sir Tristram, I both heard and saw, and notforthan we loved not inwardly well together, yet at my

love day: day appointed for the amicable settlement of a dispute.
notforthan: although.

32

mischief Sir Tristram rescued me from my death; and yet, or he and I departed, by both our assents we assigned a day that we should have met at the stony grave that Merlin set beside Camelot, and there to have done battle together; howbeit I was letted,' said Sir Palomides, 'that I might not hold my day, the which grieveth me sore; but I have a large excuse. For I was prisoner with a lord, and many other more, and that shall Sir Tristram right well understand, that I brake it not of fear of cowardice.' And then Sir Palomides told Sir Dinadan the same day that they should have met.

'So God me help,' said Sir Dinadan, 'that same day met Sir Launcelot and Sir Tristram at the same grave of stone. And there was the most mightiest battle that ever was seen in this land betwixt two knights, for they fought more than two hours. And there they both bled so much blood that all men marvelled that ever they might endure it. And so at the last, by both their assents, they were made friends and sworn brethren for ever, and no man can judge the better knight. And now is Sir Tristram made a knight of the Round Table, and he sitteth in the siege of the noble knight, Sir Marhaus.'

'By my head,' said Sir Palomides, 'Sir Tristram is far bigger than Sir Launcelot, and the hardier knight.'

'Have ye assayed them both?' said Sir Dinadan.

'I have seen Sir Tristram fight,' said Sir Palomides, 'but never Sir Launcelot, to my writing. But at the fountain where Sir Launcelot lay asleep, there with one spear he smote down Sir Tristram and me,' said Palomides, 'but at that time they knew not either other.'

'Fair knight,' said Sir Dinadan, 'as for Sir Launcelot and Sir Tristram let them be, for the worst of them will not be lightly matched of no knights that I know living.'

'No,' said Sir Palomides, 'God defend, but and I had a quarrel to the better of them both I would with as good a will fight with him as with you.'

'Sir, I require you tell me your name, and in good faith I shall hold you company till that we come to Camelot; and there shall ye have great worship now at this great tournament; for there shall be the Queen Guenever, and La Beale Isoud of Cornwall.'

'Wit you well, sir knight, for the love of La Beale Isoud I will be there, and else not, but I will not have ado in King Arthur's court.'

'Sir,' said Dinadan, 'I shall ride with you and do you service, so ye will tell me your name.'

'Sir, ye shall understand my name is Sir Palomides, brother to Safer, the good and noble knight. And Sir Segwarides and I, we be Saracens born, of father and mother.'

'Sir,' said Sir Dinadan, 'I thank you much for the telling of your name. For I am glad of that I know your name, and I promise you by the faith of my body, ye shall not be hurt by me by my will, but rather be advanced. And thereto will I help you with all my power, I promise you, doubt ye not. And certainly on my life ye shall win great worship in the court of King Arthur, and be right welcome.'

So then they dressed on their helms and put on their shields, and mounted upon their horses, and took the broad way toward Camelot. And then were they ware of a castle that was fair and rich, and also passing strong as any was within this realm.

CHAPTER 17: *How Sir Lamorak jousted with divers knights of the castle wherein was Morgan le Fay*

'Sir Palomides,' said Dinadan, 'here is a castle that I know well, and therein dwelleth Queen Morgan le Fay, King Arthur's sister; and King Arthur gave her this castle, the which he hath repenteth him sithen a thousand times, for sithen King Arthur and she have been at debate and strife; but this castle could he never get nor win of her by no manner of engine; and ever as she might she made war on King Arthur. And all dangerous knights she withholdeth with her, for to destroy all these knights that King Arthur loveth. And there shall no knight pass this way but he must joust with one knight, or with two, or with three. And if it hap that King Arthur's knight be beaten, he shall lose his horse and his harness and all that he hath, and hard if that he escape, but that he shall be prisoner.'

'So God me help,' said Palomides, 'this is a shameful custom, and a villainous usance for a queen to use, and namely to make such war upon her own lord, that is called the flower of chivalry that is Christian or heathen; and with all my heart I would destroy that shameful custom. And I will that all the world wit she shall have no service of me. And if she send out any knights, as I suppose she will, for to joust, they shall have both their hands full.'

'And I shall not fail you,' said Sir Dinadan, 'unto my puissance, upon my life.'

So as they stood on horseback afore the castle, there came a knight with a red shield, and two squires after him; and he came straight unto Sir Palomides, the good knight, and said to him, 'Fair and gentle knight errant, I require thee for the love thou owest unto knighthood, that ye will not have ado here with these men of this castle;' (for this was Sir Lamorak that thus said.) 'For I came hither to seek this deed, and it is my request; and therefore I beseech you, knight, let me deal, and if I be beaten revenge me.'

'In the name of God,' said Palomides, 'let see how ye will speed, and we shall behold you.'

Then anon came forth a knight of the castle, and proffered to joust with the knight with the red shield. Anon they encountered together, and he with the red shield smote him so hard that he bare him over to the earth. Therewith anon came another knight of the castle, and he was smitten so sore that he avoided his saddle. And forthwithal came the third knight, and the knight with the red shield smote him to the earth.

Then came Sir Palomides, and besought him that he might help him to joust.

'Fair knight,' said he unto him, 'suffer me as at this time to have my will, for and they were twenty knights I shall not doubt them.'

And ever there were upon the walls of the castle many lords and ladies that cried and said, 'Well have ye jousted, knight with the red shield.'

But as soon as the knight had smitten them down, his squire took their horses, and avoided their saddles and bridles of the horses, and turned them into the forest, and made the knights to be kept to the end of the jousts.

Right so came out of the castle the fourth knight, and freshly proffered to joust with the knight with the red shield; and he was ready, and he smote him so hard that horse and man fell to the earth, and the knight's back brake with the fall, and his neck also.

'O Jesu !' said Sir Palomides, 'That yonder is a passing good knight, and the best jouster that ever I saw.'

'By my head,' said Sir Dinadan, 'he is as good as ever was Sir Launcelot or Sir Tristram, what knight somever he be.'

CHAPTER 18: *How Sir Palomides would have jousted for Sir Lamorak with the knights of the castle*

Then forthwithal came a knight out of the castle, with a shield bended with black and with white. And anon the knight with the red shield and he encountered so hard that he smote the knight of the castle through the bended shield and through the body, and brake the horse's back.

'Fair knight,' said Sir Palomides, 'ye have overmuch on hand, therefore I pray you let me joust, for ye had need to be reposed.'

'Why sir,' said the knight, 'seem ye that I am weak and feeble? And sir, methinketh ye proffer me wrong, and to me shame, when I do well enough. I tell you now as I told you erst; for and they were twenty knights I shall beat them, and if I be beaten or slain then may ye revenge me. And if ye think that I be weary, and ye have an appetite to joust with me, I shall find you jousting enough.'

'Sir,' said Palomides, 'I said it not because I would

erst: before.

joust with you, but meseemeth that ye have overmuch on hand.'

'And therefore, and ye were gentle,' said the knight with the red shield, 'ye should not proffer me shame; therefore I require you to joust with me, and ye shall find that I am not weary.'

'Sith ye require me,' said Sir Palomides, 'take keep to yourself.'

Then they two knights came together as fast as their horses might run, and the knight smote Sir Palomides so sore on the shield that the spear went into his side a great wound, and a perilous.

And therewithal Sir Palomides avoided his saddle.

And that knight turned unto Sir Dinadan; and when he saw him coming he cried aloud, and said, 'Sir, I will not have ado with you!' but for that he let it not, but came straight upon him.

So Sir Dinadan for shame put forth his spear and all to-shivered it upon the knight. But he smote Sir Dinadan again so hard that he smote him clean from his saddle; but their horses he would not suffer his squires to meddle with, and because they were knights errant.

Then he dressed him again to the castle, and jousted with seven knights more, and there was none of them might withstand him, but he[1] bare him to the earth. And of these twelve knights he slew in plain jousts four. And the eight knights he made them to swear on the cross of a sword that they should never use the evil customs of the castle. And when he had made them to swear that oath he let them pass.

And ever stood the lords and the ladies on the castle walls crying and saying, 'Knight with the red shield, ye have marvellously well done as ever we saw knight do.'

And therewith came a knight out of the castle unarmed, and said, 'Knight with the red shield, overmuch damage hast thou done to us this day, therefore return whither thou wilt, for here are no more will have ado with thee; for we repent sore that ever thou camest here, for by thee is fordone the old custom of this castle.' And with that word he turned again into the castle, and shut the gates.

Then the knight with the red shield turned and called his squires, and so passed forth on his way, and rode a great pace.

And when he was past, Sir Palomides went to Sir Dinadan, and said, 'I had never such a shame of one knight that ever I met; and therefore I cast me to ride after him, and to be revenged with my sword, for on horseback I deem I shall get no worship of him.'

'Sir Palomides,' said Dinadan, 'ye shall not meddle with him by my counsel, for ye shall get no worship of him; and for this cause, ye have seen him this day have had overmuch to do, and overmuch travailed.'

'By Almighty Jesu,' said Palomides, 'I shall never be at ease till that I have had ado with him.'

'Sir,' said Dinadan, 'I shall give you my beholding.'

'Well,' said Palomides, 'then shall ye see how we shall redress our mights.'

So they took their horses of their varlets and rode after the knight with the red shield; and down in a valley beside a fountain they were ware where he was alit to repose him, and had done off his helm for to drink at the well.

CHAPTER 19: *How Sir Lamorak jousted with Sir Palomides, and hurt him grievously*

Then Palomides rode fast till he came nigh him. And then he said, 'Knight remember ye of the shame ye did to me right now at the castle, therefore dress thee, for I will have ado with thee.'

'Fair knight,' said he to Palomides, 'of me ye win no worship, for ye have seen this day that I have been travailed sore.'

'As for that,' said Palomides, 'I will not let, for wit ye well I will be revenged.'

'Well,' said the knight, 'I may happen to endure you.'

And therewithal he mounted upon his horse, and took a great spear in his hand ready for to joust.

'Nay,' said Palomides, 'I will not joust, for I am sure at jousting I get no prize.'

'Fair knight,' said that knight 'it would beseem a knight to joust and to fight on horseback.'

'Ye shall see what I will do,' said Palomides.

And therewith he alit down upon foot, and dressed his shield afore him and pulled out his sword. Then the knight with the red shield descended down from his horse, and dressed his shield afore him, and so he drew out his sword. And then they came together a soft pace, and wonderly they lashed together passing thick the mountenance of an hour or ever they breathed. Then they traced and traversed, and waxed wonderly wroth, and either behight other death; they hew so fast with their swords that they cut in down half their swords and mails, that the bare flesh in some place stood above their harness. And when Sir Palomides beheld his fellow's sword overhilled with his blood it grieved him sore: some while they foined, some while they struck as wild men. But at the last Sir Palomides waxed faint, because of his first wound that he had at the castle with a spear, for that wound grieved him wonderly sore.

'Fair knight,' said Palomides, 'meseemeth we have assayed either other passing sore, and if it may please thee, I require thee of thy knighthood tell me thy name.'

'Sir,' said the knight to Palomides, 'that is me loth to do, for thou hast done me wrong and no knighthood to proffer me battle, considering my great travail, but and thou wilt tell me thy name I will tell thee mine.'

'Sir,' said he, 'wit thou well my name is Palomides.'

'Ah, sir, ye shall understand my name is Sir Lamorak de Gales, son and heir unto the good knight and king, King Pellinor, and Sir Tor, the good knight, is my half brother.'

When Sir Palomides heard him say so he kneeled down and asked mercy 'for outrageously have I done to you this

behight: promised.

39

day; considering the great deeds of arms I have seen you do, shamefully and unknightly I have required you to do battle.'

'Ah, Sir Palomides,' said Sir Lamorak, 'overmuch have ye done and said to me.' And therewith he embraced him with his both hands, and said, 'Palomides, the worthy knight, in all this land is no better than ye, nor more of prowess, and me repenteth[1] sore that we should fight together.'

'So it doth not me,' said Sir Palomides, 'and yet am I sorer wounded than ye be; but as for that I shall soon thereof be whole. But certainly I would not for the fairest castle in this land, but if thou and I had met, for I shall love you the days of my life afore all other knights except my brother, Sir Safer.'

'I say the same,' said Sir Lamorak, 'except my brother, Sir Tor.'

Then came Sir Dinadan, and he made great joy of Sir Lamorak. Then their squires dressed both their shields and their harness, and stopped their wounds. And thereby at a priory they rested them all night.

CHAPTER 20: *How it was told Sir Launcelot that Dagonet chased King Mark, and how a knight overthrew him and six knights*

Now turn we again. When Sir Ganis and Sir Brandiles with his fellows came to the court of King Arthur they told the king, Sir Launcelot, and Sir Tristram, how Sir Dagonet, the fool, chased King Mark through the forest, and how the strong knight smote them down all seven with one spear. There was great laughing and japing at King Mark and at Sir Dagonet. But all these knights could not tell what knight it was that rescued King Mark. Then they asked King Mark if that he knew him and he answered and said,

'He named himself the Knight that Followed the Questing Beast, and on that name he sent one of my varlets to a place where was his mother; and when she heard from whence he came she made passing great dole, and discovered to my varlet his name, and said, "Oh, my dear son, Sir Palomides, why wilt thou not see me?" And therefore sir,' said King Mark, 'it is to understand his name is Sir Palomides, a noble knight.'

Then were all these seven knights glad that they knew his name.

Now turn we again, for on the morn they took their horses, both Sir Lamorak, Palomides, and Dinadan, with their squires and varlets, till they saw a fair castle that stood on a mountain well closed, and thither they rode; and there they found a knight that hight Galahaut, that was lord of that castle, and there they had great cheer and were well eased.

'Sir Dinadan,' said Sir Lamorak, 'what will ye do?'

'Sir,' said Dinadan, 'I will tomorrow to the court of King Arthur.'

'By my head,' said Sir Palomides, 'I will not ride these three days, for I am sore hurt, and much have I bled, and therefore I will repose me here.'

'Truly,' said Sir Lamorak, 'and I will abide here with you; and when ye ride, then will I ride, unless that ye tarry over long, then will I take my horse. Therefore I pray you, Sir Dinadan, abide and ride with us.'

'Faithfully,' said Dinadan, 'I will not abide, for I have such a talent to see Sir Tristram that I may not abide long from him.'

'Ah, Dinadan,' said Sir Palomides, 'now do I understand that ye love my mortal enemy, and therefore how should I trust you.'

'Well,' said Dinadan, 'I love my lord Sir Tristram, above all other, and him will I serve and do honour.'

'So shall I,' said Sir Lamorak, 'in all that may lie in my power.'

So on the morn Sir Dinadan rode unto the court of King Arthur; and by the way as he rode he saw where stood an errant knight, and made him ready for to joust.

'Not so,' said Dinadan, 'for I have no will to joust.'

'With me shall ye joust,' said the knight, 'or that ye pass this way.'

'Whether ask ye jousts, by love or by hate?'

The knight answered, 'Wit ye well I ask it for love, and not for hate.'

'It may well be so,' said Sir Dinadan, 'but ye proffer me hard love when ye will joust with me with a sharp spear. But, fair knight,' said Sir Dinadan, 'sith ye will joust with me, meet with me in the court of King Arthur, and there shall I joust with you.'

'Well,' said the knight, 'sith ye will not joust with me, I pray you tell me your name.'

'Sir knight,' said he, 'my name is Sir Dinadan.'

'Ah,' said the knight, 'full well know I you for a good knight and a gentle, and wit you well I love you heartily.'

'Then shall here be no jousts,' said Dinadan, 'betwixt us.'

So they departed. And the same day he came to Camelot, where lay King Arthur. And there he saluted the king and the queen, Sir Launcelot, and Sir Tristram; and all the court was glad of Sir Dinadan, for he was gentle, wise, and courteous and a good knight. And in especial the valiant knight Sir Tristram loved Sir Dinadan passing well above all other knights save Sir Launcelot. Then the king asked Sir Dinadan what adventures he had seen.

'Sir,' said Dinadan, 'I have seen many adventures, and of some King Mark knoweth, but not all.'

Then the king hearkened Sir Dinadan, how he told that Sir Palomides and he were afore the castle of Morgan le Fay, and how Sir Lamorak took the jousts afore them, and how he forjousted twelve knights, and of them four he slew, and how 'after he smote down Sir Palomides and me both.'

'I may not believe that,' said the king, 'for Sir Palomides is a passing good knight.'

'That is very truth,' said Sir Dinadan, 'but yet I saw him better proved, hand for hand.' And then he told the king all that battle, and how Sir Palomides was more weaker, and more hurt, and more lost of his blood. 'And without doubt,' said Sir Dinadan, 'had the battle longer lasted, Palomides had been slain.'

'O Jesu,' said King Arthur, 'this is to me a great marvel.'

'Sir,' said Tristram, 'marvel ye nothing thereof, for at mine advice there is not a valianter knight in the world living, for I know his might. And now I will say you, I was never so weary of knight but if it were Sir Launcelot. And there is no knight in the world except Sir Launcelot I would did so well as Sir Lamorak.'

'So God me help,' said the king, 'I would that knight, Sir Lamorak, came to this court.'

'Sir,' said Dinadan, 'he will be here in short space, and Sir Palomides both, but I fear that Palomides may not yet travel.'

CHAPTER 21: *How King Arthur let do cry a jousts, and how Sir Lamorak came in, and overthrew Sir Gawain and many other*

Then within three days after the king let make a jousting at a priory. And there made them ready many knights of the Round Table, for Sir Gawain and his brethren made them ready to joust; but Tristram, Launcelot, nor Dinadan, would not joust, but suffered Sir Gawain, for the love of King Arthur, with his brethren, to win the gree if they might.

Then on the morn they apparelled them to joust, Sir Gawain and his four brethren, and did there great deeds of arms. And Sir Ector de Maris did marvellously well, but Sir Gawain passed all that fellowship; wherefore King Arthur and all the knights gave Sir Gawain the honour at the beginning.

Right so King Arthur was ware of a knight and two squires, the which came out of a forest side, with a shield covered with leather, and then he came slyly and hurtled here and there, and anon with one spear he had smitten down two knights of the Round Table. Then with his hurtling he lost the covering of his shield, then was the king and all other ware that he bare a red shield.

'O Jesu,' said King Arthur, 'see where rideth a stout knight, he with the red shield.'

And there was noise and crying: 'Beware the knight with the red shield.'

So within a little while he had overthrown three brethren of Sir Gawain's.

'So God me help,' said King Arthur, 'meseemeth yonder is the best jouster that ever I saw.'

With that he saw him encounter with Sir Gawain, and he smite him down with so great force that he made his horse to avoid his saddle.

'How now?' said the king, 'Sir Gawain hath a fall; well were me and I knew what knight he were with the red shield.'

'I know him well,' said Dinadan, 'but as at this time ye shall not know his name.'

'By my head,' said Sir Tristram, 'he jousted better than Sir Palomides, and if ye list to know his name, wit ye well his name is Sir Lamorak de Gales.'

As they stood thus talking, Sir Gawain and he encountered together again, and there he smote Sir Gawain from his horse, and bruised him sore. And in the sight of King Arthur he smote down twenty knights, beside Sir Gawain and his brethren. And so clearly was the prize given him as a knight peerless. Then slyly and marvellously Sir Lamorak withdrew him from all the fellowship into the forest' side. All this espied King Arthur, for his eye went never from him.

Then the king, Sir Launcelot, Sir Tristram, and Sir Dinadan, took their hackneys, and rode straight after the good knight, Sir Lamorak de Gales, and there found him. And thus said the king:

'Ah, fair knight well be ye found.'

When he saw the king he put off his helm and saluted him, and when he saw Sir Tristram he alit down off his horse and ran to him to take him by the thighs, but Sir Tristram would not suffer him, but he alit or that he came, and either took other in arms, and made great joy of other.

The king was glad, and also was all the fellowship of the Round Table, except Sir Gawain and his brethren. And when they wist that he was Sir Lamorak, they had great despite at him, and were wonderly wroth with him that he had put him to dishonour that day. Then Gawain called privily in council all his brethren, and to them said thus:

'Fair brethren, here may ye see, whom that we hate King Arthur loveth, and whom that we love he hateth. And wit ye well, my fair brethren, that this Sir Lamorak will never love us, because we slew his father, King Pellinor, for we deemed that he slew our father, King of Orkney. And for the despite of Pellinor, Sir Lamorak did us a shame to our mother, therefore I will be revenged.'

'Sir,' said Sir Gawain's brethren, 'let see how ye will or may be revenged, and ye shall find us ready.'

'Well,' said Gawain, 'hold you still and we shall espy our time.'

CHAPTER 22: *How King Arthur made King Mark to be accorded with Sir Tristram, and how they departed toward Cornwall*

Now pass we our matter, and leave we Sir Gawain, and speak of King Arthur, that on a day said unto King Mark, 'Sir, I pray you give me a gift that I shall ask you.'

'Sir,' said King Mark, 'I will give you whatsomever ye desire and it be in my power.'

'Sir, gramercy,' said Arthur. 'This I will ask you, that ye will be good lord unto Sir Tristram, for he is a man of great honour; and that ye will take him with you into Cornwall, and let him see his friends, and there cherish him for my sake.'

'Sir,' said King Mark, 'I promise you by the faith of my body, and by the faith that I owe to God and to you, I shall worship him for your sake in all that I can or may.'

'Sir,' said Arthur, 'and I will forgive you all the evil will that ever I ought you, and so be that you swear that upon a book afore me.'

'With a good will,' said King Mark; and so he there sware upon a book afore him and all his knights, and therewith King Mark and Sir Tristram took either other by the hands hard knit together. But for all this King Mark thought falsely, as it proved after, for he put Sir Tristram in prison, and cowardly would have slain him.

Then soon after King Mark took his leave to ride into Cornwall, and Sir Tristram made him ready to ride with him, whereof the most part of the Round Table were wroth and heavy, and in especial Sir Launcelot, and Sir Lamorak, and Sir Dinadan, were wroth out of measure. For well they wist King Mark would slay or destroy Sir Tristram.

'Alas,' said Dinadan, 'that my lord, Sir Tristram, shall depart.'

And Sir Tristram took such sorrow that he was amazed like a fool.

'Alas,' said Sir Launcelot unto King Arthur, 'what have ye done, for ye shall lose the most man of worship that ever came into your court.'

'It was his own desire,' said Arthur, 'and therefore I might not do withal, for I have done all that I can and made them at accord.'

'Accord,' said Sir Launcelot, 'fie upon that accord, for ye shall hear that he shall slay Sir Tristram, or put him in prison, for he is the most coward and the villainest king and knight that is now living.'

And therewith Sir Launcelot departed, and came to King Mark, and said to him thus:

'Sir king, wit thou well the good knight Sir Tristram shall go with thee. Beware, I rede thee, of treason, for and thou mischief that knight by any manner of falsehood or treason, by the faith I owe to God and to the order of knighthood, I shall slay thee mine own hands.'

'Sir Launcelot,' said the king, 'overmuch have ye said to me, and I have sworn and said over largely afore King Arthur in hearing of all his knights, that I shall not slay nor betray him. It were to me overmuch shame to break my promise.'

'Ye say well,' said Sir Launcelot, 'but ye are called so false and full of treason that no man may[1] believe you. Forsooth it is known well wherefore ye came into this country, and for none other cause but for [to] slay Sir Tristram.'

So with great dole King Mark and Sir Tristram rode together, for it was by Sir Tristram's will and his means to go with King Mark, and all was for the intent to see La Beale Isoud, for without the sight of her Sir Tristram might not endure.

CHAPTER 23: *How Sir Percival was made knight of King Arthur, and how a dumb maid spake, and brought him to the Round Table*

Now turn we again unto Sir Lamorak, and speak we of his brethren, Sir Tor, which was King Pellinor's first son and begotten of Aries' wife the cowherd, for he was a bastard; and Sir Agloval was his first son begotten in wedlock; Sir Lamorak, Dornar, Percival, these were his sons too in wedlock.

So when King Mark and Sir Tristram were departed from the court there was made great dole and sorrow for the departing of Sir Tristram. Then the king and his knights made no manner of joys eight days after.

And at the eight days' end there came to the court a knight with a young squire with him. And when this knight was unarmed, he went to the king and required him to make the young squire a knight.

'Of what lineage is he come?' said King Arthur.

'Sir,' said the knight, 'he is the son of King Pellinor, that did you some time good service, and he is brother unto Sir Lamorak de Gales, the good knight.'

'Well,' said the king, 'for what cause desire ye that of me, that I should make him knight?'

'Wit you well, my lord the king, that this young squire is brother to me as well as to Sir Lamorak, and my name is Agloval.'

'Sir Agloval,' said Arthur, 'for the love of Sir Lamorak, and for his father's love, he shall be made knight tomorrow. Now tell me,' said Arthur, 'what is his name?'

'Sir,' said the knight, 'his name is Percival de Gales.'

So on the morn the king made him knight in Camelot. But the king and all the knights thought it would be long or that he proved a good knight. Then at the dinner, when the king was set at the table, and every knight after he was of prowess, the king commanded him to be set among mean knights; and so was Sir Percival set as the king commanded.

Then was there a maiden in the queen's court that was come of high blood, and she was dumb and never spake word. Right so she came straight into the hall, and went unto Sir Percival, and took him by the hand and said aloud, that the king and all the knights might hear it,

'Arise, Sir Percival, the noble knight and God's knight, and go with me;' and so he did.

And there she brought him to the right side of the Siege Perilous, and said, 'Fair knight, take here thy siege, for that siege appertaineth to thee and to none other.'

Right so she departed and asked a priest. And as she was confessed and houselled then she died.

Then the king and all the court made great joy of Sir Percival.

CHAPTER 24: *How Sir Lamorak lay with King Lot's wife, and how Sir Gaheris slew her which was his own mother*

Now turn we unto Sir Lamorak, that much there was praised. Then, by the mean of Sir Gawain and his brethren, they sent for their mother there besides, fast by a castle beside Camelot; and all was to that intent to slay Sir Lamorak. The Queen of

houselled: given the sacrament.

Orkney was there but a while, but Sir Lamorak wist of her being,[1] and was full fain; and for to make an end of this matter, he sent unto her, and there betwixt them was a night assigned that Sir Lamorak should come to her.

Thereof was ware Sir Gaheris, and there he rode afore the same night, and waited upon Sir Lamorak, and then he saw where he came all armed. And where Sir Lamorak alit he tied his horse to a privy postern, and so he went into a parlour and unarmed him; and then he went unto the queen's bed, and she made of him passing great joy, and he of her again, for either loved other passing sore.

So when the knight, Sir Gaheris, saw his time, he came to their bedside all armed, with his sword naked, and suddenly gat his mother by the hair and struck off her head. When Sir Lamorak saw the blood dash upon him all hot, the which he loved passing well, wit you well he was sore abashed and dismayed of that dolorous knight. And therewithal, Sir Lamorak leapt out of the bed in his shirt as a knight dismayed saying thus:

'Ah, Sir Gaheris, knight of the Table Round, foul and evil have ye done, and to you great shame. Alas, why have ye slain your mother that bare you? With more right ye should have slain me.'

'The offence hast thou done,' said Gaheris, 'notwithstanding a man is born to offer his service; but yet shouldst thou beware with whom thou meddlest, for thou hast put me and my brethren to a shame, and thy father slew our father; and thou to lie by our mother is too much shame for us to suffer. And as for thy father, King Pellinor, my brother Sir Gawain and I slew him.'

'Ye did him the more wrong,' said Sir Lamorak, 'for my father slew not your father, it was Balin le Savage: and as yet my father's death is not revenged.'

'Leave those words,' said Sir Gaheris, 'for and thou speak feloniously I will slay thee. But because thou art naked I am ashamed to slay thee. But wit thou well, in what place I may get thee I shall slay thee. And now my mother is quit of thee;

and withdraw thee and take thine armour, that thou were gone.'

Sir Lamorak saw there was none other boot, but fast armed him, and took his horse and rode his way making great sorrow. But for the shame and dolour he would not ride to King Arthur's court, but rode another way.

But when it was known that Gaheris had slain his mother, the king was passing wroth, and commanded him to go out of his court. Wit ye well Sir Gawain was wroth that Gaheris had slain his mother and let Sir Lamorak escape. And for this matter was the king passing wroth, and so was Sir Lamorak, and many other knights.

'Sir,' said Sir Launcelot, 'here is a great mischief befallen by felony, and by forecast treason, that your sister is thus shamefully slain. And I dare say that it was wrought by treason; and I dare say ye shall lose that good knight, Sir Lamorak, the which is great pity. I wot well and am sure, and Sir Tristram wist it, he would never more come within your court, the which should grieve you much more and all your knights.'

'God defend,' said the noble King Arthur, 'that I should lose Sir Lamorak or Sir Tristram, for then twain of my chief knights of the Table Round were gone.'

'Sir,' said Sir Launcelot, 'I am sure ye shall lose Sir Lamorak, for Sir Gawain and his brethren will slay him by one mean or other; for they among them have concluded and sworn to slay him and ever they may see their time.'

'That shall I let,' said Arthur.

CHAPTER 25: *How Sir Agravain and Sir Mordred met with a knight fleeing, and how they both were overthrown, and of Sir Dinadan*

Now leave we of Sir Lamorak, and speak of Sir Gawain's brethren, and specially of Sir Agravain and Sir Mordred.

As they rode on their adventures they met a knight fleeing, sore wounded; and they asked him what tidings.

'Fair knights,' said he, 'here cometh a knight after me that will slay me.'

With that came Sir Dinadan riding to them by adventure, but he would promise them no help. But Sir Agravain and Sir Mordred promised him to rescue him. Therewithal came that knight straight unto them, and anon he proffered to joust. That saw Sir Mordred and rode to him, but he struck Mordred over his horse's tail. That saw Sir Agravain, and straight he rode toward that knight, and right so as he served Mordred so he served Agravain, and said to them,

'Sirs, wit ye well both that I am Breunis Saunce Pité, that hath done this to you.' And yet he rode over Agravain five or six times.

When Dinadan saw this, he must needs joust with him for shame. And so Dinadan and he encountered together, that with pure strength Sir Dinadan smote him over his horse's tail. Then he took his horse and fled, for he was on foot one of the valiantest knights in Arthur's days, and a great destroyer of all good knights. Then rode Sir Dinadan unto Sir Mordred and unto Sir Agravain.

'Sir knight,' said they all, 'well have ye done, and well have ye revenged us, wherefore we pray you tell us your name.'

'Fair sirs, ye ought to know my name, the which is called Sir Dinadan.'

When they understood that it was Dinadan they were more wroth than they were before, for they hated him out of measure because of Sir Lamorak. For Dinadan had such a custom that he loved all good knights that were valiant, and he hated all those that were destroyers of good knights. And there were none that hated Dinadan but those that ever were called murderers.

Then spake the hurt knight that Breunis Saunce Pité had chased, his name was Dalan, and said, 'If thou be Dinadan thou slewest my father.'

'It may well be so,' said Dinadan, 'but then it was in my defence and at his request.'

'By my head,' said Dalan, 'thou shalt die therefore,' and therewith he dressed his spear and his shield.

And to make the shorter tale, Sir Dinadan smote him down off his horse, that his neck was nigh broken. And in the same wise he smote Sir Mordred and Sir Agravain. And after, in the quest of the Sangrail, cowardly and feloniously they slew Dinadan, the which was great damage, for he was a great bourder and a passing good knight.

And so Sir Dinadan rode to a castle that hight Beale-Valet. And there he found Sir Palomides that was not yet whole of the wound that Sir Lamorak gave him. And there Dinadan told Palomides all the tidings that he heard and saw of Sir Tristram, and how he was gone with King Mark, 'and with him he hath all his will and desire.' Therewith Sir Palomides waxed wroth, for he loved La Beale Isoud. And then he wist well that Sir Tristram enjoyed her.

CHAPTER 26: *How King Arthur, the queen, and Launcelot received letters out of Cornwall, and of the answer again*

Now leave we Sir Palomides and Sir Dinadan in the Castle of Beale-Valet, and turn we again unto King Arthur. There came a knight out of Cornwall, his name was Fergus, a fellow of the Round Table. And there he told the king and Sir Launcelot good tidings of Sir Tristram, and there were brought goodly letters, and how he left him in the Castle of Tintagel.

Then came the damosel that brought goodly letters unto King Arthur and unto Sir Launcelot, and there she had passing good cheer of the king, and of the Queen Guenever, and of Sir Launcelot. Then they wrote goodly letters again. But Sir Launcelot bad ever Sir Tristram beware of King Mark, for ever he called him in his letters King Fox, as who saith, he fareth all with wiles and treason. Whereof Sir Tristram in his heart thanked Sir Launcelot.

Then the damosel went unto La Beale Isoud, and bare her

letters from the king and from Sir Launcelot, whereof she was in passing great joy.

'Fair damosel,' said La Beale Isoud, 'how fareth my lord Arthur, and the Queen Guenever, and the noble knight, Sir Launcelot?'

She answered, and to make short tale, 'Much the better that ye and Sir Tristram be in joy.'

'God reward them,' said La Beale Isoud, 'for Sir Tristram suffereth great pain for me, and I for him.'

So the damosel departed, and brought letters to King Mark. And when he had read them, and understood them, he was wroth with Sir Tristram, for he deemed that he had sent the damosel unto King Arthur. For Arthur and Launcelot in a manner threated King Mark. And as King Mark read these letters he deemed treason by Sir Tristram.

'Damosel,' said King Mark, 'will ye ride again and bear letters from me unto King Arthur?'

'Sir,' she said, 'I will be at your commandment to ride when ye will.'

'Ye say well,' said the king; 'come again,' said the king, 'to-morn, and fetch your letters.'

Then she departed and told them how she should ride again with letters unto Arthur.

'Then we pray you,' said La Beale Isoud and Sir Tristram, 'that when ye have received your letters, that ye would come by us that we may see the privity of your letters.'

'All that I may do, madam, ye wot well I must do for Sir Tristram, for I have been long his own maiden.'

So on the morn the damosel went to King Mark to have had his letters and to depart.

'I am not advised,' said King Mark, 'as at this time to send my letters.'

Then privily and secretly he sent letters unto King Arthur, and unto Queen Guenever, and unto Sir Launcelot. So the varlet departed, and found the king and queen in Wales, at Caerleon. And as the king and the queen were at mass the varlet came with the letters. And when mass was done the king and the queen opened the letters privily by themself. And the beginning of the king's letters spake wonderly short unto King Arthur, and bad him intermit with himself and with his wife, and of his knights, for he was able enough to rule and keep his wife.

CHAPTER 27: *How Sir Launcelot was wroth with the letter that he received from King Mark, and of Dinadan which made a lay of King Mark*

When King Arthur understood the letter, he mused of many things, and thought on his sister's words, Queen Morgan le Fay, that she had said betwixt Queen Guenever and Sir Launcelot. And in this thought he studied a great while. Then he bethought him again how his sister was his own enemy, and that she hated the queen and Sir Launcelot, and so he put all that out of his thought. Then King Arthur read the letter again, and the latter clause said that King Mark took Sir Tristram for his mortal enemy; wherefore he put Arthur out of doubt he would be revenged of Sir Tristram. Then was King Arthur wroth with King Mark.

And when Queen Guenever read her letter and understood it, she was wroth out of measure, for the letter spake shame by her and by Sir Launcelot. And so privily she sent the letter unto Sir Launcelot.

And when he wist the intent of the letter he was so wroth that he laid him down on his bed to sleep, whereof Sir Dinadan was ware, for it was his manner to be privy with all good knights. And as Sir Launcelot slept he stole the letter out of his hand, and read it word by word. And then he made great sorrow for anger. And so Sir Launcelot awaked, and went to a window, and read the letter again, the which made him angry.

'Sir,' said Dinadan, 'wherefore be ye angry? Discover your

intermit: concern himself.
by her and by Sir Launcelot: about her and Sir Launcelot.

54

heart to me; for sooth ye wot well I owe you good will, how-beit I am a poor knight and a servitor unto you and to all good knights. For though I be not of worship myself I love all those that be of worship.'

'It is truth,' said Sir Launcelot, 'ye are a trusty knight, and for great trust I will show you my counsel.'

And when Dinadan understood all, he said, 'This is my counsel: set you right nought by these threats, for King Mark is so villainous, that by fair speech shall never man get of him. But ye shall see what I shall do: I will make a lay for him, and when it is made I shall make an harper to sing it afore him.'

So anon he went and made it, and taught it an harper that hight Eliot. And when he could it he taught it to many harpers. And so by the will of Sir Launcelot, and of Arthur, the harpers went straight into Wales, and into Cornwall, to sing the lay that Sir Dinadan made by King Mark, the which was the worst lay that ever harper sang with harp or with any other instruments.

CHAPTER 28: *How Sir Tristram was hurt, and of a war made to King Mark; and of Sir Tristram how he promised to rescue him*

Now turn we again unto Sir Tristram and to King Mark. As Sir Tristram was at jousts and at tournament it fortuned he was sore hurt both with a spear and with a sword, but yet he won always the degree. And for to repose him he went to a good knight that dwelled in Cornwall, in a castle, whose name was Sir Dinas le Seneschal.

Then by misfortune there came out of Sessoine a great number of men of arms, and an hideous host, and they entered nigh the Castle of Tintagel; and their captain's name was Elias, a good man of arms.

When King Mark understood his enemies were entered

when he could it: when he knew it.

unto his land he made great dole and sorrow, for in no wise by his will King Mark would not send for Sir Tristram, for he hated him deadly. So when his council was come they devised and cast many perils of the strength of their enemies. And then they concluded all at once, and said thus unto King Mark:

'Sir, wit ye well ye must send for Sir Tristram, the good knight, or else they will never be overcome. For by Sir Tristram they must be foughten withal, or else we row against the stream.'

'Well,' said King Mark, 'I will do by your counsel;' but yet he was full loth thereto, but need constrained him to send for him.

Then was he sent for in all haste that might be, that he should come to King Mark. And when he understood that King Mark had sent for him, he mounted upon a soft ambler and rode to King Mark. And when he was come the king said thus:

'Fair nephew, Sir Tristram, this is all. Here be come our enemies of Sessoine, that are here nigh hand, and without tarrying they must be met with shortly, or else they will destroy this country.'

'Sir,' said Sir Tristram, 'wit ye well all my power is at your commandment. And wit ye well, sir, these eight days I may bear none arms, for my wounds be not yet whole. And by that day I shall do what I may.'

'Ye say well,' said King Mark; 'then go ye again and repose you and make you fresh, and I shall go and meet the Sessoins with all my power.'

So the king departed unto Tintagel, and Sir Tristram went to repose him.

And the king made a great host, and departed them in three; the first part led Sir Dinas the Seneschal, and Sir Andred led the second part, and Sir Argius led the third part; and he was of the blood of King Mark. And the Sessoins had three great battles, and many good men of arms.

And so King Mark by the advice of his knights issued out

of the Castle of Tintagel upon his enemies. And Dinas, the good knight, rode out afore, and slew two knights his own hands, and then began the battles. And there was marvellous breaking of spears and smiting of swords, and slew down many good knights. And ever was Sir Dinas the Seneschal the best of King Mark's party. And thus the battle endured long with great mortality. But at the last King Mark and Sir Dinas, were they never so loth, they withdrew them to the Castle of Tintagel with great slaughter of people; and the Sessoins followed on fast, that ten of them were put within the gates and four slain with the portcullis.

Then King Mark sent for Sir Tristram by a varlet, that told him all the mortality.

Then he sent the varlet again, and bad him: 'Tell King Mark that I will come as soon as I am whole, for erst I may do him no good.' Then King Mark had his answer.

Therewith came Elias and bad the king yield up the castle: 'For ye may not hold it no while.'

'Sir Elias,' said the king, 'so will I yield up the castle if I be not soon rescued.'

Anon King Mark sent again for rescue to Sir Tristram. By then Sir Tristram was whole, and he had gotten him ten good knights of Arthur's; and with them he rode unto Tintagel.

And when he saw the great host of Sessoins he marvelled wonder greatly. And then Sir Tristram rode by the woods and by the ditches as secretly as he might, till he came nigh the gates. And there dressed a knight to him when he saw that Sir Tristram would enter; and Sir Tristram smote him down dead, and so he served three more. And every each of these ten knights slew a man of arms. So Sir Tristram entered into the Castle of Tintagel. And when King Mark wist that Sir Tristram was come he was glad of his coming, and so was all the fellowship, and of him they made great joy.

CHAPTER 29: *How Sir Tristram overcame the battle, and how Elias desired a man to fight body for body*

So on the morn Elias the captain came, and bad King Mark: 'Come out and do battle; for now the good knight Sir Tristram is entered it will be shame to thee,' said Elias, 'for to keep thy walls.'

When King Mark understood this he was wroth and said no word, but went unto Sir Tristram and asked him his counsel.

'Sir,' said Sir Tristram, 'will ye that I give him his answer?'

'I will well,' said King Mark.

Then Sir Tristram said thus to the messenger: 'Bear thy lord word from the king and me, that we will do battle with him tomorn in the plain field.'

'What is your name?' said the messenger.

'Wit thou well my name is Sir Tristram de Liones.' Therewithal the messenger departed and told his lord Elias all that he had heard.

'Sir,' said Sir Tristram unto King Mark, 'I pray you give me leave to have the rule of the battle.'

'I pray you take the rule,' said King Mark.

Then Sir Tristram let devise the battle in what manner that it should be. He let depart his host in six parties, and ordained Sir Dinas the Seneschal to have the foreward, and other knights to rule the remnant. And the same night Sir Tristram burnt all the Sessoins' ships unto the cold water.

Anon as Elias wist that, he said it was of Sir Tristram's doing: 'For he casteth that we shall never escape, mother son of us. Therefore, fair fellows, fight freely tomorrow, and miscomfort you nought; for any knight, though he be the best knight in the world, he may not have ado with us all.'

Then they ordained their battles in four parties, wonderly well apparelled and garnished with men of arms. Thus they within issued, and they without set freely upon them; and there Sir Dinas did great deeds of arms. Notforthan Sir Dinas and his fellowship were put to the worse.

With that came Sir Tristram and slew two knights with one spear; then he slew on the right hand and on the left hand, that men marvelled that ever he might do such deeds of arms. And then he might see sometime the battle was driven a bow draught from the castle, and sometime it was at the gates of the castle.

Then came Elias the captain rashing here and there, and hit King Mark so sore upon the helm that he made him to avoid the saddle. And then Sir Dinas gat King Mark again to horseback.

Therewithal came in Sir Tristram like a lion, and there he met with Elias, and he smote him so sore upon the helm that he avoided his saddle. And thus they fought till it was night, and for great slaughter and for wounded people every each party drew to their rest.

And when King Mark was come within the Castle of Tintagel he lacked of his knights an hundred, and they without lacked two hundred; and they searched the wounded men on both parties. And then they went to council; and wit you well either party were loth to fight more, so that either might escape with their worship.

When Elias the captain understood the death of his men he made great dole; and when he wist that they were loth to go to battle again he was wroth out of measure. Then Elias sent word unto King Mark, in great despite, whether he would find a knight that would fight for him body for body. And if that he might slay King Mark's knight, he to have the truage of Cornwall yearly. 'And if that his knight slay mine, I fully release my claim forever.'

Then the messenger departed unto King Mark, and told him how that his lord Elias had sent him word to find a knight to do battle with him body for body. When King Mark understood the messenger, he bad him abide and he should have his answer.

notforthan: nevertheless.

Then called he all the baronage together to wit what was the best counsel. They said all at once, 'To fight in a field we have no lust, for had not been Sir Tristram's prowess it had been likely that we never should have escaped; and therefore, sir, as we deem, it were well done to find a knight that would do battle with him, for he knightly proffereth.'

CHAPTER 30: *How Sir Elias and Sir Tristram fought together for the truage, and how Sir Tristram slew Elias in the field*

Notforthan when all this was said, they could find no knight that would do battle with him.

'Sir king,' said they all, 'here is no knight that dare fight with Elias.'

'Alas,' said King Mark, 'then am I utterly ashamed and utterly destroyed, unless that my nephew Sir Tristram will take the battle upon him.'

'Wit you well,' they said all, 'he had yesterday overmuch on hand, and he is weary for travail, and sore wounded.'

'Where is he?' said King Mark.

'Sir,' said they, 'he is in his bed to repose him.'

'Alas,' said King Mark, 'but I have the succour of my nephew Sir Tristram, I am utterly destroyed for ever.'

Therewith one went to Sir Tristram where he lay, and told him what King Mark had said. And therewith Sir Tristram arose lightly, and put on him a long gown, and came afore the king and all the lords. And when he saw them all so dismayed he asked the king and the lords what tidings were with them.

'Never worse,' said the king. And therewith he told him all how he had word of Elias to find a knight to fight for the truage of Cornwall, 'and none can I find. And as for you,' said the king 'and all the lords, we may ask no more of you for shame; for through your hardiness yesterday ye saved all our lives.'[1]

'Sir,' said Sir Tristram, 'now I understand ye would have

my succour, reason would that I should do all that lieth in my power to do, saving my worship and my life, howbeit I am sore bruised and hurt. And sithen Sir Elias proffereth so largely, I shall fight with him, or else I will be slain in the field, or else I will deliver Cornwall from the old truage. And therefore lightly call his messenger and he shall be answered, for as yet my wounds be green, and they will be sorer a seven night after than they be now; and therefore he shall have his answer that I will do battle tomorn with him.'

Then was the messenger departed brought before King Mark.

'Hark, my fellow,' said Sir Tristram, 'go fast unto thy lord, and bid him make true assurance on his part for the truage, as the king here shall make on his part; and then tell thy lord, Sir Elias, that I, Sir Tristram, King Arthur's knight, and knight of the Table Round, will as tomorn meet with thy lord on horseback, to do battle as long as my horse may endure, and after that to do battle with him on foot to the utterance.'

The messenger beheld Sir Tristram from the top to the toe; and therewithal he departed and came to his lord, and told him how he was answered of Sir Tristram.

And therewithal was made hostage on both parties, and made it as sure as it might be, that whether party had the victory, so to end. And then were both hosts assembled on both parts of the field, without the Castle of Tintagel, and there was none but Sir Trisram and Sir Elias armed.

So when the appointment was made, they departed in sunder, and they came together with all the might that their horses might run. And either knight smote other so hard that both horses and knights went to the earth. Notforthan they both lightly arose and dressed their shields on their shoulders, with naked swords in their hands, and they dashed together that it seemed a flaming fire about them. Thus they traced and traversed, and hew on helms and hauberks, and cut away many cantels of their shields, and either wounded other passing sore, so that the hot blood fell freshly upon the earth.

And by then they had foughten the mountenance of an hour, Sir Tristram waxed faint and forbled, and gave sore aback. That saw Sir Elias, and followed fiercely upon him, and wounded him in many places. And ever Sir Tristram traced and traversed, and went froward him here and there, and covered him with his shield as he might all weakly, that all men said he was overcome; for Sir Elias had given him twenty strokes against one.

Then was there laughing of the Sessoins' party, and great dole on King Mark's party.

'Alas,' said the king, 'we are ashamed and destroyed all for ever.' For as the book saith, Sir Tristram was never so matched, but if it were Sir Launcelot.

Thus as they stood and beheld both parties, that one party laughing and the other party weeping, Sir Tristram remembered him of his lady, La Beale Isoud, that looked upon him, and how he was likely never to come in her presence. Then he pulled up his shield that erst hung full low. And then he dressed up his shield unto Elias, and gave him many sad strokes, twenty against one, and all to-brake his shield and his hauberk, that the hot blood ran down to the earth.

Then began King Mark to laugh, and all Cornish men, and that other party to weep.

And ever Sir Tristram said to Sir Elias, 'Yield thee.' Then when Sir Tristram saw him so staggering on the ground, he said, 'Sir Elias, I am right sorry for thee, for thou art a passing good knight as ever I met withal, except Sir Launcelot.' Therewithal Sir Elias fell to the earth, and there died.

'What shall I do,' said Sir Tristram unto King Mark, 'for this battle is at an end?'

Then they of Elias' party departed, and King Mark took of them many prisoners, to redress the harms and the scathes that he had of them; and the remnant he sent into their country to borow out their fellows.

Then was Sir Tristram searched and well healed. Yet for all this King Mark would fain have slain Sir Tristram. But

borow: ransom.

for all that ever Sir Tristram saw or heard by King Mark, yet would he never beware of his treason, but ever he would be thereas La Beale Isoud was.

CHAPTER 31: *How at a great feast that King Mark made an harper came and sang the lay that Dinadan had made*

Now will we pass of this matter, and speak we of the harpers that Sir Launcelot and Sir Dinadan had sent into Cornwall. And at the great feast that King Mark made for joy that the Sessoins were put out of his country, then came Eliot the harper with the lay that Dinadan had made, and secretly brought it unto Sir Tristram, and told him the lay that Dinadan had made by King Mark.

And when Sir Tristram heard it, he said, 'O Lord Jesu, that Dinadan can make wonderly well and ill, there as it shall be.'

'Sir,' said Eliot, 'dare I sing this song afore King Mark?'

'Yea, on my peril,' said Sir Tristram, 'for I shall be thy warrant.'

Then at the meat came in Eliot the harper, and because he was a curious harper men heard him sing the same lay that Dinadan had made, the which spake the most villainy by King Mark of his treason that ever man heard.

When the harper had sung his song to the end King Mark was wonderly wroth, and said, 'Thou harper, how durst thou be so bold on thy head to sing this song afore me.'

'Sir,' said Eliot, 'wit you well I am a minstrel, and I must do as I am commanded of these lords that I bear the arms of. And sir, wit ye well that Sir Dinadan, a knight of the Table Round, made this song, and made me to sing it afore you.'

'Thou sayest well,' said King Mark, 'and because thou art a minstrel thou shalt go quit, but I charge thee hie thee fast out of my sight.'

So the harper departed and went to Sir Tristram, and told him how he had sped. Then Sir Tristram let make letters as goodly as he could to Launcelot and to Sir Dinadan. And so he let conduct the harper out of the country.

But to say that King Mark was wonderly wroth, he was, for he deemed that the lay that was sung afore him was made by Sir Tristram's counsel, wherefore he thought to slay him and all his well-willers in that country.

CHAPTER 32: *How King Mark slew by treason his brother Boudwin, for good service that he had done to him*

Now turn we to another matter that fell between King Mark and his brother, that was called the good Prince Boudwin, that all the people of the country loved passing well.

So it befell on a time that the miscreants Saracens landed in the country of Cornwall soon after these Sessoins were gone. And then the good Prince Boudwin, at the landing, he araised the country privily and hastily. And or it were day he let put wild fire in three of his own ships, and suddenly he pulled up the sail, and with the wind he made those ships to be driven among the navy of the Saracens. And to make short tale, those three ships set on fire all the ships, that none were saved. And at point of the day the good Prince Boudwin with all his fellowship set on the miscreants with shouts and cries, and slew to the number of forty thousand, and left none alive.

When King Mark wist this he was wonderly wroth that his brother should win such worship. And because this prince was better beloved than he in all that country, and that also Boudwin loved well Sir Tristram, therefore he thought to slay him.

And thus, hastily, as a man out of his wit, he sent for Prince Boudwin and Anglides his wife, and bad them bring their young son with them, that he might see him. All this he did to the intent to slay the child as well as his father, for he was the falsest traitor that ever was born. Alas, for his good-

araised: raised, levied.

ness and for his good deeds this gentle Prince Boudwin was slain.

So when he came with his wife Anglides, the king made them fair semblant till they had dined. And when they had dined King Mark sent for his brother and said thus:

'Brother, how sped you when the miscreants arrived by you? Meseemeth it had been your part to have sent me word, that I might have been at that journey, for it had been reason that I had had the honour and not you.'

'Sir,' said the Prince Boudwin, 'it was so that and I tarried till that I had sent for you those miscreants had destroyed my country.'

'Thou liest, false traitor,' said King Mark, 'for thou art ever about for to win worship from me, and put me to dishonour, and thou cherishest that I hate.'

And therewith he struck him to the heart with a dagger, that he never after spake word.

Then the lady Anglides made great dole, and swooned, for she saw her lord slain afore her face.

Then was there no more to do but Prince Boudwin was despoiled and brought to burials. But Anglides privily gat her husband's doublet and his shirt, and that she kept secretly.

Then was there much sorrow and crying, and great dole made Sir Tristram, Sir Dinas, Sir Fergus, and so did all knights that were there; for that prince was passingly well beloved.

So La Beale Isoud sent unto Anglides, the Prince Boudwin's wife, and bad her avoid lightly or else her young son, Alisander le Orphelin, should be slain. When she heard this, she took her horse and her child, and rode with such poor men as durst ride with her.

CHAPTER 33: *How Anglides, Boudwin's wife, escaped with her young son, Alisander le Orphelin, and came to the Castle of Arundel*

Notwithstanding, when King Mark had done this deed, yet he thought to do more vengeance; and with his sword in his hand, he sought from chamber to chamber, to seek Anglides and her young son. And when she was missed he called a good knight that hight Sadok, and charged him by pain of death to fetch Anglides again and her young son.

So Sir Sadok departed and rode after Anglides. And within ten mile he overtook her, and bad her turn again and ride with him to King Mark.

'Alas, fair knight,' she said, 'what shall ye win by my son's death or by mine? I have had overmuch harm and too great a loss.'

'Madam,' said Sadok, 'of your loss is dole and pity. But madam,' said Sadok, 'would ye depart out of this country with your son, and keep him till he be of age, that he may revenge his father's death, then would I suffer you to depart from me, so ye promise me to revenge the death of Prince Boudwin.'

'Ah, gentle knight, Jesu thank thee, and if ever my son, Alisander le Orphelin, live to be a knight, he shall have his father's doublet and his shirt with the bloody marks, and I shall give him such a charge that he shall remember it whiles he liveth.'

And therewithal Sadok departed from her, and either betook other to God.

And when Sadok came to King Mark he told him faithfully that he had drowned young Alisander her son; and thereof King Mark was full glad.

Now turn we unto Anglides, that rode both night and day by adventure out of Cornwall, and little and in few places she rested; but ever she drew southward to the seaside, till by fortune she came to a castle that is called Magouns, and now it is called Arundel, in Sussex. And the constable of the castle welcomed her, and said she was welcome to her own castle; and there was Anglides worshipfully received, for the constable's wife was nigh her cousin, and the constable's name was Bellangere; and that same constable told Anglides that the same castle was hers by right inheritance.

Thus Anglides endured years and winters, till Alisander was big and strong; there was none so wight in all that country, neither there was none that might do no manner of mastery afore him.

CHAPTER 34: *How Anglides gave the bloody doublet to Alisander, her son, the same day that he was made knight, and the charge withal*

Then upon a day Bellangere the constable came to Anglides and said, 'Madam, it were time my lord Alisander were made knight, for he is a passing strong young man.'

'Sir,' said she, 'I would he were made knight; but then must I give him the most charge that ever sinful mother gave to her child.'

'Do as ye list,' said Bellangere, 'and I shall give him warning that he shall be made knight. Now it will be well done that he may be made knight at Our Lady Day in Lent.'

'Be it so,' said Anglides, 'and I pray you make ready therefore.'

So came the constable to Alisander, and told him that he should at Our Lady Day in Lent be made knight.

'I thank God,' said Alisander; 'these are the best tidings that ever came to me.'

Then the constable ordained twenty of the greatest gentlemen's sons, and the best born men of the country, that should be made knights that same day that Alisander was made knight. So on the same day that Alisander and his twenty fellows were made knights, at the offering of the mass there came Anglides unto her son and said thus:

'O fair sweet son, I charge thee upon my blessing, and of the high order of chivalry that thou takest here this day, that thou understand what I shall say and charge thee withal.'

Therewithal she pulled out a bloody doublet and a bloody shirt, that were bebled with old blood. When Alisander saw this he start aback and waxed pale, and said, 'Fair mother, what may this mean?'

'I shall tell thee, fair son: this was thine own father's doublet and shirt, that he wore upon him that same day that he was slain.' And there she told him why and wherefore, and how 'for his goodness King Mark slew him with his dagger afore mine own eyen. And therefore this shall be your charge that I shall give thee:

CHAPTER 35: *How it was told to King Mark of Alisander, and how he would have slain Sir Sadok for saving of his life*

'Now I require thee, and charge thee upon my blessing and upon the high order of knighthood, that thou be revenged upon King Mark for the death of thy father.' And therewithal she swooned.

Then Alisander leapt to his mother, and took her up in his arms, and said, 'Fair mother, ye have given me a great charge, and here I promise you I shall be avenged upon King Mark when that I may; and that I promise to God and to you.'

So this feast was ended, and the constable, by the advice of Anglides, let purvey that Alisander was well horsed and harnessed. Then he jousted with his twenty fellows that were made knights with him, but for to make a short tale, he overthrew all those twenty, that none might withstand him a buffet.

Then one of those knights departed unto King Mark, and told him all, how Alisander was made knight, and all the charge that his mother gave him, as ye have heard afore time.

'Alas, false treason,' said King Mark, 'I weened that young traitor had been dead. Alas, whom may I trust?'

And therewithal King Mark took a sword in his hand, and sought Sir Sadok from chamber to chamber to slay him. When Sir Sadok saw King Mark come with his sword in his hand he said thus:

'Beware, King Mark, and come not nigh me; for wit thou well that I saved Alisander his life, of which I never repent me, for thou falsely and cowardly slew his father Boudwin, traitorly for his good deeds; wherefore I pray Almighty Jesu send Alisander might and strength to be revenged upon thee. And now beware King Mark of young Alisander, for he is made a knight.'

'Alas,' said King Mark, 'that ever I should hear a traitor say so afore me.'

And therewith four knights of King Mark's drew their swords to slay Sir Sadok, but anon Sir Sadok slew them all in King Mark's presence. And then Sir Sadok passed forth into his chamber, and took his horse and his harness, and rode on his way a good pace. For there was neither Sir Tristram, neither Sir Dinas, nor Sir Fergus, that would Sir Sadok any evil will.

Then was King Mark wroth, and thought to destroy Sir Alisander and Sir Sadok that had saved him; for King Mark dread and hated Alisander most of any man living.

When Sir Tristram understood that Alisander was made knight, anon forthwithal he sent him a letter, praying him and charging him that he would draw him to the court of King Arthur, and that he put him in the rule and in the hands of Sir Launcelot. So this letter was sent to Alisander from his cousin, Sir Tristram. And at that time he thought to do after his commandment.

Then King Mark called a knight that brought him the tidings from Alisander, and bad him abide still in that country.

'Sir,' said the knight, 'so must I do, for in mine own country I dare not come.'

'No force,' said King Mark, 'I shall give thee here double as much lands as ever thou hadst of thine own.'

But within short space Sir Sadok met with that false knight, and slew him. Then was King Mark wood wroth out of measure. Then he sent unto Queen Morgan le Fay, and to the Queen of Northgales, praying them in his letters that they two sorceresses would set all the country in fire with ladies that were enchantresses, and by such that were dangerous knights, as Malgrin, Breunis Saunce Pité, that by no mean Alisander le Orphelin should escape, but other he should be taken or slain. This ordinance made King Mark for to destroy Alisander.

CHAPTER 36: *How Sir Alisander won the prize at a tournament, and of Morgan le Fay: and how he fought with Sir Malgrin, and slew him*

Now turn we again unto Sir Alisander, that at his departing his mother, took with him his father's bloody shirt. So that he bare with him always till his death day, in tokening to think on his father's death.

So was Alisander purposed to ride to London, by the counsel of Sir Tristram, to Sir Launcelot. And by fortune he went by the seaside, and rode wrong. And there he won at a tournament the gree that King Carados made. And there he smote down King Carados and twenty of his knights, and also Sir Safer, a good knight that was Sir Palomides' brother, the good knight.

All this saw a damosel, and saw the best knight joust that ever she saw. And ever as he smote down knights he made them to swear to wear none harness in a twelvemonth and a day.

'This is well said,' said Morgan le Fay,[1] 'this is the knight that I would fain see.'

And so she took her palfrey, and rode a great while, and then she rested her in her pavilion. So there came four knights, two were armed, and two were unarmed, and they told Morgan le Fay their names: the first was Elias de Gomeret, the second was Car de Gomeret, those were armed; that other twain were of Camelerd, cousins unto Queen Guenever, and that one hight Guy, and that other hight Garaunt, those were unarmed.

There these four knights told Morgan le Fay how a young knight had smitten them down before a castle. 'For the maiden of that castle said that he was but late made knight, and young. But as we suppose, but if it were Sir Tristram, or Sir Launcelot, or Sir Lamorak, the good knight, there is none that might sit him a buffet with a spear.'

'Well,' said Morgan le Fay, 'I shall meet that knight or it be long time, and he dwell in that country.'

So turn we to the damosel of the castle, that when Alisander le Orphelin had forjousted the four knights, she called him to her, and said thus:

'Sir knight, wilt thou for my sake joust and fight with a knight, for my sake, of this country, that is and hath been long time an evil neighbour to me? His name is Malgrin, and he will not suffer me to be married in no manner wise for all that I can do, or any knight for my sake.'

'Damosel,' said Alisander, 'and he come whiles I am here I will fight with him, and my poor body for your sake I will jeopard.'

And therewithal she sent for him, for he was at her commandment. And when either had a sight of other, they made them ready for to joust, and they came together eagerly, and Malgrin bruised his spear upon Alisander, and Alisander smote him again so hard that he bare him quite from his saddle to the earth.

But this Malgrin arose lightly and dressed his shield and drew his sword, and bad him alight, saying, 'Though thou have the better of me on horseback, thou shalt find that I shall endure like a knight on foot.'

'It is well said,' said Alisander; and so lightly he avoided his horse and betook him to his varlet.

And then they rashed together like two boars, and laid on their helms and shields long time, by the space of three hours, that never man could say which was the better knight. And in the meanwhile came Morgan le Fay to the damosel of the castle, and they beheld the battle.

But this Malgrin was an old roted knight, and he was called one of the dangerous knights of the world to do battle on foot, but on horseback there were many better. And ever this Malgrin awaited to slay Alisander, and so wounded him wonderly sore, that it was marvel that ever he might stand, for he had bled so much blood; for Alisander fought wildly, and not wittily. And that other was a felonious knight, and awaited him, and smote him sore. And sometime they rashed together with their shields, like two boars or rams, and fell grovelling both to the earth.

'Now knight,' said Malgrin, 'hold thy hand a while, and tell me what thou art.'

'I will not,' said Alisander, 'but if me list.'

'But tell me thy name, and why thou keepest this country, or else thou shalt die of my hands. Wit thou well,' said Malgrin, 'that for this maiden's love, of this castle, I have slain ten good knights by mishap; and by outrage and orgulity of myself I have slain ten other knights.'

'So God me help,' said Alisander, 'this is the foulest confession that ever I heard knight make, nor never heard I speak of other men of such a shameful confession; wherefore it were great pity and great shame unto me that I should let thee live any longer; therefore keep thee as well as ever thou mayst, for as I am true knight, either thou shalt slay me or else I shall slay thee, I promise thee faithfully.'

Then they lashed together fiercely, and at the last Alisander smote Malgrin to the earth. And then he rased off his helm, and smote off his head lightly. And when he had done and ended this battle, anon he called to him his varlet, the which brought him his horse. And then he, weening to be strong enough, would have mounted.

roted: practised. *wittily*: cleverly.

And so she laid Sir Alisander in an horse litter, and led him into the castle, for he had no foot ne might to stand upon the earth; for he had sixteen great wounds, and in especial one of them was like to be his death.

CHAPTER 37 : *How Queen Morgan le Fay had Alisander in her castle, and how she healed his wounds*

Then Queen Morgan le Fay searched his wounds, and gave such an ointment unto him that he should have died. And on the morn when she came to him he complained him sore; and then she put other ointments upon him, and then he was out of his pain.

Then came the damosel of the castle, and said unto Morgan le Fay, 'I pray you help me that this knight might wed me, for he hath won me with his hands.'

'Ye shall see,' said Morgan le Fay, 'what I shall say.'

Then Morgan le Fay went unto Alisander, and bad in any-wise that he should 'refuse this lady, and she desire to wed you, for she is not for you.'

So the damosel came and desired of him marriage.

'Damosel,' said Orphelin, 'I thank you, but as yet I cast me not to marry in this country.'

'Sir,' she said, 'sithen ye will not marry me, I pray you inso-much as ye have won me, that ye will give me to a knight of this country that hath been my friend, and loved me many years.'

'With all my heart,' said Alisander, 'I will assent thereto.'

Then was the knight sent for, his name was Gerin le Grose. And anon he made them handfast, and wedded them.

Then came Queen Morgan le Fay to Alisander, and bad him arise, and put him in an horse litter, and gave him such a drink that in three days and three nights he waked never, but slept; and so she brought him to her own castle that at that time was called La Beale Regard. Then Morgan le Fay came to Alisander, and asked him if he would fain be whole.

'Who would be sick,' said Alisander, 'and he might be whole?'

'Well,' said Morgan le Fay, 'then shall ye promise me by your knighthood that this day twelvemonth and a day ye shall not pass the compass of this castle, and without doubt ye shall lightly be whole.'

'I assent,' said Sir Alisander. And there he made her a promise; then was he soon whole.

And when Alisander was whole, then he repented him of his oath, for he might not be revenged upon King Mark.

Right so there came a damosel that was cousin to the Earl of Pase, and she was cousin to Morgan le Fay. And by right that castle of La Beale Regard should have been hers by true inheritance. So this damosel entered into this castle where lay Alisander, and there she found him upon his bed, passing heavy and all sad.

CHAPTER 38: *How Alisander was delivered from the queen Morgan le Fay by the mean of a damosel*

'Sir knight,' said the damosel, 'and ye would be merry I could tell you good tidings.'

'Well were me,' said Alisander, 'and I might hear of good tidings, for now I stand as a prisoner by my promise.'

'Sir,' she said, 'wit ye well that ye be a prisoner, and worse than ye ween; for my lady, my cousin Queen Morgan le Fay, keepeth you here for none other intent but for to do her pleasure with you when it liked her.'

'O Jesu defend me,' said Alisander, 'from such pleasure; for I had lever cut away my hangers than I would do her such pleasure.'

'As Jesu help me,' said the damosel, 'and ye would love me and be ruled by me, I shall make your deliverance with your worship.'

'Tell me,' said Alisander, 'by what mean, and ye shall have my love.'

'Fair knight,' said she, 'this castle of right ought to be mine, and I have an uncle the which is a mighty earl, he is Earl of Pase, and of all folks he hateth most Morgan le Fay; and I shall send unto him and pray him for my sake to destroy this castle for the evil customs that be used therein; and then will he come and set wild-fire on every part of the castle, and I shall get you out at a privy postern, and there shall ye have your horse and your harness.'

'Ye say well, damosel,' said Alisander.

And then she said, 'Ye may keep the room of this castle this twelvemonth and a day, then break ye not your oath.'

'Truly, fair damosel,' said Alisander, 'ye say sooth.'

And then he kissed her, and did to her pleasance as it pleased them both at times and leisures.

So anon she sent unto her uncle and bad him come and destroy that castle, for as the book saith, he would have destroyed that castle afore time had not that damosel been.

When the earl understood her letters he sent her word again that on such a day he would come and destroy that castle.

So when that day came she showed Alisander a postern wherethrough he should flee into a garden, and there he should find his armour and his horse. When the day came that was set, thither came the Earl of Pase with four hundred knights, and set on fire all the parts of the castle, that or they ceased they left not a stone standing.

And all this while that the fire was in the castle he abode in the garden. And when the fire was done he let make a cry that he would keep that piece of earth thereas the castle of La Beale Regard was a twelvemonth and a day, from all manner knights that would come.

So it happed there was a duke that hight Ansirus, and he was of the kin of Sir Launcelot. And this knight was a great pilgrim, for every third year he would be at Jerusalem. And because he used all his life to go in pilgrimage men called him Duke Ansirus the Pilgrim. And this duke had a daughter that hight Alice, that was a passing fair woman, and because of her father she was called Alice la Beale Pilgrim.

And anon as she heard of this cry she went unto Arthur's court, and said openly in hearing of many knights, that 'what knight may overcome that knight that keepeth that piece of earth shall have me and all my lands.'

When the knights of the Round Table heard her say thus many were glad, for she was passing fair and of great rents.

Right so she let cry in castles and towns as fast on her side as Alisander did on his side. Then she dressed her pavilion straight by the piece of the earth that Alisander kept.

So she was not so soon there but there came a knight of Arthur's court that hight Sagramore le Desirous, and he proffered to joust with Alisander; and they encountered, and Sagramore le Desirous bruised his spear upon Sir Alisander, but Sir Alisander smote him so hard that he avoided his saddle.

And when La Beale Alice saw him joust so well, she thought him a passing goodly knight on horseback. And then she leapt out of her pavilion, and took Sir Alisander by the bridle, and thus she said:

'Fair knight, I require thee of thy knighthood show me thy visage.'

'I dare well,' said Alisander, 'show my visage.'

And then he put off his helm, and she saw his visage, she said, 'O sweet Jesu, thee I must love, and never other.'

'Then show me your visage,' said he.

CHAPTER 39: *How Alisander met with Alice la Beale Pilgrim, and how he jousted with two knights; and after of him and of Sir Mordred*

Then she unwimpled her visage.

And when he saw her he said, 'Here have I found my love and my lady. Truly, fair lady,' said he, 'I promise you to be your knight, and none other that beareth the life.'

'Now, gentle knight,' said she, 'tell me your name.'

'My name is,' said he, 'Alisander le Orphelin. Now, damosel, tell me your name,' said he.

'My name is,' said she, 'Alice la Beale Pilgrim. And when we be more at our heart's ease, both ye and I shall tell other of what blood we be come.' So there was great love betwixt them.

And as they thus talked there came a knight that hight Harsouse le Berbeus, and asked part of Sir Alisander's spears.

Then Sir Alisander encountered with him, and at the first Sir Alisander smote him over his horse's croup.

And then there came another knight that hight Sir Hewgon, and Sir Alisander smote him down as he did that other.

Then Sir Hewgon proffered to do battle on foot. Sir Alisander overcame him with three strokes, and there would have slain him had he not yielded him.

So then Alisander made both those knights to swear to wear none armour in a twelvemonth and a day. Then Sir Alisander alit down, and went to rest him and repose him.

Then the damosel that halp Sir Alisander out of the castle, in her play told Alice all together how he was prisoner in the castle of La Beale Regard, and there she told her how she gat him out of prison.

'Sir,' said Alice la Beale Pilgrim, 'meseemeth ye are much beholding to this maiden.'

'That is truth,' said Sir Alisander.

And there Alice told him of what blood she was come. 'Sir, wit ye well,' she said, 'that I am of the blood of King Ban, that was father unto Sir Launcelot.'

'Iwis, fair lady,' said Alisander, 'my mother told me that my father was brother unto a king, and I am nigh cousin unto Sir Tristram.'

Then this while came there three knights, that one hight Vains, and the other hight Harvis de les Marches, and the third hight Perin de la Montaine. And with one spear Sir Alisander smote them down all three, and gave them such falls that they had no list to fight upon foot. So he made them to swear to wear none arms in a twelvemonth.

So when they were departed Sir Alisander beheld his lady Alice on horseback as he stood in her pavilion. And then was he so enamoured upon her that he wist not whether he were on horseback or on foot.

Right so came the false knight Sir Mordred, and saw Sir Alisander was assotted upon his lady; and therewithal he took his horse by the bridle, and led him here and there, and had cast to have led him out of that place to have shamed him.

When the damosel that halp him out of that castle saw how shamefully he was led, anon she let arm her, and set a shield upon her shoulder; and therewith she mounted upon his horse, and gat a naked sword in her hand, and she thrust unto Alisander with all her might, and she gave him such a buffet that he thought the fire flew out of his eyen.

And when Alisander felt that stroke he looked about him, and drew his sword. And when she saw that, she fled, and so did Mordred into the forest, and the damosel fled into the pavilion.

So when Alisander understood himself how the false knight would have shamed him had not the damosel been, then was he wroth with himself that Sir Mordred was so escaped his hands. But then Sir Alisander and Alice had good game at the damosel, how sadly she hit him upon the helm.

Then Sir Alisander jousted thus day by day, and on foot he did many battles with many knights of King Arthur's court, and with many knights strangers. Therefore to tell all the battles that he did, it were overmuch to rehearse, for every day within that twelvemonth he had ado with one knight or with other, and some day he had ado with three or with four; and there was never knight that put him to the worse.

And at the twelvemonth's end he departed with his lady, Alice la Beale Pilgrim. And the damosel would never go from him, and so they went into their country of Benwick, and lived there in great joy.

CHAPTER 40: *How Sir Galahaut did do cry a jousts in Surluse, and Queen Guenever's knights should joust against all that would come*

But as the book saith, King Mark would never stint till he had slain him by treason. And by Alice he gat a child that hight Bellengerus le Beuse. And by good fortune he came to the court of King Arthur, and proved a passing good knight; and he revenged his father's death, for the false King Mark slew both Sir Tristram and Alisander falsely and feloniously.

And it happed so that Alisander had never grace ne fortune to come to King Arthur's court. For and he had comen to Sir Launcelot, all knights said that knew him, he was one of the strongest knights that was in Arthur's days, and great dole was made for him. So let we of him pass, and turn we to another tale.

So it befell that Sir Galahaut, the Haut Prince, was lord of the country of Surluse, whereof came many good knights. And this noble prince was a passing good man of arms, and ever he held a noble fellowship together. And then he came to Arthur's court and told him his intent, how this was his will, how he would let cry a jousts in the country of Surluse, the which country was within the lands of King Arthur, and there he asked leave to let cry a jousts.

'I will give you leave,' said King Arthur; 'but wit thou well,' said King Arthur, 'I may not be there.'

'Sir,' said Queen Guenever, 'please it you to give me leave to be at that jousts.'

'With right good will,' said Arthur; 'for Sir Galahaut, the Haut Prince, shall have you in governance.'

'Sir,' said Galahaut, 'I will as ye will.'

'Sir,' then [said] the queen, 'I will take with me and such knights as pleasen me best.'

'Do as ye list,' said King Arthur.

So anon she commanded Sir Launcelot to make him ready

with such knights as he thought best. So in every good town and castle of this land was made a cry, that in the country of Surluse Sir Galahaut should make a jousts that should last eight days, and how the Haut Prince, with the help of Queen Guenever's knights, should joust against all manner of men that would come. When this cry was known, kings and princes, dukes and earls, barons and noble knights, made them ready to be at that jousts. And at the day of jousting there came in Sir Dinadan disguised, and did many great deeds of arms.

CHAPTER 41: *How Sir Launcelot fought in the tournament, and how Sir Palomides did arms there for a damosel*

Then at the request of Queen Guenever and of King Bagdemagus Sir Launcelot came into the range, but he was disguised, and that was the cause that few folk knew him; and there met with him Sir Ector de Maris, his own brother, and either brake their spears upon other to their hands. And then either gat another spear. And then Sir Launcelot smote down Sir Ector de Maris, his own brother.

That saw Sir Bleoberis, and he smote Sir Launcelot such a buffet upon the helm that he wist not well where he was. Then Sir Launcelot was wroth, and smote Sir Bleoberis so sore upon the helm that his head bowed down backward. And he smote eft another buffet, that he avoided his saddle; and so he rode by, and thrust forth to the thickest.

When the King of Northgales saw Sir Ector and Bleoberis lie on the ground then was he wroth, for they came on his party against them of Surluse. So the King of Northgales ran to Sir Launcelot, and brake a spear upon him all to pieces. Therewith Sir Launcelot overtook the King of Northgales, and smote him such a buffet on the helm with his sword that he made him to avoid his horse; and anon the king was horsed again.

So both the King Bagdemagus' and the King of Northgales' party hurled to other; and then began a strong medley, but they of Northgales were far bigger.

When Sir Launcelot saw his party go to the worst he thrang into the thickest press with a sword in his hand; and there he smote down on the right hand and on the left hand, and pulled down knights and rased off their helms, that all men had wonder that ever one knight might do such deeds of arms.

When Sir Meliagaunt, that was son unto King Bagdemagus, saw how Sir Launcelot fared he marvelled greatly. And when he understood that it was he, he wist well that he was disguised for his sake. Then Sir Meliagaunt prayed a knight to slay Sir Launcelot's horse, other with sword or with spear.

At that time King Bagdemagus met with a knight that hight Sauseise, a good knight, to whom he said, 'Now fair Sauseise, encounter with my son Meliagaunt and give him large payment, for I would he were well beaten of thy hands, that he might depart out of this field.'

And then Sir Sauseise encountered with Sir Meliagaunt, and either smote other down. And then they fought on foot, and there Sauseise had won Sir Meliagaunt, had not there come rescues.

So then the Haut Prince blew to lodging, and every knight unarmed him and went to the great feast.

Then in the meanwhile there came a damosel to the Haut Prince, and complained that there was a knight that hight Goneries that withheld her all her lands. Then the knight was there present, and cast his glove to him or to any that would fight in her name. So the damosel took up the glove all heavily for default of a champion.

Then there came a varlet to her and said, 'Damosel, will ye do after me?'

'Full fain,' said the damosel.

'Then go ye unto such a knight that lieth here beside in an hermitage, and that followeth the Questing Beast, and pray him to take the battle upon him, and anon I wot well he will grant you.'

So anon she took her palfrey, and within a while she found that knight, that was Sir Palomides. And when she required him, he armed him and rode with her, and made her to go to the Haut Prince, and to ask leave for her knight to do battle.

'I will well,' said the Haut Prince.

Then the knights were ready in the field to joust on horse-back; and either gat a spear in their hands, and met so fiercely together that their spears all to-shivered. Then they flung out swords, and Sir Palomides smote Sir Goneries down to the earth. And then he rased off his helm and smote off his head.

Then they went to supper, and the damosel loved Palomides as paramour, but the book saith she was of his kin. So then Palomides disguised himself in this manner; in his shield he bare the Questing Beast, and in all his trappers. And when he was thus ready, he sent to the Haut Prince to give him leave to joust with other knights, but he was adoubted of Sir Launcelot. The Haut Prince sent him word again that he should be welcome, and that Sir Launcelot should not joust with him. Then Sir Galahaut, the Haut Prince, let cry what knight somever he were that smote down Sir Palomides should have his damosel to himself.

CHAPTER 42 : How Sir Galahaut and Palomides fought to-gether, and of Sir Dinadan and Sir Galahaut

Here beginneth the second day. Anon as Sir Palomides came into the field, Sir Galahaut, the Haut Prince, was at the range end, and met with Sir Palomides, and he with him, with great spears. And then they came so hard together that their spears all to-shivered, but Sir Galahaut smote him so hard that he bare him backward over his horse, but yet he lost not his stirrups. Then they drew their swords and lashed together many sad strokes, that many worshipful knights left their

adoubted: afraid.   range end: the end of the line of battle.

business to behold them. But at the last Sir Galahaut, the Haut Prince, smote a stroke of might unto Palomides, sore upon the helm; but the helm was so hard that the sword might not bite, but slipped and smote off the head of the horse of Sir Palomides.

When the Haut Prince wist and saw the good knight fall unto the earth he was ashamed of that stroke. And therewith he alit down off his own horse, and prayed the good knight, Palomides, to take that horse of his gift, and to forgive him that deed.

'Sir,' said Palomides, 'I thank you of your great goodness, for ever of a man of worship a knight shall never have disworship'; and so he mounted upon that horse, and the Haut Prince had another anon.

'Now,' said the Haut Prince, 'I release to you that maiden, for ye have won her.'

'Ah,' said Palomides, 'the damosel and I be at your commandment.'

So they departed, and Sir Galahaut did great deeds of arms. And right so came Dinadan and encountered with Sir Galahaut, and either came to other so fast with their spears that their spears brake to their hands. But Dinadan had weened the Haut Prince had been more weary than he was. And then he smote many sad strokes at the Haut Prince; but when Dinadan saw he might not get him to the earth he said, 'My lord, I pray you leave me, and take another.' The Haut Prince knew not Dinadan, and left goodly for his fair words.

And so they departed; but soon there came another and told the Haut Prince that it was Dinadan.

'Forsooth,' said the prince, 'therefore am I heavy that he is so escaped from me, for with his mocks and japes now shall I never have done with him.'

And then Galahaut rode fast after him, and bad him: 'Abide, Dinadan, for King Arthur's sake.'

'Nay,' said Dinadan, 'so God me help, we meet no more together this day.'

Then in that wrath the Haut Prince met with Meliagaunt,

and he smote him in the throat that and he had fallen his neck had broken; and with the same spear he smote down another knight.

Then came in they of Northgales and many strangers, and were like to have put them of Surluse to the worse, for Sir Galahaut, the Haut Prince, had ever much in hand. So there came the good knight, Semound the Valiant, with forty knights, and he beat them all aback.

Then the Queen Guenever and Sir Launcelot let blow to lodging, and every knight unarmed him, and dressed them to the feast.

CHAPTER 43: *How Sir Archade appelled Sir Palomides of treason, and how Sir Palomides slew him*

When Palomides was unarmed he asked lodging for himself and the damosel. Anon the Haut Prince commanded them to lodging. And he was not so soon in his lodging but there came a knight that hight Archade, he was brother unto Goneries that Palomides slew afore in the damosel's quarrel. And this knight, Archade, called Sir Palomides traitor, and appelled him for the death of his brother.

'By the leave of the Haut Prince,' said Palomides, 'I shall answer thee.'

When Sir Galahaut understood their quarrel he bad them go to dinner : 'And as soon as ye have dined look that either knight be ready in the field.'

So when they had dined they were armed both, and took their horses, and the queen, and the prince, and Sir Launcelot, were set to behold them; and so they let run their horses, and there Sir Palomides bare Archade on his spear over his horse's tail. And then Palomides alit and drew his sword, but Sir Archade might not arise; and there Sir Palomides rased off his helm, and smote off his head. Then the Haut Prince and Queen Guenever went unto supper.

Then King Bagdemagus sent away his son Meliagaunt be-

cause Sir Launcelot should not meet with him, for he hated
Sir Launcelot, and that knew he not.

CHAPTER 44: *Of the third day, and how Sir Palomides
jousted with Sir Lamorak, and other things*

Now beginneth the third day of jousting; and at that day
King Bagdemagus made him ready; and there came against
him King Marsil, that had in gift an island of Sir Galahaut the
Haut Prince; and this island had the name Pomitain.

Then it befell that King Bagdemagus and King Marsil of
Pomitain met together with spears, and King Marsil had such
a buffet that he fell over his horse's croup. Then came there
in a knight of King Marsil to revenge his lord, and King
Bagdemagus smote him down, horse and man, to the earth.

So there came an earl that hight Arrouse, and Sir Breunis,
and an hundred knights with them of Pomitain, and the King
of Northgales was with them; and all these were against them
of Surluse. And then there began great battle, and many
knights were cast under horses' feet. And ever King Bagdemagus did best, for he first began, and ever he held on.
Gaheris, Gawain's brother, smote ever at the face of King
Bagdemagus; and at last King Bagdemagus hurtled down
Gaheris, horse and man.

Then by adventure Sir Palomides, the good knight, met
with Sir Blamor de Ganis, Sir Bleoberis' brother. And either
smote other with great spears, that both their horses and
knights fell to the earth. But Sir Blamor had such a fall that
he had almost broken his neck, for the blood brast out at nose,
mouth, and his ears, but at the last he recovered well by good
surgeons.

Then there came in the Duke Chaleins of Clarance; and in
his governance there came a knight that hight Elis la Noire;
and there encountered with him King Bagdemagus, and he
smote Elis that he made him to avoid his saddle. So the Duke
Chaleins of Clarance did there great deeds of arms, and of so

late as he came in the third day there was no man did so well except King Bagdemagus and Sir Palomides, that the prize was given that day to King Bagdemagus. And then they blew unto lodging and unarmed them, and went to the feast.

Right so came Dinadan, and mocked and japed with King Bagdemagus that all knights laughed at him, for he was a fine japer, and well loving all good knights.

So anon as they had dined there came a varlet bearing four spears on his back; and he came to Palomides, and said thus:

'Here is a knight by hath sent you the choice of four spears, and requireth you for your lady's sake to take that one half of these spears, and joust with him in the field.'

'Tell him,' said Palomides, 'I will not fail him.'

When Sir Galahaut wist of this, he bad Palomides make him ready. So the Queen Guenever, the Haut Prince, and Sir Launcelot, they were set upon scaffolds to give the judgement of these two knights.

Then Sir Palomides and the strange knight ran so eagerly together that their spears brake to their hands. Anon withal either of them took a great spear in his hand and all to-shivered them in pieces. And then either took a greater spear, and then the knight smote down Sir Palomides, horse and man, to the earth. And as he would have passed over him the strange knight's horse stumbled and fell down upon Palomides. Then they drew their swords and lashed together wonderly sore a great while.

Then the Haut Prince and Sir Launcelot said they saw never two knights fight better than they did; but ever the strange knight doubled his strokes, and put Palomides aback; therewithal the Haut Prince cried, 'Ho!' and then they went to lodging.

And when they were unarmed they knew it was the noble knight Sir Lamorak. When Sir Launcelot knew that it was Sir Lamorak he made much of him, for above all earthly men he loved him best except Sir Tristram. Then Queen Guenever commended him, and so did all other good knights, made much of him, except Sir Gawain's brethren.

Then Queen Guenever said unto Sir Launcelot, 'Sir, I require you that and ye joust any more, that ye joust with none of the blood of my lord Arthur.'

So he promised he would not as at that time.

CHAPTER 45: *Of the fourth day, and of many great feats of arms*

Here beginneth the fourth day. Then came into the field the King with the Hundred Knights, and all they of Northgales, and the Duke Chaleins of Clarance, and King Marsil of Pomitain, and there came Safer, Palomides' brother, and there he told him tidings of his mother.

'And his name was called the Earl' – and so he appelled him afore King Arthur – 'for he made war upon our father and mother, and there I slew him in plain battle.'

So they went into the field, and the damosel with them; and there came to encounter against them Sir Bleoberis de Ganis, and Sir Ector de Maris. Sir Palomides encountered with Sir Bleoberis, and either smote other down. And in the same ways did Sir Safer and Sir Ector and the two couples did battle on foot.

Then came in Sir Lamorak, and he encountered with the King with the Hundred Knights, and smote him quite over his horse's tail. And in the same wise he served the King of Northgales, and also he smote down King Marsil. And so or ever he stint he smote down with his spear and with his sword thirty knights.

When Duke Chaleins saw Lamorak do so great prowess he would not meddle with him for shame; and then he charged all his knights in pain of death 'that none of you touch him; for it were shame to all good knights and that knight were shamed.'

Then the two kings gathered them together, and all they set upon Sir Lamorak; and he failed them not, but rashed here and there, smiting on the right hand and on the left, and rased off many helms, so that the Haut Prince and Queen Guenever said they saw never knight do such deeds of arms on horseback.

'Alas,' said Launcelot to King Bagdemagus, 'I will arm me and help Sir Lamorak.'

'And I will ride with you,' said King Bagdemagus.

And when they two were horsed they came to Sir Lamorak that stood among thirty knights; and well was him that might reach him a buffet, and ever he smote again mightily. Then came there into the press Sir Launcelot, and he threw down Sir Mador de la Porte. And with the truncheon of that spear he threw down many knights. And King Bagdemagus smote on the left hand and on the right hand marvellously well. And then the three kings fled aback.

Therewithal then Sir Galahaut let blow to lodging, and all the heralds gave Sir Lamorak the prize.

And all this while fought Palomides, Sir Bleoberis, Sir Safer, Sir Ector on foot, never were there four knights evener matched. And then they were departed, and had unto their lodging, and unarmed them, and so they went to the great feast.

But when Sir Lamorak was come into the court Queen Guenever took him in her arms and said, 'Sir, well have ye done this day.'

Then came the Haut Prince, and he made of him great joy, and so did Dinadan, for he wept for joy; but the joy that Sir Launcelot made of Sir Lamorak there might no man tell.

Then they went unto rest, and on the morn the Haut Prince let blow unto the field.

CHAPTER 46: *Of the fifth day, and how Sir Lamorak behaved him*

Here beginneth the fifth day. So it befell that Sir Palomides came in the morntide, and proffered to joust thereas King Arthur was in a castle there besides Surluse; and there encountered with him a worshipful duke, and there Sir Palomides smote him over his horse's croup. And this duke was uncle unto King Arthur. Then Sir Elis's son[1] rode unto Palomides, and Palomides served Elis in the same wise. When Sir Uwain saw this he was wroth; then he took his horse and encountered with Sir Palomides, and Palomides smote him so hard that he went to the earth, horse and man. And for to make a short tale, he smote down three brethren of Sir Gawain's, that is for to say Mordred, Gaheris, and Agravain.

'O Jesu,' said Arthur, 'this is a great despite of a Saracen that he shall smite down my blood.'

And therewithal King Arthur was wood wroth, and thought to have made him ready to joust. That espied Sir Lamorak, that Arthur and his blood were discomfit; and anon he was ready, and asked Palomides if he would any more joust.

'Why should I not?' said Palomides.

Then they hurtled together, and brake their spears, and all to-shivered them, that all the castle rang of their dints. Then either gat a greater spear in his hand, and they came so fiercely together; but Sir Palomides' spear all to-brast and Sir Lamorak did hold. Therewithal Sir Palomides lost his stirrups and lay upright on his horse's back. And then Sir Palomides returned again and took his damosel, and Sir Safer returned his way.

So when he was departed King Arthur came to Sir Lamorak and thanked him of his goodness, and prayed him to tell him his name.

'Sir,' said Lamorak, 'wit thou well, I owe you my service, but as at this time I will not abide here, for I see of mine enemies many about me.'

'Alas,' said Arthur, 'now wot I well it is Sir Lamorak de Gales. O Lamorak, abide with me, and by my crown I shall never fail thee; and not so hardy in Gawain's head, nor none of his brethren, to do thee any wrong.'

'Sir,' said Sir Lamorak, 'wrong have they done me, and to you both.'

'That is truth,' said the king, 'for they slew their own mother and my sister, the which me sore grieveth: it had been much fairer and better that ye had wedded her, for ye are a king's son as well as they.'

'O Jesu,' said the noble knight Sir Lamorak unto Arthur, 'her death shall I never forget. I promise you, and make mine vow unto God, I shall revenge her death as soon as I see time convenable. And if it were not at the reverence of your highness I should now have been revenged upon Sir Gawain and his brethren.'

'Truly,' said Arthur, 'I will make you at accord.'

'Sir,' said Lamorak, 'as at this time I may not abide with you, for I must to the jousts where is Sir Launcelot, and the Haut Prince Sir Galahaut.'

Then there was a damosel that was daughter to King Bandes. And there was a Saracen knight that hight Corsabrin, and he loved the damosel, and in no wise he would suffer her to be married; for ever this Corsabrin noised her, and named her that she was out of her mind; and thus he let her that she might not be married.

CHAPTER 47: *How Sir Palomides fought with Corsabrin for a lady, and how Palomides slew Corsabrin*

So by fortune this damosel heard tell that Palomides did much for damosels' sake; so she sent to him a pensel, and prayed him to fight with Sir Corsabrin for her love, and he should have her, and her lands of her father's that should fall to her. Then the damosel sent unto Corsabrin, and bad him go unto Sir Palomides that was a paynim as well as he, and she gave him warning that she had sent him her pensel, and if he might overcome Palomides she would wed him.

When Corsabrin wist of her deeds then was he wood wroth and angry, and rode unto Surluse where the Haut Prince was, and there he found Sir Palomides ready, the

pensel: small pennon.

which had the pensel. So there they waged battle either with other afore Galahaut.

'Well,' said the Haut Prince, 'this day must noble knights joust, and at after dinner we shall see how ye can speed.'

Then they blew to jousts; and in came Dinadan, and met with Sir Gerin, a good knight, and he threw him down over his horse's croup; and Sir Dinadan overthrew four knights more; and there he did great deeds of arms, for he was a good knight, but he was a scoffer and a japer, and the merriest knight among fellowship that was that time living. And he had such a custom that he loved every good knight, and every good knight loved him again.

So then when the Haut Prince saw Dinadan do so well he sent unto Sir Launcelot and bad him strike down Sir Dinadan: 'And when that ye have done so bring him afore me and the noble Queen Guenever.'

Then Sir Launcelot did as he was required. Then Sir Lamorak and he smote down many knights, and rased off helms, and drove all the knights afore them. And so Sir Launcelot smote down Sir Dinadan, and made his men to unarm him, and so brought him to the queen and the Haut Prince, and they laughed at Dinadan so sore that they might not stand.

'Well,' said Sir Dinadan, 'yet have I no shame, for the old shrew, Sir Launcelot, smote me down.'

So they went to dinner. All the court had good sport at Dinadan.

Then when the dinner was done they blew to the field to behold Sir Palomides and Corsabrin. Sir Palomides pitched his pensel in midst of the field; and then they hurtled together with their spears as it were thunder, and either smote other to the earth. And then they pulled out their swords, and dressed their shields, and lashed together mightily as mighty knights, that wellnigh there was no piece of harness would hold them, for this Corsabrin was a passing felonious knight.

'Corsabrin,' said Palomides, 'wilt thou release me yonder damosel and the pensel?'

Then was Corsabrin wroth out of measure, and gave Palomides such a buffet that he kneeled on his knee.

Then Palomides arose lightly, and smote him upon the helm that he fell down right to the earth. And therewith he rased off his helm and said, 'Corsabrin, yield thee or else thou shalt die of my hands.'

'Fie on thee,' said Corsabrin, 'do thy worst.' Then he smote off his head.

And therewithal came a stink of his body when the soul departed, that there might nobody abide the savour. So was the corpse had away and buried in a wood, because he was a paynim.

Then they blew unto lodging, and Palomides was unarmed. Then he went unto Queen Guenever, to the Haut Prince, and to Sir Launcelot.

'Sir,' said the Haut Prince, 'here have ye seen this day a great miracle by Corsabrin, what savour there was when the soul departed from the body. Therefore, sir, we will require you to take the baptism upon you, and I promise you all knights will set the more by you, and say more worship by you.'

'Sir,' said Palomides, 'I will that ye all know that into this land I came to be christened, and in my heart I am christened, and christened will I be. But I have made such an avow that I may not be christened till I have done seven true battles for Jesu's sake, and then will I be christened; and I trust God will take mine intent, for I mean truly.'

Then Sir Palomides prayed Queen Guenever and the Haut Prince to sup with him. And so they did, both Sir Launcelot and Sir Lamorak, and many other good knights.

So on the morn they heard their mass, and blew the field, and then knights made them ready.

CHAPTER 48: *Of the sixth day, and what was then done*

Here beginneth the sixth day. Then came therein Sir Gaheris, and there encountered with him Sir Ossaise of Surluse, and

Sir Gaheris smote him over his horse's croup. And then either party encountered with other, and there were many spears broken, and many knights cast under feet. So there came in Sir Dornard and Sir Agloval, that were brethren unto Sir Lamorak, and they met with other two knights, and either smote other so hard that all four knights and horses fell to the earth.

When Sir Lamorak saw his two brethren down he was wroth out of measure, and then he gat a great spear in his hand, and therewithal he smote down four good knights, and then his spear brake. Then he pulled out his sword, and smote about him on the right hand and on the left hand, and rased off helms and pulled down knights, that all men marvelled of such deeds of arms as he did, for he fared so that many knights fled.

Then he horsed his brethren again, and said, 'Brethren, ye ought to be ashamed to fall so off your horses! What is a knight but when he is on horseback? I set not by a knight when he is on foot, for all battles on foot are but pillers' battles. For there should no knight fight on foot but if it were for treason, or else he were driven thereto by force; therefore, brethren, sit fast on your horses, or else fight never more afore me.'

With that came in the Duke Chaleins of Clarance, and there encountered with him the Earl Ulbawes of Surluse, and either of them smote other down. Then the knights of both parties horsed their lords again, for Sir Ector and Bleoberis were on foot waiting on the Duke Chaleins. And the King with the Hundred Knights was with the Earl of Ulbawes.

With that came Gaheris and lashed to the King with the Hundred Knights, and he to him again. Then came the Duke Chaleins and departed them.

Then they blew to lodging, and the knights unarmed them and drew them to their dinner; and at the midst of their dinner in came Dinadan and began to rail.

Then he beheld the Haut Prince, that seemed wroth with

pillers: plunderers.

93

some fault that he saw; for he had a custom he loved no fish, and because he was served with fish, the which he hated, therefore he was not merry. When Sir Dinadan had espied the Haut Prince, he espied where was a fish with a great head, and that he gat betwixt two dishes, and served the Haut Prince with that fish. And then he said thus:

'Sir Galahaut, well may I liken you to a wolf, for he will never eat fish, but flesh;' then the Haut Prince laughed at his words.

'Well, well,' said Dinadan to Launcelot, 'what devil do ye in this country, for here may no mean knights win no worship for thee.'

'Sir Dinadan,' said Launcelot, 'I ensure thee I shall no more meet with thee nor with thy great spear, for I may not sit in my saddle when that spear hitteth me. And if I be happy I shall beware of that boistous body that thou bearest. Well,' said Launcelot, 'make good watch ever. God forbid that ever we meet but if it be at a dish of meat.'

Then laughed the queen and the Haut Prince, that they might not sit at their table; thus they made great joy till on the morn, and then they heard mass, and blew to field. And Queen Guenever and all the estates were set, and judges armed clean with their shields to keep the right.

CHAPTER 49: *Of the seventh battle, and how Sir Launcelot, being disguised like a maid, smote down Sir Dinadan*

Now beginneth the seventh battle. There came in the Duke Cambines, and there encountered with him Sir Aristance, that was counted a good knight, and they met so hard that either bare other down, horse and man. Then came there the Earl of Lambaile and helped the duke again to horse. Then came there Sir Ossaise of Surluse, and he smote the Earl Lambaile down from his horse. Then began they to do great deeds of arms, and many spears were broken, and many knights were cast to the earth. Then the King of Northgales and the Earl Ulbawes smote together that all the judges thought it was like mortal death.

This meanwhile Queen Guenever, and the Haut Prince, and Sir Launcelot, made there Sir Dinadan make him ready to joust.

'I would,' said Dinadan, 'ride into the field, but then one of you twain will meet with me.'

'Per dieu,' said the Haut Prince, 'ye may see how we sit here as judges with our shields, and always mayest thou behold whether we sit here or not.'

So Sir Dinadan departed and took his horse, and met with many knights, and did passing well, And as he was departed, Sir Launcelot disguised himself, and put upon his armour a maiden's garment freshly attired. Then Sir Launcelot made Sir Galihodin to lead him through the range, and all men had wonder what damosel it was. And so as Sir Dinadan came into the range, Sir Launcelot, that was in the damosel's array, gat Galihodin's spear, and ran unto Sir Dinadan.

And always Sir Dinadan looked up thereas Sir Launcelot was, and then he saw one sit in the stead of Sir Launcelot, armed. But when Dinadan saw a manner of a damosel he dread perils that it was Sir Launcelot disguised, but Sir Launcelot came on him so fast that he smote him over his horse's croup; and then great scorns gat Sir Dinadan into the forest there beside, and there they despoiled him unto his shirt, and put upon him a woman's garment, and so brought him into the field; and so they blew unto lodging. And every knight went and unarmed them.

Then was Sir Dinadan brought in among them all. And when Queen Guenever saw Sir Dinadan brought so among them all, then she laughed that she fell down, and so did all that there were.

'Well,' said Dinadan to Launcelot, 'thou art so false that I can never beware of thee.'

Then by all the assent they gave Sir Launcelot the prize, the next was Sir Lamorak de Gales, the third was Sir Palomides, the fourth was King Bagdemagus; so these four knights had the prize, and there was great joy, and great nobley in all the court.

And on the morn Queen Guenever and Sir Launcelot departed unto King Arthur, but in no wise Sir Lamorak would not go with them.

'I shall undertake,' said Sir Launcelot, 'that and ye will go with us, King Arthur shall charge Sir Gawain and his brethren never to do you hurt.'

'As for that,' said Sir Lamorak, 'I will not trust Sir Gawain nor none of his brethren; and wit ye well, Sir Launcelot, and it were not for my lord King Arthur's sake, I should match Sir Gawain and his brethren well enough. But to say that I should trust them, that shall I never, and therefore I pray you recommend me unto my lord Arthur, and unto all my lords of the Round Table. And in what place that ever I come I shall do you service to my power; and sir, it is but late that I revenged that, when my lord Arthur's kin were put to the worse by Sir Palomides.'

Then Sir Lamorak departed from Sir Launcelot, and either wept at their departing.

CHAPTER 50: *How by treason Sir Tristram was brought to a tournament for to have been slain, and how he was put in prison*

Now turn we from this matter, and speak we of Sir Tristram, of whom this book is principal of, and leave we the king and the queen, Sir Launcelot, and Sir Lamorak, and here beginneth the treason of King Mark, that he ordained against Sir Tristram.

There was cried by the coasts of Cornwall a great tournament and jousts, and all was done by Sir Galahaut the Haut Prince and King Bagdemagus, to the intent to slay Launcelot, or else utterly destroy him and shame him, because Sir Launcelot had always the higher degree; therefore this prince and this king made this jousts against Sir Launcelot. And thus their counsel was discovered unto King Mark, whereof he was full glad. Then King Mark bethought him that he would have Sir Tristram unto that tournament disguised that no man should know him, to that intent that the Haut Prince should ween that Sir Tristram were Sir Launcelot.

So at these jousts came in Sir Tristram. And at that time Sir Launcelot was not there, but when they saw a knight disguised do such deeds of arms, they weened it had been Sir Launcelot. And in especial King Mark said it was Sir Launcelot plainly.

Then they set upon him, both King Bagdemagus, and the Haut Prince, and their knights, that it was wonder that ever Sir Tristram might endure that pain. Nothwithstanding for all the pain that he had, Sir Tristram won the degree at that tournament, and there he hurt many knights and bruised them, and they hurt him and bruised him wonderly sore.

So when the jousts were all done they knew well that it was Sir Tristram de Liones; and all that were on King Mark's party were glad that Sir Tristram was hurt, and the remnant were sorry for his hurt; for Sir Tristram was not so behated as was Sir Launcelot within the realm of England.

Then came King Mark unto Sir Tristram and said, 'Fair nephew, I am sorry of your hurts.'

'Gramercy my lord,' said Sir Tristram.

Then King Mark made Sir Tristram to be put in an horse bier in great sign of love, and said, 'Fair cousin, I shall be your leech myself.'

And so he rode forth with Sir Tristram, and brought him to a castle by daylight. And then King Mark made Sir Tristram to eat. And then after he gave him a drink, the which as soon as he had drunk he fell asleep. And when it was night he made him to be carried to another castle, and there he put him in a strong prison, and there he ordained a man and a woman to give him his meat and drink. So there he was a great while.

Then was Sir Tristram missed, and no creature wist where he was become. When La Beale Isoud heard how he was missed, privily she went unto Sir Sadok, and prayed him to espy where was Sir Tristram.

Then when Sadok wist how Sir Tristram was missed, and anon espied that he was put in prison by King Mark and the traitors of Magouns, then Sadok and two of his cousins laid them in an ambushment, fast by the Castle of Tintagel, in arms.

And as by fortune, there came riding King Mark and four of his nephews, and a certain of the traitors of Magouns. When Sir Sadok espied them he brake out of the bushment, and set there upon them. And when King Mark espied Sir Sadok he fled as fast as he might, and there Sir Sadok slew all the four nephews unto King Mark. But these traitors of Magouns slew one of Sadok's cousins a great wound in the neck, but Sadok smote the other to the death.

Then Sir Sadok rode upon his way unto a castle that was called Liones, and there he espied of the treason and felony of King Mark. So they of that castle rode with Sir Sadok till that they came to a castle that hight Arbray, and there in the town they found Sir Dinas the Seneschal, that was a good knight. But when Sir Sadok had told Sir Dinas of all the treason of King Mark, he defied such a king, and said he would give up his lands that he held of him. And when he said these words all manner knights said as Sir Dinas said.

Then by his advice, and of Sir Sadok's, he let stuff all the towns and castles within the country of Liones, and assembled all the people that they might make.

CHAPTER 51: *How King Mark let do counterfeit letters from the Pope, and how Sir Percival delivered Sir Tristram out of prison*

Now turn we unto King Mark, that when he was escaped from Sir Sadok he rode unto the Castle of Tintagel, and there he made great cry and noise, and cried unto harness all that might bear arms.

Then they sought and found where were dead four cousins of King Mark's, and the traitor of Magouns. Then the king let inter them in a chapel. Then the king let cry in all the country that held of him, to go unto arms, for he understood to the war he must needs.

When King Mark heard and understood how Sir Sadok and Sir Dinas were arisen in the country of Liones, he remembered of wiles and treason. Lo thus he did: he let make and counterfeit letters from the Pope, and did make a strange clerk to bear them unto King Mark, the which letters specified that King Mark should make him ready, upon pain of cursing, with his host to come to the Pope, to help to go to Jerusalem, for to make war upon the Saracens.

When this clerk was come by the mean of the king, anon withal King Mark sent these letters unto Sir Tristram and bad him say thus: that and he would go war upon the miscreants, he should be had out of prison, and to have all his power.

When Sir Tristram understood this letter, then he said thus to the clerk, 'Ah, King Mark, ever hast thou been a traitor, and ever will be; but, clerk,' said Sir Tristram, 'say thou thus unto King Mark: since the Apostle Pope hath sent for him, bid him go thither himself; for tell him, traitor king as he is, I will not go at his commandment, get I out of prison as I may, for I see I am well rewarded for my true service.'

Then the clerk returned unto King Mark, and told him of the answer of Sir Tristram.

'Well,' said King Mark, 'yet shall he be beguiled.'

So he went into his chamber, and counterfeit letters; and the letters specified that the Pope desired Sir Tristram to come himself, to make war upon the miscreants.

When the clerk was come again to Sir Tristram and took him these letters, then Sir Tristram beheld these letters, and anon espied they were of King Mark's counterfeiting.

'Ah,' said Sir Tristram, 'false hast thou been ever, King Mark, and so wilt thou end.'

Then the clerk departed from Sir Tristram and came to King Mark again.

By then there were come four wounded knights within the Castle of Tintagel, and one of them his neck was nigh broken in twain. Another had his arm stricken away, the third was borne through with a spear, the fourth had his teeth stricken in twain. And when they came afore King Mark they cried and said, 'King, why fleest thou not, for all this country is arisen clearly against thee?'

Then was King Mark wroth out of measure.

And in the meanwhile there came into the country Sir Percival de Gales to seek Sir Tristram. And when he heard that Sir Tristram was in prison, Sir Percival made clearly the deliverance of Tristram by his knightly means. And when he was so delivered he made great joy of Sir Percival, and so each one of other. Sir Tristram said unto Sir Percival, 'And ye will abide in these marches I will ride with you.'

'Nay,' said Percival, 'in this country I may not tarry, for I must needs into Wales.'

So Sir Percival departed from Sir Tristram, and rode straight unto King Mark, and told him how he had delivered Sir Tristram; and also he told the king that he had done himself great shame for to put Sir Tristram in prison, 'for he is now the knight of most renown in this world living. And wit thou well the noblest knights of the world love Sir Tristram, and if he will make war upon you ye may not abide it.'

'That is truth,' said King Mark, 'but I may not love Sir Tristram because he loveth my queen and my wife, La Beale Isoud.'

'Ah, fie for shame' said Sir Percival, 'say ye never so more. Are ye not uncle unto Sir Tristram, and he your nephew? Ye should never think that so noble a knight as Sir Tristram is, that he would do himself so great a villainy to hold his uncle's wife; howbeit,' said Sir Percival, 'he may love your queen sinless, because she is called one of the fairest ladies of the world.'

Then Sir Percival departed from King Mark. So when he was departed King Mark bethought him of more treason:

notwithstanding King Mark granted Sir Percival never by no manner of means to hurt Sir Tristram.

So anon King Mark sent unto Sir Dinas the Seneschal that he should put down all the people that he had raised, for he sent him an oath that he would go himself unto the Pope of Rome to war upon the miscreants; 'and this is a fairer war than thus to araise the people against your king.'

When Sir Dinas understood that King Mark would go upon the miscreants, then Sir Dinas in all the haste put down all the people; and when the people were departed every man to his home, then King Mark espied 'where was Sir Tristram with La Beale Isoud; and there by treason King Mark let take him and put him in prison, contrary to his promise that he made unto Sir Percival.

When Queen Isoud understood that Sir Tristram was in prison she made as great sorrow as ever made lady or gentlewoman. Then Sir Tristram sent a letter unto La Beale Isoud, and prayed her to be his good lady; and if it pleased her to make a vessel ready for her and him, he would go with her unto the realm of Logris, that is this land.

When La Beale Isoud understood Sir Tristram's letters and his intent she sent him another, and bad him be of good comfort, for she would do make the vessel ready, and all thing to purpose. Then La Beale Isoud sent unto Sir Dinas, and to Sadok, and prayed them in anywise to take King Mark, and put him in prison, unto the time that she and Sir Tristram were departed unto the realm of Logris.

When Sir Dinas the Seneschal understood the treason of King Mark he promised her again, and sent her word that King Mark should be put in prison. And as they devised it so it was done. And then Sir Tristram was delivered out of prison; and anon in all the haste Queen Isoud and Sir Tristram went and took their counsel with that they would have with them when they departed.

CHAPTER 52 : *How Sir Tristram and La Beale Isoud came into England, and how Sir Launcelot brought them to Joyous Gard*

Then La Beale Isoud and Sir Tristram took their vessel, and came by water into this land. And so they were not in this land four days but there came a cry of a jousts and tournament that King Arthur let make. When Sir Tristram heard tell of that tournament he disguised himself, and La Beale Isoud, and rode unto that tournament. And when he came there he saw many knights joust and tourney; and so Sir Tristram dressed him to the range, and to make short conclusion, he overthrew fourteen knights of the Round Table.

When Sir Launcelot saw these knights thus overthown, Sir Launcelot dressed him to Sir Tristram. That saw La Beale Isoud how Sir Launcelot was come into the field. Then La Beale Isoud sent unto Sir Launcelot a ring, and bad him wit that it was Sir Tristram de Liones. When Sir Launcelot understood that there was Sir Tristram he was full glad, and would not joust. Then Sir Launcelot espied whither Sir Tristram yede, and after him he rode; and then either made of other great joy.

And so Sir Launcelot brought Sir Tristram and La Beale Isoud unto Joyous Gard, that was his own castle, that he had won with his own hands. And there Sir Launcelot put them in to wield for their own. And wit ye well that castle was garnished and furnished for a king and a queen royal there to have sojourned. And Sir Launcelot charged all his people to honour them and love them as they would do himself.

So Sir Launcelot departed unto King Arthur; and then he told Queen Guenever how he that jousted so well at the last tournament was Sir Tristram. And there he told her how he had with him La Beale Isoud maugre King Mark, and so Queen Guenever told all this unto King Arthur. When King Arthur wist that Sir Tristram was escaped and comen from King Mark, and had brought La Beale Isoud with him, then was he passing glad. So because of Sir Tristram King Arthur let make a cry, that on May Day should be a jousts before the Castle of Lonazep; and that castle was fast by Joyous Gard.

And thus Arthur devised, that all the knights of this land, and of Cornwall, and of North Wales, should joust against all these countries: Ireland, Scotland, and the remnant of Wales, and the country of Gore, and Surluse, and of Listinoise, and they of Northumberland, and all they that held lands of Arthur on this half the sea. When this cry was made many knights were glad and many were unglad.

'Sir,' said Launcelot unto Arthur, 'by this cry that ye have made ye will put us that be about you in great jeopardy, for there be many knights that have great envy to us; therefore when we shall meet at the day of jousts there will be hard skift among us.'

'As for that,' said Arthur, 'I care not; there shall we prove who shall be best of his hands.'

So when Sir Launcelot understood wherefore King Arthur made this jousting, then he made such purveyance that La Beale Isoud should behold the jousts in a secret place that was honest for her estate.

Now turn we unto Sir Tristram and to La Beale Isoud, how they made great joy daily together with all manner of mirths that they could devise; and every day Sir Tristram would go ride on hunting, for Sir Tristram was that time called the best chaser of the world, and the noblest blower of an horn of all manner of measures; for as books report, of Sir Tristram came all the good terms of venery and of hunting, and all the sizes and measures of blowing of an horn; and of him we had first all the terms of hawking, and which were beasts of chase and beasts of venery, and which were vermins, and all the blasts that longen to all manner of gamen. First to the uncoupling, to the seeking, to the rechate, to the flight, to the death, and to strake, and many other blasts and terms, that

skift: fate.   *rechate*: calling back of the hounds.
strake: signal with hunting horn.

all manner of gentlemen have cause to the world's end to praise Sir Tristram, and to pray for his soul.[1]

CHAPTER 53: *How by the counsel of La Beale Isoud Sir Tristram rode armed, and how he met with Sir Palomides*

So on a day La Beale Isoud said unto Sir Tristram, 'I marvel me much,' said she, 'that ye remember not yourself, how ye be here in a strange country, and here be many perilous knights; and well ye wot that King Mark is full of treason; and that ye will ride thus to chase and to hunt unarmed ye might be destroyed.'

'My fair lady and my love, I cry you mercy, I will no more do so.'

So then Sir Tristram rode daily on hunting armed, and his men bearing his shield and his spear.

So on a day a little afore the month of May, Sir Tristram chased an hart passing eagerly, and so the hart passed by a fair well. And then Sir Tristram alit and put off his helm to drink of that burbly water. Right so he heard and saw the Questing Beast come to the well. When Sir Tristram saw that beast he put on his helm, for he deemed he should hear of Sir Palomides, for that beast was his quest. Right so Sir Tristram saw where came a knight armed, upon a noble courser, and he saluted him, and they spake of many things; and this knight's name was Breunis Saunce Pité. And right so withal there came unto them the noble knight Sir Palomides, and either saluted other, and spake fair to other.

'Fair knights,' said Sir Palomides, 'I can tell you tidings.'

'What is that?' said those knights.

'Sirs, wit ye well that King Mark is put in prison by his own knights, and all was for love of Sir Tristram; for King Mark had put Sir Tristram twice in prison, and once Sir Percival delivered the noble knight Sir Tristram out of prison. And at the last time Queen La Beale Isoud delivered him, and went clearly away with him into this realm; and all this while King Mark, the false traitor, is in prison. Is this truth, said Palomides, 'then shall we hastily hear of Sir Tristram. And as for to say that I love La Beale Isoud paramours, I dare make good that I do, and that she hath my service above all other ladies, and shall have, the term of my life.'

And right so as they stood talking they saw afore them where came a knight all armed, on a great horse, and one of his men bare his shield, and the other his spears. And anon as that knight espied them he gat his shield and his spear and dressed him to joust.

'Fair fellows,' said Sir Tristram, 'yonder is a knight will joust with us, let see which of us shall encounter with him, for I see well he is of the court of King Arthur.

'It shall not be long or he be met withal,' said Sir Palomides, 'for I found never no knight in my quest of this Glasting Beast, but and he would joust I never refused him.'

'As well may I,' said Breunis Saunce Pité, 'follow that beast as ye.'

'Then shall ye do battle with me,' said Palomides.

So Sir Palomides dressed him unto that other knight, Sir Bleoberis, that was a full noble knight, nigh kin unto Sir Launcelot. And so they met so hard that Sir Palomides fell to the earth, horse and all.

Then Sir Bleoberis cried aloud and said thus: 'Make thee ready thou false traitor knight, Breunis Saunce Pité, for wit thou certainly I will have ado with thee to the utterance for the noble knights and ladies that thou hast falsely betrayed.'

When this false knight and traitor, Breunis Saunce Pité, heard him say so, he took his horse by the bridle and fled his way as fast as ever his horse might run, for sore he was of him afeared. When Sir Bleoberis saw him flee he followed fast after, through thick and through thin.

And by fortune as Sir Breunis fled, he saw even afore him three knights of the Table Round, of the which the one hight Sir Ector de Maris, the other hight Sir Percival de Gales, the third hight Sir Harry le Fise Lake, a good knight and an hardy. And as for Sir Percival, he was called that time of his time one of the best knights of the world, and the best assured. When Breunis saw these knights he rode straight unto them, and cried unto them and prayed them of rescues.

'What need have ye?' said Sir Ector.

'Ah, fair knights,' said Sir Breunis, 'here followeth me the most traitor knight, and most coward, and most of villainy; his name is Breunis Saunce Pité, and if he may get me he will slay me without mercy and pity.'

'Abide with us,' said Sir Percival, 'and we shall warrant you.'

Then were they ware of Sir Bleoberis that came riding all that he might. Then Sir Ector put himself forth to joust afore them all.

When Sir Bleoberis saw that they were four knights and he but himself, he stood in a doubt whether he would turn or hold his way. Then he said to himself, 'I am a knight of the Table Round, and rather than I should shame mine oath and my blood I will hold my way whatsoever fall thereof.'

And then Sir Ector dressed his spear, and smote either other passing sore, but Sir Ector fell to the earth. That saw Sir Percival, and he dressed his horse toward him all that he might drive, but Sir Percival had such a stroke that horse and man fell to the earth.

When Sir Harry saw that they were both to the earth then he said to himself, 'Never was Breunis of such prowess.' So Sir Harry dressed his horse, and they met together so strongly that both the horses and knights fell to the earth, but Sir Bleoberis' horse began to recover again.

That saw Sir Breunis and he came hurtling, and smote him over and over, and would have slain him as he lay on the ground.

Then Sir Harry le Fise Lake arose lightly, and took the bridle of Sir Breunis' horse, and said, 'Fie for shame! Strike never a knight when he is at the earth, for this knight may be called no shameful knight of his deeds, for yet as men may see thereas he lieth on the ground he hath done worshipfully, and put to the worse passing good knights.'

'Therefore will I not let,' said Sir Breunis.

'Thou shalt not choose,' said Sir Harry, 'as at this time.'

Then when Sir Breunis saw that he might not choose nor have his will he spake fair. Then Sir Harry let him go. And then anon he made his horse to run over Sir Bleoberis, and rashed him to the earth like if he would have slain him.

When Sir Harry saw him do so villainously he cried, 'Traitor knight, leave off for shame.'

And as Sir Harry would have taken his horse to fight with Sir Breunis, then Sir Breunis ran upon him as he was half upon his horse, and smote him down, horse and man, to the earth, and had near slain Sir Harry, the good knight.

That saw Sir Percival, and then he cried, 'Traitor knight, what dost thou?'

And when Sir Percival was upon his horse Sir Breunis took his horse and fled all that ever he might, and Sir Percival and Sir Harry followed after him fast, but ever the longer they chased the farther were they behind. Then they turned again and came to Sir Ector de Maris and to Sir Bleoberis.

'Ah, fair knights,' said Bleoberis, 'why have ye succoured that false knight and traitor?'

'Why,' said Sir Harry, 'what knight is he? For well I wot it is a false knight,' said Sir Harry, 'and a coward and a felonious knight.'

'Sir,' said Bleoberis, 'he is the most coward knight, and a devourer of ladies and a destroyer of good knights, and specially of Arthur's.'

'What is your name?' said Sir Ector.

'My name is Sir Bleoberis de Ganis.'

'Alas, fair cousin,' said Ector, 'forgive it me, for I am Sir Ector de Maris.'

Then Sir Percival and Sir Harry made great joy that they met with Bleoberis, but all they were heavy that Sir Breunis was escaped them, whereof they made great dole.

CHAPTER 54: *Of Sir Palomides, and how he met with Sir Bleoberis and with Sir Ector, and of Sir Percival*

Right so as they stood thus there came Sir Palomides, and when he saw the shield of Bleoberis lie on the earth, then said Palomides, 'He that oweth that shield let him dress him to me, for he smote me down here fast by at a fountain, and therefore I will fight for him on foot.'

'I am ready,' said Bleoberis, 'here to answer thee, for wit thou well, sir knight, it was I, and my name is Bleoberis de Ganis.'

'Well art thou met,' said Palomides, 'and wit thou well my name is Palomides the Saracen;' and either of them hated other to the death.

'Sir Palomides,' said Ector, 'wit thou well there is neither thou nor none knight that beareth the life that slayeth any of our blood but he shall die for it; therefore and thou list to fight go seek Sir Launcelot or Sir Tristram, and there shall ye find your match.'

'With them have I met,' said Palomides, 'but I had never no worship of them.'

'Was there never no manner of knight,' said Sir Ector, 'but they that ever matched with you?'

'Yes,' said Palomides, 'there was the third, a good knight as any of them, and of his age he was the best that ever I found; for and he might have lived till he had been an hardier man, there liveth no knight now such, and his name was Sir Lamorak de Gales. And as he had jousted at a tournament there he overthrew me and thirty knights more, and there he won the degree. And at his departing there met him Sir Gawain and his brethren, and with great pain they slew him feloniously, unto all good knights' great damage.'

Anon as Sir Percival heard that his brother was dead, Sir Lamorak, he fell over his horse's mane swooning, and there he made the greatest dole that ever made knight.

And when Sir Percival arose he said, 'Alas, my good and

noble brother Sir Lamorak, now shall we never meet, and I trow in all the wide world a man may not find such a knight as he was of his age; and it is too much to suffer the death of our father King Pellinor, and now the death of our good brother Sir Lamorak.'

Then in the meanwhile there came a varlet from the court of King Arthur, and told them of the great tournament that should be at Lonazep, and how these lands, Cornwall and Northgales, should be against all them that would come.

CHAPTER 55 : *How Sir Tristram met with Sir Dinadan, and of their devices, and what he said to Sir Gawain's brethren*

Now turn we unto Sir Tristram, that as he rode on hunting he met with Sir Dinadan, that was comen into that country to seek Sir Tristram. Then Sir Dinadan told Sir Tristram his name, but Sir Tristram would not tell him his name, wherefore Sir Dinadan was wroth.

'For such a foolish knight as ye are,' said Sir Dinadan, 'I saw but late this day lying by a well, and he fared as he slept; and there he lay like a fool grinning, and would not speak, and his shield lay by him, and his horse stood by him; and well I wot he was a lover.'

'Ah, fair sir,' said Sir Tristram, 'are ye not a lover?'

'Marry, fie on that craft !' said Sir Dinadan.

'That is evil said,' said Sir Tristram, 'for a knight may never be of prowess but if he be a lover.'

'It is well said,' said Sir Dinadan; 'now tell me your name, sith ye be a lover, or else I shall do battle with you.'

'As for that,' said Sir Tristram, 'it is no reason to fight with me but I tell you my name; and as for that my name shall ye not wit as at this time.'

'Fie for shame,' said Dinadan, 'art thou a knight and darst not tell thy name to me? Therefore I will fight with thee.'

'As for that,' said Sir Tristram, 'I will be advised, for I will

devices : conversations.

not do battle but if me list. And if I do battle,' said Sir Tristram, 'ye are not able to withstand me.'

'Fie on thee, coward,' said Sir Dinadan.

And thus as they hoved still, they saw a knight came riding against them.

'Lo,' said Sir Tristram, 'see where cometh a knight riding, will joust with you.'

Anon, as Sir Dinadan beheld him he said, 'That is the same doted knight that I saw lie by the well, neither sleeping ne waking.'

'Well,' said Sir Tristram, 'I know that knight well with the covered shield of azure, he is the King's son of Northumberland, his name is Epinogrus; and he is as great a lover as I know, and he loveth the King's daughter of Wales, a full fair lady. And now I suppose,' said Sir Tristram, 'and ye require him he will joust with you, and then shall ye prove whether a lover be a better knight, or ye that will not love no lady.'

'Well,' said Dinadan, 'now shalt thou see what I shall do.'

Therewithal Sir Dinadan spake on high and said, 'Sir knight, make thee ready to joust with me, for it is the custom of errant knights one to joust with other.'

'Sir,' said Epinogrus, 'is that the rule of you errant knights for to make a knight to joust will he or nill?'

'As for that,' said Dinadan, 'make thee ready, for here is for me.'

And therewithal they spurred their horses and met together so hard that Epinogrus smote down Sir Dinadan.

Then Sir Tristram rode to Sir Dinadan and said, 'How now? Meseemeth the lover hath well sped.'

'Fie on thee, coward,' said Sir Dinadan, 'and if thou be a good knight revenge me.'

'Nay,' said Sir Tristram, 'I will not joust as at this time, but take your horse and let us go hence.'

'God defend me,' said Sir Dinadan, 'from thy fellowship, for I never sped well since I met with thee;' and so they departed.

'Well,' said Sir Tristram, 'peradventure I could tell you tidings of Sir Tristram.'

'God defend me,' said Dinadan, 'from thy fellowship, for Sir Tristram were mickle the worse and he were in thy company;' and then they departed.

'Sir,' said Sir Tristram, 'yet it may happen I shall meet with you in other places.'

So rode Sir Tristram unto Joyous Gard, and there he heard in that town great noise and cry.

'What is this noise?' said Sir Tristram.

'Sir,' said they, 'here is a knight of this castle that hath been long among us, and right now he is slain with two knights, and for none other cause but that our knight said that Sir Launcelot were a better knight than Sir Gawain.'

'That was a simple cause,' said Sir Tristram, 'for to slay a good knight for to say well by his master.'

'That is little remedy to us,' said the men of the town. 'For and Sir Launcelot had been here soon we should have been revenged upon the false knights.'

When Sir Tristram heard them say so he sent for his shield and for his spear, and lightly within a while he had overtake them, and bad them turn and amend that they had misdone.

'What amends wouldst thou have?' said the one knight.

And therewith they took their course, and either met other so hard that Sir Tristram smote down that knight over his horse's tail. Then the other knight dressed him to Sir Tristram, and in the same wise he served the other knight. And then they gat off their horses as well as they might, and dressed their shields and swords to do their battle to the utterance.

'Knights,' said Sir Tristram, 'ye shall tell me of whence ye are, and what be your names, for such men ye might be ye should hard escape my hands; and ye might be such men of such a country that for all your evil deeds ye should pass quit.'

'Wit thou well, sir knight,' said they, 'we fear not to tell thee our names, for my name is Sir Agravain, and my name is Gaheris, brethren unto the good knight Sir Gawain, and we be nephews unto King Arthur.'

'Well,' said Sir Tristram, 'for King Arthur's sake I shall let you pass as at this time. But it is shame,' said Sir Tristram, 'that Sir Gawain and ye be comen of so great a blood that ye four brethren are so named as ye be, for ye be called the greatest destroyers and murderers of good knights that be now in this realm; for it is but as I heard say, that Sir Gawain and ye slew among you a better knight than ever ye were, that was the noble knight Sir Lamorak de Gales. And it had pleased God,' said Sir Tristram, 'I would I had been by Sir Lamorak at his death.'

'Then shouldst thou have gone the same way,' said Sir Gaheris.

'Fair knight,' said Sir Tristram, 'there must have been many more knights than ye are.'

And therewithal Sir Tristram departed from them toward Joyous Gard. And when he was departed they took their horses, and the one said to the other, 'We will overtake him and be revenged upon him in the despite of Sir Lamorak.'

CHAPTER 56: *How Sir Tristram smote down Sir Agravain and Sir Gaheris, and how Sir Dinadan was sent for by La Beale Isoud*

So when they had overtaken Sir Tristram, Sir Agravain bad him, 'Turn, traitor knight.'

'That is evil said,' said Sir Tristram; and therewith he pulled out his sword and smote Sir Agravain such a buffet upon the helm that he tumbled down off his horse in a swoon, and he had a grievous wound. And then he turned to Gaheris, and Sir Tristram smote his sword and his helm together with such a might that Gaheris fell out of his saddle.

And so Sir Tristram rode unto Joyous Gard, and there he alit and unarmed him.

So Sir Tristram told La Beale Isoud of all his adventure, as ye have heard tofore.

And when she heard him tell of Sir Dinadan, 'Sir,' said she, 'is not that he that made the song by King Mark?'

'That same is he,' said Sir Tristram, 'for he is the best bourder and japer, and a noble knight of his hands, and the best fellow that I know, and all good knights love his fellowship.'

'Alas, sir,' said she, 'why brought ye not him with you?'

'Have ye no care,' said Sir Tristram, 'for he rideth to seek me in this country; and therefore he will not away till he have met with me.'

And there Sir Tristram told La Beale Isoud how Sir Dinadan held against all lovers.

Right so there came in a varlet and told Sir Tristram how there was come an errant knight into the town, with such colours upon his shield.

'That is Sir Dinadan,' said Sir Tristram. 'Wit ye what ye shall do,' said Sir Tristram : 'send ye for him, my lady Isoud, and I will not be seen, and ye shall hear the merriest knight that ever ye spake withal, and the maddest talker; and I pray you heartily that ye make him good cheer.'

Then anon La Beale Isoud sent into the town, and prayed Sir Dinadan that he would come into the castle and repose him there with a lady.

'With a good will,' said Sir Dinadan; and so he mounted upon his horse and rode into the castle; and there he alit, and was unarmed, and brought into the castle.

Anon La Beale Isoud came unto him, and either saluted other; then she asked him of whence that he was.

'Madam,' said Dinadan, 'I am of the court of King Arthur, and knight of the Table Round, and my name is Sir Dinadan.'

'What do ye in this country?' said La Beale Isoud.

'Madam,' said he, 'I seek Sir Tristram the good knight, for it was told me that he was in this country.'

'It may well be,' said La Beale Isoud, 'but I am not ware of him.'

'Madam,' said Dinadan, 'I marvel of Sir Tristram and more other lovers, what aileth them to be so mad and so sotted upon women.'

'Why,' said La Beale Isoud, 'are ye a knight and be no lover? It is shame to you: wherefore ye may not be called a good knight but if ye make a quarrel for a lady.'

'God defend me,' said Dinadan, 'for the joy of love is too short, and the sorrow thereof, and what cometh thereof, dureth over long.'

'Ah,' said Le Beale Isoud, 'say ye not so, for here fast by was the good knight Sir Bleoberis, that fought with three knights at once for a damosel's sake, and he won her afore the King of Northumberland.'

'It was so,' said Sir Dinadan, 'for I know him well for a good knight and a noble, and comen of noble blood; for all be noble knights of whom he is comen of, that is Sir Launcelot du Lake.'

'Now I pray you,' said La Beale Isoud, 'tell me will ye fight for my love with three knights that do me great wrong? And insomuch as ye be a knight of King Arthur's I require you to do battle for me.'

'Then,' Sir Dinadan said, 'I shall say you ye be as fair a lady as ever I saw any, and much fairer than is my lady Queen Guenever, but wit ye well at one word, I will not fight for you with three knights, Jesu defend me.'

Then Isoud laughed, and had good game at him. So he had all the cheer that she might make him, and there he lay all that night.

And on the morn early Sir Tristram armed him, and La Beale Isoud gave him a good helm; and then he promised her that he would meet with Sir Dinadan, and they two would ride together unto Lonazep, where the tournament should be.

'And there shall I make ready for you where ye shall see the tournament.'

Then departed Sir Tristram with two squires that bare his shield and his spears that were great and long.

CHAPTER 57 : *How Sir Dinadan met with Sir Tristram, and with jousting with Sir Palomides, Sir Dinadan knew him*

Then after that Sir Dinadan departed, and rode his way a great pace until he had overtake Sir Tristram. And when Sir Dinadan had overtaken him he knew him anon, and he hated the fellowship of him above all other knights.

'Ah,' said Sir Dinadan, 'art thou that coward knight that I met with yesterday? Keep thee, for thou shalt joust with me maugre thy head.'

'Well,' said Sir Tristram, 'and I am loth to joust.'

And so they let their horses run, and Sir Tristram missed of him apurpose, and Sir Dinadan brake a spear upon Sir Tristram, and therewith Sir Dinadan dressed him to draw out his sword.

'Not so,' said Sir Tristram, 'why are ye so wroth? I will not fight.'

'Fie on thee, coward,' said Dinadan, 'thou shamest all knights.'

'As for that,' said Sir Tristram, 'I care not, for I will wait upon you and be under your protection; for because ye are so good a knight ye may save me.'

'The devil deliver me of thee,' said Sir Dinadan, 'for thou art as goodly a man of arms and of thy person as ever I saw, and the most coward that ever I saw. What wilt thou do with those great spears that thou carriest with thee?'

'I shall give them,' said Sir Tristram, 'to some good knight when I come to the tournament; and if I see you do best, I shall give them to you.'

So thus as they rode talking they saw where came an errant knight afore them, that dressed him to joust.

'Lo,' said Sir Tristram, 'yonder is one will joust; now dress thee to him.'

'Ah, shame betide thee,' said Sir Dinadan.

'Nay, not so,' said Tristram, 'for that knight beseemeth a shrew.'

'Then shall I,' said Sir Dinadan.

And so they dressed their shields and their spears, and they met together so hard that the other knight smote down Sir Dinadan from his horse.

'Lo,' said Sir Tristram, 'it had been better ye had left.'

'Fie on thee, coward,' said Sir Dinadan.

Then Sir Dinadan start up and gat his sword in his hand, and proffered to do battle on foot.

'Whether in love or in wrath?' said the other knight.

'Let us do battle in love,' said Sir Dinadan.

'What is your name,' said that knight, 'I pray you tell me.'

'Wit ye well my name is Sir Dinadan.'

'Ah, Dinadan,' said that knight, 'and my name is Gareth, the youngest brother unto Sir Gawain.'

Then either made of other great cheer, for this Gareth was the best knight of all those brethren, and he proved a good knight. Then they took their horses, and there they spake of Sir Tristram, how such a coward he was; and every word Sir Tristram heard and laughed them to scorn. Then were they ware where came a knight afore them well horsed and well armed, and he made him ready to joust.

'Fair knights,' said Sir Tristram, 'look betwixt you who shall joust with yonder knight, for I warn you I will not have ado with him.'

'Then shall I,' said Sir Gareth.

And so they encountered together, and there that knight smote down Sir Gareth over his horse's croup.

'How now,' said Sir Tristram unto Sir Dinadan. 'Dress thee now and revenge the good knight Gareth.'

'That shall I not,' said Sir Dinadan, 'for he hath stricken down a much bigger knight than I am.'

'Ah,' said Sir Tristram, 'now Sir Dinadan, I see and feel well your heart faileth you, therefore now shall ye see what I shall do.'

And then Sir Tristram hurtled unto that knight, and smote him quite from his horse. And when Sir Dinadan saw that, he marvelled greatly; and then he deemed that it was Sir

116

Tristram. Then this knight that was on foot pulled out his sword to do battle.

'What is your name?' said Sir Tristram.

'Wit ye well,' said that knight, 'my name is Sir Palomides.'

'What knight hate ye most?' said Sir Tristram.

'Sir knight,' said he, 'I hate Sir Tristram to the death, for and I may meet with him the one of us shall die.'

'Ye say well,' said Sir Tristram, 'and wit ye well that I am Sir Tristram de Liones, and now do your worst.'

When Sir Palomides heard him say so he was astonied. And then he said thus:

'I pray you, Sir Tristram, forgive me all mine evil will, and if I live I shall do you service above all other knights that be living; and thereas I have owed you evil will me sore repenteth. I wot not what aileth me, for meseemeth that ye are a good knight, and none other knight that named himself a good knight should not hate you; therefore I require you, Sir Tristram, take no displeasure at mine unkind words.'

'Sir Palomides,' said Sir Tristram, 'ye say well, and well I wot ye are a good knight, for I have seen you proved; and many great enterprises have ye taken upon you, and well achieved them; therefore,' said Sir Tristram, 'and ye have any evil will to me, now may ye right it, for I am ready at your hand.'

'Not so, my lord Sir Tristram, I will do you knightly service in all thing as ye will command.'

'And right so I will take you,' said Sir Tristram.

And so they rode forth on their ways talking of many things.

'O my lord Sir Tristram,' said Dinadan, 'foul have ye mocked me, for God knoweth I came into this country for your sake, and by the advice of my lord Sir Launcelot; and yet would not Sir Launcelot tell me the certainty of you, where I should find you.'

'Truly said Sir Tristram, 'Sir Launcelot wist well where I was, for I abode within his own castle.'

CHAPTER 58: *How they approached the Castle Lonazep, and of other devices. Of the death of Sir Lamorak*

Thus they rode until they were ware of the Castle Lonazep. And then were they ware of four hundred tents and pavilions, and marvellous great ordinance.

'So God me help,' said Sir Tristram, 'yonder I see the greatest ordinance that ever I saw.'

'Sir,' said Palomides, 'meseemeth that there was as great an ordinance at the Castle of Maidens upon the rock, where ye won the prize, for I saw myself where ye for-jousted thirty knights.'

'Sir,' said Dinadan, 'and in Surluse, at that tournament that Galahaut of the Long Isles made, the which there dured seven days, was as great a gathering as is here, for there were many nations.'

'Who was the best?' said Sir Tristram.

'Sir, it was Sir Launcelot du Lake and the noble knight, Sir Lamorak de Gales, and Sir Launcelot won the degree.'

'I doubt not,' said Sir Tristram, 'but he won the degree, so he had not been overmatched with many knights. And of the death of Sir Lamorak,' said Sir Tristram, 'it was over great pity, for I dare say he was the cleanest mighted man and the best winded of his age that was alive; for I knew him that he was the biggest knight that ever I met withal, but if it were Sir Launcelot. Alas,' said Sir Tristram, 'full woe is me for his death. And if they were not the cousins of my lord Arthur that slew him, they should die for it, and all those that were consenting to his death. And for such things,' said Sir Tristram, 'I fear to draw unto the court of my lord Arthur; I will that ye wit it,' said Sir Tristram unto Gareth.

'Sir, I blame you not,' said Gareth, 'for well I understand the vengeance of my brethren Sir Gawain, Agravain, Gaheris, and Mordred. But as for me,' said Sir Gareth, 'I meddle not of their matters, therefore there is none of them that loveth

ordinance: battle array.   *cleanest mighted*: strongest.

me. And for I understand they be murderers of good knights I left their company; and God would I had been by,' said Gareth, 'when the noble knight, Sir Lamorak, was slain.'

'Now as Jesu be my help,' said Sir Tristram, 'it is well said of you, for I had lever than all the gold betwixt this and Rome I had been there.'

'Iwis,' said Palomides, 'and so would I had been there, and yet had I never the degree at no jousts nor tournament there-as he was, but he put me to the worse, or on foot or on horse-back; and that day that he was slain he did the most deeds of arms that ever I saw knight do in all my life days. And when him was given the degree by my lord Arthur, Sir Gawain and his three brethren, Agravain, Gaheris, and Sir Mordred, set upon Sir Lamorak in a privy place, and there they slew his horse. And so they fought with him on foot more than three hours, both before him and behind him; and Sir Mordred gave him his death's wound behind him at his back, and all to-hew him; for one of his squires told me that saw it.'

'Fie upon treason,' said Sir Tristram, 'for it killeth my heart to hear this tale.'

'So it doth mine,' said Gareth; 'brethren as they be mine, I shall never love them, nor draw in their fellowship for that deed.'

'Now speak we of other deeds,' said Palomides, 'and let him be, for his life ye may not get again.'

'That is the more pity,' said Dinadan, 'for Sir Gawain and his brethren, except you Sir Gareth, haten all the good knights of the Round Table for the most part; for well I wot as they might[1] privily, they hate my lord Sir Launcelot and all his kin, and great privy despite they have at him; and that is my lord Sir Launcelot well ware of, and that causeth him to have the good knights of his kin about him.'

CHAPTER 59: *How they came to Humber bank, and how they found a ship there, wherein lay the body of King Hermance*

'Sir,' said Palomides, 'let us leave of this matter, and let us see how we shall do at this tournament. By mine advice,' said Palomides, 'let us four hold together against all that will come.'

'Not by my counsel,' said Sir Tristram, 'for I see by their pavilions there will be four hundred knights, and doubt ye not,' said Sir Tristram, 'but there will be many good knights; and be a man never so valiant nor so big, yet he may be over-matched. And so have I seen knights do many times; and when they weened best to have won worship they lost it, for manhood is not worth but if it be medled with wisdom. And as for me,' said Sir Tristram, 'it may happen I shall keep mine own head as well as another.'

So thus they rode until that they came to Humber bank, where they heard a cry and a doleful noise. Then were they ware in the wind where came a rich vessel hilled over with red silk, and the vessel landed fast by them. Therewith Sir Tristram alit and his knights. And so Sir Tristram went afore and entered into that vessel. And when he came within he saw a fair bed richly covered, and thereupon lay a dead seemly knight, all armed, save the head, was all be-bled, with deadly wounds upon him, the which seemed to be a passing good knight.

'How may this be,' said Sir Tristram, 'that this knight is thus slain?'

Then Sir Tristram was ware of a letter in the dead knight's hand.

'Master mariners,' said Sir Tristram, 'what meaneth that letter?'

'Sir,' said they, 'in that letter ye shall hear and know how he was slain, and for what cause, and what was his name. But sir,' said the mariners, 'wit ye well that no man shall take that letter and read it but if he be a good knight, and that he will faithfully promise to revenge his death, else shall there no knight see that letter open.'

'Wit ye well,' said Sir Tristram, 'that some of us may revenge his death as well as other, and if it be so as ye mariners say his death shall be revenged.'

And therewith Sir Tristram took the letter out of the knight's hand, and it said thus:

'Hermance, king and lord of the Red City, I send unto all knights errant, recommending unto you noble knights of Arthur's court. I beseech them all among them to find one knight that will fight for my sake with two brethren that I brought up of nought, and feloniously and traitorly they have slain me; wherefore I beseech one good knight to revenge my death. And he that revenged my death I will that he have my Red City and all my castles.'

'Sir,' said the mariners, 'wit ye well this king and knight that here lieth was a full worshipful man and of full great prowess, and full well he loved all manner knights errants.'

'So God me help,' said Sir Tristram, 'here is a piteous case, and full fain would I take this enterprise upon me; but I have made such a promise that needs I must be at this great tournament, or else I am shamed. For well I wot for my sake in especial my lord Arthur let make this jousts and tournament in this country; and well I wot that many worshipful people will be there at that tournament for to see me; therefore I fear for me to take this enterprise upon me that I shall not come again by time to this jousts.'

'Sir,' said Palomides, 'I pray you give me this enterprise, and ye shall see me achieve it worshipfully, other else I shall die in this quarrel.'

'Well,' said Sir Tristram, 'and this enterprise I give you, with this, that ye be with me at this tournament that shall be as this day seven night.'

'Sir,' said Palomides, 'I promise you that I shall be with you by that day if I be unslain or unmaimed.'

CHAPTER 60: *How Sir Tristram with his fellowship came and were with an host which after fought with Sir Tristram; and other matters*

Then departed Sir Tristram, Gareth, and Sir Dinadan, and left Sir Palomides in the vessel; and so Sir Tristram beheld the mariners how they sailed overlong Humber. And when Sir Palomides was out of their sight they took their horses and beheld about them. And then were they ware of a knight that came riding against them unarmed, and nothing about him but a sword. And when this knight came nigh them he saluted them, and they him again.

'Fair knights,' said that knight, 'I pray you insomuch as ye be knights errant, that ye will come and see my castle, and take such as ye find there; I pray you heartily.'

And so they rode with him until his castle, and there they were brought into the hall, that was well apparelled; and so they were there unarmed, and set at a board; and when this knight saw Sir Tristram, anon he knew him. And then this knight waxed pale and wroth at Sir Tristram.

When Sir Tristram saw his host make such cheer he marvelled and said, 'Sir, mine host, what cheer make you?'

'Wit thou well,' said he, 'I fare the worse for thee, for I know thee Sir Tristram de Liones, thou slewest my brother; and therefore I give thee summons I will slay thee and ever I may get thee at large.'

'Sir knight,' said Sir Tristram, 'I am never advised that ever I slew any brother of yours, and if ye say that I did I will make amends unto my power.'

'I will none amends,' said the knight, 'but keep thee from me.'

So when he had dined Sir Tristram asked his arms, and departed. And so they rode on their ways, and within a while Sir Dinadan saw where came a knight well armed and well horsed, without shield.

'Sir Tristram,' said Sir Dinadan, 'take keep to yourself, for

122

I dare undertake yonder cometh your host that will have ado with you.'

'Let him come,' said Sir Tristram, 'I shall abide him as well as I may.'

Anon the knight when he came nigh Sir Tristram he cried and bad him abide and keep him. So they hurtled together, but Sir Tristram smote the other knight so sore that he bare him over his horse's croup. That knight arose lightly and took his horse again, and so rode fiercely to Sir Tristram, and smote him twice hard upon the helm.

'Sir knight,' said Sir Tristram, 'I pray you leave off and smite me no more, for I would be loth to deal with you and I might choose, for I have your meat and your drink within my body.'

For all that he would not leave; and then Sir Tristram gave him such a buffet upon the helm that he fell up-so-down from his horse, that the blood brast out at the ventails of his helm, and so he lay still, likely to be dead.

Then Sir Tristram said, 'Me repenteth of this buffet that I smote so sore, for as I suppose he is dead.'

And so they left him and rode on their ways. So they had not ridden but a while, but they saw riding against them two full likely knights, well armed and well horsed, and goodly servants about them. The one was Berrant le Apres, and he was called the King with the Hundred Knights, and the other was Sir Segwarides, which were renowned two noble knights. So as they came either by other the king looked upon Sir Dinadan that at that time he had Sir Tristram's helm upon his shoulder, the which helm the king had seen tofore with the Queen of Northgales, and that queen the king loved as paramour; and that helm the Queen of Northgales had given to La Beale Isoud, and the Queen La Beale Isoud gave it to Sir Tristram.

'Sir knight,' said Berrant, 'where had ye that helm?'

'What would ye?' said Sir Dinadan.

'For I will have ado with thee,' said the king, 'for the love
ventails: vents.

of her that owed that helm, and therefore keep you.'

So they departed and came together with all their mights of their horses, and there the King with the Hundred Knights smote Sir Dinadan, horse and all, to the earth; and then he commanded his servant: 'Go and take thou his helm off, and keep it.' So the varlet went to unbuckle his helm.

'What helm? What wilt thou do?' said Sir Tristram. 'Leave that helm.'

'To what intent,' said the king, 'will ye, sir knight, meddle with that helm?'

'Wit you well,' said Sir Tristram, 'that helm shall not depart from me or it be dearer bought.'

'Then make you ready,' said Sir Berrant unto Sir Tristram.

So they hurtled together, and there Sir Tristram smote him down over his horse's tail; and then the king arose lightly, and gat his horse lightly again. And then he struck fiercely at Sir Tristram many great strokes. And then Sir Tristram gave Sir Berrant such a buffet upon the helm that he fell down over his horse sore stonied.

'Lo,' said Dinadan, 'that helm is unhappy to us twain, for I had a fall for it, and now, sir king, have ye another fall.'

Then Segwarides asked, 'Who shall joust with me?'

'I pray thee,' said Sir Gareth unto Dinadan, 'let me have this jousts.'

'Sir,' said Dinadan, 'I pray you take it as for me.'

'That is no reason,' said Tristram, 'for this jousts should be yours.'

'At a word,' said Dinadan, 'I will not thereof.'

Then Gareth dressed him to Sir Segwarides, and there Sir Segwarides smote Gareth and his horse to the earth.

'Now,' said Sir Tristram to Dinadan, 'joust with yonder knight.'

'I will not thereof,' said Dinadan.

'Then will I,' said Sir Tristram.

And then Sir Tristram ran to him, and gave him a fall; and so they left them on foot, and Sir Tristram rode unto Joyous Gard, and there Sir Gareth would not of his courtesy have gone into this castle, but Sir Tristram would not suffer him to depart. And so they alit and unarmed them, and had great cheer. But when Dinadan came afore La Beale Isoud he cursed the time that ever he bare Sir Tristram's helm, and there he told her how Sir Tristram had mocked him. Then was there laughing and japing at Sir Dinadan, that they wist not what to do with him.

CHAPTER 61 : *How Palomides went for to fight with two brethren for the death of King Hermance*

Now will we leave them merry within Joyous Gard, and speak we of Sir Palomides. Then Sir Palomides sailed evenlong Humber to the coasts of the sea, where was a fair castle. And at that time it was early in the morning, afore day. Then the mariners went unto Sir Palomides that slept fast.

'Sir knight,' said the mariners, 'ye must arise, for here is a castle there ye must go into.'

'I assent me,' said Sir Palomides; and therewithal he arrived.

And then he blew his horn that the mariners had given him. And when they within the castle heard that horn they put forth many knights; and there they stood upon the walls, and said with one voice, 'Welcome be ye to this castle.'

And then it waxed clear day, and Sir Palomides entered into the castle. And within a while he was served with many divers meats. Then Sir Palomides heard about him much weeping and great dole.

'What may this mean?' said Sir Palomides. 'I love not to hear such a sorrow, and fain I would know what it meaneth.'

Then there came afore him one whose name was Sir Ebel, that said thus :

'Wit ye well, sir knight, this dole and sorrow is here made every day, and for this cause: we had a king that hight Hermance, and he was king of the Red City, and this king that was lord was a noble knight, large and liberal of his

125

expense; and in the world he loved nothing so much as he did errant knights of King Arthur's court, and all jousting, hunting, and all manner of knightly games; for so kind a king and knight had never the rule of poor people as he was; and because of his goodness and gentleness we bemoan him, and ever shall. And all kings and estates may beware by our lord, for he was destroyed in his own default; for had he cherished them of his blood he had yet lived with great riches and rest: but all estates may beware by our king. But alas,' said Ebel, 'that we shall give all other warning by his death.'

'Tell me,' said Palomides, 'and in what manner was your lord slain, and by whom.'

'Sir,' said Sir Ebel, 'our king brought up of children two men that now are perilous knights; and these two knights our king had so in charity that he loved no man nor trusted no man of his blood, nor none other that was about him. And by these two knights our king was governed, and so they ruled him peaceably and his lands, and never would they suffer none of his blood to have no rule with our king. And also he was so free and so gentle, and they so false and deceivable, that they ruled him peaceably; and that espied the lords of our king's blood, and departed from him unto their own livelihood. Then when these two traitors understood that they had driven all the lords of his blood from him, they were not pleased with that rule, but when they thought to have more as ever it is an old saw: "Give a churl rule and thereby he will not be sufficed"; for whatsomever he be that is ruled by a villain born, and the lord of the soil to be a gentleman born, that same villain shall destroy all the gentlemen about him: therefore all estates and lords, beware whom ye take about you. And if ye be a knight of King Arthur's court remember this tale, for this is the end and conclusion. My lord and king rode unto the forest hereby by the advice of these traitors, and there he chased at the red deer, armed at all pieces full like a good knight; and so for labour he waxed dry, and then he alit, and drank at a well; and when he was alit, by the assent of these two traitors, that one that hight

Helius he suddenly smote our king through the body with a spear, and so they left him there. And when they were departed, then by fortune I came to the well, and found my lord and king wounded to the death. And when I heard his complaint, I let bring him to the water side, and in that same ship I put him alive; and when my lord King Hermance was in that vessel, he required me for the true faith I owed unto him for to write a letter in this manner:

CHAPTER 62: *The copy of the letter written for to revenge the king's death, and how Sir Palomides fought for to have the battle*

' "Recommending unto King Arthur and to all his knights errant, beseeching them all that insomuch as I, King Hermance, king of the Red City, thus am slain by felony and treason, through two knights of mine own, and of mine own bringing up and of mine own making, that some worshipful knight will revenge my death, insomuch I have been ever to my power well willing unto Arthur's court. And who that will adventure his life with these two traitors for my sake in one battle, I, King Hermance, king of the Red City, freely give him all my lands and rents that ever I wielded in my life."

'This letter,' said Ebel, 'I wrote by my lord's commandment, and then he received his Creator; and when he was dead, he commanded me or ever he were cold to put that letter fast in his hand. And then he commanded me to put forth that same vessel down Humber, and I should give these mariners in commandment never to stint until that they came unto Logris, where all the noble knights shall assemble at this time. "And there shall some good knight have pity on me to revenge my death, for there was never king nor lord falslier ne traitorlier slain than I am here to my death." Thus was the complaint of our King Hermance. Now,' said Sir Ebel, 'ye know all how our lord was betrayed, we require you for God's sake have pity upon his death, and worshipfully revenge his death, and then may ye wield all these lands. For we all wit well that and ye may slay these two traitors, the Red City and all those that be therein will take you for their lord.'

'Truly,' said Sir Palomides, 'it grieveth my heart for to hear you tell this doleful tale; and to say the truth I saw the same letter that ye speak of, and one of the best knights on the earth read that letter to me, and by his commandment I came hither to revenge your king's death; and therefore have done, and let me wit where I shall find those traitors, for I shall never be at ease in my heart till I be in hands with them.'

'Sir,' said Sir Ebel, 'then take your ship again, and that ship must bring you unto the Delectable Isle, fast by the Red City, and we in this castle shall pray for you, and abide your again-coming. For this same castle, and ye speed well, must needs be yours; for our King Hermance let make this castle for the love of the two traitors, and so we kept it with strong hand, and therefore full sore are we threated.'

'Wot ye what ye shall do,' said Sir Palomides: 'whatsomever come of me, look ye keep well this castle. For and it misfortune me so to be slain in this quest I am sure there will come one of the best knights of the world for to revenge my death, and that is Sir Tristram de Liones, or else Sir Launcelot du Lake.'

Then Sir Palomides departed from that castle. And as he came nigh the city, there came out of a ship a goodly knight armed against him, with his shield on his shoulder, and his hand upon his sword. And anon as he came nigh Sir Palomides he said, 'Sir knight, what seek ye here? Leave this quest for it is mine, and mine it was or ever it was yours, and therefore I will have it.'

'Sir knight,' said Palomides, 'it may well be that this quest was yours or it was mine, but when the letter was take out of the dead king's hand, at that time by likelihood there was no knight had undertake to revenge the death of the king.

And so at that time I promised to revenge his death, and so I shall or else I am ashamed.'

'Ye say well,' said the knight, 'but wit ye well then will I fight with you, and who be the better knight of us both, let him take the battle upon hand.'

'I assent me' said Sir Palomides.

And then they dressed their shields, and pulled out their swords, and lashed together many sad strokes as men of might; and this fighting was more than [an] hour, but at the last Sir Palomides waxed big and better winded, so that then he smote that knight such a stroke that he made him to kneel upon his knees.

Then that knight spake on high and said, 'Gentle knight, hold thy hand.'

Sir Palomides was goodly and withdrew his hand.

Then this knight said, 'Wit ye well, knight, that thou art better worthy to have this battle than I, and require thee of knighthood tell me thy name.'

'Sir, my name is Palomides, a knight of King Arthur's, and of the Table Round, that hither I came to revenge the death of this dead king.'

CHAPTER 63: *Of the preparation of Sir Palomides and the two brethren that should fight with him*

'Well be ye found,' said the knight to Palomides, 'for of all knights that be alive, except three, I had levest have you. The first is Sir Launcelot du Lake, and Sir Tristram de Liones, the third is my nigh cousin, Sir Lamorak de Gales. And I am brother unto King Hermance that is dead, and my name is Sir Hermind.'

'Ye say well,' said Sir Palomides, 'and ye shall see how I shall speed; and if I be there slain go ye to my lord Sir Launcelot, or else to my lord Sir Tristram, and pray them to revenge my death, for as for Sir Lamorak him shall ye never see in this world.'

'Alas,' said Sir Hermind, 'how may that be?'

'He is slain,' said Sir Palomides, 'by Sir Gawain and his brethren.'

'So God me help,' said Hermind, 'there was not one for one that slew him.'

'That is truth,' said Sir Palomides, 'for they were four dangerous knights that slew him, as Sir Gawain, Sir Agravain, Sir Gaheris, and Sir Mordred, but Sir Gareth, the fifth brother was away, the best knight of them all.' And so Sir Palomides told Hermind all the manner, and how they slew Sir Lamorak all only by treason.

So Sir Palomides took his ship, and arrived up at the Delectable Isle. And in the meanwhile Sir Hermind that was the king's brother, he arrived up at the Red City, and there he told them how there was comen a knight of King Arthur's to avenge King Hermance's death : 'And his name is Sir Palomides, the good knight, that for the most part he followeth the Beast Glatisant.'

Then all the city made great joy, for mickle had they heard of Sir Palomides, and of his noble prowess. So let they ordain a messenger, and sent unto the two brethren, and bad them to make them ready, for there was a knight comen that would fight with them both. So the messenger went unto them where they were at a castle there beside; and there he told them how there was a knight comen of King Arthur's court to fight with them both at once.

'He is welcome,' said they; 'but tell us, we pray you, if it be Sir Launcelot or any of his blood?'

'He is none of that blood,' said the messenger.

'Then we care the less,' said the two brethren, 'for with none of the blood of Sir Launcelot we keep not to have ado withal.'

'Wit ye well,' said the messenger, 'that his name is Sir Palomides, that yet is unchristened, a noble knight.'

'Well,' said they, 'and he be now unchristened he shall never be christened.'

So they appointed to be at the city within two days.

And when Sir Palomides was come to the city they made passing great joy of him, and then they beheld him, and saw that he was well made, cleanly and bigly, and unmaimed of his limbs, and neither too young nor too old. And so all the people praised him. And though he was not christened yet he believed in the best manner, and was full faithful and true of his promise, and well conditioned; and because he made his avow that he would never be christened unto the time that he had achieved the Beast Glatisant, the which was a full wonderful beast, and a great signification, for Merlin prophesied much of that beast. And also Sir Palomides avowed never to take full christendom unto the time that he had done seven battles within the lists.

So within the third day there came to the city these two brethren, the one hight Helius, the other Helake, the which were men of great prowess; howbeit that they were false and full of treason, and but poor men born, yet were they noble knights of their hands. And with them they brought forty knights, to that intent that they should be big enough for the Red City. Thus came the two brethren with great bobaunce and pride, for they had put the Red City in fear and damage. Then they were brought to the lists, and Sir Palomides came into the place and said thus:

'Be ye the two brethren, Helius and Helake, that slew your king and lord, Sir Hermance, by felony and treason, for whom that I am comen hither to revenge his death?'

'Wit thou well,' said Sir Helius and Sir Helake, 'that we are the same knights that slew King Hermance; and wit thou well, Sir Palomides, Saracen, that we shall handle thee so or thou depart that thou shalt wish that thou werst christened.'

'It may well be,' said Sir Palomides, 'for yet I would not die or I were christened; and yet so am I not afeared of you both, but I trust to God that I shall die a better Christian man than any of you both; and doubt ye not,' said Sir Palomides, 'either ye or I shall be left dead in this place.'

bobaunce: boasting.

CHAPTER 64: *Of the battle between Sir Palomides and the two brethren, and how the two brethren were slain*

Then they departed, and the two brethren came against Sir Palomides, and he against them, as fast as their horses might run. And by fortune Sir Palomides smote Helake through his shield and through the breast more than a fathom.

All this while Sir Helius held up his spear, and for pride and orgulity he would not smite Sir Palomides with his spear; but when he saw his brother lie on the earth, and saw he might not help himself, then he said unto Sir Palomides, 'Help thyself.' And therewith he came hurtling unto Sir Palomides with his spear, and smote him quite from his saddle. Then Sir Helius rode over Sir Palomides twice or thrice.

And therewith Sir Palomides was ashamed, and gat the horse of Sir Helius by the bridle, and therewithal the horse reared, and Sir Palomides halp after, and so they fell both to the earth; but anon Sir Helius start up lightly, and there he smote Sir Palomides a great stroke upon the helm, that he kneeled upon his own knee. Then they lashed together many sad strokes, and traced and traversed now backward, now sideling, hurtling together like two boars, and that same time they fell both grovelling to the earth.

Thus they fought still without any reposing two hours, and never breathed; and then Sir Palomides waxed faint and weary, and Sir Helius waxed passing strong, and doubled his strokes, and drove Sir Palomides overthwart and endlong all the field, that they of the city when they saw Sir Palomides in this case they wept and cried, and made great dole, and the other party made as great joy.

'Alas,' said the men of the city, 'that this noble knight should thus be slain for our king's sake.'

And as they were thus weeping and crying, Sir Palomides that had suffered an hundred strokes, that it was wonder that he stood on his feet, at the last Sir Palomides beheld as he might the common people, how they wept for him; and then he said to himself, 'Ah, fie for shame, Sir Palomides, why hangest thou thy head so low;' and therewith he bare up his shield, and looked Sir Helius in the visage, and he smote him a great stroke upon the helm, and after that another and another.

And then he smote Sir Helius with such a might that he fell to the earth grovelling; and then he rased off his helm from his head, and there he smote him such a buffet that he departed his head from the body.

And then were the people of the city the joyfullest people that might be. So they brought him to his lodging with great solemnity, and there all the people became his men. And then Sir Palomides prayed them all to take keep unto all the lordship of King Hermance: 'For, fair sirs, wit ye well I may not as at this time abide with you, for I must in all haste be with my lord King Arthur at the Castle of Lonazep, the which I have promised.'

Then was the people full heavy at his departing, for all that city proffered Sir Palomides the third part of their goods so that he would abide with them; but in no wise as at that time he would not abide.

And so Sir Palomides departed, and so he came unto the castle thereas Sir Ebel was lieutenant. And when they in the castle wist how Sir Palomides had sped, there was a joyful meyne; and so Sir Palomides departed, and came to the Castle of Lonazep.

And when he wist that Sir Tristram was not there he took his way over Humber, and came unto Joyous Gard, whereas Sir Tristram was and La Beale Isoud. Sir Tristram had commanded that what knight errant came within the Joyous Gard, as in the town, that they should warn Sir Tristram. So there came a man of the town, and told Sir Tristram how there was a knight in the town, a passing goodly man.

'What manner of man is he,' said Sir Tristram, 'and what sign beareth he?'

So the man told Sir Tristram all the tokens of him.

'That is Palomides,' said Dinadan.

133

'It may well be,' said Sir Tristram. 'Go ye to him,' said Sir Tristram unto Dinadan.

So Dinadan went unto Sir Palomides, and there either made of other great joy, and so they lay together that night. And on the morn early came Sir Tristram and Sir Gareth, and took them in their beds, and so they arose and brake their fast.

CHAPTER 65: *How Sir Tristram and Sir Palomides met Breunis Saunce Pité, and how Sir Tristram and La Beale Isoud went unto Lonazep*

And then Sir Tristram desired Sir Palomides to ride into the fields and woods. So they were accorded to repose them in the forest. And when they had played them a great while they rode unto a fair well; and anon they were ware of an armed knight that came riding against them, and there either saluted other.

Then this armed knight spake to Sir Tristram, and asked what were these knights that were lodged in Joyous Gard.

'I wot not what they are,' said Sir Tristram.

'What knights be ye?' said that knight. 'For meseemeth ye be no knights errant, because ye ride unarmed.'

'Whether we be knights or not we list not to tell thee our name.'

'Wilt thou not tell me thy name?' said that knight; 'Then keep thee, for thou shalt die of my hands.' And therewith he got his spear in his hands, and would have run Sir Tristram through.

That saw Sir Palomides, and smote his horse traverse in midst of the side, that man and horse fell to the earth. And therewith Sir Palomides alit and pulled out his sword to have slain him.

'Let be,' said Sir Tristram, 'slay him not, the knight is but a fool, it were shame to slay him. But take away his spear,'

traverse: crossways.

said Sir Tristram, 'and let him take his horse and go where that he will.'

So when this knight arose he groaned sore of the fall, and so he took his horse, and when he was up he turned then his horse, and required Sir Tristram and Sir Palomides to tell him what knights they were.

'Now wit ye well,' said Sir Tristram, 'that my name is Sir Tristram de Liones, and this knight's name is Sir Palomides.'

When he wist what they were he took his horse with the spurs, because they should not ask him his name, and so rode fast away through thick and thin. Then came there by them a knight with a bended shield of azure, whose name was Epinogrus, and he came toward them a great wallop.

'Whither are ye riding?' said Sir Tristram.

'My fair lords,' said Epinogrus, 'I follow the falsest knight that beareth the life; wherefore I require you tell me whether ye saw him, for he beareth a shield with a case of red over it.'

'So God me help,' said Tristram, 'such a knight departed from us not a quarter of an hour agone; we pray you tell us his name.'

'Alas,' said Epinogrus, 'why let ye him escape from you? And he is so great a foe unto all errant knights; his name is Breunis Saunce Pité.'

'Ah, fie for shame,' said Sir Palomides, 'alas that ever he escaped mine hands, for he is the man in the world that I hate most.'

Then every knight made great sorrow to other; and so Epinogrus departed and followed the chase after him.

Then Sir Tristram and his three fellows rode unto Joyous Gard; and there Sir Tristram talked unto Sir Palomides of his battle, how he sped at the Red City, and as ye have heard afore so was it ended.

'Truly,' said Sir Tristram, 'I am glad ye have well sped, for ye have done worshipfully. Well,' said Sir Tristram, 'we must forward to-morn.'

And then he devised how it should be; and Sir Tristram devised to send his two pavilions to set them fast by the well of Lonazep, 'and therein shall be the Queen La Beale Isoud.'

'It is well said,' said Sir Dinadan, but when Sir Palomides heard of that his heart was ravished out of measure: notwithstanding he said but little.

So when they came to Joyous Gard Sir Palomides would not have gone into the castle, but as Sir Tristram took him by the finger, and led him into the castle. And when Sir Palomides saw La Beale Isoud he was ravished so that he might unnethe speak. So they went unto meat, but Palomides might not eat, and there was all the cheer that might be had.

And on the morn they were apparelled to ride toward Lonazep. So Sir Tristram had three squires, and La Beale Isoud had three gentlewomen, and both the queen and they were richly apparelled; and other people had they none with them, but varlets to bear their shields and their spears. And thus they rode forth.

So as they rode they saw afore them a rout of knights; it was the knight Galihodin with twenty knights with him.

'Fair fellows,' said Galihodin, 'yonder comen four knights, and a rich and a well fair lady: I am in will to take that lady from them.'

'That is not of the best counsel,' said one of Galihodin's men, 'but send ye to them and wit what they will say.'

And so it was done. There came a squire unto Sir Tristram, and asked them whether they would joust or else to lose their lady.

'Not so,' said Sir Tristram, 'tell your lord I bid him come as many as we be, and win her and take her.'

'Sir,' said Palomides, 'and it please you let me have this deed, and I shall undertake them all four.'

'I will that ye have it,' said Sir Tristram, 'at your pleasure. Now go and tell your lord Galihodin, that this same knight will encounter with him and his fellows.'

CHAPTER 66: *How Sir Palomides jousted with Sir Gali-hodin, and after with Sir Gawain, and smote them down*

Then this squire departed and told Galihodin; and then he dressed his shield, and put forth a spear, and Sir Palomides another; and there Sir Palomides smote Galihodin so hard that he smote both horse and man to the earth. And there he had an horrible fall.

And then came there another knight, and in the same wise he served him; and so he served the third and the fourth, that he smote them over their horses' croups, and always Sir Palomides' spear was whole. Then came six knights more of Galihodin's men, and would have been avenged upon Sir Palomides.

'Let be,' said Sir Galihodin, 'not so hardy, none of you all meddle with this knight, for he is a man of great bounty and honour, and if he would, ye were not able to meddle with him.'

And right so they held them still. And ever Sir Palomides was ready to joust; and when he saw they would no more he rode unto Sir Tristram.

'Right well have ye done,' said Sir Tristram, 'and worshipfully have ye done as a good knight should.'

This Galihodin was nigh cousin unto Galahaut, the Haut Prince; and this Galihodin was a king within the country of Surluse.

So as Sir Tristram, Sir Palomides, and La Beale Isoud rode together they saw afore them four knights, and every man had his spear in his hand: the first was Sir Gawain, the second Sir Uwain, the third Sir Sagramore le Desirous, and the fourth was Dodinas le Savage.

When Sir Palomides beheld them, that the four knights were ready to joust, he prayed Sir Tristram to give him leave to have ado with them all so long as he might hold him on horseback. 'And if that I be smitten down I pray you revenge me.'

'Well,' said Sir Tristram, 'I will as ye will, and ye are not so fain to have worship but I would as fain increase your worship.'

And therewithal Sir Gawain put forth his spear, and Sir Palomides another; and so they came so eagerly together that Sir Palomides smote Sir Gawain to the earth, horse and all; and in the same wise he served Uwain, Sir Dodinas, and Sagramore. All these four knights Sir Palomides smote down with divers spears.

And then Sir Tristram departed toward Lonazep. And when they were departed then came thither Galihodin with his ten knights unto Sir Gawain, and there he told him all how he had sped.

'I marvel,' said Sir Gawain, 'what knights they be, that are so arrayed in green.'

'And that knight upon the white horse smote me down,' said Galihodin, 'and my three fellows.'

'And so he did to me,' said Gawain; 'and well I wot,' said Sir Gawain, 'that either he upon the white horse is Sir Tristram or else Sir Palomides, and that gay beseen lady is Queen Isoud.'

Thus they talked of one thing and of other. And in the meanwhile Sir Tristram passed on till that he came to the well where his two pavilions were set; and there they alighted, and there they saw many pavilions and great array.

Then Sir Tristram left there Sir Palomides and Sir Gareth with La Beale Isoud, and Sir Tristram and Sir Dinadan rode to Lonazep to hearken tidings; and Sir Tristram rode upon Sir Palomides' white horse. And when he came into the castle Sir Dinadan heard a great horn blow, and to the horn drew many knights.

Then Sir Tristram asked a knight, 'What meaneth the blast of that horn?'

'Sir,' said that knight, 'it is all those that shall hold against King Arthur at this tournament. The first is the King of Ireland, and the King of Surluse, the King of Listinoise, the King of Northumberland, and the king of the best part of

Wales, with many other countries. And these draw them to a council, to understand what governance they shall be of.'

But the King of Ireland, whose name was Marhalt, and father to the good knight Sir Marhaus that Sir Tristram slew, had all the speech that Sir Tristram might hear it. He said, 'Lords and fellows, let us look to ourself, for wit ye well King Arthur is sure of many good knights, or else he would not with so few knights have ado with us; therefore by my counsel let every king have a standard and a cognisance by himself, that every knight draw to their natural lord, and then may every king and captain help his knights if they have need.'

When Sir Tristram had heard all their counsel he rode unto King Arthur for to hear of his counsel.

CHAPTER 67: *How Sir Tristram and his fellowship came unto the Tournament of Lonazep; and of divers jousts and matters*

But Sir Tristram was not so soon come into the place, but Sir Gawain and Sir Galihodin went to King Arthur, and told him : 'That same green knight in the green harness with the white horse smote us two down, and six of our fellows this same day.'

'Well,' said Arthur. And then he called Sir Tristram and asked him what was his name.

'Sir,' said Sir Tristram, 'ye shall hold me excused as at this time, for ye shall not wit my name.' And there Sir Tristram returned and rode his way.

'I have marvel,' said Arthur, 'that yonder knight will not tell me his name, but go thou, Griflet le Fise de Dieu, and pray him to speak with me betwixt us.'

Then Sir Griflet rode after him and overtook him, and said him that King Arthur prayed him for to speak with him secretly apart.

'Upon this covenant,' said Sir Tristram, 'I will speak with

him: that I will turn again so that ye will ensure me not to desire to hear my name.'

'I shall undertake,' said Sir Griflet, 'that he will not greatly desire it of you.'

So they rode together until they came to King Arthur.

'Fair sir,' said King Arthur, 'what is the cause ye will not tell me your name?'

'Sir,' said Sir Tristram, 'without a cause I will not hide my name.'

'Upon what party will ye hold?' said King Arthur.

'Truly, my lord,' said Sir Tristram, 'I wot not yet on what party I will be on, until I come to the field, and thereas my heart giveth me, there will I hold; but tomorrow ye shall see and prove on what party I shall come.'

And therewithal he returned and went to his pavilions.

And upon the morn they armed them all in green, and came into the field; and there young knights began to joust, and did many worshipful deeds.

Then spake Gareth unto Sir Tristram, and prayed him to give him leave to break his spear, for him thought shame to bear his spear whole again.

When Sir Tristram heard him say so he laughed, and said, 'I pray you do your best.'

Then Sir Gareth gat a spear and proffered to joust. That saw a knight that was nephew unto the King of the Hundred Knights; his name was Selises, and a good man of arms. So this knight Selises then dressed him unto Sir Gareth, and they two met together so hard that either smote other down, horse and all, to the earth, so they were both bruised and hurt; and there they lay till the King with the Hundred Knights halp Selises up, and Sir Tristram and Sir Palomides halp up Gareth again.

And so they rode with Sir Gareth unto their pavilions, and then they pulled off his helm. And when La Beale Isoud saw Sir Gareth bruised in the face she asked him what ailed him.

'Madam,' said Sir Gareth, 'I had a great buffet, and as I suppose I gave another, but none of my fellows, God thank them, would not rescue me.'

'Forsooth,' said Palomides, 'it longed not to none of us as this day to joust, for there have not this day jousted no proved knights, and needly ye would joust. And when the other party saw ye proffered yourself to joust they sent one to you, a passing good knight of his age, for I know him well, his name is Selises; and worshipfully ye met with him, and neither of you are dishonoured, and therefore refresh yourself that ye may be ready and whole to joust to-morrow.'

'As for that,' said Gareth, 'I shall not fail you and I may bestride mine horse.'

CHAPTER 68: *How Sir Tristram and his fellowship jousted, and of the noble feats that they did in that tourneying*

'Now upon what party,' said Tristram, 'is it best we be withal as to-morn?'

'Sir,' said Palomides, 'ye shall have mine advice to be against King Arthur as to-morn, for on his party will be Sir Launcelot and many good knights of his blood with him. And the more men of worship that they be, the more worship we shall win.'

'That is full knightly spoken,' said Sir Tristram; 'and right so as ye counsel me, so will we do.'

'In the name of God,' said they all.

So that night they were lodged with the best. And on the morn when it was day they were arrayed all in green trappers, shields and spears, and La Beale Isoud in the same colour, and her three damosels. And right so these four knights came into the field endlong and through. And so they led La Beale Isoud thither as she should stand and behold all the jousts in a bay window; but always she was wimpled that no man might see her visage. And then these three knights rode straight unto the party of the King of Scots.

When King Arthur had seen him do all this he asked Sir Launcelot what were these knights and that queen.

'Sir,' said Launcelot, 'I cannot say you in certain, but if Sir Tristram be in this country, or Sir Palomides, wit ye well it be they in certain, and La Beale Isoud.'

Then Arthur called to him Sir Kay and said, 'Go lightly and wit how many knights there be here lacking of the Table Round, for by the sieges thou mayest know.'

So went Sir Kay and saw by the writing in the sieges that there lacked ten knights, 'and these be their names that be not here: Sir Tristram, Sir Palomides, Sir Percival, Sir Gaheris, Sir Epinogrus, Sir Mordred, Sir Dinadan, Sir La Cote Male Taile, and Sir Pelleas the noble knight.'

'Well,' said Arthur, 'some of these I dare undertake are here this day against us.'

Then came therein two brethren, cousins unto Sir Gawain, the one hight Sir Edward, that other hight Sir Sadok, the which were two good knights; and they asked of King Arthur that they might have the first jousts, for they were of Orkney.

'I am pleased,' said King Arthur.

Then Sir Edward encountered with the King of Scots, in whose party was Sir Tristram and Sir Palomides; and Sir Edward smote the King of Scots quite from his horse, and Sir Sadok smote down the King of North Wales, and gave him a wonder great fall, that there was a great cry on King Arthur's party, and that made Sir Palomides passing wroth. And so Sir Palomides dressed his shield and his spear, and with all his might he met with Sir Edward of Orkney, that he smote him so hard that his horse might not stand on his feet, and so they hurtled to the earth; and then with the same spear Sir Palomides smote down Sir Sadok over his horse's croup.

'O Jesu!' said Arthur, 'What knight is that arrayed all in green? He jousteth mightily.'

'Wit you well,' said Sir Gawain, 'he is a good knight, and yet shall ye see him joust better or he depart. And yet shall ye see,' said Sir Gawain, 'another bigger knight, in the same colour, than he is; for that same knight,' said Sir Gawain, 'that smote down right now my four cousins, he smote me down within these two days, and seven fellows more.'

This meanwhile as they stood thus talking there came into the place Sir Tristram upon a black horse, and or ever he stint he smote down with one spear four good knights of Orkney that were of the kin of Sir Gawain; and Sir Gareth and Sir Dinadan every each of them smote down a good knight.

'Jesu!' said Arthur, 'yonder knight upon the black horse doth mightily and marvellously well.'

'Abide you,' said Sir Gawain. 'That knight with the black horse began not yet.'

Then Sir Tristram made to horse again the two kings that Edward and Sadok had unhorsed at the beginning. And then Sir Tristram drew his sword and rode into the thickest of the press against them of Orkney; and there he smote down knights, and rashed off helms, and pulled away their shields, and hurtled down many knights: he fared so that Sir Arthur and all knights had great marvel when they saw one knight do so great deeds of arms. And Sir Palomides failed not upon the other side, but did so marvellously well that all men had wonder. For there King Arthur likened Sir Tristram that was on the black horse like to a wood lion, and likened Sir Palomides upon the white horse unto a wood leopard, and Sir Gareth and Sir Dinadan unto eager wolves. But the custom was such among them that none of the kings would help other, but all the fellowship of every standard to help other as they might; but ever Sir Tristram did so much deeds of arms that they of Orkney waxed weary of him, and so withdrew them unto Lonazep.

CHAPTER 69: *How Sir Tristram was unhorsed and smitten down by Sir Launcelot, and after that Sir Tristram smote down King Arthur*

Then was the cry of heralds and all manner of common people: 'The green knight hath done marvellously, and beaten all them of Orkney.' And there the heralds numbered that Sir Tristram that sat upon the black horse had smitten down with spears and swords thirty knights; and Sir Palomides had smitten down twenty knights, and the most part of these fifty knights were of the house of King Arthur and proved knights.

'So God me help,' said Arthur unto Sir Launcelot, 'this is a great shame to us to see four knights beat so many knights of mine; and therefore make you ready, for we will have ado with them.'

'Sir,' said Launcelot, 'wit ye well that there are two passing good knights, and great worship were it not to us now to have ado with them, for they have this day sore travailed.'

'As for that,' said Arthur, 'I will be avenged; and therefore take with you Sir Bleoberis and Sir Ector, and I will be the fourth,' said Arthur.

'Sir,' said Launcelot, 'ye shall find me ready, and my brother Sir Ector, and my cousin Sir Bleoberis.'

And so when they were ready and on horseback, 'Now choose,' said Sir Arthur unto Sir Launcelot, 'with whom that ye will encounter withal.'

'Sir,' said Launcelot, 'I will meet with the green knight upon the black horse;' (that was Sir Tristram) 'and my cousin Sir Bleoberis shall match the green knight upon the white horse;' (that was Sir Palomides) 'and my brother Sir Ector shall match with the green knight upon the white horse,' (that was Sir Gareth).

'Then must I,' said Sir Arthur, 'have ado with the green knight upon the grizzled horse,' (and that was Sir Dinadan).

'Now every man take heed to his fellow,' said Sir Launcelot.

And so they trotted on together, and there encountered Sir Launcelot against Sir Tristram. So Sir Launcelot smote Sir Tristram so sore upon the shield that he bare horse and man to the earth; but Sir Launcelot weened that it had been Sir Palomides, and so he passed forth. And then Sir Bleoberis encountered with Sir Palomides, and he smote him so hard upon the shield that Sir Palomides and his white horse rustled to the earth. Then Sir Ector de Maris smote Sir Gareth so hard that down he fell off his horse. And the noble King Arthur encountered with Sir Dinadan, and he smote him quite from his saddle. And then the noise turned awhile how the green knights were slain down.

When the King of Northgales saw that Sir Tristram had a fall, then he remembered him how great deeds of arms Sir Tristram had done. Then he made ready many knights, for the custom and cry was such, that what knight were smitten down, and might not be horsed again by his fellows other by his own strength, that as that day he should be prisoner unto the party that had smitten him down.

So came in the King of Northgales, and he rode straight unto Sir Tristram; and when he came nigh him he alit down suddenly and betook Sir Tristram his horse, and said thus:

'Noble knight, I know thee not of what country that thou art, but for the noble deeds that thou hast done this day take there my horse, and let me do as well I may; for as Jesu me help thou art better worthy to have mine horse than I myself.'

'Gramercy,' said Sir Tristram, 'and if I may [I] shall quit you; look that ye go not far from us, and as I suppose, I shall win you another horse.'

And therewith Sir Tristram mounted upon his horse, and there he met with King Arthur, and he gave him such a buffet upon the helm with his sword that King Arthur had no power to keep his saddle. And then Sir Tristram gave the King of Northgales King Arthur's horse: then was there great press about King Arthur for to horse him again; but Sir Palomides would not suffer King Arthur to be horsed again, but ever Sir Palomides smote on the right hand and on the left hand mightily as a noble knight.

And this meanwhile Sir Tristram rode through the thickest of the press, and smote down knights on the right hand and on the left hand, and rased off helms, and so passed forth unto his pavilions, and left Sir Palomides on foot; and Sir Tristram changed his horse and disguised himself all in red, horse and harness.

CHAPTER 70: *How Sir Tristram changed his harness and it was all red, and how he demeaned him, and how Sir Palomides slew Launcelot's horse*

And when the Queen La Beale Isoud saw that Sir Tristram was unhorsed, and she wist not where he was, then she wept greatly. But Sir Tristram when he was ready came dashing lightly into the field, and then La Beale Isoud espied him. And so he did great deeds of arms; with one spear that was great Sir Tristram smote down five knights or ever he stint.

Then Sir Launcelot espied him readily, that it was Sir Tristram, and then he repented him that he had smitten him down; and so Sir Launcelot went out of the press to repose him and lightly he came again.

And now when Sir Tristram came into the press, through his great force he put Sir Palomides upon his horse, and Sir Gareth, and Sir Dinadan, and then they began to do marvellously; but Sir Palomides nor none of his two fellows knew not who had holpen them on horseback again. But ever Sir Tristram was nigh them and succoured them, and they not him, because he was changed into red armour. And all this while Sir Launcelot was away.

So when La Beale Isoud knew Sir Tristram again upon his horseback she was passing glad, and then she laughed and made good cheer. And as it happened, Sir Palomides looked up toward her where she lay in the window, and he espied how she laughed; and therewith he took such a rejoicing that he smote down, what with his spear and with his sword, all that ever he met; for through the sight of her he was so enamoured in her love that he seemed at that time, that and both Sir Tristram and Sir Launcelot had been both against him they should have won no worship of him; and in his heart, as the book saith, Sir Palomides wished that with his worship he might have ado with Sir Tristram before all men, because of La Beale Isoud.

Then Sir Palomides began to double his strength, and he did so marvellously that all men had wonder of him, and ever he cast up his eye unto La Beale Isoud. And when he saw her make such cheer he fared like a lion, that there might no man withstand him.

And then Sir Tristram beheld him, how that Sir Palomides bestirred him; and then he said unto Sir Dinadan, 'So God me help, Sir Palomides is a passing good knight and a well enduring, but such deeds saw I him never do, nor never heard I tell that ever he did so much in one day.'

'It is his day,' said Dinadan; and he would say no more unto Sir Tristram; but to himself he said, 'And if ye knew for whose love he doth all those deeds of arms, soon would Sir Tristram abate his courage.'

'Alas,' said Sir Tristram, 'that Sir Palomides is not christened.' So said King Arthur, and so said all those that beheld him.

Then all people gave him the prize, as for the best knight that day, that he passed Sir Launcelot other Sir Tristram.

'Well,' said Dinadan to himself, 'all this worship that Sir Palomides hath here this day he may thank the Queen Isoud, for had she been away this day Sir Palomides had not gotten the prize this day.'

Right so came into the field Sir Launcelot du Lake, and saw and heard the noise and cry and the great worship that Sir Palomides had. He dressed him against Sir Palomides, with a great mighty spear and a long, and thought to smite him down. And when Sir Palomides saw Sir Launcelot come upon him so fast, he ran upon Sir Launcelot as fast with his sword as he might; and as Sir Launcelot should have stricken him he smote his spear aside, and smote it atwo with his sword. And Sir Palomides rashed unto Sir Launcelot, and thought to have put him to a shame; and with his sword he smote his horse's neck that Sir Launcelot rode upon, and then Sir Launcelot fell to the earth.

Then was the cry huge and great: 'See how Sir Palomides the Saracen hath smitten down Sir Launcelot's horse.'

Right then were there many knights wroth with Sir Palomides because he had done that deed; therefore many knights held there against that it was unknightly done in a tournament to kill an horse wilfully, but that it had been done in plain battle, life for life.

CHAPTER 71: *How Sir Launcelot said to Sir Palomides, and how the prize of that day was given unto Sir Palomides*

When Sir Ector de Maris saw Sir Launcelot his brother have such a despite, and so set on foot, then he gat a spear eagerly, and ran against Sir Palomides, and he smote him so hard that he bare him quite from his horse. That saw Sir Tristram, that was in red harness, and he smote down Sir Ector de Maris quite from his horse.

Then Sir Launcelot dressed his shield upon his shoulder, and with his sword naked in his hand, and so came straight upon Sir Palomides fiercely and said, 'Wit thou well thou hast done me this day the greatest despite that ever any worshipful knight did to me in tournament or in jousts, and therefore I will be avenged upon thee, therefore take keep to yourself.'

'Ah mercy, noble knight,' said Palomides, 'and forgive me mine unkindly deeds, for I have no power nor might to withstand you, and I have done so much this day that well I wot I did never so much, nor never shall in my life days; and therefore, most noble knight, I require thee spare me as at this day, and I promise you I shall ever be your knight while

I live: and ye put me from my worship now, ye put me from the greatest worship that ever I had or ever shall have in my life days.'

'Well,' said Sir Launcelot, 'I see, for to say thee sooth, ye have done marvellously well this day; and I understand a part for whose love ye do it, and well I wot that love is a great mistress. And if my lady were here as she nis not, wit you well, Sir Palomides,[1] ye should not bear away the worship. But beware your love be not discovered, for and Sir Tristram may know it ye will repent it. And sithen my quarrel is not here, ye shall have this day the worship as for me; considering the great travail and pain that ye have had this day, it were no worship for me to put you from it.'

And therewithal Sir Launcelot suffered Sir Palomides to depart. Then Sir Launcelot by great force and might gat his own horse maugre twenty knights. So when Sir Launcelot was horsed he did many marvels, and so did Sir Tristram, and Sir Palomides in like wise. Then Sir Launcelot smote down with a spear Sir Dinadan, and the King of Scotland, and the King of Wales, and the King of Northumberland, and the King of Listinoise. So then Sir Launcelot and his fellows smote down well a forty knights.

Then came the King of Ireland and the King of the Strait Marches to rescue Sir Tristram and Sir Palomides. There began a great medley, and many knights were smitten down on both parties; and always Sir Launcelot spared Sir Tristram, and he spared him. And Sir Palomides would not meddle with Sir Launcelot, and so there was hurtling here and there.

And then King Arthur sent out many knights of the Table Round; and Sir Palomides was ever in the foremost front, and Sir Tristram did so strongly well that the king and all other had marvel.

And then the king let blow to lodging; and because Sir Palomides began first, and never he went nor rode out of the field to repose, but ever he was doing marvellously well other on foot or on horseback, and longest during, King Arthur and all the kings gave Sir Palomides the honour and the gree as for that day.

Then Sir Tristram commanded Sir Dinadan to fetch the queen, La Beale Isoud, and bring her to his two pavilions that stood by the well. And so Dinadan did as he was commanded. But when Sir Palomides understood and wist that Sir Tristram was in the red armour, and on the red horse, wit ye well that he was glad, and so was Sir Gareth and Sir Dinadan, for they all weened that Sir Tristram had been taken prisoner.

And then every knight drew to his inn. And then King Arthur and every knight spake of those knights; but above all men they gave Sir Palomides the prize, and all knights that knew Sir Palomides had wonder of his deeds.

'Sir,' said Sir Launcelot unto Arthur, 'as for Sir Palomides, and he be the green knight, I dare say as for this day he is best worthy to have the degree, for he reposed him never, ne never changed his weeds, and he began first and longest held on. And yet well I wot,' said Sir Launcelot, 'that there was a better knight than he, and that shall be proved or we depart, upon pain of my life.'

Thus they talked on either party; and so Sir Dinadan railed with Sir Tristram and said, 'What the devil is upon thee this day? For Sir Palomides' strength feebled never this day, but ever he doubled his strength.

CHAPTER 72: *How Sir Dinadan provoked Sir Tristram to do well*

'And thou, Sir Tristram, farest all this day as though thou hadst been asleep, and therefore I call thee coward.'

'Well, Dinadan,' said Sir Tristram, 'I was never called coward or now of no earthly knight in my life; and wit thou well, sir, I call myself never the more coward though Sir Launcelot gave me a fall, for I outcept him of all knights. And doubt ye not Sir Dinadan, and Sir Launcelot have a

outcept: except.

quarrel good, he is too over good for any knight that now is
living; and yet of his sufferance, largess, bounty, and courtesy, I call him knight peerless;' and so Sir Tristram was in
manner wroth with Sir Dinadan. But all this language Sir
Dinadan said because he would anger Sir Tristram, for to
cause him to awake his spirits and to be wroth; for well
knew Sir Dinadan that and Sir Tristram were thoroughly
wroth Sir Palomides should not get the prize upon the morn.
And for this intent Sir Dinadan said all this railing and language against Sir Tristram.

'Truly,' said Sir Palomides, 'as for Sir Launcelot, of his
noble knighthood, courtesy, and prowess, and gentleness, I
know not his peer; for this day,' said Sir Palomides, 'I did
full uncourteously unto Sir Launcelot, and full unknightly,
and full knightly and courteously he did to me again; for and
he had been as ungentle to me as I was to him, this day I had
won no worship. And therefore,' said Palomides, 'I shall be
Sir Launcelot's knight whiles my life lasteth.'

This talking was in the houses of kings. But all kings, lords,
and knights, said, of clear knighthood, and of pure strength,
of bounty, of courtesy, Sir Launcelot and Sir Tristram bare
the prize above all knights that ever were in Arthur's days.
And there were never knights in Arthur's days did half so
many deeds as they did; as the book saith, no ten knights did
not half the deeds that they did, and there was never knight
in their days that required Sir Launcelot or Sir Tristram of
any quest, so it were not to their shame, but they performed
their desire.

CHAPTER 73 : How King Arthur and Sir Launcelot came to
see La Beale Isoud, and how Palomides smote down King
Arthur

So on the morn Sir Launcelot departed, and Sir Tristram
was ready, and La Beale Isoud with Sir Palomides and Sir
Gareth. And so they rode all in green full freshly beseen

unto the forest. And Sir Tristram left Sir Dinadan sleeping in his bed. And so as they rode it happed the king and Launcelot stood in a window, and saw Sir Tristram ride and Isoud.

'Sir,' said Launcelot, 'yonder rideth the fairest lady of the world except your queen, Dame Guenever.'

'Who is that?' said Sir Arthur.

'Sir,' said he, 'it is Queen Isoud that, out-taken my lady your queen, she is makeless.'

'Take your horse,' said Arthur, 'and array you at all rights as I will do, and I promise you,' said the king, 'I will see her.'

Then anon they were armed and horsed, and either took a spear and rode unto the forest.

'Sir,' said Launcelot, 'it is not good that ye go too nigh them, for wit ye well there are two as good knights as now are living, and therefore, sir, I pray you be not too hasty. For peradventure there will be some knights be displeased and we come suddenly upon them.'

'As for that,' said Arthur, 'I will see her, for I take no force whom I grieve.'

'Sir,' said Launcelot, 'ye put yourself in great jeopardy.'

'As for that,' said the king, 'we will take the adventure.'

Right so anon the king rode even to her, and saluted her, and said, 'God you save.'

'Sir,' said she, 'ye are welcome.'

Then the king beheld her, and liked her wonderly well.

With that came Sir Palomides unto Arthur, and said, 'Uncourteous knight, what seekest thou here? Thou art uncourteous to come upon a lady thus suddenly, therefore withdraw thee.'

Sir Arthur took none heed of Sir Palomides' words, but ever he looked still upon Queen Isoud. Then was Sir Palomides wroth, and therewith he took a spear, and came hurtling upon King Arthur, and smote him down with a spear.

When Sir Launcelot saw that despite of Sir Palomides, he said to himself, 'I am loth to have ado with yonder knight, and not for his own sake but for Sir Tristram. And one thing

out-taken: excepted.

I am sure of, if I smite down Sir Palomides I must have ado with Sir Tristram, and that were overmuch for me to match them both, for they are two noble knights; notwithstanding whether I live or I die needs must I revenge my lord, and so will I whatsomever befall of me.'

And therewith Sir Làuncelot cried to Sir Palomides, 'Keep thee from me.'

And then Sir Launcelot and Sir Palomides rashed together with two spears strongly, but Sir Launcelot smote Sir Palomides so hard that he went quite out of his saddle, and had a great fall.

When Sir Tristram saw Sir Palomides have that fall, he said to Sir Launcelot, 'Sir knight, keep thee, for I must joust with thee.'

'As for to joust with me,' said Sir Launcelot, 'I will not fail you, for no dread I have of you; but I am loth to have ado with you and I might choose, for I will that ye wit that I must revenge my special lord that was unhorsed unwarly and unknightly. And therefore, though I revenged that fall, take ye no displeasure therein, for he is to me such a friend that I may not see him shamed.'

Anon Sir Tristram understood by his person and by his knightly words that it was Sir Launcelot du Lake, and verily Sir Tristram deemed that it was King Arthur, he that Sir Palomides had smitten down. And then Sir Tristram put his spear from him, and put Sir Palomides again on horseback, and Sir Launcelot put King Arthur on horseback and so departed.

'So God me help,' said Sir Tristram unto Palomides, 'ye did not worshipfully when ye smote down that knight so suddenly as ye did. And wit ye well ye did yourself great shame, for the knights came hither of their gentleness to see a fair lady; and that is every good knight's part, to behold a fair lady; and ye had not ado to play such masteries afore my lady. Wit thou well it will turn to anger, for he that ye smote down was King Arthur, and that other was the good knight Sir Launcelot. But I shall not forget the words of Sir Launcelot when that he called him a man of great worship, thereby I wist that it was King Arthur. And as for Sir Launcelot, and there had been five hundred knights in the meadow, he would not have refused them, and yet he said he would refuse me. By that again I wist that it was Sir Launcelot, for ever he forbeareth me in every place, and showeth me great kindness; and of all knights, I out-take none, say what men will say, he beareth the flower of all chivalry, say it him whosomever will. And he be well angered, and that him list to do his utterance without any favour, I know him not alive but Sir Launcelot is over hard for him, be it on horseback or on foot.'

'I may never believe,' said Palomides, 'that King Arthur will ride so privily as a poor errant knight.'

'Ah,' said Sir Tristram, 'ye know not my lord Arthur, for all knights may learn to be a knight of him. And therefore ye may be sorry,' said Sir Tristram, 'of your unkindly deeds to so noble a king.'

'And a thing that is done may not be undone,' said Palomides.

Then Sir Tristram sent Queen Isoud unto her lodging in the priory, there to behold all the tournament.

CHAPTER 74: *How the second day Palomides forsook Sir Tristram and went to the contrary party against him*

Then there was a cry unto all knights, that when they heard an horn blow they should make jousts as they did the first day. And like as the brethren Sir Edward and Sir Sadok began the jousts the first day, Sir Uwain the King's son Uriens and Sir Lucan de Butler began the jousts the second day.

And at the first encounter Sir Uwain smote down the King's son of Scots; and Sir Lucan ran against the King of Wales, and they brake their spears all to pieces; and they were so fierce both, that they hurtled together that both fell to the earth. Then they of Orkney horsed again Sir Lucan.

And then came in Sir Tristram de Liones; and then Sir Tristram smote down Sir Uwain and Sir Lucan; and Sir Palomides smote down other two knights; and Sir Gareth smote down other two knights.

Then said Sir Arthur unto Sir Launcelot, 'See yonder three knights do passingly well, and namely the first that jousted.'

'Sir,' said Launcelot, 'that knight began not yet, but ye shall see him this day do marvellously.'

And then came into the place the Duke's son of Orkney, and then they began to do many deeds of arms.

When Sir Tristram saw them so begin, he said to Palomides, 'How feel ye yourself? May ye do this day as ye did yesterday?'

'Nay,' said Palomides, 'I feel myself so weary, and so sore bruised of the deeds of yesterday, that I may not endure as I did yesterday.'

'That me repenteth,' said Sir Tristram, 'for I shall lack you this day.'

Sir Palomides said, 'Trust not to me, for I may not do as I did.' All these words said Palomides for to beguile Sir Tristram.

'Sir,' said Sir Tristram unto Sir Gareth, 'then must I trust upon you; wherefore I pray you be not far from me to rescue me.'

'And need be,' said Sir Gareth, 'I shall not fail you in all that I may do.'

Then Sir Palomides rode by himself; and then in despite of Sir Tristram he put himself in the thickest press among them of Orkney, and there he did so marvellous deeds of arms that all men had wonder of him, for there might none stand him a stroke.

When Sir Tristram saw Sir Palomides do such deeds, he marvelled and said to himself, 'He is weary of my company.' So Sir Tristram beheld him a great while and did but little else, for the noise and cry was so huge and great that Sir Tristram marvelled from whence came the strength that Sir Palomides had there in the field.

'Sir,' said Sir Gareth unto Sir Tristram, 'remember ye not

of the words that Sir Dinadan said to you yesterday, when he called you a coward; forsooth, sir, he said it for none ill, for ye are the man in the world that he most loveth, and all that he said was for your worship. And therefore,' said Sir Gareth to Sir Tristram, 'let me know this day what ye be; and wonder ye not so upon Sir Palomides, for he enforceth himself to win all the worship and honour from you.'

'I may well believe it,' said Sir Tristram. 'And sithen I understand his evil will and his envy, ye shall see, if that I enforce myself, that the noise shall be left that now is upon him.'

Then Sir Tristram rode into the thickest of the press, and then he did so marvellously well, and did so great deeds of arms, that all men said that Sir Tristram did double so much deeds of arms as Sir Palomides had done aforehand. And then the noise went plain from Sir Palomides, and all the people cried upon Sir Tristram.

'O Jesu,' said the people. 'See how Sir Tristram smiteth down with his spear so many knights. And see,' said they all, 'how many knights he smiteth down with his sword, and of how many knights he rashed off their helms and their shields;' and so he beat them all of Orkney afore him.

'How now?' said Sir Launcelot unto King Arthur, 'I told you that this day there would a knight play his pageant. Yonder rideth a knight ye may see he doth knightly, for he hath strength and wind.'

'So God me help,' said Arthur to Launcelot, 'ye say sooth, for I saw never a better knight, for he passeth far Sir Palomides.'

'Sir, wit ye well,' said Launcelot, 'it must be so of right, for it is himself, that noble knight Sir Tristram.'

'I may right well believe it,' said Arthur.

But when Sir Palomides heard the noise and the cry was turned from him, he rode out on a part and beheld Sir Tristram. And when Sir Palomides saw Sir Tristram do so marvellously well he wept passingly sore for despite, for he wist well he should no worship win that day; for well knew Sir

Palomides when Sir Tristram would put forth his strength and his manhood he should get but little worship that day.

CHAPTER 75: *How Sir Tristram departed out of the field, and awaked Sir Dinadan, and changed his array into black*

Then came King Arthur, and the King of Northgales, and Sir Launcelot du Lake; and Sir Bleoberis, Sir Bors de Ganis, Sir Ector de Maris, these three knights came into the field with Sir Launcelot. And then Sir Launcelot with the three knights of his kin did so great deeds of arms that all the noise began upon Sir Launcelot. And so they beat the King of Wales and the King of Scots far aback, and made them to avoid the field; but Sir Tristram and Sir Gareth abode still in the field and endured all that ever there came, that all men had wonder that any knight might endure so many strokes. But ever Sir Launcelot, and his three kinsmen by the commandment of Sir Launcelot, forbare Sir Tristram.

Then said Sir Arthur, 'Is that Sir Palomides that endureth so well?'

'Nay,' said Sir Launcelot, 'wit ye well it is the good knight Sir Tristram, for yonder ye may see Sir Palomides beholdeth and hoveth, and doth little or nought. And sir, ye shall understand that Sir Tristram weeneth this day to beat us all out of the field. And as for me,' said Sir Launcelot, 'I shall not beat him, beat him whoso will. Sir,' said Launcelot unto Arthur, 'ye may see how Sir Palomides hoveth yonder, as though he were in a dream; wit ye well he is full heavy that Tristram doth such deeds of arms.'

'Then is he but a fool,' said Arthur, 'for never was Sir Palomides, nor never shall be, of such prowess as Sir Tristram. And if he have any envy at Sir Tristram, and cometh in with him upon his side he is a false knight.'

As the King and Sir Launcelot thus spake, Sir Tristram rode privily out of the press, that none espied him but La Beale Isoud and Sir Palomides, for they two would not let off their eyen upon Sir Tristram. And when Sir Tristram came to his pavilions he found Sir Dinadan in his bed asleep.

'Awake,' said Tristram, 'ye ought to be ashamed so to sleep when knights have ado in the field.'

Then Sir Dinadan arose lightly and said, 'Sir, what will ye that I shall do?'

'Make you ready,' said Sir Tristram, 'to ride with me into the field.'

So when Sir Dinadan was armed he looked upon Sir Tristram's helm and on his shield, and when he saw so many strokes upon his helm and upon his shield he said, 'In good time was I thus asleep, for had I been with you I must needs for shame there have followed you; more for shame than any prowess that is in me; that I see well now by those strokes that I should have been truly beaten as I was yesterday.'

'Leave your japes,' said Sir Tristram, 'and come off, that we were in the field again.'

'What,' said Sir Dinadan, 'is your heart up? Yesterday ye fared as though ye had dreamed.'

So then Sir Tristram was arrayed in black harness.

'O Jesu,' said Dinadan, 'what aileth you this day? Meseemeth ye be wilder than ye were yesterday.'

Then smiled Sir Tristram and said to Dinadan, 'Await well upon me; if ye see me overmatched look that ye be ever behind me, and I shall make you ready way by God's grace.'

So Sir Tristram and Sir Dinadan took their horses.

All this espied Sir Palomides, both their going and their coming, and so did La Beale Isoud, for she knew Sir Tristram above all other.

CHAPTER 76: *How Sir Palomides changed his shield and armour for to hurt Sir Tristram, and how Sir Launcelot did to Sir Tristram*

Then when Sir Palomides saw that Sir Tristram was disguised, then he thought to do him a shame. So Sir Palomides rode to a knight that was sore wounded, that sat under a fair well from the field.

'Sir knight,' said Sir Palomides, 'I pray you to lend me your armour and your shield, for mine is over well known in this field, and that hath done me great damage; and ye shall have mine armour and my shield that is as sure as yours.'

'I will well,' said the knight, 'that ye have mine armour and my shield, if they may do you any avail.'

So Sir Palomides armed him hastily in that knight's armour and his shield that shone as any crystal or silver, and so he came riding into the field. And then there was neither Sir Tristram nor none of King Arthur's party that knew Sir Palomides.

And right so as Sir Palomides was come into the field Sir Tristram smote down three knights, even in the sight of Sir Palomides. And then Sir Palomides rode against Sir Tristram, and either met other with great spears, that they brast to their hands. And then they dashed together with swords eagerly.

Then Sir Tristram had marvel what knight he was that did battle so knightly with him. Then was Sir Tristram wroth, for he felt him passing strong, so that he deemed he might not have ado with the remnant of the knights, because of the strength of Sir Palomides.

So they lashed together and gave many sad strokes together, and many knights marvelled what knight he might be that so encountered with the black knight, Sir Tristram. Full well knew La Beale Isoud that there was Sir Palomides that fought with Sir Tristram, for she espied all in her window where that she stood, as Sir Palomides changed his harness with the wounded knight. And then she began to weep so heartily for the despite of Sir Palomides that there she swooned.

Then came in Sir Launcelot with the knights of Orkney. And when the other party had espied Sir Launcelot, they cried, 'Return, return, here cometh Sir Launcelot du Lake.'

So there came knights and said, 'Sir Launcelot ye must

needs fight with yonder knight in the black harness,' (that was Sir Tristram), 'for he hath almost overcome that good knight that fighteth with him with the silver shield,' (that was Sir Palomides).

Then Sir Launcelot rode betwixt Sir Tristram and Sir Palomides, and Sir Launcelot said to Palomides, 'Sir knight, let me have the battle, for ye have need to be reposed.'

Sir Palomides knew Sir Launcelot well, and so did Sir Tristram, but because Sir Launcelot was far hardier knight than himself therefore he was glad, and suffered Sir Launcelot to fight with Sir Tristram. For well wist he that Sir Launcelot knew not Sir Tristram, and there he hoped that Sir Launcelot should beat or shame Sir Tristram, whereof Sir Palomides was full fain. And so Sir Launcelot gave Sir Tristram many sad strokes, but Sir Launcelot knew not Sir Tristram, but Sir Tristram knew well Sir Launcelot. And thus they fought long together, that La Beale Isoud was well nigh out of her mind for sorrow.

Then Sir Dinadan told Sir Gareth how that knight in the black harness was Sir Tristram; 'and this is Launcelot that fighteth with him, that must needs have the better of him for Sir Tristram hath had too much travail this day.'

'Then let us smite him down,' said Sir Gareth.

'So it is better that we do,' said Sir Dinadan, 'than Sir Tristram be shamed, for yonder hoveth the strong knight with the silver shield to fall upon Sir Tristram if need be.'

Then forthwith Gareth rashed upon Sir Launcelot, and gave him a great stroke upon his helm so hard that he was astonied. And then came Sir Dinadan with a spear, and he smote Sir Launcelot such a buffet that horse and all fell to the earth.

'O Jesu,' said Sir Tristram to Sir Gareth and Sir Dinadan, 'Fie for shame, why did ye smite down so good a knight as he is, and namely when I had ado with him? Now ye do yourself great shame, and him no disworship, for I held him reasonable hot though ye had not holpen me.'

Then came Sir Palomides that was disguised, and smote down Sir Dinadan from his horse. Then Sir Launcelot, because Sir Dinadan had smitten him aforehand, then Sir Launcelot assailed Sir Dinadan passing sore, and Sir Dinadan defended him mightily. But well understood Sir Tristram that Sir Dinadan might not endure Sir Launcelot, wherefore Sir Tristram was sorry.

Then came Sir Palomides fresh upon Sir Tristram. And when Sir Tristram saw him come, he thought to deliver him at once, because that he would help Sir Dinadan, because he stood in great peril with Sir Launcelot. Then Sir Tristram hurtled unto Sir Palomides and gave him a great buffet, and then Sir Tristram gat Sir Palomides and pulled him down underneath him. And so fell Sir Tristram with him; and Sir Tristram leapt up lightly and left Sir Palomides, and went betwixt Sir Launcelot and Dinadan, and then they began to do battle together.

Right so Sir Dinadan gat Sir Tristram's horse, and said on high that Sir Launcelot might hear it, 'My lord Sir Tristram, take your horse.'

And when Sir Launcelot heard him name Sir Tristram, 'O Jesu,' said Launcelot, 'what have I done? I am dishonoured. Ah, my lord Sir Tristram,' said Launcelot, 'why were ye disguised? Ye have put yourself in great peril this day; but I pray you noble knight to pardon me, for and I had known you we had not done this battle.'

'Sir,' said Sir Tristram, 'this is not the first kindness ye showed me.'

So they were both horsed again. Then all the people on the one side gave Sir Launcelot the honour and the degree, and on the other side all the people gave to the noble knight Sir Tristram the honour and the degree; but Launcelot said nay thereto :

'For I am not worthy to have this honour, for I will report me unto all knights that Sir Tristram hath been longer in the field than I, and he hath smitten down many more knights this day than I have done. And therefore I will give Sir Tristram my voice and my name, and so I pray all my lords and fellows so to do.'

Then there was the whole voice of dukes and earls, barons and knights, that 'Sir Tristram this day is proved the best knight.'

CHAPTER 77: *How Sir Tristram departed with La Beale Isoud, and how Palomides followed and excused him*

Then they blew unto lodging, and Queen Isoud was led unto her pavilions. But wit you well she was wroth out of measure with Sir Palomides, for she saw all his treason from the beginning to the ending. And all this while neither Sir Tristram, neither Sir Gareth nor Dinadan, knew not of the treason of Sir Palomides; but afterward ye shall hear that there befell the greatest debate betwixt Sir Tristram and Sir Palomides that might be.

So when the tournament was done, Sir Tristram, Gareth, and Dinadan, rode with La Beale Isoud to these pavilions. And ever Sir Palomides rode with them in their company disguised as he was. But when Sir Tristram had espied him that he was the same knight with the shield of silver that held him so hot that day,

'Sir knight,' said Sir Tristram, 'wit ye well here is none that hath need of your fellowship, and therefore I pray you depart from us.'

Sir Palomides answered again as though he had not known Sir Tristram, 'Wit you well, sir knight, from this fellowship will I never depart, for one of the best knights of the world commanded me to be in this company, and till he discharge me of my service I will not be discharged.'

By that Sir Tristram knew that it was Sir Palomides.

'Ah, Sir Palomides,' said the noble knight Sir Tristram, 'are ye such a knight? Ye have been named wrong, for ye have long been called a gentle knight, and as this day ye have showed me great ungentleness, for ye had almost brought me

unto my death. But, as for you, I suppose I should have done
well enough, but Sir Launcelot with you was overmuch; for
I know no knight living but Sir Launcelot is over good for
him, and he will do his uttermost.'

'Alas,' said Sir Palomides, 'are ye my lord Sir Tristram?'

'Yea, sir, and that ye know well enough.'

'By my knighthood,' said Palomides, 'until now I knew you
not; I weened that ye had been the King of Ireland, for well
I wot ye bare his arms.'

'His arms I bare,' said Sir Tristram, 'and that will I stand
by, for I won them once in a field of a full noble knight, his
name was Sir Marhaus; and with great pain I won that
knight, for there was none other recover, but Sir Marhaus
died through false leeches; and yet was he never yielden to
me.'

'Sir,' said Palomides, 'I weened ye had been turned upon
Sir Launcelot's party, and that caused me to turn.'

'Ye say well,' said Sir Tristram, 'and so I take you, and I
forgive you.'

So then they rode into their pavilions; and when they were
alit they unarmed them and washed their faces and hands,
and so yode unto meat, and were set at their table.

But when Isoud saw Sir Palomides she changed then her
colours, and for wrath she might not speak. Anon Sir Tristram espied her countenance and said,

'Madam, for what cause make ye us such cheer? We have
been sore travailed this day.'

'Mine own lord,' said La Beale Isoud, 'for God's sake be ye
not displeased with me, for I may none otherwise do; for I
saw this day how ye were betrayed and nigh brought to your
death. Truly, sir, I saw every deal, how and in what wise, and
therefore, sir, how should I suffer in your presence such a
felon and traitor as Sir Palomides; for I saw him with mine
eyen how he beheld you when ye went out of the field. For
ever he hoved still upon his horse till he saw you come in
againward. And then forthwithal I saw him ride to the hurt
knight, and changed harness with him, and then straight I

saw him how he rode into the field. And anon as he had found you he encountered with you, and thus wilfully Sir Palomides did battle with you; and as for him, sir, I was not greatly afraid, but I dread sore Launcelot, that knew you not.'

'Madam,' said Palomides, 'ye may say whatso ye will, I may not contrary you, but by my knighthood I knew not Sir Tristram.'

'Sir Palomides,' said Sir Tristram, 'I will take your excuse, but well I wot ye spared me but little, but all is pardoned on my part.'

Then La Beale Isoud held down her head and said no more at that time.

CHAPTER 78: *How King Arthur and Sir Launcelot came into their pavilions as they sat at supper, and of Palomides*

And therewithal two knights armed came unto the pavilion, and there they alit both, and came in armed at all pieces.

'Fair knights,' said Sir Tristram, 'ye are to blame to come thus armed at all pieces upon me while we are at our meat; if ye would anything when we were in the field there might ye have eased your hearts.'

'Not so,' said one of those knights, 'we come not for that intent, but wit ye well Sir Tristram, we be come hither as your friends.'

'And I am come here,' said the one, 'for to see you, and this knight is come for to see La Beale Isoud.'

Then said Sir Tristram, 'I require you do off your helms that I may see you.'

'That will we do at your desire,' said the knights.

And when their helms were off, Sir Tristram thought that he should know them.

Then said Sir Dinadan privily unto Sir Tristram, 'Sir, that is Sir Launcelot du Lake that spake unto you first, and the other is my lord King Arthur.'

Then said Sir Tristram unto La Beale Isoud, 'Madam arise, for here is my lord, King Arthur.'

Then the king and the queen kissed, and Sir Launcelot and Sir Tristram braced either other in arms, and then there was joy without measure; and at the request of La Beale Isoud, King Arthur and Launcelot were unarmed, and then there was merry talking.

'Madam,' said Sir Arthur, 'it is many a day sithen that I have desired to see you, for ye have been praised so far; and now I dare say ye are the fairest that ever I saw, and Sir Tristram is as fair and as good a knight as any that I know; therefore me beseemeth ye are well beset together.'

'Sir, God thank you,' said the noble knight, Sir Tristram, and Isoud; 'of your great goodness and largess ye are peerless.'

Thus they talked of many things and of all the whole jousts.

'But for what cause,' said King Arthur, 'were ye, Sir Tristram, against us? Ye are a knight of the Table Round; of right ye should have been with us.'

'Sir,' said Sir Tristram, 'here is Dinadan, and Sir Gareth your own nephew, caused me to be against you.'

'My lord Arthur,' said Gareth, 'I may well bear the blame, but it were Sir Tristram's own deeds.'

'That may I repent,' said Dinadan, 'for this unhappy Sir Tristram brought us to this tournament, and many great buffets he caused us to have.'

Then the king and Launcelot laughed that they might not sit.

'What knight was that,' said Arthur, 'that held you so short, this with the shield of silver?'

'Sir,' said Sir Tristram, 'here he sitteth at this board.'

'What,' said Arthur, 'was it Sir Palomides?'

'Wit ye well it was he,' said La Beale Isoud.

'So God me help,' said Arthur, 'that was unknightly done of you of so good a knight, for I have heard many people call you a courteous knight.'

'Sir,' said Palomides, 'I knew not Sir Tristram, for he was so disguised.'

'So God me help,' said Launcelot, 'it may well be, for I knew not Sir Tristram.'

'But I marvel why ye turned on our party.'

'That was done for the same cause,' said Launcelot.

'As for that,' said Sir Tristram, 'I have pardoned him, and I would be right loth to leave his fellowship, for I love right well his company.'

So they left off and talked of other things. And in the evening King Arthur and Sir Launcelot departed unto their lodging; but wit ye well Sir Palomides had envy heartily, for all that night he had never rest in his bed, but wailed and wept out of measure.

So on the morn Sir Tristram, Gareth, and Dinadan arose early, and then they went unto Sir Palomides' chamber, and there they found him fast asleep, for he had all night watched, and it was seen upon his cheeks that he had wept full sore.

'Say nothing,' said Sir Tristram, 'for I am sure he hath taken anger and sorrow for the rebuke that I gave to him, and La Beale Isoud.'

CHAPTER 79: *How Sir Tristram and Sir Palomides did the next day, and how King Arthur was unhorsed*

Then Sir Tristram let call Sir Palomides, and bad him make him ready, for it was time to go to the field. When they were ready they were armed, and clothed all in red, both Isoud and all they; and so they led her passing freshly through the field, into the priory where was her lodging.

And then they heard three blasts blow, and every king and knight dressed him unto the field. And the first that was ready to joust was Sir Palomides and Sir Kainus le Strange, a knight of the Table Round. And so they two encountered together, but Sir Palomides smote Sir Kainus so hard that he

smote him quite over his horse's croup. And forthwithal Sir
Palomides smote down another knight, and brake then his
spear, and pulled out his sword and did wonderly well. And
then the noise began greatly upon Sir Palomides.

'Lo,' said King Arthur, 'yonder Palomides beginneth to
play his pageant. So God me help,' said Arthur, 'he is a passing good knight.'

And right as they stood talking thus, in came Sir Tristram
as thunder, and he encountered with Sir Kay the Seneschal,
and there he smote him down quite from his horse; and with
that same spear Sir Tristram smote down three knights more,
and then he pulled out his sword and did marvellously. Then
the noise and cry changed from Sir Palomides and turned to
Sir Tristram, and all the people cried, 'O Tristram, O Tristram.' And then was Sir Palomides clean forgotten.

'How now,' said Launcelot unto Arthur, 'yonder rideth a
knight that playeth his pageants.'

'So God me help,' said Arthur to Launcelot, 'ye shall see
this day that yonder two knights shall here do this day
wonders.'

'Sir,' said Launcelot, 'the one knight waiteth upon the
other, and enforceth himself through envy to pass the noble
knight Sir Tristram, and he knoweth not of the privy envy
the which Sir Palomides hath to him; for all that the noble
Sir Tristram doth is through clean knighthood.'

And then Sir Gareth and Dinadan did wonderly great deeds
of arms, as two noble knights, so that King Arthur spake of
them great honour and worship; and the kings and knights
of Sir Tristram's side did passingly well, and held them truly
together.

Then Sir Arthur and Sir Launcelot took their horses and
dressed them, and gat into the thickest of the press. And
there Sir Tristram unknowing smote down King Arthur, and
then Sir Launcelot would have rescued him, but there were
so many upon Sir Launcelot that they pulled him down from
his horse. And then the King of Ireland and the King of
Scots with their knights did their pain to take King Arthur

and Sir Launcelot prisoner. When Sir Launcelot heard them say so, he fared as it had been an hungry lion, for he fared so that no knight durst nigh him.

Then came Sir Ector de Maris, and he bare a spear against Sir Palomides, and brast it upon him all to-shivers. And then Sir Ector came again and gave Sir Palomides such a dash with a sword that he stooped down upon his saddle bow. And forthwithal Sir Ector pulled down Sir Palomides under his feet; and then Sir Ector de Maris gat Sir Launcelot du Lake an horse, and brought it to him, and bad him mount upon him; but Sir Palomides leapt afore and gat the horse by the bridle, and leapt into the saddle.

'So God me help,' said Launcelot, 'ye are better worthy to have that horse than I.'

Then Sir Ector brought Sir Launcelot another horse.

'Gramercy,' said Launcelot unto his brother.

And so when he was horsed again, with one spear he smote down four knights. And then Sir Launcelot brought to King Arthur one of the best of the four horses. Then Sir Launcelot with King Arthur and a few of his knights of Sir Launcelot's kin did marvellous deeds; for that time, as the book recordeth, Sir Launcelot smote down and pulled down thirty knights. Notwithstanding the other party held them so fast together that King Arthur and his knights were overmatched.

And when Sir Tristram saw that, what labour King Arthur and his knights, and in especial the noble deeds that Sir Launcelot did with his own hands, he marvelled greatly.

CHAPTER 80: *How Sir Tristram turned to King Arthur's side, and how Sir Palomides would not*

Then Sir Tristram called unto him Sir Palomides, Sir Gareth, and Sir Dinadan, and said thus to them:

'My fair fellows, wit ye well that I will turn unto King Arthur's party, for I saw never so few men do so well, and it will be shame unto us knights that be of the Round Table to see our lord King Arthur, and that noble knight Sir Launcelot, to be dishonoured.'

'It will be well done,' said Sir Gareth and Sir Dinadan.

'Do your best,' said Palomides, 'for I will not change my party that I came in withal.'

'That is for my sake,' said Sir Tristram. 'God speed you in your journey.'

And so departed Sir Palomides from them. Then Sir Tristram, Gareth, and Dinadan, turned with Sir Launcelot. And then Sir Launcelot smote down the King of Ireland quite from his horse; and so Sir Launcelot smote down the King of Scots, and the King of Wales; and then Sir Arthur ran unto Sir Palomides and smote him quite from his horse; and then Sir Tristram bare down all that he met. Sir Gareth and Sir Dinadan did there as noble knights; then all the parties began to flee.

'Alas,' said Palomides, 'that ever I should see this day, for now have I lost all the worship that I won.'

And then Sir Palomides went his way wailing, and so withdrew him till he came to a well, and there he put his horse from him, and did off his armour, and wailed and wept like as he had been a wood man.

Then many knights gave the prize to Sir Tristram, and there were many that gave the prize unto Sir Launcelot.

'Fair lords,' said Sir Tristram, 'I thank you of the honour ye would give me, but I pray you heartily that ye would give your voice to Sir Launcelot, for by my faith,' said Sir Tristram, 'I will give Sir Launcelot my voice.'

But Sir Launcelot would not have it, and so the prize was given betwixt them both.

Then every man rode to his lodging, and Sir Bleoberis and Sir Ector rode with Sir Tristram and La Beale Isoud unto their pavilions.

Then as Sir Palomides was at the well wailing and weeping, there came by him fleeing the King of Wales and of Scotland, and they saw Sir Palomides in that arage.

'Alas,' said they, 'that so noble a man as ye be should be in this array.'

And then those kings gat Sir Palomides' horse again, and made him to arm him and mount upon his horse, and so he rode with them, making great dole. So when Sir Palomides came nigh the pavilions thereas Sir Tristram and La Beale Isoud was in, then Sir Palomides prayed the two kings to abide him there the while that he spake with Sir Tristram.

And when he came to the port of the pavilions, Sir Palomides said on high, 'Where art thou, Sir Tristram de Liones?'

'Sir,' said Dinadan, 'that is Palomides.'

'What, Sir Palomides, will ye not come in here among us?'

'Fie on thee, traitor,' said Palomides, 'for wit you well and it were daylight as it is night I should slay thee mine own hands. And if ever I may get thee,' said Palomides, 'thou shalt die for this day's deed.'

'Sir Palomides,' said Sir Tristram, 'ye wit me with wrong, for had ye done as I did ye had won worship. But sithen ye give me so large warning I shall be well ware of you.'

'Fie on thee, traitor,' said Palomides, and therewith departed.

Then on the morn Sir Tristram, Bleoberis, and Sir Ector de Maris, Sir Gareth, Sir Dinadan, what by water and what by land, they brought La Beale Isoud unto Joyous Gard, and there reposed them a seven night, and made all the mirths and disports that they could devise.

And King Arthur and his knights drew unto Camelot, and Sir Palomides rode with the two kings; and ever he made the greatest dole that any man could think, for he was not all only so dolorous for the departing from La Beale Isoud, but he was a part as sorrowful to depart from the fellowship of Sir Tristram; for Sir Tristram was so kind and so gentle that when Sir Palomides remembered him thereof he might never be merry.

CHAPTER 81: *How Sir Bleoberis and Sir Ector reported to Queen Guenever of the beauty of La Beale Isoud*

So at the seven nights' end Sir Bleoberis and Sir Ector departed from Sir Tristram and from the queen; and these two good knights had great gifts; and Sir Gareth and Sir Dinadan abode with Sir Tristram.

And when Sir Bleoberis and Sir Ector were comen thereas the Queen Guenever was lodged, in a castle by the seaside, and through the grace of God the queen was recovered of her malady, then she asked the two knights from whence they came. They said that they came from Sir Tristram and from La Beale Isoud.

'How doth Sir Tristram,' said the queen, 'and La Beale Isoud?'

'Truly,' said those two knights, 'he doth as a noble knight should do; and as for the Queen Isoud, she is peerless of all ladies; for to speak of her beauty, bounty, and mirth, and of her goodness, we saw never her match as far as we have ridden and gone.'

'O mercy Jesu,' said Queen Guenever, 'so saith all the people that have seen her and spoken with her. God would that I had part of her conditions; and it is misfortuned me of my sickness while that tournament endured. And as I suppose I shall never see in all my life such an assembly of knights and ladies as ye have done.'

Then the knights told her how Palomides won the degree at the first day with great noblesse; and the second day Sir Tristram won the degree; and the third day Sir Launcelot won the degree.

'Well,' said Queen Guenever, 'who did best all these three days?'

'So God me help,' said these knights, 'Sir Launcelot and Sir Tristram had least dishonour. And wit ye well Sir Palomides did passing well and mightily; but he turned against the party that he came in withal, and that caused him to lose a great part of his worship, for it seemed that Sir Palomides is passing envious.'

'Then shall he never win worship,' said Queen Guenever, 'for and it happeth an envious man once to win worship he shall be dishonoured twice therefore; and for this cause all men of worship hate an envious man, and will show him no favour, and he that is courteous, and kind, and gentle, hath favour in every place.'

CHAPTER 82: *How Epinogrus complained by a well, and how Sir Palomides came and found him, and of their both sorrows*

Now leave we off this matter and speak we of Sir Palomides, that rode and lodged him with the two kings, whereof the kings were heavy. Then the King of Ireland sent a man of his to Sir Palomides, and gave him a great courser, and the King of Scotland gave him great gifts; and fain they would have had Sir Palomides to have abiden with them, but in no wise he would abide; and so he departed, and rode as adventures would guide him, till it was nigh noon.

And then in a forest by a well Sir Palomides saw where lay a fair wounded knight and his horse bounden by him; and that knight made the greatest dole that ever he heard man make, for ever he wept, and therewith he sighed as though he would die.

Then Sir Palomides rode near him and saluted him mildly and said, 'Fair knight, why wail ye so? Let me lie down and wail with you, for doubt not I am much more heavier than ye are; for I dare say,' said Palomides, 'that my sorrow is an hundred-fold more than yours is, and therefore let us complain either to other.'

'First,' said the wounded knight, 'I require you tell me your name, for and thou be none of the noble knights of the Round Table thou shalt never know my name, whatsomever come of me.'

'Fair knight,' said Palomides, 'such as I am, be it better or be it worse, wit thou well that my name is Sir Palomides, son and heir unto King Astlabor, and Sir Safer and Sir Segwarides are my two brethren; and wit thou well as for myself I was never christened, but my two brethren are truly christened.'

'O noble knight,' said that knight, 'well is me that I have met with you; and wit ye well my name is Epinogrus, the King's son of Northumberland. Now sit down,' said Epinogrus, 'and let us either complain to other.'

Then Sir Palomides began his complaint: 'Now shall I tell you,' said Palomides, 'what woe I endure. I love the fairest queen and lady that ever bare life, and wit ye well her name is La Beale Isoud, King Mark's wife of Cornwall.'

'That is great folly,' said Epinogrus, 'for to love Queen Isoud, for one of the best knights of the world loveth her, that is Sir Tristram de Liones.'

'That is truth,' said Palomides, 'for no man knoweth that matter better than I do, for I have been in Sir Tristram's fellowship this month, and with La Beale Isoud together; and alas,' said Palomides, 'unhappy man that I am, now have I lost the fellowship of Sir Tristram for ever, and the love of La Beale Isoud for ever, and I am never like to see her more, and Sir Tristram and I be either to other mortal enemies.'

'Well,' said Epinogrus, 'sith that ye loved La Beale Isoud, loved she you ever again by anything that ye could think or wit, or else did ye rejoice her ever in any pleasure?'

'Nay, by my knighthood,' said Palomides, 'I never espied that ever she loved me more than all the world, nor never had I pleasure with her, but the last day she gave me the greatest rebuke that ever I had, the which shall never go from my heart. And yet I well deserved that rebuke, for I did not knightly, and therefore I have lost the love of her and of Sir Tristram for ever. And I have many times enforced myself to do many deeds for La Beale Isoud's sake, and she was the causer of my worship-winning. Alas,' said Sir Palomides, 'now have I lost all the worship that ever I won, for never shall me befall such prowess as I had in the fellowship of Sir Tristram.'

CHAPTER 83: *How Sir Palomides brought Sir Epinogrus his lady*

'Nay, nay,' said Epinogrus, 'your sorrow is but japes to my sorrow; for I rejoiced my lady and won her with my hands, and lost her again: alas that day! Thus first I won her,' said Epinogrus: 'my lady was an earl's daughter, and as the earl and two knights came from the Tournament of Lonazep, for her sake I set upon this earl and on his two knights, my lady there being present; and so by fortune there I slew the earl and one of the knights, and the other knight fled, and so that night I had my lady. And on the morn as she and I reposed us at this well side there came there to me an errant knight, his name was Sir Helior le Preuse, an hardy knight, and this Sir Helior challenged me to fight for my lady. And then we went to battle first upon horse and after on foot, but at the last Sir Helior wounded me so that he left me for dead, and so he took my lady with him; and thus my sorrow is more than yours, for I have rejoiced and ye rejoiced never.'

'That is truth,' said Palomides, 'but sith I can never recover myself I shall promise you if I can meet with Sir Helior I shall get you your lady again, or else he shall beat me.'

Then Sir Palomides made Sir Epinogrus to take his horse, and so they rode to an hermitage, and there Sir Epinogrus rested him.

And in the meanwhile Sir Palomides walked privily out to rest him under the leaves, and there beside he saw a knight come riding with a shield that he had seen Sir Ector de Maris bear aforehand; and there came after him a ten knights, and so these ten knights hoved under the leaves for heat.

And anon after there came a knight with a green shield and therein a white lion, leading a lady upon a palfrey. Then this knight with the green shield that seemed to be master of the ten knights, he rode fiercely after Sir Helior, for it was he that hurt Sir Epinogrus. And when he came nigh Sir Helior he bad him defend his lady.

'I will defend her,' said Helior, 'unto my power.'

And so they ran together so mightily that either of these knights smote other down, horse and all, to the earth; and then they won up lightly and drew their swords and their shields, and lashed together mightily more than an hour. All this Sir Palomides saw and beheld.

But ever at the last the knight with Sir Ector's shield was bigger, and at the last this knight smote Sir Helior down, and then that knight unlaced his helm to have stricken off his head. And then he cried mercy, and prayed him to save his life, and bad him take his lady.

Then Sir Palomides dressed him up, because he wist well that that same lady was Epinogrus' lady, and he promised him to help him. Then Sir Palomides went straight to that lady, and took her by the hand, and asked her whether she knew a knight that hight Epinogrus.

'Alas,' she said, 'that ever he knew me or I him, for I have for his sake lost my worship, and also his life grieveth me most of all.'

'Not so, lady,' said Palomides, 'come on with me, for here is Epinogrus in this hermitage.'

'Ah! well is me,' said the lady, 'and he be alive.'

'Whither wilt thou with that lady?' said the knight with Sir Ector's shield.

'I will do with her what me list,' said Palomides.

'Wit you well,' said that knight, 'thou speakest over large, though thou seemest me to have at advantage, because thou sawest me do battle but late. Thou weenest, sir knight, to have that lady away from me so lightly? Nay, think it never not; and thou were as good a knight as is Sir Launcelot, or as is Sir Tristram, or Sir Palomides, but thou shalt win her dearer than ever did I.'

And so they went unto battle upon foot, and there they gave many sad strokes, and either wounded other passing sore, and thus they fought still more than an hour. Then Sir Palomides had marvel what knight he might be that was so strong and so well breathed during, and thus said Palomides:

'Knight, I require thee tell me thy name.'

'Wit thou well,' said that knight, 'I dare tell thee my name, so that thou wilt tell me thy name.'

'I will,' said Palomides.

'Truly,' said that knight, 'my name is Safer, son of King Astlabor, and Sir Palomides and Sir Segwarides are my brethren.'

'Now, and wit thou well, my name is Sir Palomides.'

Then Sir Safer kneeled down upon his knees, and prayed him of mercy; and then they unlaced their helms and either kissed other weeping.

And in the meanwhile Sir Epinogrus arose out of his bed, and heard them by the strokes, and so he armed him to help Sir Palomides if need were.

CHAPTER 84: *How Sir Palomides and Sir Safer were assailed*

Then Sir Palomides took the lady by the hand and brought her to Sir Epinogrus, and there was great joy betwixt them, for either swooned for joy.

When they were met, 'Fair knight and lady,' said Sir Safer, 'it were pity to depart you; Jesu send you joy either of other.'

'Gramercy, gentle knight,' said Epinogrus; 'and much more thank be to my lord, Sir Palomides, that thus hath through his prowess made me to get my lady.'

Then Sir Epinogrus required Sir Palomides and Sir Safer, his brother, to ride with them unto his castle, for the safeguard of his person.

'Sir,' said Palomides, 'we will be ready to conduct you because that ye are sore wounded.'

And so was Epinogrus and his lady horsed, and his lady behind him upon a soft ambler. And then they rode unto his castle, where they had great cheer and joy, as great as ever Sir Palomides and Sir Safer had in their life days.

So on the morn Sir Safer and Sir Palomides departed, and rode as fortune led them, and so they rode all that day until afternoon. And at the last they heard a great weeping and a great noise down in a manor.

'Sir,' said then Sir Safer, 'let us wit what noise this is.'

'I will well,' said Sir Palomides.

And so they rode forth till that they came to a fair gate of a manor, and there sat an old man saying his prayers and beads. Then Sir Palomides and Sir Safer alit and left their horses, and went within the gates, and there they saw full many goodly men weeping.

'Fair sirs,' said Palomides, 'wherefore weep ye and make this sorrow?'

Anon one of the knights of the castle beheld Sir Palomides and knew him, and then went to his fellows and said, 'Fair fellows, wit ye well all, we have in this castle the same knight that slew our lord at Lonazep, for I know him well; it is Sir Palomides.'

Then they went unto harness, all that might bear harness, some on horseback and some on foot, to the number of three score. And when they were ready they came freshly upon Sir Palomides and upon Sir Safer with a great noise, and said thus,

'Keep thee, Sir Palomides, for thou art known, and by right thou must be dead, for thou hast slain our lord; and therefore wit ye well we will slay thee, therefore defend thee.'

Then Sir Palomides and Sir Safer, the one set his back to the other, and gave many great strokes, and took many great strokes; and thus they fought with a twenty knights and forty gentlemen and yeomen nigh two hours.

But at the last though they were loth, Sir Palomides and Sir Safer were taken and yielden, and put in a strong prison; and within three days twelve knights passed upon them, and they found Sir Palomides guilty, and Sir Safer not guilty, of their lord's death. And when Sir Safer should be delivered there was great dole betwixt Sir Palomides and him, and many piteous complaints that Sir Safer made at his departing, there is no maker can rehearse the tenth part.

'Fair brother,' said Palomides, 'let be thy dolour and thy sorrow. And if I be ordained to die a shameful death, welcome be it; but and I had wist of this death that I am deemed unto, I should never have been yielden.'

So Sir Safer departed from his brother with the greatest dolour and sorrow that ever made knight.

And on the morn they of the castle ordained twelve knights to ride with Sir Palomides unto the father of the same knight that Sir Palomides slew; and so they bound his legs under an old steed's belly. And then they rode with Sir Palomides unto a castle by the seaside, that hight Pelownes, and there Sir Palomides should have justice. Thus was their ordinance; and so they rode with Sir Palomides fast by the castle of Joyous Gard. And as they passed by that castle there came riding out of that castle by them one that knew Sir Palomides. And when that knight saw Sir Palomides bounden upon a crooked courser, the knight asked Sir Palomides for what cause he was led so.

'Ah, my fair fellow and knight,' said Palomides, 'I ride toward my death for the slaying of a knight at a tournament of Lonazep; and if I had not departed from my lord Sir Tristram, as I ought not to have done, now might I have been sure to have had my life saved; but I pray you, sir knight, recommend me unto my lord, Sir Tristram, and unto my lady, Queen Isoud, and say to them if ever I trespassed to them I ask them forgiveness. And also I beseech you recommend me unto my lord, King Arthur, and to all the fellowship of the Round Table, unto my power.'

Then that knight wept for pity of Sir Palomides; and therewithal he rode unto Joyous Gard as fast as his horse might run, and lightly that knight descended down off his horse and went unto Sir Tristram, and there he told him all as ye have heard, and ever the knight wept as he had been mad.

CHAPTER 85: *How Sir Tristram made him ready to rescue Sir Palomides, but Sir Launcelot rescued him or he came*

When Sir Tristram heard how Sir Palomides went to his death, he was heavy to hear that, and said, 'Howbeit that I am wroth with Sir Palomides, yet will not I suffer him to die so shameful a death, for he is a full noble knight.'

And then anon Sir Tristram was armed and took his horse and two squires with him, and rode a great pace toward the Castle of Pelownes where Sir Palomides was judged to death.

And these twelve knights that led Sir Palomides passed by a well whereas Sir Launcelot was, which was alit there, and had tied his horse to a tree, and taken off his helm to drink of that well; and when he saw these knights, Sir Launcelot put on his helm and suffered them to pass by him. And then was he ware of Sir Palomides bounden, and led shamefully to his death.

'O Jesu,' said Launcelot, 'What misadventure is befall him that he is thus led toward his death? Forsooth,' said Launcelot, 'it were shame to me to suffer this noble knight so to die and I might help him, therefore I will help him whatsomever come of it, or else I shall die for Sir Palomides' sake.'

And then Sir Launcelot mounted upon his horse, and gat his spear in his hand, and rode after the twelve knights that led Sir Palomides.

'Fair knights,' said Sir Launcelot, 'whither lead ye that knight? It beseemeth him full ill to ride bounden.'

Then these twelve knights suddenly turned their horses and said to Sir Launcelot, 'Sir knight, we counsel thee not to meddle with this knight, for he hath deserved death, and unto death he is judged.'

'That me repenteth,' said Launcelot, 'that I may not borow him with fairness, for he is over good a knight to die such a shameful death. And therefore, fair knights,' said Sir Launcelot, 'keep you as well as ye can, for I will rescue that knight or die for it.'

Then they began to dress their spears, and Sir Launcelot smote the foremost down, horse and man, and so he served three more with one spear; and then that spear brast, and therewithal Sir Launcelot drew his sword, and then he smote on the right hand and on the left hand. Then within a while he left none of those twelve knights, but he had laid them to the earth, and the most part of them were sore wounded.

And then Sir Launcelot took the best horse that he found, and loosed Sir Palomides and set him upon that horse; and so they returned again unto Joyous Gard, and then was Sir Palomides ware of Sir Tristram how he came riding. And when Sir Launcelot saw him he knew him well, but Sir Tristram knew not him because Sir Launcelot had on his shoulder a golden shield. So Sir Launcelot made him ready to joust with Sir Tristram, that Sir Tristram should not ween that he were Sir Launcelot.

Then Sir Palomides cried aloud to Sir Tristram, 'O my lord, I require you joust not with this knight, for this good knight hath saved me from my death.'

When Sir Tristram heard him say so he came a soft trotting pace toward them.

And then Sir Palomides said, 'My lord, Sir Tristram, much am I beholding unto you of your great goodness, that would proffer your noble body to rescue me undeserved, for I have greatly offended you. Notwithstanding,' said Sir Palomides, 'here met we with this noble knight that worshipfully and manly rescued me from twelve knights, and smote them down all and wounded them sore.'

CHAPTER 86: *How Sir Tristram and Launcelot, with Palomides, came to Joyous Gard. Of Palomides and Sir Tristram*

'Fair knight,' said Sir Tristram unto Sir Launcelot, 'of whence be ye?'

'I am a knight errant,' said Sir Launcelot, 'that rideth to seek many adventures.'

'What is your name?' said Sir Tristram.

'Sir, at this time I will not tell you.'

Then Sir Launcelot said unto Sir Tristram and to Palomides, 'Now either of you are met together I will depart from you.'

'Not so,' said Sir Tristram; 'I pray you of knighthood to ride with me unto my castle.'

'Wit you well,' said Sir Launcelot, 'I may not ride with you, for I have many deeds to do in other places, that at this time I may not abide with you.'

'Ah, mercy Jesu,' said Sir Tristram, 'I require you as ye be a true knight to the order of knighthood, play you with me this night.'

Then Sir Tristram had a grant of Sir Launcelot; howbeit though he had not desired him he would have ridden with them, other soon have come after them; for Sir Launcelot came for none other cause into that country but for to see Sir Tristram.

And when they were come within Joyous Gard they alit, and their horses were led into a stable; and then they unarmed them. And when Sir Launcelot was unhelmed, Sir Tristram and Sir Palomides knew him. Then Sir Tristram took Sir Launcelot in arms, and so did La Beale Isoud; and Palomides kneeled down upon his knees and thanked Sir Launcelot. When Sir Launcelot saw Sir Palomides kneel he lightly took him up and said thus:

'Wit thou well Sir Palomides, I and any knight in this land, of worship ought of very right succour and rescue so noble a knight as ye are proved and renowned, throughout all this realm endlong and overthwart.'

And then was there joy among them, and the oftener that Sir Palomides saw La Beale Isoud the heavier he waxed day by day.

Then Sir Launcelot within three or four days departed, and with him rode Sir Ector de Maris; and Dinadan and Sir Palomides were there left with Sir Tristram a two months and more. But ever Sir Palomides faded and mourned, that all men had marvel wherefore he faded so away.

So upon a day, in the dawning, Sir Palomides went into the forest by himself alone; and there he found a well, and then he looked into the well, and in the water he saw his own visage, how he was disturbed and defaded, nothing like that he was.

'What may this mean?' said Sir Palomides, and thus he said to himself: 'Ah, Palomides, Palomides, why art thou defaded, thou that was wont to be called one of the fairest knights of the world? I will no more lead this life, for I love that I may never get nor recover.'

And therewithal he laid him down by the well. And then he began to make a rhyme of La Beale Isoud and him. And in the meanwhile Sir Tristram was that same day ridden into the forest to chase the hart of grease; but Sir Tristram would not ride on hunting never more unarmed, because of Sir Breunis Saunce Pité. And so as Sir Tristram rode into that forest up and down, he heard one sing marvellously loud, and that was Sir Palomides that lay by the well.

And then Sir Tristram rode softly thither, for he deemed there was some knight errant that was at the well. And when Sir Tristram came nigh him he descended down from his horse and tied his horse fast till a tree, and then he came near him on foot; and anon he was ware where lay Sir Palomides by the well and sang loud and merrily; and ever the complaints were of that noble queen, La Beale Isoud, the which was marvellously and wonderfully well said, and full dolefully and piteously made. And all the whole song the noble knight, Sir Tristram, heard from the beginning to the ending, the which grieved and troubled him sore. But then at the last, when Sir Tristram had heard all Sir Palomides' complaints, he was wroth out of measure, and thought for to slay him thereas he lay.

Then Sir Tristram remembered himself that Sir Palomides

hart of grease: fat deer.

was unarmed, and of the noble name that Sir Palomides had, and the noble name that himself had, and then he made a restraint of his anger; and so he went unto Sir Palomides a soft pace and said, 'Sir Palomides, I have heard your complaint, and of thy treason that thou hast owed me so long, and wit thou well therefore thou shalt die; and if it were not for shame of knighthood thou shouldest not escape my hands, for now I know well thou hast awaited me with treason. Tell me,' said Sir Tristram, 'how thou wilt acquit thee?'

'Sir,' said Palomides, 'thus I will acquit me: as for Queen La Beale Isoud, ye shall wit well that I love her above all other ladies in this world; and well I wot it shall befall me as for her love as befell the noble knight Sir Kehydius, that died for the love of La Beale Isoud. And now, Sir Tristram, I will that ye wit that I have loved La Beale Isoud many a day, and she hath been the causer of my worship, and else I had been the most simplest knight in the world. For by her, and because of her, I have won the worship that I have; for when I remembered me of La Beale Isoud I won the worship wheresomever I came for the most part; and yet had I never reward nor bounty of her the days of my life, and yet have I been her knight guerdonless. And therefore, Sir Tristram, as for any death I dread not, for I had as leve die as to live. And if I were armed as thou art, I should lightly do battle with thee.'

'Well have ye uttered your treason,' said Tristram.

'I have done to you no treason,' said Palomides, 'for love is free for all men, and though I have loved your lady, she is my lady as well as yours; howbeit I have wrong if any wrong be, for ye rejoice her, and have your desire of her, and so had I never nor never am like to have, and yet shall I love her to the uttermost days of my life as well as ye.'

CHAPTER 87: *How there was a day set between Sir Tristram and Sir Palomides for to fight, and how Sir Tristram was hurt*

Then said Sir Tristram, 'I will fight with you to the uttermost.'

'I grant,' said Palomides, 'for in a better quarrel keep I never to fight, for and I die of your hands, of a better knight's hands may I not be slain. And sithen I understand that I shall never rejoice La Beale Isoud, I have as good will to die as to live.'

'Then set ye a day,' said Sir Tristram, 'that we shall do battle.'

'This day fifteen days,' said Palomides, 'will I meet with you hereby, in the meadow under Joyous Gard.'

'Fie for shame,' said Sir Tristram, 'Will ye set so long day? Let us fight to-morn.'

'Not so,' said Palomides, 'for I am meagre, and have been long sick for the love of La Beale Isoud, and therefore I will repose me till I have my strength again.'

So then Sir Tristram and Sir Palomides promised faithfully to meet at the well that day fifteen days.

'I am remembered,' said Sir Tristram to Palomides, 'that ye brake me once a promise when that I rescued you from Breunis Saunce Pité and nine knights; and then ye promised me to meet me at the peron and the grave besides Camelot, whereas at that time ye failed of your promise.'

'Wit you well,' said Palomides unto Sir Tristram, 'I was at that day in prison, so that I might not hold my promise.'

'So God me help,' said Sir Tristram, 'and ye had holden your promise this work had not been here now at this time.'

Right so departed Sir Tristram and Sir Palomides. And so Sir Palomides took his horse and his harness, and he rode unto King Arthur's court; and there Sir Palomides gat him four knights and four sergeants-of-arms, and so he returned againward unto Joyous Gard.

And in the meanwhile Sir Tristram chased and hunted at all manner of venery; and about three days afore the battle should be, as Sir Tristram chased an hart, there was an archer shot at the hart, and by misfortune he smote Sir Tristram in the thick of the thigh, and the arrow slew Sir Tristram's horse and hurt him.

When Sir Tristram was so hurt he was passing heavy, and wit ye well he bled sore; and then he took another horse, and rode unto Joyous Gard with great heaviness, more for the promise that he had made with Sir Palomides, as to do battle with him within three days after, than for any hurt of his thigh. Wherefore there was neither man ne woman that could cheer him with anything that they could make to him, neither Queen La Beale Isoud; for ever he deemed that Sir Palomides[1] had smitten him so that he should not be able to do battle with him at the day set.

CHAPTER 88: *How Sir Palomides kept his day for to have foughten, but Sir Tristram might not come; and other things*

But in no wise there was no knight about Sir Tristram that would believe that ever Sir Palomides would hurt Sir Tristram, neither by his own hands nor by none other consenting. Then when the fifteenth day was come, Sir Palomides came to the well with four knights with him of Arthur's court, and three sergeants-of-arms. And for this intent Sir Palomides brought the knights with him and the sergeants-of-arms, for they should bear record of the battle betwixt Sir Tristram and Sir Palomides. And the one sergeant brought in his helm, the other his spear, the third his sword. So thus Palomides came into the field, and there he abode nigh two hours; and then he sent a squire unto Sir Tristram, and desired him to come into the field to hold his promise.

When the squire was come to Joyous Gard, anon as Sir Tristram heard of his coming he let command that the squire should come to his presence there as he lay in his bed.

'My lord Sir Tristram,' said Palomides' squire, 'wit you well my lord, Palomides, abideth you in the field, and he would wit whether ye would do battle or not.'

'Ah, my fair brother,' said Sir Tristram, 'wit thou well that I am right heavy for these tidings; therefore tell Sir Palomides and I were well at ease I would not lie here, nor he should have no need to send for me and I might other ride or go; and for thou shalt say that I am no liar' – Sir Tristram showed him his thigh that the wound was six inches deep. 'And now thou hast seen my hurt, tell thy lord that this is no feigned matter, and tell him that I had lever than all the gold of King Arthur that I were whole; and tell Palomides as soon as I am whole I shall seek him endlong and overthwart, and that I promise you as I am true knight; and if ever I may meet with him, he shall have battle of me his fill.'

And with this the squire departed; and when Palomides wist that Tristram was hurt he was glad and said, 'Now I am sure I shall have no shame, for I wot well I should have had hard handling of him, and by likely I must needs have had the worse, for he is the hardest knight in battle that now is living except Sir Launcelot.'

And then departed Sir Palomides whereas fortune led him, and within a month Sir Tristram was whole of his hurt. And then he took his horse, and rode from country to country, and all strange adventures he achieved wheresomever he rode; and always he enquired for Sir Palomides, but of all that quarter of summer Sir Tristram could never meet with Sir Palomides. But thus as Sir Tristram sought and enquired after Sir Palomides Sir Tristram achieved many great battles, wherethrough all the noise fell to Sir Tristram, and it ceased of Sir Launcelot; and therefore Sir Launcelot's brethren and his kinsmen would have slain Sir Tristram because of his fame.

But when Sir Launcelot wist how his kinsmen were set, he said to them openly, 'Wit you well, that and the envy of you all be so hardy to wait upon my lord, Sir Tristram, with any hurt, shame, or villainy, as I am true knight I shall slay the best of you with mine own hands. Alas, fie for shame, should ye for his noble deeds await upon him to slay him. Jesu defend,' said Launcelot, 'that ever any noble knight as Sir Tristram is should be destroyed with treason.'

Of this, noise and fame sprang into Cornwall, and among them of Liones, whereof they were passing glad, and made great joy. And then they of Liones sent letters unto Sir Tristram of recommendation, and many great gifts to maintain Sir Tristram's estate; and ever between, Sir Tristram resorted unto Joyous Gard whereas La Beale Isoud was that loved him as her life.

Here endeth the tenth book which is of Sir Tristram.
And here followeth the eleventh book
which is of Sir Launcelot

Book XI

CHAPTER 1: *How Sir Launcelot rode on his adventure, and how he helped a dolorous lady from her pain, and how that he fought with a dragon*

Now leave we Sir Tristram de Liones, and speak we of Sir Launcelot du Lake, and of Sir Galahad, Sir Launcelot's son, how he was gotten, and in what manner, as the book of French rehearseth.

Afore the time that Sir Galahad was gotten or born, there came in an hermit unto King Arthur upon Whitsunday, as the knights sat at the Table Round. And when the hermit saw the Siege Perilous, he asked the king and all the knights why that siege was void.

Sir Arthur and all the knights answered, 'There shall never none sit in that siege but one, but if he be destroyed.'

Then said the hermit, 'Wot ye what is he?'

'Nay,' said Arthur and all the knights, 'we wot not who is he that shall sit therein.'

'Then wot I,' said the hermit, 'for he that shall sit there is unborn and ungotten, and this same year he shall be gotten that shall sit there in that Siege Perilous, and he shall win the Sangrail.' When this hermit had made this mention he departed from the court of King Arthur.

And then after this feast Sir Launcelot rode on his adventure, till on a time by adventure he passed over the Pounte of Corbin; and there he saw the fairest tower that ever he saw, and thereunder was a fair town full of people; and all the people, men and women, cried at once, 'Welcome, Sir Launcelot du Lake, the flower of all knighthood, for by thee all we shall be holpen out of danger.'

pounte: bridge.

'What mean ye,' said Sir Launcelot, 'that ye cry so upon me?'

'Ah, fair knight,' said they all, 'here is within this tower a dolorous lady that hath been there in pains many winters and days, for ever she boileth in scalding water; and but late,' said all the people, 'Sir Gawain was here and he might not help her, and so he left her in pain.'

'So may I,' said Sir Launcelot, 'leave her in pain as well as Sir Gawain did.'

'Nay,' said the people, 'we know well that it is Sir Launcelot that shall deliver her.'

'Well,' said Launcelot, 'then show me what I shall do.'

Then they brought Sir Launcelot into the tower; and when he came to the chamber thereas this lady was, the doors of iron unlocked and unbolted. And so Sir Launcelot went into the chamber that was as hot as any stew. And there Sir Launcelot took the fairest lady by the hand that ever he saw, and she was naked as a needle; and by enchantment Queen Morgan le Fay and the Queen of Northgales had put her there in that pains, because she was called the fairest lady of that country; and there she had been five years, and never might she be delivered out of her great pains unto the time the best knight of the world had taken her by the hand.

Then the people brought her clothes. And when she was arrayed, Sir Launcelot thought she was the fairest lady of the world, but if it were Queen Guenever.

Then this lady said to Sir Launcelot, 'Sir, if it please you will ye go with me hereby into a chapel that we may give loving and thanking unto God?'

'Madam,' said Sir Launcelot, 'cometh on with me, I will go with you.'

So when they came there and gave thankings to God all the people, both learned and lewd, gave thankings unto God and him, and said, 'Sir knight, since ye have delivered this lady, ye shall deliver us from a serpent that is here in a tomb.'

Then Sir Launcelot took his shield and said, 'Bring me

thither, and what I may do unto the pleasure of God and you I will do.'

So when Sir Launcelot came thither he saw written upon the tomb letters of gold that said thus: HERE SHALL COME A LEOPARD OF KINGS' BLOOD, AND HE SHALL SLAY THIS SERPENT, AND THIS LEOPARD SHALL ENGENDER A LION IN THIS FOREIGN COUNTRY, THE WHICH LION SHALL PASS ALL OTHER KNIGHTS.

So then Sir Launcelot lift up the tomb, and there came out an horrible and a fiendly dragon, spitting fire out of his mouth. Then Sir Launcelot drew his sword and fought with the dragon long, and at the last with great pain Sir Launcelot slew that dragon.

Therewithal came King Pelles, the good and noble knight, and saluted Sir Launcelot, and he him again.

'Fair knight,' said the king, 'what is your name? I require you of your knighthood tell me!'

CHAPTER 2 : How Sir Launcelot came to Pelles, and of the Sangrail, and how he begat Galahad on Elaine, King Pelles' daughter

'Sir,' said Launcelot, 'wit you well my name is Sir Launcelot du Lake.'

'And my name is,' said the king, 'Pelles, king of the foreign country, and cousin nigh unto Joseph of Arimathea.'

And then either of them made much of other, and so they went into the castle to take their repast. And anon there came in a dove at a window, and in her mouth there seemed a little censer of gold. And therewithal there was such a savour as all the spicery of the world had been there. And forthwithal there was upon the table all manner of meats and drinks that they could think upon.

So came in a damosel passing fair and young, and she bare a vessel of gold betwixt her hands; and thereto the king kneeled devoutly, and said his prayers, and so did all that were there.

'O Jesu!' said Sir Launcelot, 'What may this mean?'

'This is,' said the king, 'the richest thing that any man hath living. And when this thing goeth about, the Round Table shall be broken; and wit thou well,' said the king, 'this is the holy Sangrail that ye have here seen.'

So the king and Sir Launcelot led their life the most part of that day. And fain would King Pelles have found the mean to have had Sir Launcelot to have lain by his daughter, fair Elaine. And for this intent: the king knew well that Sir Launcelot should get a child upon his daughter, the which should be named Sir Galahad, the good knight, by whom all the foreign country should be brought out of danger, and by him the Holy Grail should be achieved.

Then came forth a lady that hight Dame Brisen, and she said unto the king, 'Sir, wit ye well Sir Launcelot loveth no lady in the world but all only Queen Guenever; and therefore work ye by counsel, and I shall make him to lie with your daughter, and he shall not wit but that he lieth with Queen Guenever.'

'O fair lady, Dame Brisen,' said the king, 'hope ye to bring this about?'

'Sir,' said she, 'upon pain of my life let me deal;' for this Brisen was one of the greatest enchantresses that was at that time in the world living.

Then anon by Dame Brisen's wit she made one to come to Sir Launcelot that he knew well. And this man brought him a ring from Queen Guenever like as it had come from her, and such one as she was wont for the most part to wear; and when Sir Launcelot saw that token wit ye well he was never so fain.

'Where is my lady?' said Sir Launcelot.

'In the Castle of Case,' said the messenger, 'but five mile thence.'

Then Sir Launcelot thought to be there the same night. And then this Brisen by the commandment of King Pelles let send Elaine to this castle with twenty-five knights unto the Castle of Case. Then Sir Launcelot against night rode unto that castle, and there anon he was received worshipfully with such people to his seeming as were about Queen Guenever secret. So when Sir Launcelot was alit, he asked where the queen was. So Dame Brisen said she was in her bed; and then the people were avoided, and Sir Launcelot was led unto his chamber.

And then Dame Brisen brought Sir Launcelot a cupful of wine; and anon as he had drunken that wine he was so assotted and mad that he might make no delay, but withouten any let he went to bed; and he weened that maiden Elaine had been Queen Guenever. Wit you well that Sir Launcelot was glad, and so was that lady Elaine that she had gotten Sir Launcelot in her arms. For well she knew that same night should be gotten upon her Galahad that should prove the best knight of the world; and so they lay together until undern on the morn; and all the windows and holes of that chamber were stopped that no manner of day might be seen.

And then Sir Launcelot remembered him, and he arose up and went to the window.

CHAPTER 3: *How Sir Launcelot was displeased when he knew that he had lain by Elaine, and how she was delivered of Galahad*

And anon as he had unshut the window the enchantment was gone; then he knew himself that he had done amiss.

'Alas,' he said, 'that I have lived so long; now I am shamed.'

So then he gat his sword in his hand and said, 'Thou traitoress, what art thou that I have lain by all this night? Thou shalt die right here of my hands.'

Then this fair lady Elaine skipped out of her bed all naked, and kneeled down afore Sir Launcelot, and said, 'Fair courteous knight, comen of kings' blood, I require you have mercy upon me, and as thou art renowned the most noble knight of

the world, slay me not, for I have in my womb him by thee
that shall be the most noblest knight of the world.'

'Ah, false traitoress,' said Sir Launcelot, 'why hast thou
betrayed me? Anon tell me what thou art.'

'Sir,' she said, 'I am Elaine, the daughter of King Pelles.'

'Well,' said Sir Launcelot, 'I will forgive you this deed;' and
therewith he took her up in his arms, and kissed her, for she
was as fair a lady, and thereto lusty and young, and as wise,
as any was that time living. 'So God me help,' said Sir Launcelot, 'I may not wit this to you; but her that made this
enchantment upon me as between you and me, and I may
find her, that same Lady Brisen, she shall lose her head for
witchcrafts, for there was never knight deceived so as I am
this night.'

And so Sir Launcelot arrayed him, and armed him, and
took his leave mildly at that lady young Elaine, and so he
departed.

Then she said, 'My lord Sir Launcelot, I beseech you see me
as soon as ye may, for I have obeyed me unto the prophecy
that my father told me. And by his commandment to fulfil
this prophecy I have given the greatest riches and the fairest
flower that ever I had, and that is my maidenhood that I
shall never have again; and therefore, gentle knight, owe me
your goodwill.'

And so Sir Launcelot arrayed him and was armed, and took
his leave mildly at that young lady Elaine; and so he departed, and rode till he came to the Castle of Corbin, where
her father was.

And as fast as her time came she was delivered of a fair
child, and they christened him Galahad; and wit ye well that
child was well kept and well nourished, and he was named
Galahad because Sir Launcelot was so named at the fountain
stone; and after that, the Lady of the Lake confirmed him Sir
Launcelot du Lake.

Then after this lady was delivered and churched there
came a knight unto her, his name was Sir Bromel la Pleche,
the which was a great lord; and he had loved that lady long,

and he evermore desired her to wed her; and so by no mean she could put him off, till on a day she said to Sir Bromel,

'Wit thou well, sir knight, I will not love you, for my love is set upon the best knight of the world.'

'Who is he?' said Sir Bromel.

'Sir,' she said, 'it is Sir Launcelot du Lake that I love and none other, and therefore woo me no longer.'

'Ye say well,' said Sir Bromel, 'and sithen ye have told me so much, ye shall have but little joy of Sir Launcelot, for I shall slay him wheresomever I meet him.'

'Sir,' said the Lady Elaine, 'do to him no treason.'

'Wit ye well, my lady,' said Bromel, 'and I promise you this twelvemonth I shall keep the Pounte of Corbin for Sir Launcelot's sake, that he shall neither come ne go unto you, but I shall meet with him.

CHAPTER 4: *How Sir Bors came to Dame Elaine and saw Galahad, and how he was fed with the Sangrail*

Then as it fell by fortune and adventure, Sir Bors de Ganis, that was nephew unto Sir Launcelot, came over that bridge; and there Sir Bromel and Sir Bors jousted, and Sir Bors smote Sir Bromel such a buffet that he bare him over his horse's croup.

And then Sir Bromel as an hardy knight pulled out his sword, and dressed his shield to do battle with Sir Bors. And then Sir Bors alit and avoided his horse, and there they dashed together many sad strokes; and long thus they fought, till at the last Sir Bromel was laid to the earth, and there Sir Bors began to unlace his helm to slay him. Then Sir Bromel cried Sir Bors mercy, and yielded him.

'Upon this covenant thou shalt have thy life,' said Sir Bors, 'so thou go unto Sir Launcelot upon Whitsunday that next cometh, and yield thee unto him as knight recreant.'

'I will do it,' said Sir Bromel, and that he sware upon the cross of the sword.

And so he let him depart, and Sir Bors rode unto King Pelles, that was within Corbin. And when the king and Elaine his daughter wist that Sir Bors was nephew unto Sir Launcelot, they made him great cheer.

Then said Dame Elaine, 'We marvel where Sir Launcelot is, for he came never here but once.'

'Marvel not,' said Sir Bors, 'for this half year he hath been in prison with Queen Morgan le Fay, King Arthur's sister.'

'Alas,' said Dame Elaine, 'that me repenteth.'

And ever Sir Bors beheld that child in her arms, and ever him seemed it was passing like Sir Launcelot.

'Truly,' said Elaine, 'wit ye well this child he gat upon me.'

Then Sir Bors wept for joy, and he prayed to God it might prove as good a knight as his father was.

And so came in a white dove, and she bare a little censer of gold in her mouth, and there was all manner of meats and drinks; and a maiden bare that Sangrail, and she said openly, 'Wit you well, Sir Bors, that this child is Galahad, that shall sit in the Siege Perilous, and achieve the Sangrail, and he shall be much better than ever was Sir Launcelot du Lake, that is his own father.'

And then they kneeled down and made their devotions, and there was such a savour as all the spicery in the world had been there. And when the dove took her flight, the maiden vanished with the Sangrail as she came.

'Sir,' said Sir Bors unto King Pelles, 'this castle may be named the Castle Adventurous, for here be many strange adventures.'

'That is sooth,' said the king, 'for well may this place be called the adventurous place, for there come but few knights here that go away with any worship; be he never so strong, here he may be proved; and but late Sir Gawain, the good knight, gat but little worship here. For I let you wit,' said King Pelles, 'here shall no knight win no worship but if he be of worship himself and of good living, and that loveth God and dreadeth God, and else he getteth no worship here, be he never so hardy.'

'That is wonderful thing,' said Sir Bors. 'What ye mean in this country I wot not, for ye have many strange adventures, and therefore I will lie in this castle this night.'

'Ye shall not do so,' said King Pelles, 'by my counsel, for it is hard and ye escape without a shame.'

'I shall take the adventure that will befall me,' said Sir Bors.

'Then I counsel you,' said the king, 'to be confessed clean.'

'As for that,' said Sir Bors, 'I will be shriven with a good will.'

So Sir Bors was confessed, and for all women Sir Bors was a virgin, save for one, that was the daughter of King Brandegoris, and on her he gat a child that hight Helin, and save for her Sir Bors was a clean maiden.

And so Sir Bors was led unto bed in a fair large chamber, and many doors were shut about the chamber. When Sir Bors espied all those doors, he avoided all the people, for he might have nobody with him; but in no wise Sir Bors would unarm him, but so he laid him down upon the bed.

And right so he saw come in a light, that he might well see a spear great and long that came straight upon him pointling, and to Sir Bors seemed that the head of the spear burnt like a taper. And anon or Sir Bors wist, the spear head smote him into the shoulder an handbreath in deepness, and that wound grieved Sir Bors passing sore.

And then he laid him down again for pain; and anon therewithal there came a knight armed with his shield on his shoulder and his sword in his hand, and he bad Sir Bors: 'Arise, sir knight, and fight with me.'

'I am sore hurt,' he said, 'but yet I shall not fail thee.'

And then Sir Bors start up and dressed his shield; and then they lashed together mightily a great while; and at the last Sir Bors bare him backward until that he came unto a chamber door, and there that knight yede into that chamber and rested him a great while. And when he had reposed him he came out freshly again, and began new battle with Sir Bors mightily and strongly.

CHAPTER 5: *How Sir Bors made Sir Pedivere to yield him, and of marvellous adventures that he had, and how he achieved them*

Then Sir Bors thought he should no more go into that chamber to rest him, and so Sir Bors dressed him betwixt the knight and that chamber door, and there Sir Bors smote him down, and then that knight yielded him.

'What is your name?' said Sir Bors.

'Sir,' said he, 'my name is Pedivere of the Strait Marches.'

So Sir Bors made him to swear at Whitsunday next coming to be at the court of King Arthur, and yield him there as a prisoner as an overcome knight by the hands of Sir Bors. So thus departed Sir Pedivere of the Strait Marches.

And then Sir Bors laid him down to rest, and then he heard and felt much noise in that chamber, and then Sir Bors espied that there came in, he wist not whether at the doors nor windows, shot of arrows and of quarrels so thick that he marvelled, and many fell upon him and hurt him in the bare places.

And then Sir Bors was ware where came in an hideous lion; so Sir Bors dressed him unto the lion, and anon the lion bereft him his shield, and with his sword Sir Bors smote off the lion's head.

Right so Sir Bors forthwithal saw a dragon in the court passing horrible, and there seemed letters of gold written in his forehead; and Sir Bors thought that the letters made a signification of King Arthur.

Right so there came an horrible leopard and an old, and there they fought long, and did great battle together. And at the last the dragon spit out of his mouth as it had been an hundred dragons; and lightly all the small dragons slew the old dragon and tare him all to pieces.

Anon withal there came an old man into the hall, and he sat him down in a fair chair, and there seemed to be two

quarrels: short arrows.

197

adders about his neck; and then the old man had an harp, and there he sang an old song how Joseph of Arimathea came into this land. Then when he had sungen, the old man bad Sir Bors go from thence.

'For here shall ye have no more adventures; and full worshipfully have ye done, and better shall ye do hereafter.'

And then Sir Bors seemed that there came the whitest dove with a little golden censer in her mouth. And anon therewithal the tempest ceased and passed, that afore was marvellous to hear. So was all that court full of good savours. Then Sir Bors saw four children bearing four fair tapers, and an old man in the midst of the children with a censer in his one hand,[1] and a spear in his other hand, and that spear was called the spear of vengeance.

CHAPTER 6: *How Sir Bors departed; and how Sir Launcelot was rebuked of the queen Guenever, and of his excuse*

'Now,' said that old man to Sir Bors, 'go ye to your cousin, Sir Launcelot, and tell him of this adventure the which had been most convenient for him of all earthly knights; but sin is so foul in him he may not achieve such holy deeds, for had not been his sin he had passed all the knights that ever were in his days; and tell thou Sir Launcelot, of all worldly adventures he passeth in manhood and prowess all other, but in these spiritual matters he shall have many his better.'

And then Sir Bors saw four gentlewomen come by him, poorly beseen; and he saw where that they entered into a chamber where was great light as it were a summer light; and the women kneeled down afore an altar of silver with four pillars, and as it had been a bishop kneeled down afore that table of silver. And as Sir Bors looked over his head he saw a sword like silver naked hoving over his head, and the clearnes thereof smote so in his eyen that as at that time Sir Bors was blind; and there he heard a voice that said, 'Go hence, thou Sir Bors, for as yet thou art not worthy for to be in this place.'

And then he yede backward to his bed till on the morn.

And on the morn King Pelles made great joy of Sir Bors; and then he departed and rode to Camelot, and there he found Sir Launcelot du Lake, and told him of the adventures that he had seen with King Pelles at Corbin.

So the noise sprang in Arthur's court that Launcelot had gotten a child upon Elaine, the daughter of King Pelles, wherefore Queen Guenever was wroth, and gave many rebukes to Sir Launcelot, and called him false knight. And then Sir Launcelot told the queen all, and how he was made to lie by her by enchantment in likeness of the queen. So the queen held Sir Launcelot excused.

And as the book saith, King Arthur had been in France, and had made war upon the mighty king Claudas, and had won much of his lands. And when the king was come again he let cry a great feast, that all lords and ladies of all England should be there, but if it were such as were rebellious against him.

CHAPTER 7: *How Dame Elaine, Galahad's mother, came in great estate to Camelot, and how Launcelot behaved him there*

And when Dame Elaine, the daughter of King Pelles, heard of this feast she went to her father and required him that he would give her leave to ride to that feast.

The king answered, 'I will well ye go thither, but in any wise as ye love me and will have my blessing, that ye be well beseen in the richest wise; and look that ye spare not for no cost; ask and ye shall have all that you needeth.'

Then by the advice of Dame Brisen, her maiden, all thing was apparelled unto the purpose, that there was never no lady more richlier beseen. So she rode with twenty knights, and ten ladies, and gentlewomen, to the number of an hundred horses. And when she came to Camelot, King Arthur and Queen Guenever said, and all the knights, that Dame Elaine was the fairest and the best beseen lady that ever was seen in that court.

And anon as King Arthur wist that she was come he met her and saluted her, and so did the most part of all the knights of the Round Table, both Sir Tristram, Sir Bleoberis, and Sir Gawain, and many more that I will not rehearse.

But when Sir Launcelot saw her he was so ashamed, and that because he drew his sword on the morn when he had lain by her, that he would not salute her nor speak to her; and yet Sir Launcelot thought she was the fairest woman that ever he saw in his life days.

But when Dame Elaine saw Sir Launcelot that would not speak unto her she was so heavy that she weened her heart would have to-brast, for wit you well, out of measure she loved him.

And then Elaine said unto her woman, Dame Brisen, 'The unkindness of Sir Launcelot slayeth me near.'

'Ah, peace, madam,' said Dame Brisen, 'I will undertake that this night shall he lie with you, and ye would hold you still.'

'That were me lever,' said Dame Elaine, 'than all the gold that is above the earth.'

'Let me deal,' said Dame Brisen.

So when Elaine was brought unto Queen Guenever either made other good cheer by countenance, but nothing with hearts. But all men and women spake of the beauty of Dame Elaine, and of her great riches.

Then at night the queen commanded that Dame Elaine should sleep in a chamber nigh her chamber, and all under one roof; and so it was done as the queen commanded. Then the queen sent for Sir Launcelot and bad him come to her chamber that night: 'Or else I am sure,' said the queen, 'that ye will go to your lady's bed, Dame Elaine, by whom ye gat Galahad.'

'Ah, madam,' said Sir Launcelot, 'never say ye so, for that I did was against my will.'

'Then,' said the queen, 'look that ye come to me when I send for you.'

'Madam' said Launcelot, 'I shall not fail you, but I shall be ready at your commandment.'

This bargain was soon done and made between them, but Dame Brisen knew it by her crafts, and told it to her lady, Dame Elaine.

'Alas,' said she, 'how shall I do?'

'Let me deal,' said Dame Brisen, 'for I shall bring him by the hand even to your bed, and he shall ween that I am Queen Guenever's messenger.'

'Now well is me,' said Dame Elaine, 'for all the world I love not so much as I do Sir Launcelot.'

CHAPTER 8: *How Dame Brisen by enchantment brought Sir Launcelot to Dame Elaine's bed, and how Queen Guenever rebuked him*

So when time came that all folks were abed, Dame Brisen came to Sir Launcelot's bed's side and said, 'Sir Launcelot du Lake, sleep you? My lady, Queen Guenever, lieth and awaiteth upon you.'

'O my fair lady,' said Sir Launcelot, 'I am ready to go with you where ye will have me.'

So Sir Launcelot threw upon him a long gown, and his sword in his hand; and then Dame Brisen took him by the finger and led him to her lady's bed, Dame Elaine; and then she departed and left them in bed together. Wit you well the lady was glad, and so was Sir Launcelot, for he weened that he had had another in his arms.

Now leave we them kissing and clipping, as was kindly thing; and now speak we of Queen Guenever that sent one of her women unto Sir Launcelot's bed; and when she came

kindly: natural.

there she found the bed cold, and he was away; so she came to the queen and told her all.

'Alas,' said the queen, 'where is that false knight become?'

Then the queen was nigh out of her wit, and then she writhed and weltered as a mad woman, and might not sleep a four or five hours. Then Sir Launcelot had a condition that he used of custom, he would clatter in his sleep, and speak oft of his lady, Queen Guenever. So as Sir Launcelot had waked as long as it had pleased him, then by course of kind he slept, and Dame Elaine both. And in his sleep he talked and clattered as a jay, of the love that had been betwixt Queen Guenever and him. And so as he talked so loud the queen heard him there as she lay in her chamber; and when she heard him so clatter she was nigh wood and out of her mind, and for anger and pain wist not what to do. And then she coughed so loud that Sir Launcelot awaked, and he knew her heming. And then he knew well that he lay not by the queen; and therewith he leapt out of his bed as he had been a wood man, in his shirt, and the queen met him in the floor; and thus she said:

'False traitor knight that thou art, look thou never abide in my court, and avoid my chamber, and not so hardy, thou false traitor knight that thou art, that ever thou come in my sight!'

'Alas,' said Sir Launcelot; and therewith he took such an heartly sorrow at her words that he fell down to the floor in a swoon. And therewithal Queen Guenever departed.

And when Sir Launcelot awoke of his swoon, he leapt out at a bay window into a garden, and there with thorns he was all to-cratched in his visage and his body; and so he ran forth he wist not whither, and was wild wood as ever was man; and so he ran two year, and never man might have grace to know him.

CHAPTER 9: *How Dame Elaine was commanded by Queen Guenever to avoid the court, and how Sir Launcelot became mad*

Now turn we unto Queen Guenever and to the fair Lady Elaine, that when Dame Elaine heard the queen so to rebuke Sir Launcelot, and also she saw how he swooned, and how he leapt out at a bay window, then she said unto Queen Guenever, 'Madam, ye are greatly to blame for Sir Launcelot, for now have ye lost him, for I saw and heard by his countenance that he is mad for ever. Alas, madam, ye do great sin, and to yourself great dishonour, for ye have a lord of your own, and therefore it is your part to love him; for there is no queen in this world hath such another king as ye have. And if ye were not I might have the love of my lord Sir Launcelot; and cause I have to love him for he had my maidenhood, and by him I have borne a fair son, and his name is Galahad, and he shall be in his time the best knight of the world.'

'Dame Elaine,' said the queen, 'when it is daylight I charge you and command you to avoid my court; and for the love ye owe unto Sir Launcelot discover not his counsel, for and ye do, it will be his death.'

'As for that,' said Dame Elaine, 'I dare undertake he is marred for ever, and that have ye made; for ye nor I are like to rejoice him, for he made the most piteous groans when he leapt out at yonder bay window that ever I heard man make. Alas,' said fair Elaine, and 'Alas,' said the Queen Guenever, 'for now I wot well we have lost him for ever.'

So on the morn Dame Elaine took her leave to depart, and she would no longer abide. Then King Arthur brought her on her way with more than an hundred knights through a forest. And by the way she told Sir Bors de Ganis all how it betid that same night, and how Sir Launcelot leapt out at a window araged out of his wit.

'Alas,' said Sir Bors, 'Where is my lord, Sir Launcelot, become?'

'Sir,' said Elaine, 'I wot nere.'

'Alas,' said Sir Bors, 'betwixt you both ye have destroyed that good knight.'

'As for me,' said Dame Elaine, 'I said never nor did never thing that should in any wise displease him, but with the rebuke that Queen Guenever gave him I saw him swoon to the earth; and when he awoke he took his sword in his hand, naked save his shirt, and leapt out at a window with the grisliest groan that ever I heard man make.'

'Now farewell, Dame Elaine,' said Sir Bors, 'and hold my lord Arthur with a tale as long as ye can, for I will turn again to Queen Guenever and give her a hete; and I require you, as ever ye will have my service, make good watch and espy if ever ye may see my lord Sir Launcelot.'

'Truly,' said fair Elaine, 'I shall do all that I may do, for as fain would I know and wit where he is become, as you, or any of his kin, or Queen Guenever; and cause great enough have I thereto as well as any other. And wit ye well,' said fair Elaine to Sir Bors, 'I would lose my life for him rather than he should be hurt; but alas, I cast me never for to see him, and the chief causer of this is Dame Guenever.'

'Madam,' said Dame Brisen, the which had made the enchantment before betwixt Sir Launcelot and her, 'I pray you heartily, let Sir Bors depart, and hie him with all his might as fast as he may to seek Sir Launcelot, for I warn you he is clean out of his mind; and yet he shall be well holpen and but by miracle.'

Then wept Dame Elaine, and so did Sir Bors de Ganis; and so they departed, and Sir Bors rode straight unto Queen Guenever. And when she saw Sir Bors she wept as she were wood.

'Fie on your weeping,' said Sir Bors de Ganis, 'for ye weep never but when there is no boot. Alas,' said Sir Bors, 'that ever Sir Launcelot's kin saw you, for now have ye lost the best knight of our blood, and he that was all our leader and

hete: reproach.

our succour; and I dare say and make it good that all kings, Christian nor heathen, may not find such a knight, for to speak of his nobleness and courtesy, with his beauty and his gentleness. Alas,' said Sir Bors, 'what shall we do that be of his blood?'

'Alas,' said Ector de Maris.

'Alas,' said Lionel.

CHAPTER 10: *What sorrow Queen Guenever made for Sir Launcelot, and how he was sought by knights of his kin*

And when the queen heard them say so she fell to the earth in a dead swoon. And then Sir Bors took her up, and dawed her; and when she was awaked she kneeled afore the three knights, and held up both their hands, and besought them to seek him. 'And spare not for no goods but that he be founden, for I wot he is out of his mind.'

And Sir Bors, Sir Ector, and Sir Lionel departed from the queen, for they might not abide no longer for sorrow. And then the queen sent them treasure enough for their expenses, and so they took their horses and their armour, and departed. And then they rode from country to country, in forests, and in wilderness, and in wastes; and ever they laid watch both at forests and at all manner of men as they rode, to hearken and spere after him, as he that was a naked man, in his shirt, with a sword in his hand.

And thus they rode nigh a quarter of a year, endlong and overthwart, in many places, forests and wilderness, and ofttimes were evil lodged for his sake; and yet for all their labour and seeking could they never hear word of him. And wit you well these three knights were passing sorry. Then at the last Sir Bors and his fellows met with a knight that hight Sir Melion de Tartare.

'Now fair knight,' said Sir Bors, 'whither be ye away?' For they knew either other afore time.

dawed: revived.

'Sir,' said Melion, 'I am in the way toward the court of King Arthur.'

'Then we pray you,' said Sir Bors, 'that ye will tell my lord Arthur, and my lady, Queen Guenever, and all the fellowship of the Round Table, that we cannot in no wise hear tell where Sir Launcelot is become.'

Then Sir Melion departed from them, and said that he would tell the king, and the queen, and all the fellowship of the Round Table, as they had desired him. So when Sir Melion came to the court of King Arthur he told the king, and the queen, and all the fellowship of the Round Table, what Sir Bors had said of Sir Launcelot.

Then Sir Gawain, Sir Uwain, Sir Sagramore le Desirous, Sir Agloval, and Sir Percival de Gales took upon them by the great desire of King Arthur, and in especial by the queen, to seek throughout all England, Wales, and Scotland, to find Sir Launcelot, and with them rode eighteen knights more to bear them fellowship; and wit ye well, they lacked no manner of spending; and so were they three and twenty knights.

Now turn we to Sir Launcelot, and speak we of his care and woe, and what pain he there endured; for cold, hunger, and thirst, he had plenty.

And thus as these noble knights rode together, they by one assent departed, and then they rode by two, by three, and by four, and by five, and ever they assigned where they should meet. And so Sir Agloval and Sir Percival rode together unto their mother that was a queen in those days. And when she saw her two sons, for joy she wept tenderly. And then she said,

'Ah, my dear sons, when your father was slain he left me four sons, of the which now be twain slain. And for the death of my noble son, Sir Lamorak, shall my heart never be glad.'

And then she kneeled down upon her knees tofore Agloval and Sir Percival, and besought them to abide at home with her.

'Ah, sweet mother,' said Sir Percival, 'we may not, for we come of kings' blood of both parties, and therefore, mother, it is our kind to haunt arms and noble deeds.'

'Alas my sweet sons,' then she said, 'for your sakes I shall lose my liking and lust, and then wind and weather I may not endure, what for the death of your father, King Pellinor, that was shamefully slain by the hands of Sir Gawain, and his brother, Sir Gaheris: and they slew him not manly but by treason. Ah, my dear sons, this is a piteous complaint for me of your father's death, considering also the death of Sir Lamorak, that of knighthood had but few fellows. Now, my dear sons, have this in your mind.'

Then there was but weeping and sobbing in the court when they should depart, and she fell in swooning in midst of the court.

CHAPTER 11 : *How a servant of Sir Agloval's was slain, and what vengeance Sir Agloval and Sir Percival did therefore*

And when she was awaked she sent a squire after them with spending enough. And so when the squire had overtake them, they would not suffer him to ride with them, but sent him home again to comfort their mother, praying her meekly of her blessing.

And so this squire was benighted, and by misfortune he happened to come to a castle where dwelled a baron. And so when the squire was come into the castle, the lord asked him from whence he came, and whom he served.

'My lord,' said the squire, 'I serve a good knight that is called Sir Agloval.' The squire said it to good intent, weening unto him to have been more forborne for Sir Agloval's sake, than he had said he had served the queen, Agloval's mother.

'Well, my fellow,' said the lord of that castle, 'for Sir Agloval's sake thou shalt have evil lodging, for Sir Agloval slew my brother, and therefore thou shalt die on part of payment.'

And then that lord commanded his men to have him away and slay him; and so they did, and so pulled him out of the castle, and there they slew him without mercy. Right so on the morn came Sir Agloval and Sir Percival riding by a churchyard, where men and women were busy, and beheld the dead squire, and they thought to bury him.

'What is there,' said Sir Agloval, 'that ye behold so fast?'

A good man start forth and said, 'Fair knight, here lieth a squire slain shamefully this night.'

'How was he slain, fair fellow?' said Sir Agloval.

'My fair sir,' said the man, 'the lord of this castle lodged this squire this night; and because he said he was servant unto a good knight that is with King Arthur, his name is Sir Agloval, therefore the lord commanded to slay him, and for this cause is he slain.'

'Gramercy,' said Sir Agloval, 'and ye shall see his death revenged lightly; for I am that same knight for whom this squire was slain.'

Then Sir Agloval called unto him Sir Percival, and bad him alight lightly; and so they alit both, and betook their horses to their men, and so they yede on foot into the castle. And all so soon as they were within the castle gate Sir Agloval bad the porter : 'Go thou unto thy lord and tell him that I am Sir Agloval for whom this squire was slain this night.'

Anon the porter told this to his lord, whose name was Goodewin.

Anon he armed him, and then he came into the court and said, 'Which of you is Sir Agloval?'

'Here I am,' said Agloval. 'For what cause slewest thou this night my mother's squire?'

'I slew him,' said Sir Goodewin, 'because of thee, for thou slewest my brother, Sir Gawdelin.'

'As for thy brother,' said Sir Agloval, 'I avow it I slew him, for he was a false knight and a betrayer of ladies and of good knights; and for the death of my squire thou shalt die.'

'I defy thee,' said Sir Goodewin.

Then they lashed together as eagerly as it had been two lions, and Sir Percival he fought with all the remnant that would fight. And within a while Sir Percival had slain all that would withstand him; for Sir Percival dealt so his strokes that were so rude that there durst no man abide him.

And within a while Sir Agloval had Sir Goodewin at the earth, and there he unlaced his helm, and struck off his head. And then they departed and took their horses; and then they let carry the dead squire unto a priory, and there they interred him.

CHAPTER 12: *How Sir Percival departed secretly from his brother, and how he loosed a knight bounden with a chain, and other things*

And when this was done they rode into many countries, ever inquiring after Sir Launcelot, but never they could hear of him; and at the last they came to a castle that hight Cardican, and there Sir Percival and Sir Agloval were lodged together.

And privily about midnight Sir Percival came to Agloval's squire and said, 'Arise and make thee ready, for ye and I will ride away secretly.'

'Sir,' said the squire, 'I would full fain ride with you where ye would have me, but and my lord, your brother, take me he will slay me.'

'As for that care thou not, for I shall be thy warrant.'

And so Sir Percival rode till it was after noon, and then he came upon a bridge of stone, and there he found a knight that was bounden with a chain fast about the waist unto a pillar of stone.

'O fair knight,' said that bounden knight, 'I require thee loose me of my bonds.'

'What knight are ye,' said Sir Percival, 'and for what cause are ye so bounden?'

'Sir, I shall tell you,' said that knight: 'I am a knight of the Table Round, and my name is Sir Persides; and thus by adventure I came this way, and here I lodged in this castle at the bridge foot, and therein dwelleth an uncourteous lady;

and because she proffered me to be her paramour, and I refused her, she set her men upon me suddenly or ever I might come to my weapon; and thus they bound me, and here I wot well I shall die but if some man of worship break my bands.'

'Be ye of good cheer,' said Sir Percival, 'and because ye are a knight of the Round Table as well as I, I trust to God to break your bands.'

And therewith Sir Percival pulled out his sword and struck at the chain with such a might that he cut atwo the chain, and through Sir Persides' hauberk and hurt him a little.

'O Jesu!' said Sir Persides, 'That was a mighty stroke as ever I felt one, for had not the chain been ye had slain me.'

And therewithal Sir Persides saw a knight coming out of a castle all that ever he might fling.

'Beware, sir,' said Sir Persides, 'yonder cometh a man that will have ado with you.'

'Let him come,' said Sir Percival.

And so he met with that knight in midst of the bridge; and Sir Percival gave him such a buffet that he smote him quite from his horse and over a part of the bridge, that had not been a little vessel under the bridge, that knight had been drowned.

And then Sir Percival took the knight's horse and made Sir Persides to mount up him; and so they rode unto the castle, and bad the lady deliver Sir Persides' servants, or else he would slay all that ever he found; and so for fear she delivered them all. Then was Sir Percival ware of a lady that stood in that tower.

'Ah, madam,' said Sir Percival, 'what use and custom is that in a lady to destroy good knights but if they will be your paramour? Forsooth this is a shameful custom of a lady, and if I had not a great matter in my hand I should fordo your evil customs.'

And so Sir Persides brought Sir Percival unto his own castle, and there he made him great cheer all that night.

And on the morn, when Sir Percival had heard mass and broken his fast, he bad Sir Persides ride unto King Arthur:

'And tell the king how that ye met with me; and tell my brother, Sir Agloval, how I rescued you; and bid him seek not after me, for I am in the quest to seek Sir Launcelot du Lake, and though he seek me he shall not find me; and tell him I will never see him nor the court till I have found Sir Launcelot. Also tell Sir Kay the Seneschal, and to Sir Mordred, that I trust to Jesu to be of as great worthiness as either of them, for tell them I shall never forget their mocks and scorns that they did to me that day that I was made knight; and tell them I will never see that court till men speak more worship of me than ever men did of any of them both.'

And so Sir Persides departed from Sir Percival, and then he rode unto King Arthur, and told there of Sir Percival.

And when Sir Agloval heard him speak of his brother Sir Percival, he said, 'He departed from me unkindly.'

CHAPTER 13: *How Sir Percival met with Sir Ector, and how they fought long, and each had almost slain other*

'Sir,' said Sir Persides, 'on my life he shall prove a noble knight as any now is living.'

And when he saw Sir Kay and Sir Mordred, Sir Persides said thus:

'My fair lords both, Sir Percival greeteth you well both, and he sent you word by me that he trusteth to God or ever he come to the court again to be of as great noblesse as ever were ye both, and more men to speak of his noblesse than ever they did you.'

'It may well be,' said Sir Kay and Sir Mordred, 'but at that time when he was made knight he was full unlike to prove a good knight.'

'As for that,' said King Arthur, 'he must needs prove a good knight, for his father and his brethren were noble knights.'

And now will we turn unto Sir Percival that rode long; and in a forest he met a knight with a broken shield and a broken helm; and as soon as either saw other readily they made them ready to joust, and so hurtled together with all the might of their horses, and they together so hard, that Sir Percival was smitten to the earth. And then Sir Percival arose lightly, and cast his shield on his shoulder and drew his sword, and bad the other knight: 'Alight, and do we battle unto the uttermost.'

'Will ye more?' said that knight.

And therewith he alit, and put his horse from him; and then they came together an easy pace, and there they lashed together with noble swords, and sometime they struck and sometime they foined, and either gave other many great wounds. Thus they fought near half a day, and never rested but right little, and there was none of them both that had less wounds than fifteen, and they bled so much that it was marvel they stood on their feet. But this knight that fought with Sir Percival was a proved knight and a wise fighting knight, and Sir Percival was young and strong, not knowing in fighting as the other was.

Then Sir Percival spoke first, and said, 'Sir knight, hold thy hand a while still, for we have foughten for a simple matter, and quarrel overlong, and therefore I require thee tell me thy name, for I was never or this time matched.'

'So God me help,' said that knight, 'and never or this time was there never knight that wounded me so sore as thou hast done, and yet have I foughten in many battles; and now shalt thou wit that I am a knight of the Table Round, and my name is Sir Ector de Maris, brother unto the good knight, Sir Launcelot du Lake.'

'Alas,' said Sir Percival, 'and my name is Sir Percival de Gales that hath made my quest to seek Sir Launcelot, and now I am siker that I shall never finish my quest, for ye have slain me with your hands.'

'It is not so,' said Sir Ector, 'for I am slain by your hands, and may not live. Therefore I require you,' said Sir Ector unto Sir Percival, 'ride ye hereby to a priory and bring me a priest that I may receive my Saviour, for I may not live. And when ye come to the court of King Arthur tell not my brother, Sir Launcelot, how that ye slew me, for then he would be your mortal enemy, but ye may say that I was slain in my quest as I sought him.'

'Alas,' said Sir Percival, 'ye say that thing that never will be, for I am so faint for bleeding that I may unnethe stand, how should I then take my horse?'

CHAPTER 14: *How by miracle they were both made whole by the coming of the holy vessel of Sangrail*

Then they made both great dole out of measure.

'This will not avail,' said Sir Percival.

And then he kneeled down and made his prayer devoutly unto Almighty Jesu, for he was one of the best knights of the world that at that time was, in whom the very faith stood most in.

Right so there came by the holy vessel of the Sangrail with all manner of sweetness and savour; but they could not readily see who that bare that vessel, but Sir Percival had a glimmering of the vessel and of the maiden that bare it, for she was a perfect clean maiden; and forthwithal they both were as whole of hide and limb as ever they were in their life days: then they gave thankings to God with great mildness.

'O Jesu,' said Sir Percival, 'what may this mean, that we be thus healed, and right now we were at the point of dying?'

'I wot full well,' said Sir Ector, 'what it is: it is an holy vessel that is borne by a maiden, and therein is part of the holy blood of Our Lord Jesu Christ, blessed mote he be. But it may not be seen,' said Sir Ector, 'but if it be by a perfect man.'

'So God me help,' said Sir Percival, 'I saw a damosel, as me thought, all in white, with a vessel in both her hands, and forthwithal I was whole.'

So then they took their horses and their harness, and

amended their harness as well as they might that was broken; and so they mounted upon their horses, and rode talking together.

And there Sir Ector de Maris told Sir Percival how he had sought his brother, Sir Launcelot, long, and never could hear witting of him: 'In many strange adventures have I been in this quest.'

And so either told other of their adventures.

Here endeth the eleventh book,
And here followeth the
twelfth book.

Book XII

CHAPTER 1: *How Sir Launcelot in his madness took a sword and fought with a knight, and leapt into a bed*

And now leave we of a while of Sir Ector and of Sir Percival, and speak we of Sir Launcelot that suffered and endured many sharp showers, that ever ran wild wood from place to place, and lived by fruit and such as he might get, and drank water two year; and other clothing had he but little but his shirt and his breeches.

Thus as Sir Launcelot wandered here and there he came in a fair meadow where he found a pavilion; and thereby, upon a tree, there hung a white shield, and two swords hung thereby, and two spears leaned there by a tree. And when Sir Launcelot saw the swords, anon he leapt to the one sword, and took it in his hand, and drew it out. And then he lashed at the shield, that all the meadow rang of the dints, that he gave such a noise as ten knights had foughten together.

Then came forth a dwarf, and leapt unto Sir Launcelot, and would have had the sword out of his hand. And then Sir Launcelot took him by the both shoulders and threw him to the ground upon his neck, that he had almost broken his neck; and therewithal the dwarf cried help.

Then came forth a likely knight, and well apparelled in scarlet furred with minever. And anon as he saw Sir Launcelot he deemed that he should be out of his wit.

And then he said with fair speech, 'Good man, lay down that sword, for as meseemeth thou hadst more need of sleep and of warm clothes than to wield that sword.'

'As for that,' said Sir Launcelot, 'come not too nigh, for and thou do, wit thou well I will slay thee.'

showers: misfortunes.   *minever*: fur trimming.

215

And when the knight of the pavilion saw that, he start backward within the pavilion. And then the dwarf armed him lightly; and so the knight thought by force and might to take the sword from Sir Launcelot, and so he came stepping out; and when Sir Launcelot saw him come so all armed with his sword in his hand, then Sir Launcelot flew to him with such a might, and hit him upon the helm such a buffet, that the stroke troubled his brains, and therewith the sword brake in three. And the knight fell to the earth as he had been dead, the blood brasting out of his mouth, the nose, and the ears.

And then Sir Launcelot ran into the pavilion, and rashed even into the warm bed; and there was a lady in that bed, and she gat her smock, and ran out of the pavilion. And when she saw her lord lie at the ground like to be dead, then she cried and wept as she had been mad. Then with her noise the knight awaked out of his swoon, and looked up weakly with his eyen; and then he asked her, where was that mad man that had given him such a buffet, 'For such a buffet had I never of man's hand.'

'Sir,' said the dwarf, 'it is not worship to hurt him, for he is a man out of his wit; and doubt ye not he hath been a man of great worship, and for some heartly sorrow that he hath taken, he is fallen mad; and me beseemeth,' said the dwarf, 'he resembleth much unto Sir Launcelot, for him I saw at the great tournament beside Lonazep.'

'Jesu defend,' said that knight, 'that ever that noble knight, Sir Launcelot, should be in such a plight; but whatsomever he be,' said that knight, 'harm will I none do him.' And this knight's name was Bliant.

Then he said unto the dwarf, 'Go thou fast on horseback, unto my brother, Sir Selivant, that is at the Castle Blank, and tell him of mine adventure, and bid him bring with him an horse litter, and then will we bear this knight unto my castle.'

CHAPTER 2: *How Sir Launcelot was carried in an horse litter, and after, Sir Launcelot rescued Sir Bliant, his host*

So the dwarf rode fast, and he came again and brought Sir Selivant with him, and six men with an horse litter; and so they took up the feather bed with Sir Launcelot, and so carried all away with them unto the Castle Blank, and he never awaked till he was within the castle. And then they bound his hands and his feet, and gave him good meats and good drinks, and brought him again to his strength and his fairness; but in his wit they could not bring him again, nor to know himself. Thus was Sir Launcelot there more than a year and a half, honestly arrayed and fair faren withal.

Then upon a day this lord of that castle, Sir Bliant, took his arms, on horseback, with a spear, to seek adventures. And as he rode in a forest there met him two knights adventurous, the one was Breunis Saunce Pité, and his brother, Sir Bertelot; and these two ran both at once upon Sir Bliant, and brake their spears upon his body. And then they drew out swords and made great battle, and fought long together. But at the last Sir Bliant was sore wounded, and felt himself faint; and then he fled on horseback toward his castle.

And they came hurling under the castle whereas Sir Launcelot lay in a window, and saw how two knights laid upon Sir Bliant with their swords. And when Sir Launcelot saw that, yet as wood as he was, he was sorry for his lord, Sir Bliant. And then Sir Launcelot brake the chains from his legs and off his arms, and in the breaking he hurt his hands sore; and so Sir Launcelot ran out at a postern, and there he met with the two knights that chased Sir Bliant; and there he pulled down Sir Bertelot with his bare hands from his horse, and therewithal he wrothe his sword out of his hand; and so he leapt unto Sir Breunis, and gave him such a buffet upon the head that he tumbled backward over his horse's croup.

And when Sir Bertelot saw there his brother have such a

fall, he gat a spear in his hand, and would have run Sir Launcelot through : that saw Sir Bliant, and struck off the hand of Sir Bertelot. And then Sir Breunis and Sir Bertelot gat their horses and fled away.

When Sir Selivant came and saw what Sir Launcelot had done for his brother, then he thanked God, and so did his brother, that ever they did him any good. But when Sir Bliant saw that Sir Launcelot was hurt with the breaking of his irons, then was he heavy that ever he bound him.

'Bind him no more,' said Sir Selivant, 'for he is happy and gracious.'

Then they made great joy of Sir Launcelot, and they bound him no more; and so he abode there an half year and more.

And on the morn early Sir Launcelot was ware where came a great boar with many hounds nigh him. But the boar was so big there might no hounds tear him; and the hunters came after, blowing their horns, both upon horseback and some upon foot; and then Sir Launcelot was ware where one alit and tied his horse to a tree, and leaned his spear against the tree.

CHAPTER 3 : *How Sir Launcelot fought against a boar and slew him, and how he was hurt, and brought to an hermitage*

So came Sir Launcelot and found the horse bounden till a tree, and a spear leaning against a tree, and a sword tied to the saddle bow; and then Sir Launcelot leapt into the saddle and gat that spear in his hand, and then he rode after the boar; and then Sir Launcelot was ware where the boar set his arse to a tree fast by an hermitage. Then Sir Launcelot ran at the boar with his spear, and therewith the boar turned him nimbly, and rove out the lungs and the heart of the horse, so that Launcelot fell to the earth; and, or ever Sir Launcelot might get from the horse, the boar rove him on the brawn of the thigh up to the hough bone. And then Sir

Launcelot was wroth, and up he gat upon his feet, and drew his sword, and he smote off the boar's head at one stroke.

And therewithal came out the hermit, and saw him have such a wound. Then the hermit came to Sir Launcelot and bemoaned him, and would have had him home unto his hermitage; but when Sir Launcelot heard him speak, he was so wroth with his wound that he ran upon the hermit to have slain him, and the hermit ran away. And when Sir Launcelot might not overget him, he threw his sword after him, for Sir Launcelot might then no further for bleeding; then the hermit turned again, and asked Sir Launcelot how he was hurt.

'Fellow,' said Sir Launcelot, 'this boar hath bitten me sore.'

'Then come with me,' said the hermit, 'and I shall heal you.'

'Go thy way,' said Sir Launcelot, 'and deal not with me.'

Then the hermit ran his way, and there he met with a good knight with many men.

'Sir,' said the hermit, 'here is fast by my place the good-liest man that ever I saw, and he is sore wounded with a boar, and yet he hath slain the boar. But well I wot,' said the hermit, 'and he be not holpen, that goodly man shall die of that wound, and that were great pity.'

Then that knight at the desire of the hermit gat a cart, and in that cart that knight put the boar and Sir Launcelot, for Sir Launcelot was so feeble that they might right easily deal with him; and so Sir Launcelot was brought unto the hermitage; and there the hermit healed him of his wound. But the hermit might not find Sir Launcelot's sustenance, and so he impaired and waxed feeble, both of his body and of his wit; for the default of his sustenance he waxed more wooder than he was aforehand.

And then upon a day Sir Launcelot ran his way into the forest; and by adventure he came to the city of Corbin, where Dame Elaine was, that bare Galahad, Sir Launcelot's son. And so when he was entered into the town he ran through

hough : back part of the knee joint.

the town to the castle; and then all the young men of that city ran after Sir Launcelot, and there they threw turves at him, and gave him many sad strokes. And ever as Sir Launcelot might overreach any of them, he threw them so that they would never come in his hands no more; for of some he brake the legs and the arms, and so fled into the castle; and then came out knights and squires and rescued Sir Launcelot.

And when they beheld him and looked upon his person, they thought they saw never so goodly a man. And when they saw so many wounds upon him, all they deemed that he had been a man of worship. And then they ordained him clothes to his body, and straw underneath him, and a little house. And then every day they would throw him meat, and set him drink, but there was but few would bring him meat to his hands.

CHAPTER 4: *How Sir Launcelot was known by Dame Elaine, and was borne into a chamber and after healed by the Sangrail*

So it befell that King Pelles had a nephew, his name was Castor; and so he desired of the king to be made knight, and so at the request of this Castor the king made him knight at the feast of Candlemas. And when Sir Castor was made knight, that same day he gave many gowns. And then Sir Castor sent for the fool – that was Sir Launcelot. And when he was come afore Sir Castor, he gave Sir Launcelot a robe of scarlet and all that longed unto him. And when Sir Launcelot was so arrayed like a knight, he was the seemliest man in all the court, and none so well made.

So when he saw his time he went into the garden, and there Sir Launcelot laid him down by a well and slept. And so at after noon Dame Elaine and her maidens came into the garden to play them; and as they roamed up and down one of Dame Elaine's maidens espied where lay a goodly man by the well sleeping, and anon showed him to Dame Elaine.

'Peace,' said Dame Elaine, 'and say no word.'

And then she brought Dame Elaine where he lay. And when that she beheld him, anon she fell in remembrance of him, and knew him verily for Sir Launcelot; and therewithal she fell on weeping so heartily that she sank even to the earth; and when she had thus wept a great while, then she arose and called her maidens and said she was sick.

And so she yede out of the garden, and she went straight to her father, and there she took him apart by herself; and then she said, 'O father, now have I need of your help, and but if that ye help me farewell my good days for ever.'

'What is that, daughter?' said King Pelles.

'Sir,' she said, 'thus is it: in your garden I went for to sport, and there by the well I found Sir Launcelot du Lake sleeping.'

'I may not believe that,' said King Pelles.

'Sir,' she said, 'truly he is there, and meseemeth he should be distract out of his wit.'

'Then hold you still,' said the king, 'and let me deal.'

Then the king called to him such as he most trusted, a four persons, and Dame Elaine, his daughter. And when they came to the well and beheld Sir Launcelot, anon Dame Brisen knew him.

'Sir,' said Dame Brisen, 'we must be wise how we deal with him, for this knight is out of his mind, and if we awake him rudely what he will do we all know not; but ye shall abide, and I shall throw such an enchantment upon him that he shall not awake within the space of an hour;' and so she did.

Then within a little while after, the king commanded that all people should avoid that none should be in that way there as the king would come. And so when this was done, these four men and these ladies laid hand on Sir Launcelot, and so they bare him into a tower, and so into a chamber where was the holy vessel of the Sangrail, and by force Sir Launcelot was laid by that holy vessel; and there came an holy man and unhilled that vessel, and so by miracle and by virtue of that holy vessel Sir Launcelot was healed and recovered. And when that he was awaked he groaned and sighed, and complained greatly that he was passing sore.

CHAPTER 5 : *How Sir Launcelot, after that he was whole and had his mind, he was ashamed, and how that Elaine desired a castle for him*

And when Sir Launcelot saw King Pelles and Elaine, he waxed ashamed and said thus :

'O Lord Jesu, how I came here? For God's sake, my lord, let me wit how I came here.'

'Sir,' said Dame Elaine, 'into this country ye came like a madman, clean out of your wit, and here have ye been kept as a fool; and no creature here knew what ye were, until by fortune a maiden of mine brought me unto you whereas ye lay sleeping by a well, and anon as I verily beheld you I knew you. And then I told my father, and so were ye brought afore this holy vessel, and by the virtue of it thus were ye healed.'

'O Jesu, mercy,' said Sir Launcelot; 'if this be sooth, how many there be that knowen of my woodness?'

'So God me help,' said Elaine, 'no more but my father, and I, and Dame Brisen.'

'Now for Christ's love,' said Sir Launcelot, 'keep it in counsel, and let no man know it in the world, for I am sore ashamed that I have been thus miscarried; for I am banished out of the country of Logris forever, that is for to say the country of England.'

And so Sir Launcelot lay more than a fortnight or ever that he might stir for soreness. And then upon a day he said unto Dame Elaine these words :

'Lady Elaine, for your sake I have had much travail, care, and anguish, it needeth not to rehearse it, ye know how. Notwithstanding I know well I have done foul to you when that I drew my sword to you, to have slain you, upon the morn when I had lain with you. And all was the cause, that ye and Dame Brisen made me for to lie by you maugre mine head; and as ye say, that night Galahad your son was begotten.'

'That is truth,' said Dame Elaine.

'Now will ye for my love,' said Sir Launcelot, 'go unto your father and get me a place of him wherein I may dwell? For in the court of King Arthur may I never come.'

'Sir,' said Dame Elaine, 'I will live and die with you, and only for your sake; and if my life might not avail you and my death might avail you, wit you well I would die for your sake. And I will go to my father, and I am sure there is nothing that I can desire of him but I shall have it. And where ye be, my lord Sir Launcelot, doubt ye not but I will be with you with all the service that I may do.'

So forthwithal she went to her father and said, 'Sir, my lord, Sir Launcelot, desireth to be here by you in some castle of yours.'

'Well daughter,' said the king, 'sith it is his desire to abide in these marches he shall be in the Castle of Bliant, and there shall ye be with him, and twenty of the fairest ladies that be in this country, and they shall all be of the great blood, and ye shall have ten knights with you; for, daughter, I will that ye wit we all be honoured by the blood of Sir Launcelot.'

CHAPTER 6: *How Sir Launcelot came into the Joyous Isle, and there he named himself Le Chevaler Mal Fet*

Then went Dame Elaine unto Sir Launcelot, and told him all how her father had devised for him and her. Then came the knight Sir Castor, that was nephew unto King Pelles, unto Sir Launcelot, and asked him what was his name.

'Sir,' said Sir Launcelot, 'my name is Le Chevaler Mal Fet, that is to say the knight that hath trespassed.'

'Sir,' said Sir Castor, 'it may well be so, but ever meseemeth your name should be Sir Launcelot du Lake, for or now I have seen you.'

'Sir,' said Launcelot, 'ye are not as a gentle knight: I put case my name were Sir Launcelot, and that it list me not to discover my name, what should it grieve you here to keep my counsel, and ye not hurt thereby? But wit thou well an ever it lie in my power I shall grieve you, and that I promise you truly.'

Then Sir Castor kneeled down and besought Sir Launcelot of mercy: 'For I shall never utter what ye be while that ye be in these parts.'

Then Sir Launcelot pardoned him.

And then after this King Pelles with ten knights, and Dame Elaine, and twenty ladies, rode unto the Castle of Bliant that stood in an island beclosed in iron,[1] with a fair water deep and large. And when they were there Sir Launcelot let call it the Joyous Isle; and there was he called none otherwise but Le Chevaler Mal Fet, 'the knight that hath trespassed'.

Then Sir Launcelot let make him a shield all of sable, and a queen crowned in the midst, all of silver, and a knight clean armed kneeling afore her. And every day once, for any mirths that all the ladies might make him, he would once every day look toward the realm of Logris, where King Arthur and Queen Guenever was. And then would he fall upon a weeping as his heart should to-brast.

So it fell that time Sir Launcelot heard of a jousting fast by his castle, within three leagues. Then he called unto him a dwarf, and he bad him go unto that jousting: 'And or ever the knights depart, look thou make there a cry, in hearing of all the knights, that there is one knight in the Joyous Isle, that is the Castle of Bliant, and say his name is Le Chevaler Mal Fet, that will joust against knights that will come. And who that putteth that knight to the worse shall have a fair maid and a gerfalcon.'

CHAPTER 7: *Of a great tourneying in the Joyous Isle, and how Sir Percival and Sir Ector came thither, and Sir Percival fought with him*

So when this cry was made, unto Joyous Isle drew knights to the number of five hundred; and wit ye well there was never seen in Arthur's days one knight that did so much deeds of arms as Sir Launcelot did three days together; for as the book maketh truly mention, he had the better of all the five hundred knights, and there was not one slain of them. And after that Sir Launcelot made them all a great feast.

And in the meanwhile came Sir Percival de Gales and Sir Ector de Maris under that castle that was called the Joyous Isle. And as they beheld that gay castle they would have gone to that castle, but they might not for the broad water, and bridge could they find none. Then they saw on the other side a lady with a sperhawk in her hand, and Sir Percival called unto her, and asked that lady who was in that castle.

'Fair knights,' she said, 'here within this castle is the fairest lady in this land, and her name is Elaine. Also we have in this castle the fairest knight and the mightiest man that is I dare say living, and he called himself Le Chevaler Mal Fet.'

'How came he into these marches?' said Sir Percival.

'Truly,' said the damosel, 'he came into this country like a mad man, with dogs and boys chasing him through the city of Corbin, and by the holy vessel of the Sangrail he was brought into his wit again; but he will not do battle with no knight, but by undern or by noon. And if ye list to come into the castle,' said the lady, 'ye must ride unto the further side of the castle and there shall ye find a vessel that will bear you and your horse.'

Then they departed, and came unto the vessel. And then Sir Percival alit, and said to Sir Ector de Maris:

'Ye shall abide me here until that I wit what manner a knight he is; for it were shame unto us, inasmuch as he is

sperhawk: sparrowhawk.

but one knight, an we should both do battle with him.'

'Do ye as ye list,' said Sir Ector,' and here I shall abide you until that I hear of you.'

Then passed Sir Percival the water, and when he came to the castle gate he bad the porter: 'Go thou to the good knight within the castle, and tell him here is come an errant knight to joust with him.'

'Sir,' said the porter, 'ride ye within the castle, and there is a common place for jousting, that lords and ladies may behold you.'

So anon as Sir Launcelot had warning he was soon ready; and there Sir Percival and Sir Launcelot encountered with such a might, and their spears were so rude, that both the horses and the knights fell to the earth. Then they avoided their horses and flung out noble swords, and hew away cantels of their shields, and hurtled together with their shields like two boars, and either wounded other passing sore. At the last Sir Percival spake first when they had foughten there more than two hours.

'Fair knight,' said Sir Percival, 'I require thee tell me thy name, for I met never with such a knight.'

'Sir,' said Sir Launcelot, 'my name is Le Chevaler Mal Fet. Now tell me your name,' said Sir Launcelot, 'I require you, gentle knight.'

'Truly,' said Sir Percival, 'my name is Sir Percival de Gales, that was brother unto the good knight, Sir Lamorak de Gales, and King Pellinor was our father, and Sir Agloval is my brother.'

'Alas,' said Sir Launcelot, 'what have I done to fight with you that art a knight of the Round Table, that sometime was your fellow?'

CHAPTER 8: *How each of them knew other, and of their courtesy, and how his brother Sir Ector came him, and of their joy*

And therewithal Sir Launcelot kneeled down upon his knees, and threw away his shield and his sword from him. When Sir Percival saw him do so he marvelled what he meaned. And then thus he said:

'Sir knight, whatsomever thou be, I require thee upon the high order of knighthood, tell me thy true name.'

Then he said, 'So God me help, my name is Sir Launcelot du Lake, King Ban's son of Benwick.'

'Alas,' said Sir Percival, 'what have I done? I was sent by the queen for to seek you, and so I have sought you nigh this two year, and yonder is Sir Ector de Maris, your brother, abideth me on the other side of the yonder water. Now, for God's sake,' said Sir Percival, 'forgive me mine offences that I have here done.'

'It is soon forgiven,' said Sir Launcelot.

Then Sir Percival sent for Sir Ector de Maris, and when Sir Launcelot had a sight of him, he ran unto him and took him in his arms; and then Sir Ector kneeled down, and either wept upon other, that all had pity to behold them.

Then came Dame Elaine, and she there made them great cheer as might lie in her power; and there she told Sir Ector and Sir Percival how and in what manner Sir Launcelot came into that country, and how he was healed; and there it was known how long Sir Launcelot was with Sir Bliant and with Sir Selivant, and how he first met with them, and how he departed from them because of a boar; and how the hermit healed Sir Launcelot of his great wound, and how that he came to Corbin.

CHAPTER 9: *How Sir Bors and Sir Lionel came to King Brandegoris, and how Sir Bors took his son Helin le Blank, and of Sir Launcelot*

Now leave we Sir Launcelot in the Joyous Isle with the lady Dame Elaine, and Sir Percival and Sir Ector playing with them, and turn we to Sir Bors de Ganis and Sir Lionel, that had sought Sir Launcelot nigh by the space of two year, and never could they hear of him. And as they thus rode, by adventure they came to the house of Brandegoris, and there Sir Bors was well known, for he had gotten a child upon the king's daughter fifteen year tofore, and his name was Helin le Blank. And when Sir Bors saw that child it liked him passing well. And so those knights had good cheer of the King Brandegoris.

And on the morn Sir Bors came afore King Brandegoris and said, 'Here is my son Helin le Blank, that as it is said he is my son; and sith it is so, I will that ye wit that I will have him with me unto the court of King Arthur.'

'Sir,' said the king, 'ye may well take him with you, but he is over tender of age.'

'As for that,' said Sir Bors, 'I will have him with me, and bring him to the house of most worship of the world.'

So when Sir Bors should depart there was made great sorrow for the departing of Helin le Blank, and great weeping was there made. But Sir Bors and Sir Lionel departed, and within a while they came to Camelot, where was King Arthur.

And when King Arthur understood that Helin le Blank was Sir Bors' son, and nephew unto King Brandegoris, then King Arthur let him make knight of the Round Table; and so he proved a good knight and an adventurous.

Now will we turn to our matter of Sir Launcelot. It befell upon a day Sir Ector and Sir Percival came to Sir Launcelot and asked him what he would do, and whether he would go with them unto King Arthur or not.

'Nay,' said Sir Launcelot, 'that may not be by no mean, for I was so entreated[1] at the court that I cast me never to come there more.'

'Sir,' said Sir Ector, 'I am your brother, and ye are the man in the world that I love most; and if I understood that it were your disworship, ye may understand I would never counsel you thereto; but King Arthur and all his knights, and in especial Queen Guenever, made such dole and sorrow that it was marvel to hear and see. And ye must remember the great worship and renown that ye be of, how that ye have been more spoken of than any other knight that is now living; for there is none that beareth the name now but ye and Sir Tristram. Therefore brother,' said Sir Ector, 'make you ready to ride to the court with us, and I daresay there was never knight better welcome to the court than ye; and I wot well, and can make it good,' said Sir Ector, 'it hath cost my lady, the queen, twenty thousand pound the seeking of you.'

'Well brother,' said Sir Launcelot, 'I will do after your counsel, and ride with you.'

So then they took their horses and made them ready, and took their leave at King Pelles and at Dame Elaine. And when Sir Launcelot should depart Dame Elaine made great sorrow.

'My lord, Sir Launcelot,' said Dame Elaine, 'at this same feast of Pentecost shall your son and mine, Galahad, be made knight, for he is fully now fifteen winter old.'

'Do as ye list,' said Sir Launcelot. 'God give him grace to prove a good knight.'

'As for that,' said Dame Elaine, 'I doubt not he shall prove the best man of his kin except one.'

'Then shall he be a man good enough,' said Sir Launcelot.

CHAPTER 10: *How Sir Launcelot with Sir Percival and Sir Ector came to the court, and of the great joy of him*

Then they departed, and within five days' journey they came to Camelot, that is called in English, Winchester. And when Sir Launcelot was come among them, the king and all the knights made great joy of him.

And there Sir Percival de Gales and Sir Ector de Maris began and told the whole adventures: that Sir Launcelot had been out of his mind the time of his absence, and how he called himself Le Chevaler Mal Fet, the knight that had trespassed; and in three days Sir Launcelot smote down five hundred knights.

And ever as Sir Ector and Sir Percival told these tales of Sir Launcelot, Queen Guenever wept as she should have died. Then the queen made great cheer.

'O Jesu,' said King Arthur, 'I marvel for what cause ye, Sir Launcelot, went out of your mind. I and many other deem it was for the love of fair Elaine, the daughter of King Pelles, by whom ye are noised that ye have gotten a child, and his name is Galahad, and men say he shall do marvels.'

'My lord,' said Sir Launcelot, 'if I did any folly I have that I sought.'

And therewithal the king spake no more. But all Sir Launcelot's kin knew for whom he went out of his mind.

And then there were great feasts made and great joy; and many great lords and ladies, when they heard that Sir Launcelot was come to the court again, they made great joy.

CHAPTER 11: *How La Beale Isoud counselled Sir Tristram to go unto the court, to the great feast of Pentecost*

Now will we leave of this matter, and speak we of Sir Tristram, and of Sir Palomides that was the Saracen unchristened. When Sir Tristram was come home unto Joyous Gard from his adventures, all this while that Sir Launcelot was thus missed, two year and more, Sir Tristram bare the renown through all the realm of Logris, and many strange adventures befell him, and full well and manly and worshipfully he brought them to an end.

So when he was come home La Beale Isoud told him of the great feast that should be at Pentecost next following, and there she told him how Sir Launcelot had been missed two year, and all that while he had been out of his mind, and how he was holpen by the holy vessel, the Sangrail.

'Alas,' said Sir Tristram, 'that caused some debate betwixt him and Queen Guenever.'

'Sir,' said Dame Isoud, 'I know it all, for Queen Guenever sent me a letter in the which she wrote me all how it was, for to require you to seek him. And now, blessed be God,' said La Beale Isoud, 'he is whole and sound and come again to the court.'

'Thereof am I glad,' said Sir Tristram, 'and now shall ye and I make us ready, for both ye and I will be at the feast.'

'Sir,' said Isoud, 'and it please you I will not be there, for through me ye be marked of many good knights, and that caused you to have much more labour for my sake than needeth you.'

'Then will I not be there,' said Sir Tristram, 'but if ye be there.'

'God defend,' said La Beale Isoud, 'for then shall I be spoken of shame among all queens and ladies of estate; for ye that are called one of the noblest knights of the world, and ye a knight of the Round Table, how may ye be missed at that feast? What shall be said among all knights? "See how Sir Tristram hunteth, and hawketh, and cowereth within a castle with his lady, and forsaketh your worship. Alas," shall some say, "it is pity that ever he was made knight, or that ever he should have the love of a lady." Also what shall queens and ladies say of me? It is pity that I have my life, that I will hold so noble a knight as ye are from his worship.'

'So God me help,' said Sir Tristram unto La Beale Isoud, 'it is passing well said of you and nobly counselled; and now I well understand that ye love me; and like as ye have counselled me I will do a part thereafter. But there shall no man nor child ride with me, but myself. And so will I ride on Tuesday next coming, and no more harness of war but my spear and my sword.'

CHAPTER 12: *How Sir Tristram departed unarmed and met with Sir Palomides, and how they smote each other, and how Sir Palomides forbare him*

And so when the day came Sir Tristram took his leave at La Beale Isoud, and she sent with him four knights, and within half a mile he sent them again. And within a mile after Sir Tristram saw afore him where Sir Palomides had stricken down a knight, and almost wounded him to the death. Then Sir Tristram repented him that he was not armed, and then he hoved still.

With that Sir Palomides knew Sir Tristram, and cried on high, 'Sir Tristram, now be we met, for or we depart we will redress our old sores !'

'As for that ,' said Sir Tristram, 'there was yet never Christian man might make his boast that ever I fled from him; and wit ye well, Sir Palomides, thou that art a Saracen shall never make thy boast that Sir Tristram de Liones shall flee from thee.'

And therewith Sir Tristram made his horse to run, and with all his might he came straight upon Sir Palomides, and brast his spear upon him an hundred pieces. And forthwithal Sir Tristram drew his sword. And then he turned his horse and struck at Palomides six great strokes upon his helm; and then Sir Palomides stood still, and beheld Sir Tristram, and marvelled of his woodness, and of his folly.

And then Sir Palomides said to himself, 'And Sir Tristram were armed, it were hard to cease him of this battle, and if I turn again and slay him I am ashamed wheresomever that I go.'

Then Sir Tristram spake and said, 'Thou coward knight, what castest thou to do; why wilt thou not do battle with me? For have thou no doubt I shall endure all thy malice.'

'Ah, Sir Tristram,' said Palomides, 'full well thou wotest I may not fight with thee for shame, for thou art here naked and I am armed, and if I slay thee, dishonour shall be mine. And well thou wotest,' said Sir Palomides to Sir Tristram, 'I know thy strength and thy hardiness to endure against a good knight.'

'That is truth,' said Sir Tristram. 'I understand thy valiantness well.'

'Ye say well,' said Sir Palomides; 'now, I require you, tell me a question that I shall say to you.'

'Tell me what it is,' said Sir Tristram, 'and I shall answer you the truth, as God me help.'

'I put case,' said Sir Palomides, 'that ye were armed at all rights as well as I am, and I naked as ye be, what would you do to me now, by your true knighthood?'

'Ah,' said Sir Tristram, 'now I understand thee well, Sir Palomides, for now must I say mine own judgement, and as God me bless, that I shall say shall not be said for no fear that I have of thee. But this is all: wit Sir Palomides, as at this time thou shouldest depart from me, for I would not have ado with thee.'

'No more will I,' said Palomides, 'and therefore ride forth on thy way.'

'As for that I may choose,' said Sir Tristram, 'other to ride or to abide. But Sir Palomides,' said Sir Tristram, 'I marvel of one thing, that thou that art so good a knight, that thou wilt not be christened, and thy brother, Sir Safer, hath been christened many a day.'

CHAPTER 13: *How that Sir Tristram gat him harness of a knight which was hurt, and how he overthrew Sir Palomides*

'As for that,' said Sir Palomides, 'I may not yet be christened, for one avow that I have made many years agone, howbeit in my heart I believe in Jesu Christ and his mild mother Mary; but I have but one battle to do, and when that is done I will be baptised with a good will.'

'By my head,' said Tristram, 'as for one battle thou shalt not seek it no longer. For God defend,' said Sir Tristram, 'that through my default thou shouldst longer live thus a Saracen, for yonder is a knight that ye, Sir Palomides, have hurt and smitten down. Now help me that I were armed in his armour, and I shall soon fulfil thine avows.'

'As ye will,' said Palomides, 'so it shall be.'

So they rode both unto that knight that sat upon a bank, and then Sir Tristram saluted him, and he weakly saluted him again.

'Sir knight,' said Sir Tristram, 'I require you tell me your right name.'

'Sir,' he said, 'my name is Sir Galleron of Galway, and knight of the Table Round.'

'So God me help,' said Sir Tristram, 'I am right heavy of your hurts; but this is all, I must pray you to lend me all your whole armour, for ye see I am unarmed, and I must do battle with this knight.'

'Sir,' said the hurt knight, 'ye shall have it with a good will; but ye must beware, for I warn you that knight is wight. Sir,' said Galleron, 'I pray you tell me your name, and what is that knight's name that hath beaten me.'

'Sir, as for my name it is Sir Tristram de Liones, and as for the knight's name that hath hurt you is Sir Palomides, brother to the good knight Sir Safer, and yet is Sir Palomides unchristened.'

'Alas,' said Sir Galleron, 'that is pity that so good a knight and so noble a man of arms should be unchristened.'

234

'So God me help,' said Sir Tristram, 'other he shall slay me or I him, but that he shall be christened or ever we depart in sunder.'

'My lord Sir Tristram,' said Sir Galleron, 'your renown and worship is well known through many realms, and God save you this day from senship and shame.'

Then Sir Tristram unarmed Galleron, the which was a noble knight, and had done many deeds of arms, and he was a large knight of flesh and bone. And when he was unarmed he stood upon his feet, for he was bruised in the back with a spear; yet so as Sir Galleron might, he armed Sir Tristram. And then Sir Tristram mounted upon his own horse, and in his hand he gat Sir Galleron's spear; and therewithal Sir Palomides was ready.

And so they came hurtling together, and either smote other in midst of their shields; and therewithal Sir Palomides' spear brake, and Sir Tristram smote down the horse; and Sir Palomides as soon as he might avoided his horse, and dressed his shield, and pulled out his sword. That saw Sir Tristram, and therewithal he alit and tied his horse till a tree.

CHAPTER 14: *How Sir Tristram and Sir Palomides fought long together, and after accorded, and Sir Tristram made him to be christened*

And then they came together as two wild boars, lashing together, tracing and traversing as noble men that oft had been well proved in battle; but ever Sir Palomides dread the might of Sir Tristram, and therefore he suffered him to breathe him. Thus they fought more than two hours, but often Sir Tristram smote such strokes at Sir Palomides that he made him to kneel; and Sir Palomides brake and cut away many pieces of Sir Tristram's shield; and then Sir Palomides wounded Sir Tristram, for he was a well fighting man.

Then Sir Tristram was wood wroth out of measure, and

senship: censure.

rashed upon Sir Palomides with such a might that Sir Palomides fell grovelling to the earth; and therewithal he leapt up lightly upon his feet, and then Sir Tristram wounded Palomides sore through the shoulder. And ever Sir Tristram fought still in like hard, and Sir Palomides failed not, but gave him many sad strokes. And at the last Sir Tristram doubled his strokes, and by fortune Sir Tristram smote Sir Palomides' sword out of his hand, and if Sir Palomides had stooped for his sword he had been slain. Then Palomides stood still and beheld his sword with a sorrowful heart.

'How now,' said Sir Tristram unto Palomides. 'Now have I thee at advantage as thou haddest me this day; but it shall never be said in no court, nor among good knights, that Sir Tristram shall slay any knight that is weaponless; and therefore take thou thy sword, and let us make an end of this battle.'

'As for to do this battle,' said Palomides, 'I dare right well end it, but I have no great lust to fight no more. And for this cause,' said Palomides: 'mine offence to you is not so great but that we may be friends. All that I have offended is and was for the love of La Beale Isoud. And as for her, I dare say she is peerless above all other ladies, and also I proffered her never no dishonour; and by her I have gotten the most part of my worship, and sithen I offended never as to her own person. And as for the offence that I have done, it was against your own person, and for that offence ye have given me this day many sad strokes, and some I have given you again; and now I dare say I felt never man of your might, nor so well breathed, but if it were Sir Launcelot du Lake. Wherefore I require you, my lord, forgive me all that I have offended unto you; and this same day have me to the next church, and first let me be clean confessed, and after see you now that I be truly baptised. And then will we all ride together unto the court of Arthur, that we be there at the high feast.'

'Now take your horse,' said Sir Tristram, 'and as ye say so it shall be, and all thine evil will God forgive it you, and

I do. And here within this mile is the suffragan of Carlisle that shall give you the sacrament of baptism.'

Then they took their horses and Sir Galleron rode with them. And when they came to the suffragan Sir Tristram told him their desire. Then the suffragan let fill a great vessel with water, and when he had hallowed it he then confessed clean Sir Palomides, and Sir Tristram and Sir Galleron were his godfathers.

And then soon after they departed, riding toward Camelot, where King Arthur and Queen Guenever was, and for the most part all the knights of the Round Table. And so the king and all the court were glad that Sir Palomides was christened. And at the same feast in came Galahad and sat in the Siege Perilous. And so therewithal departed and dissevered all the knights of the Round Table. And Sir Tristram returned again unto Joyous Gard, and Sir Palomides followed the Questing Beast.

Here endeth the second book of Sir Tristram that was drawn out of French into English. But here is no rehearsal of the third book. And here followeth the noble tale of the Sangrail, that called is the holy vessel; and the signification of the blessed blood of Our Lord Jesu Christ, blessed mote it be, the which was brought into this land by Joseph of Arimathea. Therefore on all sinful souls blessed Lord have thou mercy.

*Explicit liber xii. Et incipit
Decimustercius.*

Book XIII

CHAPTER 1: *How at the vigil of the feast of Pentecost entered into the hall before King Arthur a damosel, and desired Sir Launcelot for to come and dub a knight, and how he went with her*

At the vigil of Pentecost, when all the fellowship of the Round Table were comen unto Camelot and there heard their service, and the tables were set ready to the meat, right so entered into the hall a full fair gentlewoman on horseback, that had ridden full fast, for her horse was all besweat.

Then she there alit, and came before the king and saluted him; and he said, 'Damosel, God thee bless.'

'Sir,' said she, 'for God's sake say me where Sir Launcelot is.'

'Yonder ye may see him,' said the king.

Then she went unto Launcelot and said, 'Sir Launcelot, I salute you on King Pelles' behalf, and I require you come on with me hereby into a forest.'

Then Sir Launcelot asked her with whom she dwelled.

'I dwell,' said she, 'with King Pelles.'

'What will ye with me?' said Launcelot.

'Ye shall know,' said she, 'when ye come thither.'

'Well,' said he, 'I will gladly go with you.'

So Sir Launcelot bad his squire saddle his horse and bring his arms; and in all haste he did his commandment.

Then came the queen unto Launcelot, and said, 'Will ye leave us at this high feast?'

'Madam,' said the gentlewoman, 'wit ye well he shall be with you tomorn by dinner time.'

'If I wist,' said the queen, 'that he should not be with us here tomorn he should not go with you by my good will.'

238

Right so departed Sir Launcelot with the gentlewoman, and rode until that he came into a forest and into a great valley, where they saw an abbey of nuns; and there was a squire ready and opened the gates, and so they entered and descended off their horses; and there came a fair fellowship about Sir Launcelot, and welcomed him, and were passing glad of his coming.

And then they led him unto the abbess's chamber and unarmed him; and right so he was ware upon a bed lying two of his cousins, Sir Bors and Sir Lionel, and then he waked them; and when they saw him they made great joy.

'Sir,' said Sir Bors unto Sir Launcelot, 'what adventure hath brought you hither, for we weened tomorn to have found you at Camelot?'

'As God me help,' said Sir Launcelot, 'a gentlewoman brought me hither, but I know not the cause.'

In the meanwhile that they thus stood talking together, therein came twelve nuns that brought with them Galahad, the which was passing fair and well made, that unnethe in the world men might not find his match: and all those ladies wept.

'Sir,' said they all, 'we bring you here this child the which we have nourished, and we pray you to make him a knight, for of a more worthier man's hand may he not receive the order of knighthood.'

Sir Launcelot beheld the young squire and saw him seemly and demure as a dove, with all manner of good features, that he weened of his age never to have seen so fair a man of form.

Then said Sir Launcelot, 'Cometh this desire of himself?'

He and all they said yea.

'Then shall he,' said Sir Launcelot, 'receive the high order of knighthood as tomorn at the reverence of the high feast.'

That night Sir Launcelot had passing good cheer; and on the morn at the hour of prime, at Galahad's desire, he made him knight and said, 'God make him a good man, for of beauty faileth you not as any that liveth.'

CHAPTER 2: How the letters were found written in the Siege Perilous, and of the marvellous adventure of the sword in a stone

'Now fair sir,' said Sir Launcelot, 'will ye come with me unto the court of King Arthur?'

'Nay,' said he, 'I will not go with you as at this time.'

Then he departed from them and took his two cousins with him, and so they came unto Camelot by the hour of undern on Whitsunday. By that time the king and queen were gone to the minster to hear their service. Then the king and the queen were passing glad of Sir Bors and Sir Lionel, and so was all the fellowship.

So when the king and all the knights were come from service, the barons espied in the sieges of the Round Table all about, written with golden letters: HERE OUGHT TO SIT HE, and: HE OUGHT TO SIT HERE.

And thus they went so long till that they came to the Siege Perilous, where they found letters newly written of gold which said: FOUR HUNDRED WINTERS AND FOUR-AND-FIFTY ACCOMPLISHED AFTER THE PASSION OF OUR LORD JESU CHRIST OUGHT THIS SIEGE TO BE FUL-FILLED.

Then all they said, 'This is a marvellous thing and an adventurous.'

'In the name of God,' said Sir Launcelot; and then accounted the term of the writing from the birth of Our Lord unto that day. 'It seemeth me,' said Sir Launcelot, 'this siege ought to be fulfilled this same day, for this is the feast of Pentecost after the four hundred and four-and-fifty year; and if it would please all parties, I would none of these letters were seen this day, till he be come that ought to achieve this adventure.'

Then made they to ordain a cloth of silk, for to cover these letters in the Siege Perilous. Then the king bad haste unto dinner.

'Sir,' said Sir Kay the Steward, 'if ye go now to your meat ye shall break your old custom of your court, for ye have not used on this day to sit at your meat or that ye have seen some adventure.'

'Ye say sooth,' said the king, 'but I had so great joy of Sir Launcelot and of his cousins, which be come to the court whole and sound, so that I bethought me not of mine old custom.'

So, as they stood speaking, in came a squire and said unto the king, 'Sir, I bring unto you marvellous tidings.'

'What be they?' said the king.

'Sir, there is here beneath at the river a great stone which I saw float above the water, and therein I saw sticking a sword.'

The king said, 'I will see that marvel.'

So all the knights went with him, and when they came unto the river they found there a stone floating, as it were of red marble, and therein stuck a fair rich sword, and in the pommel thereof were precious stones wrought with subtle letters of gold. Then the barons read the letters which said in this wise: NEVER SHALL MAN TAKE ME HENCE, BUT ONLY HE BY WHOSE SIDE I OUGHT TO HANG, AND HE SHALL BE THE BEST KNIGHT OF THE WORLD.

When the king had seen the letters, he said unto Sir Launcelot, 'Fair sir, this sword ought to be yours, for I am sure ye be the best knight of the world.'

Then Sir Launcelot answered full soberly, 'Certes sir, it is not my sword; also, sir, wit ye well I have no hardiness to set my hand to, for it longed not to hang by my side. Also, who that assayeth to take the sword and faileth of it, he shall receive a wound by that sword that he shall not be whole long after. And I will that ye wit that this same day shall the adventures of the Sangrail, that is called the holy vessel, begin.'

CHAPTER 3: *How Sir Gawain assayed to draw out the sword, and how an old man brought in Galahad*

'Now, fair nephew,' said the king unto Sir Gawain, 'assay ye, for my love.'

'Sir,' he said, 'save your good grace I shall not do that.'

'Sir,' said the king, 'assay to take the sword and at my commandment.'

'Sir,' said Gawain, 'your commandment I will obey.'

And therewith he took up the sword by the handles, but he might not stir it.

'I thank you,' said the king to Sir Gawain.

'My lord Sir Gawain,' said Sir Launcelot, 'now wit ye well this sword shall touch you so sore that ye shall will ye had never set your hand thereto for the best castle of this realm.'

'Sir,' he said, 'I might not withsay mine uncle's will and commandment.'

But when the king heard this he repented it much, and said unto Sir Percival that he should assay, for his love.

And he said, 'Gladly, for to bear Sir Gawain fellowship.'

And therewith he set his hand on the sword and drew it strongly, but he might not move it. Then were there no more that durst be so hardy to set their hands thereto.

'Now may ye go to your dinner,' said Sir Kay unto the king, 'for a marvellous adventure have ye seen.'

So the king and all went unto the court, and every knight knew his own place, and set him therein, and young men that were knights served them.

So when they were served, and all sieges fulfilled save only the Siege Perilous, anon there befell a marvellous adventure, that all the doors and windows of the palace shut by themself. Notforthan the hall was not greatly darked; and therewith they abashed both one and other.

Then King Arthur spake first and said, 'By God, fair fellows and lords, we have seen this day marvels, but or night I suppose we shall see greater marvels.'

In the meanwhile came in a good old man, and an ancient, clothed all in white, and there was no knight knew from whence he came. And with him he brought a young knight, both on foot, in red arms, without sword or shield, save a scabbard hanging by his side. And these words he said:

'Peace be with you, fair lords.'

Then the old man said unto Arthur, 'Sir, I bring here a young knight, the which is of kings' lineage, and of the kindred of Joseph of Arimathea, whereby the marvels of this court, and of strange realms, shall be fully accomplished.'

CHAPTER 4: *How the old man brought Galahad to the Siege Perilous and set him therein, and how all the knights marvelled*

The king was right glad of his words, and said unto the good man, 'Sir, ye be right welcome, and the young knight with you.'

Then the old man made the young man to unarm him, and he was in a coat of red sendal, and bare a mantle upon his shoulder that was furred with ermine, and put that upon him. And the old knight said unto the young knight, 'Sir, followeth me.'

And anon he led him unto the Siege Perilous, where beside sat Sir Launcelot; and the good man lift up the cloth, and found there letters that said thus:

THIS IS THE SIEGE OF GALAHAD, THE HAUT PRINCE.

'Sir,' said the old knight, 'wit ye well that place is yours.'

And then he set him down surely in that siege. And then he said to the old man, 'Sir, ye may now go your way, for well have ye done that ye were commanded to do; and recommend me unto my grandsire, King Pelles, and unto my lord Petchere, and say them on my behalf, I shall come and see them as soon as ever I may.'

So the good man departed; and there met him twenty noble squires, and so took their horses and went their way.

Then all the knights of the Table Round marvelled greatly of Sir Galahad, that he durst sit there in that Siege Perilous, and was so tender of age; and wist not from whence he came but all only by God; and said, 'This is he by whom the Sangrail shall be achieved, for there sat never none but he, but he were mischieved.'

Then Sir Launcelot beheld his son and had great joy of him.

Then Bors told his fellows, 'Upon pain of my life this young knight shall come unto great worship.'

This noise was great in all the court, so that it came to the queen. Then she had marvel what knight it might be that durst adventure him to sit in the Siege Perilous. Many said unto the queen he resembled much unto Sir Launcelot.

'I may well suppose,' said the queen, 'that Sir Launcelot begat him on King Pelles' daughter, by the which he was made to lie by, by enchantment, and his name is Galahad. I would fain see him,' said the queen, 'for he must needs be a noble man, for so is his father that him begat, I report me unto all the Table Round.'

So when the meat was done that the king and all were risen, the king yede unto the Siege Perilous and lift up the cloth, and found there the name of Galahad; and then he showed it unto Sir Gawain, and said, 'Fair nephew, now have we among us Sir Galahad, the good knight that shall worship us all; and upon pain of my life he shall achieve the Sangrail, right as Sir Launcelot had done us to understand.'

Then came King Arthur unto Galahad and said, 'Sir, ye be welcome, for ye shall move many good knights to the quest of the Sangrail, and ye shall achieve that never knights might bring to an end.'

Then the king took him by the hand, and went down from the palace to show Galahad the adventures of the stone.

CHAPTER 5: *How King Arthur showed the stone hoving on the water to Galahad, and how he drew out the sword.*

The queen heard thereof, and came after with many ladies, and showed them the stone where it hoved on the water.

'Sir,' said the king unto Sir Galahad, 'here is a great marvel as ever I saw, and right good knights have assayed and failed.'

'Sir,' said Galahad, 'that is no marvel, for this adventure is not theirs but mine; and for the surety of this sword I brought none with me, for here by my side hangeth the scabbard.'

And anon he laid his hand on the sword, and lightly drew it out of the stone, and put it in the sheath, and said unto the king, 'Now it goeth better than it did aforehand.'

'Sir,' said the king, 'a shield God shall send you.'

'Now have I that sword that sometime was the good knight's, Balin le Savage, and he was a passing good man of his hands; and with this sword he slew his brother Balan, and that was great pity, for he was a good knight, and either slew other through a dolorous stroke that Balin gave unto my grandfather King Pelles, the which is not yet whole, nor not shall be till I heal him.'

Therewith the king and all espied where came riding down the river a lady on a white palfrey toward them. Then she saluted the king and the queen, and asked if that Sir Launcelot was there.

And then he answered himself, 'I am here, fair lady.'

Then she said all with weeping, 'How your great doing is changed sith this day in the morn.'

'Damosel, why say ye so?' said Launcelot.

'I say you sooth,' said the damosel, 'for ye were this day the best knight of the world, but who should say so now, he should be a liar, for there is now one better than ye, and well it is proved by the adventures of the sword whereto ye durst not set to your hand; and that is the change and leaving of your name. Wherefore I make unto you a remembrance, that ye shall not ween from henceforth that ye be the best knight of the world.'

'As touching unto that,' said Launcelot, 'I know well I was never the best.'

'Yes,' said the damosel, 'that were ye, and are yet, of any sinful man of the world. And sir king, Nacien, the hermit, sendeth thee word, that thee shall befall the greatest worship that ever befell king in Britain; and I say you wherefore: for this day the Sangrail appeared in thy house and fed thee and all thy fellowship of the Round Table.' So she departed and went that same way that she came.

CHAPTER 6: *How King Arthur had all the knights together for to joust in the meadow beside Winchester or they departed*

'Now,' said the king, 'I am sure at this quest of the Sangrail shall all ye of the Table Round depart, and never shall I see you again whole together; therefore I will see you all whole together in the meadow of Camelot to joust and to tourney, that after your death men may speak of it that such good knights were wholly together such a day.'

As unto that counsel and at the king's request they accorded all, and took on their harness that longed unto jousting. But all this moving of the king was for this intent, for to see Galahad proved; for the king deemed he should not lightly come again unto the court after his departing. So were they assembled in the meadow both more and less.

Then Sir Galahad, by the prayer of the king and the queen, did upon him a noble jesseraunte, and also he did on his helm, but shield would he take none for no prayer of the king.

And then Sir Gawain and other knights prayed him to take a spear. Right so he did; and the queen was in a tower with all her ladies, for to behold that tournament.

Then Sir Galahad dressed him in midst of the meadow, and began to break spears marvellously, that all men had wonder

246

of him; for he there surmounted all other knights, for within a while he had defouled many good knights of the Table Round save twain, that was Sir Launcelot and Sir Percival.

CHAPTER 7: *How the queen desired to see Galahad; and after, all the knights were replenished with the Holy Sangrail, and how all they avowed the enquest of the same*

Then the king, at the queen's request, made him to alight and to unlace his helm, that the queen might see him in the visage.

When she beheld him she said, 'Soothly I dare well say that Sir Launcelot begat him, for never two men resembled more in likeness, therefore it nis no marvel though he be of great prowess.'

So a lady that stood by the queen said, 'Madam, for God's sake ought he of right to be so good a knight?'

'Yea, forsooth,' said the queen, 'for he is of all parties come of the best knights of the world and of the highest lineage; for Sir Launcelot is come but of the eighth degree from Our Lord Jesu Christ, and Sir Galahad is of the ninth degree from Our Lord Jesu Christ, therefore I dare say they be the greatest gentlemen of the world.'

And then the king and all estates went home unto Camelot, and so went to evensong to the great minster, and so after upon that to supper, and every knight sat in his own place as they were toforehand.

Then anon they heard cracking and crying of thunder, that them thought the place should all to-drive. In the midst of this blast entered a sunbeam more clearer by seven times than ever they saw day, and all they were alighted of the grace of the Holy Ghost. Then began every knight to behold other, and either saw other, by their seeming, fairer than ever they saw afore. Notforthan there was no knight might speak one word a great while, and so they looked every man on other as they had been dumb.

Then there entered into the hall the Holy Grail covered with white samite, but there was none might see it, nor who bare it. And there was all the hall fulfilled with good odours, and every knight had such meats and drinks as he best loved in this world. And when the Holy Grail had been borne through the hall, then the holy vessel departed suddenly, that they wist not where it became; then had they all breath to speak.

And then the king yielded thankings to God, of His good grace that he had sent them. 'Certes,' said the king, 'we ought to thank Our Lord Jesu greatly for that he hath showed us this day, at the reverence of this high feast of Pentecost.'

'Now,' said Sir Gawain, 'we have been served this day of what meats and drinks we thought on; but one thing beguiled us, we might not see the Holy Grail, it was so preciously covered. Wherefore I will make here avow, that tomorn, without longer abiding, I shall labour in the quest of the Sangrail, that I shall hold me out a twelvemonth and a day, or more if need be, and never shall I return again unto the court till I have seen it more openly than it hath been seen here; and if I may not speed I shall return again as he that may not be against the will of Our Lord Jesu Christ.'

When they of the Table Round heard Sir Gawain say so, they arose up the most part and made such avows as Sir Gawain had made. Anon as King Arthur heard this he was greatly displeased, for he wist well they might not again-say their avows.

'Alas,' said King Arthur unto Sir Gawain, 'ye have nigh slain me with the avow and promise that ye have made; for through you ye have bereft me the fairest fellowship and the truest of knighthood that ever were seen together in any realm of the world; for when they depart from hence I am sure they all shall never meet more in this world, for they shall die many in the quest. And so it forthinketh me a little, for I have loved them as well as my life, wherefore it shall grieve me right sore, the departition of this fellowship; for I have had an old custom to have them in my fellowship.'

CHAPTER 8: *How great sorrow was made of the king and ladies for the departing of the knights, and how they departed*

And therewith the tears fell in his eyen. And then he said, 'Gawain, Gawain, ye have set me in great sorrow, for I have great doubt that my true fellowship shall never meet here more again.'

'Ah,' said Sir Launcelot, 'comfort yourself; for it shall be unto us a great honour and much more than if we died in any other places, for of death we be siker.'

'Ah, Launcelot,' said the king, 'the great love that I have had unto you all the days of my life maketh me to say such doleful words; for never Christian king had never so many worthy men at his table as I have had this day at the Round Table, and that is my great sorrow.'

When the queen, ladies, and gentlewomen, wist these tidings, they had such sorrow and heaviness that there might no tongue tell it, for those knights had held them in honour and charity. But among all other Queen Guenever made great sorrow.

'I marvel,' said she, 'my lord would suffer them to depart from him.'

Thus was all the court troubled for the love of the departition of those knights. And many of those ladies that loved knights would have gone with their lovers; and so had they done, had not an old knight come among them in religious clothing; and then he spake all on high and said:

'Fair lords, which have sworn in the quest of the Sangrail, thus sendeth you Nacien, the hermit, word, that none in this quest lead lady nor gentlewoman with him, for it is not to do in so high a service as they labour in; for I warn you plain, he that is not clean of his sins he shall not see the mysteries of Our Lord Jesus Christ.'

And for this cause they left these ladies and gentlewomen. After this the queen came unto Galahad and asked him of whence he was, and of what country. He told her of whence he was. And son unto Launcelot, she said he was. As to that, he said neither yea or nay.

'So God me help,' said the queen, 'of your father, ye need not to shame you, for he is the goodliest knight, and of the best men of the world comen, and of the strain, of all parties, of kings. Wherefore ye ought of right to be, of your deeds, a passing good man; and certainly,' she said, 'ye resemble him much.'

Then Sir Galahad was a little ashamed and said, 'Madam, sith ye know in certain, wherefore do ye ask it me? For he that is my father shall be known openly and all betimes.'

And then they went to rest them. And in the honour of the highness of Galahad he was led into King Arthur's chamber, and there rested in his own bed.

And as soon as it was day the king arose, for he had no rest of all that night for sorrow. Then he went unto Gawain and to Sir Launcelot that were arisen for to hear mass.

And then the king again said, 'Ah Gawain, Gawain, ye have betrayed me; for never shall my court be amended by you, but ye will never be sorry for me as I am for you.' And therewith the tears began to run down by his visage. And therewith the king said, 'Ah, knight Sir Launcelot, I require thee thou counsel me, for I would that this quest were undone and it might be.'

'Sir,' said Sir Launcelot, 'ye saw yesterday so many worthy knights that then were sworn that they may not leave it in no manner of wise.'

'That wot I well,' said the king, 'but it shall so heavy me at their departing that I wot well there shall no manner of joy remedy me.'

And then the king and the queen went unto the minster.

So anon Launcelot and Gawain commanded their men to bring their arms. And when they all were armed save their shields and their helms, then they came to their fellowship, which were all ready in the same wise, for to go to the minster to hear their service.

Then after the service was done the king would wit how many had undertake the quest of the Holy Grail; and to account them he prayed them all. Then found they by the tale an hundred and fifty, and all were knights of the Table Round. And then they put on their helms and departed, and recommended them all wholly unto the queen; and there was weeping and great sorrow.

Then the queen departed into her chamber and held her that no man should perceive her great sorrows. When Sir Launcelot missed the queen he went till her chamber, and when she saw him she cried aloud, 'O Launcelot, Launcelot, ye have betrayed me and put me to the death, for to leave thus my lord.'

'Ah, madam, I pray you be not displeased, for I shall come again as soon as I may with my worship.'

'Alas,' said she, 'that ever I saw you; but he that suffered death upon the cross for all mankind be unto you good conduct and safety, and all the whole fellowship.'

Right so departed Sir Launcelot, and found his fellowship that abode his coming. And so they mounted on their horses and rode through the street of Camelot; and there was weeping of rich and poor, and the king turned away and might not speak for weeping.

So within a while they came to a city, and a castle that hight Vagon. There they entered into the castle, and the lord thereof was an old man that hight Vagon, and he was a good man of his living and set open the gates, and made them all the cheer that he might. And so on the morn they were all accorded that they should depart every each from other; and on the morn they departed with weeping cheer, and every knight took the way that him liked best.

tale: reckoning.

CHAPTER 9: *How Galahad gat him a shield, and how they sped that presumed to take down the said shield*

Now rideth Galahad yet withouten shield, and so rode four days without any adventure. And at the fourth day after evensong he came to a white abbey, and there was he received with great reverence, and led unto a chamber, and there was he unarmed; and then was he ware of two knights of the Table Round, one was Sir Bagdemagus, and Sir Uwain.

And when they saw him they went unto Galahad and made of him great solace, and so they went unto supper.

'Sirs,' said Sir Galahad, 'what adventure brought you hither?'

'Sir,' they said all, 'it is told us that within this place is a shield that no man may bear about his neck but he be mischieved other dead within three days, or maimed for ever.'

'Ah sir,' said King Bagdemagus, 'I shall bear it tomorn for to assay this adventure.'

'In the name of God,' said Galahad.

'Sir,' said Bagdemagus, 'and I may not achieve the adventure of this shield ye shall take it upon you, for I am sure ye shall not fail.'

'Sir,' said Galahad, 'I right well agree me thereto, for I have no shield.'

So on the morn they arose and heard mass. Then Bagdemagus asked where the adventurous shield was. Anon a monk led him behind an altar where the shield hung as white as any snow, but in the midst was a red cross.

'Sirs,' said the monk, 'this shield ought not to be hanged about no knight's neck but he be the worthiest knight of the world, and therefore I counsel you knights to be well advised.'

'Well,' said Bagdemagus, 'I wot well I am not the best knight of the world, but I shall assay to bear it,' and so bare it out of the minster; and then he said unto Galahad, 'And it please you to abide here still, till ye wit how that I speed.'

'I shall abide you,' said Galahad.

Then King Bagdemagus took with him a good squire, to bring tidings unto Sir Galahad how he sped. Then when they had ridden two mile and came in a fair valley afore an hermitage, and then they saw a knight come from that part in white armour, horse and all; and he came as fast as his horse might run, with his spear in his rest, and Sir Bagdemagus dressed his spear against him and brake it upon the white knight. But the other struck him so hard that he brast the mails, and shove him through the right shoulder, for the shield covered him not as at that time; and so he bare him from his horse.

And therewith he alit and took the white shield from him, saying, 'Knight, thou hast done thyself great folly, for this shield ought not to be borne but by him that shall have no peer that liveth.'

And then he came to Bagdemagus' squire and said, 'Bear this shield unto the good knight Sir Galahad, that thou left in the abbey, and greet him well by me.'

'Sir,' said the squire, 'what is your name?'

'Take thou no heed of my name,' said the knight, 'for it is not for thee to know nor for none earthly man.'

'Now, fair sir,' said the squire, 'at the reverence of Jesu Christ, tell me for what cause this shield may not be borne but if the bearer thereof be mischieved.'

'Now sith thou hast conjured me so,' said the knight, 'this shield behoveth unto no man but unto Galahad.'

And the squire went unto Bagdemagus and asked whether he were sore wounded or not.

'Yea forsooth,' said he, 'I shall escape hard from the death.'

Then he fetched his horse, and brought him with great pain unto an abbey. Then was he taken down softly and unarmed, and laid in a bed, and there was looked to his wounds. And as the book telleth, he lay there long, and escaped hard with the life.

CHAPTER 10: *How Galahad departed with the shield, and how King Evelake had received this shield of Joseph of Arimathea*

'Sir Galahad,' said the squire, 'that knight that wounded Bagdemagus sendeth you greeting, and bad that ye should bear this shield, wherethrough great adventures should befall.'

'Now blessed be good and fortune,' said Galahad.

And then he asked his arms, and mounted upon his horse, and hung the white shield about his neck, and commended them unto God. And Sir Uwain said he would bear him fellowship if it pleased him.

'Sir,' said Galahad, 'that may ye not, for I must go alone, save this squire shall bear me fellowship:' and so departed Uwain.

Then within a while came Galahad thereas the white knight abode him by the hermitage, and every each saluted other courteously.

'Sir,' said Galahad, 'by this shield be many marvels fallen?'

'Sir,' said the knight, 'it befell after the passion of Our Lord Jesu Christ thirty-two year, that Joseph of Arimathea, the gentle knight, the which took down Our Lord off the holy Cross, at that time he departed from Jerusalem with a great party of his kindred with him. And so he laboured till that they came to a city that hight Sarras. And at that same hour that Joseph came to Sarras there was a king that hight Evelake, that had great war against the Saracens, and in especial against one Saracen, the which was King Evelake's cousin, a rich king and a mighty, which marched nigh this land, and his name was called Tolleme la Feintes. So on a day these two met to do battle.

'Then Joseph, the son of Joseph of Arimathea, went to King Evelake and told him he should be discomfit and slain, but if he left his belief of the old law and believe upon the new law. And then there he showed him the right belief of the Holy Trinity, to the which he agreed unto with all his heart; and there this shield was made for King Evelake, in the name of Him that died upon the Cross. And then through his good belief he had the better of King Tolleme. For when Evelake was in the battle there was a cloth set afore the shield, and when he was in the greatest peril he let put away the cloth, and then his enemies saw a figure of a man on the cross, wherethrough they all were discomfit.

'And so it befell that a man of King Evelake's was smitten his hand off, and bare that hand in his other hand; and Joseph called that man unto him and bad him go with good devotion touch the cross. And as soon as that man had touched the cross with his hand it was as whole as ever it was tofore. Then soon after there fell a great marvel, that the cross of the shield at one time vanished away that no man wist where it became. And then King Evelake was baptised, and for the most part all the people of that city.

'So, soon after Joseph would depart, and King Evelake would go with him whether he would or nold. And so by fortune they came into this land, that at that time was called Great Britain; and there they found a great felon paynim, that put Joseph into prison. And so by fortune tidings came unto a worthy man that hight Mondrames,[1] and he assembled all his people for the great renown he had heard of Joseph; and so he came into the land of Great Britain and disinherited this felon paynim and consumed him, and therewith delivered Joseph out of prison. And after that all the people were turned to the Christian faith.

CHAPTER 11: *How Joseph made a cross on the white shield with his blood, and how Galahad was by a monk brought to a tomb*

'Not long after that Joseph was laid in his deadly bed. And when King Evelake saw that, he made such sorrow, and said, "For thy love I have left my country, and sith ye shall depart out of this world, leave me some token of yours that I may think on you."

'Joseph said, "That will I do full gladly; now bring me your shield that I took you when ye went into battle against King Tolleme."

'Then Joseph bled sore at the nose, so that he might not by no mean be staunched. And there upon that shield he made a cross of his own blood. "Now may ye see a remembrance that I love you, for ye shall never see this shield but ye shall think on me, and it shall be always as fresh as it is now. And never shall man bear this shield about his neck but he shall repent it, unto the time that Galahad, the good knight, bear it; and the last of my lineage shall have it about his neck, that shall do many marvellous deeds."

"Now," said King Evelake, "where shall I put this shield, that this worthy knight may have it?"

"Ye shall leave it thereas Nacien, the hermit, shall be put after his death; for thither shall that good knight come the fifteenth day after that he shall receive the order of knighthood": and so that day that they set is this time that he have his shield, and in the same abbey lieth Nacien, the hermit.'

And then the white knight vanished away.

Anon as the squire had heard these words, he alit off his hackney and kneeled down at Galahad's feet, and prayed him that he might go with him till he had made him knight.

'If I would not refuse you?'

'Then will ye make me a knight?' said the squire. 'And that order, by the grace of God, shall be well set in me.'

So Sir Galahad granted him, and turned again unto the abbey there they came from; and there men made great joy of Sir Galahad. And anon as he was alit there was a monk brought him unto a tomb in a churchyard, where there was such a noise that who that heard it should verily nigh be mad or lose his strength; 'and sir,' they said, 'we deem it is a fiend.'

CHAPTER 12: *Of the marvel that Sir Galahad saw and heard in the tomb, and how he made Melias knight*

'Now lead me thither,' said Galahad.

And so they did, all armed save his helm.

'Now,' said the good man, 'go to the tomb and lift it up.'

So he did, and heard a great noise; and piteously he said, that all men might hear it, 'Sir Galahad, the servant of Jesu Christ, come thou not nigh me, for thou shalt make me go again there where I have been so long.'

But Galahad was nothing afraid, but lift up the stone; and there came out so foul a smoke, and after he saw the foulest figure leap thereout that ever he saw in the likeness of a man; and then he blessed him and wist well it was a fiend.

Then heard he a voice say, 'Galahad, I see there environ about thee so many angels that my power may not dere thee.'

Right so Sir Galahad saw a body all armed lie in that tomb, and beside him a sword.

'Now, fair brother,' said Galahad, 'let us remove this body, for it is not worthy to lie in this churchyard, for he was a false Christian man.'

And therewith they all departed and went to the abbey.

And anon as he was unarmed a good man came and set him down by him and said, 'Sir, I shall tell you what betokeneth all that ye saw in the tomb; for that covered body betokeneth the duress of the world, and the great sin that Our Lord found in the world. For there was such wretchedness that the father loved not the son, nor the son loved not the father; and that was one of the causes that Our Lord took flesh and blood of a clean maiden, for our sins were so great at that time that wellnigh all was wickedness.'

'Truly,' said Galahad, 'I believe you right well.'

So Sir Galahad rested him there that night; and upon the

duress: affliction.

257

morn he made the squire knight, and asked him his name, and of what kindred he was come.

'Sir,' said he, 'men calleth me Melias de Lile, and I am the son of the King of Denmark.'

'Now, fair sir,' said Galahad, 'sith that ye be come of kings and queens, now look that knighthood be well set in you, for ye ought to be a mirror unto all chivalry.'

'Sir,' said Sir Melias, 'ye say sooth. But, sir, sithen ye have made me a knight ye must of right grant me my first desire that is reasonable.'

'Ye say sooth,' said Galahad.

Melias said, 'Then that ye will suffer me to ride with you in this quest of the Sangrail, till that some adventure depart us.'

'I grant you, sir.'

Then men brought Sir Melias his armour and his spear and his horse, and so Sir Galahad and he rode forth all that week or they found any adventure.

And then upon a Monday in the morning, as they were departed from an abbey, they came to a cross which departed two ways, and in that cross were letters written that said thus:

'Now, ye knights errant, the which goeth to seek knights adventurous, see here two ways; that one way defendeth thee that thou ne go that way, for he shall not go out of the way again but if he be a good man and a worthy knight; and if thou go on the left hand, thou shalt not lightly there win prowess, for thou shalt in this way be soon assayed.'

'Sir,' said Melias to Galahad, 'if it like you to suffer me to take the way on the left hand, tell me, for there I shall well prove my strength.'

'It were better,' said Galahad, 'ye rode not that way, for I deem I should better escape in that way than ye.'

'Nay, my lord, I pray you let me have that adventure.'

'Take it in God's name,' said Galahad.

CHAPTER 13: *Of the adventure that Melias had, and how Galahad revenged him, and how Melias was carried into an abbey*

And then rode Melias into an old forest, and therein he rode two days and more. And then he came into a fair meadow, and there was a fair lodge of boughs. And then he espied in that lodge a chair, wherein was a crown of gold, subtly wrought. Also there were cloths covered upon the earth, and many delicious meats set thereon. Sir Melias beheld this adventure, and thought it marvellous, but he had no hunger, but of the crown of gold he took much keep; and therewith he stooped down and took it up, and rode his way with it.

And anon he saw a knight came riding after him that said, 'Knight, set down that crown which is not yours, and therefore defend you.'

Then Sir Melias blessed him and said, 'Fair Lord of Heaven, help and save Thy new-made knight.'

And then they let their horses run as fast as they might, so that the other knight smote Sir Melias through hauberk and through the left side, that he fell to the earth nigh dead. And then he took the crown and went his way; and Sir Melias lay still and had no power to stir.

In the meanwhile by fortune there came Sir Galahad and found him there in peril of death. And then he said,

'Ah, Melias, who hath wounded you? Therefore it had been better to have ridden the other way.'

And when Sir Melias heard him speak, 'Sir,' he said, 'for God's love let me not die in this forest, but bear me unto the abbey here beside, that I may be confessed and have my rites.'

'It shall be done,' said Galahad, 'but where is he that hath wounded you?'

With that Sir Galahad heard in the leaves cry on high: 'Knight, keep thee from me.'

'Ah sir,' said Melias, 'beware, for that is he that hath slain me.'

Sir Galahad answered: 'Sir knight, come on your peril.'

Then either dressed to other, and came together as fast as their horses might run, and Galahad smote him so that his spear went through his shoulder, and smote him down off his horse, and in the falling Galahad's spear brake. With that came out another knight out of the leaves, and brake a spear upon Galahad or ever he might turn him. Then Galahad drew out his sword and smote off the left arm of him, so that it fell to the earth. And then he fled, and Sir Galahad sued fast after him.

And then he turned again unto Sir Melias, and there he alit and dressed him softly on his horse tofore him, for the truncheon of his spear was in his body; and Sir Galahad start up behind him, and held him in his arms, and so brought him to the abbey, and there unarmed him and brought him to his chamber. And then he asked his Saviour.

And when he had received Him he said unto Sir Galahad, 'Sir, let death come when it pleased him.'

And therewith he drew out the truncheon of the spear out of his body; and then he swooned.

Then came there an old monk which sometime had been a knight, and beheld Sir Melias. And anon he ransacked him; and then he said unto Sir Galahad; 'I shall heal him of this wound, by the grace of God, within the term of seven weeks.'

Then was Sir Galahad glad, and unarmed him, and said he would abide there three days. And then he asked Sir Melias how it stood with him. Then he said he was turned unto helping, God be thanked.

CHAPTER 14: *How Galahad departed, and how he was commanded to go to the Castle of Maidens to destroy the wicked custom*

'Now will I depart,' said Galahad, 'for I have much on hand, for many good knights be full busy about it, and this knight and I were in the same quest of the Sangrail.'

'Sir,' said the good man, 'for his sin he was thus wounded; and I marvel,' said the good man, 'how ye durst take upon you so rich a thing as the high order of knighthood without clean confession, and that was the cause ye were bitterly wounded. For the way on the right hand betokeneth the highway of Our Lord Jesus Christ, and the way of a good true good liver. And the other way betokeneth the way of sinners and of misbelievers. And when the devil saw your pride and presumption, for to take you in the quest of the Sangrail, that made you to be overthrown, for it may not be achieved but by virtuous living. Also, the writing on the cross was a signification of heavenly deeds, and of knightly deeds in God's works, and no knightly deeds in worldly works. And pride is head of all deadly sins, that caused this knight to depart from Galahad. And where thou tookest the crown of gold thou sinnest in covetise and in theft: all this were no knightly deeds. And this Galahad, the holy knight, the which fought with the two knights, the two knights signifyen the two deadly sins which were wholly in this knight Melias; and they might not withstand you, for ye are without deadly sin.'

Now departed Galahad from thence, and betaught them all unto God.

Sir Melias said; 'My lord Galahad, as soon as I may ride I shall seek you.'

'God send you health,' said Galahad, and so took his horse and departed, and rode many journeys forward and backward, as adventure would lead him.

And at the last it happened him to depart from a place or a castle the which was named Abblasoure; and he had heard no mass, the which he was wont ever to hear or ever he departed out of any castle or place, and kept that for a custom. Then Sir Galahad came unto a mountain where he found an old chapel, and found there nobody, for all, all was desolate; and there he kneeled tofore the altar, and besought God of wholesome counsel. So as he prayed he heard a voice that said, 'Go thou now, thou adventurous knight, to the Castle of Maidens, and there do thou away the[1] wicked customs.'

CHAPTER 15: *How Sir Galahad fought with the knights of
the castle, and destroyed the wicked custom*

When Sir Galahad heard this he thanked God, and took his
horse; and he had not ridden but half a mile, he saw in a
valley afore him a strong castle with deep ditches, and there
ran beside it a fair river that hight Severn; and there he met
with a man of great age, and either saluted other, and Galahad asked him the castle's name.

'Fair sir,' said he, 'it is the Castle of Maidens.'

'That is a cursed castle,' said Galahad, 'and all they that be
conversant therein, for all pity is out thereof, and all hardiness and mischief is therein.'

'Therefore, I counsel you, sir knight, to turn again.'

'Sir,' said Galahad, 'wit you well I shall not turn again.'

Then looked Sir Galahad on his arms that nothing failed
him, and then he put his shield afore him; and anon there
met him seven fair maidens, the which said unto him, 'Sir
knight, ye ride here in a great folly, for ye have the water to
pass over.'

'Why should I not pass the water?' said Galahad.

So rode he away from them and met with a squire that
said, 'Knight, those knights in the castle defyen you, and
defenden you ye go no further till that they wit what ye
would.'

'Fair sir,' said Galahad, 'I come for to destroy the wicked
custom of this castle.'

'Sir, and ye will abide by that ye shall have enough to do.'

'Go you now,' said Galahad, 'and haste my needs.'

Then the squire entered into the castle. And anon after
there came out of the castle seven knights, and all were
brethren.

And when they saw Galahad they cried, 'Knight, keep
thee, for we assure thee nothing but death.'

'Why,' said Galahad, 'will ye all have ado with me at once?'

conversant: living.

'Yea,' said they, 'thereto mayest thou trust.'

Then Galahad put forth his spear and smote the foremost to the earth, that near he brake his neck. And therewithal the other smote him on his shield great strokes, so that their spears brake. Then Sir Galahad drew out his sword, and set upon them so hard that it was marvel to see it, and so through great force he made them to forsake the field; and Galahad chased them till they entered into the castle, and so passed through the castle at another gate.

And there met Sir Galahad an old man clothed in religious clothing, and said, 'Sir, have here the keys of this castle.'

Then Sir Galahad opened the gates, and saw so much people in the streets that he might not number them, and all said, 'Sir, ye be welcome, for long have we abiden here our deliverance.'

Then came to him a gentlewoman and said, 'These knights be fled, but they will come again this night, and here to begin again their evil custom.'

'What will ye that I shall do?' said Galahad.

'Sir,' said the gentlewoman, 'that ye send after all the knights hither that hold their lands of this castle, and make them to swear for to use the customs that were used heretofore of old time.'

'I will well,' said Galahad.

And there she brought him an horn of ivory, bounden with gold richly, and said, 'Sir, blow this horn which will be heard two mile about this castle.'

When Sir Galahad had blown the horn he set him down upon a bed.

Then came a priest to Galahad, and said, 'Sir, it is past a seven year agone that these seven brethren came into this castle, and harboured with the lord of this castle, that hight the Duke Lianour, and he was lord of all this country. And when they espied the duke's daughter, that was a full fair woman, then by their false covin they made debate betwixt themself, and the duke of his goodness would have departed

covin: conspiracy.

them, and there they slew him and his eldest son. And then they took the maiden and the treasure of the castle. And then by great force they held all the knights of this castle against their will under their obeisance, and in great service and truage, robbing and pilling the poor common people of all that they had. So it happened on a day the duke's daughter said, "Ye have done unto me great wrong to slay mine own father, and my brother, and thus to hold our lands: notforthan," she said, "ye shall not hold this castle for many years, for by one knight ye shall be overcomen." Thus she prophesied seven years agone.

' "Well," said the seven knights, "sithen ye say so, there shall never lady nor knight pass this castle but they shall abide maugre their heads, or die therefore, till that knight be come by whom we shall lose this castle." And therefore is it called the Maidens' Castle, for they have devoured many maidens.'

'Now,' said Galahad, 'is she here for whom this castle was lost?'

'Nay sir,' said the priest, 'she was dead within these three nights after that she was thus enforced; and sithen have they kept their younger sister, which endureth great pains with more other ladies.'

By this were the knights of the country comen, and then he made them do homage and fealty to the king's daughter, and set them in great ease of heart. And in the morn there came one to Galahad and told him how that Gawain, Gareth, and Uwain, had slain the seven brethren.

'I suppose well,' said Sir Galahad, and took his armour and his horse, and commended them unto God.

CHAPTER 16: *How Sir Gawain came to the abbey for to follow Galahad, and how he was shriven to an hermit*

Now, saith the tale, after Sir Gawain departed, he rode many journeys, both toward and froward. And at the last he came to the abbey where Sir Galahad had the white shield, and there Sir Gawain learned the way to sue after Sir Galahad; and so he rode to the abbey where Melias lay sick and there Sir Melias told Sir Gawain of the marvellous adventures that Sir Galahad did.

'Certes,' said Sir Gawain, 'I am not happy that I took not the way that he went, for and I may meet with him I will not depart from him lightly, for all marvellous adventures Sir Galahad achieveth.'

'Sir,' said one of the monks, 'he will not of your fellow-ship.'

'Why?' said Sir Gawain.

'Sir,' said he, 'for ye be wicked and sinful, and he is full blessed.'

Right as they thus stood talking there came in riding Sir Gareth. And then they made joy either of other. And on the morn they heard mass, and so departed.

And by the way they met with Sir Uwain les Avoutres, and there Sir Uwain told Sir Gawain how he had met with none adventure sith he departed from the court.

'Nor we,' said Sir Gawain. And either promised other of those three knights not to depart while they were in that quest, but if fortune caused it.

So they departed and rode by fortune till that they came by the Castle of Maidens; and there the seven brethren espied the three knights, and said, 'Sithen we be flemed by one knight from this castle, we shall destroy all the knights of King Arthur's that we may overcome, for the love of Sir Galahad.'

And therewith the seven knights set upon the three knights, and by fortune Sir Gawain slew one of the brethren, and each one of his fellows slew another, and so slew the remnant. And then they took the way under the castle, and there they lost the way that Sir Galahad rode, and there every each of them departed from other.

And Sir Gawain rode till he came to an hermitage, and

flemed: put to flight.

there he found the good man saying his evensong of Our Lady; and there Sir Gawain asked harbour for charity, and the good man granted it him gladly. Then the good man asked him what he was.

'Sir,' he said, 'I am a knight of King Arthur's that am in the quest of the Sangrail, and my name is Sir Gawain.'

'Sir,' said the good man, 'I would wit how it standeth betwixt God and you.'

'Sir,' said Sir Gawain, 'I will with a good will show you my life if it please you.' And there he told the hermit how 'a monk of an abbey called me wicked knight.'

'He might well say it,' said the hermit, 'for when ye were first made knight you should have taken you to knightly deeds and virtuous living, and ye have done the contrary, for ye have lived mischievously many winters; and Sir Galahad is a maid, and sinner never, and that is the cause he shall achieve where he goeth that ye nor none such shall not attain, nor none in your fellowship, for ye have used the most untruest life that ever I heard knight live. For certes had ye not been so wicked as ye are, never had the seven brethren been slain by you and your two fellows. For Sir Galahad himself alone beat them all seven the day tofore, but his living is such he shall slay no man lightly. Also I may say you the Castle of Maidens betokenen the good souls that were in prison afore the Incarnation of Jesu Christ. And the seven knights betokenen the seven deadly sins that reigned that time in the world; and I may liken the good Galahad unto the son of the High Father, that lit within a maid, and bought all the souls out of thrall: so did Sir Galahad deliver all the maidens out of the woeful castle. Now, Sir Gawain,' said the good man, 'thou must do penance for thy sin.'

'Sir, what penance shall I do?'

'Such as I will give,' said the good man.

'Nay,' said Sir Gawain, 'I may do no penance; for we knights adventurous oft sufferen great woe and pain.'

'Well,' said the good man, and then he held his peace.

And on the morn Sir Gawain departed from the hermit,

and betaught him unto God. And by adventure he met with Sir Agloval and Sir Griflet, two knights of the Table Round. And they two rode four days without finding of any adventure, and at the fifth day they departed. And every each held as befell them by adventure.

Here leaveth the tale of Sir Gawain and his fellows, and speak we of Sir Galahad.

CHAPTER 17: *How Sir Galahad met with Sir Launcelot and with Sir Percival, and smote them down, and departed from them*

So when Sir Galahad was departed from the Castle of Maidens he rode till he came to a waste forest, and there he met with Sir Launcelot and Sir Percival, but they knew him not, for he was new disguised. Right so Sir Launcelot, his father, dressed his spear and brake it upon Sir Galahad, and Galahad smote him so again that he smote down horse and man. And then he drew his sword, and dressed him unto Sir Percival, and smote him so on the helm, that it rove to the coif of steel; and had not the sword swerved Sir Percival had been slain, and with the stroke he fell out of his saddle.

This jousts was done tofore the hermitage where a recluse dwelled. And when she saw Sir Galahad ride, she said, 'God be with thee, best knight of the world. Ah certes,' said she, all aloud that Launcelot and Percival might hear it, 'and yonder two knights had known thee as well as I do they would not have encountered with thee.'

Then Sir Galahad heard her say so, he was adread to be known; therewith he smote his horse with his spurs and rode a great pace toward them.

Then perceived they both that he was Galahad; and up they gat on their horses, and rode fast after him, but in a while he was out of their sight. And then they turned again with heavy cheer.

'Let us spere some tidings,' said Percival, 'at yonder recluse.'

'Do as ye list,' said Sir Launcelot.

When Sir Percival came to the recluse she knew him well enough, and Sir Launcelot both.

But Sir Launcelot rode overthwart and endlong in a wild forest, and held no path but as wild adventure led him. And at the last he came to a stony cross which departed two ways in waste land; and by the cross was a stone that was of marble, but it was so dark that Sir Launcelot might not wit what it was.

Then Sir Launcelot looked by him, and saw an old chapel, and there he weened to have found people; and Sir Launcelot tied his horse till a tree, and there he did off his shield and hung it upon a tree. And then he went to the chapel door, and found it waste and broken. And within he found a fair altar, full richly arrayed with cloth of clean silk, and there stood a fair clean candlestick, which bare six great candles, and the candlestick was of silver. And when Sir Launcelot saw this light he had great will for to enter into the chapel, but he could find no place where he might enter; then was he passing heavy and dismayed. Then he returned and came to his horse and did off his saddle and bridle, and let him pasture, and unlaced his helm, and ungirt his sword, and laid him down to sleep upon his shield tofore the cross.

CHAPTER 18: *How Sir Launcelot, half sleeping and half waking, saw a sick man borne in a litter, and how he was healed by the Sangrail*

And so he fell asleep; and half waking and sleeping he saw come by him two palfreys all fair and white, the which bare a litter, therein lying a sick knight. And when he was nigh the cross he there abode still. All this Sir Launcelot saw and beheld, for he slept not verily; and he heard him say,

'O sweet Lord, when shall this sorrow leave me? And when shall the holy vessel come by me, wherethrough I shall be blessed? For I have endured thus long, for little trespass.'

A full great while complained the knight thus, and always Sir Launcelot heard it.

With that Sir Launcelot saw the candlestick with the six tapers come before the cross, and he saw nobody that brought it. Also there came a table of silver, and the holy vessel of the Sangrail, which Launcelot had seen aforetime in King Petchere's house.

And therewith the sick knight sat him up, and held up both his hands, and said, 'Fair sweet Lord, which is here within this holy vessel, take heed unto me that I may be whole of this malady.'

And therewith on his hands and on his knees he went so nigh that he touched the holy vessel and kissed it, and anon he was whole; and then he said, 'Lord God, I thank Thee, for I am healed of this sickness.'

So when the holy vessel had been there a great while it went unto the chapel with the chandelier and the light, so that Launcelot wist not where it was become; for he was overtaken with sin that he had no power to rise against the holy vessel; wherefore after that many men said of him shame, but he took repentance after that.

Then the sick knight dressed him up and kissed the cross; anon his squire brought him his arms, and asked his lord how he did.

'Certes,' said he, 'I thank God right well, through the holy vessel I am healed. But I have marvel of this sleeping knight that had no power to awake when this holy vessel was brought hither.'

'I dare right well say,' said the squire, 'that he dwelleth in some deadly sin whereof he was never confessed.'

'By my faith,' said the knight, 'whatsomever he be he is unhappy, for as I deem he is of the fellowship of the Round Table, the which is entered into the quest of the Sangrail.'

'Sir,' said the squire, 'here I have brought you all your arms save your helm and your sword, and therefore by mine *against*: in the presence of.

assent now may ye take this knight's helm and his sword:' and so he did.

And when he was clean armed he took Sir Launcelot's horse, for he was better than his; and so departed they from the cross.

CHAPTER 19: *How a voice spake to Sir Launcelot, and how he found his horse and his helm borne away, and after went afoot*

Then anon Sir Launcelot waked, and sat him up, and bethought him what he had seen there, and whether it were dreams or not.

Right so heard he a voice that said, 'Sir Launcelot, more harder than is the stone, and more bitter than is the wood, and more naked and barer than is the leaf of the fig tree; therefore go thou from hence, and withdraw thee from this holy place.'

And when Sir Launcelot heard this he was passing heavy and wist not what to do, and so departed sore weeping, and cursed the time that he was born. For then he deemed never to have had worship more. For those words went to his heart, till that he knew wherefore he was called so.

Then Sir Launcelot went to the cross and found his helm, his sword, and his horse taken away. And then he called himself a very wretch, and most unhappy of all knights; and there he said,

'My sin and my wickedness have brought me unto great dishonour. For when I sought worldly adventures for worldly desires, I ever achieved them and had the better in every place, and never was I discomfit in no quarrel, were it right or wrong. And now I take upon me the adventures of holy things, and now I see and understand that mine old sin hindereth me and shameth me, so that I had no power to stir nor speak when the holy blood appeared afore me.'

So thus he sorrowed till it was day, and heard the fowls

sing; then somewhat he was comforted. But when Sir Launcelot missed his horse and his harness then he wist well God was displeased with him. Then he departed from the cross on foot into a forest; and so by prime he came to an high hill, and found an hermitage and a hermit therein which was going unto mass.

And then Launcelot kneeled down and cried on Our Lord mercy for his wicked works. So when mass was done Launcelot called him, and prayed him for charity for to hear his life.

'With a good will,' said the good man. 'Sir,' said he, 'be ye of King Arthur's court and of the fellowship of the Round Table?'

'Yea forsooth, and my name is Sir Launcelot du Lake that hath been right well said of, and now my good fortune is changed, for I am the most wretch of the world.'

The hermit beheld him and had marvel how he was so abashed.

'Sir,' said the hermit, 'ye ought to thank God more than any knight living, for He hath caused you to have more worldly worship than any knight that now liveth. And for your presumption to take upon you in deadly sin for to be in His presence, where His flesh and His blood was, that caused you ye might not see it with worldly eyen; for He will not appear where such sinners be, but if it be unto their great hurt and unto their great shame; and there is no knight living now that ought to ken God so great thank as ye, for He hath given you beauty, seemliness, and great strength above all other knights; and therefore ye are the more beholding unto God than any other man, to love Him and dread Him, for your strength and manhood will little avail you and God be against you.'

ken . . . thank: express thanks.

CHAPTER 20: *How Sir Launcelot was shriven, and what sorrow he made, and of good examples which were showed to him*

Then Sir Launcelot wept with heavy cheer, and said, 'Now I know well ye say me sooth.'

'Sir,' said the good man, 'hide none old sin from me.'

'Truly,' said Sir Launcelot, 'that were me full loth to discover. For this fourteen year I never discovered one thing that I have used, and that may I now wit my shame and my disadventure.' And then he told there that good man all his life. And how he had loved a queen unmeasurably and out of measure long. 'And all my great deeds of arms that I have done, I did for the most part for the queen's sake, and for her sake would I do battle were it right or wrong; and never did I battle all only for God's sake, but for to win worship and to cause me to be the better beloved, and little or nought I thanked God of it.'

Then Sir Launcelot said, 'I pray you counsel me.'

'I will counsel you,' said the hermit, 'if ye will ensure me that ye will never come in that queen's fellowship as much as ye may forbear.'

And then Sir Launcelot promised him he nold, by the faith of his body.

'Look that your heart and your mouth accord,' said the good man, 'and I shall ensure you ye shall have more worship than ever ye had.'

'Holy father,' said Sir Launcelot, 'I marvel of the voice that said to me marvellous words, as ye have heard toforehand.'

'Have ye no marvel,' said the good man, 'thereof, for it seemeth well God loveth you; for men may understand a stone is hard of kind, and namely one more than another; and that is to understand by thee, Sir Launcelot, for thou wilt not leave thy sin for no goodness that God hath sent thee; therefore thou art more than any stone, and never wouldst thou be made nesh nor by water nor by fire, and that is the heat of the Holy Ghost may not enter in thee.

'Now take heed, in all the world men shall not find one knight to whom Our Lord hath given so much of grace as He hath given you, for He hath given you fairness with seemliness, He hath given thee wit, discretion to know good from evil, He hath given thee prowess and hardiness, and given thee to work so largely that thou hast had at all days the better wheresomever thou came; and now Our Lord will suffer thee no longer, but that thou shalt know Him whether thou wilt or nilt. And why the voice called thee bitterer than wood, for where overmuch sin dwelleth, there may be but little sweetness, wherefore thou art likened to an old rotten tree.

'Now have I showed thee why thou art harder than the stone and bitterer than the tree. Now shall I show thee why thou art more naked and barer than the fig tree. It befell that Our Lord on Palm Sunday preached in Jerusalem, and there He found in the people that all hardness was harboured in them, and there He found in all the town not one that would harbour him. And then He went without the town, and found in the midst of the way a fig tree, the which was right fair and well garnished of leaves, but fruit had it none. Then Our Lord cursed the tree that bare no fruit; that betokeneth the fig tree unto Jerusalem, that had leaves and no fruit. So thou, Sir Launcelot, when the Holy Grail was brought afore thee, He found in thee no fruit, nor good thought nor good will, and defouled with lechery.'

'Certes,' said Sir Launcelot, 'all that you have said is true, and from henceforward I cast me, by the grace of God, never to be so wicked as I have been, but as to follow knighthood and to do feats of arms.'

Then the good man joined Sir Launcelot such penance as he might do and to sue knighthood, and so assoiled him, and prayed Sir Launcelot to abide with him all that day.

nesh: soft. *joined*: enjoined. *assoiled*: absolved.

'I will well,' said Sir Launcelot, 'for I have neither helm, ne horse, ne sword.'

'As for that,' said the good man, 'I shall help you or tomorn at even of an horse, and all that longed unto you.'

And then Sir Launcelot repented him greatly.

Here leaveth off the history of Sir Launcelot.
And here followeth of Sir Percival
de Gales which is the fourteenth
book

Book XIV

CHAPTER 1: *How Sir Percival came to a recluse and asked her counsel, and how she told him that she was his aunt*

Now saith the tale, that when Sir Launcelot was ridden after Sir Galahad, the which had all these adventures above said, Sir Percival turned again unto the recluse, where he deemed to have tidings of that knight that Launcelot followed. And so he kneeled at her window, and the recluse opened it and asked Sir Percival what he would.

'Madam,' he said, 'I am a knight of King Arthur's court, and my name is Sir Percival de Gales.'

When the recluse heard his name she had great joy of him, for mickle she had loved him tofore any other knight, for she ought to do so, for she was his aunt. And then she commanded the gates to be opened, and there he had all the cheer that she might make him, and all that was in her power was at his commandment.

So on the morn Sir Percival went to the recluse and asked her if she knew that knight with the white shield.

'Sir,' said she, 'why would ye wit?'

'Truly, madam,' said Sir Percival, 'I shall never be well at ease till that I know of that knight's fellowship, and that I may fight with him, for I may not leave him so lightly, for I have the shame yet.'

'Ah, Percival,' said she, 'would ye fight with him? I see well ye have great will to be slain as your father was, through outrageousness.'

'Madam,' said Sir Percival, 'it seemeth by your words that ye know me.'

'Yea,' said she, 'I well ought to know you, for I am your aunt, although I be in a priory place. For some called me sometime the Queen of the Waste Lands, and I was called the queen of most riches in the world; and it pleased me never my riches so much as doth my poverty.'

Then Sir Percival wept for very pity when that he knew it was his aunt.

'Ah, fair nephew,' said she, 'when heard ye tidings of your mother?'

'Truly,' said he, 'I heard none of her, but I dream of her much in my sleep; and therefore I wot not whether she be dead or alive.'

'Certes, fair nephew,' said she, 'your mother is dead, for after your departing from her she took such a sorrow that anon, after she was confessed, she died.'

'Now, God have mercy on her soul,' said Sir Percival. 'It sore forthinketh me; but all we must change the life. Now, fair aunt, tell me what is the knight? I deem it be he that bare the red arms on Whitsunday.'

'Wit you well,' said she, 'that this is he, for otherwise ought he not to do, but to go in red arms, and that same knight hath no peer, for he worketh all by miracle, and he shall never be overcome of none earthly man's hand.'

CHAPTER 2: *How Merlin likened the Round Table to the world, and how the knights that should achieve the Sangrail should be known*

'Also Merlin made the Round Table in tokening of round-ness of the world, for by the Round Table is the world signi-fied by right, for all the world, Christian and heathen, re-pairen unto the Round Table; and when they are chosen to be of the fellowship of the Round Table they think them more blessed and more in worship than if they had gotten half the world; and ye have seen that they have lost their fathers and their mothers, and all their kin, and their wives and their children, for to be of your fellowship. It is well seen by you; for since ye departed from your mother ye would never see her, ye found such fellowship at the Round Table.

'When Merlin had ordained the Round Table he said, by them which should be fellows of the Round Table the truth of the Sangrail should be well known. And men asked him how men might know them that should best do and to achieve the Sangrail. Then he said there should be three white bulls that should achieve it, and the two should be maidens, and the third should be chaste. And that one of the three should pass his father as much as the lion passeth the leopard, both of strength and hardiness. They that heard Merlin say so said thus unto Merlin:

"Sithen there shall be such a knight, thou shouldest ordain by thy crafts a siege, that no man should sit in it but he all only that shall pass all other knights."

'Then Merlin answered that he would do so. And then he made the Siege Perilous, in the which Galahad sat in at his meat on Whitsunday last past.'

'Now, madam,' said Sir Percival, 'so much have I heard of you that by my good will I will never have ado with Sir Galahad but by way of kindness; and for God's love, fair aunt, can ye teach me some way where I may find him? For much would I love the fellowship of him.'

'Fair nephew,' said she, 'ye must ride unto a castle the which is called Goothe, where he hath a cousin germain, and there may ye be lodged this night. And as he teacheth you, sueth after as fast as ye can; and if he can tell you no tidings of him, ride straight unto the Castle of Carbonek, where the Maimed King is there lying, for there shall ye hear true tidings of him.'

CHAPTER 3: *How Sir Percival came into a monastery, where he found King Evelake, which was an old man*

Then departed Sir Percival from his aunt, either making great sorrow. And so he rode till evensong time. And then he heard a clock smite; and then he was ware of an house closed well with walls and deep ditches, and there he knocked at the gate and was let in, and he alit and was led unto a chamber, and soon he was unarmed.

And there he had right good cheer all that night; and on the morn he heard his mass, and in the monastery he found a priest ready at the altar. And on the right side he saw a pew closed with iron, and behind the altar he saw a rich bed and a fair, as of cloth of silk and gold. Then Sir Percival espied that therein was a man or a woman, for the visage was covered; then he left off his looking and heard his service. And when it came to the sacring, he that lay within that perclose dressed him up, and uncovered his head; and then him beseemed a passing old man, and he had a crown of gold upon his head, and his shoulders were naked and unhilled unto his navel. And then Sir Percival espied his body was full of great wounds, both on the shoulders, arms, and visage.

And ever he held up his hands against Our Lord's body, and cried, 'Fair, sweet Father, Jesu Christ, forget not me.'

And so he lay down, but always he was in his prayers and orisons; and him seemed to be of the age of three hundred winter.

And when the mass was done the priest took Our Lord's body and bare it to the sick king. And when he had used it he did off his crown, and commanded the crown to be set on the altar. Then Sir Percival asked one of the brethren what he was.

'Sir,' said the good man, 'ye have heard much of Joseph of Arimathea, how he was sent by Jesu Christ into this land for to teach and preach the holy Christian faith; and therefore he suffered many persecutions the which the enemies of Christ did unto him, and in the city of Sarras he converted a king whose name was Evelake. And so this king came with Joseph into this land, and ever he was busy to be thereas the Sangrail was; and on a time he nighed it so nigh that Our Lord was displeased with him, but ever he followed it more

sacring: consecration.   *perclose*: enclosure.

278

and more, till God struck him almost blind. Then this king cried mercy, and said, "Fair Lord, let me never die till the good knight of my blood of the ninth degree be come, that I may see him openly that he shall achieve the Sangrail, that I may kiss him."

CHAPTER 4: *How Sir Percival saw many men of arms bearing a dead knight, and how he fought against them*

'When the king thus had made his prayers he heard a voice that said, "Heard be thy prayers, for thou shalt not die till he have kissed thee. And when that knight shall come the clearness of your eyen shall come again, and thou shalt see openly, and thy wounds shall be healed, and erst shall they never close."

'And this befell of King Evelake, and this same king hath lived this three hundred winters this holy life, and men say the knight is in the court that shall heal him. Sir,' said the good man, 'I pray you tell me what knight that ye be, and if ye be of King Arthur's court and of the Table Round.'

'Yea, forsooth,' said he, 'and my name is Sir Percival de Gales.'

And when the good man understood his name he made great joy of him.

And then Sir Percival departed and rode till the hour of noon. And he met in a valley about a twenty men of arms, which bare in a bier a knight deadly slain. And when they saw Sir Percival they asked him of whence he was.

And he answered, 'Of the court of King Arthur.'

Then they cried all at once, 'Slay him !'

Then Sir Percival smote the first to the earth and his horse upon him. And then seven of the knights smote upon his shield all at once, and the remnant slew his horse so that he fell to the earth. So had they slain him or taken him had not the good knight, Sir Galahad, with the red arms, come there by adventure into those parts.

And when he saw all those knights upon one knight, he cried, 'Save me that knight's life.'

And then he dressed him toward the twenty men of arms as fast as his horse might drive, with his spear in the rest, and smote the foremost horse and man to the earth. And when his spear was broken he set his hand to his sword, and smote on the right hand and on the left hand that it was marvel to see, and at every stroke he smote one down or put him to a rebuke, so that they would fight no more but fled to a thick forest, and Sir Galahad followed them. And when Sir Percival saw him chase them so, he made great sorrow that his horse was away. And then he wist well it was Sir Galahad.

And then he cried aloud, 'Ah fair knight, abide and suffer me to do thankings unto thee, for much have ye done for me.'

But ever Sir Galahad rode so fast that at the last he passed out of his sight. And as fast as Sir Percival might he went after him on foot, crying. And then he met with a yeoman riding upon an hackney, the which led in his hand a great steed blacker than any bear.

'Ah, fair friend,' said Sir Percival, 'as ever as I may do for you, and to be your true knight in the first place ye will require me, that ye will lend me that black steed, that I might overtake a knight the which rideth afore me.'

'Sir knight,' said the yeoman, 'I pray you hold me excused of that, for that I may not do. For wit ye well, the horse is such a man's horse, that and I lent it you or any man, that he would slay me.'

'Alas,' said Sir Percival, 'I had never so great sorrow as I have had for losing of yonder knight.'

'Sir,' said the yeoman, 'I am right heavy for you, for a good horse would beseem you well; but I dare not deliver you this horse but if ye would take him from me.'

'That will I not do,' said Sir Percival.

And so they departed; and Sir Percival sat him down under a tree, and made sorrow out of measure. And as he was there,

there came a knight riding on the horse that the yeoman led, and he was clean armed.

CHAPTER 5: *How a yeoman desired him to get again an horse, and how Sir Percival's hackney was slain, and how he gat an horse*

And anon the yeoman came pricking after as fast as ever he might, and asked Sir Percival if he saw any knight riding on his black steed.

'Yea, sir, forsooth,' said he. 'Why, sir, ask ye me that?'

'Ah, sir, that steed he hath benome me with strength; wherefore my lord will slay me in what place he findeth me.'

'Well,' said Sir Percival, 'what wouldst thou that I did? Thou seest well that I am on foot, but and I had a good horse I should bring him soon again.'

'Sir,' said the yeoman, 'take mine hackney and do the best ye can, and I shall sue you on foot to wit how that ye shall speed.'

Then Sir Percival alit upon that hackney, and rode as fast as he might, and at the last he saw that knight. And then he cried, 'Knight, turn again!'

And he turned and set his spear against Sir Percival, and he smote the hackney in the midst of the breast that he fell down dead to the earth, and there he had a great fall, and the other rode his way.

And then Sir Percival was wood wroth, and cried, 'Abide, wicked knight; coward and false-hearted knight, turn again and fight with me on foot!'

But he answered not, but passed on his way. When Sir Percival saw he would not turn he cast away his helm and sword, and said, 'Now am I a very wretch, cursed and most unhappy above all other knights.'

So in this sorrow he abode all that day till it was night;

benome: taken away.

and then he was faint, and laid him down and slept till it was midnight.

And then he awaked and saw afore him a woman which said unto him right fiercely, 'Sir Percival, what dost thou here?'

He answered, 'I do neither good nor great ill.'

'If thou wilt ensure me,' said she, 'that thou wilt fulfil my will when I summon thee, I shall lend thee mine own horse which shall bear thee whither thou wilt.'

Sir Percival was glad of her proffer, and ensured her to fulfil all her desire.

'Then abideth me here, and I shall go fetch you an horse.'

And so she came soon again and brought an horse with her that was inly black.[1]

When Percival beheld that horse he marvelled that it was so great and so well apparelled; and notforthan he was so hardy, and he leapt upon him, and took none heed of himself. And so anon as he was upon him he thrust to him with his spurs, and so rode by a forest, and the moon shone clear.

And within an hour and less he bare him four days' journey thence, until he came to a rough water the which roared, and his horse would have borne him into it.

CHAPTER 6: *Of the great danger that Sir Percival was in by his horse, and how he saw a serpent and a lion fight*

And when Sir Percival came nigh the brim, and saw the water so boistous, he doubted to overpass it. And then he made a sign of the cross in his forehead. When the fiend felt him so charged he shook off Sir Percival, and he went into the water crying and roaring, making great sorrow, and it seemed unto him that the water burnt.

Then Sir Percival perceived it was a fiend, the which would have brought him unto his perdition. Then he commended himself unto God, and prayed Our Lord to keep him from all such temptations; and so prayed all that night till on the morn that it was day; then he saw that he was in a wild mountain the which was closed with the sea nigh all about, that he might see no land about him which might relieve him, but wild beasts. And then he went into a valley, and there he saw a young serpent bring a young lion by the neck, and so he came by Sir Percival.

With that came a great lion crying and roaring after the serpent. And as fast as Sir Percival saw this he marvelled, and hied him thither, but anon the lion had overtake the serpent and began battle with him. And then Sir Percival thought to help the lion for he was the more natural beast of the two; and therewith he drew his sword, and set his shield afore him, and there he gave the serpent such a buffet that he had a deadly wound. When the lion saw that, he made no resemblant to fight with him, but made him all the cheer that a beast might make a man.

Then Percival perceived that, and cast down his shield which was broken; and then he did off his helm for to gather wind, for he was greatly enchafed with the serpent: and the lion went alway about him fawning as a spaniel. And then he stroked him on the neck and on the shoulders. And then he thanked God of the fellowship of that beast.

And about noon the lion took his little whelp and trussed him and bare him there he came from. Then was Sir Percival alone. And as the tale telleth, he was one of the men of the world at that time which most believed in Our Lord Jesu Christ, for in those days there were but few folks that believed in God perfectly. For in those days the son spared not the father no more than a stranger.

And so Sir Percival comforted himself in Our Lord Jesu, and besought God no temptation should bring him out of God's service, but to endure as his true champion. Thus when Sir Percival had prayed he saw the lion come toward him, and then he couched down at his feet.

And so all that night the lion and he slept together; and

enchafed: heated.   *trussed*: bundled.

283

when Sir Percival slept he dreamed a marvellous dream, that there two ladies met with him, and that one sat upon a lion, and that other sat upon a serpent, and that one of them was young, and the other was old; and the youngest him thought said, 'Sir Percival, my lord saluteth thee, and sendeth thee word that thou array thee and make thee ready, for tomorn thou must fight with the strongest champion of the world. And if thou be overcome thou shalt not be quit for losing of any of thy members, but thou shalt be shamed for ever to the world's end.' And then he asked her what was her lord. And she said the greatest lord of all the world; and so she departed suddenly that he wist not where.

CHAPTER 7: *Of that vision that Sir Percival saw, and how his vision was expounded, and of his lion*

Then came forth the other lady that rode upon the serpent, and she said, 'Sir Percival, I complain me of you that ye have done unto me, and have not offended unto you.'

'Certes, madam,' he said, 'unto you nor no lady I never offended.'

'Yes,' said she, 'I shall tell you why. I have nourished in this place a great while a serpent, which served me a great while, and yesterday ye slew him as he gat his prey. Say me for what cause ye slew him, for the lion was not yours.'

'Madam,' said Sir Percival, 'I know well the lion was not mine, but I did it for the lion is of more gentler nature than the serpent, and therefore I slew him; meseemeth I did not amiss against you. Madam,' said he, 'what would ye that I did?'

'I would,' said she, 'for the amends of my beast that ye become my man.'

And then he answered, 'That will I not grant you.'

'No,' said she, 'truly ye were never but my servant since ye received the homage of Our Lord Jesu Christ. Therefore, I ensure you in what place I may find you without keeping I shall take you as he that sometime was my man.'

And so she departed from Sir Percival and left him sleeping, the which was sore travailed of his advision. And on the morn he arose and blessed him, and he was passing feeble.

Then was Sir Percival ware in the sea, and saw a ship come sailing toward him; and Sir Percival went unto the ship and found it covered within and without with white samite. And at the board stood an old man clothed in a surplice, in likeness of a priest.

'Sir,' said Sir Percival, 'ye be welcome.'

'God keep you,' said the good man. 'Sir,' said the old man, 'of whence be ye?'

'Sir,' said Sir Percival, 'I am of King Arthur's court, and a knight of the Table Round, the which am in the quest of the Sangrail; and here am I in great duress, and never like to escape out of this wilderness.'

'Doubt not,' said the good man, 'and ye be so true a knight as the order of chivalry requireth, and of heart as ye ought to be, ye should not doubt that none enemy should slay you.'

'What are ye?' said Sir Percival.

'Sir,' said the old man, 'I am of a strange country, and hither I come to comfort you.'

'Sir,' said Sir Percival, 'what signifieth my dream that I dreamed this night?'

And there he told him altogether: 'She which rode upon the lion betokeneth the new law of holy church, that is to understand, faith, good hope, belief, and baptism. For she seemed younger than the other it is great reason, for she was born in the resurrection and the passion of Our Lord Jesu Christ. And for great love she came to thee to warn thee of thy great battle that shall befall thee.'

'With whom,' said Sir Percival, 'shall I fight?'

'With the most champion of the world,' said the old man; 'for as the lady said, but if thou quit thee well thou shalt not be quit by losing of one member, but thou shalt be shamed to the world's end. And she that rode on the serpent signifieth the old law, and that serpent betokeneth a fiend. And why she blamed thee that thou slewest her servant, it betokeneth nothing the serpent that thou slewest; [that] [1] betokeneth the devil that thou rodest upon to the rock, and when thou madest a sign of the cross, there thou slewest him, and put away his power. And when she asked thee amends and to become her man, and thou saidst thou wouldst not, that was to make thee to believe on her and leave thy baptism.'

So he commanded Sir Percival to depart, and so he leapt over the board and the ship, and all went away he wist not whither. Then he went up unto the rock and found the lion which always kept him fellowship, and he stroked him upon the back and had great joy of him.

CHAPTER 8: *How Sir Percival saw a ship coming to himward, and how the lady of the ship told him of her disheritance*

By that Sir Percival had abiden there till mid-day he saw a ship came rowing in the sea as all the wind of the world had driven it. And so it drove under that rock. And when Sir Percival saw this he hied him thither, and found the ship covered with silk more blacker than any bear, and therein was a gentlewoman of great beauty, and she was clothed richly that none might be better.

And when she saw Sir Percival she said, 'Who brought you in this wilderness where ye be never like to pass hence, for ye shall die here for hunger and mischief?'

'Damosel,' said Sir Percival, 'I serve the best man of the world, and in his service he will not suffer me to die, for who that knocketh shall enter, and who that asketh shall have, and who seeketh him he hideth him not.'

But then she said, 'Sir Percival, wot ye what I am?'

'Yea,' said he.

'Now who taught you my name?' said she.

'Now,' said Sir Percival, 'I know you better than ye ween.'

'And I came out of the waste forest where I found the red knight with the white shield,' said the damosel.

'Ah, damosel,' said he, 'with that knight would I meet passing fain.'

'Sir knight,' said she, 'and ye will ensure me by the faith that ye owe unto knighthood that ye shall do my will what time I summon you, and I shall bring you unto that knight.'

'Yea,' said he, 'I shall promise you to fulfil your desire.'

'Well,' said she, 'now shall I tell you. I saw him in the forest chasing two knights unto a water, the which is called Mortaise; and they drove him into that water for dread of death, and the two knights passed over, and the red knight passed after, and there his horse was drenched, and he, through great strength, escaped unto the land:' thus she told him, and Sir Percival was passing glad thereof. Then she asked him if he had ate any meat late.

'Nay, madam, truly I ate no meat nigh this three days, but late here I spake with a good man that fed me with his good words and holy, and refreshed me greatly.'

'Ah, sir knight,' said she, 'that same man is an enchanter and a multiplier of words. For and ye believe him ye shall plainly be shamed, and die in this rock for pure hunger, and be eaten with wild beasts; and ye be a young man and a goodly knight, and I shall help you and ye will.'

'What are ye,' said Sir Percival, 'that proffered me thus great kindness?'

'I am,' said she, 'a gentlewoman that am disherited, which was sometime the richest woman of the world.'

'Damosel,' said Sir Percival, 'who hath disherited you? For I have great pity of you.'

'Sir.' said she, 'I dwelled with the greatest man of the world, and he made me so fair and clear that there was none like me; and of that great beauty I had a little pride more than I ought to have had. Also I said a word that pleased him not. And then he would not suffer me to be any longer in his

drenched: drowned.

company, and so drove me from mine heritage, and so disherited me, and he had never pity of me nor of none of my council, nor of my court. And sithen, sir knight, it hath befallen me so, and through me and mine I have benome him many of his men and made them to become my men. For they ask never nothing of me but I give it them, that and much more. Thus I and all my servants were against him night and day. Therefore I know now no good knight, nor no good man, but I get them on my side and I may. And for that I know that thou art a good knight, I beseech you to help me; and for ye be a fellow of the Round Table, wherefore ye ought not to fail no gentlewoman which is disherited, and she besought you of help.'

CHAPTER 9: *How Sir Percival promised her help, and how he required her of love, and how he was saved from the fiend*

Then Sir Percival promised her all the help that he might; and then she thanked him.

And at that time the weather was hot. Then she called unto her a gentlewoman and bad her bring forth a pavilion; and so she did, and pitched it upon the gravel.

'Sir,' said she, 'may now ye rest you in this heat of the day.'

Then he thanked her, and she put off his helm and his shield, and there he slept a great while.

And then he awoke and asked her if she had any meat, and she said; 'Yea, also ye shall have enough.'

And so there was set enough upon the table, and thereon so much that he had marvel, for there was all manner of meats that he could think on. Also he drank there the strongest wine that ever he drank, him thought, and therewith he was a little chafed more than he ought to be; with that he beheld the gentlewoman, and him thought she was the fairest creature that ever he saw.

And then Sir Percival proffered her love, and prayed her

that she would be his. Then she refused him, in a manner, when he required her, for the cause he should be the more ardent on her, and ever he ceased not to pray her of love.

And when she saw him well enchafed, then she said, 'Sir Percival, wit you well I shall not fulfil your will but if ye swear from henceforth ye shall be my true servant, and to do nothing but that I shall command you. Will ye ensure me this as ye be a true knight?'

'Yea,' said he, 'fair lady, by the faith of my body.'

'Well,' said she, 'now shall ye do with me what so it please you; and now wit ye well ye are the knight in the world that I have most desire to.'

And then two squires were commanded to make a bed in midst of the pavilion. And anon she was unclothed and laid therein. And then Sir Percival laid him down by her naked; and by adventure and grace he saw his sword lie on the ground naked, in whose pommel was a red cross and the sign of the crucifix therein, and bethought him on his knighthood and his promise made toforehand unto the good man; then he made a sign of the cross in his forehead, and therewith the pavilion turned up-so-down, and then it changed unto a smoke, and a black cloud, and then he was adread and cried aloud:

CHAPTER 10: *How Sir Percival for penance rove himself through the thigh; and how she was known for the devil*

'Fair sweet father, Jesu Christ, ne let me not be shamed, the which was nigh lost had not thy good grace been.'

And then he looked into a ship, and saw her enter therein, which said, 'Sir Percival, ye have betrayed me.'

And so she went with the wind roaring and yelling, that it seemed all the water burnt after her.

Then Sir Percival made great sorrow, and drew his sword unto him, saying, 'Sithen my flesh will be my master I shall punish it;' and therewith he rove himself through the thigh that the blood start about him, and said, 'O good Lord, take this in recompensation of that I have done against Thee, my Lord.'

So then he clothed him and armed him, and called himself a wretch, saying, 'How nigh was I lost, and to have lost that I should never have gotten again, that was my virginity, for that may never be recovered after it is once lost.' And then he stopped his bleeding wound with a piece of his shirt.

Thus as he made his moan he saw the same ship come from Orient that the good man was in the day afore, and the noble knight was ashamed with himself, and therewith he fell in a swoon. And when he awoke he went unto him weakly, and there he saluted this good man.

And then he asked Sir Percival, 'How hast thou done sith I departed?'

'Sir,' said he, 'here was a gentlewoman and led me into deadly sin.' And there he told him altogether.

'Knew ye not the maid?' said the good man.

'Sir,' said he, 'nay, but well I wot the fiend sent her hither to shame me.'

'O good knight,' said he, 'thou art a fool, for that gentlewoman was the master fiend of hell, the which hath power above all devils, and that was the old lady that thou sawest in thine advision riding on the serpent.'

Then he told Sir Percival how Our Lord Jesu Christ beat him out of heaven for his sin, the which was the most brightest angel of heaven, and therefore he lost his heritage: 'And that was the champion that thou foughtest withal, the which had overcome thee had not the grace of God been. Now beware Sir Percival, and take this for an example.'

And then the good man vanished away. Then Sir Percival took his arms, and entered into the ship, and so departed from thence.

Here endeth the fourteenth book, which is of Sir Percival. And here followeth of Sir Launcelot, which is the fifteenth book

Book XV

CHAPTER 1 : *How Sir Launcelot came into a chapel, where he found dead, in a white shirt, a man of religion, of an hundred winter old*

When the hermit had kept Sir Launcelot three days, the hermit gat him an horse, an helm, and a sword. And then he departed about the hour of noon. And then he saw a little house.

And when he came near he saw a chapel, and there beside he saw an old man that was clothed all in white full richly; and then Sir Launcelot said, 'God save you.'

'God keep you,' said the good man, 'and make you a good knight.'

Then Sir Launcelot alit and entered into the chapel, and there he saw an old man dead, in a white shirt of passing fine cloth.

'Sir,' said the good man, 'this man that is dead ought not to be in such clothing as ye see him in, for in that he brake the oath of his order, for he hath been more than an hundred winter a man of a religion.'

And then the good man and Sir Launcelot went into the chapel; and the good man took a stole about his neck, and a book, and then he conjured on that book; and with that they saw in an hideous figure and horrible, that there was no man so hard-hearted nor so hard but he should have been afeared.

Then said the fiend, 'Thou hast travailed me greatly; now tell me what thou wilt with me.'

'I will,' said the good man, 'that thou tell me how my fellow became dead, and whether he be saved or damned.'

Then he said with an horrible voice, 'He is not lost but saved.'

'How may that be?' said the good man; 'It seemed to me that he lived not well, for he brake his order to wear a shirt where he ought to wear none, and who that trespasseth against our order doth not well.'

'Not so,' said the fiend, 'this man that lieth here dead was come of a great lineage. And there was a lord that hight the Earl de Vale, that held great war against this man's nephew, the which hight Aguarus. And so this Aguarus saw the earl was bigger than he. Then he went for to take counsel of his uncle, the which lieth here dead as ye may see. And then he asked leave, and went out of his hermitage for to maintain his nephew against the mighty earl; and so it happed that this man that lieth here dead did so much by his wisdom and hardiness that the earl was take, and three of his lords, by force of this dead man.

CHAPTER 2: *Of a dead man, how men would have hewn him, and it would not be, and how Sir Launcelot took the hair of the dead man*

'Then was there peace betwixt the earl and this Aguarus, and great surety that the earl should never war against him. Then this dead man that here lieth came to this hermitage again; and then the earl made two of his nephews for to be avenged upon this man. So they came on a day, and found this dead man at the sacring of his mass, and they abode him till he had said mass. And then they set upon him and drew out swords to have slain him; but there would no sword bite on him more than upon a gad of steel, for the High Lord which he served, He him preserved. Then made they a great fire, and did off all his clothes, and the hair off his back. And then this dead man hermit said unto them, "Ween you to burn me? It shall not lie in your power nor to perish me as much as a thread and there were any on my body."

' "No," said one of them, "it shall be assayed."

gad: rod. *hair*: hairshirt.

'And then they dispoiled him, and put upon him this shirt, and cast him in a fire, and there he lay all that night till it was day in that fire, and was not dead, and so in the morn I came and found him him dead; but I found neither thread nor skin tamed, and so took him out of the fire with great fear, and led him here as ye may see. And now may ye suffer me to go my way, for I have said you the sooth.'

And then he departed with a great tempest. Then was the good man and Sir Launcelot more gladder than they were tofore. And then Sir Launcelot dwelled with that good man that night.

'Sir,' said the good man, 'be ye not Sir Launcelot du Lake?'

'Yea, sir,' said he.

'What seek ye in this country?'

'Sir,' said Sir Launcelot, 'I go to seek the adventures of the Sangrail.'

'Well,' said he, 'seek it ye may well, but though it were here ye shall have no power to see it no more than a blind man should see a bright sword, and that is long on your sin, and else ye were more abler than any man living.'

And then Sir Launcelot began to weep.

Then said the good man, 'Were ye confessed sith ye entered¹ into the quest of the Sangrail?'

'Yea, sir,' said Sir Launcelot.

Then upon the morn when the good man had sung his mass, then they buried the dead man.

Then Sir Launcelot said, 'Father, what shall I do?'

'Now,' said the good man, 'I require you take this hair that was this holy man's and put it next thy skin, and it shall prevail thee greatly.'

'Sir, and I will do it,' said Sir Launcelot.

'Also I charge you that ye eat no flesh as long as ye be in the quest of the Sangrail, nor ye shall drink no wine, and that ye hear mass daily and ye may do it.'

So he took the hair and put it upon him, and so departed at evensong-time.

long on your sin: due to your sin.

And so rode he into a forest, and there he met with a gentlewoman riding upon a white palfrey, and then she asked him, 'Sir knight, whither ride ye?'

'Certes, damosel,' said Launcelot, 'I wot not whither I ride but as fortune leadeth me.'

'Ah, Sir Launcelot,' said she, 'I wot what adventure ye seek, for ye were afore time nearer than ye be now, and yet shall ye see it more openly than ever ye did, and that shall ye understand in short time.'

Then Sir Launcelot asked her where he might be harboured that night.

'Ye shall not find this day nor night, but tomorn ye shall find harbour good, and ease of that ye be in doubt of.'

And then he commended her unto God. Then he rode till that he came to a cross, and took that for his host as for that night.

CHAPTER 3: *Of a vision that Sir Launcelot had, and how he told it to an hermit, and desired counsel of him*

And so he put his horse to pasture, and did off his helm and his shield, and made his prayers unto the cross that he never fall in deadly sin again. And so he laid him down to sleep.

And anon as he was asleep it befell him there an advision, that there came a man afore him all by compass of stars, and that man had a crown of gold on his head, and that man led in his fellowship seven kings and two knights. And all these worshipped the cross, kneeling upon their knees, holding up their hands toward the heaven. And all they said, 'Fair sweet Father of Heaven, come and visit us, and yield unto us every each as we have deserved.'

Then looked Launcelot up to the heaven, and him seemed the clouds did open, and an old man came down, with a company of angels, and alit among them, and gave unto every each his blessing, and called them his servants, and good and true knights. And when this old man had said thus he came to one of those knights, and said, 'I have lost all that I have set in thee, for thou hast ruled thee against me as a warrior, and used wrong wars with vain glory, more for the pleasure of the world than to please me, therefore thou shalt be confounded without thou yield me my treasure.'

All this advision saw Sir Launcelot at the cross. And on the morn he took his horse and rode till mid-day; and there by adventure he met with the same knight that took his horse, helm, and his sword, when he slept when the Sangrail appeared afore the cross.

When Sir Launcelot saw him he saluted him not fair, but cried on high, 'Knight, keep thee, for thou hast done to me great unkindness.'

And then they put afore them their spears, and Sir Launcelot came so fiercely upon him that he smote him and his horse down to the earth, that he had nigh broken his neck. Then Sir Launcelot took the knight's horse that was his own aforehand, and descended from the horse he sat upon, and mounted upon his own horse, and tied the knight's own horse to a tree, that he might find that horse when that he was arisen.

Then Sir Launcelot rode till night, and by adventure he met an hermit, and each of them saluted other; and there he rested with that good man all night, and gave his horse such as he might get.

Then said the good man unto Launcelot, 'Of whence be ye?'

'Sir,' said he, 'I am of Arthur's court, and my name is Sir Launcelot du Lake that am in the quest of the Sangrail, and therefore I pray you to counsel me of a vision which I had at the cross.' And so he told him all.

CHAPTER 4: *How the hermit expounded to Sir Launcelot his vision and told him that Sir Galahad was his son*

'Lo, Sir Launcelot,' said the good man, 'there thou mightest understand the high lineage that thou art comen of, and thine advision betokeneth.

'After the passion of Jesu Christ forty year, Joseph of Arimathea preached the victory of King Evelake, that he had in the battles the better of his enemies. And of the seven kings and the two knights: the first of them is called Nappus, an holy man; and the second hight Nacien, in remembrance of his grandsire, and in him dwelled Our Lord Jesu Christ; and the third was called Helias le Grose; and the fourth hight Lisais; and the fifth hight Jonas, he departed out of his country and went into Wales, and took there the daughter of Manuel, whereby he had the land of Gaul, and he came to dwell in this country. And of him came King Launcelot thy grandsire, the which there wedded the King's daughter of Ireland, and he was as worthy a man as thou art, and of him came King Ban, thy father, the which was the last of the seven kings. And by thee, Sir Launcelot, it signifieth that the angels said thou were none of the seven fellowships. And the last was the ninth knight, he was signified to a lion, for he should pass all manner of earthly knights, that is Sir Galahad, the which thou gat on King Pelles' daughter; and thou ought to thank God more than any other man living, for of a sinner earthly thou hast no peer as in knighthood, nor never shall be. But little thank hast thou given to God for all the great virtues that God hath lent thee.'

'Sir,' said Launcelot, 'ye say that that good knight is my son.'

'That oughtest thou to know and no man better,' said the good man, 'for thou knewest the daughter of King Pelles fleshly, and on her thou begattest Galahad, and that was he that at the feast of Pentecost sat in the Siege Perilous; and therefore make thou it known openly that he is one of thy begetting on King Pelles' daughter, for that will be your worship and honour, and to all thy kindred. And I counsel you in no place press not upon him to have ado with him.'

'Well,' said Launcelot, 'meseemeth that good knight should pray for me unto the High Father, that I fall not to sin again.'

'Trust thou well,' said the good man, 'thou farest mickle the better for his prayer; but the son shall not bear the wickedness of the father, nor the father shall not bear the wickedness of the son, but every each shall bear his own burden. And therefore beseech thou only God, and he will help thee in all thy needs.'

And then Sir Launcelot and he went to supper, and so laid him to rest, and the hair pricked so Sir Launcelot's skin which grieved him full sore, but he took it meekly, and suffered the pain.

And so on the morn he heard his mass and took his arms, and so took his leave.

CHAPTER 5: *How Sir Launcelot jousted with many knights, and he was taken*

And then mounted upon his horse, and rode into a forest, and held no highway. And as he looked afore him he saw a fair plain, and beside that a fair castle, and afore the castle were many pavilions of silk and of diverse hue. And him seemed that he saw there five hundred knights riding on horseback; and there were two parties: they that were of the castle were all on black horses and their trappers black, and they that were without were all on white horses and trappers, and every each hurtled to other that it marvelled Sir Launcelot. And at the last him thought they of the castle were put to the worse.

Then thought Sir Launcelot for to help there the weaker party in increasing of his chivalry. And so Sir Launcelot thrust in among the party of the castle, and smote down a knight, horse and man, to the earth. And then he rashed here and there, and did marvellous deeds of arms. And then he drew out his sword, and struck many knights to the earth, so that all those that saw him marvelled that ever one knight might do so great deeds of arms.

But always the white knights held them nigh about Sir Launcelot, for to tire him and wind him. But at the last, as a man may not ever endure, Sir Launcelot waxed so faint of fighting and travailing, and was so weary of his great deeds, but he might not lift up his arms for to give one stroke, so that he weened never to have borne arms; and then they all took and led him away into a forest, and there made him to alight and to rest him.

And then all the fellowship of the castle were overcome for the default of him.

Then they said all unto Sir Launcelot, 'Blessed be God that ye be now of our fellowship, for we shall hold you in our prison;' and so they left him with few words.

And then Sir Launcelot made great sorrow, 'For never or now was I never at tournament nor jousts but I had the best, and now I am shamed.' And then he said, 'Now I am sure that I am more sinfuller than ever I was.'

Thus he rode sorrowing, and half a day he was out of despair, till that he came into a deep valley. And when Sir Launcelot saw he might not ride up into the mountain, he there alit under an apple tree, and there he left his helm and his shield, and put his horse unto pasture. And then he laid him down to sleep.

And then him thought there came an old man afore him, the which said, 'Ah, Launcelot of evil faith and poor belief, wherefore is thy will turned so lightly toward thy deadly sin?' And when he had said thus he vanished away, and Launcelot wist not where he was become.

Then he took his horse, and armed him; and as he rode by the way he saw a chapel where was a recluse, which had a window that she might see up to the altar. And all aloud she called Launcelot, for that he seemed a knight errant. And then he came, and she asked him what he was, and of what place, and where about he went to seek.

CHAPTER 6: *How Sir Launcelot told his vision unto a woman, and how she expounded it unto him*

And then he told her all together word by word, and the truth how it befell him at the tournament. And after told her his advision that he had had that night in his sleep, and prayed her to tell him what it might mean, for he was not well content with it.

'Ah, Launcelot,' said she, 'as long as ye were knight of earthly knighthood ye were the most marvellous man of the world, and most adventurous. Now,' said the lady, 'sithen ye be set among the knights of heavenly adventures, if adventure fell thee contrary at that tournament have thou no marvel, for that tournament yesterday was but a tokening of Our Lord. And notforthan there was none enchantment, for they at the tournament were earthly knights. The tournament was a token to see who should have most knights, other Eliazar, the son of King Pelles, or Argustus, the son of King Harlon. But Eliazar was all clothed in white, and Argustus was covered in black, the which were comen. All what this betokeneth I shall tell you.

'The day of Pentecost, when King Arthur held his court, it befell that earthly kings and knights took a tournament together, that is to say the quest of the Sangrail. The earthly knights were they the which were clothed all in black, and the covering betokeneth the sins whereof they be not confessed. And they with the covering of white betokeneth virginity, and they that chose chastity. And thus was the quest begun in them. Then thou beheld the sinners and the good men, and when thou sawest the sinners overcome, thou inclinest to that party for bobaunce and pride of the world, and all that must be left in that quest, for in this quest thou shalt have many fellows and thy betters. For thou art so feeble of evil trust and good belief, this made it when thou were there where they took thee and led thee into the forest.

'And anon there appeared the Sangrail unto the white knights, but thou was so feeble of good belief and faith that thou mightest not abide it for all the teaching of the good man, but anon thou turnest to the sinners, and that caused thy misadventure that thou shouldst know good from evil and vain glory of the world, the which is not worth a pear. And for great pride thou madest great sorrow that thou haddest not overcome all the white knights with the covering of white by whom was betokened virginity and chastity; and therefore God was wroth with you, for God loveth no such deeds in this quest. And this advision signifieth that thou were of evil faith and of poor belief, the which will make thee to fall into the deep pit of hell if thou keep thee not.

'Now have I warned thee of thy vain glory and of thy pride, that thou hast many times erred against thy Maker. Beware of everlasting pain, for of all earthly knights I have most pity of thee, for I know well thou hast not thy peer of any earthly sinful man.' And so she commanded Sir Launcelot to dinner.

And after dinner he took his horse and commended her to God, and so rode into a deep valley, and there he saw a river and an high mountain. And through the water he must needs pass, the which was hideous; and then in the name of God he took it with good heart.

And when he came over he saw an armed knight, horse and man black as any bear; without any word he smote Sir Launcelot's horse to the earth; and so he passed on, he wist not where he was become. And then he took his helm and his shield, and thanked God of his adventure.

*Here leaveth off the story of Sir Launcelot,
and speak we of Sir Gawain, the
which is the sixteenth book*

Book XVI

CHAPTER 1: *How Sir Gawain was nigh weary of the quest of Sangrail, and of his marvellous dream*

When Sir Gawain was departed from his fellowship he rode long without any adventure. For he found not the tenth part of adventure as he was wont to do. For Sir Gawain rode from Whitsuntide until Michaelmas and found none adventure that pleased him.

So on a day it befell Gawain met with Sir Ector de Maris, and either made great joy of other that it were marvel to tell. And so they told every each other, and complained them greatly that they could find none adventure.

'Truly,' said Sir Gawain unto Sir Ector, 'I am nigh weary of this quest, and loth I am to follow further in strange countries.'

'One thing marvelled me,' said Sir Ector, 'I have met with twenty knights, fellows of mine, and all they complain as I do.'

'I have marvel,' said Sir Gawain, 'where that Sir Launcelot, your brother, is.'

'Truly,' said Sir Ector, 'I cannot hear of him, nor of Sir Galahad, Percival, nor Sir Bors.'

'Let them be,' said Sir Gawain, 'for they four have no peers. And if one thing were not in Sir Launcelot he had no fellow of none earthly man; but he is as we be, but if he took more pain upon him. But and these four be met together they will be loth that any man meet with them; for and they fail of the Sangrail it is in waste of all the remnant to recover it.'

Thus as Ector and Gawain rode more than eight days, and on a Saturday they found an old chapel, the which was wasted that there seemed no man thither repaired; and there they alit, and set their spears at the door, and in they entered into the chapel, and there made their orisons a great while, and then sat them down in the sieges of the chapel. And as they spake of one thing and other, for heaviness they fell asleep, and there befell them both marvellous adventures.

Sir Gawain him seemed he came into a meadow full of herbs and flowers, and there he saw a rack of bulls, an hundred and fifty, that were proud and black, save three of them were all white, and one had a black spot, and the other two were so fair and so white that they might be no whiter. And these three bulls which were so fair were tied with two strong cords. And the remnant of the bulls said among them, 'Go we hence to seek better pasture.' And so some went, and some came again, but they were so lean that they might not stand upright; and of the bulls that were so white, that one came again and no more. But when this white bull was come again among these other there rose up a great cry for lack of wind that failed them; and so they departed one here and another there: this advision befell Gawain that night.

CHAPTER 2: *Of the vision of Sir Ector, and how he jousted with Sir Uwain les Avoutres, his sworn brother*

But to Ector de Maris befell another vision the contrary. For it seemed him that his brother, Sir Launcelot, and he alit out of a chair and leapt upon two horses, and the one said to the other, 'Go we seek that we shall not find.' And him thought that a man beat Sir Launcelot, and despoiled him, and clothed him in another array, the which was all full of knots, and set him upon an ass, and so he rode till he came to the fairest well that ever he saw; and Sir Launcelot alit and would have drunk of that well. And when he stooped to drink of the water the water sank from him. And when Sir Launcelot saw that, he turned and went thither as he had[1] come from.

And in the meanwhile he trowed that himself, Sir Ector[2]

rack: i.e. feeding rack.

rode till that he came to a rich man's house where there was a wedding. And there he saw a king the which said, 'Sir knight, here is no place for you.' And then he turned again unto the chair that he came from.

Thus within a while both Gawain and Ector awaked, and either told other of their advision, the which marvelled them greatly.

'Truly,' said Ector, 'I shall never be merry till I hear tidings of my brother Launcelot.'

Now as they sat thus talking they saw an hand showing unto the elbow, and was covered with red samite, and upon that hung a bridle not right rich, and held within the fist a great candle which burned right clear, and so passed afore them, and entered into the chapel, and then vanished away and they wist not where.

And anon came down a voice which said, 'Knights full of evil faith and of poor belief, these two things have failed you, and therefore ye may not come to the adventures of the Sangrail.'

Then first spake Gawain and said, 'Ector, have ye heard these words?'

'Yea truly,' said Sir Ector, 'I heard all. Now go we,' said Sir Ector, 'unto some hermit that will tell us of our advision, for it seemeth me we labour all in vain.'

And so they departed and rode into a valley, and there met with a squire which rode on an hackney, and they saluted him fair.

'Sir,' said Gawain, 'can thou teach us to any hermit?'

'Here is one in a little mountain, but it is so rough there may no horse go thither, and therefore ye must go upon foot; there shall ye find a poor house, and there is Nacien the hermit, which is the holiest man in this country.'

And so they departed either from other. And then in a valley they met with a knight all armed, which proffered them to joust as far as he saw them.

'In the name of God,' said Sir Gawain, 'sith I departed from Camelot there was none proffered me to joust but once.'

'And now, sir,' said Ector, 'let me joust with him.'

'Nay,' said Gawain, 'ye shall not but if I be beat; it shall not forthink me then if ye go after me.'

And then either embraced other to joust and came together as fast as their horses might run, and brast their shields and the mails, and the one more than the other; and Gawain was wounded in the left side, but the other knight was smitten through the breast, and the spear came out on the other side, and so they fell both out of their saddles, and in the falling they brake both their spears. Anon Gawain arose and set his hand to his sword, and cast his shield afore him. But all for naught was it, for the knight had no power to rise against him.

Then said Gawain, 'Ye must yield you as an overcome man, or else I may slay you.'

'Ah, sir knight,' said he, 'I am but dead, for God's sake and of your gentleness lead me here unto an abbey that I may receive my Creator.'

'Sir,' said Gawain, 'I know no house of religion hereby.'

'Sir,' said the knight, 'set me on an horse tofore you, and I shall teach you.'

Gawain set him up in the saddle, and he leapt up behind him for to sustain him, and so came to an abbey where they were well received; and anon he was unarmed, and received his Creator.

Then he prayed Gawain to draw out the truncheon of the spear out of his body. Then Gawain asked him what he was, that knew him not.

'I am,' said he, 'of King Arthur's court, and was a fellow of the Round Table, and we were brethren sworn together; and now Sir Gawain, thou hast slain me, and my name is Uwain les Avoutres, that sometime was son unto King Uriens, and was in the quest of the Sangrail; and now forgive it thee God, for it shall ever be said that the one sworn brother hath slain the other.'

CHAPTER 3: *How Sir Gawain and Sir Ector came to an hermitage to be confessed, and how they told to the hermit their visions*

'Alas,' said Gawain, 'that ever this misadventure is befallen me.'

'No force,' said Uwain, 'sith I shall die this death, of a much more worshipfuller man's hand might I not die; but when ye come to the court recommend me unto my lord, King Arthur, and all those that be left alive, and for old brotherhood think on me.'

Then began Gawain to weep, and Ector also.

And then Uwain himself and Sir Gawain drew out the truncheon of the spear, and anon departed the soul from the body. Then Sir Gawain and Sir Ector buried him as men ought to bury a king's son, and made writen upon his name, and by whom he was slain.

Then departed Gawain and Ector as heavy as they might for their misadventure, and so rode till that they came to the rough mountain, and there they tied their horses and went on foot to the hermitage. And when they were come up they saw a poor house, and beside the chapel a little courtelage, where Nacien the hermit gathered worts, as he which had tasted none other meat of a great while. And when he saw the errant knights he came toward them and saluted them, and they him again.

'Fair lords,' said he, 'what adventure brought you hither?'

'Sir,' said Gawain, 'to speak with you for to be confessed.'

'Sir,' said the hermit, 'I am ready.'

Then they told him so much that he wist well what they were. And then he thought to counsel them if he might.

Then began Gawain first and told him of his advision that he had had in the chapel, and Ector told him all as it is afore rehearsed.

'Sir,' said the hermit unto Sir Gawain, 'the fair meadow and the rack therein ought to be understand the Round

Table, and by the meadow ought to be understand humility and patience, those be the things which be always green and quick; for men may no time overcome humility and patience, therefore was the Round Table founden; and the chivalry hath been at all times so by the fraternity which was there that she might not be overcomen; for men said she was founded in patience and in humility. At the rack ate an hundred and fifty bulls; but they ate not in the meadow, for their hearts should be set in humility and patience, and the bulls were proud and black save only three. By the bulls is to understand the fellowship of the Round Table, which for their sin and their wickedness be black. Blackness is to say without good or virtuous works. And the three bulls which were white save only one that was spotted: and two white betokenen Sir Galahad and Sir Percival, for they be maidens clean and without spot; and the third that had a spot signifieth Sir Bors de Ganis, which trespassed but once in his virginity, but sithen he kept himself so well in chastity that all is forgiven him and his misdeeds. And why those three were tied by the necks, they be three knights in virginity and chastity, and there is no pride smitten in them. And the black bulls which said, 'Go we hence,' they were those which at Pentecost at the high feast took upon them to go in the quest of the Sangrail without confession: they might not enter in the meadow of humility and patience. And therefore they returned into waste countries, that signifieth death, for there shall die many of them: every each of them shall slay other for sin, and they that shall escape shall be so lean that it shall be marvel to see them. And of the three bulls without spot, the one shall come again, and the other two never.'

CHAPTER 4: *How the hermit expounded their vision*

Then spake Nacien unto Ector: 'Sooth it is that Launcelot and ye came down off one chair: the chair betokeneth mas-

tership and lordship which ye came down from. But ye two
knights,' said the hermit, 'ye go to seek that ye shall never
find, that is the Sangrail; for it is the secret thing of Our
Lord Jesu Christ. What is to mean that Sir Launcelot fell
down off his horse: he hath left pride and taken him to
humility, for he had cried mercy loud for his sin, and sore
repented him, and Our Lord hath clothed him in his clothing
which is full of knots, that is the hair that he weareth daily.
And the ass that he rideth upon is a beast of humility, for
God would not ride upon no steed, nor upon no palfrey; so in
example that an ass betokeneth meekness, that thou sawest
Sir Launcelot ride on in thy sleep. And the well whereas the
water sank from him when he should have taken thereof, and
when he saw he might not have it, he returned thither from
whence he came, for the well betokeneth the high grace of
God, the more men desire it to take it the more shall be their
desire. So when he came nigh the Sangrail, he meeked him
that he held him not a man worthy to be so nigh the holy
vessel, for he had been so defouled in deadly sin by the space
of many years; yet when he kneeled to drink of the well,
there he saw great providence of the Sangrail. And for he
had served so long the devil, he shall have vengeance four
and twenty days long, for that he hath been the devil's servant four and twenty years. And then soon after he shall
return unto Camelot out of this country, and he shall say a
part of such things as he hath found.

'Now will I tell you what betokeneth the hand with the
candle and the bridle: that is to understand the holy ghost
where charity is ever, and the bridle signifieth abstinence.
For when she is bridled in Christian man's heart she holdeth
him so short that he falleth not in deadly sin. And the candle
which showeth clearness and sight signifieth the right way of
Jesu Christ. And when he went and said, "Knights of poor
faith and of wicked belief, these three things failed, charity,
abstinence, and truth;" therefore ye may not attain that high
adventure of the Sangrail.'

CHAPTER 5: *Of the good counsel that the hermit gave to them*

'Certes,' said Gawain, 'soothly have ye said, that I see it openly. Now, I pray you, good man and holy father, tell me why we met not with so many adventures as we were wont to do, and commonly have the better.'

'I shall tell you gladly,' said the good man: 'the adventure of the Sangrail which ye and many other have undertake the quest of it and find it not, the cause is for it appeareth not to sinners. Wherefore marvel not though ye fail thereof, and many other. For ye be an untrue knight, and a great murderer, and to good men signifieth other things than murder. For I dare say as sinful as Sir Launcelot hath been, sith that he went into the quest of the Sangrail he slew never man, nor nought shall, till that he come unto Camelot again, for he hath taken upon him for to forsake sin. And nere were that he nis not stable, but by his thought he is likely to turn again, he should be next to achieve it save Galahad, his son. But God knoweth his thought and his unstableness, and yet shall he die right an holy man, and no doubt he hath no fellow of no earthly sinful man.'

'Sir,' said Gawain, 'it seemeth me by your words that for our sins it will not avail us to travel in this quest.'

'Truly,' said the good man, 'there be an hundred such as ye be that never shall prevail, but to have shame.'

And when they had heard these voices they commended him unto God.

Then the good man called Gawain, and said, 'It is long time passed sith that ye were made knight, and never sithen thou servedst thy Maker, and now thou art so old a tree that in thee is neither leaf ne fruit; wherefore bethink thee that thou yield to Our Lord the bare rind, sith the fiend hath the leaves and the fruit.'

'Sir,' said Gawain, 'and I had leisure I would speak with

nere were that he nis not stable: were it not that he is not steadfast.

you, but my fellow here, Sir Ector, is gone, and abideth me yonder beneath the hill.'

'Well,' said the good man, 'thou were better to be counselled.'

Then departed Gawain and came to Ector, and so took their horses and rode till they came to a forester's house, which harboured them right well. And on the morn they departed from their host, and rode long or they could find any adventure.

CHAPTER 6: *How Sir Bors met with an hermit, and how he was confessed to him, and of his penance enjoined to him*

When Bors was departed from Camelot he met with a religious man riding on an ass, and Sir Bors saluted him. Anon the good man knew him that he was one of the knights errant that was in the quest of the Sangrail.

'What are ye?' said the good man.

'Sir,' said he, 'I am a knight that fain would be counselled in the quest of the Sangrail, for he shall have much earthly worship that may bring it to an end.'

'Certes,' said the good man, 'that is sooth, for he shall be the best knight of the world, and the fairest of all the fellowship. But wit you well there shall none attain it but by cleanness, that is pure confession.'

So rode they together till that they came to an hermitage. And there he prayed Bors to dwell all that night with him. And so he alit and put away his armour, and prayed him that he might be confessed; and so they went into the chapel, and there he was clean confessed, and they ate bread and drank water together.

'Now,' said the good man, 'I pray thee that thou eat none other till that thou sit at the table where the Sangrail shall be.'

'Sir,' said he, 'I agree me thereto, but how wit ye that I shall sit there?'

'Yes,' said the good man, 'that know I, but there shall be but few of your fellows with you.'

'All is welcome,' said Sir Bors, 'that God sendeth me.'

'Also,' said the good man, 'instead of a shirt, and in sign of chastisement, ye shall wear a garment; therefore I pray you do off all your clothes and your shirt': and so he did.

And then he took him a scarlet coat, so that should be instead of his shirt till he had fulfilled the quest of the Sangrail; and the good man found him in so marvellous a life and so stable, that he marvelled and felt that he was never corrupt in fleshly lusts, but in one time that he begat Helin le Blank. Then he armed him, and took his leave, and so departed.

And so a little from thence he looked up into a tree, and there he saw a passing great bird upon an old tree, and it was passing dry, without leaves; and the bird sat above, and had birds, the which were dead for hunger. So smote he himself with his beak, the which was great and sharp. And so the great bird bled till that he died among his birds. And the young birds tooken the life by the blood of the great bird. When Bors saw this he wist well it was a great tokening; for when he saw the great bird arose not, then he took his horse and yede his way. So by evensong, by adventure he came to a strong tower and an high, and there was he lodged gladly.

CHAPTER 7: *How Sir Bors was lodged with a lady, and how he took on him for to fight against a champion for her land*

And when he was unarmed they led him into an high tower where was a lady, young, lusty, and fair. And she received him with great joy, and made him to sit down by her, and so was he set to sup with flesh and many dainties. And when Sir Bors saw that, he bethought him on his penance, and bad a squire to bring him water. And so he brought him, and he made sops therein and ate them.

'Ah,' said the lady, 'I trow ye like not my meat.'

'Yes, truly,' said Sir Bors, 'God thank you, madam, but I may eat none other meat this day.'

Then she spake no more as at that time, for she was loth to displease him. Then after supper they spake of one thing and other.

With that came a squire and said, 'Madam, ye must purvey you tomorn for a champion, for else your sister will have this castle and also your lands, except ye can find a knight that will fight tomorn in your quarrel against Pridam le Noire.'

Then she made sorrow and said, 'Ah, Lord God, wherefore granted Ye to hold my land, whereof I should now be disherited without reason and right?'

And when Sir Bors had heard her say thus, he said, 'I shall comfort you.'

'Sir,' said she, 'I shall tell you there was here a king that hight Aniause, which held all this land in his keeping. So it mishapped he loved a gentlewoman a great deal elder than I. So took he her all this land to her keeping, and all his men to govern; and she brought up many evil customs whereby she put to death a great part of his kinsmen. And when he saw that, he let chase her out of this land, and betook it me, and all this land in my domains. But anon as that worthy king was dead, this other lady began to war upon me, and hath destroyed many of my men, and turned them against me, that I have wellnigh no man left me; and I have nought else but this high tower that she left me. And yet she hath promised me to have this tower, without I can find a knight to fight with her champion.'

'Now tell me,' said Sir Bors, 'what is that Pridam le Noire?'

'Sir,' said she, 'he is the most doubted man of this land.'

'Now may ye send her word that ye have found a knight that shall fight with that Pridam le Noire in God's quarrel and yours.'

Then that lady was not a little glad, and sent word that she was purveyed, and that night Bors had good cheer; but in no bed he would come, but laid him on the floor, nor never would do otherwise till that he had met with the quest of the Sangrail.

CHAPTER 8: *Of a vision which Sir Bors had that night, and how he fought and overcame his adversary*

And anon as he was asleep him befell a vision, that there came to him two birds, the one as white as a swan, and the other was marvellous black; but it was not so great as the other, but in the likeness of a raven.

Then the white bird came to him, and said: 'And thou wouldst give me meat and serve me I should give thee all the riches of the world, and I shall make thee as fair and as white as I am.'

So the white bird departed, and there came the black bird to him, and said, 'And thou wolt, serve me tomorrow and have me in no despite though I be black, for wit thou well that more availeth my blackness than the other's whiteness.' And then he departed.

And he had another vision: him thought that he came to a great place which seemed a chapel, and there he found a chair set on the left side, which was wormeaten and feeble. And on the right hand were two flowers like a lily, and the one would have benome the others whiteness, but a good man departed them that the one[1] touched not the other; and then out of every each flower came out many flowers, and fruit great plenty. Then him thought the good man said; 'Should not he do great folly that would let these two flowers perish for to succour the rotten tree, that it fell not to the earth?'

'Sir,' said he, 'it seemeth me that this wood might not avail.'

'Now keep thee,' said the good man, 'that thou never see such adventure befall thee.'

Then he awaked and made a sign of the cross in midst of the forehead, and so rose and clothed him.

And there came the lady of the place, and she saluted him, and he her again, and so went to a chapel and heard their service. And there came a company of knights, that the lady had sent for, to lead Sir Bors unto battle. Then asked he his arms. And when he was armed she prayed him to take a little morsel to dine.

'Nay, madam,' said he, 'that shall I not do till I have done my battle, by the grace of God.'

And so he leaped upon his horse, and departed all the knights and men with him.

And as soon as these two ladies met together, she which Bors should fight for complained her, and said, 'Madam, ye have done me wrong to bereave me of my lands that King Aniause gave me, and full loth I am there should be any battle.'

'Ye shall not choose,' said the other lady, 'or else your knight withdraw him.'

Then there was the cry made, which party had the better of the two knights, that his lady should rejoice all the land.

Now departed the one knight here, and the other there. Then they came together with such a raundon that they pierced their shields and their hauberks, and the spears flew in pieces, and they wounded either other sore. Then hurtled they together, so that they fell both to the earth, and their horses betwixt their legs; and anon they arose, and set hands to their swords, and smote each one other upon the heads, that they made great wounds and deep, that the blood went out of their bodies. For there found Sir Bors greater defence in that knight more than he weened. For that Pridam was a passing good knight, and he wounded Sir Bors full evil, and he him again; but ever this Pridam held the stour in like hard. That perceived Sir Bors, and suffered him till he was nigh attaint. And then he ran upon him more and more, and the other went back for dread of death. So in his withdrawing he fell upright, and Sir Bors drew his helm so strongly that he rent it from his head, and gave him great strokes with the

attaint: exhausted.

313

flat of his sword upon the visage, and bad him yield or he should slay him.

Then he cried him mercy and said, 'Fair knight, for God's love slay me not, and I shall ensure thee never to war against thy lady, but be alway toward her.'

Then Bors let him be; then the old lady fled with all her knights.

CHAPTER 9: *How the lady was returned to her lands by the battle of Sir Bors, and of his departing, and how he met Sir Lionel taken and beaten with thorns, and also a maid which should have been devoured*

So then came Bors to all those that held lands of his lady, and said he should destroy them but if they did such service unto her as longed to their lands. So they did their homage, and they that would not were chased out of their lands.

Then befell that young lady to come to her estate again, by the mighty prowess of Sir Bors de Ganis. So when all the country was well set in peace, then Sir Bors took his leave and departed; and she thanked him greatly, and would have given him great riches, but he refused it.

Then he rode all that day till night, and came to an harbour to a lady which knew him well enough, and made of him great joy.

Upon the morn, as soon as the day appeared, Bors departed from thence, and so rode into a forest unto the hour of midday, and there befell him a marvellous adventure. So he met at the departing of the two ways two knights that led Lionel, his brother, all naked, bounden upon a strong hackney, and his hands bounden tofore his breast. And every each of them held in his hands thorns wherewith they went beating him so sore that the blood trailed down more than in an hundred places of his body, so that he was all blood tofore and behind, but he said never a word; as he which was great of heart he suffered all that ever they did to him as though he had felt none anguish.

Anon Sir Bors dressed him to rescue him that was his brother; and so he looked upon the other side of him, and saw a knight which brought a fair gentlewoman, and would have set her in the thickest place of the forest for to have been the more surer out of the way from them that sought him.

And she which was nothing assured, cried with an high voice, 'Saint Mary succour your maid.'

And anon she espied where Sir Bors came riding. And when she came nigh him she deemed him a knight of the Round Table, whereof she hoped to have some comfort; and then she conjured him; by the faith that he ought 'unto Him in whose service thou art entered in, and for the faith ye owe unto the high order of knighthood, and for the noble King Arthur's sake, that I suppose that made thee knight, that thou help me, and suffer me not to be shamed of this knight.'

When Bors heard her say thus he had so much sorrow there he nist not what to do. 'For if I let my brother be in adventure he must be slain, and that would I not for all the earth. And if I help not the maid she is shamed for ever, and also she shall lose her virginity the which she shall never get again.'

Then lift he up his eyen and said weeping, 'Fair sweet Lord Jesu Christ, whose liege man I am, keep Lionel, my brother, that these knights slay him not, and for pity of You, and for Mary's sake, I shall succour this maid.'

CHAPTER 10: *How Sir Bors left to rescue his brother, and rescued the damosel; and how it was told him that Lionel was dead*

Then dressed he him unto the knight the which had the gentlewoman, and then he cried, 'Sir knight, let your hand off that maiden, or ye be but dead.'

And then he set down the maiden, and was armed at all pieces save he lacked his spear. Then he dressed his shield, and drew out his sword, and Bors smote him so hard that it went through his shield and habergeon on the left shoulder. And through great strength he beat him down to the earth, and at the pulling out of Bors' spear there he swooned.

Then came Bors to the maid and said, 'How seemeth it you? Of this knight ye be delivered at this time.'

'Now sir,' said she, 'I pray you lead me thereas this knight had me.'

'So shall I do gladly,' and took the horse of the wounded knight, and set the gentlewoman upon him, and so brought her as she desired.

'Sir knight,' said she, 'ye have better sped than ye weened, for and I had lost my maidenhead, five hundred men should have died for it.'

'What knight was he that had you in the forest?'

'By my faith,' said she, 'he is my cousin. So wot I never with what engine the fiend enchafed him, for yesterday he took me from my father privily; for I nor none of my father's men mistrusted him not, and if he had had my maidenhead he should have died for the sin, and his body shamed and dishonoured for ever.'

Thus as she stood talking with him there came twelve knights seeking after her, and anon she told them all how Bors had delivered her; then they made great joy, and besought him to come to her father, a great lord, and he should be right welcome.

'Truly,' said Bors, 'that may not be at this time, for I have a great adventure to do in this country.'

So he commended them unto God and departed. Then Sir Bors rode after Lionel, his brother, by the trace of their horses, thus he rode seeking a great while.

Then he overtook a man clothed in a religious clothing, and rode on a strong black horse blacker than a berry, and said, 'Sir knight, what seek you?'

habergeon: coat of mail.   *engine*: evil device.

'Sir,' said he, 'I seek my brother that I saw within a while beaten with two knights.'

'Ah, Bors, discomfort you not, ne fall into no wanhope, for I shall tell you tidings such as they be, for truly he is dead.'

Then showed he him a new slain body lying in a bush, and it seemed him well that it was the body of Lionel; and then he made such a sorrow that he fell to the earth all in a swoon, and lay a great while there.

And when he came to himself he said, 'Fair brother, sith the company of you and me is departed shall I never have joy in my heart, and now He which I have take unto my master, He be my help.' And when he had said thus he took his body lightly in his arms, and put it upon the arson of his saddle.

And then he said to the man, 'Canst thou tell me unto some chapel where that I may bury this body?'

'Come on,' said he, 'here is one fast by;' and so long they rode till they saw a fair tower, and afore it there seemed an old feeble chapel.

And then they alit both, and put him into a tomb of marble.

CHAPTER 11: *How Sir Bors told his dream to a priest, which he had dreamed, and of the counsel that the priest gave to him*

'Now leave we him here,' said the good man, 'and go we to our harbour till tomorrow; we will come here again to do him service.'

'Sir,' said Bors, 'be ye a priest?'

'Yea forsooth,' said he.

'Then I pray you tell me a dream that befell to me the last night.'

'Say on,' said he.

Then he began so much to tell him of the great bird in the

wanhope: despair.

forest, and after told him of his birds, one white, another black, and of the rotten tree, and of the white flowers.

'Sir, I shall tell you a part now, and the other deal to-morrow. The white fowl betokeneth a gentlewoman, fair and rich, which loved thee paramours, and hath loved thee long; and if thou warn her love she shall go die anon, if thou have no pity on her. That signifieth the great bird, the which shall make thee to warn her. Now for no fear that thou hast, ne for no dread that thou hast of God, thou shalt not warn her, but thou wouldst not do it for to be holden chaste, for to conquer the loos of the vain glory of the world; for that shall befall thee now and thou warn her, that Launcelot, the good knight, thy cousin, shall die. And therefore men shall now say that thou art a manslayer, both of thy brother, Sir Lionel, and of thy cousin, Sir Launcelot du Lake, the which thou mightest have saved and rescued easily, but thou ween-edst to rescue a maid which pertaineth nothing to thee. Now look thou whether it had been a greater harm of thy brother's death, or else to have suffered her to have lost her maiden-hood.'

Then asked he him, 'Hast thou heard the tokens of thy dream the which I have told to you?'

'Yea forsooth,' said Sir Bors, 'all your exposition and de-claring of my dream I have well understand and heard.'

Then said the man in this black clothing, 'Then is it in thy default if Sir Launcelot, thy cousin, die.'

'Sir,' said Bors, 'that were me loth, for wit ye well there is nothing in the world but I had lever do it than to see my lord, Sir Launcelot du Lake, to die in my default.'

'Choose ye now the one or the other,' said the good man.

And then he led Sir Bors into an high tower, and there he found knights and ladies; those ladies said he was welcome, and so they unarmed him. And when he was in his doublet men brought him a mantle furred with ermine, and put it about him; and then they made him such cheer that he had forgotten all his sorrow and anguish, and only set his heart in these delights and dainties, and took no thought more for

his brother Sir Lionel, neither of Sir Launcelot du Lake, his
cousin. And anon came out of a chamber to him the fairest
lady that ever he saw, and more richer beseen than ever he
saw Queen Guenever or any other estate.

'Lo,' said they, 'Sir Bors, here is the lady unto whom we
owe all our service, and I trow she be the richest lady and the
fairest of all the world, and the which loveth you best above
all other knights, for she will have no knight but you.'

And when he understood that language he was abashed.
Notforthan she saluted him, and he her; and then they sat
down together and spake of many things, in so much that she
besought him to be her love, for she had loved him above all
earthly men, and she should make him richer than ever was
man of his age.

When Bors understood her words he was right evil at ease,
which in no manner would not break chastity, so wist not he
how to answer her.

CHAPTER 12: *How the devil in a woman's likeness would
have had Sir Bors to have lain by her, and how by God's grace
he escaped*

'Alas,' said she, 'Bors, shall ye not do my will?'

'Madam,' said Bors, 'there is no lady in this world whose
will I will fulfil as of this thing, for my brother lieth dead
which was slain right late.'

'Ah Bors,' said she, 'I have loved you long for the great
beauty I have seen in you, and the great hardiness that I
have heard of you, that needs ye must lie by me this night,
and therefore I pray you grant it me.'

'Truly,' said he, 'I shall not do it in no manner wise.'

Then she made him such sorrow as though she would have
died. 'Well Bors,' said she, 'unto this have ye brought me,
nigh to mine end.' And therewith she took him by the hand,
and bad him behold her. 'And ye shall see how I shall die
for your love.'

'Ah,' said then he, 'that shall I never see.'

Then she departed and went up into an high battlement, and led with her twelve gentlewomen; and when they were above, one of the gentlewomen cried, and said, 'Ah, Sir Bors, gentle knight have mercy on us all, and suffer my lady to have her will, and if ye do not we must suffer death with our lady, for to fall down off this high tower, and if ye suffer us thus to die for so little a thing all ladies and gentlewomen will say of you dishonour.'

Then looked he upward, they seemed all ladies of great estate, and richly and well beseen. Then had he of them great pity; not for that he was [not]¹ uncounselled in himself that lever he had they all had lost their souls than he his, and with that they fell adown all at once unto the earth. And when he saw that, he was all abashed, and had thereof great marvel. With that he blessed his body and his visage.

And anon he heard a great noise and a great cry, as though all the fiends of hell had been about him; and therewith he saw neither tower ne lady, ne gentlewoman, nor no chapel where he brought his brother to.

Then held he up both his hands to the heaven, and said, 'Fair Father God, I am grievously escaped;' and then he took his arms and his horse and rode on his way.

Then he heard a clock smite on his right hand; and thither he came to an abbey on his right hand, closed with high walls, and there was let in. Then they supposed that he was one of the quest of the Sangrail, so they led him into a chamber and unarmed him.

'Sirs,' said Sir Bors, 'if there be any holy man in this house I pray you let me speak with him.'

Then one of them led him unto the abbot, which was in a chapel. And then Sir Bors saluted him, and he him again.

'Sir,' said Bors, 'I am a knight errant;' and told him all the adventure which he had seen.

'Sir knight,' said the abbot, 'I wot not what ye be, for I weened never that a knight of your age might have been so strong in the grace of Our Lord Jesu Christ. Notforthan ye shall go unto your rest, for I will not counsel you this day, it is too late, and tomorrow I shall counsel you as I can.'

CHAPTER 13: *Of the holy communication of an abbot to Sir Bors, and how the abbot counselled him*

And that night was Sir Bors served richly; and on the morn early he heard mass, and the abbot came to him, and bad him good morrow, and Bors to him again.

And then he told him he was a fellow of the quest of the Sangrail, and how he had charge of the holy man to eat bread and water.

'Then Our Lord Jesu Christ showed him unto you in the likeness of a fowl that suffered great anguish for us, since He was put upon the cross, and bled His heart blood for mankind: there was the token and the likeness of the Sangrail that appeared afore you, for the blood that the great fowl bled revived the chickens from death to life. And by the bare tree is betokened the world which is naked and without fruit but if it come of Our Lord. Also the lady for whom ye fought for, and King Aniause which was lord there tofore, betokeneth Jesu Christ which is King of the world.

'And that ye fought with the champion for the lady, this it betokeneth: for when ye took the battle for the lady, by her shall ye understand the new law of Jesu Christ and Holy Church; and by the other lady ye shall understand the old law and the fiend, which all day warreth against Holy Church, therefore ye did your battle with right. For ye be Jesu Christ's knights, therefore ye ought to be defenders of Holy Church. And by the black bird might ye understand Holy Church, which sayeth "I am black," but he is fair. And by the white bird might men understand the fiend, and I shall tell you how the swan is white withoutforth, and black within: it is hypocrisy which is without yellow or pale, and seemeth withoutforth the servants of Jesu Christ,

321

but they be within so horrible of filth and sin, and beguile the world evil.

'Also when the fiend appeared to thee in likeness of a man of religion, and blamed thee that thou left thy brother for a lady, so led thee where thou seemed thy brother was slain, but he is yet alive; and all was for to put thee in error, and bring thee unto wanhope and lechery, for he knew thou were tender hearted, and all was for thou shouldst not find the blessed adventure of the Sangrail. And the third fowl betokeneth the strong battle against the fair ladies which were all devils.

'Also the dry tree and the white lily: the dry tree betokeneth thy brother Lionel, which is dry without virtue, and therefore many men ought to call him the rotten tree, and the wormeaten tree, for he is a murderer and doth contrary to the order of knighthood. And the two white flowers signifyen two maidens, the one is a knight which was wounded the other day, and the other is the gentlewoman which ye rescued; and why the other flower drew nigh the other, that was the knight which would have defouled her and himself both. And Sir Bors, ye had been a great fool and in great peril for to have seen those two flowers perish for to succour the rotten tree, for and they had sinned together they had been damned; and for that ye rescued them both, men might call you a very knight and servant of Jesu Christ.'

CHAPTER 14: *How Sir Bors met with his brother Sir Lionel, and how Sir Lionel would have slain Sir Bors*

Then went Sir Bors from thence and commended the abbot unto God. And then he rode all that day, and harboured with an old lady. And on the morn he rode to a castle in a valley, and there he met with a yeoman going a great pace toward a forest.

'Say me,' said Sir Bors, 'canst thou tell me of any adventure?'

'Sir,' said he, 'here shall be under this castle a great and a marvellous tournament.'

'Of what folks shall it be?' said Sir Bors.

'The Earl of Plains shall be in the one party, and the Lady's nephew of Hervin on the other party.'

Then Bors thought to be there if he might meet with his brother Sir Lionel, or any other of his fellowship, which were in the quest of the Sangrail.

And then he turned to an hermitage that was in the entry of the forest. And when he was come thither he found there Sir Lionel, his brother, which sat all armed at the entry of the chapel door for to abide there harbour till on the morn that the tournament shall be. And when Sir Bors saw him he had great joy of him, that it were marvel to tell of his joy.

And then he alit off his horse, and said, 'Fair sweet brother, when came ye hither?'

Anon as Lionel saw him he said, 'Ah Bors, ye may not make none avaunt, but as for you I might have been slain; when ye saw two knights leading me away beating me, ye left me for to succour a gentlewoman, and suffered me in peril of death; for never erst ne did no brother to another so great an untruth. And for that misdeed now I ensure you but death, for well have ye deserved it; therefore keep thee from henceforward, and that shall ye find as soon as I am armed.'

When Sir Bors understood his brother's wrath he kneeled down to the earth and cried him mercy, holding up both his hands, and prayed him to forgive him his evil will.

'Nay,' said Lionel, 'that shall never be and I may have the higher hand, that I make mine avow to God, thou shalt have death for it, for it were pity ye lived any longer.'

Right so he went in and took his harness, and mounted upon his horse, and came tofore him and said, 'Bors, keep thee from me, for I shall do to thee as I would to a felon or a traitor, for ye be the untruest knight that ever came out of so worthy an house as was King Bors' de Ganis which was our father, therefore start upon thy horse, and so shall ye be most at your advantage. And but if ye will I will run upon you there as ye stand upon foot, and so the shame shall be mine and the harm yours, but of that shame ne reck I nought.'

When Sir Bors saw that he must fight with his brother or else to die, he nist what to do; then his heart counselled him not thereto, inasmuch as Lionel was born or he, wherefore he ought to bear him reverence; yet kneeled he down afore Lionel's horse's feet, and said; 'Fair sweet brother, have mercy upon me and slay me not, and have in remembrance the great love which ought to be between us twain.'

What Sir Bors said to Lionel he rought not, for the fiend had brought him in such a will that he should slay him. Then when Lionel saw he would none other, and that he would not have risen to give him battle, he rashed over him so that he smote Bors with his horse's feet, upward to the earth, and hurt him so sore that he swooned of distress, the which he felt in himself to have died without confession. So when Lionel saw this, he alit off his horse to have smitten off his head. And so he took him by the helm, and would have rent it from his head.

Then came the hermit running unto him, which was a good man and of great age, and well had heard all the words that were between them, and so fell down upon Sir Bors.

CHAPTER 15: *How Sir Colgrevaunce fought against Sir Lionel for to save Sir Bors, and how the hermit was slain*

Then he said to Lionel, 'Ah gentle knight, have mercy upon me and on thy brother, for if thou slay him thou shalt be dead of sin, and that were sorrowful, for he is one of the worthiest knights of the world, and of the best conditions.'

'So God me help,' said Lionel, 'sir priest, but if ye flee from him I shall slay you, and he shall never the sooner be quit.'

'Certes,' said the good man, 'I have lever ye slay me than him, for my death shall not be great harm, not half so much as of his.'

rought: cared. *upward*: supine.

'Well,' said Lionel, 'I am agreed;' and set his hand to his sword and smote him so hard that his head yede backward. Not for that he restrained him of his evil will, but took his brother by the helm, and unlaced it to have stricken off his head, and had slain him without fail.

But it so happed, Colgrevaunce, a fellow of the Round Table, came at that time thither as Our Lord's will was. And when he saw the good man slain he marvelled much what it might be. And then he beheld Lionel would have slain his brother, and knew Sir Bors which he loved right well.

Then start he down and took Lionel by the shoulders, and drew him strongly aback from Bors, and said, 'Lionel, will ye slay your brother, the worthiest knight of the world one? And that should no good man suffer.'

'Why,' said Lionel, 'will ye let me? Therefore if ye intermit you in this I shall slay you, and him after.'

'Why,' said Colgrevaunce, 'is this sooth that ye will slay him?'

'Slay him will I,' said he, 'whoso say the contrary, for he hath done so much against me that he hath well deserved it.'

And so ran upon him, and would have smitten him through the head, and Sir Colgrevaunce ran betwixt them, and said, 'And ye be so hardy to do so more, we two shall meddle together.'

When Lionel understood his words he took his shield afore him, and asked him what that he was. And he told him, Colgrevaunce, one of his fellows.

Then Lionel defied him, and gave him a great stroke through the helm. Then he drew his sword, for he was a passing good knight, and defended him right manfully.

So long dured the battle that Bors rose up all anguishly, and beheld Colgrevaunce, the good knight, fought with his brother for his quarrel; then was he full sorry and heavy and thought if Colgrevaunce slay him that was his brother he should never have joy; and if his brother slew Colgrevaunce 'the shame should ever be mine.'

Then would he have risen to have departed them, but he

had not so much might to stand on foot; so he abode him so long till Colgrevaunce had the worse, for Lionel was of great chivalry and right hardy, for he had pierced the hauberk and the helm, that he abode but death, for he had lost much of his blood that it was marvel that he might stand upright.

Then beheld he Sir Bors which sat dressing him upward and said, 'Ah, Bors, why come ye not to cast me out of peril of death, wherein I have put me to succour you which were right now nigh the death?'

'Certes,' said Lionel, 'that shall not avail you, for none of you shall bear others warrant, but that ye shall die both of my hand.'

When Bors heard that he did so much, he rose and put on his helm. Then perceived he first the hermit priest which was slain, then made he a marvellous sorrow upon him.

CHAPTER 16: *How Sir Lionel slew Sir Colgrevaunce, and how after he would have slain Sir Bors*

Then oft Colgrevaunce cried upon Sir Bors, 'Why will ye let me die here for your sake? If it please you that I die for you the death, it will please me the better for to save a worthy man.'

With that word Sir Lionel smote off the helm from his head.

Then Colgrevaunce saw that he might not escape; then he said, 'Fair sweet Jesu, that I have misdone have mercy upon my soul, for such sorrow that my heart suffereth for goodness, and for alms deed that I would have done here, be to me a lygement of penance unto my soul's health.'

At these words Lionel smote him so sore that he bare him to the earth. So when he had slain Colgrevaunce he ran upon his brother as a fiendly man, and gave him such a stroke that he made him stoop.

And he that was full of humility prayed him for God's

lygement: alleviation.

love to leave this battle, 'For and it befell, fair brother, that I slew you or ye me, we should be dead of that sin.'

'Never God me help but if I have on you mercy, and I may have the better hand.'

Then drew Bors his sword, all weeping, and said, 'Fair brother, God knoweth mine intent. Ah, fair brother, ye have done full evil this day to slay such an holy priest the which never trespassed. Also ye have slain a gentle knight, and one of our fellows. And well wot ye that I am not afeared of you greatly, but I dread the wrath of God, and this is an unkindly war, therefore God show miracle upon us both. Now God have mercy upon me though I defend my life against my brother;' with that Bors lift up his hand and would have smitten his brother.

CHAPTER 17: *How there came a voice which charged Sir Bors to touch not him, and of a cloud that came between them*

And then he heard a voice that said, 'Flee Bors, and touch him not, or else thou shall slay him.'

Right so alit a cloud betwixt them in likeness of a fire and a marvellous flame, that both their two shields burnt. Then were they sore afraid, that they fell both to the earth, and lay there a great while in a swoon. And when they came to themself, Bors saw that his brother had no harm; then he held up both his hands, for he dread God had taken vengeance upon him.

With that he heard a voice say, 'Bors, go hence, and bear thy brother no longer fellowship, but take thy way, anon right to the sea, for Sir Percival abideth thee there.'

Then he said to his brother, 'Fair sweet brother, forgive me for God's love all that I have trespassed unto you.'

Then he answered, 'God forgive it thee and I do gladly.'

So Sir Bors departed from him and rode the next way to the sea. And at the last by fortune he came to an abbey which was nigh the sea.

That night Bors rested him there; and in his sleep there

came a voice to him and bad him go to the sea. Then he start up and made a sign of the cross in the midst of his forehead, and took his harness, and made ready his horse, and mounted upon him; and at a broken wall he rode out, and rode so long till that he came to the sea.

And on the strand he found a ship covered all with white samite, and he alit, and betook him to Jesu Christ. And as soon as he entered into the ship, the ship departed into the sea, and went so fast that him seemed the ship went flying, but it was soon dark so that he might know no man, and so he slept till it was day.

Then he awaked, and saw in midst of the ship a knight lie all armed save his helm. Then knew he that it was Sir Percival of Wales, and then he made of him right great joy; but Sir Percival was abashed of him, and he asked him what he was.

'Ah, fair sir,' said Bors, 'know ye me not?'

'Certes,' said he, 'I marvel how ye came hither, but if Our Lord brought ye hither Himself.'

Then Sir Bors smiled and did off his helm. Then Percival knew him, and either made great joy of each other, that it was marvel to hear.

Then Bors told him how he came into the ship, and by whose admonishment; and either told other of their temptations, as ye have heard toforehand. So went they downward in the sea, one while backward, another while forward, and every each comforted other, and oft were in their prayers.

Then said Sir Percival; 'We lack nothing but Galahad, the good knight.'

And thus endeth the sixteenth book, which is of Sir Gawain, Ector de Maris, and Sir Bors de Ganis, and Sir Percival. And here followeth the seventeenth book, which is of the noble knight Sir Galahad

Book XVII

How Sir Galahad fought at a tournament, and how he was known of Sir Gawain and of Sir Ector de Maris

Now saith this story, when Galahad had rescued Percival from the twenty knights, he yede then into a waste forest wherein he rode many journeys; and he found many adventures the which he brought to an end, whereof the story maketh here no mention.

Then he took his way to the sea on a day, and it befell as he passed by a castle where was a wonder tournament, but they without had done so much that they within were put to the worse, yet were they within good knights enough, when Galahad saw that those within were at so great a mischief that men slew them at the entry of the castle, then he thought to help them, and put a spear forth and smote the first that he flew to the earth, and the spear brake to pieces. Then he drew his sword and smote thereas they were thickest and so he did wonderful deeds of arms that all they marvelled.

Then it happed that Gawain and Sir Ector de Maris were with the knights without. But when they espied the white shield with the red cross the one said to the other, 'Yonder is the good knight, Sir Galahad, the Haut Prince: now he should be a great fool which should meet with him to fight.'

So by adventure he came to Sir Gawain, and he smote him so hard that he clave his helm and the coif of iron unto his head, so that Gawain fell to the earth; but the stroke was so great that it slanted down to the earth and carved the horse's shoulder in two. When Ector saw Gawain down he drew him aside, and thought it no wisdom for to abide him, and also for natural love, that he was his uncle.

Thus through his great hardiness he beat aback all the knights without. And then they within came out and chased them all about. But when Galahad saw there would none turn again he stole away privily so that none wist where he was become.

'Now by my head,' said Gawain to Ector, 'now are the wonders true that were said of Launcelot du Lake, that the sword which stuck in the stone should give me such a buffet that I would not have it for the best castle in this world; and soothly now it is proved true, for never ere had I such a stroke of man's hand.'

'Sir,' said Ector, 'meseemeth your quest is done.'

'And yours is not done,' said Gawain, 'but mine is done, I shall seek no further.'

Then Gawain was borne into a castle and unarmed him, and laid him in a rich bed, and a leech found that he might live, and to be whole within a month. Thus Gawain and Ector abode together, for Sir Ector would not away till Gawain were whole.

And the good knight, Galahad, rode so long till he came that night to the Castle of Carbonek : and it befell him thus that he was benighted in an hermitage. So the good man was fain when he saw he was a knight errant.

Then when they were at rest there came a gentlewoman knocking at the door, and called Galahad, and so the good man came to the door to wit what she would.

Then she called the hermit, 'Sir Ulfin, I am a gentlewoman that would speak with the knight which is with you.'

Then the good man awaked Galahad, and bad him : 'Arise, and speak with a gentlewoman that seemeth hath great need of you.'

Then Galahad went to her and asked her what she would.

'Galahad,' said she, 'I will that ye arm you, and mount upon your horse and follow me, for I shall show you within these three days the highest adventure that ever any knight saw.'

Anon Galahad armed him, and took his horse, and commended him to God, and bad the gentlewoman go, and he would follow thereas she liked.

CHAPTER 2: *How Sir Galahad rode with a damosel, and came to the ship whereas Sir Bors and Sir Percival were in*

So she rode as fast as her palfrey might bear her, till that she came to the sea, the which was called Collibe. And at the night they came unto a castle in a valley, closed with a running water, and with strong walls and high; and so she entered into the castle with Galahad, and there had he great cheer, for the lady of that castle was the damosel's lady.

So when he was unarmed, then said the damosel, 'Madam, shall we abide here all this day?'

'Nay,' said she, 'but till he hath dined and till he hath slept a little.'

So he ate and slept a while till that the maid called him, and armed him by torchlight. And when the maid was horsed and he both, the lady took Galahad a fair shield and rich; and so they departed from the castle till they came to the seaside; and there they found the ship where Bors and Percival were in, the which cried on the ship's board, 'Sir Galahad, ye be welcome, we have abiden you long.'

And when he heard them he asked them what they were.

'Sir,' said she, 'leave your horse here, and I shall leave mine;' and took their saddles and their bridles with them, and made a cross on them, and so entered into the ship.

And the two knights received them both with great joy, and every each knew other ; and so the wind arose, and drove them through the sea in a marvellous place. And within a while it dawed. Then did Galahad off his helm and his sword, and asked of his fellows from whence came that fair ship.

'Truly,' said they, 'ye wot as well as we but of God's grace;' and then they told every each to other of all their hard adventures, and of their great temptations.

dawed: dawned.

'Truly,' said Galahad, 'ye are much bounden to God, for ye have escaped great adventures; and had not the gentlewoman been I had not comen here, for as for you I weened never to have found you in these strange countries.'

'Ah Galahad,' said Bors, 'if Launcelot, your father, were here then were we well at ease, for then meseemed we failed nothing.'

'That may not be,' said Galahad, 'but if it pleased Our Lord.'

By then the ship went from the land of Logris, and by adventure it arrived up betwixt two rocks passing great and marvellous; but there they might not land, for there was a swallow of the sea, save there was another ship, and upon it they might go without danger.

'Go we thither,' said the gentlewoman, 'and there shall we see adventures, for so is Our Lord's will.'

And when they came thither they found the ship rich enough, but they found neither man ne woman therein. But they found in the end of the ship two fair letters written, which said a dreadful word and a marvellous:

'Thou man, which shall enter into this ship, beware thou be in steadfast belief, for I am Faith, and therefore beware how thou enterest, for and thou fail I shall not help thee.'

Then said the gentlewoman, 'Percival, wot ye what I am?'
'Certes,' said [he], 'nay, to my witting.'

'Wit you well,' said she, 'that I am thy sister, which am daughter of King Pellinor, and therefore wit ye well ye are the man in the world that I most love; and if ye be not in perfect belief of Jesu Christ enter not in no manner of wise, for then should ye perish the ship, for he is so perfect he will suffer no sinner in him.'

When Percival understood that she was his very sister he was inwardly glad, and said, 'Fair sister, I shall enter therein, for if I be a miscreature or an untrue knight there shall I perish.'

swallow: whirlpool.

CHAPTER 3: *How Sir Galahad entered into the ship, and of a fair bed therein, with other marvellous things, and of a sword*

In the meanwhile Galahad blessed him, and entered therein; and then next the gentlewoman, and then Sir Bors and Sir Percival. And when they were in, it was so marvellous fair and rich that they marvelled; and in midst of the ship was a fair bed, and Galahad went thereto, and found there a crown of silk.

And at the feet was a sword, rich and fair, and it was drawn out of the sheath half a foot and more; and the sword was of divers fashions, and the pommel was of stone, and there was in him all manner of colours that any man might find, and every each of the colours had divers virtues; and the scales of the haft were of two ribs of divers beasts, the one beast was a serpent which was conversant in Caledonia, and is called the serpent of the fiend; and the bone of him is of such a virtue that there is no hand that handleth him shall never be weary nor hurt. And the other beast is a fish which is not right great, and haunteth the flood of Euphrates; and that fish is called Ertanax, and his bones be of such a manner of kind that who that handleth them shall have so much will that he shall never be weary, and he shall not think on joy nor sorrow that he hath had, but only that thing that he beholdeth before him.

AND AS FOR THIS SWORD THERE SHALL NEVER MAN BEGRIP HIM AT THE HANDLES BUT ONE, BUT HE SHALL PASS ALL OTHER.

'In the name of God,' said Percival, 'I shall assay to handle it.'

So he set his hand to the sword, but he might not begrip it.

'By my faith,' said he, 'now have I failed.'

Bors set his hand thereto and failed.

Then Galahad beheld the sword and saw letters like blood that said:

LET SEE WHO SHALL ASSAY TO DRAW ME OUT OF MY SHEATH, BUT IF HE BE MORE HARDIER THAN ANY OTHER; AND WHO THAT DRAWETH ME, WIT YE WELL THAT HE SHALL NEVER FAIL OF SHAME OF HIS BODY, OR TO BE WOUNDED TO THE DEATH.

'By my faith,' said Galahad, 'I would draw this sword out of the sheath, but the offending is so great that I shall not set my hand thereto.'

'Now sirs,' said the gentlewoman, 'wit ye well that the drawing of this sword is warned to all men save all only to you. Also this ship arrived in the realm of Logris; and that time was deadly war between King Labor, which was father unto the Maimed King, and King Hurlame, which was a Saracen. But then was he newly christened, so that men held him afterward one of the wittiest men of the world.

'And so upon a day it befell that King Labor and King Hurlame had assembled their folk upon the sea where this ship was arrived; and there King Hurlame was discomfit, and his men slain; and he was afeared to be dead, and fled to his ship, and there found this sword and drew it, and came out and found King Labor, the man in the world of all Christendom in whom was then the greatest faith. And when King Hurlame saw King Labor he dressed this sword, and smote him upon the helm so hard that he clave him and his horse to the earth with the first stroke of his sword.

'And it was in the realm of Logris; and so befell great pestilence and great harm to both realms. For sithen increased neither corn, ne grass, nor well-nigh no fruit, ne in the water was no fish; wherefore men callen it, the lands of the two marches, the Waste Land, for that dolorous stroke.

'And when King Hurlame saw this sword so carving, he turned again to fetch the scabbard, and so came into this ship and entered, and put up the sword in the sheath. And as soon as he had done it he fell down dead afore the bed. Thus was the sword proved, that none ne drew it but he were dead or maimed. So lay he there till a maiden came into the ship and

wittiest: wisest.

cast him out, for there was no man so hardy of the world to enter into that ship[1] for the defence.'

CHAPTER 4: *Of the marvels of the sword and of the scabbard*

And then beheld they the scabbard, it seemed to be of a serpent's skin, and thereon were letters of gold and silver, And the girdle was but poorly to come to, and not able to sustain such a rich sword. And the letters said:

'He which shall wield me ought to be more harder than any other, if he bear me as truly as me ought to be borne. For the body of him which I ought to hang by, he shall not be shamed in no place while he is girt with this girdle; nor never none be so hardy to do away this girdle; for it ought not to be done away but by the hands of a maid, and that she be a king's daughter and queen's, and she must be a maid all the days of her life, both in will and in deed. And if she break her virginity she shall die the most villainous death that ever died any woman.'

'Sir,' said Percival, 'turn this sword that we may see what is on the other side.' And it was red as blood, with black letters as any coal, which said:

'He that shall praise me most, most shall he find me to blame at a great need; and to whom I should be most debonair shall I be most felon, and that shall be at one time.'

'Fair brother,' said she to Percival, 'it befell after a forty year after the passion of Jesu Christ that Nacien, the brother-in-law of King Mordrains, was borne into a town more than fourteen days' journey from his country, by the commandment of Our Lord, into an isle, into the parts of the West, that men cleped the Isle of Turnance. So befell it that he found this ship at the entry of a rock, and he found the bed and this sword as we have heard now. Notforthan he had not so much hardiness to draw it; and there he

debonair: gracious.

dwelled an eight days, and at the ninth day there fell a great wind which departed him out of the isle, and brought him to another isle by a rock, and there he found the greatest giant that ever man might see. Therewith came that horrible giant to slay him; and then he looked about him and might not flee, and he had nothing to defend him with. So he ran to his sword, and when he saw it naked he praised it much, and then he shook it, and therewith he brake it in the midst. ·

' "Ah," said Nacien, "the thing that I most praised ought I now most to blame," and therewith he threw the pieces of his sword over his bed.

'And after he leapt over the board to fight with the giant, and slew him. And anon he entered the ship again, and the wind arose, and drove him through the sea, that by adventure he came to another ship where King Mordrains was, which had been tempted full evil with a fiend in the port of perilous rock.

'And when that one saw the other they made great joy of other, and either told other of their adventure, and how the sword failed him at his most need. When Mordrains saw the sword he praised it much: "But the breaking was not to do but by wickedness of thyself-ward, for thou art in some sin."

'And there he took the sword, and set the pieces together, and they soldered as fair as ever they were tofore; and there put he the sword in the sheath, and laid it down on the bed.

'Then heard they a voice that said, "Go out of this ship a little while, and enter into the other, for dread ye fall in deadly sin, for and ye be found in deadly sin ye may not escape but perish;" and so they went into the other ship.

'And as Nacien went over the board he was smitten with a sword on the right foot, that he fell down noseling to the ship's board; and therewith he said, "O God, how am I hurt."

'And then there came a voice and said, "Take thou that for thy forfeit that thou didst in drawing of this sword, therefore thou receivest a wound, for thou were never worthy to handle it, the writing maketh mention."

'In the name of God,' said Galahad, 'ye are right wise of these works.'

CHAPTER 5: *How King Pelles was smitten through both thighs because he drew the sword, and other marvellous histories*

'Sir,' said she, 'there was a king that hight Pelles, the Maimed King. And while he might ride he supported much Christendom and Holy Church. So upon a day he hunted in a wood of his which lasted unto the sea; and at the last he lost his hounds and his knights save only one: and there he and his knight went till that they came toward Ireland, and there he found the ship.

'And when he saw the letters and understood them, yet he entered, for he was right perfect of his life, but his knight had none hardiness to enter; and there found he this sword, and drew it out as much as ye may see. So therewith entered a spear wherewith he was smit him through both the thighs, and never sith might he be healed, ne nought shall tofore we come to him. Thus,' said she, 'was not King Pelles, your grandsire, maimed for his hardiness?'

'In the name of God, damosel,' said Galahad.

So they went toward the bed to behold all about it, and above the head there hung two swords. Also there were two spindles which were as white as any snow, and other that were as red as blood, and other above green as any emerald: of these three colours were the spindles, and of natural colour within, and without any painting.

'These spindles,' said the damosel, 'were when sinful Eve came to gather fruit, for which Adam and she were put out of paradise, she took with her the bough on which the apple hung on. Then perceived she that the branch was fair and green, and she remembered her the loss which came from the tree. Then she thought to keep the branch as long as she might. And for she had no coffer to keep it in, she put it in

337

the earth. So by the will of Our Lord the branch grew to a great tree within a little while, and was as white as any snow, branches, boughs, and leaves: that was a token a maiden planted it. But after God came to Adam, and bad him know his wife fleshly as nature required. So lay Adam with his wife under the same tree; and anon the tree which was white [was] full green as any grass, and all that came out of it; and in the same time that they meddled together there was Abel begotten: thus was the tree long of green colour.

'And so it befell many days after, under the same tree Cain slew Abel, whereof befell great marvel. For anon as Abel had received the death under the green tree, he lost the green colour and became red; and that was in tokening of the blood. And anon all the plants died thereof, but the tree grew and waxed marvellously fair, and it was the fairest tree and the most delectable that any man might behold and see; and so died the plants that grew out of it tofore that Abel was slain under it.

'So long dured the tree till that Solomon, King David's son, reigned, and held the land after his father. This Solomon was wise, and knew all the virtues of stones and trees, and so he knew the course of the stars and many other divers things. This Solomon had an evil wife, wherethrough he weened that there had been no good women, and so he despised them in his books. So answered a voice him once: "Solomon, if heaviness come to a man by a woman, ne reck thou never; for yet shall there come a woman whereof there shall come greater joy to man an hundred times more than this heaviness giveth sorrow; and that woman shall be born of thy lineage." Then when Solomon heard these words he held himself but a fool, and the truth he perceived by old books. Also the Holy Ghost showed him the coming of the glorious Virgin Mary. Then asked he of the voice, if it should be in the yard of his lineage. "Nay," said the voice, "but there shall come a man which shall be a maid, and the last of your blood, and he shall be as good a knight as Duke Joshua, thy brother-in-law.

yard: branch.

338

CHAPTER 6: *How Solomon took David's sword by the counsel of his wife, and of other matters marvellous*

'"Now have I certified thee of that thou stoodest in doubt."

'Then was Solomon glad that there should come any such of his lineage; but ever he marvelled and studied who that should be, and what his name might be. His wife perceived that he studied, and thought she would know it at some season; and so she waited her time, and asked of him the cause of his studying, and there he told her all together how the voice told him.

' "Well," said she, "I shall let make a ship of the best wood and most durable that men may find."

'So Solomon sent for all the carpenters of the land, and the best. And when they had made the ship the lady said to Solomon : "Sir," said she, "since it is so that this knight ought to pass all knights of chivalry which have been tofore him and shall come after him, moreover I shall tell you," said she, "ye shall go into Our Lord's temple, where is King David's sword, your father, the which is the marvelloust and the sharpest that ever was taken in any knight's hand. Therefore take that, and take off the pommel, and thereto make ye a pommel of precious stones, that it be so subtly made that no man perceive it but that they be all one; and after make there an hilt so marvellously and wonderly that no man may know it; and after make a marvellous sheath. And when ye have made all this I shall let make a girdle thereto such as shall please me."

'All this King Solomon did let make as she devised, both the ship and all the remnant. And when the ship was ready in the sea to sail, the lady let make a great bed and marvellous rich, and set her upon the bed's head, covered with silk, and laid the sword at the feet, and the girdles were of hemp, and therewith the king was angry.

' "Sir, wit ye well," said she, "that I have none so high a thing which were worthy to sustain so high a sword, and a maid shall bring other knights hereto, but I wot not when it shall be, ne what time."

'And there she let make a covering to the ship, of cloth of silk that should never rot for no manner of weather. Yet went that lady and made a carpenter to come to the tree which Abel was slain under.

' "Now," said she, "carve me out of this tree as much wood as will make me a spindle."

' "Ah madam," said he, "this is the tree the which our first mother planted."

' "Do it," said she, "or else I shall destroy thee."

'Anon as he began to work there came out drops of blood; and then would he have left, but she would not suffer him, and so he took away as much wood as might make a spindle: and so she made him to take as much of the green tree and of the white tree. And when these three spindles were shapen she made them to be fastened upon the selar of the bed.

'When Solomon saw this, he said to his wife, "Ye have done marvellously, for though all the world were here right now, he could not devise wherefore all this was made, but Our Lord Himself; and thou that hast done it wotest not what it shall betoken."

' "Now let it be," said she, "for ye shall hear tidings sooner than ye ween."

'Now shall ye hear a wonderful tale of King Solomon and his wife.

CHAPTER 7: A wonderful tale of King Solomon and his wife

'That night lay Solomon before the ship with little fellowship. And when he was asleep him thought there come from heaven a great company of angels, and alit into the ship, and took water which was brought by an angel, in a vessel of silver, and sprent all the ship. And after he came to the sword,

selar: canopy. sprent: sprinkled.

and drew letters on the hilt. And after went to the ship's board, and wrote there other letters which said: "Thou man that wilt enter within me, beware that thou be full within the faith, for I ne am but Faith and Belief."

'When Solomon espied these letters he was abashed, so that he durst not enter, and so drew him aback; and the ship was anon shoven in the sea, and he went so fast that he lost sight of him within a little while.

'And then a little voice said, "Solomon, the last knight of thy lineage shall rest in this bed."

'Then went Solomon and awaked his wife, and told her of the adventures of the ship.'

Now saith the history that a great while the three fellows beheld the bed and the three spindles. Then they were at certain that they were of natural colours without painting. Then they lift up a cloth which was above the ground, and there found a rich purse by seeming. And Percival took it, and found therein a writ and so he read it, and devised the manner of the spindles and of the ship, whence it came, and by whom it was made.

'Now,' said Galahad, 'where shall we find the gentlewoman that shall make new girdles to the sword?'

'Fair sir,' said Percival's sister, 'dismay you not, for by the leave of God I shall let make a girdle to the sword, such one as shall long thereto.'

And then she opened a box, and took out girdles which were seemly wrought with golden threads, and upon that were set full precious stones, and a rich buckle of gold.

'Lo, lords,' said she, 'here is a girdle that ought to be set about the sword. And wit ye well the greatest part of this girdle was made of my hair, which I loved well while that I was a woman of the world. But as soon as I wist that this adventure was ordained me I clipped off my hair, and made this girdle in the name of God.'

'Ye be well found,' said Sir Bors, 'for certes ye have put us out of great pain, wherein we should have entered ne had your tidings been.'

341

Then went the gentlewoman and set it on the girdle of the sword.

'Now,' said the fellowship, 'what is the name of the sword, and what shall we call it?'

'Truly,' said she, 'the name of the sword is the Sword with the Strange Girdles; and the sheath, Mover of Blood; for no man that hath blood in him ne shall never see the one part of the sheath which was made of the tree of life.'

Then they said to Galahad, 'In the name of Jesu Christ, and pray you that ye gird you with this sword which hath been desired so much in the realm of Logris.'

'Now let me begin,' said Galahad, 'to grip this sword for to give you courage; but wit ye well it longeth no more to me than it doth to you.'

And then he gripped about it with his fingers a great deal; and then she girt him about the middle with the sword.

'Now reck I not though I die, for now I hold me one of the blessed maidens of the world, which hath made the worthiest knight of the world.'

'Damosel,' said Galahad, 'ye have done so much that I shall be your knight all the days of my life.'

Then they went from that ship, and went to the other. And anon the wind drove them into the sea a great pace, but they had no victual: but it befell that they came on the morn to a castle that men call Carteloise, that was in the marches of Scotland.

And when they had passed the port, the gentlewoman said, 'Lords, here be men arriven that, and they wist that ye were of King Arthur's court, ye should be assailed anon.'

'Damosel,' said Galahad, 'He that cast us out of the rock shall deliver us from them.'

CHAPTER 8: *How Galahad and his fellows came to a castle, and how they were foughten withal, and how they slew their adversaries, and other matters*

So it befell as they spoken thus there came a squire by them, and asked what they were; and they said they were of King Arthur's house.

'Is that sooth?' said he. 'Now by my head,' said he, 'ye be ill arrayed;' and then turned he again unto the cliff fortress.

And within a while they heard an horn blow. Then a gentlewoman came to them, and asked them of whence they were; and they told her.

'Fair lords,' said she, 'for God's love turn again if ye may, for ye be come unto your death.'

'Nay,' they said, 'we will not turn again, for He shall help us in whose service we be entered in.'

Then as they stood talking there came knights well armed, and bad them yield them or else die.

'That yielding,' said they, 'shall be noyous to you.'

And therewith they let their horses run, and Sir Percival smote the foremost to the earth, and took his horse, and mounted thereupon, and the same did Galahad. Also Bors served another so, for they had no horses in that country, for they left their horses when they took their ship in other countries.

And so when they were horsed then began they to set upon them; and they of the castle fled into the strong fortress, and the three knights after them into the castle, and so alit on foot, and with their swords slew them down, and gat into the hall. Then when they beheld the great multitude of people that they had slain, they held themself great sinners.

'Certes,' said Bors, 'I ween and God had loved them that we should not have had power to have slain them thus. But they have done so much against Our Lord that He would not suffer them to reign no longer.'

noyous: troublesome.

'Say ye not so,' said Galahad, 'for if they misdid against God, the vengeance is not ours, but to Him which hath power thereof.'

So came there out of a chamber a good man which was a priest, and bare God's body in a cup. And when he saw them which lay dead in the hall he was all abashed; and Galahad did off his helm and kneeled down, and so did his two fellows.,

'Sir,' said they, 'have ye no dread of us, for we be of King Arthur's court.'

Then asked the good man how they were slain so suddenly, and they told it him.

'Truly,' said the good man, 'and ye might live as long as the world might endure, ne might ye have done so great an alms deed as this.'

'Sir,' said Galahad, 'I repent me much, inasmuch as they were christened.'

'Nay, repent you not,' said he, 'for they were not christened, and I shall tell you how that I wot of this castle. Here was Lord Earl Hernox not but one year, and he had three sons, good knights of arms, and a daughter, the fairest gentlewoman that men knew. So those three knights loved their sister so sore that they burnt in love, and so they lay by her, maugre her head. And for she cried to her father they slew her, and took their father and put him in prison, and wounded him nigh to the death, but a cousin of hers rescued him. And then did they great untruth : they slew clerks and priests, and made beat down chapels, that Our Lord's service might not be served ne said. And this same day her father sent to me for to be confessed and houselled; but such shame had never man as I had this day with the three brethren, but the earl bad me suffer, for he said they should not long endure, for three servants of Our Lord should destroy them, and now it is brought to an end. And by this may ye wit that Our Lord is not displeased with your deeds.'

'Certes,' said Galahad, 'and it had not pleased Our Lord, never should we have slain so many men in so little a while.'

And then they brought the Earl Hernox out of prison into the midst of the hall, that knew Galahad anon, and yet he saw him never afore but by revelation of Our Lord.

CHAPTER 9: *How the three knights, with Percival's sister, came into the waste forest, and of an hart and four lions, and other things*

Then began he to weep right tenderly, and said, 'Long have I abiden your coming, but for God's love hold me in your arms, that my soul may depart out of my body in so good a man's arms as ye be.'

'Gladly,' said Galahad.

And then one said on high, that all heard, 'Galahad, well hast thou avenged me on God's enemies. Now behoveth thee to go to the Maimed King as soon as thou mayest, for he shall receive by thee health which he hath abiden so long.'

And therewith the soul departed from the body, and Galahad made him to be buried as him ought to be. Right so departed the three knights, and Percival's sister with them.

And so they came into a waste forest, and there they saw afore them a white hart which four lions led. Then they took them to assent for to follow after for to know whither they repaired; and so they rode after a great pace till that they came to a valley, and thereby was an hermitage where a good man dwelled, and the hart and the lions entered also. So when they saw all this they turned to the chapel, and saw the good man in a religious weed and in the armour of Our Lord, for he would sing mass of the Holy Ghost; and so they entered in and heard mass.

And at the secrets of the mass they three saw the hart become a man, the which marvelled them, and set him upon the altar in a rich siege; and saw the four lions were changed, the one to the form of a man, the other to the form of a lion, and the third to an eagle, and the fourth was changed unto an ox. Then took they their siege where the hart sat, and went out through a glass window, and there was nothing

345

perished nor broken; and they heard a voice say, 'In such a manner entered the Son of God in the womb of a maid Mary, whose virginity ne was perished ne hurt.'

And when they heard these words they fell down to the earth and were astonied; and therewith was a great clearness. And when they were come to theirself again they went to the good man and prayed him that he would say them truth.

'What thing have ye seen?' said he.

And they told him all that they had seen.

'Ah lords,' said he, 'ye be welcome; now wot I well ye be the good knights the which shall bring the Sangrail to an end; for ye be they unto whom Our Lord shall show great secrets, And well ought Our Lord be signified to an hart, for the hart when he is old he waxeth young again in his white skin. Right so cometh again Our Lord from death to life, for He lost earthly flesh that was the deadly flesh, which He had taken in the womb of the Blessed Virgin Mary; and for that cause appeared Our Lord as a white hart without spot. And the four that were with Him is to understand the four evangelists which set in writing a part of Jesu Christ's deeds that He did sometime when He was among you an earthly man; for wit ye well never erst ne might no knight know the truth, for ofttimes or this Our Lord showed Him unto good men and unto good knights, in likeness of an hart, but I suppose from henceforth ye shall see no more.'

And then they joyed much, and dwelled there all that day. And upon the morrow when they had heard mass they departed and commended the good man to God: and so they came to a castle and passed by.

So there came a knight armed after them and said, 'Lords, hark what I shall say to you:

CHAPTER 10: *How they were desired of a strange custom, the which they would not obey, wherefore they fought and slew many knights*

'This gentlewoman that ye lead with you is a maid?'

'Sir,' said she, 'a maid I am.'

Then he took her by the bridle and said, 'By the Holy Cross, ye shall not escape me tofore ye have yielden the custom of this castle.'

'Let her go,' said Percival, 'ye be not wise, for a maid in what place she cometh is free.'

So in the meanwhile there came out a ten or twelve knights armed, out of the castle, and with them came gentlewomen which held a dish of silver. And then they said, 'This gentlewoman must yield us the custom of this castle.'

'Sir,' said a knight, 'what maid passeth hereby shall give this dish full of blood of her right arm.'

'Blame have he,' said Galahad, 'that brought up such customs, and so God me save, I ensure you of this gentlewoman ye shall fail while that I live.'

'So God me help,' said Percival, 'I had lever be slain.'

'And I also,' said Sir Bors.

'By my troth,' said the knight, 'then shall ye die, for ye may not endure against us though ye were the best knights of the world.'

Then let they run each other, and the three fellows beat the ten knights, and then set their hands to their swords and beat them down and slew them. Then there came out of the castle a three score knights armed.

'Fair lords,' said the three fellows, 'have mercy on yourself and have not ado with us.'

'Nay, fair lords,' said the knights of the castle, 'we counsel you to withdraw you, for ye be the best knights of the world, and therefore do no more, for ye have done enough. We will let you go with this harm, but we must needs have the custom.'

'Certes,' said Galahad, 'for nought speak ye.'

'Well,' said they, 'will ye die?'

'We be not yet come thereto,' said Galahad.

Then began they to meddle together, and Galahad, with the strange girdles, drew his sword, and smote on the right hand and on the left hand, and slew what that ever abode him, and did such marvels that there was none that saw him they weened he had been none earthly man, but a monster. And his two fellows halp him passing well, and so they held the journey every each in like hard till it was night: then must they needs depart.

So came in a good knight, and said to the three fellows, 'If ye will come in tonight and take such harbour as here is ye shall be right welcome and we shall ensure you by the faith of our bodies, and as we be true knights, to leave you in such estate tomorrow as we find you, without any falsehood. And as soon as ye know of the custom we dare say ye will accord.'

'Therefore for God's love,' said the gentlewoman, 'go thither and spare not for me.'

'Go we,' said Galahad; and so they entered into the chapel.

And when they were alit they made great joy of them. So within a while the three knights asked the custom of the castle and wherefore it was.

'What it is,' said they, 'we will say you sooth:

CHAPTER 11: *How Sir Percival's sister bled a dish full of blood for to heal a lady, wherefore she died; and how that the body was put in a ship*

'There is in this castle a gentlewoman which we and this castle is hers, and many other. So it befell many years agone there fell upon her a malady; and when she had lain a great while she fell unto a mesel, and of no leech she could have no remedy. But at the last an old man said and she might have a dish full of blood of a maid and a clean virgin in will and

mesel: sickness.

in work, and a king's daughter, that blood should be her health, and for to anoint her withal; and for this thing was this custom made.'

'Now,' said Percival's sister, 'fair knights, I see well that this gentlewoman is but dead.'

'Certes,' said Galahad, 'and ye bleed so much ye may die.'

'Truly,' said she, 'and I die for to heal her I shall get me great worship and soul's health, and worship to my lineage, and better is one harm than twain. And therefore there shall be no more battle, but tomorn I shall yield you your custom of this castle.'

And then there was great joy more than there was tofore, for else had there been mortal war upon the morn; notwithstanding she would none other, whether they would or nold. That night were the three fellows eased with the best; and on the morn they heard mass, and Sir Percival's sister bad bring forth the sick lady. So she was, the which was evil at ease.

Then said she, 'Who shall let me blood?'

So one came forth and let her blood, and she bled so much that the dish was full.

Then she lift up her hand and blessed her; and then she said to the lady, 'Madam, I am come to the death for to make you whole, for God's love pray for me.' With that she fell in a swoon.

Then Galahad and his two fellows start up to her, and lift her up and staunched her, but she had bled so much that she might not live.

Then she said when she was awaked, 'Fair brother Percival, I die for the healing of this lady, so I require you that ye bury me not in this country, but as soon as I am dead put me in a boat at the next haven, and let me go as adventure will lead me; and as soon as ye three come to the City of Sarras, there to achieve the Holy Grail, ye shall find me under a tower arrived, and there bury me in the spiritual place; for I say you so much, there Galahad shall be buried, and ye also, in the same place.'

Then Percival understood these words, and granted it her, weeping.

And then said a voice, 'Lords and fellows, tomorrow at the hour of prime ye three shall depart every each from other, till the adventure bring you to the Maimed King.'

Then asked she her Saviour; and as soon as she had received it the soul departed from the body.

So the same day was the lady healed, when she was anointed withal. Then Sir Percival made a letter of all that she had holpen them as in strange adventures, and put it in her right hand, and so laid her in a barge, and covered it with black silk; and so the wind arose, and drove the barge from the land, and all knights beheld it till it was out of their sight.

Then they drew all to the castle, and so forthwith there fell a sudden tempest and a thunder, lait, and rain, as all the earth would have broken. So half the castle turned up-so-down. So it passed evensong or the tempest was ceased.

Then they saw afore them a knight armed and wounded hard in the body and in the head, that said, 'O God, succour me for now it is need.'

After this knight came another knight and a dwarf, which cried to them afar, 'Stand, ye may not escape!'

Then the wounded knight held up his hands to God that he should not die in such tribulation.

'Truly,' said Galahad, 'I shall succour him for His sake that he calleth upon.'

'Sir,' said Bors, 'I shall do it, for it is not for you, for he is but one knight.'

'Sir,' said he, 'I grant.'

So Sir Bors took his horse, and commended him to God, and rode after, to rescue the wounded knight.

Now turn we to the two fellows.

lait: lightning.

CHAPTER 12: *How Galahad and Percival found in a castle many tombs of maidens that had bled to death*

Now saith the story that all night Galahad and Percival were in a chapel in their prayers, for to save Sir Bors. So on the morrow they dressed them in their harness toward the castle, to wit what was fallen of them therein. And when they came there they found neither man ne woman that he ne was dead by the vengeance of Our Lord.

With that they heard a voice that said, 'This vengeance is for blood-shedding of maidens.'

Also they found at the end of the chapel a churchyard, and therein might they see a three score fair tombs, and that place was so fair and so delectable that it seemed them there had been none tempest, for there lay the bodies of all the good maidens which were martyred for the sick lady's sake. Also they found the names of every each, and of what blood they were come, and all were of kings' blood, and twelve of them were kings' daughters. Then they departed and went into a forest.

'Now,' said Percival unto Galahad, 'we must depart, so pray we Our Lord that we may meet together in short time;' then they did off their helms and kissed together, and wept at their departing.

CHAPTER 13: *How Sir Launcelot entered into the ship where Sir Percival's sister lay dead, and how he met with Sir Galahad, his son*

Now saith the history, that when Launcelot was come to the water of Mortaise, as it is rehearsed before, he was in great peril, and so he laid him down and slept and took the adventure that God would send him.

So when he was asleep there came a vision unto him and said, 'Launcelot, arise up and take thine armour, and enter into the first ship that thou shalt find.'

And when he heard these words he start up and saw great clearness about him. And then he lift up his hand and blessed him, and so took his arms and made him ready; and so by adventure he came by a strand, and found a ship the which was without sail or oar.

And as soon as he was within the ship there he felt the most sweetness that ever he felt, and he was fulfilled with all thing that he thought on or desired.

Then he said, 'Fair sweet Father, Jesu Christ, I wot not in what joy I am, for this joy passeth all earthly joys that ever I was in.'

And so in this joy he laid him down to the ship's board, and slept till day. And when he awoke he found there a fair bed, and therein lying a gentlewoman dead, the which was Sir Percival's sister.

And as Launcelot devised her, he espied in her right hand a writ, the which he read, the which told him all the adventures that ye have heard tofore, and of what lineage she was come. So with this gentlewoman Sir Launcelot was a month and more. If ye would ask how he lived, He that fed the people of Israel with manna in desert, so was he fed; for every day when he had said his prayers he was sustained with the grace of the Holy Ghost.

So on a night he went to play him by the water side, for he was somewhat weary of the ship. And then he listened and heard an horse come, and one riding upon him. And when he came nigh he seemed a knight. And so he let him pass, and went thereas the ship was; and there he alit, and took the saddle and the bridle and put the horse from him, and went into the ship.

And then Launcelot dressed unto him, and said, 'Ye be welcome.'

And he answered and saluted him again, and asked him, 'What is your name? For much my heart giveth unto you.'

'Truly,' said he, 'my name is Launcelot du Lake.'

'Sir,' said he, 'then be ye welcome, for ye were the beginner of me in this world.'

'Ah,' said he, 'are ye Galahad?'

'Yea, forsooth,' said he; and so he kneeled down and asked him his blessing, and after took off his helm and kissed him.

And there was great joy between them, for there is no tongue can tell the joy that they made either of other, and many a friendly word spoken between, as kind would, the which is no need here to be rehearsed. And there every each told other of their adventures and marvels that were befallen to them in many journeys sith that they departed from the court.

Anon, as Galahad saw the gentlewoman dead in the bed, he knew her well enough, and told great worship of her, that she was the best maid living, and it was great pity of her death. But when Launcelot heard how the marvellous sword was gotten, and who made it, and all the marvels rehearsed afore, then he prayed Galahad, his son, that he would show him the sword, and so he did; and anon he kissed the pommel, and the hilts, and the scabbard.

'Truly,' said Launcelot, 'never erst knew I of so high adventures done, and so marvellous and strange.'

So dwelt Launcelot and Galahad within that ship half a year, and served God daily and nightly with all their power; and often they arrived in isles far from folk, where there repaired none but wild beasts, and there they found many strange adventures and perillous, which they brought to an end; but for those adventures were with wild beasts, and not in the quest of the Sangrail, therefore the tale maketh here no mention thereof, for it would be too long to tell of all those adventures that befell them.

CHAPTER 14: *How a knight brought to Sir Galahad an horse, and bad him come from his father, Sir Launcelot*

So after, on a Monday, it befell that they arrived in the edge of a forest tofore a cross; and then saw they a knight armed all in white, and was richly horsed, and led in his right hand a white horse; and so he came to the ship, and saluted the two knights on the High Lord's behalf, and said, 'Galahad, sir, ye have been long enough with your father, come out of the ship, and start upon this horse, and go where the adventures shall lead thee in the quest of the Sangrail.'

Then he went to his father and kissed him sweetly, and said, 'Fair sweet father, I wot not when I shall see you more till I see the body of Jesu Christ.'

'I pray you,' said Launcelot, 'pray ye to the High Father that He hold me in His service.'

And so he took his horse, and there they heard a voice that said, 'Think for to do well, for the one shall never see the other before the dreadful day of doom.'

'Now, son Galahad,' said Launcelot, 'since we shall depart, and never see other, I pray to the High Father to conserve me and you both.'

'Sir,' said Galahad, 'no prayer availeth so much as yours.'

And therewith Galahad entered into the forest. And the wind arose, and drove Launcelot more than a month throughout the sea, where he slept but little, but prayed to God that he might see some tidings of the Sangrail.

So it befell on a night, at midnight, he arrived afore a castle, on the back side, which was rich and fair, and there was a postern opened toward the sea, and was open without any keeping, save two lions kept the entry; and the moon shone clear.

Anon Sir Launcelot heard a voice that said, 'Launcelot, go out of this ship and enter into the castle, where thou shalt see a great part of thy desire.'

Then he ran to his arms, and so armed him, and so went to the gate and saw the lions. Then set he hand to his sword and drew it. Then there came a dwarf suddenly, and smote him on the arm so sore that the sword fell out of his hand.

Then heard he a voice say, 'O man of evil faith and poor belief, wherefore trowest thou more on thy harness than in thy Maker, for He might more avail thee than thine armour, in whose service that thou art set.'

Then said Launcelot, 'Fair Father Jesu Christ, I thank thee of Thy great mercy that Thou reprovest me of my misdeed; now see I well that Ye hold me for Your servant.'

Then took he again his sword and put it up in his sheath, and made a cross in his forehead, and came to the lions, and they made semblant to do him harm. Notwithstanding he passed by them without hurt, and entered into the castle to the chief fortress, and there were they all at rest.

Then Launcelot entered in so armed, for he found no gate nor door but it was open. And at the last he found a chamber whereof the door was shut, and he set his hand thereto to have opened it, but he might not.

CHAPTER 15 : *How Sir Launcelot was tofore the door of the chamber wherein the Holy Sangrail was*

Then he enforced him mickle to undo the door. Then he listened and heard a voice which sang so sweetly that it seemed none earthly thing; and him thought the voice said, 'Joy and honour be to the Father of Heaven.'

Then Launcelot kneeled down tofore the chamber, for well wist he that there was the Sangrail within that chamber. Then said he,

'Fair sweet Father, Jesu Christ, if ever I did thing that pleased Thee, Lord for Thy pity ne have me not in despite for my sins done aforetime, and that Thou show me something of that I seek.'

And with that he saw the chamber door open, and there came out a great clearness, that the house was as bright as all the torches of the world had been there. So came he to the chamber door, and would have entered.

And anon a voice said to him, 'Flee, Launcelot, and enter not, for thou oughtest not to do it; and if thou enter thou shalt forthink it.'

Then he withdrew him aback right heavy. Then looked he up in the midst of the chamber, and saw a table of silver, and the holy vessel, covered with red samite, and many angels about it, whereof one held a candle of wax burning, and the other held a cross, and the ornaments of an altar. And before the holy vessel he saw a good man clothed as a priest. And it seemed that he was at the sacring of the mass. And it seemed to Launcelot that above the priest's hands were three men, whereof the two put the youngest by likeness between the priest's hands; and so he lift it up right high, and it seemed to show so to the people. And then Launcelot marvelled not a little, for him thought the priest was so greatly charged of the figure that him seemed that he should fall to the earth.

And when he saw none about him that would help him, then came he to the door a great pace, and said, 'Fair Father Jesu Christ, ne take it for no sin though I help the good man which hath great need of help.'

Right so entered he into the chamber, and came toward the table of silver; and when he came nigh he felt a breath, that him thought it was intermeddled with fire, which smote him so sore in the visage that him thought it burnt his visage; and therewith he fell to the earth, and had no power to arise, as he that was so araged, that had lost the power of his body, and his hearing, and his seeing. Then felt he many hands about him, which took him up and bare him out of the chamber door, without any amending of his swoon, and left him there, seeming dead to all people.

So upon the morrow when it was fair day they within were arisen, and found Launcelot lying afore the chamber door. All they marvelled how that he came in, and so they looked upon him, and felt his pulse to wit whether there were any life in him; and so they found life in him, but he might not stand nor stir no member that he had. And so they took him by every part of the body, and bare him into a chamber, and laid him in a rich bed, far from all folk; and so he lay four days. Then the one said he was alive, and the other said, 'Nay.'

'In the name of God,' said an old man, 'for I do you verily to wit he is not dead, but he is so full of life as the mightiest

of you all; and therefore I counsel you that he be well kept
till God send him life again.'

CHAPTER 16: *How Sir Launcelot had lain four and twenty*
days and as many nights as a dead man, and other divers
matters

In such manner they kept Launcelot four and twenty days
and all so many nights, that ever he lay still as a dead man;
and at the twenty-fifth day befell him after midday that he
opened his eyen.

And when he saw folk he made great sorrow, and said,
'Why have ye awaked me, for I was more at ease than I am
now. O Jesu Christ, who might be so blessed that might see
openly Thy great marvels of secretness there where no sinner
may be !'

'What have ye seen?' said they about him.

'I have seen,' said he, 'so great marvels that no tongue may
tell, and more than any heart can think, and had not my sin[1]
been here afore me I had seen much more.'

Then they told him how he had lain there four and twenty
days and nights. Then him thought it was punishment for
the four and twenty years that he had been a sinner, wherefore Our Lord put him in penance four and twenty days and
nights.

Then looked Sir Launcelot afore him, and saw the hair
which he had borne nigh a year, for that he forthought him
right much that he had broken his promise unto the hermit,
which he had avowed to do. Then they asked how it stood
with him.

'Forsooth,' said he, 'I am whole of body, thanked be Our
Lord; therefore, sirs, for God's love tell me where I am.'

Then said they all that he was in the Castle of Carbonek.

Therewith came a gentlewoman and brought him a shirt
of small linen cloth, but he changed not there, but took the
hair to him again.

357

'Sir,' said they, 'the quest of the Sangrail is achieved now right in you, that never shall ye see of the Sangrail no more than ye have seen.'

'Now I thank God,' said Launcelot, 'of His great mercy of that I have seen, for it sufficeth me; for as I suppose no man in this world hath lived better than I have done to achieve that I have done.'

And therewith he took the hair and clothed him in it, and above that he put a linen shirt, and after a robe of scarlet, fresh and new. And when he was so arrayed they marvelled all, for they knew him that he was Launcelot, the good knight.

And then they said all, 'O my lord Sir Launcelot, be that ye?'

And he said, 'Truly I am he.'

Then came word to King Pelles that the knight that had lain so long dead was Sir Launcelot. Then was the king right glad, and went to see him. And when Launcelot saw him come he dressed him against him, and there made the king great joy of him. And there the king told him tidings that his fair daughter was dead.

Then Launcelot was right heavy of it, and said, 'Sir, me forthinketh the death of your daughter, for she was a full fair lady, fresh and young. And well I wot she bare the best knight that is now on earth, or that ever was sith God was born.'

So the king held him there four days, and on the morrow he took his leave at King Pelles and at all the fellowship, and thanked them of the great labour.

Right so as they sat at their dinner in the chief sale, then was so befall that the Sangrail had fulfilled the tables with all manner of meats that any heart might think. So as they sat they saw all the doors and the windows of the place were shut without man's hand, whereof they were all abashed, and none wist what to do.

And then it happed suddenly that a knight came to the chief door and knocked, and cried, 'Undo the door.'

sale: hall.

But they would not.

And ever he cried, 'Undo !' but they would not.

And at last it noyed them so much that the king himself arose and came to a window there where the knight called.

Then he said, 'Sir knight, ye shall not enter at this time while the Sangrail is here, and therefore go into another; for certes ye be none of the knights of the quest, but one of them which hath served the fiend, and hast left the service of Our Lord.'

And he was passing wroth at the king's words.

'Sir knight,' said the king, 'since ye would so fain enter, say me of what country ye be.'

'Sir,' said he, 'I am of the realm of Logris, and my name is Ector de Maris, and brother unto my lord, Sir Launcelot.'

'In the name of God,' said the king, 'me forthinketh of that I have said, for your brother is here within.'

And when Ector de Maris understood that his brother was there, for he was the man in the world that he most dread and loved, and then he said, 'Ah God, now doubleth my sorrow and shame. Full truly said the good man of the hill unto Gawain and to me of our dreams.'

Then went he out of the court as fast as his horse might, and so throughout the castle.

CHAPTER 17: *How Sir Launcelot returned toward Logris, and of other adventures which he saw in the way*

Then King Pelles came to Sir Launcelot and told him tidings of his brother, whereof he was sorry, that he wist not what to do.

So Sir Launcelot departed, and took his arms, and said he would go see the realm of Logris, 'which I have not seen in a twelvemonth.' And therewith he commended the king to God, and so rode through many realms.

And at the last he came to a white abbey, and there they

made him that night great cheer; and on the morn he arose and heard mass.

And afore an altar he found a rich tomb, which was newly made; and then he took heed, and saw the sides written with gold which said: HERE LIETH KING BAGDEMAGUS OF GORE, WHICH KING ARTHUR'S NEPHEW SLEW; and named him, Sir Gawain.

Then was not he a little sorry, for Launcelot loved him much more than any other, and had it been any other than Gawain he should not have escaped from death to life; and said to himself, 'Ah Lord God, this is a great hurt unto King Arthur's court, the loss of such a man.'

And then he departed and came to the abbey where Galahad did the adventure of the tombs, and won the white shield with the red cross; and there had he great cheer all that night.

And on the morn he turned unto Camelot, where he found King Arthur and the queen. But many of the knights of the Round Table were slain and destroyed more than half. And so three were come home, Sir Ector, Gawain and Lionel, and many other that needen not to be rehearsed. And all the court was passing glad of Sir Launcelot, and the king asked him many tidings of his son Galahad.

And there Launcelot told the king of his adventures that had befallen him since he departed. And also he told him of the adventures of Galahad, Percival, and Bors, which that he knew by the letter of the dead damosel, and as Galahad had told him.

'Now God would,' said the king, 'that they were all three here.'

'That shall never be,' said Launcelot, 'for two of them shall ye never see, but one of them shall come again.'

Now leave we this story and speak of Galahad.

CHAPTER 18: *How Galahad came to King Mordrains, and of other matters and adventures*

Now saith the story that Galahad rode many journeys in vain. And at the last he came to the abbey where King Mordrains was, and when he heard that, he thought he would abide to see him. And upon the morn, when he had heard mass, Galahad came unto King Mordrains, and anon the king saw him, which had lain blind of long time.

And then he dressed him against him, and said, 'Galahad, the servant of Jesu Christ, whose coming I have abiden so long, now embrace me and let me rest on thy breast, so that I may rest between thine arms, for thou art a clean virgin above all knights, as the flower of the lily in whom virginity is signified, and thou art the rose the which is the flower of all good virtue, and in colour of fire. For the fire of the Holy Ghost is take so in thee that my flesh which was all dead of oldness is become young again.'

Then Galahad heard his words, then he embraced him and all his body.

Then said he: 'Fair Lord Jesu Christ, now I have my will. Now I require Thee, in this point that I am in, Thou come and visit me.'

And anon Our Lord heard his prayer; therewith the soul departed from the body.

And then Galahad put him in the earth as a king ought to be, and so departed and so came into a perilous forest where he found the well the which boiled with great waves, as the tale telleth tofore. And as soon as Galahad set his hand thereto, it ceased so that it burnt no more, and the heat departed. For that it burnt it was a sign of lechery, the which was that time much used. But that heat might not abide his pure virginity. And this was taken in the country for a miracle. And so ever after was it called Galahad's well.

Then by adventure he came into the country of Gore, and into the abbey where Launcelot had been toforehand, and found the tomb of King Bagdemagus, but he was founder thereof Joseph of Arimathea's son, and the tomb of Simeon where Launcelot had failed. Then he looked into a croft under the minster, and there he saw a tomb which burnt full marvellously. Then asked he the brethren what it was.

'Sir,' said they, 'a marvellous adventure that may not be brought unto none end but by him that passeth of bounty and of knighthood all them of the Round Table.'

'I would,' said Galahad, 'that ye would lead me thereto.'

'Gladly,' said they.

And so they led him till a cave. And he went down upon greces, and came nigh the tomb. And then the flaming failed, and the fire stanched, the which many a day had been great.

Then came there a voice that said, 'Much are ye behold to thank Our Lord, the which hath given you a good hour, that ye may draw out the souls of earthly pain, and to put them into the joys of paradise. I am of your kindred, the which have dwelled in this heat this three hundred four and fifty winter to be purged of the sin that I did against Joseph of Arimathea.'

Then Galahad took the body in his arms and bare it into the minster. And that night lay Galahad in the abbey; and on the morn he gave him service, and put him in the earth afore the high altar.

CHAPTER 19: *How Sir Percival and Sir Bors met with Sir Galahad, and how they came to the Castle of Carbonek, and other matters*

So departed he from thence, and commended the brethren to God; and so he rode five days till that he came to the Maimed King. And ever followed Percival the five days, asking where he had been; and so one told him how the adventures of Logris were achieved.

So on a day it befell that they came out of a great forest,

greces: stairs.

and there they met at traverse with Sir Bors, the which rode alone. It is none need to tell if they were glad; and them he saluted, and they yielded him honour and good adventure, and every each told other.

Then said Bors, 'It is more than a year and an half that I ne lay ten times where men dwelled, but in wild forests and in mountains, but God was ever my comfort.'

Then rode they a great while till that they came to the Castle of Carbonek. And when they were entered within the castle King Pelles knew them; then there was great joy, for they wist well by their coming that they had fulfilled the quest of the Sangrail.

Then Eliazar, King Pelles' son, brought tofore them the broken sword wherewith Joseph was stricken through the thigh. Then Bors set his hand thereto, if that he might have soldered it again; but it would not be. Then he took it to Percival, but he had no more power thereto than he.

'Now have ye it again,' said Percival to Galahad, 'for and it be ever achieved by any bodily man ye must do it.'

And then he took the pieces and set them together, and they seemed that they had never been broken, and as well as it had been first forged. And when they within espied that the adventure of the sword was achieved, then they gave the sword to Bors, for it might not be better set; for he was a good knight and a worthy man.

And a little afore even the sword arose great and marvellous, and was full of great heat that many men fell for dread. And anon alit a voice among them, and said, 'They that ought not to sit at the table of Jesu Christ arise, for now shall very knights be fed.'

So they went thence, all save King Pelles and Eliazar, his son, the which were holy men, and a maid which was his niece; and so these three fellows and they three were there, no more.

Anon they saw knights all armed came in at the hall door, and did off their helms and their arms, and said unto Galahad, 'Sir, we have hied right much for to be with you at this table where the holy meat shall be departed.'

Then said he, 'Ye be welcome, but of whence be ye?'

So three of them said they were of Gaul, and other three said they were of Ireland, and the other three said they were of Denmark.

So as they sat thus there came out a bed of tree, of a chamber, the which four gentlewomen brought; and in the bed lay a good man sick, and a crown of gold upon his head; and there in the midst of the place they set him down, and went again their way.

Then he lift up his head, and said, 'Galahad, knight, ye be welcome, for much have I desired your coming, for in such anguish I have been long. But now I trust to God the term is come that my pain shall be allayed, that I shall pass out of this world so as it was promised me long ago.'

Therewith a voice said, 'There be two among you that be not in the quest of the Sangrail, and therefore depart ye.'

CHAPTER 20: *How Galahad and his fellows were fed of the Holy Sangrail, and how Our Lord appeared to them, and other things*

Then King Pelles and his son departed. And therewithal beseemed them that there came a man, and four angels from heaven, clothed in likeness of a bishop, and had a cross in his hand; and these four angels bare him up in a chair, and set him down before the table of silver whereupon the Sangrail was; and it seemed that he had in the midst of his forehead letters the which said, 'See ye here Joseph, the first bishop of Christendom, the same which Our Lord succoured in the city of Sarras in the spiritual place.'

Then the knights marvelled, for that bishop was dead more than three hundred year tofore.

tree: wood.

'O knights,' said he, 'marvel not, for I was sometime an earthly man.'

With that they heard the chamber door open, and there they saw angels; and two bare candles of wax, and the third a towel, and the fourth a spear which bled marvellously, that three drops fell within a box which he held with his other hand. And they set the candles upon the table, and the third the towel upon the vessel, and the fourth the holy spear even upright upon the vessel.

And then the bishop made semblant as though he would have gone to the sacring of the mass. And then he took an *ubblye* which was made in likeness of bread. And at the lifting up there came a figure in likeness of a child, and the visage was as red and as bright as any fire, and smote himself into the bread, so that they all saw it that the bread was formed of a fleshly man; and then he put it into the holy vessel again, and then he did that longed to a priest to do to a mass.

And then he went to Galahad and kissed him, and bad him go and kiss his fellows : and so he did anon.

'Now,' said he, 'servants of Jesu Christ, ye shall be fed afore this table with sweetmeats that never knights tasted.'

And when he had said, he vanished away. And they set them at the table in great dread, and made their prayers.

Then looked they and saw a man come out of the holy vessel, that had all the signs of the passion of Jesu Christ, bleeding all openly, and said, 'My knights, and my servants, and my true children, which be come out of deadly life into spiritual life, I will now no longer hide me from you, but ye shall see now a part of my secrets and of my hid things : now holdeth and receiveth the high meat which ye have so much desired.'

Then took he himself the holy vessel and came to Galahad; and he kneeled down, and there he received his Saviour, and after him so received all his fellows; and they thought it so sweet that it was marvellous to tell.

ubblye : oblation.

Then said he to Galahad, 'Son, wotest thou what I hold betwixt my hands?'

'Nay,' said he, 'but if Ye will tell me.'

'This is,' said he, 'the holy dish wherein I ate the lamb on Sher-Thursday. And now hast thou seen that thou most desired to see, but yet hast thou not seen it so openly as thou shalt see it in the city of Sarras in the spiritual place. Therefore thou must go hence and bear with thee this holy vessel; for this night it shall depart from the realm of Logris, that it shall never be seen more here. And wotest thou wherefore? For he is not served nor worshipped to his right by them of this land, for they be turned to evil living; therefore I shall disherit them of the honour which I have done them. And therefore go ye three tomorrow unto the sea, where ye shall find your ship ready, and with you take the sword with the strange girdles, and no more with you but Sir Percival and Sir Bors. Also I will that ye take with you of the blood of this spear for to anoint the Maimed King, both his legs and all his body, and he shall have his health.'

'Sir,' said Galahad, 'why shall not these other fellows go with us?'

'For this cause: for right as I departed my apostles one here and another there, so I will that ye depart; and two of you shall die in my service, but one of you shall come again and tell tidings.' Then gave he them his blessing and vanished away.

CHAPTER 21: *How Galahad anointed with the blood of the spear the Maimed King, and of other adventures*

And Galahad went anon to the spear which lay upon the table, and touched the blood with his fingers, and came after to the Maimed King and anointed his legs.

And therewith he clothed him anon, and start upon his feet out of his bed as an whole man, and thanked Our Lord

Sher-Thursday: Thursday before Easter.

that He had healed him. And that was not to the world-ward, for anon he yielded him to a place of religion of white monks, and was a full holy man.

That same night about midnight came a voice among them which said, 'My sons and not my chief sons, my friends and not my warriors, go ye hence where ye hope best to do and as I bad you.'

'Ah, thanked be Thou, Lord, that Thou wilt vouchsafe to call us, Thy sinners. Now may we well prove that we have not lost our pains.'

And anon in all haste they took their harness and departed.

But the three knights of Gaul, one of them hight Claudine, King Claudas' son, and the other two were great gentlemen, then prayed Galahad to every each of them, that if they come to King Arthur's court that they should 'salute my lord, Sir Launcelot, my father, and of them of the Round Table;' and prayed them if that they came on that part that they should not forget it.

Right so departed Galahad, Percival and Bors with him; and so they rode three days, and then they came to a rivage, and found the ship whereof the tale speaketh of tofore. And when they came to the board they found in the midst the table of silver which they had left with the Maimed King, and the Sangrail which was covered with red samite.

Then were they glad to have such things in their fellowship; and so they entered and made great reverence thereto; and Galahad fell in his prayer long time to Our Lord, that at what time he asked, that he should pass out of this world.

So much he prayed till a voice said to him, 'Galahad, thou shalt have thy request; and when thou askest the death of thy body thou shalt have it, and then shalt thou find the life of the soul.'

Percival heard this, and prayed him, of fellowship that was between them, to tell him wherefore he asked such things.

'That shall I tell you,' said Galahad; 'the other day when we saw a part of the adventures of the Sangrail I was in such

rivage: shore.

a joy of heart, that I trow never man was that was earthly. And therefore I wot well, when my body is dead my soul shall be in great joy to see the Blessed Trinity every day, and the Majesty of Our Lord, Jesu Christ.'

So long were they in the ship that they said to Galahad, 'Sir, in this bed ought ye to lie, for so saith the scripture.'

And so he laid him down and slept a great while; and when he awaked he looked afore him and saw the city of Sarras. And as they would have landed they saw the ship wherein Percival had put his sister in.

'Truly,' said Percival, 'in the name of God, well hath my sister holden us covenant.'

Then took they out of the ship the table of silver, and he took it to Percival and to Bors, to go tofore, and Galahad came behind. And right so they went to the city, and at the gate of the city they saw an old man crooked. Then Galahad called him and bad him help to bear this heavy thing.

'Truly,' said the old man, 'it is ten year ago that I might not go but with crutches.'

'Care thou not,' said Galahad, 'and arise up and show thy good will.'

And so he assayed, and found himself as whole as ever he was. Then ran he to the table, and took one part against Galahad. And anon arose there great noise in the city, that a cripple was made whole by knights marvels that entered into the city.

Then anon after, the three knights went to the water, and brought up into the palace Percival's sister, and buried her as richly as a king's daughter ought to be.

And when the king of the city, which was cleped Estorause, saw the fellowship, he asked them of whence they were, and what thing it was that they had brought upon the table of silver. And they told him the truth of the Sangrail, and the power which that God had set there.

Then the king was a tyrant, and was come of the line of paynims, and took them and put them in prison in a deep hole.

CHAPTER 22: *How they were fed with the Sangrail while they were in prison, and how Galahad was made king*

But as soon as they were there Our Lord sent them the Sangrail, through whose grace they were always fulfilled while that they were in prison.

So at the year's end it befell that this King Estorause lay sick, and felt that he should die. Then he sent for the three knights, and they came afore him; and he cried them mercy of that he had done to them, and they forgave it him goodly; and he died anon.

When the king was dead all the city was dismayed, and wist not who might be their king. Right so as they were in counsel there came a voice among them, and bad them choose the youngest knight of them three to be their king: 'For he shall well maintain you and all yours.'

So they made Galahad king by all the assent of the whole city, and else they would have slain him. And when he was come to behold the land, he let make above the table of silver a chest of gold and of precious stones, that hilled the holy vessel. And every day early the three fellows would come afore it, and make their prayers.

Now at the year's end, and the self day after Galahad had borne the crown of gold, he arose up early and his fellows, and came to the palace, and saw tofore them the holy vessel, and a man kneeling on his knees in likeness of a bishop, that had about him a great fellowship of angels as it had been Jesu Christ himself; and then he arose and began a mass of Our Lady.

And when he came to the sacrament of the mass, and had done, anon he called Galahad, and said to him, 'Come forth the servant of Jesu Christ, and thou shalt see that thou hast much desired to see.'

And then he began to tremble right hard when the deadly flesh began to behold the spiritual things.

Then he held up his hands toward heaven and said, 'Lord,

I thank Thee, for now I see that that hath been my desire many a day. Now, blessed Lord, would I not longer live, if it might please Thee, Lord.'

And therewith the good man took Our Lord's body betwixt his hands, and proffered it to Galahad, and he received it right gladly and meekly.

'Now wotest thou what I am?' said the good man.

'Nay,' said Galahad.

'I am Joseph of Arimathea,[1] the which Our Lord hath sent here to thee to bear thee fellowship; and wotest thou wherefore that He hath sent me more than any other? For thou hast resembled [me] in two things; in that thou hast seen the marvels of the Sangrail, in that thou hast been a clean maiden, as I have been and am.'

And when he had said these words Galahad went to Percival and kissed him, and commended him to God; and so he went to Sir Bors and kissed him, and commended him to God, and said, 'Fair lord, salute me to my lord, Sir Launcelot, my father, and as soon as ye see him, bid him remember of this unstable world.'

And therewith he kneeled down tofore the table and made his prayers, and then suddenly his soul departed to Jesu Christ, and a great multitude of angels bare his soul up to heaven, that the two fellows might well behold it. Also the two fellows saw come from heaven an hand, but they saw not the body. And then it came right to the vessel, and took it and the spear, and so bare it up to heaven. Sithen was there never man so hardy to say that he had seen the Sangrail.

CHAPTER 23: *Of the sorrow that Percival and Bors made when Galahad was dead: and of Percival how he died, and other matters*

When Percival and Bors saw Galahad dead they made as much sorrow as ever did two men. And if they had not been good men they might lightly have fallen in despair. And the people of the country and of the city were right heavy. And then he was buried; and as soon as he was buried Sir Percival yielded him to an hermitage out of the city, and took a religious clothing. And Bors was alway with him, but never changed he his secular clothing, for that he purposed him to go again into the realm of Logris.

Thus a year and two months lived Sir Percival in the hermitage a full holy life, and then passed out of this world; and Bors let bury him by his sister and by Galahad in the spiritualities.

When Bors saw that he was in so far countries as in the parts of Babylon he departed from Sarras, and armed him and came to the sea, and entered into a ship; and so it befell him in good adventure he came into the realm of Logris; and he rode so fast till he came to Camelot where the king was.

And then was there great joy made of him in the court, for they weened all he had been dead, forasmuch as he had been so long out of the country.

And when they had eaten, the king made great clerks to come afore him, that they should chronicle of the high adventures of the good knights. When Bors had told him of the adventures of the Sangrail, such as had befall him and his three fellows, that was Launcelot, Percival, Galahad, and himself, there Launcelot told the adventures of the Sangrail that he had seen. All this was made in great books, and put up in almeries at Salisbury.

And anon Sir Bors said to Sir Launcelot, 'Galahad, your own son, saluted you by me, and after you King Arthur and all the court, and so did Sir Percival, for I buried them with mine own hands in the city of Sarras. Also, Sir Launcelot, Galahad prayed you to remember of this unsiker world as ye behight him when ye were together more than half a year.'

'This is true,' said Launcelot; 'now I trust to God his prayer shall avail me.'

Then Launcelot took Sir Bors in his arms, and said, 'Gentle cousin, ye are right welcome to me, and all that ever I may

almeries: libraries.

do for you and for yours ye shall find my poor body ready at all times, whiles the spirit is in it, and that I promise you faithfully, and never to fail. And wit ye well, gentle cousin, Sir Bors, that ye and I will never depart in sunder whilst our lives may last.'

'Sir,' said he, 'I will as ye will.'

Thus endeth the history of the Sangrail, that was briefly drawn out of French into English, the which is a story chronicled for one of the truest and the holiest that is in this world, the which is the xvii. book.

And here followeth the
eighteenth book

Book XVIII

CHAPTER 1: *Of the joy King Arthur and the queen had of the achievement of the Sangrail; and how Launcelot fell to his old love again*

So after the quest of the Sangrail was fulfilled, and all knights that were left alive were comen again unto the Table Round, as the Book of the Sangrail maketh mention, then was there great joy in the court; and in especial King Arthur and Queen Guenever made great joy of the remnant that were comen home, and passing glad was the king and the queen of Sir Launcelot and of Sir Bors, for they had been passing long away in the quest of the Sangrail.

Then, as the book saith, Sir Launcelot began to resort unto Queen Guenever again, and forgat the promise and the perfection that he made in the quest. For, as the book saith, had not Sir Launcelot been in his privy thoughts and in his minds so set inwardly to the queen as he was in seeming outward to God, there had no knight passed him in the quest of the Sangrail; but ever his thoughts were privily on the queen, and so they loved together more hotter than they did toforehand, and had such privy draughts together, that many in the court spake of it, and in especial Sir Agravain, Sir Gawain's brother, for he was ever open-mouthed.

So befell that Sir Launcelot had many resorts of ladies and damosels that daily resorted unto him, that besought him to be their champion, and in all such matters of right Sir Launcelot applied him daily to do for the pleasure of Our Lord, Jesu Christ. And ever as much as he might he withdrew him from the company and fellowship of Queen Guenever, for to eschew the slander and noise; wherefore the queen waxed wroth with Sir Launcelot.

And upon a day she called Sir Launcelot unto her chamber, and said thus:

'Sir Launcelot, I see and feel daily that thy love beginneth to slake, for thou hast no joy to be in my presence, but ever thou art out of this court, and quarrels and matters thou hast nowadays for ladies and gentlewomen more than ever thou were wont to have aforehand.'

'Ah madam,' said Launcelot, 'in this ye must hold me excused for divers causes; one is, I was but late in the quest of the Sangrail; and I thank God of His great mercy, and never of my desert, that I saw in that my quest as much as ever saw any sinful man, and so was it told me. And if I had not had my privy thoughts to return to your love again as I do, I had seen as great mysteries as ever saw my son Galahad, other Percival, or Sir Bors; and therefore, madam, I was but late in that quest. Wit ye well, madam, it may not be yet lightly forgotten the high service in whom I did my diligent labour.

'Also, madam, wit ye well that there be many men speaken of our love in this court, and have you and me greatly in a-wait, as Sir Agravain and Sir Mordred; and madam, wit ye well I dread them more for your sake than for any fear I have of them myself, for I may happen to escape and rid myself in a great need, where ye must abide all that will be said unto you. And then if that ye fall in any distress through wilful folly, then is there none other remedy or help but by me and my blood.

'And wit ye well, madam, the boldness of you and me will bring us to great shame and slander; and that were me loth to see you dishonoured. And that is the cause I take upon me more for to do for damosels and maidens than ever I did tofore, that men should understand my joy and my delight is my pleasure to have ado for damosels and maidens.'

slake: abate.

CHAPTER 2: *How the queen commanded Sir Launcelot to avoid the court, and of the sorrow that Launcelot made*

All this while the queen stood still and let Sir Launcelot say what he would. And when he had all said she brast out on weeping, and so she sobbed and wept a great while. And when she might speak she said, 'Launcelot, now I well understand that thou art a false recreant knight and a common lecher, and lovest and holdest other ladies, and by me thou hast disdain and scorn. For wit thou well,' she said, 'now I understand thy falsehood, and therefore shall I never love thee no more. And never be thou so hardy to come in my sight; and right here I discharge thee this court, that thou never come within it; and I forfend thee my fellowship, and upon pain of thy head that thou see me no more.'

Right so Sir Launcelot departed with great heaviness, that unnethe he might sustain himself for great dole-making. Then he called Sir Bors, Sir Ector de Maris, and Sir Lionel, and told them how the queen had forfended him the court, and so he was in will to depart into his own country.

'Fair sir,' said Sir Bors de Ganis, 'ye shall not depart out of this land by mine advice. Ye must remember in what honour ye are renowned, and called the noblest knight of the world; and many great matters ye have in hand. And women in their hastiness will do ofttimes that sore repenteth them; and therefore by mine advice ye shall take your horse, and ride to the good hermitage here beside Windsor, that sometime was a good knight, his name is Sir Brastias, and there shall ye abide till I send you word of better tidings.'

'Brother,' said Sir Launcelot, 'wit ye well I am full loth to depart out of this realm, but the queen hath defended me so highly, that meseemeth she will never be my good lady as she hath been.'

'Say ye never so,' said Sir Bors, 'for many times or this

forfend: forbid.

375

time she hath been wroth with you, and after it she was the first that repented it.'

'Ye say well,' said Launcelot, 'for now will I do by your counsel, and take mine horse and my harness, and ride to the hermit, Sir Brastias, and there will I repose me until I hear some manner of tidings from you, but, fair brother, I pray you get me the love of my lady, Queen Guenever, and ye may.'

'Sir,' said Sir Bors, 'ye need not to move me of such matters, for well ye wot I will do what I may to please you.'

And then the noble knight, Sir Launcelot, departed with right heavy cheer suddenly, that none earthly creature wist of him, nor where he was become, but Sir Bors. So when Sir Launcelot was departed, the queen outward made no manner of sorrow in showing to none of his blood nor to none other. But wit ye well, inwardly, as the book saith, she took great thought, but she bare it out with a proud countenance as though she felt nothing nor danger.

CHAPTER 3: *How at a dinner that the queen made there was a knight poisoned, which Sir Mador laid on the queen*

And then the queen let make a privy dinner in London unto the knights of the Round Table. And all was for to show outward that she had as great joy in all other knights of the Table Round as she had in Sir Launcelot. All only at that dinner she had Sir Gawain and his brethren, that is for to say Sir Agravain, Sir Gaheris, Sir Gareth, and Sir Mordred. Also there was Sir Bors de Ganis, Sir Blamor de Ganis, Sir Bleoberis de Ganis, Sir Galihud, Sir Galihodin, Sir Ector de Maris, Sir Lionel, Sir Palomides, Sir Safer his brother, Sir La Cote Male Taile, Sir Persant, Sir Ironside, Sir Brandiles, Sir Kay le Seneschal, Sir Mador de la Porte, Sir Patrise, a knight of Ireland, Aliduke, Sir Astamore, and Sir Pinel le Savage, the which was cousin to Sir Lamorak de Gales, the good knight that Sir Gawain and his brethren slew by treason.

And so these four and twenty knights should dine with the queen in a privy place by themself, and there was made a great feast of all manner of dainties. But Sir Gawain had a custom that he used daily at dinner and at supper, that he loved well all manner of fruit, and in especial apples and pears. And therefore whosomever dined or feasted Sir Gawain would commonly purvey for good fruit for him, and so did the queen for to please Sir Gawain; she let purvey for him all manner of fruit. For Sir Gawain was a passing hot knight of nature, and this Pinel hated Sir Gawain because of his kinsman Sir Lamorak de Gales; and therefore for pure envy and hate Sir Pinel enpoisoned certain apples for to enpoison Sir Gawain.

And so this was well unto the end of the meat; and so it befell by misfortune a good knight named Patrise, cousin unto Sir Mador de la Porte, to take a poisoned apple. And when he had eaten it he swelled so till he brast, and there Sir Patrise fell down suddenly dead among them. Then every knight leapt from the board ashamed, and araged for wrath, nigh out of their wits. For they wist not what to say; considering Queen Guenever made the feast and dinner, they all had suspicion unto her.

'My lady, the queen,' said Gawain, 'wit ye well, madam, that this dinner was made for me, for all folks that knowen my condition understand that I love well fruit, and now I see well I had near been slain; therefore, madam, I dread me lest ye will be shamed.'

Then the queen stood still and was sore abashed, that she nist not what to say.

'This shall not so be ended,' said Sir Mador de la Porte, 'for here have I lost a full noble knight of my blood; and therefore upon this shame and despite I will be revenged to the utterance.' And there openly Sir Mador appelled the queen of the death of his cousin, Sir Patrise.

Then stood they all still, that none would speak a word against him, for they all had great suspicion unto the queen because she let make that dinner. And the queen was so abashed that she could none other ways do, but wept so heartily that she fell in a swoon. With this noise and cry came to them King Arthur, and when he wist of that trouble he was a passing heavy man.

CHAPTER 4: How Sir Mador appeached the queen of treason, and there was no knight would fight for her at the first time

And ever Sir Mador stood still afore the king, and ever he appelled the queen of treason; for the custom was such that time that all manner of shameful death was called treason.

'Fair lords,' said King Arthur, 'me repenteth of this trouble, but the case is so I may not have ado in this matter, for I must be a rightful judge; and that repenteth me that I may not do battle for my wife, for as I deem this deed came never by her. And therefore I suppose she shall not be all distained, but that some good knight shall put his body in jeopardy for my queen rather than she shall be burnt in a wrong quarrel. And therefore, Sir Mador, be not so hasty, for it may happen she shall not be all friendless; and therefore desire thou thy day of battle, and she shall purvey her of some good knight that shall answer you, or else it were to me great shame, and to all my court.'

'My gracious lord,' said Sir Mador, 'ye must hold me excused, for though ye be our king in that degree, ye are but a knight as we are, and ye are sworn unto knighthood as well as we; and therefore I beseech you that ye be not displeased, for there is none of the four and twenty knights that were bidden to this dinner but all they have great suspicion unto the queen. What say ye all, my lords?' said Sir Mador.

Then they answered by and by that they could not excuse the queen; for why she made the dinner, and other it must come by her or by her servants.

'Alas,' said the queen, 'I made this dinner for a good in-
distained: dishonoured.

tent, and never for none evil, so Almighty God me help in my right, as I was never purposed to do such evil deeds, and that I report me unto God.'

'My lord, the king,' said Sir Mador, 'I require you as ye be a righteous king give me a day that I may have justice.'

'Well,' said the king, 'I give the day this day fifteen days that thou be ready armed on horseback in the meadow beside Winchester.¹ And if it so fall that there be any knight to encounter with you, there mayest thou do the best, and God speed the right. And if it so fall that there be no knight at that day, then must my queen be burnt, and there she shall be ready to have her judgement.'

'I am answered,' said Sir Mador.

And every knight went where it liked them. So when the king and the queen were together the king asked the queen how this case befell.

The queen answered, 'So God me help, I wot not how nor in what manner.'

'Where is Sir Launcelot?' said King Arthur; 'And he were here he would not grudge to do battle for you.'

'Sir,' said the queen, 'I wot not where he is, but his brother and his kinsmen deem that he be not within this realm.'

'That me repenteth,' said King Arthur, 'for and he were here he would soon stint this strife. Then I will counsel you,' said the king, 'and unto Sir Bors: "That ye will do battle for her for Sir Launcelot's sake,"² and upon my life he will not refuse you. For well I see,' said the king, 'that none of these four and twenty knights that were with you at your dinner where Sir Patrise was slain, that will do battle for you, nor none of them will say well of you, and that shall be a great slander for you in this court.'

'Alas,' said the queen, 'and I may not do withal, but now I miss Sir Launcelot, for and he were here he would put me soon to my heart's ease.'

'What aileth you,' said the king, 'ye cannot keep Sir Launcelot upon your side? For wit ye well,' said the king,' who that hath Sir Launcelot upon his part hath the most man of worship in the world upon his side. Now go your way,' said the king unto the queen, 'and require Sir Bors to do battle for you for Sir Launcelot's sake.'

CHAPTER 5: *How the queen required Sir Bors to fight for her, and how he granted upon condition; and how he warned Sir Launcelot thereof*

So the queen departed from the king, and sent for Sir Bors into her chamber. And when he was come she besought him of succour.

'Madam,' said he, 'what would ye that I did? For I may not with my worship have ado in this matter, because I was at the same dinner, for dread that any of those knights would have me in suspicion. Also, Madam,' said Sir Bors, 'now miss ye Sir Launcelot, for he would not have failed you neither in right nor in wrong, as ye have well proved when ye have been in danger; and now ye have driven him out of this country, by whom ye and all we were daily worshipped by; therefore, madam, I marvel how ye dare for shame require me to do any thing for you, in so much ye have chased him out of your country by whom we were borne up and honoured.'

'Alas, fair knight,' said the queen, 'I put me wholly in your grace, and all that is done amiss I will amend as ye will counsel me.' And therewith she kneeled down upon both her knees, and besought Sir Bors to have mercy upon her: 'Other I shall have a shameful death, and thereto I never offended.'

Right so came King Arthur, and found the queen kneeling afore Sir Bors; then Sir Bors pulled her up and said,

'Madam, ye do me great dishonour.'

'Ah, gentle knight,' said the king, 'have mercy upon my queen, courteous knight, for I am now in certain she is untruly defamed. And therefore, courteous knight,' said the king, 'promise her to do battle for her, I require you for the love of Sir Launcelot.'

'My lord,' said Sir Bors, 'ye require me the greatest thing

that any man may require me; and wit ye well if I grant to do battle for the queen I shall wrath many of my fellowship of the Table Round. But as for that,' said Bors, 'I will grant my lord that for my lord Sir Launcelot's sake, and for your sake I will at that day be the queen's champion unless that there come by adventure a better knight than I am to do battle for her.'

'Will ye promise me this,' said the king, 'by your faith?'

'Yea sir,' said Sir Bors, 'of that I will not fail you, nor her both, but if there came a better knight than I am, and then shall he have the battle.'

Then was the king and the queen passing glad, and so departed, and thanked him heartily. So then Sir Bors departed secretly upon a day, and rode unto Sir Launcelot thereas he was with the hermit, Sir Brastias, and told him of all their adventure.

'Ah Jesu,' said Sir Launcelot, 'this is come happily as I would have it, and therefore I pray you make you ready to do battle, but look that ye tarry till ye see me come, as long as ye may. For I am sure Mador is an hot knight when he is enchafed, for the more ye suffer him the hastier will he be to battle.'

'Sir,' said Bors, 'let me deal with him, doubt ye not ye shall have all your will.'

Then departed Sir Bors from him and came to the court again. Then was it noised in all the court that Sir Bors should do battle for the queen; wherefore many knights were displeased with him, that he would take upon him to do battle in the queen's quarrel; for there were but few knights in all the court but they deemed the queen was in the wrong, and that she had done that treason. So Sir Bors answered thus to his fellows of the Table Round:

'Wit ye well, my fair lords, it were shame to us all and we suffered to see the most noble queen of the world to be shamed openly, considering her lord and our lord is the man of most worship in the world, and most christened, and he hath ever worshipped us all in all places.'

Many answered him again: 'As for our most noble King Arthur, we love him and honour him as well as ye do, but as for Queen Guenever we love her not, because she is a destroyer of good knights.'

'Fair lords,' said Sir Bors, 'meseemeth ye say not as ye should say, for never yet in my days knew I never nor heard say that ever she was a destroyer of any good knight. But at all times as far as ever I could know she was a maintainer of good knights; and ever she hath been large and free of her goods to all good knights, and the most bounteous lady of her gifts and her good grace, that ever I saw or heard speak of. And therefore it were shame,' said Sir Bors, 'to us all to our most noble king's wife, and we suffered her to be shamefully slain. And wit ye well,' said Sir Bors, 'I will not suffer it, for I dare say so much, the queen is not guilty of Sir Patrise's death, for she owed him never none ill will, nor none of the four and twenty knights that were at that dinner; for I dare say for good love she bad us to dinner, and not for no mal engine, and that I doubt not shall be proved hereafter, for howsomever the game goeth, there was treason among us.'

Then some said to Sir Bors, 'We may well believe your words.'

And so some of them were well pleased, and some were not so.

CHAPTER 6: *How at the day Sir Bors made him ready for to fight for the queen; and when he should fight how another discharged him*

The day came on fast until the even that the battle should be. Then the queen sent for Sir Bors and asked him how he was disposed.

'Truly madam,' said he, 'I am disposed in likewise as I promised you, that is for to say I shall not fail you, unless by adventure there come a better knight than I am to do battle for you, then, madam, am I discharged of my promise.'

'Will ye,' said the queen, 'that I tell my lord Arthur thus?'
'Do as it shall please you, madam.'

Then the queen went unto the king and told him the answer of Sir Bors.

'Have ye no doubt,' said the king, 'of Sir Bors, for I call him now one of the best knights of the world, and the most profitliest man.'

And thus it passed on until the morn, and the king and the queen and all manner of knights that were there at that time drew them unto the meadow beside Winchester where the battle should be. And so when the king was come with the queen and many knights of the Round Table, then the queen was put there in the constable's ward, and a great fire made about an iron stake, that and Sir Mador de la Porte had the better, she should be burnt: such custom was used in those days, that neither for favour, neither for love nor affinity, there should be none other but righteous judgement, as well upon a king as upon a knight, and as well upon a queen as upon another poor lady.

So in this meanwhile came in Sir Mador de la Porte, and took his oath afore the king, that the queen did this treason until his cousin Sir Patrise, and unto his oath he would prove it with his body, hand for hand, who that would say the contrary.

Right so came in Sir Bors de Ganis, and said that 'as for Queen Guenever she is in the right, and that will I make good with my hands that she is not culpable of this treason that is put upon her.'

'Then make thee ready,' said Sir Mador, 'and we shall prove whether thou be in the right or I.'

'Sir Mador,' said Sir Bors, 'wit thou well I know you for a good knight. Notforthan I shall not fear you so greatly, but I trust to God I shall be able to withstand your malice. But thus much have I promised my lord Arthur and my lady the queen, that I shall do battle for her in this case to the uttermost, unless that there come a better knight than I am and discharge me.'

'Is that all?' said Sir Mador, 'other come thou off and do battle with me, or else say nay.'

'Take your horse,' said Sir Bors, 'and as I suppose, ye shall not tarry long but ye shall be answered.'

Then either departed to their tents and made them ready to horseback as they thought best. And anon Sir Mador came into the field with his shield on his shoulder and his spear in his hand; and so rode about the place crying unto Arthur: 'Bid your champion come forth and he dare.'

Then was Sir Bors ashamed and took his horse and came to the lists' end.

And then was he ware where came from a wood there fast by a knight all armed, upon a white horse, with a strange shield of strange arms; and he came riding all that he might run, and so he came to Sir Bors, and said thus:

'Fair knight, I pray you be not displeased, for here must a better knight than ye are have this battle, therefore I pray you withdraw you. For wit ye well I have had this day a right great journey, and this battle ought to be mine, and so I promised you when I spake with you last, and with all my heart I thank you of your good will.'

Then Sir Bors rode unto King Arthur and told him how there was a knight come that would have the battle for to fight for the queen.

'What knight is he?' said the king.

'I wot not,' said Sir Bors, 'but such covenant he made with me to be here this day. Now my lord,' said Sir Bors, 'here am I discharged.'

CHAPTER 7: *How Sir Launcelot fought against Sir Mador for the queen, and how he overcame Sir Mador, and discharged the queen*

Then the king called to that knight, and asked him if he would fight for the queen.

Then he answered to the king, 'Therefore came I hither,

and therefore, sir king,' he said, 'tarry me no longer, for I may not tarry. For anon as I have finished this battle I must depart hence, for I have ado many matters elsewhere. For wit you well,' said that knight, 'this is dishonour to you all knights of the Round Table, to see and know so noble a lady and so courteous a queen as Queen Guenever is, thus to be rebuked and shamed amongst you.'

Then they all marvelled what knight that might be that so took the battle upon him. For there was not one that knew him, but if it were Sir Bors.

Then said Sir Mador de la Porte unto the king, 'Now let me wit with whom I shall have ado withal.'

And then they rode to the lists' end, and there they couched their spears, and ran together with all their mights, and Sir Mador's spear brake all to pieces, but the other's spear held, and bare Sir Mador's horse and all backward to the earth a great fall. But mightily and suddenly he avoided his horse and put his shield afore him, and then drew his sword, and bad the other knight alight and do battle with him on foot.

Then that knight descended from his horse lightly like a valiant man, and put his shield afore him and drew his sword; and so they came eagerly unto battle, and either gave other many great strokes, tracing and traversing, rasing and foining, and hurtling together with their swords as it were wild boars. Thus were they fighting nigh an hour, for this Sir Mador was a strong knight, and mightily proved in many strong battles. But at the last this knight smote Sir Mador grovelling upon the earth, and the knight stepped near him to have pulled Sir Mador flatling upon the ground; and therewith suddenly Sir Mador arose, and in his rising he smote that knight through the thick of the thighs that the blood ran out fiercely.

And when he felt himself so wounded, and saw his blood, he let him arise upon his feet. And then he gave him such a buffet upon the helm that he fell to the earth flatling, and therewith he strode to him to have pulled off his helm off his head. And then Sir Mador prayed that knight to save his life, and so he yielded him as overcome, and released the queen of his quarrel.

'I will not grant thee thy life,' said that knight, 'only that thou freely release the queen for ever, and that no mention be made upon Sir Patrise's tomb that ever Queen Guenever consented to that treason.'

'All this shall be done,' said Sir Mador, 'I clearly discharge my quarrel for ever.'

Then the knights parters of the lists took up Sir Mador, and led him to his tent, and the other knight went straight to the stairfoot where sat King Arthur; and by that time was the queen come to the king, and either kissed other heartily.

And when the king saw that knight, he stooped down to him, and thanked him, and in likewise did the queen; and the king prayed him to put off his helm, and to repose him, and to take a sop of wine. And then he put off his helm to drink, and then every knight knew him that it was Sir Launcelot du Lake.

Anon as the king[1] wist that, he took the queen in his hand, and yode unto Sir Launcelot, and said, 'Sir, gramercy of your great travail that ye have had this day for me and for my queen.'

'My lord,' said Sir Launcelot, 'wit ye well I ought of right ever to be in your quarrel, and in my lady the queen's quarrel, to do battle; for ye are the man that gave me the high order of knighthood, and that day my lady, your queen, did me great worship, and else I had been shamed; for that same day ye made me knight, through my hastiness I lost my sword, and my lady, your queen, found it, and lapped it in her train, and gave me my sword when I had need thereto, and else had I been shamed among all knights; and therefore, my lord Arthur, I promised her at that day ever to be her knight in right other in wrong.'

'Gramercy,' said the king, 'for this journey; and wit ye well,' said the king, 'I shall acquit your goodness.'

And ever the queen beheld Sir Launcelot, and wept so tenderly that she sank almost to the ground for sorrow that he had done to her so great goodness where she showed him great unkindness.

Then the knights of his blood drew unto him, and there either of them made great joy of other. And so came all the knights of the Table Round that were there at that time, and welcomed him. And then Sir Mador was had to leech craft, and Sir Launcelot was healed of his wound. And then there was made great joy and mirths in that court.

CHAPTER 8: *How the truth was known by the Maiden of the Lake, and of divers other matters*

And so it befell that the Damosel of the Lake, her name was Nimue, the which wedded the good knight Sir Pelleas, and so she came to the court; for ever she did great goodness unto King Arthur and to all his knights through her sorcery and enchantments. And so when she heard how the queen was an angered for the death of Sir Patrise, then she told it openly that she was never guilty; and there she disclosed by whom it was done, and named him, Sir Pinel; and for what cause he did it, there it was openly disclosed; and so the queen was excused, and the knight Pinel fled into his country.

Then was it openly known that Sir Pinel enpoisoned the apples at the feast to that intent to have destroyed Sir Gawain, because Sir Gawain and his brethren destroyed Sir Lamorak de Gales, to the which Sir Pinel was cousin unto.

Then was Sir Patrise buried in the church of Westminster in a tomb, and thereupon was written: HERE LIETH SIR PATRISE OF IRELAND, SLAIN BY SIR PINEL LE SAVAGE, THAT ENPOISONED APPLES TO HAVE SLAIN SIR GAWAIN, AND BY MISFORTUNE SIR PATRISE ATE ONE OF THOSE APPLES, AND THEN SUDDENLY HE BRAST. Also there was written upon the tomb that Queen Guenever was appelled of treason of the death of Sir Patrise, by Sir Mador de la Porte; and there was made mention how Sir Launcelot fought with him for Queen Guenever, and overcame him in plain battle. All this was written upon the tomb of Sir Patrise in excusing of the queen.

And then Sir Mador sued daily and long, to have the queen's good grace; and so by the means of Sir Launcelot he caused him to stand in the queen's good grace, and all was forgiven.

Thus it passed on till Our Lady Day, Assumption. Within a fifteen days of that feast the king let cry a great jousts and a tournament that should be at that day at Camelot, that is Winchester; and the king let cry that he and the King of Scots would joust against all that would come against them.

And when this cry was made, thither came many knights. So there came thither the King of Northgales, and King Agwisance of Ireland, and the King with the Hundred Knights, and Galahaut, the Haut Prince, and the King of Northumberland, and many other noble dukes and earls of divers countries.

So King Arthur made him ready to depart to these jousts, and would have had the queen with him, but at that time she would not, she said, for she was sick and might not ride at that time.

'That me repenteth,' said the king, 'for this seven year ye saw not such a noble fellowship together except at Whitsuntide when Galahad departed from the court.'

'Truly,' said the queen to the king, 'ye must hold me excused, I may not be there, and that me repenteth.'

And many deemed the queen would not be there because of Sir Launcelot du Lake, for Sir Launcelot would not ride with the king, for he said that he was not whole of the wound the which Sir Mador had given him; wherefore the king was heavy and passing wroth.

And so he departed toward Winchester with his fellowship; and so by the way the king lodged in a town called Astolat, that is now in English called Guildford, and there the king lay in the castle. So when the king was departed the queen called Sir Launcelot to her, and said thus:

'Sir Launcelot, ye are greatly to blame thus to hold you

behind my lord; what, trow ye, what will your enemies and mine say and deem? Nought else but, "See how Sir Launcelot holdeth him ever behind the king, and so doth the queen, for that they would have their pleasure together." And thus will they say,' said the queen to Sir Launcelot, 'have ye no doubt thereof.'

CHAPTER 9: *How Sir Launcelot rode to Astolat, and received a sleeve to bear upon his helm at the request of a maid*

'Madam,' said Sir Launcelot, 'I allow your wit, it is of late come since ye were wise. And therefore, madam, at this time I will be ruled by your counsel, and this night I will take my rest, and tomorrow betime I will take my way toward Winchester. But wit you well,' said Sir Launcelot to the queen, 'that at that jousts I will be against the king, and against all his fellowship.'

'Ye may there do as ye list,' said the queen, 'but by my counsel ye shall not be against your king and your fellowship. For therein be full many hard knights of your blood, as ye wot well enough, it needeth not to rehearse them.'

'Madam,' said Sir Launcelot, 'I pray you that ye be not displeased with me, for I will take the adventure that God will send me.'

And so upon the morn early Sir Launcelot heard mass and brake his fast, and so took his leave of the queen and departed. And then he rode so much until he came to Astolat, that is Guildford; and there it happed him in the eventide he came to an old baron's place that hight Sir Bernard of Astolat. And as Sir Launcelot entered into his lodging, King Arthur espied him as he did walk in a garden beside the castle, how he took his lodging, and knew him full well.

'It is well,' said King Arthur unto the knights that were with him in that garden beside the castle, 'I have now espied one knight that will play his play at the jousts to the which we be gone toward; I undertake he will do marvels.'

389

'Who is that, we pray you tell us?' said many knights that were there at that time.

'Ye shall not wit for me,' said the king, 'as at this time.' And so the king smiled, and went to his lodging.

So when Sir Launcelot was in his lodging, and unarmed him in his chamber, the old baron and hermit came to him making his reverence, and welcomed him in the best manner; but the old knight knew not Sir Launcelot.

'Fair sir,' said Sir Launcelot to his host, 'I would pray you to lend me a shield that were not openly known, for mine is well known.'

'Sir,' said his host, 'ye shall have your desire, for me-seemeth ye be one of the likeliest knights of the world, and therefore I shall show you friendship. Sir, wit you well I have two sons that were but late made knights, and the eldest hight Sir Tirre, and he was hurt that same day he was made knight, that he may not ride, and his shield ye shall have; for that is not known I dare say but here, and in no place else. And my youngest son hight Lavaine, and if it please you, he shall ride with you unto that jousts; and he is of his age strong and wight, for much my heart giveth unto you that ye should be a noble knight, therefore I pray you, tell me your name,' said Sir Bernard.

'As for that,' said Sir Launcelot, 'ye must hold me excused as at this time, and if God give me grace to speed well at the jousts I shall come again and tell you. But I pray you,' said Sir Launcelot, 'in any wise let me have your son, Sir Lavaine, with me, and that I may have your brother's shield.'

'All this shall be done,' said Sir Bernard.

This old baron had a daughter that time that was called that time the Fair Maiden of Astolat. And ever she beheld Sir Launcelot wonderfully; and as the book saith, she cast such a love unto Sir Launcelot that she could never withdraw her love, wherefore she died, and her name was Elaine le Blank. So thus as she came to and fro she was so hot in her love that she besought Sir Launcelot to wear upon him at the jousts a token of hers.

'Fair damosel,' said Sir Launcelot, 'and if I grant you that, ye may say I do more for your love than ever I did for lady or damosel.'

Then he remembered him he would go to the jousts disguised. And because he had never fore that time borne no manner of token of no damosel, then he bethought him that he would bear one of her, that none of his blood thereby might know him, and then he said, 'Fair maiden, I will grant you to wear a token of yours upon mine helmet, and therefore what it is, show it me.'

'Sir,' she said, 'it is a red sleeve of mine of scarlet, well embroidered with great pearls:' and so she brought it him.

So Sir Launcelot received it, and said, 'Never did I erst so much for no damosel.'

And then Sir Launcelot betook the fair maiden his shield in keeping, and prayed her to keep that until that he came again; and so that night he had merry rest and great cheer, for ever the damosel Elaine was about Sir Launcelot all the while she might be suffered.

CHAPTER 10: *How the tourney began at Winchester, and what knights were at the jousts; and other things*

So upon a day, on the morn, King Arthur and all his knights departed, for their king had tarried three days to abide his noble knights. And so when the king was ridden, Sir Launcelot and Sir Lavaine made them ready to ride, and either of them had white shields, and the red sleeve Sir Launcelot let carry with him. And so they took their leave at Sir Bernard, the old baron, and at his daughter, the Fair Maiden of Astolat. And then they rode so long till that they came to Camelot, that time called Winchester; and there was great press of kings, dukes, earls, and barons, and many noble knights. But there Sir Launcelot was lodged privily by the means of Sir Lavaine with a rich burgess, that no man in that town was ware what they were. And so they reposed them there till

Our Lady Day, Assumption, as the great feast should be.

So then trumpets blew unto the field, and King Arthur was set on high upon a scaffold to behold who did best. But as the French book saith, the king would not suffer Sir Gawain to go from him, for never had Sir Gawain the better and Sir Launcelot were in the field; and many times was Sir Gawain rebuked when Launcelot came into any jousts disguised. Then some of the kings, as King Agwisance of Ireland and the King of Scots, were that time turned upon the side of King Arthur. And then on the other party was the King of Northgales, and the King with the Hundred Knights, and the King of Northumberland, and Sir Galahaut, the Haut Prince. But these three kings and this duke were passing weak to hold against King Arthur's party, for with him were the noblest knights of the world.

So then they withdrew them either party from other, and every man made him ready in his best manner to do what he might. Then Sir Launcelot made him ready, and put the red sleeve upon his head, and fastened it fast; and so Sir Launcelot and Sir Lavaine departed out of Winchester privily, and rode until a little leaved wood behind the party that held against King Arthur's party, and there they held them still till the parties smote together. And then came in the King of Scots and the King of Ireland on Arthur's party, and against them came the King of Northumberland, and the King with the Hundred Knights smote down the King of Northumberland, and the King with the Hundred Knights smote down King Agwisance of Ireland. Then Sir Palomides that was on Arthur's party encountered with Sir Galahaut, and either of them smote down other, and either party halp their lords on horseback again. So there began a strong assail upon both parties.

And then came in Sir Brandiles, Sir Sagramore le Desirous, Sir Dodinas le Savage, Sir Kay le Seneschal, Sir Griflet le Fise de Dieu, Sir Mordred, Sir Meliot de Logris, Sir Ozanna le Cure Hardy, Sir Safer, Sir Epinogrus, Sir Galleron of Galway. All these fifteen knights were knights of the Table Round. So these with more other came in together, and beat aback the King of Northumberland and the King of Northgales.

When Sir Launcelot saw this, as he hoved in a little leaved wood, then he said unto Sir Lavaine, 'See yonder is a company of good knights, and they hold them together as boars that were chafed with dogs.'

'That is truth,' said Sir Lavaine.

CHAPTER 11: *How Sir Launcelot and Sir Lavaine entered in the field against them of King Arthur's court, and how Launcelot was hurt*

'Now,' said Sir Launcelot, 'and ye will help me a little, ye shall see yonder fellowship that chaseth now these men in our side, that they shall go as fast backward as they went forward.'

'Sir, spare not,' said Sir Lavaine, 'for I shall do what I may.'

Then Sir Launcelot and Sir Lavaine came in at the thickest of the press, and there Sir Launcelot smote down Sir Brandiles, Sir Sagramore, Sir Dodinas, Sir Kay, Sir Griflet and all this he did with one spear; and Sir Lavaine smote down Sir Lucan the Butler and Sir Bedevere. And then Sir Launcelot gat another spear and there he smote down Sir Agravain, Sir Gaheris, and Sir Mordred, and Sir Meliot de Logris; and Sir Lavaine smote Ozanna le Cure Hardy. And then Sir Launcelot drew his sword, and there he smote on the right hand and on the left hand, and by great force he unhorsed Sir Safer, Sir Epinogrus, and Sir Galleron, and then the knights of the Table Round withdrew them aback, after they had gotten their horses as well as they might.

'O mercy Jesu,' said Sir Gawain, 'what knight is yonder that doth so marvellous deeds of arms in that field?'

'I wot[1] what he is,' said King Arthur, 'but as at this time I will not name him.'

'Sir,' said Sir Gawain, 'I would say it were Sir Launcelot

by his riding and his buffets that I see him deal, but ever
meseemeth it should not be he for that he beareth the red
sleeve upon his head, for I wist him never bear token at no
jousts of lady nor gentlewoman.'

'Let him be,' said King Arthur, 'he will be better known
and do more or ever he depart.'

Then the party that was against King Arthur were well
comforted, and then they held them together that beforehand
were sore rebuked. Then Sir Bors, Sir Ector de Maris, and Sir
Lionel called unto them the knights of their blood, as Sir
Blamor de Ganis, Sir Bleoberis, Sir Aliduke, Sir Galihud, Sir
Galihodin, Sir Bellengerus le Beuse. So these nine knights of
Sir Launcelot's kin thrust in mightily, for they were all noble
knights; and they, of great hate and despite that they had
unto him, thought to rebuke that noble knight Sir Launcelot,
and Sir Lavaine, for they knew them not; and so they came
hurling together, and smote down many knights of Northgales and of Northumberland.

And when Sir Launcelot saw them fare so, he gat a spear
in his hand; and there encountered with him all at once Sir
Bors, Sir Ector, and Sir Lionel, and all they three smote him
at once with their spears. And with force of themself they
smote Sir Launcelot's horse to the earth; and by misfortune
Sir Bors smote Sir Launcelot through the shield into the side,
and the spear brake, and the head left still in his side.

When Sir Lavaine saw his master lie on the ground, he ran
to the King of Scots and smote him to the earth; and by great
force he took his horse, and brought him to Sir Launcelot,
and maugre of them all he made him to mount upon that
horse. And then Launcelot gat a spear in his hand, and there
he smote Sir Bors, horse and man, to the earth. In the same
wise he served Sir Ector and Sir Lionel; and Sir Lavaine smote
down Sir Blamor de Ganis. And then Sir Launcelot drew his
sword, for he felt himself so sore hurt that he weened there
to have had his death. And then he smote Sir Bleoberis such
a buffet on the helmet that he fell down to the earth in a
swoon. And in the same wise he served Sir Aliduke and Sir

Galihud. And Sir Lavaine smote down Sir Bellengerus, that was the son of Alisander le Orphelin. And by this was Sir Bors horsed, and then he came with Sir Ector and Sir Lionel, and all they three smote with swords upon Sir Launcelot's helmet. And when he felt their buffets and his wound, the which was so grievous, then he thought to do what he might while he might endure. And then he gave Sir Bors such a buffet that he made him bow his head passing low; and therewithal rased off his helm, and might have slain him; and so pulled him down, and in the same wise he served Sir Ector and Sir Lionel. For as the book saith he might have slain them, but when he saw their visages his heart might not serve him thereto, but left them there. And then afterward he hurled into the thickest press of them all, and did there the marvelloust deeds of arms that ever man saw or heard speak of, and ever Sir Lavaine, the good knight, with him. And there Sir Launcelot with his sword smote down and pulled down, as the French book maketh mention, more than thirty knights, and the most part were of the Table Round; and Sir Lavaine did full well that day, for he smote down ten knights of the Table Round.

CHAPTER 12: *How Sir Launcelot and Sir Lavaine departed out of the field, and in what jeopardy Launcelot was*

'Mercy Jesu,' said Sir Gawain to Arthur, 'I marvel what knight that he is with the red sleeve.'

'Sir,' said King Arthur, 'he will be known or he depart.'

And then the king blew unto lodging, and the prize was given by heralds unto the knight with the white shield that bare the red sleeve.

Then came the King with the Hundred Knights, the King of Northgales, and the King of Northumberland, and Sir Galahaut, the Haut Prince, and said unto Sir Launcelot, 'Fair knight, God thee bless, for much have ye done this day for us, therefore we pray you that ye will come with us that ye may receive the honour and the prize as ye have worshipfully deserved it.'

'My fair lords,' said Launcelot, 'wit you well if I have deserved thank I have sore bought it, and that me repenteth, for I am like never to escape with my life; therefore, fair lords, I pray you that ye will suffer me to depart where me liketh, for I am sore hurt. I take none force of none honour, for I had lever to repose me than to be lord of all the world.'

And therewithal he groaned piteously, and rode a great wallop away-ward from them until he came under a wood's side. And when he saw that he was from the field nigh a mile, that he was sure he might not be seen, then he said with an high voice, 'O gentle knight, Sir Lavaine, help me that this truncheon were out of my side, for it sticketh so sore that it nigh slayeth me.'

'O mine own lord,' said Sir Lavaine, 'I would fain do that might please you, but I dread me sore and I pull out the truncheon that ye shall be in peril of death.'

'I charge you,' said Sir Launcelot, 'as ye love me, draw it out.'

And therewithal he descended from his horse, and right so did Sir Lavaine and forthwithal Sir Lavaine drew the truncheon out of his side, and gave a great shriek and a marvellous grisly groan, and the blood brast out nigh a pint at once, that at the last he sank down upon his buttocks, and so swooned pale and deadly.

'Alas,' said Sir Lavaine, 'what shall I do?'

And then he turned Sir Launcelot into the wind, but so he lay there nigh half an hour as he had been dead.

And so at the last Sir Launcelot cast up his eyen, and said, 'O Lavaine, help me that I were on my horse, for here is fast by within this two mile a gentle hermit that sometime was a full noble knight and a great lord of possessions. And for great goodness he hath taken him to wilful poverty, and forsaken many lands, and his name is Sir Baudwin of Britain, and he is a full noble surgeon and a good leech. Now let see, help me up that I were there, for ever my heart giveth me that I shall never die of my cousin germain's hands.'

And then with great pain Sir Lavaine halp him upon his horse. And then they rode a great wallop together, and ever Sir Launcelot bled that it ran down to the earth; and so by fortune they came to that hermitage the which was under a wood, and a great cliff on the other side, and a fair water running under it.

And then Sir Lavaine beat on the gate with the butt of his spear, and cried fast, 'Let in for Jesu's sake.'

And there came a fair child to them, and asked them what they would.

'Fair son,' said Sir Lavaine, 'go and pray thy lord, the hermit, for God's sake to let in here a knight that is full sore wounded; and this day tell thy lord I saw him do more deeds of arms than ever I heard say that any man did.'

So the child went in lightly, and then he brought the hermit, the which was a passing good man. When Sir Lavaine saw him he prayed him for God's sake of succour.

'What knight is he?' said the hermit. 'Is he of the house of King Arthur, or not?'

'I wot not,' said Sir Lavaine, 'what is he, nor what is his name, but well I wot I saw him do marvellously this day as of deeds of arms.'

'On whose party was he?' said the hermit.

'Sir,' said Sir Lavaine, 'he was this day against King Arthur, and there he won the prize of all the knights of the Round Table.'

'I have seen the day,' said the hermit, 'I would have loved him the worse because he was against my lord, King Arthur, for sometime I was one of the fellowship of the Round Table, but I thank God now I am otherwise disposed. But where is he? Let me see him.'

Then Sir Lavaine brought the hermit to him.

CHAPTER 13 : *How Launcelot was brought to an hermit for to be healed of his wound, and of other matters*

And when the hermit beheld him, as he sat leaning upon his saddle bow ever bleeding piteously, and ever the knight hermit thought that he should know him, but he could not bring him to knowledge because he was so pale for bleeding.

'What knight are ye,' said the hermit, 'and where were ye born?'

'My fair lord,' said Sir Launcelot, 'I am a stranger and a knight adventurous, that laboureth throughout many realms for to win worship.'

Then the hermit advised him better, and saw by a wound on his cheek that he was Sir Launcelot.

'Alas,' said the hermit, 'mine own lord why layne you your name from me? Forsooth I ought to know you of right, for ye are the most noblest knight of the world, for well I know you for Sir Launcelot.'

'Sir,' said he, 'sith ye know me help me and ye may, for God's sake, for I would be out of this pain at once, other to death or to life.'

'Have ye no doubt,' said the hermit, 'ye shall live and fare right well.'

And so the hermit called to him two of his servants, and so he and his servants bare him into the hermitage, and lightly unarmed him, and laid him in his bed. And then anon the hermit staunched his blood, and made him to drink good wine, so that Sir Launcelot was well refreshed and knew himself; for in these days it was not the guise of hermits as is nowadays, for there were none hermits in those days but that they had been men of worship and of prowess; and those hermits held great household, and refreshed people that were in distress.

Now turn we unto King Arthur, and leave we Sir Launcelot in the hermitage. So when the kings were comen together

layne: conceal.

on both parties, and the great feast should be holden, King Arthur asked the King of Northgales and their fellowship, where was that knight that bare the red sleeve:

'Bring him afore me that he may have his laud, and honour, and the prize, as it is right.'

Then spake Sir Galahaut, the Haut Prince, and the King with the Hundred Knights:

'We suppose that knight is mischieved, and that he is never like to see you nor none of us all, and that is the greatest pity that ever we wist of any knight.'

'Alas,' said Arthur, 'how may this be, is he so hurt? What is his name?' said King Arthur.

'Truly,' said they all, 'we know not his name, nor from whence he came, nor whither he would.'

'Alas,' said the king, 'these be to me the worst tidings that came to me this seven year, for I would not for all the lands I wield to know and wit it were so that that noble knight were slain.'

'Know ye him?' said they all.

'As for that,' said Arthur, 'whether I know him or know him not, ye shall not know for me what man he is, but Almighty Jesu send me good tidings of him.'

And so said they all.

'By my head,' said Sir Gawain, 'if it so be that the good knight be so sore hurt, it is great damage and pity to all this land, for he is one of the noblest knights that ever I saw in a field handle a spear or a sword; and if he may be found I shall find him, for I am sure he nis not far from this town.'

'Bear you well,' said King Arthur, 'and ye may find him, unless that he be in such a plight that he may not wield himself.'

'Jesu defend,' said Sir Gawain, 'but wit I shall what he is, and I may find him.'

Right so Sir Gawain took a squire with him upon hackneys, and rode all about Camelot within six or seven mile, but so he came again and could hear no word of him.

Then within two days King Arthur and all the fellowship

returned unto London again. And so as they rode by the way it happed Sir Gawain at Astolat to lodge with Sir Bernard thereas was Sir Launcelot lodged. And so as Sir Gawain was in his chamber to repose him Sir Bernard, the old baron, came unto him, and his daughter Elaine, to cheer him and to ask him what tidings, and who did best at that tournament of Winchester.

'So God me help,' said Sir Gawain, 'there were two knights that bare two white shields, but the one of them bare a red sleeve upon his head, and certainly he was one of the best knights that ever I saw joust in field. For I dare say,' said Sir Gawain, 'that one knight with the red sleeve smote down forty knights of the Table Round, and his fellow did right well and worshipfully.'

'Now blessed be God,' said the Fair Maiden of Astolat, 'that that knight sped so well, for he is the man in the world that I first loved, and truly he shall be last that ever I shall love.'

'Now, fair maid,' said Sir Gawain, 'is that good knight your love?'

'Certainly sir,' said she, 'wit ye well he is my love.'

'Then know ye his name?' said Sir Gawain.

'Nay truly,' said the damosel, 'I know not his name nor from whence he cometh, but to say that I love him, I promise you and God that I love him.'

'How had ye knowledge of him first?' said Sir Gawain.

CHAPTER 14: *How Sir Gawain was lodged with the lord of Astolat, and there had knowledge that it was Sir Launcelot that bare the red sleeve*

Then she told him as ye have heard tofore, and how her father betook him her brother to do him service, and how her father lent him her brother's, Sir Tirre's, shield: 'And here with me he left his own shield.'

'For what cause did he so?' said Sir Gawain.

'For this cause,' said the damosel, 'for his shield was too well known among many noble knights.'

'Ah fair damosel,' said Sir Gawain, 'please it you let me have a sight of that shield.'

'Sir,' said she, 'it is in my chamber, covered with a case, and if ye will come with me ye shall see it.'

'Not so,' said Sir Bernard till his daughter, 'let send for it.'

So when the shield was comen, Sir Gawain took off the case, and when he beheld that shield he knew anon that it was Sir Launcelot's shield, and his own arms.

'Ah Jesu mercy,' said Sir Gawain, 'now is my heart more heavier than ever it was tofore.'

'Why?' said Elaine.

'For I have great cause,' said Sir Gawain. 'Is that knight that oweth this shield your love?'

'Yea truly,' said she, 'my love he is, God would I were his love.'

'So God me speed,' said Sir Gawain, 'fair damosel ye have right, for and he be your love ye love the most honourable knight of the world, and the man of most worship.'

'So me thought ever,' said the damosel, 'for never or that time, for no knight that ever I saw, loved I never none erst.'

'God grant,' said Sir Gawain, 'that either of you may rejoice other, but that is in a great adventure. But truly,' said Sir Gawain unto the damosel, 'ye may say ye have a fair grace, for why I have known that noble knight this four and twenty year, and never or that day, I nor none other knight, I dare make good, saw nor heard say that ever he bare token or sign of no lady, gentlewoman, ne maiden, at no jousts nor tournament. And therefore, fair maiden,' said Sir Gawain, 'ye are much beholden to him to give him thanks. But I dread me,' said Sir Gawain, 'that ye shall never see him in this world, and that is great pity that ever was of earthly knight.'

'Alas,' said she, 'how may this be, is he slain?'

'I say not so,' said Sir Gawain, 'but wit ye well he is grievously wounded, by all manner of signs, and by men's sight more likelier to be dead than to be alive; and wit ye well he is the noble knight, Sir Launcelot, for by this shield I know him.'

'Alas,' said the Fair Maiden of Astolat, 'how may this be, and what was his hurt?'

'Truly,' said Sir Gawain, 'the man in the world that loved him best hurt him so; and I dare say,' said Sir Gawain, 'and that knight that hurt him knew the very certainty that he had hurt Sir Launcelot, it would be the most sorrow that ever came to his heart.'

'Now fair father,' said then Elaine, 'I require you give me leave to ride and to seek him, or else I wot well I shall go out of my mind, for I shall never stint till that I find him and my brother, Sir Lavaine.'

'Do as it liketh you,' said her father, 'for me sore repenteth of the hurt of that noble knight.'

Right so the maid made her ready, and before Sir Gawain,[1] making great dole.

Then on the morn Sir Gawain came to King Arthur, and told him how he had found Sir Launcelot's shield in the keeping of the Fair Maiden of Astolat.

'All that knew I aforehand,' said King Arthur, 'and that caused me I would not suffer you to have ado at the great jousts, for I espied,' said King Arthur, 'when he came in till his lodging full late in the evening in Astolat. But marvel have I,' said Arthur, 'that ever he would bear any sign of any damosel, for or now I never heard say nor knew that ever he bare any token of none earthly woman.'

'By my head,' said Sir Gawain, 'the Fair Maiden of Astolat loveth him marvellously well; what it meaneth I cannot say, and she is ridden after to seek him.'

So the king and all came to London, and there Sir Gawain openly disclosed to all the court that it was Sir Launcelot that jousted best.

CHAPTER 15: *Of the sorrow that Sir Bors had for the hurt of Launcelot; and of the anger that the queen had because Launcelot bare the sleeve*

And when Sir Bors heard that, wit ye well he was an heavy man, and so were all his kinsmen. But when Queen Guenever wist that Sir Launcelot bare the red sleeve of the Fair Maiden of Astolat she was nigh out of her mind for wrath. And then she sent for Sir Bors de Ganis in all the haste that might be. So when Sir Bors was come tofore the queen, then she said,

'Ah Sir Bors, have ye heard say how falsely Sir Launcelot hath betrayed me?'

'Alas madam,' said Sir Bors, 'I am afeared he hath betrayed himself and us all.'

'No force,' said the queen, 'though he be destroyed, for he is a false traitor knight.'

'Madam,' said Sir Bors, 'I pray you say ye not so, for wit you well I may not hear such language of him.'

'Why Sir Bors,' said she, 'should I not call him traitor when he bare the red sleeve upon his head at Winchester, at the great jousts?'

'Madam,' said Sir Bors, 'that sleeve-bearing repenteth me sore, but I dare say he did it to none evil intent, but for this cause he bare the red sleeve that none of his blood should know him. For or then we nor none of us all never knew that ever he bare token or sign of maid, lady, ne gentlewoman.'

'Fie on him!' said the queen, 'Yet for all his pride and bobaunce there ye proved yourself his better.'

'Nay madam, say ye never more so, for he beat me and my fellows, and might have slain us and he had would.'

'Fie on him,' said the queen, 'for I heard Sir Gawain say before my lord Arthur that it were marvel to tell the great love that is between the Fair Maiden of Astolat and him.'

'Madam,' said Sir Bors, 'I may not warn Sir Gawain to say what it pleased him; but I dare say, as for my lord, Sir Launcelot, that he loveth no lady, gentlewoman, nor maid, but all he loveth in like much. And therefore madam,' said Sir Bors, 'ye may say what ye will, but wit ye well I will haste me to seek him, and find him wheresomever he be, and God send me good tidings of him.'

And so leave we them there, and speak we of Sir Launcelot that lay in great peril.

So as fair Elaine came to Winchester she sought there all about, and by fortune Sir Lavaine was ridden to play him, to enchafe his horse. And anon as Elaine saw him she knew him, and then she cried aloud until him. And when he heard her anon he came to her, and then she asked her brother how did 'my lord, Sir Launcelot.'

'Who told you, sister, that my lord's name was Sir Launcelot?'

Then she told him how Sir Gawain by his shield knew him. So they rode together till that they came to the hermitage, and anon she alit. So Sir Lavaine brought her in to Sir Launcelot; and when she saw him lie so sick and pale in his bed she might not speak, but suddenly she fell to the earth down suddenly in a swoon, and there she lay a great while.

And when she was relieved, she shrieked[1] and said, 'My lord, Sir Launcelot, alas why be ye in this plight?' And then she swooned again.

And then Sir Launcelot prayed Sir Lavaine to take her up: 'And bring her to me.'

And when she came to herself Sir Launcelot kissed her, and said, 'Fair maiden, why fare ye thus? Ye put me to pain; wherefore make ye no more such cheer, for and ye be come to comfort me ye be right welcome; and of this little hurt that I have I shall be right hastily whole by the grace of God. But I marvel,' said Sir Launcelot, 'who told you my name?'

Then the fair maiden told him all how Sir Gawain was lodged with her father: 'And there by your shield he discovered your name.'

'Alas,' said Sir Launcelot, 'that me repenteth that my name is known, for I am sure it will turn unto anger.'

And then Sir Launcelot compassed in his mind that Sir

Gawain would tell Queen Guenever how he bare the red sleeve, and for whom; that he wist well would turn into great anger.

So this maiden Elaine never went from Sir Launcelot, but watched him day and night, and did such attendance to him, that the French book saith there was never woman did more kindlier for man than she.

Then Sir Launcelot prayed Sir Lavaine to make aspies in Winchester for Sir Bors if he came there, and told him by what tokens he should know him, by a wound in his forehead. 'For well I am sure,' said Sir Launcelot, 'that Sir Bors will seek me, for he is the same good knight that hurt me.'

CHAPTER 16: *How Sir Bors sought Launcelot and found him in the hermitage, and of the lamentation between them*

Now turn we unto Sir Bors de Ganis that came unto Winchester to seek after his cousin Sir Launcelot. And so when he came to Winchester, anon there were men that Sir Lavaine had made to lie in a watch for such a man, and anon Sir Lavaine had warning; and then Sir Lavaine came to Winchester and found Sir Bors, and there he told him what he was, and with whom he was, and what was his name.

'Now fair knight,' said Sir Bors, 'I require you that ye will bring me to my lord, Sir Launcelot.'

'Sir,' said Sir Lavaine, 'take your horse, and within this hour ye shall see him.'

And so they departed, and came to the hermitage. And when Sir Bors saw Sir Launcelot lie in his bed pale and discoloured, anon Sir Bors lost his countenance, and for kindness and pity he might not speak, but wept tenderly a great while. And then when he might speak he said thus:

'O my lord, Sir Launcelot, God you bless, and send you hasty recover; and full heavy am I of my misfortune and of mine unhappiness, for now I may call myself unhappy. And I dread me that God is greatly displeased with me, that he would suffer me to have such a shame for to hurt you that are all our leader, and all our worship; and therefore I call myself unhappy. Alas that ever such a caitiff knight as I am should have power by unhappiness to hurt the most noblest knight of the world. Where I so shamefully set upon you and overcharged you, and where ye might have slain me, ye saved me; and so did not I, for I and your blood did to you our utterance. I marvel,' said Sir Bors, 'that my heart or my blood would serve me, wherefore my lord, Sir Launcelot, I ask your mercy.'

'Fair cousin,' said Sir Launcelot, 'ye be right welcome; and wit ye well, overmuch ye say for to please me the which pleaseth me not, for why I have the same sought; for I would with pride have overcome you all, and there in my pride I was near slain, and that was in mine own default, for I might have give you warning of my being there. And then had I had no hurt, for it is an old said saw, there is hard battle thereas kin and friends do battle either against other, there may be no mercy but mortal war. Therefore, fair cousin,' said Sir Launcelot, 'let this speech overpass, and all shall be welcome that God sendeth; and let us leave off this matter and let us speak of some rejoicing, for this that is done may not be undone; and let us find a remedy how soon that I may be whole.'

Then Sir Bors leaned upon his bedside, and told Sir Launcelot how the queen was passing wroth with him, because he wore the red sleeve at the great jousts; and there Sir Bors told him all how Sir Gawain discovered it: 'By your shield that ye left with the Fair Maiden of Astolat.'

'Then is the queen wroth,' said Sir Launcelot, 'and therefore am I right heavy, for I deserved no wrath, for all that I did was because I would not be known.'

'Right so excused I you,' said Sir Bors, 'but all was in vain, for she said more largelier to me than I to you now. But is this she,' said Sir Bors, 'that is so busy about you, that men call the Fair Maiden of Astolat?'

caitiff: wretched.

'She it is,' said Sir Launcelot, 'that by no means I cannot put her from me.'

'Why should ye put her from you?' said Sir Bors, 'She is a passing fair damosel, and a well beseen, and well taught; and God would, fair cousin,' said Sir Bors, 'that ye could love her, but as to that I may not, nor I dare not, counsel you. But I see well,' said Sir Bors, 'by her diligence about you that she loveth you entirely.'

'That me repenteth,' said Sir Launcelot.

'Sir,' said Sir Bors, 'she is not the first that hath lost her pain upon you, and that is the more pity.'

And so they talked of many more things. And so within three days or four Sir Launcelot was big and strong again.

CHAPTER 17: *How Sir Launcelot armed him to assay if he might bear arms, and how his wounds brast out again*

Then Sir Bors told Sir Launcelot how there was sworn a great tournament and jousts betwixt King Arthur and the King of Northgales, that should be upon All Hallowmass Day, beside Winchester.

'Is that truth?' said Sir Launcelot. 'Then shall ye abide with me still a little while until that I be whole, for I feel myself right big and strong.'

'Blessed be God,' said Sir Bors.

Then were they there nigh month together, and ever this maiden Elaine did ever her diligent labour night and day unto Sir Launcelot, that there was never child nor wife more meeker to her father and husband than was that Fair Maiden of Astolat; wherefore Sir Bors was greatly pleased with her.

So upon a day, by the assent of Sir Launcelot, Sir Bors, and Sir Lavaine, they made the hermit to seek in woods for divers herbs, and so Sir Launcelot made fair Elaine to gather herbs for him to make him a bain. In the meanwhile Sir Launcelot made him to arm him at all pieces; and there he thought to assay his armour and his spear, for his hurt or not.

And so when he was upon his horse he stirred him fiercely, and the horse was passing lusty and fresh because he was not laboured a month afore. And then Sir Launcelot couched that spear in the rest. That courser leapt mightily when he felt the spurs; and he that was upon him the which was the noblest horse of the world, strained him mightily and stably, and kept still the spear in the rest; and therewith Sir Launcelot strained himself so straitly, with so great force, to get the horse forward, that the bottom of his wound brast both within and without; and therewithal the blood came out so fiercely that he felt himself so feeble, that he might not sit upon his horse.

And then Sir Launcelot cried unto Sir Bors, 'Ah, Sir Bors and Sir Lavaine, help, for I am come to mine end.'

And therewith he fell down on the one side to the earth like a dead corpse. And then Sir Bors and Sir Lavaine came to him with sorrow making out of measure. And so by fortune the maiden Elaine heard their mourning, and then she came thither; and when she found Sir Launcelot there armed in that place she cried and wept as she had been wood; and then she kissed him, and did what she might to awake him.

And then she rebuked her brother and Sir Bors, and called them false traitors, why they would take him out of his bed; there she cried, and said she would appel them of his death.

With this came the holy hermit, Sir Baudwin of Britain, and when he found Sir Launcelot in that plight he said but little, but wit ye well he was wroth; and then he bad them: 'Let us have him in.'

And so they all bare him unto the hermitage, and unarmed him, and laid him in his bed; and evermore his wound bled piteously, but he stirred no limb of him. Then the knight hermit put a thing in his nose and a little deal of water in his mouth. And then Sir Launcelot waked of his swoon, and then the hermit staunched his bleeding. And when he might speak he asked Sir Launcelot why he put his life in jeopardy.

'Sir,' said Sir Launcelot, 'because I weened I had been

straitly: severely.

strong, and also Sir Bors told me that there should be at All Hallowmass a great jousts betwixt King Arthur and the King of Northgales, and therefore I thought to assay it myself, whether I might be there or not.'

'Ah, Sir Launcelot,' said the hermit, 'your heart and your courage will never be done until your last day, but ye shall do now by my counsel. Let Sir Bors depart from you, and let him do at that tournament what he may. And by the grace of God,' said the knight hermit, 'by that the tournament be done and ye come hither again, Sir Launcelot shall be as whole as ye, so that he will be governed by me.'

CHAPTER 18: *How Sir Bors returned and told tidings of Sir Launcelot; and of the tourney, and to whom the prize was given*

Then Sir Bors made him ready to depart from Sir Launcelot; and then Sir Launcelot said, 'Fair cousin, Sir Bors, recommend me unto all them unto whom me ought to recommend me unto. And I pray you, enforce yourself at that jousts that ye may be best, for my love; and here shall I abide at the mercy of God till ye come again.'

And so Sir Bors departed and came to the court of King Arthur, and told them in what place he had left Sir Launcelot.

'That me repenteth,' said the king, 'but since he shall have his life we all may thank God.'

And there Sir Bors told the queen in what jeopardy Sir Launcelot was when he would assay his horse. 'And all that he did, madam, was for the love of you, because he would have been at this tournament.'

'Fie on him, recreant knight,' said the queen, 'for wit ye well I am right sorry and he shall have his life.'

'His life shall he have,' said Sir Bors, 'and who that would otherwise except you, madam, we that be of his blood should help to short their lives. But madam,' said Sir Bors, 'ye have been ofttimes displeased with my lord, Sir Launcelot, but at all times at the end ye find him a true knight,' And so he departed.

And then every knight of the Round Table that were there at that time present made them ready to be at that jousts at All Hallowmass, and thither drew many knights of divers countries. And as All Hallowmass drew near, thither came the King of Northgales, and the King with the Hundred Knights, and Sir Galahaut, the Haut Prince of Surluse, and thither came King Agwisance of Ireland, and the King of Scots. So these three kings came on King Arthur's party.

And so that day Sir Gawain did great deeds of arms, and began first. And the heralds numbered that Sir Gawain smote down twenty knights. Then Sir Bors de Ganis came in the same time, and he was numbered that he smote down twenty knights; and therefore the prize was given betwixt them both, for they began first and longest endured. Also Sir Gareth, as the book saith, did that day great deeds of arms, for he smote down and pulled down thirty knights. But when he had done these deeds he tarried not but so departed, and therefore he lost his prize. And Sir Palomides did great deeds of arms that day, for he smote down twenty knights, but he departed suddenly, and men deemed Sir Gareth and he rode together to some manner adventures.

So when this tournament was done Sir Bors departed, and rode till he came to Sir Launcelot, his cousin; and then he found him walking on his feet, and there either made great joy of other; and so Sir Bors told Sir Launcelot of all the jousts like as ye have heard.

'I marvel,' said Sir Launcelot, 'that Sir Gareth, when he had done such deeds of arms, that he would not tarry.'

'Thereof we marvelled all,' said Sir Bors, 'for but if it were you, or Sir Tristram, or Sir Lamorak de Gales, I saw never knight bear down so many in so little a while as did Sir Gareth; and anon as he was gone we wist not where.'

'By my head,' said Sir Launcelot, 'he is a noble knight, and a mighty man and well breathed; and if he were well assayed,' said Sir Launcelot, 'I would deem he were good enough for any knight that beareth the life; and he is a gentle knight, courteous, true, and bounteous, meek, and mild, and in him is no manner of mal engine, but plain, faithful, and true.'

So then they made them ready to depart from the hermit. And so upon a morn they took their horses and Elaine le Blank with them; and when they came to Astolat there were they well lodged, and had great cheer of Sir Bernard, the old baron, and of Sir Tirre, his son. And so upon the morn when Sir Launcelot should depart, fair Elaine brought her father with her, and Sir Lavaine, and Sir Tirre, and thus she said:

CHAPTER 19: *Of the great lamentation of the Fair Maid of Astolat when Launcelot should depart, and how she died for his love*

'My lord, Sir Launcelot, now I see ye will depart; now fair knight and courteous knight, have mercy upon me, and suffer me not to die for thy love.'

'What would ye that I did?' said Sir Launcelot.

'I would have you to my husband,' said Elaine.

'Fair damosel, I thank you,' said Sir Launcelot, 'but truly,' said he, 'I cast me never to be wedded man.'

'Then, fair knight,' said she, 'will ye be my paramour?'

'Jesu defend me,' said Sir Launcelot, 'for then I rewarded your father and your brother full evil for their great goodness.'

'Alas,' said she, 'then must I die for your love.'

'Ye shall not so,' said Sir Launcelot, 'for wit ye well, fair maiden, I might have been married and I had would, but I never applied me to be married yet; but because, fair damosel, that ye love me as ye say ye do, I will for your good will and kindness show you some goodness, and that is this, that wheresomever ye will beset your heart upon some good knight that will wed you, I shall give you together a thousand pound yearly to you and to your heirs; thus much will I give you, fair madam, for your kindness, and always, while I live, to be your own knight.'

'Of all this,' said the maiden, 'I will none, for but if ye will wed me, or else be my paramour at the least, wit ye well, Sir Launcelot, my good days are done.'

'Fair damosel,' said Sir Launcelot, 'of these two things ye must pardon me.'

Then she shrieked shrilly, and fell down in a swoon; and then women bare her into her chamber, and there she made over much sorrow; and then Sir Launcelot would depart, and there he asked Sir Lavaine what he would do.

'What should I do,' said Sir Lavaine, 'but follow you, but if ye drive me from you, or command me to go from you.'

Then came Sir Bernard to Sir Launcelot and said to him, 'I cannot see but that my daughter Elaine will die for your sake.'

'I may not do withal,' said Sir Launcelot, 'for that me sore repenteth, for I report me to yourself, that my proffer is fair; and me repenteth,' said Sir Launcelot, 'that she loveth me as she doth; I was never the causer of it, for I report me to your son I early ne late proffered her bounty nor fair behests; and as for me,' said Sir Launcelot, 'I dare do all that a knight should do that she is a clean maiden for me, both for deed and for will. And I am right heavy of her distress, for she is a full fair maiden, good, gentle, and well taught.'

'Father,' said Sir Lavaine, 'I dare make good she is a clean maiden as for my lord Sir Launcelot; but she doth as I do, for sithen I first saw my lord Sir Launcelot, I could never depart from him, nor nought I will and I may follow him.'

Then Sir Launcelot took his leave, and so they departed, and came unto Winchester. And when Arthur wist that Sir Launcelot was come whole and sound the king made great joy of him, and so did Sir Gawain and all the knights of the Round Table except Sir Agravain and Sir Mordred. Also Queen Guenever was wood wroth with Sir Launcelot, and would by no means speak with him, but estranged herself from him; and Sir Launcelot made all the means that he might for to speak with the queen, but it would not be.

Now speak we of the Fair Maiden of Astolat that made such sorrow day and night that she never slept, ate, nor drank, and ever she made her complaint unto Sir Launcelot. So when she had thus endured a ten days, that she feebled so that she must needs pass out of this world, then she shrived her clean, and received her Creator. And ever she complained still upon Sir Launcelot. Then her ghostly father bad her leave such thoughts.

Then she said, 'Why should I leave such thoughts? Am I not an earthly woman? And all the while the breath is in my body I may complain me, for my belief is I do none offence though I love an earthly man; and I take God to my record I loved never none but Sir Launcelot du Lake, nor never shall, and a clean maiden I am for him and for all other; and sithen it is the sufferance of God that I shall die for the love of so noble a knight, I beseech the High Father of Heaven to have mercy upon my soul, and upon mine innumerable pains that I suffered may be allegiance of part of my sins. For sweet Lord Jesu,' said the fair maiden, 'I take Thee to record, on Thee I was never great offencer against Thy laws; but that I loved this noble knight, Sir Launcelot, out of measure, and of my self, good Lord, I might not withstand the fervent love wherefore I have my death.'

And then she called her father, Sir Bernard, and her brother, Sir Tirre, and heartily she prayed her father that her brother might write a letter like as she did indite it; and so her father granted her.

And when the letter was written word by word like as she devised then she prayed her father that she might be watched until she were dead. 'And while my body is hot let this letter be put in my right hand, and my hand bound fast with the letter until that I be cold; and let me be put in a fair bed with all the richest clothes that I have about me, and so let my bed and all my richest clothes be laid with me in a chariot unto the next place where Thames is; and there let me be put within a barget, and but one man with me, such as ye trust to steer me thither, and that my barget be covered with black samite over and over: thus father I beseech you let it be done.'

So her father granted it her faithfully, all thing should be done like as she had devised. Then her father and her brother made great dole, for when this was done anon she died. And so when she was dead the corpse and the bed all was led the next way unto Thames, and there a man, and the corpse, and all, were put into Thames; and so the man steered the barget unto Westminster, and there he rowed a great while to and fro or any espied it.

CHAPTER 20: *How the corpse of the Maid of Astolat arrived tofore King Arthur, and of the burying, and how Sir Launcelot offered the mass-penny*

So by fortune King Arthur and the Queen Guenever were speaking together at a window, and so as they looked into Thames they espied this black barget, and had marvel what it meant. Then the king called Sir Kay, and showed it him.

'Sir,' said Sir Kay, 'wit you well there is some new tidings.'

'Go thither,' said the king to Sir Kay, 'and take with you Sir Brandiles and Agravain, and bring me ready word what is there.'

Then these four knights departed and came to the barget and went in; and there they found the fairest corpse lying in a rich bed, and a poor man sitting in the barget's end, and no word would he speak. So these four knights returned unto the king again, and told him what they found.

'That fair corpse will I see,' said the king.

And so then the king took the queen by the hand, and went thither. Then the king made the barget to be holden fast, and then the king and the queen entered with certain knights with them; and there he saw the fairest woman lie in a rich bed, covered unto her middle with many rich clothes, and all was of cloth of gold, and she lay as though she had smiled. Then the queen espied a letter in her right hand, and told it to the king. Then the king took it and said, 'Now am I sure this letter will tell what she was, and why she is come hither.'

So then the king and the queen went out of the barget, and so commanded a certain to await upon the barget. And so when the king was come within his chamber, he called many knights about him, and said that he would wit openly what was written within that letter. Then the king brake it, and made a clerk to read it, and this was the intent of the letter:

'Most noble knight, Sir Launcelot, now hath death made us two at debate for your love. I was your lover, that men called the Fair Maiden of Astolat; therefore unto all ladies I make my moan, yet pray for my soul and bury me at least, and offer ye my mass-penny; this is my last request. And a clean maiden I died, I take God to witness, pray for my soul, Sir Launcelot, as thou art peerless.'

This was all the substance in the letter. And when it was read, the king, the queen, and all the knights wept for pity of the doleful complaints. Then was Sir Launcelot sent for; and when he was come King Arthur made the letter to be read to him. And when Sir Launcelot heard it word by word, he said,

'My lord Arthur, wit ye well I am right heavy of the death of this fair damosel. God knoweth I was never causer of her death by my willing, and that will I report me to her own brother: here he is, Sir Lavaine. I will not say nay,' said Sir Launcelot, 'but that she was both fair and good, and much I was beholden unto her, but she loved me out of measure.'

'Ye might have showed her,' said the queen, 'some bounty and gentleness that might have preserved her life.'

'Madam,' said Sir Launcelot, 'she would none other ways be answered but that she would be my wife, other else my paramour; and of these two I would not grant her, but I proffered her, for her good love that she showed me, a thousand pound yearly to her, and to her heirs, and to wed any manner knight that she could find best to love in her heart. For madam,' said Sir Launcelot, 'I love not to be constrained to love; for love must arise of the heart, and not by no constraint.'

'That is truth,' said the king, 'and many knight's love is free in himself, and never will be bounden, for where he is bounden he looseth himself.' Then said the king unto Sir Launcelot, 'It will be your worship that ye oversee that she be interred worshipfully.'

'Sir,' said Sir Launcelot, 'that shall be done as I can best devise.'

And so many knights yede thither to behold that fair maiden. And so upon the morn she was interred richly, and Sir Launcelot offered her mass-penny; and all the knights of the Table Round that were there at that time offered with Sir Launcelot. And then the poor man went again with the barget. Then the queen sent for Sir Launcelot, and prayed him of mercy, for why that she had been wroth with him causeless.

'This is not the first time,' said Sir Launcelot, 'that ye had been displeased with me causeless, but, madam, ever I must suffer you, but what sorrow I endure I take no force.'

So this passed on all that winter, with all manner of hunting and hawking, and jousts and tourneys were many betwixt many great lords, and ever in all places Sir Lavaine gat great worship, so that he was nobly renowned among many knights of the Table Round.

CHAPTER 21: *Of great jousts done all a Christmas, and of a great jousts and tourney ordained by King Arthur, and of Sir Launcelot*

Thus it passed on till Christmas, and then every day there was jousts made for a diamond: who that jousted best should have a diamond. But Sir Launcelot would not joust but if it were at a great jousts cried. But Sir Lavaine jousted there all that Christmas passingly well, and best was praised, for there were but few that did so well. Wherefore all manner of knights deemed that Sir Lavaine should be made knight of the Table Round at the next feast of Pentecost.

So at after Christmas King Arthur let call unto him many knights, and there they advised together to make a party and a great tournament and jousts. And the King of Northgales said to Arthur, he would have on his party King Agwisance of Ireland, and the King with the Hundred Knights, and the King of Northumberland, and Sir Galahaut, the Haut Prince. And so these four kings and this mighty duke took part against King Arthur and the knights of the Table Round.

And the cry was made that the day of the jousts should be beside Westminster upon Candlemas Day, whereof many knights were glad, and made them ready to be at that jousts in the freshest manner. Then Queen Guenever sent for Sir Launcelot, and said thus:

'I warn you that ye ride no more in no jousts nor tournaments but that your kinsmen may know you. And at these jousts that shall be ye shall have of me a sleeve of gold; and I pray you for my sake enforce yourself there, that men may speak of you worship; but I charge you as ye will have my love, that ye warn your kinsmen that ye will bear that day the sleeve of gold upon your helmet.'

'Madam,' said Sir Launcelot, 'it shall be done.'

And so either made great joy of other. And when Sir Launcelot saw his time he told Sir Bors that he would depart, and have no more with him but Sir Lavaine, unto the good hermit that dwelt in that Forest of Windsor; his name was Sir Brastias; and there he thought to repose him, and take all the rest that he might, because he would be fresh at that day of jousts.

So Sir Launcelot and Sir Lavaine departed, that no creature wist where he was become, but the noble men of his blood. And when he was come to the hermitage, wit you well he had good cheer. And so daily Sir Launcelot would go to a well fast by the hermitage, and there he would lie down, and see the well spring and burble, and sometime he slept there.

So at that time there was a lady dwelt in that forest, and she was a great huntress, and daily she used to hunt, and ever she bare her bow with her; and no men went never with her, but always women, and they were shooters, and could well kill a deer, both at the stalk and at the trist; and they daily bare bows and arrows, horns and wood knives, and many good dogs they had, both for the string and for a bait.[1]

So it happed this lady the huntress had abated her dog for the bow at a barren hind, and so this barren hind took the flight over hedges and woods. And ever this lady and part of her women costed the hind, and checked it by the noise of the hounds, to have met with the hind at some water; and so it happed, the hind came to the well whereas Sir Launcelot was sleeping and slumbering.

And so when the hind came to the well, for heat she went to soil, and there she lay a great while; and the dogs came after, and umbecast about, for she had lost the very perfect feute of the hind. Right so came that lady the huntress, that knew by the dog that she had, that the hind was at the soil in that well; and there she came stiffly and found the hind, and she put a broad arrow in her bow, and shot at the hind, and over-shot the hind; and so by misfortune the arrow smote Sir Launcelot in the thick of the buttock, over the barbs.

When Sir Launcelot felt himself so hurt, he hurled up woodly, and saw the lady that had smitten him. And when he saw she was a woman, he said thus: 'Lady or damosel, what that thou be, in an evil time bear ye a bow; the devil made you a shooter.'

CHAPTER 22: *How Sir Launcelot after that he was hurt of a gentlewoman came to an hermit, and of other matters*

'Now mercy, fair sir,' said the lady, 'I am a gentlewoman that useth here in this forest hunting, and God knoweth I saw you not; but as here was a barren hind at the soil in this trist: hunting station.   *costed*: followed.   *umbecast*: cast around. *stiffly*: resolutely.

well, and I weened to have done well, but my hand swerved.'

'Alas,' said Sir Launcelot, 'ye have mischieved me.'

And so the lady departed, and Sir Launcelot as he might pulled out the arrow, and left that head still in his buttock, and so he went weakly to the hermitage ever more bleeding as he went. And when Sir Lavaine and the hermit espied that Sir Launcelot was hurt, wit you well they were passing heavy, but Sir Lavaine wist not how that he was hurt nor by whom. And then were they wroth out of measure. Then with great pain the hermit gat out the arrow's head out of Sir Launcelot's buttock, and much of his blood he shed, and the wound was passing sore, and unhappily smitten, for it was in such a place that he might not sit in no saddle.

'Have mercy, Jesu,' said Sir Launcelot, 'I may call myself the most unhappiest man that liveth, for ever when I would fainest have worship there befalleth me ever some unhappy thing. Now so Jesu me help,' said Sir Launcelot, 'and if no man would but God, I shall be in the field upon Candlemas Day at the jousts, whatsomever fall of it.'

So all that might be gotten to heal Sir Launcelot was had. So when the day was come Sir Launcelot let devise that he was arrayed, and Sir Lavaine, and their horses, as though they had been Saracens; and so they departed and came nigh to the field.

The King of Northgales with an hundred knights with him, and the King of Northumberland brought with him an hundred good knights, and King Agwisance of Ireland brought with him an hundred good knights ready to joust, and Sir Galahaut, the Haut Prince, brought with him an hundred good knights, and the King with the Hundred Knights brought with him as many, and all these were proved good knights.

Then came in King Arthur's party; and there came in the King of Scots with an hundred knights, and King Uriens of Gore brought with him an hundred knights, and King Howel of Brittanny brought with him an hundred knights, and Cha-

whatsomever fall of it: whatever may happen as a result.

leins of Clarance brought with him an hundred knights, and King Arthur himself came into the field with two hundred knights, and the most part were knights of the Table Round, that were proved noble knights; and there were old knights set in scaffolds for to judge, with the queen, who did best.

CHAPTER 23 : How Sir Launcelot behaved him at the jousts, and other men also

Then they blew to the field; and there the King of Northgales encountered with the King of Scots, and there the King of Scots had a fall; and the King of Ireland smote down King Uriens; and the King of Northumberland smote down King Howel of Brittany; and Sir Galahaut, the Haut Prince, smote down Chaleins of Clarance. And then King Arthur was wood wroth, and ran to the King with the Hundred Knights, and there King Arthur smote him down; and after with that same spear King Arthur smote down three other knights.

And then when his spear was broken King Arthur did passingly well; and so therewithal came in Sir Gawain and Sir Gaheris, Sir Agravain and Sir Mordred, and there every each of them smote down a knight, and Sir Gawain smote down four knights; and then there began a strong medley, for then there came in the knights of Launcelot's blood, and Sir Gareth and Sir Palomides with them, and many knights of the Table Round, and they began to hold the four kings and the mighty duke so hard that they were discomfit; but this Duke Galahaut, the Haut Prince, was a noble knight, and by his mighty prowess of arms he held the knights of the Table Round strait enough.

All this doing saw Sir Launcelot, and then he came into the field with Sir Lavaine as it had been thunder. And then anon Sir Bors and the knights of his blood espied Sir Launcelot, and said to them all, 'I warn you beware of him with the sleeve of gold upon his head, for he is himself Sir Launcelot du Lake.' And for great goodness Sir Bors warned Sir Gareth.

'I am well apayed,' said Sir Gareth, 'that I may know him.'

'But who is he,' said they all, 'that rideth with him in the same array?'

'That is the good and gentle knight Sir Lavaine,' said Sir Bors.

So Sir Launcelot encountered with Sir Gawain, and there by force Sir Launcelot smote down Sir Gawain and his horse to the earth, and so he smote down Sir Agravain and Sir Gaheris, and also he smote down Sir Mordred, and all this was with one spear.

Then Sir Lavaine met with Sir Palomides, and either met other so hard and so fiercely that both their horses fell to the earth. And then were they horsed again, and then met Sir Launcelot with Sir Palomides, and there Sir Palomides had a fall; and so Sir Launcelot or ever he stint, as fast as he might get spears, he smote down thirty knights, and the most part of them were knights of the Table Round; and ever the knights of his blood withdrew them, and made them ado in other places where Sir Launcelot came not.

And then King Arthur was wroth when he saw Sir Launcelot do such deeds; and then the king called unto him Sir Gawain, Sir Mordred, Sir Kay, Sir Griflet, Sir Lucan the Butler, Sir Bedevere, Sir Palomides, Sir Safer, his brother; and so the king with these nine knights made them ready to set upon Sir Launcelot, and upon Sir Lavaine. All this espied Sir Bors and Sir Gareth.

'Now I dread me sore,' said Sir Bors, 'that my lord, Sir Launcelot, will be hard matched.'

'By my head,' said Sir Gareth, 'I will ride unto my lord Sir Launcelot, for to help him, fall of him what fall may, for he is the same man that made me knight.'

'Ye shall not so,' said Sir Bors, 'by my counsel, unless that ye were disguised.'

'Ye shall see me disguised,' said Sir Gareth; and therewithal he espied a Welsh knight where he was to repose him, and he was sort hurt afore, hurt by Sir Gawain, and to him

apayed: pleased.

421

Sir Gareth rode, and prayed him of his knighthood to lend him his shield for his.

'I will well,' said the Welsh knight.

And when Sir Gareth had his shield, the book saith it was green, with a maiden that seemed in it.

Then Sir Gareth came driving to Sir Launcelot all that he might and said, 'Knight, keep thyself, for yonder cometh King Arthur with nine noble knights with him to put you to a rebuke, and so I am come to bear you fellowship for old love ye have showed me.'

'Gramercy,' said Sir Launcelot.

'Sir,' said Sir Gareth, 'encounter ye with Sir Gawain, and I shall encounter with Sir Palomides; and let Sir Lavaine match with the noble King Arthur. And when we have delivered them, let us three hold us sadly together.'

Then came King Arthur with his nine knights with him, and Sir Launcelot encountered with Sir Gawain, and gave him such a buffet that the arson of his saddle brast, and Sir Gawain fell to the earth. Then Sir Gareth encountered with the good knight Sir Palomides, and he gave him such a buffet that both his horse and he dashed to the earth. Then encountered King Arthur with Sir Lavaine, and there either of them smote other to the earth, horse and all, that they lay a great while.

Then Sir Launcelot smote down Sir Agravain, and Sir Gaheris, and Sir Mordred; and Sir Gareth smote down Sir Kay, and Sir Safer, and Sir Griflet. And then Sir Lavaine was horsed again, and he smote down Sir Lucan the Butler and Sir Bedevere; and then there began great throng of good knights. Then Sir Launcelot hurtled here and there, and rased and pulled off helms, so that at that time there might none sit him a buffet with spear nor with sword; and Sir Gareth did such deeds of arms that all men marvelled what knight he was with the green shield, for he smote down that day and pulled down more than thirty knights. And, as the French book saith, Sir Launcelot marvelled, when he beheld Sir Gareth do such deeds, what knight he might be. And Sir Lavaine pulled down and smote down twenty knights. Also Sir Launcelot knew not Sir Gareth, for and Sir Tristram de Liones, other Sir Lamorak de Gales had been alive, Sir Launcelot would have deemed he had been one of them twain.

So ever as Sir Launcelot, Sir Gareth, Sir Lavaine fought, and on the one side Sir Bors, Sir Ector de Maris, Sir Lionel, Sir Lamorak de Gales, Sir Bleoberis, Sir Galihud, Sir Galihodin, Sir Pelleas, and with more other of King Ban's blood fought upon another party, and held the King with the Hundred Knights and the King of Northumberland right strait.

CHAPTER 24: *How King Arthur marvelled much of the jousting in the field, and how he rode and found Sir Launcelot*

So this tournament and this jousts dured long, till it was near night, for the knights of the Round Table relieved ever unto King Arthur; for the king was wroth out of measure that he and his knights might not prevail that day.

Then Sir Gawain said to the king, 'I marvel where all this day Sir Bors de Ganis and his fellowship of Sir Launcelot's blood, I marvel all this day they be not about you: it is for some cause,' said Sir Gawain.

'By my head,' said Sir Kay, 'Sir Bors is yonder all this day upon the right hand of this field, and there he and his blood do more worshipfully than we do.'

'It may well be,' said Sir Gawain, 'but I dread me ever of guile; for on pain of my life,' said Sir Gawain, 'this knight with the red sleeve of gold is himself Sir Launcelot, I see well by his riding and by his great strokes; and the other knight in the same colours is the good young knight, Sir Lavaine. Also that knight with the green shield is my brother, Sir Gareth, and yet he hath disguised himself, for no man shall never make him be against Sir Launcelot, because he made him knight.'

'By my head,' said Arthur, 'nephew, I believe you; therefore tell me now what is your best counsel.'

'Sir,' said Sir Gawain, 'ye shall have my counsel: let blow unto lodging, for and he be Sir Launcelot du Lake, and my brother, Sir Gareth, with him, with the help of that good young knight, Sir Lavaine, trust me truly it will be no boot to strive with them but if we should fall ten or twelve upon one knight, and that were no worship, but shame.'

'Ye say truth,' said the king; 'and for to say sooth,' said the king, 'it were shame to us so many as we be to set upon them any more; for wit ye well,' said King Arthur, 'they be three good knights, and namely that knight with the sleeve of gold.'

So then they blew unto lodging; but forthwithal King Arthur let send unto the four kings, and to the mighty duke, and prayed them that the knight with the sleeve of gold depart not from them, but that the king may speak with him. Then forthwithal King Arthur alit and unarmed him, and took a little hackney and rode after Sir Launcelot, for ever he had a spy upon him. And so he found him among the four kings and the duke; and there the king prayed them all unto supper, and they said they would with good will. And when they were unarmed then King Arthur knew Sir Launcelot, Sir Lavaine, and Sir Gareth.

'Ah, Sir Launcelot,' said King Arthur, 'this day ye have heated me and my knights.'

So they yede unto Arthur's lodging all together, and there was a great feast and great revel, and the prize was given unto Sir Launcelot; and by heralds they named him that he had smitten down fifty knights, and Sir Gareth five-and-thirty, and Sir Lavaine four-and-twenty knights.

Then Sir Launcelot told the king and the queen how the lady huntress shot him in the Forest of Windsor, in the buttock, with an broad arrow, and how the wound thereof was that time six inches deep, and in like long. Also Arthur blamed Sir Gareth because he left his fellowship and held with Sir Launcelot.

'My lord,' said Sir Gareth, 'he made me a knight, and when I saw him so hard bestad, methought it was my worship to help him, for I saw him do so much, and so many noble knights against him; and when I understood that he was Sir Launcelot du Lake, I shamed to see so many knights against him alone.'

'Truly,' said King Arthur unto Sir Gareth, 'ye say well, and worshipfully have ye done and to yourself great worship; and all the days of my life,' said King Arthur unto Sir Gareth, 'wit you well I shall love you, and trust you the more better. For ever,' said Arthur 'it is a worshipful knight's deed to help another worshipful knight when he seeth him in a great danger; for ever a worshipful man will be loth to see a worshipful shamed; and he that is of no worship, and fareth with cowardice, never shall he show gentleness, nor no manner of goodness where he seeth a man in any danger, for then ever will a coward show no mercy; and always a good man will do ever to another man as he would be done to himself.'

So then there were great feasts unto kings and dukes, and revel, game, and play, and all manner of noblesse was used; and he that was courteous, true, and faithful, to his friend was that time cherished.

CHAPTER 25 : *How true love is likened to summer*

And thus it passed on from Candlemas until after Easter, that the month of May was come, when every lusty heart beginneth to blossom, and to bring forth fruit; for like as herbs and trees bringen forth fruit and flourish in May, in likewise every lusty heart that is in any manner a lover, springeth and flourisheth in lusty deeds. For it giveth unto all lovers courage, that lusty month of May, in something to constrain him to some manner of thing more in that month than in any other month, for diverse causes. For then all herbs and trees renewen a man and woman, and in likewise lovers callen again to their mind old gentleness and old service, and many kind deeds that were forgotten by negligence.

For like as winter rasure doth alway erase and deface green summer, so fareth it by unstable love in man and woman. For in many persons there is no stability; for we may see all day, for a little blast of winter's rasure, anon we shall deface and lay apart true love for little or nought, that cost much thing; this is no wisdom nor stability, but it is feebleness of nature and great disworship, whomsoever useth this.

Therefore, like as May month flowereth and flourisheth in many gardens, so in likewise let every man of worship flourish his heart in this world, first unto God, and next unto the joy of them that he promised his faith unto; for there was never worshipful man nor worshipful woman, but they loved one better than another; and worship in arms may never be foiled, but first reserve the honour to God, and secondly the quarrel must come of thy lady : and such love I call virtuous love.

But nowadays men cannot love seven night but they must have all their desires : that love may not endure by reason; for where they be soon accorded and hasty, heat soon it cooleth. Right so fareth love nowadays, soon hot soon cold: this is no stability. But the old love was not so; men and women could love together seven years, and no licours lusts were between them, and then was love, truth, and faithfulness : and lo, in likewise was used love in King Arthur's days.

Wherefore I liken love nowadays unto summer and winter; for like as the one is hot and the other cold, so fareth love nowadays; therefore all ye that be lovers call unto your remembrance the month of May, like as did Queen Guenever, for whom I make here a little mention, that while she lived she was a true lover, and therefore she had a good end.

Explicit liber Octodecimus.
And here followeth
liber xix

rasure : destruction. *licours* : lecherous.

Book XIX

CHAPTER 1: *How Queen Guenever rode on Maying with certain knights of the Round Table and clad all in green*

So it befell in the month of May, Queen Guenever called unto her knights of the Table Round; and she gave them warning that early upon the morrow she would ride on Maying into woods and fields beside Westminster: 'And I warn you that there be none of you but that he be well horsed, and that ye all be clothed in green, other in silk other in cloth; and I shall bring with me ten ladies, and every knight shall have a lady behind him, and every knight shall have a squire and two yeomen, and I will that ye all be well horsed.'

So they made them ready in the freshest manner. And these were the names of the knights: Sir Kay le Seneschal, Sir Agravain, Sir Brandiles, Sir Sagramore le Desirous, Sir Dodinas le Savage, Sir Ozanna le Cure Hardy, Sir Ladinas of the Forest Savage, Sir Persant of Inde, Sir Ironside, that was called the Knight of the Red Launds, and Sir Pelleas, the lover; and these ten knights made them ready in the freshest manner to ride with the queen.

And so upon the morn they took their horses with the queen, and rode on Maying in woods and meadows as it pleased them, in great joy and delights; for the queen had cast to have been again with King Arthur at the furthest by ten of the clock, and so was that time her purpose.

Then there was a knight that hight Meliagaunt, and he was son unto King Bagdemagus, and this knight had at that time a castle of the gift of King Arthur within seven mile of Westminster. And this knight, Sir Meliagaunt, loved passing well Queen Guenever, and so had he done long and many years. And the book saith he had lain in a wait for to steal

away the queen, but evermore he forbare for because of Sir
Launcelot; for in no wise he would meddle with the queen
and Sir Launcelot were in her company, other else and he
were near hand her.

And that time was such a custom, the queen rode never
without a great fellowship of men of arms about her, and
they were many good knights, and the most part were young
men that would have worship; and they were called the
Queen's Knights, and never in no battle, tournament, nor
jousts, they bare none of them no manner of knowledging of
their own arms, but plain white shields, and thereby they
were called the Queen's Knights. And then when it happed
any of them to be of great worship by his noble deeds, then
at the next feast of Pentecost, if there were any slain or dead,
as there was none year that there failed but some were dead,
then was there chosen in his stead that was dead, the most
men of worship that were called the Queen's Knights. And
thus they came up all first, or they were renowned men of
worship, both Sir Launcelot and all the remnant of them.

But this knight, Sir Meliagaunt, had espied the queen well
and her purpose, and how Sir Launcelot was not with her,
and how she had no man of arms with her but the ten noble
knights all arrayed in green for Maying. Then he purveyed
him a twenty men of arms and an hundred archers for to
destroy the queen and her knights, for he thought that time
was best season to take the queen.

CHAPTER 2: How Sir Meliagaunt took the queen and all
her knights, which were sore hurt in fighting

So as the queen had Mayed and all her knights, all were be-
dashed with herbs, mosses and flowers, in the best manner
and freshest. Right so came out of a wood Sir Meliagaunt
with an eight score men well harnessed, as they should fight
in a battle of arrest, and bad the queen and her knights abide,
for maugre their heads they should abide.

'Traitor knight,' said Queen Guenever, 'what cast thou for to do? Wilt thou shame thyself? Bethink thee how thou art a king's son, and knight of the Table Round, and thou to be about to dishonour the noble king that made thee knight; thou shamest all knighthood and thyself, and me I let thee wit shalt thou never shame, for I had lever cut mine own throat in twain rather than thou shouldest dishonour me.'

'As for all this language,' said Meliagaunt, 'be it as it be may, for wit you well, madam, I have loved you many a year, and never or now could I get you at such an advantage as I do now, and therefore I will take you as I find you.'

Then spake all the ten noble knights at once and said, 'Sir Meliagaunt, wit thou well ye are about to jeopard your worship to dishonour, and also ye cast to jeopard our persons howbeit we be unarmed. Ye have us at a great avail, for it seemeth by you that ye have laid watch upon us; but rather than ye should put the queen to a shame and us all, we had as leve to depart from our lives, for and if we other ways did, we were shamed for ever.'

Then said Sir Meliagaunt, 'Dress you as well ye can, and keep the queen.'

Then the ten knights of the Table Round drew their swords, and the other let run at them with their spears, and the ten knights manly abode them, and smote away their spears that no spear did them none harm. Then they lashed together with swords, and anon Sir Kay, Sir Sagramore, Sir Agravain, Sir Dodinas, Sir Ladinas, and Sir Ozanna were smitten to the earth with grimly wounds. Then Sir Brandiles, and Sir Persant, Sir Ironside, Sir Pelleas, fought long, and they were sore wounded, for these ten knights, or ever they were laid to the ground, slew forty men of the boldest and the best of them.

So when the queen saw her knights thus dolefully wounded, and needs must be slain at the last, then for pity and sorrow she cried Sir Meliagaunt, 'Slay not my noble knights, and I will go with thee upon this covenant, that thou save them, and suffer them not to be no more hurt, with this, that they be led with me wheresomever thou leadest me, for I will rather slay myself than I will go with thee, unless that these my noble knights may be in my presence.'

'Madam,' said Meliagaunt, 'for your sake they shall be led with you into mine own castle, with that ye will be ruled, and ride with me.'

Then the queen prayed the four knights to leave their fighting, and she and they would not depart.

'Madam,' said Sir Pelleas, 'we will do as ye do, for as for me I take no force of my life nor death.'

For as the French book saith, Sir Pelleas gave such buffets there that none armour might hold him.

CHAPTER 3: *How Sir Launcelot had word how the queen was taken, and how Sir Meliagaunt laid a bushment for Launcelot*

Then by the queen's commandment they left battle, and dressed the wounded knights on horseback, some sitting, some overthwart their horses, that it was pity to behold them. And then Sir Meliagaunt charged the queen and all her knights that none of all her fellowship should depart from her; for full sore he dread Sir Launcelot du Lake, lest he should have any knowledging.

All this espied the queen, and privily she called unto her a child of her chamber that was swiftly horsed, to whom she said, 'Go thou, when thou seest thy time, and bear this ring unto Sir Launcelot du Lake, and pray him as he loveth me that he will see me and rescue me, if ever he will have joy of me; and spare not thy horse,' said the queen, 'neither for water, neither for land.'

So the child espied his time, and lightly he took his horse with the spurs, and departed as fast as he might. And when Sir Meliagaunt saw him so flee, he understood that it was by the queen's commandment for to warn Sir Launcelot. Then they that were best horsed chased him and shot at him, but from them all the child went suddenly.

And then Sir Meliagaunt said to the queen, 'Madam, ye are about to betray me, but I shall ordain for Sir Launcelot that he shall not come lightly at you.'

And then he rode with her, and they all, to his castle, in all the haste that they might. And by the way Sir Meliagaunt laid in an ambushment the best archers that he might get in his country, to the number of thirty, to await upon Sir Launcelot, charging them that if they saw such a manner of knight come by the way upon a white horse, that in any wise they slay his horse, 'but in no manner of wise have not ado with him bodily, for he is over-hard to be overcomen.' So this was done, and they were comen to his castle, but in no wise the queen would never let none of the ten knights and her ladies out of her sight, but always they were in her presence;[1] for the book saith, Sir Meliagaunt durst make no masteries, for dread of Sir Launcelot, insomuch he deemed that he had warning.

So when the child was departed from the fellowship of Sir Meliagaunt, within a while he came to Westminster, and anon he found Sir Launcelot. And when he had told his message, and delivered him the queen's ring,

'Alas,' said Sir Launcelot, 'now am I shamed for ever, unless that I may rescue that noble lady from dishonour.'

Then eagerly he asked his armour; and ever the child told Sir Launcelot how the ten knights fought marvellously, and how Sir Pelleas, and Sir Ironside, and Sir Brandiles, and Sir Persant of Inde, fought strongly, but namely Sir Pelleas, there might none withstand him; and how they all fought till at the last they were laid to the earth; and then the queen made appointment for to save their lives, and go with Sir Meliagaunt.

'Alas,' said Sir Launcelot, 'that most noble lady, that she should be so destroyed; I had lever,' said Sir Launcelot, 'than all France, that I had been there, were well armed.'

So when Sir Launcelot was armed and upon his horse, he prayed the child of the queen's chamber to warn Sir Lavaine how suddenly he was departed, and for what cause. 'And pray him as he loveth me, that he will hie him after me, and that he stint not until he come to the castle where Sir Meliagaunt abideth, or dwelleth; for there,' said Sir Launcelot, 'he shall hear of me and I am a man living, and rescue the queen and the ten knights the which he traitorously hath taken, and that shall I prove upon his head, and all them that hold with him.'

CHAPTER 4: *How Sir Launcelot's horse was slain, and how Sir Launcelot rode in a cart for to rescue the queen*

Then Sir Launcelot rode as fast as he might, and the book saith he took the water at Westminster Bridge, and made his horse to swim over Thames unto Lambeth. And then within a while he came to the same place thereas the ten noble knights fought with Sir Meliagaunt. And then Sir Launcelot followed the track until that he came to a wood, and there was a strait way, and there the thirty archers bad Sir Launcelot turn again, and follow no longer that track.

'What commandment have ye thereto,' said Sir Launcelot, 'to cause me that am a knight of the Round Table to leave my right way?'

'This way shalt thou leave other else thou shalt go it on thy foot, for wit thou well thy horse shall be slain.'

'That is little mastery,' said Sir Launcelot, 'to slay mine horse; but as for myself, when my horse is slain, I give right nought for you, not and ye were five hundred more.'

So then they shot Sir Launcelot's horse, and smote him with many arrows; and then Sir Launcelot avoided his horse, and went on foot; but there were so many ditches and hedges betwixt them and him that he might not meddle with none of them.

'Alas for shame,' said Launcelot, 'that ever one knight should betray another knight; but it is an old saw, "A good man is never in danger but when he is in the danger of a coward." '

Then Sir Launcelot went a while, and then he was foul cumbered of his armour, his shield, and his spear, and all that longed unto him. Wit ye well he was full sore annoyed, and full loth he was for to leave anything that longed unto him, for he dread sore the treason of Sir Meliagaunt. Then by fortune there came by him a chariot that came thither for to fetch wood.

'Say me, carter,' said Sir Launcelot, 'what shall I give thee to suffer me to leap into thy chariot, and that thou bring me unto a castle within this two mile?'

'Thou shalt not come within my chariot,' said the carter, 'for I am sent for to fetch wood, for my lord, Sir Meliagaunt.'

'With him would I speak.'

'Thou shalt not go with me,' said the carter.

Then Sir Launcelot leapt to him, and gave him such a buffet that he fell to the earth stark dead. Then the other carter, his fellow, was afeared, and weened to have gone the same way; and then he cried, 'Fair lord, save my life, and I shall bring you where ye will.'

'Then I charge thee,' said Sir Launcelot, 'that thou drive me and this chariot even unto Sir Meliagaunt's gate.'

'Leap up into the chariot,' said the carter, 'and ye shall be there anon.'

So the carter drove on a great wallop, and Sir Launcelot's horse followed the chariot, with more than a forty arrows broad and rough in him.

And more than an hour and an half Dame Guenever was awaiting in a bay window with her ladies, and espied an armed knight standing in a chariot.

'See, madam,' said a lady, 'where rideth in a chariot a goodly armed knight; I suppose he rideth unto hanging.'

'Where?' said the queen.

Then she espied by his shield that he was there himself, Sir Launcelot du Lake. And then she was ware where came his horse ever after that chariot, and ever he trod his guts and his paunch under his feet.

'Alas,' said the queen, 'now I see well and prove, that well is him that hath a trusty friend. Ha, ha, most noble knight,' said Queen Guenever, 'I see well thou art hard bestad when thou ridest in a chariot.'

Then she rebuked that lady that likened Sir Launcelot to ride in a chariot to hanging. 'It was foul mouthed,' said the queen, 'and evil likened, so for to liken the most noble knight of the world unto such a shameful death. O Jesu defend him and keep him,' said the queen, 'from all mischievous end.'

By this was Sir Launcelot comen to the gates of the castle, and there he descended down, and cried, that all the castle rang of it, 'Where art thou, false traitor, Sir Meliagaunt, and knight of the Table Round? Now come forth here, thou traitor knight, thou and thy fellowship with thee; for here I am, Sir Launcelot du Lake, that shall fight with you.'

And therewithal he bare the gate wide open upon the porter, and smote him under his ear with his gauntlet, that his neck brast in sunder.

CHAPTER 5: *How Sir Meliagaunt required forgiveness of the queen, and how she appeased Sir Launcelot; and other matters*

When Sir Meliagaunt heard that Sir Launcelot was there he ran unto Queen Guenever, and fell upon his knee, and said, 'Mercy, madam, now I put me wholly into your grace.'

'What aileth you now?' said Queen Guenever. 'Forsooth I might well wit some good knight would revenge me though my lord Arthur wist not of this your work.'

'Madam,' said Sir Meligaunt, 'all this that is amiss on my part shall be amended right as yourself will devise, and wholly I put me in your grace.'

'What would ye that I did?' said the queen.

'I would no more,' said Meliagaunt, 'but that ye would

take all in your own hands, and that ye will rule my lord Sir Launcelot; and such cheer as may be made him in this poor castle ye and he shall have until to-morn, and then may ye and all they return unto Westminster; and my body and all that I have I shall put in your rule.'

'Ye say well,' said the queen, 'and better is peace than ever war, and the less noise the more is my worship.'

Then the queen and her ladies went down unto the knight, Sir Launcelot, that stood wroth out of measure in the inner court, to abide battle; and ever he bad: 'Thou traitor knight come forth.'

Then the queen came to him and said, 'Sir Launcelot, why be ye so moved?'

'Ha, madam,' said Sir Launcelot, 'why ask ye me that question? Meseemeth,' said Sir Launcelot, 'ye ought to be more wroth than I am, for ye have the hurt and the dishonour, for wit ye well, madam, my hurt is but little for the killing of a mare's son, but the despite grieveth me much more than all my hurt.'

'Truly,' said the queen, 'ye say truth; but heartily I thank you,' said the queen, 'but ye must come in with me peaceable, for all thing is put in my hand, and all that is evil shall be for the best, for the knight full sore repenteth him of the misadventure that is befallen him.'

'Madam,' said Sir Launcelot, 'sith it is so that ye be accorded with him, as for me I may not be against it, howbeit Sir Meliagaunt hath done full shamefully to me, and cowardly. Ah madam,' said Sir Launcelot, 'and I had wist ye would have been so soon accorded with him I would not have made such haste unto you.'

'Why say ye so?' said the queen, 'Do ye forthink yourself of your good deeds? Wit you well,' said the queen, 'I accorded never unto him for favour nor love that I had unto him, but for to lay down every shameful noise.'

'Madam,' said Sir Launcelot, 'ye understand full well I was never willing nor glad of shameful slander nor noise; and there is neither king, queen, ne knight, that beareth the life, except my lord King Arthur, and you, madam should let me, but I should make Sir Meliagaunt's heart full cold or ever I departed from hence.'

'That wot I well,' said the queen, 'but what will ye more? Ye shall have all thing ruled as ye list to have it.'

'Madam,' said Sir Launcelot, 'so ye be pleased I care not, as for my part ye shall soon please.'

Right so the queen took Sir Launcelot by the bare hand, for he had put off his gauntlet, and so she went with him till her chamber; and then she commanded him to be unarmed. And then Sir Launcelot asked where were the ten knights that were wounded sore; so she showed them unto Sir Launcelot, and there they made great joy of the coming of him, and Sir Launcelot made great dole of their hurts, and bewailed them greatly. And there Sir Launcelot told them how cowardly and traitorly Meliagaunt set archers to slay his horse, and how he was fain to put himself in a chariot. Thus they complained every each to other; and full fain they would have been revenged, but they peaced themself because of the queen.

Then, as the French book saith, Sir Launcelot was called many a day after le Chevaler du Chariot, and did many deeds, and great adventures he had. And so leave we of this tale le Chevaler du Chariot, and turn we to this tale.

So Sir Launcelot had great cheer with the queen, and then Sir Launcelot made a promise with the queen that the same night Sir Launcelot should come to a window outward toward a garden; and that window was barred with iron, and there Sir Launcelot promised to meet her when all folks were asleep.

So then came Sir Lavaine driving to the gates, crying, 'Where is my lord, Sir Launcelot du Lake?'

Then was he sent for, and when Sir Lavaine saw Sir Launcelot, he said, 'My lord, I found well how ye were hard bestad, for I have found your horse that was slain with arrows.'

'As for that,' said Sir Launcelot, 'I pray you, Sir Lavaine, speak ye of other matters, and let ye this pass, and we shall right it another time when we best may.'

CHAPTER 6: *How Sir Launcelot came in the night to the queen, and how Sir Meliagaunt appeached the queen of treason*

Then the knights that were hurt were searched, and soft salves were laid to their wounds; and so it passed on till supper time, and all the cheer that might be made them there was done unto the queen and all her knights. Then when season was, they went unto their chambers, but in no wise the queen would not suffer the wounded knights to be from her, but that they were laid within draughts by her chamber, upon beds and pillows, that she herself might see to them, that they wanted nothing.

So when Sir Launcelot was in his chamber that was assigned unto him, he called unto him Sir Lavaine, and told him that night he must go speak with his lady, Dame Guenever.

'Sir,' said Sir Lavaine, 'let me go with you and it please you, for I dread me sore of the treason of Sir Meliagaunt.'

'Nay,' said Sir Launcelot, 'I thank you, but I will have nobody with me.'

Then Sir Launcelot took his sword in his hand, and privily went to a place where he had espied a ladder toforehand, and that he took under his arm, and bare it through the garden, and set it up to the window, and there anon the queen was ready to meet him. And then they made either to other their complaints of many diverse things, and then Sir Launcelot wished that he might have comen in to her.

'Wit ye well,' said the queen, 'I would as fain as ye, that ye might come in to me.'

'Would ye, madam,' said Sir Launcelot, 'with your heart that I were with you?'

'Yea, truly,' said the queen.

draughts: adjoining rooms.

'Now shall I prove my might,' said Sir Launcelot, 'for your love.'

And then he set his hands upon the bars of iron, and he pulled at them with such a might that he brast them clean out of the stone walls, and therewithal one of the bars of iron cut the brawn of his hands throughout to the bone; and then he leapt into the chamber to the queen.

'Make ye no noise,' said the queen, 'for my wounded knights lie here fast by me.'

So, to pass upon this tale, Sir Launcelot went unto bed with the queen, and he took no force of his hurt hand, but took his pleasance and his liking until it was in the dawning of the day; and wit ye well he slept not but watched, and when he saw his time that he might tarry no longer he took his leave and departed at the window, and put it together as well as he might again, and so departed unto his own chamber; and there he told Sir Lavaine how he was hurt.

Then Sir Lavaine dressed his hand and staunched it, and put upon it a glove, that it should not be espied; and so the queen lay long in her bed until it was nine of the clock.

Then Sir Meliagaunt went to the queen's chamber, and found her ladies there ready clothed.

'Jesu mercy,' said Sir Meliagaunt, 'what aileth you, madam, that ye sleep thus long?'

And right therewithal he opened the curtain for to behold her; and then was he ware where she lay, and all the sheet and pillow was bebled with the blood of Sir Launcelot and of his hurt hand. When Sir Meliagaunt espied that blood, then he deemed in her that she was false to the king, and that some of the wounded knights had lain by her all that night.

'Ah, madam,' said Sir Meliagaunt, 'now I have founden you a false traitress unto my lord Arthur; for now I prove well it was not for nought that ye laid these wounded knights within the bounds of your chamber; therefore I will call you of treason before my lord, King Arthur. And now I have proved you, madam, with a shameful deed; and that they be all false, or some of them, I will make good, for a wounded knight this night hath lain by you.'

'That is false,' said the queen, 'and that I will report me unto them all.'

Then when the ten knights heard Sir Meliagaunt's words, they spake all in one voice and said to Sir Meliagaunt, 'Thou sayest falsely, and wrongfully puttest upon us such a deed, and that we will make good any of us; choose which thou list of us when we are whole of our wounds.'

'Ye shall not,' said Sir Meliagaunt. 'Away with your proud language, for here ye may all see,' said Sir Meliagaunt, 'that by the queen this night a wounded knight hath lain.'

Then were they all ashamed when they saw that blood; and wit you well Sir Meliagaunt was passing glad that he had the queen at such an advantage, for he deemed by that to hide his treason. So with this rumour came in Sir Launcelot, and found them all at a great array.

CHAPTER 7: *How Sir Launcelot answered for the queen, and waged battle against Sir Meliagaunt; and how Sir Launcelot was taken in a trap*

'What array is this?' said Sir Launcelot.

Then Sir Meliagaunt told them what he had found, and showed them the queen's bed.

'Truly,' said Sir Launcelot, 'ye did not your part nor knightly, to touch a queen's bed while it was drawn, and she lying therein; for I dare say my lord Arthur himself would not have displayed her curtains, she being within her bed, unless that it had pleased him to have lain down by her; and therefore ye have done unworshipfully and shamefully to yourself.'

'I wot not what ye mean,' said Sir Meliagaunt, 'but well I am sure there hath one of her wounded knights lain by her this night, and therefore I will prove with my hands that she is a traitress unto my lord Arthur.'

'Beware what ye do,' said Launcelot, 'for and ye say so, and ye will prove it, it will be taken at your hands.'

'My lord, Sir Launcelot,' said Meliagaunt, 'I rede you beware what ye do; for though ye are never so good a knight, as ye wot well ye are renowned the best knight of the world, yet should ye be advised to do battle in a wrong quarrel, for God will have a stroke in every battle.'

'As for that,' said Sir Launcelot, 'God is to be dread; but as to that I say nay plainly, that this night there lay none of these ten wounded knights with my lady Queen Guenever, and that will I prove with my hands, that ye say untruly in that now.'

'Hold,' said Sir Meliagaunt, 'here is my glove that she is traitress unto my lord, King Arthur, and that this night one of the wounded knights lay with her.'

'And I receive your glove,' said Sir Launcelot.

And so they were sealed with their signets, and delivered unto the ten knights.

'At what day shall we do battle together?' said Sir Launcelot.

'This day eight days,' said Sir Meliagaunt, 'in the field beside Westminster.'

'I am agreed,' said Sir Launcelot.

'But now,' said Sir Meliagaunt, 'sithen it is so that we must fight together, I pray you, as ye be a noble knight, await me with no treason, nor none villainy the meanwhile, nor none for you.'

'So God me help,' said Sir Launcelot, 'ye shall right well wit I was never of no such conditions, for I report me to all knights that ever have known me, I fared never with no treason, nor I loved never the fellowship of no man that fared with treason.'

'Then let us go to dinner,' said Meliagaunt, 'and after dinner ye and the queen and ye may ride all to Westminster.'

'I will well,' said Sir Launcelot.

Then Sir Meliagaunt said to Sir Launcelot, 'Pleaseth it you to see the estures of this castle?'

estures: rooms.

'With a good will,' said Sir Launcelot.

And then they went together from chamber to chamber, for Sir Launcelot dread no perils; for ever a man of worship and of prowess dreadeth least always perils, for they ween every man be as they be; but ever he that fareth with treason putteth oft a man in great danger. So it befell upon Sir Launcelot that no peril dread, as he went with Sir Meliagaunt he trod on a trap and the board rolled, and there Sir Launcelot fell down more than ten fathom into a cave full of straw; and then Sir Meliagaunt departed and made no fare as that he nist where he was. And when Sir Launcelot was thus missed they marvelled where he was become; and then the queen and many of them deemed that he was departed as he was wont to do, suddenly. For Sir Meliagaunt made suddenly to put away aside Sir Lavaine's horse, that they might all understand that Sir Launcelot was departed suddenly.

So it passed on till after dinner; and then Sir Lavaine would not stint until that he ordained litters for the wounded knights, that they might be lead in them; and so with the queen and them all, both ladies and gentlewomen and other, went unto Westminster; and there the knights told King Arthur how Meliagaunt had appelled the queen of high treason, and how Sir Launcelot had received the glove of him; 'and this day eight days they shall do battle afore you.'

'By my head,' said King Arthur, 'I am afeared Sir Meliagaunt hath taken upon him a great charge; but where is Sir Launcelot?' said the king.

'Sir,' said they all, 'we wot not where he is, but we deem he is ridden to some adventures, as he is ofttimes wont to do, for he hath Sir Lavaine's horse.'

'Let him be,' said the king, 'he will be founden, but if he be trapped with some treason.'

CHAPTER 8: *How Sir Launcelot was delivered out of prison by a lady, and took a white courser and came for to keep his day*

So leave we Sir Launcelot lying within that cave in great pain; and every day there came a lady and brought him his meat and his drink, and wooed him, to have lain by him; and ever the noble knight, Sir Launcelot, said her nay.

'Sir Launcelot,' said she, 'ye are not wise, for ye may never out of this prison, but if ye have my help; and also your lady, Queen Guenever, shall be burnt in your default, unless that ye be there at the day of battle.'

'God defend,' said Sir Launcelot, 'that she should be burnt in my default; and if it be so,' said Sir Launcelot, 'that I may not be there, it shall be well understand, both at the king and at the queen, and with all men of worship, that I am dead, sick, other in prison. For all men that know me will say for me that I am in some evil case and I be not there that day; and well I wot there is some good knight other of my blood, or some other that loveth me, that will take my quarrel in hand; and therefore,' said Sir Launcelot, 'wit ye well ye shall not fear me; and if there were no more women in all this land but ye, I will not have ado with you.'

'Then art thou shamed,' said the lady, 'and destroyed for ever.'

'As for world's shame, Jesu defend me, and as for my distress, it is welcome whatsover it be that God sendeth me.'

So she came to him the same day that the battle should be, and said, 'Sir Launcelot, methinketh ye are too hard-hearted, but wouldest thou but kiss me once I should deliver thee, and thine armour, and the best horse that is within Sir Meliagaunt's stable.'

'As for to kiss you,' said Sir Launcelot, 'I may do that and lose no worship; and wit ye well and I understood there were any disworship for to kiss you I would not do it.' Then he kissed her, and then she gat him, and brought him to his armour. And when he was armed, she brought him to a stable, where stood twelve good coursers, and bad him choose the best. Then Sir Launcelot looked upon a white courser the which liked him best; and anon he commanded the keepers fast to saddle him with the best saddle of war that there was; and so it was done as he bad.

Then gat he his spear in his hand, and his sword by his side, and commended the lady unto God, and said, 'Lady, for this good deed I shall do you service if ever it be in my power.'

CHAPTER 9: *How Sir Launcelot came the same time that Sir Meliagaunt abode him in the field and dressed him to battle*

Now leave we Sir Launcelot wallop all that he might, and speak we of Queen Guenever that was brought to a fire to be burnt; for Sir Meliagaunt was sure, him thought, that Sir Launcelot should not be at that battle; therefore he ever cried upon King Arthur to do him justice, other else bring forth Sir Launcelot du Lake.

Then was the king and all the court full sore abashed and shamed that the queen should be burnt in the default of Sir Launcelot.

'My lord Arthur,' said Sir Lavaine, 'ye may understand that it is not well with my lord Sir Launcelot, for and he were alive, so he be not sick other in prison, wit ye well he would be here; for never heard ye that ever he failed his part for whom he should do battle for. And therefore,' said Sir Lavaine, 'my lord, King Arthur, I beseech you give me license to do battle here this day for my lord and master, and for to save my lady, the queen.'

'Gramercy gentle Sir Lavaine,' said King Arthur, 'for I dare say all that Sir Meliagaunt putteth upon my lady the queen is wrong, for I have spoken with all the ten wounded knights, and there is not one of them, and he were whole and able to

do battle, but he would prove upon Sir Meliagaunt's body
that it is false that he putteth upon my queen.'

'So shall I,' said Sir Lavaine, 'in the defence of my lord, Sir
Launcelot, and ye will give me leave.'

'Now I give you leave,' said King Arthur, 'and do your
best, for I dare well say there is some treason done to Sir
Launcelot.'

Then was Sir Lavaine armed and horsed, and suddenly at
the lists' end he rode to perform this battle; and right as the
heralds should cry, 'Lesses les aler,'[1] right so came in Sir
Launcelot driving with all the force of his horse.

And then Arthur cried, 'Ho !' and 'Abide !'

Then was Sir Launcelot called on horseback tofore King
Arthur, and there he told openly tofore the king and all, how
Sir Meliagaunt had served him first and last. And when the
king, and the queen, and all the lords, knew of the treason of
Sir Meliagaunt they were all ashamed on his behalf. Then
was Queen Guenever sent for, and set by the king in great
trust of her champion.

And then there was no more else to say, but Sir Launcelot
and Sir Meliagaunt dressed them unto battle, and took their
spears; and so they came together as thunder, and there Sir
Launcelot bare him down quite over his horse's croup. And
then Sir Launcelot alit and dressed his shield on his shoulder,
with his sword in his hand, and Sir Meliagaunt in the same
wise dressed him unto him, and there they smote many great
strokes together; and at the last Sir Launcelot smote him such
a buffet upon the helmet that he fell on the one side to the
earth.

And then he cried upon him aloud, 'Most noble knight, Sir
Launcelot du Lake, save my life, for I yield me unto you, and
I require you, as ye be a knight and fellow of the Table
Round, slay me not, for I yield me as overcomen; and whether
I shall live or die I put me in the king's hands and yours.'

Then Sir Launcelot wist not what to do, for he had had
lever than all the good of the world he might have been
revenged upon Sir Meliagaunt; and Sir Launcelot looked up

to the queen Guenever, if he might espy by any sign or countenance what she would have done. And then the queen wagged her head upon Sir Launcelot, as though she would say, 'Slay him.' Full well knew Sir Launcelot by the wagging of her head that she would have him dead; then Sir Launcelot bad him rise for shame and perform that battle to the utterance.

'Nay,' said Sir Meliagaunt, 'I will never arise until ye take me as yielden and recreant.'

'I shall proffer you large proffers,' said Sir Launcelot, 'that is for to say, I shall unarm my head and my left quarter of my body, all that may be unarmed, and let bind my left hand behind me, so that it shall not help me, and right so I shall do battle with you.'

Then Sir Meliagaunt start up upon his legs, and said on high, 'My lord Arthur, take heed to this proffer, for I will take it, and let him be disarmed and bounden according to his proffer.'

'What say ye,' said King Arthur unto Sir Launcelot, 'will ye abide by your proffer?'

'Yea, my lord,' said Sir Launcelot, 'I will never go from that I have once said.'

Then the knights parters of the field disarmed Sir Launcelot, first his head, and sithen his left arm, and his left side, and they bound his left arm behind his back, without shield or anything, and then they were put together. Wit you well there was many a lady and knight marvelled that Sir Launcelot would jeopardy himself in such wise.

Then Sir Meliagaunt came with his sword all on high, and Sir Launcelot showed him openly his bare head and the bare left side; and when he weened to have smitten him upon the bare head, then lightly he avoided the left leg and the left side, and put his right hand and his sword to that stroke, and put it aside with great sleight; and then with great force Sir Launcelot smote him on the helmet such a buffet that the stroke carved the head in two parts.

Then there was no more to do, but he was drawn out of

the field. And at the great instance of the knights of the Table Round, the king suffered him to be interred, and the mention made upon him, who slew him, and for what cause he was slain; and then the king and the queen made more of Sir Launcelot du Lake, and more he was cherished, than ever he was aforehand.

CHAPTER 10: *How Sir Urré came into Arthur's court for to be healed of his wounds, and how King Arthur would begin to handle him*

Then as the French book maketh mention, there was a good knight in the land of Hungary, his name was Sir Urré, and he was an adventurous knight, and in all places where he might hear of any deeds of worship there would he be.

So it happened in Spain there was an earl's son, his name was Alphegus, and at a great tournament in Spain this Sir Urré, knight of Hungary, and Sir Alphegus of Spain encountered together for very envy; and so either undertook other to the utterance. And by fortune Sir Urré slew Sir Alphegus, the earl's son of Spain, but this knight that was slain had given Sir Urré, or ever he was slain, seven great wounds, three on the head, and four on his body and upon his left hand. And this Sir Alphegus had a mother, the which was a great sorceress; and she, for the despite of her son's death, wrought by her subtle crafts that Sir Urré should never be whole, but ever his wounds should one time fester and another time bleed, so that he should never be whole until the best knight of the world had searched his wounds: and thus she made her avaunt, wherethrough it was known that Sir Urré should never be whole.

Then his mother let make an horse litter, and put him therein under two palfreys; and then she took Sir Urré's sister with him, a full fair damosel, whose name was Felelolie; and then she took a page with him to keep their horses, and so they led Sir Urré through many countries. For as the

French book saith, she led him so seven year through all lands christened, and never she could find no knight that might ease her son.

So she came into Scotland and into the bounds of England, and by fortune she came nigh the feast of Pentecost until King Arthur's court, that at that time was holden at Carlisle. And when she came there, then she made it openly to be known how that she was come into that land for to heal her son. Then King Arthur let call that lady, and asked her the cause why she brought that hurt knight into that land.

'My most noble king,' said that lady, 'wit you well I brought him hither for to be healed of his wounds, that of all this seven year he might not be whole.'

And then she told the king where he was wounded, and of whom; and how his mother had discovered in her pride how she had wrought that by enchantment so that he should never be whole until the best knight of the world had searched his wounds. 'And so I have passed through all the lands christened to have him healed, except this land. And if I fail to heal him here in this land, I will never take more pain upon me, and that is pity, for he was a good knight, and of great nobleness.'

'What is his name?' said Arthur.

'My good and gracious lord,' she said, 'his name is Sir Urré of the Mount.'

'In good time,' said the king, 'and sith ye are come into this land, ye are right welcome; and wit you well here shall your son be healed, and ever any Christian man may heal him. And for to give all other men of worship courage, I myself will assay to handle your son, and so shall all the kings, dukes, and earls that be here present with me at this time; thereto will I command them, and well I wot they shall obey and do after my commandment. And wit you well,' said King Arthur unto Urré's sister, 'I shall begin to handle him, and search unto my power, not presuming upon me that I am so worthy to heal your son by my deeds, but I will courage other men of worship to do as I will do.'

And then the king commanded all the kings, dukes, and earls, and all noble knights of the Round Table that were there that time present, to come into the meadow of Carlisle. And so at that time there were but an hundred and ten of the Round Table, for forty knights were that time away. And so here we must begin at King Arthur, as is kindly to begin at him that was the most man of worship that was christened at that time.

CHAPTER 11: *How King Arthur handled Sir Urré, and after him many other knights of the Round Table*

Then King Arthur looked upon Sir Urré, and the king thought he was a full likely man when he was whole; and then King Arthur made him to be take down off the litter and laid him upon the earth, and there was laid a cushion of gold that he should kneel upon.

And then noble Arthur said, 'Fair knight, me repenteth of thy hurt, and for to courage all other noble knights I will pray thee softly to suffer me to handle your wounds.'

'Most noble christened king,' said Urré, 'do as ye list, for I am at the mercy of God, and at your commandment.'

So then Arthur softly handled him, and then some of his wounds renewed upon bleeding.

Then the King Clarivaus of Northumberland searched, and it would not be. And then Sir Berrant le Apres that was called the King with the Hundred Knights, he assayed and failed; and so did King Uriens of the land of Gore; so did King Agwisance of Ireland; so did King Nentres of Garlot; so did King Carados of Scotland; so did the Duke Galahaut, the Haut Prince; so did Constantine, that was Sir Carados' son of Cornwall; so did Duke Chaleins of Clarance; so did the Earl Ulbawes; so did the Earl Lambaile; so did the Earl Aristause. Then came in Sir Gawain with his three sons, Sir Gingalin, Sir Florence, and Sir Lovel, these two were begotten upon Sir Brandiles' sister; and all they failed. Then came in Sir Agravain, Sir Gaheris, Sir Mordred, and the good knight, Sir Gareth, that was of very knighthood worth all the brethren.

So came knights of Launcelot's kin, but Sir Launcelot was not that time in the court, for he was that time upon his adventures. Then Sir Lionel, Sir Ector de Maris, Sir Bors de Ganis, Sir Blamor de Ganis, Sir Bleoberis de Ganis, Sir Gahalatine, Sir Galihodin, Sir Menaduke, Sir Villiars the Valiant, Sir Hebes le Renoumes. All these were of Sir Launcelot's kin, and all they failed.

Then came in Sir Sagramore le Desirous, Sir Dodinas le Savage, Sir Dinadan, Sir Breunor le Noire, that Sir Kay named La Cote Male Taile, and Sir Kay le Seneschal, Sir Kainus de Stranges, Sir Meliot de Logris, Sir Petipase of Winchelsea, Sir Galleron of Galway, Sir Melion of the Mountain, Sir Cardok, Sir Uwain les Avoutres, and Sir Ozanna le Cure Hardy. Then came in Sir Astamor, and Sir Grummor Grummorson, Sir Crosselm, Sir Servause le Breuse, that was called a passing strong knight, for as the book saith, the chief lady of the lake feasted Sir Launcelot and Servause le Breuse, and when she had feasted them both at sundry times she prayed them to give her a boon. And they granted it her. And then she prayed Sir Servause that he would promise her never to do battle against Sir Launcelot du Lake, and in the same wise she prayed Sir Launcelot never to do battle against Sir Servause, and so either promised her. For the French book saith, that Sir Servause had never courage nor lust to do battle against no man, but if it were against giants, and against dragons, and wild beasts.

So we pass unto them that at the king's request made them all that were there at that high feast, as of the knights of the Table Round, for to search Sir Urré. To that intent the king did it: to wit which was the noblest knight among them.

Then came Sir Agloval, Sir Durnore, Sir Tor, that was begotten upon Aries the cowherd's wife, but he was

449

begotten afore Aries wedded her (and King Pellinor begat them all, first Sir Tor, Sir Agloval, Sir Durnore, Sir Lamorak, the most noblest knight one that ever was in Arthur's days as for a worldly knight, and Sir Percival that was peerless except Sir Galahad in holy deeds, but they died in the quest of the Sangrail).

Then came Sir Griflet le Fise de Dieu, Sir Lucan the Butler, Sir Bedevere his brother, Sir Brandiles, Sir Constantine, Sir Cador's son of Cornwall, that was king after Arthur's days, and Sir Clegis, Sir Sadok, Sir Dinas le Seneschal of Cornwall, Sir Fergus, Sir Driant, Sir Lambegus, Sir Clarrus of Cleremont, Sir Cloddrus, Sir Hectimere, Sir Edward of Caernarvon, Sir Dinas, Sir Priamus, that was christened by Sir Tristram the noble knight, and these three were brethren; Sir Helin le Blank that was son to Sir Bors, he begat him upon King Brandegoris' daughter, and Sir Brian de Listinoise; Sir Gauter, Sir Arnold, Sir Gilmer, were three brethren that Sir Launcelot won upon a bridge in Sir Kay's arms; Sir Gumret le Petite, Sir Bellengerus le Beuse, that was son to the good knight, Sir Alisander le Orphelin, that was slain by the treason of King Mark. (Also that traitor king slew the noble knight Sir Tristram, as he sat harping afore his lady La Beale Isoud, with a trenchant glaive, for whose death was much bewailing of every knight that ever were in Arthur's days; there was never none so bewailed as was Sir Tristram and Sir Lamorak, for they were traitorously slain, Sir Tristram by King Mark, and Sir Lamorak by Sir Gawain and his brethren. And this Sir Bellengerus revenged the death of his father Alisander and Sir Tristram, slew King Mark, and La Beale Isoud died swooning upon the cross of Sir Tristram, whereof was great pity. And all that were with King Mark that were consenting to the death of Sir Tristram were slain, as Sir Andred and many other.)

Then came Sir Hebes, Sir Morganor, Sir Sentraille, Sir Suppinabiles, Sir Bellengerus le Orgulous, that the good knight Sir Lamorak won in plain battle; Sir Nerovens and Sir Plenorius, two good knights that Sir Launcelot won; Sir

Darras, Sir Harry le Fise Lake, Sir Erminide, brother to King Hermance, for whom Sir Palomides fought at the Red City with two brethren; and Sir Selises of the Dolorous Tower, Sir Edward of Orkney, Sir Ironside, that was called the noble Knight of the Red Launds that Sir Gareth won for the love of Dame Lyonesse, Sir Arrok de Grevaunt, Sir Degrane Saunce Velany that fought with the giant of the black lowe, Sir Epinogrus, that was the King's son of Northumberland, Sir Pelleas that loved the lady Ettard, and he had died for her love had not been one of the ladies of the lake, her name was Dame Nimue, and she wedded Sir Pelleas, and she saved him that he was never slain, and he was a full noble knight; and Sir Lamiel of Cardiff that was a great lover. Sir Plaine de Fors, Sir Melias de Lile, Sir Borre le Cure Hardy that was King Arthur's son, Sir Mador de la Porte, Sir Colgrevaunce, Sir Hervis de la Forest Savage, Sir Marrok, the good knight that was betrayed with his wife, for she made him seven year a werewolf, Sir Persant, Sir Pertelope, his brother, that was called the Green Knight, and Sir Perimones, brother to them both that was called the Red Knight, that Sir Gareth won when he was called Beaumains.

All these hundred knights and ten searched Sir Urré's wounds by the commandment of King Arthur.

CHAPTER 12: *How Sir Launcelot was commanded by Arthur to handle his wounds, and anon he was all whole, and how they thanked God*

'Mercy Jesu,' said King Arthur, 'where is Sir Launcelot du Lake that he is not here at this time?'

Thus, as they stood and spake of many things, there was espied Sir Launcelot that came riding toward them, and told the king.

'Peace,' said the king, 'let no manner thing be said until he be come to us.'

So when Sir Launcelot espied King Arthur, he descended

from his horse and came to the king, and saluted him and them all.

Anon as the maid, Sir Urré's sister, saw Sir Launcelot, she ran to her brother there as he lay in his litter, and said, 'Brother, here is come a knight that my heart giveth greatly unto.'

'Fair sister,' said Sir Urré, 'so doth my heart light against him, and certainly I hope now to be healed, for my heart giveth unto him more than to all these that have searched me.'

Then said Arthur unto Sir Launcelot, 'Ye must do as we have done;' and told Sir Launcelot what they had done, and showed him them all, that had searched him.

'Jesu defend me,' said Sir Launcelot, 'when so many kings and knights have assayed and failed, that I should presume upon me to achieve that all ye, my lords, might not achieve.'

'Ye shall not choose,' said King Arthur, 'for I will command you for to do as we all have done.'

'My most renowned lord,' said Sir Launcelot, 'ye know well I dare not nor may not disobey your commandment, but and I might or durst, wit you well I would not take upon me to touch that wounded knight in that intent that I should pass all other knights; Jesu defend me from that shame.'

'Ye take it wrong,' said King Arthur, 'ye shall not do it for no presumption, but for to bear us fellowship insomuch ye be a fellow of the Table Round; and wit you well,' said King Arthur, 'and ye prevail not and heal him, I dare say there is no knight in this land may heal him, and therefore I pray you, do as we have done.'

And then all the kings and knights for the most part prayed Sir Launcelot to search him; and then the wounded knight, Sir Urré, set him up weakly, and prayed Sir Launcelot heartily, saying, 'Courteous knight, I require thee for God's sake heal my wounds, for methinketh ever sithen ye came here my wounds grieven me not.'

'Ah, my fair lord,' said Sir Launcelot, 'Jesu would that I

might help you; I shame me sore that I should be thus rebuked, for never was I able in worthiness to do so high a thing.'

Then Sir Launcelot kneeled down by the wounded knight saying. 'My lord Arthur, I must do your commandment, the which is sore against my heart.' And then he held up his hands, and looked into the east, saying secretly unto himself, 'Thou blessed Father, Son, and Holy Ghost, I beseech Thee of Thy mercy, that my simple worship and honesty be saved, and Thou blessed Trinity, Thou mayst give power to heal this sick knight by Thy great virtue and grace of Thee, but, good Lord, never of myself.'

And then Sir Launcelot prayed Sir Urré to let him see his head; and then devoutly kneeling he ransacked the three wounds, that they bled a little, and forthwithal the wounds fair healed, and seemed as they had been whole a seven year. And in likewise he searched his body of other three wounds, and they healed in likewise; and then the last of all he searched the which was in his hand, and anon it healed fair.

Then King Arthur and all the kings and knights kneeled down and gave thankings and lovings unto God and to his blessed mother. And ever Sir Launcelot wept as he had been a child that had been beaten.

Then King Arthur let array priests and clerks in the most devoutest manner, to bring in Sir Urré within Carlisle, with singing and loving to God. And when this was done, the king let clothe him in the richest manner that could be thought; and then were there but few better made knights in all the court, for he was passingly well made and bigly. And Arthur asked Sir Urré how he felt himself.

'My good lord,' he said, 'I felt myself never so lusty.'

'Will ye joust and do deeds of arms?' said King Arthur.

'Sir,' said Urré, 'and I had all that longed unto jousts I would be soon ready.'

CHAPTER 13: *How there was a party made of an hundred knights against an hundred knights; and of other matters*

Then Arthur made a party of hundred knights to be against an hundred knights. And so upon the morn they jousted for a diamond, but there jousted none of the dangerous knights; and so for to shorten this tale, Sir Urré and Sir Lavaine jousted best that day, for there was none of them but he overthrew and pulled down thirty knights; and then by the assent of all the kings and lords, Sir Urré and Sir Lavaine were made knights of the Table Round.

And Sir Lavaine cast his love unto Dame Felelolie, Sir Urré's sister, and then they were wedded together with great joy, and King Arthur gave to every each of them a barony of lands.

And this Sir Urré would never go from Sir Launcelot, but he and Sir Lavaine awaited evermore upon him; and they were in all the court accounted for good knights, and full desirous in arms; and many noble deeds they did, for they would have no rest, but ever sought adventures. Thus they lived in all that court with great noblesse and joy long time.

But every night and day Sir Agravain, Sir Gawain's brother, awaited Queen Guenever and Sir Launcelot du Lake to put them to a rebuke and shame.

And so I leave here of this tale, and overleap[1] great books of Sir Launcelot du Lake, what great adventures he did when he was called le Chevaler du Chariot. For as the French book saith, because of despite that knights and ladies called him 'the knight that rode in the chariot' like as he were judged to the gallows, therefore in despite of all them that named him so, he was carried in a chariot a twelvemonth, for, but little after that he had slain Sir Meliagaunt in the queen's quarrel, he never in a twelvemonth came on horseback. And as the French book saith, he did that twelvemonth more than forty battles. And because I have lost the very matter of le Chevaler du Chariot, I depart from the tale of Sir Launcelot, and here I go unto the morte of King Arthur; and that caused Sir Agravain.

Explicit liber xix.
And hereafter followeth the most
piteous history of the morte of
King Arthur, the which is
the twentieth book

morte: death.

Book XX

How Sir Agravain and Sir Mordred were busy upon Sir Gawain for to disclose the love between Sir Launcelot and Queen Guenever

In May when every lusty heart flourisheth and burgeoneth, for as the season is lusty to behold and comfortable, so man and woman rejoicen and gladden of summer coming with his fresh flowers: for winter with his rough winds and blasts causeth a lusty man and woman to cower, and sit fast by the fire.

So in this season, as in the month of May, it befell a great anger and unhap that stinted not till the flower of chivalry of all the world was destroyed and slain; and all was long upon two unhappy knights, the which were named Agravain and Sir Mordred, that were brethren unto Sir Gawain. For this Sir Agravain and Sir Mordred had ever a privy hate unto the queen Dame Guenever and to Sir Launcelot, and daily and nightly they ever watched upon Sir Launcelot.

So it mishapped, Sir Gawain and all his brethren were in King Arthur's chamber; and then Sir Agravain said thus openly, and not in no counsel, that many knights might hear it, 'I marvel that we all be not ashamed both to see and to know how Sir Launcelot lieth daily and nightly by the queen, and all we know it so; and it is shamefully suffered of us all, that we all should suffer so noble a king as King Arthur is so to be shamed.'

Then spake Sir Gawain, and said, 'Brother Sir Agravain, I pray you and charge you move no such matters no more afore me, for wit you well,' said Sir Gawain, 'I will not be of your counsel.'

'So God me help,' said Sir Gaheris and Sir Gareth, 'we

456

will not be knowing, brother Agravain, of your deeds.'

'Then will I,' said Sir Mordred.

'I leve well that,' said Sir Gawain, 'for ever unto all unhappiness, brother Sir Mordred, thereto will ye grant; and I would that ye left all this, and made you not so busy, for I know,' said Sir Gawain, 'what will fall of it.'

'Fall of it what fall may,' said Sir Agravain, 'I will disclose it to the king.'

'Not by my counsel,' said Sir Gawain, 'for and there rise war and wrack betwixt Sir Launcelot and us, wit you well brother, there will many kings and great lords hold with Sir Launcelot. Also, brother Sir Agravain,' said Sir Gawain, 'ye must remember how ofttimes Sir Launcelot hath rescued the king and the queen; and the best of us all had been full cold at the heart root had not Sir Launcelot been better than we, and that hath he proved himself full oft. And as for my part,' said Sir Gawain, 'I will never be against Sir Launcelot for one day's deed, when he rescued me from King Carados of the Dolorous Tower, and slew him, and saved my life. Also, brother Sir Agravain and Sir Mordred, in like wise Sir Launcelot rescued you both, and threescore and two, from Sir Turquin. Methinketh brother, such kind deeds and kindness should be remembered.'

'Do as ye list,' said Sir Agravain, 'for I will layne it no longer.'

With these words came to them King Arthur.

'Now brother, stint your noise,' said Sir Gawain.

'We will not,' said Sir Agravain and Sir Mordred.

'Will ye so?' said Sir Gawain. 'Then God speed you, for I will not hear your tales ne be of your counsel.'

'No more will I,' said Sir Gareth and Sir Gaheris, 'for we will never say evil by that man; for because,' said Sir Gareth, 'Sir Launcelot made me knight, by no manner owe I to say ill of him;' and therewithal they three departed, making great dole.

'Alas,' said Sir Gawain and Sir Gareth, 'now is this realm

leve: believe.

457

wholly mischieved, and the noble fellowship of the Round Table shall be disperpled.'

So they departed.

CHAPTER 2: *How Sir Agravain disclosed their love to King Arthur, and how King Arthur gave them licence to take him*

And then Sir Arthur asked them what noise they made.

'My lord,' said Agravain, 'I shall tell you that I may keep no longer. Here is I, and my brother Sir Mordred, brake unto my brother Sir Gawain, Sir Gaheris, and to Sir Gareth, how this we know all, that Sir Launcelot holdeth your queen, and hath done long; and we be your sister's sons, and we may suffer it no longer, and all we wot that ye should be above Sir Launcelot; and ye are the king that made him knight, and therefore we will prove it, that he is a traitor to your person.'

'If it be so,' said Sir Arthur, 'wit you well he is none other, but I would be loth to begin such a thing but I might have proofs upon it; for Sir Launcelot is an hardy knight, and all ye know he is the best knight among us all; and but if he be taken with the deed, he will fight with him that bringeth up the noise, and I know no knight that is able to match him. Therefore and it be sooth as ye say, I would he were taken with the deed.'

For as the French book saith, the king was full loth thereto, that any noise should be upon Sir Launcelot and his queen; for the king had a deeming, but he would not hear of it, for Sir Launcelot had done so much for him and the queen so many times, that wit ye well the king loved him passingly well.

'My lord,' said Sir Agravain, 'ye shall ride to-morn on hunting, and doubt ye not Sir Launcelot will not go with you. Then when it draweth toward night, ye may send the queen word that ye will lie out all that night, and so may ye send for your cooks, and then upon pain of death we shall take him that night with the queen, and other we shall bring him to you dead or quick.'

'I will well,' said the king; 'then I counsel you,' said the king, 'take with you sure fellowship.'

'Sir,' said Agravain, 'my brother, Sir Mordred, and I, will take with us twelve knights of the Round Table.'

'Beware' said King Arthur, 'for I warn you ye shall find him wight.'

'Let us deal,' said Sir Agravain and Sir Mordred.

So on the morn King Arthur rode on hunting, and sent word to the queen that he would be out all that night. Then Sir Agravain and Sir Mordred gat to them twelve knights, and did themself in a chamber in the Castle of Carlisle, and these were their names: Sir Colgrevaunce, Sir Mador de la Porte, Sir Gingalin, Sir Meliot de Logris, Sir Petipase of Winchelsea, Sir Galleron of Galway, Sir Melion of the Mountain, Sir Astamore, Sir Gromore Somir Jaure, Sir Curselaine, Sir Florence, Sir Lovel. So these twelve knights were with Sir Mordred and Sir Agravain, and all they were of Scotland, other of Sir Gawain's kin, other well-willers to his brethren.

So when the night came, Sir Launcelot told Sir Bors how he would go that night and speak with the queen.

'Sir,' said Sir Bors, 'ye shall not go this night by my counsel.'

'Why?' said Sir Launcelot.

'Sir,' said Sir Bors, 'I dread me ever of Sir Agravain, that waiteth you daily to do you shame and us all; and never gave my heart against no going, that ever ye went to the queen, so much as now; for I mistrust that the king is out this night from the queen because peradventure he hath lain some watch for you and the queen, and therefore I dread me sore of treason.'

'Have ye no dread,' said Sir Launcelot, 'for I shall go and come again, and make no tarrying.'

'Sir,' said Sir Bors, 'that me repenteth, for I dread me sore that your going out this night shall wrath us all.'

'Fair nephew,' said Sir Launcelot, 'I marvel much why ye

say thus, sithen the queen hath sent for me; and wit ye well I will not be so much a coward, but she shall understand I will see her good grace.'

'God speed you well,' said Sir Bors, 'and send you sound and safe again.'

CHAPTER 3: *How Sir Launcelot was espied in the queen's chamber, and how Sir Agravain and Sir Mordred came with twelve knights to slay him*

So Sir Launcelot departed, and took his sword under his arm, and so in his mantle that noble knight put himself in great jeopardy; and so he passed till he came to the queen's chamber, and then Sir Launcelot was lightly put into the chamber.

And then, as the French book saith, the queen and Launcelot were together. And whether they were abed or at other manner of disports, me list not hereof make no mention, for love that time was not as is nowadays.

But thus as they were together, there came Sir Agravain and Sir Mordred, with twelve knights with them of the Round Table, and they said with crying voice, 'Traitor knight, Sir Launcelot du Lake, now art thou taken.'

And thus they cried with a loud voice, that all the court might hear it; and they all fourteen were armed at all points as they should fight in a battle.

'Alas,' said Queen Guenever, 'now are we mischieved both.'

'Madam,' said Sir Launcelot, 'is there here any armour within your chamber, that I might cover my poor body withal? And if there be any give it me, and I shall soon stint their malice, by the grace of God.'

'Truly,' said the queen, 'I have none armour, shield, sword, nor spear; wherefore I dread me sore our long love is come to a mischievous end, for I hear by their noise there be many noble knights, and well I wot they be surely armed; against them ye may make no resistance. Wherefore ye are likely to be slain, and then shall I be burnt. For and ye might escape them,' said the queen, 'I would not doubt but that ye would rescue me in what danger that ever I stood in.'

'Alas,' said Sir Launcelot, 'in all my life thus was I never bestad, that I should be thus shamefully slain for lack of mine armour.'

But ever in one Sir Agravain and Sir Mordred cried, 'Traitor knight, come out of the queen's chamber, for wit thou well thou art so beset that thou shalt not escape.'

'O Jesu mercy,' said Sir Launcelot, 'this shameful cry and noise I may not suffer, for better were death at once than thus to endure this pain.'

Then he took the queen in his arms, and kissed her, and said, 'Most noble Christian queen, I beseech you as ye have been ever my special good lady, and I at all times your true poor knight unto my power, and as I never failed you in right nor in wrong, sithen the first day King Arthur made me knight, that ye will pray for my soul if that I here be slain, for well I am assured that Sir Bors, mine nephew, and all the remnant of my kin, with Sir Lavaine and Sir Urré, that they will not fail you to rescue you from the fire; and therefore, mine own lady, recomfort yourself, whatsomever come of me, that ye go with Sir Bors, my nephew, and Sir Urré, and they all will do you all the pleasure that they can or may, that ye shall live like a queen upon my lands.'

'Nay, Launcelot,' said the queen, 'wit thou well I will never live after thy days, but and thou be slain I will take my death as meekly for Jesus Christ's sake as ever did any Christian queen.'

'Well, madam,' said Launcelot, 'sith it is so that the day is come that our love must depart, wit you well I shall sell my life as dear as I may; and a thousandfold,' said Sir Launcelot, 'I am more heavier for you than for myself. And now I had lever than to be lord of all Christendom, that I had sure armour upon me, that men might speak of my deeds or ever I were slain.'

'Truly,' said the queen, 'I would and it might please God that they would take me and slay me, and suffer you to escape.'

'That shall never be,' said Sir Launcelot, 'God defend me from such a shame, but Jesu be thou my shield and mine armour!'

CHAPTER 4: *How Sir Launcelot slew Sir Colgrevaunce, and armed him in his harness, and after slew Sir Agravain, and twelve of his fellows*

And therewith Sir Launcelot wrapped his mantle about his arm well and surely; and by then they had gotten a great form out of the hall, and therewithal they rashed at the door.

'Fair lords,' said Sir Launcelot, 'leave your noise and your rashing, and I shall set open this door, and then may ye do with me what it liketh you.'

'Come off then,' said they all, 'and do it, for it availeth thee not to strive against us all; and therefore let us into this chamber, and we shall save thy life until thou come to King Arthur.'

Then Launcelot unbarred the door, and with his left hand he held it open a little, so that but one man might come in at once; and so there came striding a good knight, a much man and large, and his name was Colgrevaunce of Gore, and he with a sword struck at Sir Launcelot mightily; and he put aside the stroke and gave him such a buffet upon the helmet, that he fell grovelling dead within the chamber door.

And then Sir Launcelot with great might drew that dead knight within the chamber door; and Sir Launcelot with help of the queen and her ladies was lightly armed in Sir Colgrevaunce's armour.

And ever stood Sir Agravain and Sir Mordred crying, 'Traitor knight, come out of the queen's chamber.'

'Leave your noise,' said Sir Launcelot unto Sir Agravain, 'for wit you well, Sir Agravain, ye shall not prison me this night; and therefore and ye do by my counsel, go ye all from this chamber door, and make not such crying and such manner of slander as ye do; for I promise you by my knighthood, and ye will depart and make no more noise, I shall as to-morn appear afore you all before the king, and then let it be seen which of you all, other else ye all, that will accuse me of treason; and there I shall answer you as a knight should, that hither I came to the queen for no manner of mal engine, and that will I prove and make it good upon you within my hands.'

'Fie on thee, traitor,' said Sir Agravain and Sir Mordred, 'we will have thee maugre thy head, and slay thee if we list; for we let thee wit we have the choice of King Arthur to save thee or to slay thee.'

'Ah sirs,' said Sir Launcelot, 'is there none other grace with you? Then keep yourself.'

So then Sir Launcelot set all open the chamber door, and mightily and knightly he strode in amongst them; and anon at the first buffet he slew Sir Agravain. And twelve of his fellows after, within a little while after, he laid them cold to the earth, for there was none of the twelve that might stand Sir Launcelot one buffet. Also Sir Launcelot wounded Sir Mordred, and he fled with all his might.

And then Sir Launcelot returned again unto the queen, and said, 'Madam, now wit you well all our true love is brought to an end, for now will King Arthur ever be my foe; and therefore, madam, and it like you that I may have you with me, I shall save you from all manner adventures dangerous.'

'That is not best,' said the queen. 'Meseemeth now ye have done so much harm, it will be best ye hold you still with this. And if ye see that as to-morn they will put me unto the death, then may ye rescue me as ye think best.'

'I will well,' said Sir Launcelot, 'for have ye no doubt, while I am living I shall rescue you.' And then he kissed her, and either gave other a ring; and so there he left the queen, and went until his lodging.

CHAPTER 5: *How Sir Launcelot came to Sir Bors, and told him how he had sped, and in what adventure he had been, and how he had escaped*

When Sir Bors saw Sir Launcelot he was never so glad of his home coming as he was then.

'Jesu mercy,' said Sir Launcelot, 'why be ye all armed? What meaneth this?'

'Sir,' said Sir Bors, 'after ye were departed from us, we all that be of your blood and your well-willers were so dretched that some of us leapt out of our beds naked, and some in their dreams caught naked swords in their hands; therefore,' said Sir Bors, 'we deem there is some great strife at hand; and then we all deemed that ye were betrapped with some treason, and therefore we made us thus ready, what need that ever ye were in.'

'My fair nephew,' said Sir Launcelot unto Sir Bors, 'now shall ye wit all, that this night I was more harder bestad than[1] ever I was in my life, and yet I escaped.' And so he told them all how and in what manner, as ye have heard tofore. 'And therefore, my fellows,' said Sir Launcelot, 'I pray you all that ye will be of good heart in what need somever I stand, for now is war come to us all.'

'Sir,' said Bors, 'all is welcome that God sendeth us, and we have had much weal with you and much worship, and therefore we will take the woe with you as we have taken the weal.'

'And therefore,' they said all, there were many good knights, 'look ye take no discomfort, for there nis no bands of knights under heaven but we shall be able to grieve them as much as they may us. And therefore discomfort not yourself by no manner, and we shall gather together that we love, and that loveth us, and what that ye will have done shall be done. And therefore, Sir Launcelot,' said they, 'we will take the woe with the weal.'

'Gramercy,' said Sir Launcelot, 'of your good comfort, for

in my great distress, my fair nephew, ye comfort me greatly, and much I am beholding unto you. But this, my fair nephew, I would that ye did in all haste that ye may, or it be forth days, that ye will look in their lodging that be lodged here nigh about the king, which will hold with me, and which will not, for now I would know which were my friends from my foes.'

'Sir,' said Sir Bors, 'I shall do my pain, and or it be seven of the clock I shall wit of such as ye have said before, who will hold with you.'

Then Sir Bors called unto him Sir Lionel, Sir Ector de Maris, Sir Blamor de Ganis, Sir Bleoberis de Ganis, Sir Gahalantine, Sir Galihodin, Sir Galihud, Sir Menaduke, Sir Villiars the Valiant, Sir Hebes le Renoumes, Sir Lavaine, Sir Urré of Hungary, Sir Nerovens, Sir Plenorious (these two knights Sir Launcelot made, and the one he won upon a bridge, and therefore they would never be against him), and Harry le Fise du Lake, and Sir Selises of the Dolorous Tower, and Sir Melias de Lile, and Sir Bellengerus le Beuse, that was Sir Alisander's son le Orphelin, because his mother Alice la Beale Pellerin and she was kin unto Sir Launcelot, and he held with him. So there came Sir Palomides and Sir Safer, his brother, to hold with Sir Launcelot, and Sir Clegis, Sir Sadok, and Sir Dinas, Sir Clarrus of Cleremont. So these two-and-twenty knights drew them together, and by then they were armed on horseback, and promised Sir Launcelot to do what he would. Then there fell to them, what of North Wales and of Cornwall, for Sir Lamorak's sake and for Sir Tristram's sake, to the number of a four-score knights.

'My lords,' said Sir Launcelot, 'wit you well I have been ever since I came into this country well willed unto my lord, King Arthur, and unto my lady, Queen Guenever, unto my power; and this night because my lady the queen sent for me to speak with her, I suppose it was made by treason, howbeit I dare largely excuse her person, notwithstanding I was there by a forecast near slain, but as Jesu provided me I escaped all their malice and treason.' And then that noble knight Sir

Launcelot told them all how he was hard bestad in the queen's chamber, and how and in what manner he escaped from them. 'And therefore,' said Sir Launcelot, 'wit you well, my fair lords, I am sure there nis but war unto me and mine. And for because I have slain this night these knights, I wot well as is Sir Agravain, Sir Gawain's brother, and at the least twelve of his fellows, for this cause now I am sure of mortal war, for these knights were sent and ordained by King Arthur to betray me. And therefore the king will in this heat and malice judge the queen to the fire, and that may not I suffer, that she should be burnt for my sake; for and I may be heard and suffered and so taken, I will fight for the queen, that she is a true lady unto her lord; but the king in his heat I dread me will not take me as I ought to be taken.'

CHAPTER 6: *Of the counsel and advice which was taken by Sir Launcelot and by his friends for to save the queen*

'My lord, Sir Launcelot,' said Sir Bors, 'by mine advice ye shall take the woe with the weal, and take it in patience, and thank God of it. And sithen it is fallen as it is, I counsel you keep yourself, for and ye will yourself, there is no fellowship of knights christened that shall do you wrong. Also I will counsel you my lord, Sir Launcelot, that and my lady, Queen Guenever, be in distress, insomuch as she is in pain for your sake, that ye knightly rescue her; and ye did otherwise, all the world will speak of you shame to the world's end. Insomuch as ye were taken with her, whether ye did right or wrong, it is now your part to hold with the queen, that she be not slain and put to a mischievous death, for and she so die the shame shall be yours.'

'Jesu defend me from shame,' said Sir Launcelot, 'and keep and save my lady the queen from villainy and shameful death, and that she never be destroyed in my default; wherefore my fair lords, my kin, and my friends,' said Sir Launcelot, 'what will ye do?'

Then they said all, 'We will do as ye will do.'

'I put this to you,' said Sir Launcelot, 'that if my lord Arthur by evil counsel will to-morn in his heat put my lady the queen to the fire there to be burnt, now I pray you counsel me what is best to do.'

Then they said all at once with one voice, 'Sir, us thinketh best that ye knightly rescue the queen, insomuch as she shall be burnt it is for your sake; and it is to suppose, and ye might be handled, ye should have the same death, or a more shamefuller death. And sir, we say all, that ye have many times rescued her from death for other men's quarrels, us seemeth it is more your worship that ye rescue the queen from this peril, insomuch she hath it for your sake.'

Then Sir Launcelot stood still, and said, 'My fair lords, wit you well I would be loth to do that thing that should dishonour you or my blood, and wit you well I would be loth that my lady, the queen, should die a shameful death; but and it be so that ye will counsel me to rescue her, I must do much harm or I rescue her; and peradventure I shall there destroy some of my best friends, that should much repent me; and peradventure there be some, and they could well bring it about, or disobey my lord King Arthur, they would soon come to me, the which I were loth to hurt. And if so be that I rescue her, where shall I keep her?'

'That shall be the least care of us all,' said Sir Bors. 'How did the noble knight Sir Tristram, by your good will? Kept not he with him La Beale Isoud near three year in Joyous Gard? The which was done by your althers device, and that same place is your own; and in likewise may ye do and ye list, and take the queen lightly away, if it so be the king will judge her to be burnt; and in Joyous Gard ye may keep her long enough until the heat of the king be past. And then shall ye bring again the queen to the king with great worship; and then peradventure ye shall have thank for her bringing home, and love and thank where other shall have maugre.'

'That is hard to do,' said Sir Launcelot, 'for by Sir Tristram I may have a warning, for when by means of treaties, Sir Tristram brought again La Beale Isoud unto King Mark from Joyous Gard, look what befell on the end, how shamefully that false traitor King Mark slew him as he sat harping afore his lady La Beale Isoud, with a grounden glaive he thrust him in behind to the heart. It grieveth me,' said Sir Launcelot, 'to speak of his death, for all the world may not find such a knight.'

'All this is truth,' said Sir Bors, 'but there is one thing shall courage you and us all, ye know well King Arthur and King Mark were never like of conditions, for there was never yet man could prove King Arthur untrue of his promise.'

So to make short tale, they were all consented that for better other for worse, if so were that the queen were on that morn brought to the fire, shortly they all would rescue her. And so by the advice of Sir Launcelot, they put them all in an ambushment in a wood, as nigh Carlisle as they might, and there they abode still, to wit what the king would do.

CHAPTER 7: *How Sir Mordred rode hastily to the king, to tell him of the affray and death of Sir Agravain and the other knights*

Now turn we again unto Sir Mordred, that when he was escaped from the noble knight, Sir Launcelot, he anon gat his horse and mounted upon him, and rode unto King Arthur, sore wounded and smitten, and all forbled; and there he told the king all how it was, and how they were all slain save himself all only.

'Jesu mercy, how may this be?' said the king. 'Took ye him in the queen's chamber?'

'Yea, so God me help,' said Sir Mordred, 'there we found him unarmed, and there he slew Colgrevaunce, and armed him in his armour;' and all this he told the king from the beginning to the ending.

'Jesu mercy,' said the king, 'he is a marvellous knight of

prowess. Alas, me sore repenteth,' said the king, 'that ever
Sir Launcelot should be against me. Now I am sure the noble
fellowship of the Round Table is broken for ever, for with
him will many a noble knight hold; and now it is fallen so,'
said the king, 'that I may not with my worship but the queen
must suffer the death.'

So then there was made great ordinance in this heat, that
the queen must be judged to the death. And the law was such
in those days that whatsomever they were, of what estate or
degree, if they were found guilty of treason, there should be
none other remedy but death; and either the men[1] or the taking with the deed should be causer of their hasty judgement.
And right so was it ordained for Queen Guenever, because
Sir Mordred was escaped sore wounded, and the death of
thirteen knights of the Round Table, these proofs and ex-
periences caused King Arthur to command the queen to the
fire there to be burnt.

Then spake Sir Gawain, and said, 'My lord Arthur, I would
counsel you not to be over-hasty, but that ye would put it in
respite, this judgement of my lady the queen, for many
causes. One it is, though it were so that Sir Launcelot were
found in the queen's chamber, yet it might be so that he
came thither for none evil; for ye know my lord,' said Sir
Gawain, 'that the queen is much beholden unto Sir Launcelot, more than unto any other knight, for ofttimes he hath
saved her life, and done battle for her when all the court refused the queen; and peradventure she sent for him for goodness and for none evil, to reward him for his good deeds that
he had done to her in times past. And peradventure my lady,
the queen, sent for him to that intent that Sir Launcelot
should come to her good grace privily and secretly, weening
to her that it was best so to do, in eschewing and dreading of
slander; for ofttimes we do many things that we ween it be
for the best, and yet peradventure it turneth to the worst. For
I dare say,' said Sir Gawain, 'my lady, your queen, is to you
both good and true; and as for Sir Launcelot,' said Sir Gawain,
'I dare say he will make it good upon any knight living that

will put upon himself villainy or shame, and in like wise he will make good for my lady, Dame Guenever.'

'That I believe well,' said King Arthur, 'but I will not that way with Sir Launcelot, for he trusteth so much upon his hands and his might that he doubteth no man; and therefore for my queen he shall never fight more, for she shall have the law. And if I may get Sir Launcelot, wit you well he shall have a shameful death.'

'Jesu defend,' said Sir Gawain, 'that I may never see it.'

'Why say ye so?' said King Arthur. 'Forsooth ye have no cause to love Sir Launcelot, for this night last past he slew your brother, Sir Agravain, a full good knight, and almost he had slain your other brother, Sir Mordred, and also there he slew thirteen noble knights; and also, Sir Gawain, remember ye he slew two sons of yours, Sir Florence and Sir Lovel.'

'My lord,' said Sir Gawain, 'of all this I have knowledge, of whose deaths I repent me sore; but insomuch I gave them warning, and told my brethren and my sons aforehand what would fall in the end, insomuch they would not do by my counsel, I will not meddle me thereof, nor revenge me nothing of their deaths; for I told them it was no boot to strive with Sir Launcelot. Howbeit I am sorry of the death of my brethren and of my sons, for they are the causers of their own death; for ofttimes I warned my brother Sir Agravain, and I told him the perils the which be now fallen.'

CHAPTER 8: *How Sir Launcelot and his kinsmen rescued the queen from the fire, and how he slew many knights*

Then said the noble King Arthur to Sir Gawain, 'Dear nephew, I pray you make you ready in your best armour, with your brethren, Sir Gaheris and Sir Gareth, to bring my queen to the fire, there to have her judgement and receive the death.'

'Nay, my most noble lord,' said Sir Gawain, 'that will I never do; for wit you well I will never be in that place where so noble a queen as is my lady, Dame Guenever, shall take a shameful end. For wit ye well,' said Sir Gawain, 'my heart will never serve me to see her die; and it shall never be said that ever I was of your counsel of her death.'

Then said the king to Sir Gawain, 'Suffer your brother Sir Gaheris and Sir Gareth to be there.'

'My lord,' said Sir Gawain, 'wit you well they will be loth to be there present, because of many adventures the which be like there to fall, but they are young and full unable to say you nay.'

Then spake Sir Gaheris, and the good knight Sir Gareth, unto Sir Arthur: 'Sir, ye may well command us to be there, but wit you well it shall be sore against our will; but and we be there by your straight commandment ye shall plainly hold us there excused: we will be there in peaceable wise, and bear none harness of war upon us.'

'In the name of God,' said the king, 'then make you ready, for she shall soon have her judgement anon.'

'Alas,' said Sir Gawain, 'that ever I should endure to see this woeful day.'

So Sir Gawain turned him and wept heartily, and so he went into his chamber.

And then the queen was led forth without Carlisle, and there she was despoiled into her smock. And so then her ghostly father was brought to her, to be shriven of her misdeeds. Then was there weeping, and wailing, and wringing of hands, of many lords and ladies, but there were but few in comparison that would bear any armour for to strength the death of the queen.

Then was there one that Sir Launcelot had sent unto that place for to espy what time the queen should go unto her death; and anon as he saw the queen despoiled into her smock, and so shriven, then he gave Sir Launcelot warning.

Then was there but spurring and plucking up of horses, and right so they came to the fire. And who that stood against them, there were they slain; there might none withstand Sir Launcelot, so all that bare arms and withstood them, there were they slain, full many a noble knight. For there was slain Sir Belliance le Orgulous, Sir Segwarides, Sir Griflet, Sir Brandiles, Sir Agloval, Sir Tor; Sir Gauter, Sir Gilmere, Sir Arnold, three brethren; Sir Damas, Sir Priamus, Sir Kay the Stranger, Sir Driant, Sir Lambegus, Sir Hermind; Sir Pertelope, Sir Perimones, two brethren that were called the Green Knight and the Red Knight.

And so in this rashing and hurling, as Sir Launcelot thrang here and there, it mishapped him to slay Gaheris and Sir Gareth, the noble knight, for they were unarmed and unware. For as the French book saith, Sir Launcelot smote Sir Gareth and Sir Gaheris upon the brainpans, wherethrough they were slain in the field; howbeit in very truth Sir Launcelot saw them not, and so were they found dead among the thickest of the press.

Then when Sir Launcelot had thus done, and slain and put to flight all that would withstand him, then he rode straight unto Dame Guenever, and made a kirtle and a gown to be cast upon her; and then he made her to be set behind him, and prayed her to be of good cheer.

Wit you well the queen was glad that she was escaped from the death. And then she thanked God and Sir Launcelot; and so he rode his way with the queen, as the French book saith, unto Joyous Gard, and there he kept her as a noble knight should do; and many great lords and some kings sent Sir Launcelot many good knights, and many noble knights drew unto Sir Launcelot. When this was known openly, that King Arthur and Sir Launcelot were at debate, many knights were glad of their debate, and many were full heavy of their debate.

CHAPTER 9: *Of the sorrow and lamentation* [*of King Arthur*] *for the death of his nephews and other good knights, and also for the queen, his wife*

So turn we again unto King Arthur, that when it was told him how and in what manner of wise the queen was taken away from the fire, and when he heard of the death of his noble knights, and in especial for Sir Gaheris' and Sir Gareth's death, then the king swooned for pure sorrow.

And when he awoke of his swoon, then he said, 'Alas, that ever I bare crown upon my head! For now have I lost the fairest fellowship of noble knights that ever held Christian king together. Alas, my good knights be slain away from me: now within these two days I have lost forty knights, and also the noble fellowship of Sir Launcelot and his blood, for now I may never hold them together no more with my worship. Alas that ever this war began. Now fair fellows,' said the king, 'I charge you that no man tell Sir Gawain of the death of his two brethren; for I am sure,' said the king, 'when Sir Gawain heareth tell that Sir Gareth is dead he will go nigh out of his mind. Mercy Jesu,' said the king, 'why slew he Sir Gareth and Sir Gaheris? For I dare say as for Sir Gareth he loved Sir Launcelot above all men earthly.'

'That is truth,' said some knights, 'but they were slain in the hurtling as Sir Launcelot thrang in the thick of the press; and as they were unarmed he smote them and wist not whom that he smote, and so unhappily they were slain.'

'The death of them,' said Arthur, 'will cause the greatest mortal war that ever was; I am sure, wist Sir Gawain that Sir Gareth were slain, I should never have rest of him till I had destroyed Sir Launcelot's kin and himself both, other else he to destroy me. And therefore,' said the king, 'wit you well my heart was never so heavy as it is now, and much more I am sorrier for my good knights' loss than for the loss of my fair queen; for queens I might have enow, but such a fellowship of good knights shall never be together in no company. And now I dare say,' said King Arthur, 'there was never Christian king held such a fellowship together; and alas that ever Sir Launcelot and I should be at debate. Ah Agravain, Agravain,' said the king, 'Jesu forgive it thy soul, for thine evil will that thou and thy brother Sir Mordred hadst unto Sir Launcelot hath caused all this sorrow;' and ever among these complaints the king wept and swooned.

Then there came one unto Sir Gawain, and told him how the queen was led away with Sir Launcelot, and nigh a twenty-four knights slain.

'O Jesu defend my brethren,' said Sir Gawain, 'for full well wist I that Sir Launcelot would rescue her, other else he would die in that field; and to say the truth he had not been a man of worship had he not rescued the queen that day, insomuch she should have been burnt for his sake. And as in that,' said Sir Gawain, 'he hath done but knightly, and as I would have done myself and I had stand in like case. But where are my brethren?' said Sir Gawain, 'I marvel I hear not of them.'

'Truly,' said that man, 'Sir Gareth and Sir Gaheris be slain.'

'Jesu defend!' said Sir Gawain. 'For all the world I would not that they were slain, and in especial my good brother, Sir Gareth.'

'Sir,' said the man, 'he is slain, and that is great pity.'

'Who slew him?' said Sir Gawain.

'Sir,' said the man, 'Launcelot slew them both.'

'That may I not believe,' said Sir Gawain, 'that ever he slew my brother, Sir Gareth; for I dare say my brother Gareth loved him better than me, and all his brethren, and the king both. Also I dare say, and Sir Launcelot had desired my brother, Sir Gareth, with him he would have been with him against the king and us all, and therefore I may never believe that Sir Launcelot slew my brother.'

'Sir,' said this man, 'it is noised that he slew him.'

CHAPTER 10: How King Arthur at the request of Sir Gawain concluded to make war against Sir Launcelot, and laid siege to his castle called Joyous Gard

'Alas,' said Sir Gawain, 'now is my joy gone.' And then he fell down and swooned, and long he lay there as he had been dead. And then, when he arose of his swoon, he cried out sorrowfully, and said, 'Alas!'

And right so Sir Gawain ran to the king, crying and weeping: 'O King Arthur, mine uncle, my good brother Sir Gareth is slain, and so is my brother Sir Gaheris, the which were two noble knights.'

Then the king wept, and he both; and so they fell on swooning.

And when they were revived then spake Sir Gawain: 'Sir, I will go see my brother, Sir Gareth.'

'Ye may not see him,' said the king, 'for I caused him to be interred, and Sir Gaheris both; for I well understood that ye would make over-much sorrow, and the sight of Sir Gareth should have caused your double sorrow.'

'Alas, my lord,' said Sir Gawain, 'how slew he my brother, Sir Gareth? Mine own good lord I pray you tell me.'

'Truly,' said the king, 'I shall tell you as it is told me, Sir Launcelot slew him and Sir Gaheris both.'

'Alas,' said Sir Gawain, 'they bare none arms against him, neither of them both.'

'I wot not how it was,' said the king, 'but as it is said, Sir Launcelot slew them both in the thickest of the press and knew them not; and therefore let us shape a remedy for to revenge their deaths.'

'My king, my lord, and mine uncle,' said Sir Gawain, 'wit you well now I shall make you a promise that I shall hold by my knighthood, that from this day I shall never fail Sir Launcelot until the one of us have slain the other. And therefore I require you, my lord and king, dress you to the war, for wit you well I will be revenged upon Sir Launcelot;

and therefore, as ye will have my service and my love, now haste you thereto, and assay your friends. For I promise unto God,' said Sir Gawain, 'for the death of my brother, Sir Gareth, I shall seek Sir Launcelot throughout seven kings' realms, but I shall slay him or else he shall slay me.'

'Ye shall not need to seek him so far,' said the king, 'for as I hear say, Sir Launcelot will abide me and you in the Joyous Gard; and much people draweth unto him, as I hear say.'

'That may I believe,' said Sir Gawain. 'But my lord,' he said, 'assay your friends, and I will assay mine.'

'It shall be done,' said the king, 'and as I suppose I shall be big enough to draw him out of the biggest tower of his castle.'

So then the king sent letters and writs throughout all England, both in the length and breadth, for to assummon all his knights. And so unto Arthur drew many knights, dukes, and earls, so that he had a great host. And when they were assembled, the king informed them how Sir Launcelot had bereft him his queen. Then the king and all his host made them ready to lay siege about Sir Launcelot, where he lay within Joyous Gard.

Thereof heard Sir Launcelot, and purveyed him of many good knights, for with him held many knights; and some for his own sake, and some for the queen's sake. Thus they were on both parties well furnished and garnished of all manner of thing that longed to the war. But King Arthur's host was so big that Sir Launcelot would not abide him in the field, for he was full loth to do battle against the king; but Sir Launcelot drew him to his strong castle with all manner of victual, and as many noble men as he might suffice within the town and the castle.

Then came King Arthur with Sir Gawain with an huge host, and laid a siege all about Joyous Gard, both at the town and at the castle, and there they made strong war on both parties. But in no wise Sir Launcelot would ride out, nor go out of his castle, of long time; neither he would none of his good knights to issue out, neither none of the town nor of the castle, until fifteen weeks were past.

CHAPTER 11 : *Of the communication between King Arthur and Sir Launcelot, and how King Arthur reproved him*

Then it befell upon a day in harvest time, Sir Launcelot looked over the walls and spake on high unto King Arthur and Sir Gawain :

'My lords both, wit ye well all is in vain that ye make at this siege, for here win ye no worship but maugre and dishonour; for and it list me to come myself out and my good knights, I should full soon make an end of this war.'

'Come forth,' said Arthur unto Launcelot, 'and thou darst, and I promise thee I shall meet thee in midst of the field.'

'God defend me,' said Sir Launcelot, 'that ever I should encounter with the most noble king that made me knight.'

'Fie upon thy fair language,' said the king, 'for wit you well and trust it, I am thy mortal foe, and ever will to my death day; for thou hast slain my good knights, and full noble men of my blood, that I shall never recover again. Also thou hast lain by my queen, and holden her many winters, and sithen like a traitor taken her from me by force.'

'My most noble lord and king,' said Sir Launcelot, 'ye may say what ye will, for ye wot well with yourself will I not strive; but thereas ye say I have slain your good knights, I wot well that I have done so, and that me sore repenteth; but I was enforced to do battle with them in saving of my life, or else I must have suffered them to have slain me. And as for my lady, Queen Guenever, except your person of your highness, and my lord Sir Gawain, there is no knight under heaven that dare make it good upon me that ever I was traitor unto your person. And where it please you to say that I have holden my lady your queen years and winters, unto that I shall ever make a large answer, and prove it upon any knight that beareth the life, except your person and Sir Gawain,

that my lady, Queen Guenever, is a true lady unto your
person as any is living unto her lord, and that will I make
good with my hands. Howbeit it hath liked her good grace
to have me in charity, and to cherish me more than any other
knight; and unto my power I again have deserved her love,
for ofttimes, my lord, ye have consented that she should be
burnt and destroyed, in your heat, and then it fortuned me
to do battle for her; and or I departed from her adversary
they confessed their untruth, and she full worshipfully excused. And at such times, my lord Arthur,' said Sir Launcelot,
'ye loved me, and thanked me when I saved your queen from
the fire; and then ye promised me for ever to be my good
lord; and now methinketh ye reward me full ill for my good
service. And my good lord, meseemeth I had lost a great part
of my worship in my knighthood and I had suffered my
lady, your queen, to have been burnt, and insomuch she
should have been burnt for my sake. For sithen I have done
battles for your queen in other quarrels than in mine own,
meseemeth now I had more right to do battle for her in right
quarrel. And therefore my good and gracious lord,' said Sir
Launcelot, 'take your queen unto your good grace, for she is
both fair, true, and good.'

'Fie on thee, false recreant knight,' said Sir Gawain. 'I let
thee wit my lord, mine uncle, King Arthur, shall have his
queen and thee, maugre thy visage, and slay you both
whether it please him.'

'It may well be,' said Sir Launcelot, 'but wit you well, my
lord Sir Gawain, and me list to come out of this castle ye
should win me and the queen more harder than ever ye won
a strong battle.'

'Fie on thy proud words,' said Sir Gawain; 'as for my lady,
the queen, I will never say of her shame. But thou, false and
recreant knight,' said Sir Gawain, 'what cause hadst thou to
slay my good brother Sir Gareth, that loved thee more than
all[1] my kin? Alas thou madest him knight thine own hands;
why slew thou him that loved thee so well?'

'For to excuse me,' said Sir Launcelot, 'it helpeth me not,

but by Jesu, and by the faith that I owe to the high order of knighthood, I should with as good will have slain my nephew, Sir Bors de Ganis, at that time. But alas that ever I was so unhappy,' said Launcelot, 'that I had not seen Sir Gareth and Sir Gaheris.'

'Thou liest, recreant knight,' said Sir Gawain, 'thou slewest him in despite of me; and therefore, wit thou well I shall make war to thee, and all the while that I may live.'

'That me repenteth,' said Sir Launcelot; 'for well I understand it helpeth not to seek none accordment while ye, Sir Gawain, are so mischievously set. And if ye were not, I would not doubt to have the good grace of my lord Arthur.'

'I believe it well, false recreant knight,' said Sir Gawain; 'for thou hast many long days overlead me and us all, and destroyed many of our good knights.'

'Ye say as it pleaseth you,' said Sir Launcelot; 'and yet may it never be said on me, and openly proved, that ever I by forecast of treason slew no good knight, as my lord, Sir Gawain, ye have done; and so did I never, but in my defence that I was driven thereto, in saving of my life.'

'Ah, false knight,' said Sir Gawain, 'that thou meanest by Sir Lamorak: wit thou well I slew him.'

'Ye slew him not yourself,' said Sir Launcelot; 'it had been overmuch on hand for you to have slain him, for he was one of the best knights christened of his age, and it was great pity of his death.'

CHAPTER 12: *How the cousins and kinsmen of Sir Launcelot excited him to go out to battle, and how they made them ready*

'Well, well,' said Sir Gawain to Launcelot, 'sithen thou enbraidest me of Sir Lamorak, wit thou well I shall never leave thee till I have thee at such avail that thou shalt not escape my hands.'

overlead: oppressed. *forecast*: intention. *enbraidest*: upbraid.

'I trust you well enough,' said Sir Launcelot, 'and ye may get me I get but little mercy.'

But as the French book saith, the noble King Arthur would have taken his queen again, and have been accorded with Sir Launcelot, but Sir Gawain would not suffer him by no manner of mean. And then Sir Gawain made many men to blow upon Sir Launcelot; and all at once they called him false recreant knight.

Then when Sir Bors de Ganis, Sir Ector de Maris, and Sir Lionel, heard this outcry, they called to them Sir Palomides, Sir Safer's brother, and Sir Lavaine, with many more of their blood, and all they went unto Sir Launcelot, and said thus:

'My lord Sir Launcelot, wit ye well we have great scorn of the great rebukes that we heard Gawain say to you; wherefore we pray you, and charge you as ye will have our service, keep us no longer within these walls; for wit you well plainly, we will ride into the field and do battle with them; for ye fare as a man that were afeared, and for all your fair speech it will not avail you. For wit you well Sir Gawain will not suffer you to be accorded with King Arthur, and therefore fight for your life and your right, and ye dare.'

'Alas,' said Sir Launcelot, 'for to ride out of this castle, and to do battle, I am full loth.' Then Sir Launcelot spake on high unto Sir Arthur and Sir Gawain:

'My lords, I require you and beseech you, sithen that I am thus required and conjured to ride into the field, that neither you, my lord King Arthur, nor you Sir Gawain, come not into the field.'

'What shall we do then?' said Sir Gawain. 'Is this the king's quarrel with thee to fight? And it is my quarrel to fight with thee, Sir Launcelot, because of the death of my brother Sir Gareth.'

'Then must I needs unto battle,' said Sir Launcelot. 'Now wit you well, my lord Arthur and Sir Gawain, ye will repent it whensomever I do battle with you.'

And so then they departed either from other; and then either party made them ready on the morn for to do battle, and great purveyance was made on both sides; and Sir Gawain let purvey many knights for to wait upon Sir Launcelot, for to overset him and to slay him

And on the morn at undern Sir Arthur was ready in the field with three great hosts. And then Sir Launcelot's fellowship came out at three gates, in a full good array; and Sir Lionel came in the foremost battle, and Sir Launcelot came in the middle, and Sir Bors came out at the third gate. Thus they came in order and rule, as full noble knights; and always Sir Launcelot charged all his knights in any wise to save King Arthur and Sir Gawain.

CHAPTER 13 : *How Sir Gawain jousted and smote down Sir Lionel, and how Sir Launcelot horsed King Arthur*

Then came forth Sir Gawain from the king's host, and he came before and proffered to joust. And Sir Lionel was a fierce knight, and lightly he encountered with Sir Gawain; and there Sir Gawain smote Sir Lionel throughout the body, that he dashed to the earth like as he had been dead; and then Sir Ector de Maris and other more bare him into the castle.

Then there began a great stour, and much people was slain; and ever Sir Launcelot did what he might to save the people on King Arthur's party, for Sir Palomides, and Sir Bors, and Sir Safer overthrew many knights, for they were deadly knights. And Sir Blamor de Ganis, and Sir Bleoberis de Ganis, with Sir Bellengerus le Beuse, these six knights did much harm; and ever King Arthur was nigh about Sir Launcelot to have slain him, and Sir Launcelot suffered him, and would not strike again.

So Sir Bors encountered with King Arthur, and there with a spear Sir Bors smote him down; and so he alit and drew his sword, and said to Sir Launcelot,

'Shall I make an end of this war?' And that he meant to have slain King Arthur.

'Not so hardy,' said Sir Launcelot, 'upon pain of thy head, that thou touch him no more, for I will never see that most noble king that made me knight neither slain ne shamed.'

And therewithal Sir Launcelot alit off his horse and took up the king and horsed him again, and said thus:

'My lord Arthur, for God's love stint this strife, for ye get here no worship, and I would do mine utterance, but always I forbear you, and ye nor none of yours forbeareth me; my lord, remember what I have done in many places, and now I am evil rewarded.'

Then when King Arthur was on horseback, he looked upon Sir Launcelot, and then the tears brast out of his eyen, thinking on the great courtesy that was in Sir Launcelot more than in any other man; and therewith the king rode his way, and might no longer behold him, and said, 'Alas, that ever this war began.'

And then either parties of the battles withdrew them to repose them, and buried the dead, and to the wounded men they laid soft salves; and thus they endured that night till on the morn.

And on the morn by undern they made them ready to do battle. And then Sir Bors led the forward. So upon the morn there came Sir Gawain as brim as any boar, with a great spear in his hand. And when Sir Bors saw him he thought to revenge his brother Sir Lionel of the despite that Sir Gawain did him the other day. And so they that knew either other fewtered their spears, and with all their mights of their horses and themself, they met together so feloniously that either bare other through, and so they fell both to the earth; and then the battles joined, and there was much slaughter on both parties.

Then Sir Launcelot rescued Sir Bors, and sent him into the castle; but neither Sir Gawain nor Sir Bors died not of their wounds, for they were all holpen. Then Sir Lavaine and Sir Urré prayed Sir Launcelot to do his pain, and fight as they had done: 'For we see ye forbear and spare, and that doth

brim: fierce.

much harm; therefore we pray you spare not your enemies no more than they do you.'

'Alas,' said Sir Launcelot, 'I have no heart to fight against my lord Arthur, for ever meseemeth I do not as I ought to do.'

'My lord,' said Sir Palomides, 'though ye spare them all this day they will never can you thank; and if they may get you at avail ye are but dead.'

So then Sir Launcelot understood that they said him truth; and then he strained himself more than he did aforehand, and because his nephew Sir Bors was sore wounded.

And then within a little while, by evensong time, Sir Launcelot and his party better stood, for their horses went in blood past the fetlocks, there was so much people slain. And then for pity Sir Launcelot withheld his knights, and suffered King Arthur's party for to withdraw them aside. And then Sir Launcelot's party withdrew them into his castle, and either parties buried the dead, and put salve unto the wounded men. So when Sir Gawain was hurt, they on King Arthur's party were not so orgulous as they were toforehand to do battle.

Of this war was noised through all Christendom, and at the last it was noised afore the Pope; and he considering the great goodness of King Arthur, and of Sir Launcelot, that was called the most noblest knights of the world, wherefore the Pope called unto him a noble clerk that at that time was there present (the French book saith, it was the Bishop of Rochester), and the Pope gave him bulls under lead unto King Arthur of England, charging him upon pain of interdicting of all England, that he take his queen Dame Guenever unto him again, and accord with Sir Launcelot.

can you thank: express thanks.

CHAPTER 14: *How the Pope sent down his bulls to make peace, and how Sir Launcelot brought the queen to King Arthur*

So when this Bishop was come to Carlisle he showed the king these bulls. And when the king understood these bulls he nist what to do: full fain he would have been accorded with Sir Launcelot, but Sir Gawain would not suffer him; but as for to have the queen, thereto he agreed. But in nowise Sir Gawain would not suffer the king to accord with Sir Launcelot; but as for the queen he consented. And then the Bishop had of the king his great seal, and his assurance as he was a true anointed king that Sir Launcelot should come safe, and go safe, and that the queen should not be spoken unto of the king, nor of none other, for no thing done afore time past; and of all these appointments the Bishop brought with him sure assurance and writing, to show Sir Launcelot.

So when the Bishop was come to Joyous Gard, there he showed Sir Launcelot how the Pope had written to Arthur and unto him, and there he told him the perils if he withheld the queen from the king.

'It was never in my thought,' said Launcelot, 'to withhold the queen from my lord Arthur; but, insomuch she should have been dead for my sake, meseemeth it was my part to save her life, and put her from that danger, till better recover might come. And now I thank God,' said Sir Launcelot, 'that the Pope hath made her peace; for God knoweth,' said Sir Launcelot, 'I will be a thousandfold more gladder to bring her again, than ever I was of her taking away; with this, I may be sure to come safe and go safe, and that the queen shall have her liberty as she had before; and never for no thing that hath been surmised afore this time, she never from this day stand in no peril. For else,' said Sir Launcelot, 'I dare adventure me to keep her from an harder shower than ever I kept her.'

'It shall not need you,' said the Bishop, 'to dread so much;

for wit you well, the Pope must be obeyed, and it were not the Pope's worship nor my poor honesty to wit you distressed, neither the queen, neither in peril, nor shamed.'

And then he showed Sir Launcelot all his writing, both from the Pope and from King Arthur.

'This is sure enough,' said Sir Launcelot, 'for full well I dare trust my lord's own writing and his seal, for he was never shamed of his promise. Therefore,' said Sir Launcelot unto the Bishop, 'ye shall ride unto the king afore, and recommend me unto his good grace, and let him have knowledging that this same day eight days, by the grace of God, I myself shall bring my lady, Queen Guenever, unto him. And then say ye unto my most redoubted king, that I will say largely for the queen, that I shall none except for dread nor fear, but the king himself, and my lord Sir Gawain, and that is more for the king's love than for himself.'

So the Bishop departed and came to the king at Carlisle, and told him all how Sir Launcelot answered him; and then the tears brast out of the king's eyen.

Then Sir Launcelot purveyed him an hundred knights, and all were clothed in green velvet, and their horses trapped to their heels; and every knight held a branch of olive in his hand, in tokening of peace. And the queen had four and twenty gentlewomen following her in the same wise; and Sir Launcelot had twelve coursers following him, and on every courser sat a young gentleman, and all they were arrayed in green velvet, with sarpes of gold about their quarters, and the horse trapped in the same wise down to the heels, with many ouches, set with stones and pearls in gold, to the number of a thousand. And she and Sir Launcelot were clothed in white cloth of gold tissue: and right so as ye have heard, as the French book maketh mention, he rode with the queen from Joyous Gard to Carlisle.

And so Sir Launcelot rode throughout Carlisle, and so in the castle, that all men might behold; and wit you well there was many a weeping eyen. And then Sir Launcelot himself alit

sarpes: chains.   ouches: clasps.

and avoided his horse, and took the queen, and so led her where King Arthur was in his seat: and Sir Gawain sat afore him, and many other great lords. So when Sir Launcelot saw the king and Sir Gawain, then he led the queen by the arm, and then he kneeled down, and the queen both. Wit you well then was there many bold knight there with King Arthur that wept as tenderly as though they had seen all their kin afore them. So the king sat still, and said no word. And when Sir Launcelot saw his countenance, he arose and pulled up the queen with him, and thus he spake full knightly:

CHAPTER 15: *Of the deliverance of the queen to the king by Sir Launcelot, and what language Sir Gawain had to Sir Launcelot*

'My most redoubted king, ye shall understand, by the Pope's commandment and yours, I have brought to you my lady the queen, as right requireth; and if there be any knight, of whatsomever degree that he be, except your person, that will say or dare say but that she is true and clean to you, I here myself, Sir Launcelot du Lake, will make it good upon his body, that she is a true lady unto you; but liars ye have listened, and that hath caused debate betwixt you and me. For time hath been, my lord Arthur, that ye have been greatly pleased with me when I did battle for my lady, your queen; and full well ye know, my most noble king, that she hath been put to great wrong or this time; and sithen it pleased you at many times that I should fight for her, me-seemeth, my good lord, I had more cause to rescue her from the fire, insomuch she should have been burnt for my sake. For they that told you those tales were liars, and so it fell upon them; for by likelihood had not the might of God been with me, I might never have endured fourteen knights, and they armed and afore purposed, and I unarmed and not purposed. For I was sent for unto my lady your queen, I wot not for what cause; but I was not so soon within the chamber

486

door, but anon Sir Agravain and Sir Mordred called me traitor and recreant knight.'

'They called thee right,' said Sir Gawain.

'My lord Sir Gawain,' said Sir Launcelot, 'in their quarrel they proved themself not in the right.'

'Well well, Sir Launcelot,' said the king, 'I have given thee no cause to do to me as thou hast done, for I have worshipped thee and thine more than any of all my knights.'

'My good lord,' said Sir Launcelot, 'so ye be not displeased, ye shall understand I and mine have done you oft better service than any other knights have done, in many diverse places; and where ye have been full hard bestad divers times, I have myself rescued you from many dangers; and ever unto my power I was glad to please you, and my lord Sir Gawain; both in jousts, and tournaments, and in battles set, both on horseback and on foot, I have often rescued you, and my lord Sir Gawain, and many more of your knights in many diverse places. For now I will make avaunt,' said Sir Launcelot, 'I will that ye all wit that yet I found never no manner of knight but that I was overhard for him, and I had done my utterance, thanked be God; howbeit I have been matched with good knights, as Sir Tristram and Sir Lamorak, but ever I had a favour unto them and a deeming what they were. And I take God to record,' said Sir Launcelot, 'I never was wroth nor greatly heavy with no good knight and I saw him busy about to win worship; and glad I was ever when I found any knight that might endure me on horseback and on foot: howbeit Sir Carados of the Dolorous Tower was a full noble knight and a passing strong man, and that wot ye, my lord Sir Gawain; for he might well be called a noble knight when he by fine force pulled you out of your saddle, and bound you overthwart afore him to his saddle bow; and there, my lord Sir Gawain, I rescued you, and slew him afore your sight. Also I found his brother, Sir Turquin, in likewise leading Sir Gaheris, your brother, bounden afore him; and there I rescued your brother and slew that Turquin, and delivered three-score-and-four of my lord Arthur's knights out of his prison.

And now I dare say,' said Sir Launcelot, 'I met never with so strong knights, nor so well fighting, as was Sir Carados and Sir Turquin, for I fought with them to the uttermost. And therefore,' said Sir Launcelot unto Sir Gawain, 'meseemeth ye ought of right to remember this; for, and I might have your good will, I would trust to God to have my lord Arthur's good grace.'

CHAPTER 16: *Of the communication between Sir Gawain and Sir Launcelot, with much other language*

'The king may do as he will,' said Sir Gawain, 'but wit thou well, Sir Launcelot, thou and I shall never be accorded while we live, for thou hast slain three of my brethren; and two of them ye slew traitorly and piteously, for they bare none harness against thee, nor none would bear.'

'God would they had been armed,' said Sir Launcelot, 'for then had they been alive. And wit ye well Sir Gawain, as for Sir Gareth, I love none of my kinsmen so much as I did him; and ever while I live,' said Sir Launcelot, 'I will bewail Sir Gareth's death, not all only for the great fear I have of you, but many causes causen me to be sorrowful. One is, for I made him knight; another is, I wot well he loved me above all other knights; and the third is, he was passing noble, true, courteous, and gentle, and well conditioned; the fourth is, I wist well, anon as I heard that Sir Gareth was dead, I should never after have your love, but everlasting war betwixt us; and also I wist well that ye would cause my noble lord Arthur for ever to be my mortal foe. And as Jesu be my help,' said Sir Launcelot, 'I slew never Sir Gareth nor Sir Gaheris by my will; but alas that ever they were unarmed that unhappy day.

'But thus much I shall offer me,' said Sir Launcelot, 'if it may please the king's good grace, and you, my lord Sir Gawain, I shall first begin at Sandwich, and there I shall go in my shirt, bare foot; and at every ten miles' end I will found and gar make an house of religion, of what order that ye will assign me, with an whole convent, to sing and read, day and night, in especial for Sir Gareth's sake and Sir Gaheris. And this shall I perform from Sandwich unto Carlisle; and every house shall have sufficient livelihood. And this shall I perform while I have any livelihood in Christendom; and there nis none of all these religious places, but they shall be performed, furnished and garnished in all things as an holy place ought to be, I promise you faithfully. And this, Sir Gawain, methinketh were more fairer, holier, and more better to their souls, than ye, my most noble king, and you, Sir Gawain, to war upon me, for thereby shall ye get none avail.'

Then all knights and ladies that were there wept as they were mad, and the tears fell on King Arthur's cheeks.

'Sir Launcelot,' said Sir Gawain, 'I have right well heard thy speech, and thy great proffers, but wit thou well, let the king do as it pleased him, I will never forgive my brothers' death, and in especial the death of my brother, Sir Gareth. And if mine uncle, King Arthur, will accord with thee, he shall lose my service, for wit thou well thou art both false to the king and to me.'

'Sir,' said Launcelot, 'he beareth not the life that may make that good; and if ye, Sir Gawain, will charge me with so high a thing, ye must pardon me, for then needs must I answer you.'

'Nay,' said Sir Gawain, 'we are past that at this time, and that caused the Pope, for he hath charged mine uncle, the king, that he shall take his queen again, and to accord with thee, Sir Launcelot, as for this season, and therefore thou shalt go safe as thou camest. But in this land thou shalt not abide past fifteen days, such summons I give thee: so the king and we were consented and accorded or thou camest. And else,' said Sir Gawain, 'wit thou well thou shouldst not have comen here, but if it were maugre thy head. And if it were not for the Pope's commandment,' said Sir Gawain, 'I should do battle

gar make: have made.

with mine own body against thy body, and prove it upon thee, that thou hast been both false unto mine uncle King Arthur, and to me both; and that shall I prove upon thy body, when thou art departed from hence, wheresomever I find thee.'

CHAPTER 17: *How Sir Launcelot departed from the king and from Joyous Gard over seaward, and what knights went with him*

Then Sir Launcelot sighed, and therewith the tears fell on his cheeks, and then he said thus:

'Alas, most noble Christian realm, whom I have loved above all other realms, and in thee I have gotten a great part of my worship, and now I shall depart in this wise. Truly me repenteth that ever I came in this realm, that should be thus shamefully banished undeserved and causeless; but fortune is so variant, and the wheel so moveable, there nis none constant abiding, and that may be proved by many old chronicles, of noble Ector, and Troilus, and Alisander, the mighty Conqueror, and many more other; when they were most in their royalty, they alit lowest. And so fareth it by me,' said Sir Launcelot, 'for in this realm I had worship, and by me and mine all the whole Round Table hath been increased more in worship by me and mine blood than by any other. And therefore wit thou well, Sir Gawain, I may live upon my lands as well as any knight that here is. And if ye, most redoubted king, will come upon my lands with Sir Gawain to war upon me, I must endure you as well as I may. But as to you, Sir Gawain, if that ye come there, I pray you charge me not with treason nor felony, for and ye do, I must answer you.'

'Do thou thy best,' said Sir Gawain; 'therefore hie thee fast that thou were gone, and wit thou well we shall soon come after, and break the strongest castle that thou hast, upon thy head.'

'That shall not need,' said Sir Launcelot, 'for and I were as orgulous set as ye are, wit you well I should meet you in the midst of the field.'

'Make thou no more language,' said Sir Gawain, 'but deliver the queen from thee, and pick thee lightly out of this court.'

'Well,' said Sir Launcelot, 'and I had wist of this short-coming, I would have advised me twice or that I had comen hither; for and the queen had been so dear to me as ye noise her, I durst have kept her from the fellowship of the best knights under heaven.'

And then Sir Launcelot said unto Guenever, in hearing of the king and them all, 'Madam, now I must depart from you and this noble fellowship for ever; and sithen it is so, I beseech you to pray for me, and say me well; and if ye be hard bestad by any false tongues, lightly my lady send me word, and if any knight's hands may deliver you by battle, I shall deliver you.'

And therewithal Sir Launcelot kissed the queen; and then he said all openly, 'Now let see what he be in this place that dare say the queen is not true unto my lord Arthur, let see who will speak and he dare speak.'

And therewith he brought the queen to the king, and then Sir Launcelot took his leave and departed; and there was neither king, duke, ne earl, baron ne knight, lady nor gentlewoman, but all they wept as people out of their mind, except Sir Gawain.

And when the noble Sir Launcelot took his horse to ride out of Carlisle, there was sobbing and weeping for pure dole of his departing; and so he took his way unto Joyous Gard. And then ever after he called it the Dolorous Gard.

And thus departed Sir Launcelot from the court for ever. And so when he came to Joyous Gard he called his fellowship unto him, and asked them what they would do. Then they answered all wholly together with one voice, they would as he would do.

'My fair fellows,' said Sir Launcelot, 'I must depart out of this most noble realm, and now I shall depart it grieveth me sore, for I shall depart with no worship, for a flemed man departed never out of a realm with no worship; and that is my heaviness, for ever I fear after my days that men shall chronicle upon me that I was flemed out of this land; and else, my fair lords, be ye sure, and I had not dread shame, my lady, Queen Guenever, and I should never have departed.'

Then spake many noble knights, as Sir Palomides, Sir Safer his brother, and Sir Bellengerus le Beuse, and Sir Urré, with Sir Lavaine, with many other:

'Sir, and ye be so disposed to abide in this land we will never fail you; and if ye list not to abide in this land there nis none of the good knights that here be will fail you, for many causes. One is, all we that be not of your blood shall never be welcome to the court. And sithen it liked us to take a part with you in your distress and heaviness in this realm, wit you well it shall like us as well to go in other countries with you, and there to take such part as ye do.'

'My fair lords,' said Sir Launcelot, 'I well understand you, and as I can, thank you: and ye shall understand, such livelihood as I am born unto I shall depart with you in this manner of wise; that is for to say I shall depart all my livelihood and all my lands freely among you, and I myself will have as little as any of you, for have I sufficient that may long to my person, I will ask none other rich array; and I trust to God to maintain you on my lands as well as ever were maintained any knights.'

Then spake all the knights at once: 'He have shame that will leave you; for we all understand in this realm will be now no quiet, but ever strife and debate, now the fellowship of the Round Table is broken; for by the noble fellowship of the Round Table was King Arthur upborne, and by their noblesse the king and all his realm was in quiet and rest, and a great part,' they said all, 'was because of your noblesse.'

CHAPTER 18: *How Sir Launcelot passed over the sea, and how he made great lords of the knights that went with him*

'Truly,' said Sir Launcelot, 'I thank you all of your good saying; howbeit, I wot well, in me was not all the stability of this realm, but in that I might I did my devoir; and well I am sure I knew many rebellions in my days that by me were peaced, and I trow we all shall hear of them in short space, and that me sore repenteth. For ever I dread me,' said Sir Launcelot, 'that Mordred will make trouble, for he is passing envious and applieth him to trouble.'

So they were accorded to go with Sir Launcelot to his lands; and to make short tale, they trussed and paid all that would ask them; and wholly an hundred knights departed with Sir Launcelot at once, and made their avows they would never leave him for weal nor for woe.

And so they shipped at Cardiff, and sailed unto Benwick: some men call it Bayonne, and some men call it Beaune, where the wine of Beaune is. But to say the sooth, Sir Launcelot and his nephews were lords of all France, and of all the lands that longed unto France; he and his kindred rejoiced it all through Sir Launcelot's noble prowess.

And then Sir Launcelot stuffed and furnished and garnished all his noble towns and castles. Then all the people of those lands came to Sir Launcelot on foot and hands. And so when he had stabled all these countries, he shortly called a parliament; and there he crowned Sir Lionel, King of France; and Sir Bors, crowned him king of all King Claudas' lands; and Sir Ector de Maris, that was Sir Launcelot's youngest brother, he crowned him King of Benwick, and king of all Guienne, that was Sir Launcelot's own land. And he made Sir Ector prince of them all, and thus he departed.

Then Sir Launcelot advanced all his noble knights, and first he advanced them of his blood; that was Sir Blamor, he made him Duke of Limousin in Guienne, and Sir Bleoberis

trussed: equipped.

493

he make him Duke of Poitiers, and Sir Gahalantine he made him Duke of Auvergne, and Sir Galihodin he made him Duke of Saintonge, and Sir Galihud he made him Earl of Périgord, and Sir Menaduke he made him Earl of Rouerge, and Sir Villiars the Valiant he made him Earl of Béearn, and Sir Hebes le Renoumes he made him Earl of Comminges, and Sir Lavaine he made him Earl of Armagnac, and Sir Urré he made him Earl of Estrake, and Sir Nerovens he made him Earl of Pardiac, and Sir Plenorius he made Earl of Foix, and Sir Selises of the Dolorous Tower he made him Earl of Marsan, and Sir Melias de Lile he made him Earl of Tursan, and Sir Bellengerus le Beuse he made Earl of the Launds, and Sir Palomides he made him Duke of the Provence, and Sir Safer he made him Duke of Languedoc, and Sir Clegis he gave him the Earldom of Agen, and Sir Sadok he gave the Earldom of Surlat, and Sir Dinas le Seneschal he made him Duke of Anjou, and Sir Clarrus he made him Duke of Normandy. Thus Sir Launcelot rewarded his noble knights and many more, that meseemeth it were too long to rehearse.

CHAPTER 19: *How King Arthur and Sir Gawain made a great host ready to go over sea to make war on Sir Launcelot*

So leave we Sir Launcelot in his lands, and his noble knights with him, and return we again unto King Arthur and to Sir Gawain, that made a great host ready, to the number of threescore thousand; and all thing was made ready for their shipping to pass over the sea, and so they shipped at Cardiff.

And there King Arthur made Sir Mordred chief ruler of all England, and also he put Queen Guenever under his governance; because Sir Mordred was King Arthur's son, he gave him the rule of his land and of his wife; and so the king passed the sea and landed upon Sir Launcelot's lands, and there he burnt and wasted, through the vengeance of Sir Gawain, all that they might overrun.

When this word came to Sir Launcelot, that King Arthur

and Sir Gawain were landed upon his lands, and made a full great destruction and waste, then spake Sir Bors, and said:

'My lord Sir Launcelot, it is shame that we suffer them thus to ride over our lands, for wit you well, suffer ye them as long as ye will, they will do you no favour and they may handle you.'

Then said Sir Lionel that was ware and wise, 'My lord Sir Launcelot, I will give this counsel: let us keep our strong walled towns until they have hunger and cold, and blow on their nails; and then let us freshly set upon him, and shred them down as sheep in a field, that aliens may take example for ever how they land upon our lands.'

Then spake King Bagdemagus to Sir Launcelot: 'Sir, your courtesy will shend us all, and thy courtesy hath waked all this sorrow; for and they thus over our lands ride, they shall by process bring us all to nought whilst we thus in holes us hide.'

Then said Sir Galihud unto Sir Launcelot, 'Sir, here be knights come of kings' blood, that will not long droop, and they are within these walls; therefore give us leave, like as we be knights, to meet them in the field, and we shall slay them, that they shall curse the time that ever they came into this country.'

Then spake seven brethren of North Wales, and they were seven noble knights; a man might seek in seven kings' lands or he might find such seven knights. Then they all said at once, 'Sir Launcelot, for Christ's sake let us out ride with Sir Galihud, for we be never wont to cower in castles nor in noble towns.'

Then spake Sir Launcelot, that was master and governor of them all: 'My fair lords, wit you well I am full loth to ride out with my knights for shedding of Christian blood; and yet my lands I understand be full bare for to sustain any host awhile, for the mighty wars that whilom made King Claudas upon this country, upon my father King Ban, and on mine uncle King Bors; howbeit we will as at this time keep our strong walls, and I shall send a messenger unto my lord

Arthur, a treaty for to take; for better is peace than always war.'

So Sir Launcelot sent forth a damosel and a dwarf with her, requiring King Arthur to leave his warring upon his lands; and so she start upon a palfrey, and the dwarf ran by her side.

And when she came to the pavilion of King Arthur, there she alit; and there met her a gentle knight, Sir Lucan the Butler, and said, 'Fair damosel, come ye from Sir Launcelot du Lake?'

'Yea sir,' she said, 'therefore I come hither to speak with my lord the king.'

'Alas,' said Sir Lucan, 'my lord Arthur would love Launcelot, but Sir Gawain will not suffer him.' And then he said, 'I pray to God, damosel, ye may speed well, for all we that be about the king would Sir Launcelot did best of any knight living.'

And so with this Lucan led the damosel unto the king where he sat with Sir Gawain, for to hear what she would say. So when she had told her tale, the water ran out of the king's eyen, and all the lords were full glad for to advise the king as to be accorded with Sir Launcelot, save all only Sir Gawain, and he said, 'My lord mine uncle, what will ye do? Will ye now turn again now ye are passed thus far upon this journey? All the world will speak of you villainy.'

'Nay,' said Arthur, 'wit thou well, Sir Gawain, I will do as ye will advise me; and yet meseemeth,' said Arthur, 'his fair proffers were not good to be refused; but sithen I am comen so far upon this journey, I will that ye give the damosel her answer, for I may not speak to her for pity, for her proffers be so large.'

CHAPTER 20: *What message Sir Gawain sent to Sir Launce-lot; and King Arthur laid seige to Benwick, and other matters*

Then Sir Gawain said to the damosel thus:

'Damosel, say ye to Sir Launcelot that it is waste labour now to sue to mine uncle; for tell him, and he would have made any labour for peace, he should have made it or this time, for tell him now it is too late; and say that I, Sir Gawain, so send him word, that I promise him by the faith I owe unto God and to knighthood, I shall never leave him till he have slain me or I him.'

So the damosel wept and departed, and there were many weeping eyen; and so Sir Lucan brought the damosel to her palfrey, and so she came to Sir Launcelot where he was among all his knights.

And when Sir Launcelot had heard this answer, then the tears ran down by his cheeks. And then his noble knights strode about him, and said, 'Sir Launcelot, wherefore make ye such cheer. Think what ye are, and what men we are, and let us noble knights match them in midst of the field.'

'That may be lightly done,' said Sir Launcelot, 'but I was never so loth to do battle, and therefore I pray you, fair sirs, as ye love me, be ruled as I will have you, for I will always flee that noble king that made me knight. And when I may no further, I must needs defend me, and that will be more worship for me and us all than to compare with that noble king whom we have all served.'

Then they held their language, and as that night they took their rest. And upon the morn early, in the dawning of the day, as knights looked out, they saw the city of Benwick besieged round about; and fast they began to set up ladders, and then they defied them out of the town, and beat them from the walls wightly.

Then came forth Sir Gawain well armed upon a stiff steed,

stiff: strong.

and he came before the chief gate, with his spear in his hand, crying, 'Sir Launcelot, where art thou? Is there none of you proud knights dare break a spear with me?'

Then Sir Bors made him ready, and came forth out of the town, and there Sir Gawain encountered with Sir Bors. And at that time he smote Sir Bors down from his horse, and almost he had slain him; and so Sir Bors was rescued and borne into the town.

Then came forth Sir Lionel, brother to Sir Bors, and thought to revenge him; and either fewtered their spears, and ran together; and there they met spitefully, but Sir Gawain had such grace that he smote Sir Lionel down, and wounded him there passing sore; and then Sir Lionel was rescued and borne into the town.

And this Sir Gawain came every day, and he failed not but that he smote down one knight or other. So thus they endured half a year, and much slaughter was of people on both parties.

Then it befell upon a day, Sir Gawain came afore the gates armed at all pieces on a noble horse, with a great spear in his hand; and then he cried with a loud voice, 'Where art thou now, thou false traitor, Sir Launcelot? Why hidest thou thyself within holes and walls like a coward? Look out now, thou false traitor knight, and here I shall revenge upon thy body the death of my three brethren.'

All this language heard Sir Launcelot every deal; and his kin and his knights drew about him, and all they said at once to Sir Launcelot, 'Sir Launcelot, now must ye defend you like a knight, or else ye be shamed for ever; for, now ye be called upon treason, it is time for you to stir, for ye have slept over-long and suffered over-much.'

'So God me help,' said Sir Launcelot, 'I am right heavy of Sir Gawain's words, for now he charged me with a great charge; and therefore I wot it as well as ye, that I must defend me, or else to be recreant.'

Then Sir Launcelot bad saddle his strongest horse, and bad let fetch his arms, and bring all unto the gate of the tower;

and then Sir Launcelot spake on high unto King Arthur, and said, 'My lord Arthur, and noble king that made me knight, wit you well I am right heavy for your sake, that ye thus sue upon me; and always I forbare you, for and I would have been vengeable, I might have met you in midst of the field, and there to have made your boldest knights full tame. And now I have forborne half a year, and suffered you and Sir Gawain to do what ye would do; and now may I endure it no longer, for now must I needs defend myself, insomuch Sir Gawain hath appelled me of treason; the which is greatly against my will that ever I should fight against any of your blood, but now I may not forsake it, I am driven thereto as a beast till a bay.'

Then Sir Gawain said, 'Sir Launcelot, and thou darst do battle, leave thy babbling and come off, and let us ease our hearts.'

Then Sir Launcelot armed him lightly, and mounted upon his horse, and either of the knights gat great spears in their hands, and the host without stood still all apart, and the noble knights came out of the city by a great number insomuch that when Arthur saw the number of men and knights, he marvelled, and said to himself, 'Alas, that ever Sir Launcelot was against me, for now I see he hath forborne me.'

And so the covenant was made, there should no man nigh them, nor deal with them, till the one were dead or yielden.

CHAPTER 21: *How Sir Launcelot and Sir Gawain did battle together, and how Sir Gawain was overthrown and hurt.*

Then Sir Gawain and Sir Launcelot departed a great way in sunder, and then they came together with all their horses' might as they might run, and either smote other in midst of their shields; but the knights were so strong, and their spears so big, that their horses might not endure their buffets, and so their horses fell to the earth; and then they avoided their horses, and dressed their shields afore them. Then they stood together and gave many sad strokes on divers places of their bodies, that the blood brast out on many sides and places.

Then had Sir Gawain such a grace and gift that an holy man had given to him, that every day in the year, from undern till high noon, his might increased those three hours as much as thrice his strength, and that caused Sir Gawain to win great honour. And for his sake King Arthur made an ordinance, that all manner of battles for any quarrels that should be done afore King Arthur should begin at undern; and all was done for Sir Gawain's love, that by likelihood, if Sir Gawain were on the one part, he should have the better in battle while his strength endured three hours; but there were but few knights that time living that knew this advantage that Sir Gawain had, but King Arthur all only.

Thus Sir Launcelot fought with Sir Gawain, and when Sir Launcelot felt his might evermore increase, Sir Launcelot wondered and dread him sore to be shamed. For as the French book saith, Sir Launcelot weened, when he felt Sir Gawain double his strength, that he had been a fiend and none earthly man; wherefore Sir Launcelot traced and traversed, and covered himself with his shield, and kept his might and his braid during three hours; and that while Sir Gawain gave him many sad brunts, and many sad strokes, that all the knights that beheld Sir Launcelot marvelled how that he might endure him; but full little understood they that travail that Sir Launcelot had for to endure him.

And then when it was past noon Sir Gawain had no more but his own might. Then Sir Launcelot felt him so come down, then he stretched him up and stood near Sir Gawain, and said thus:

'My lord Sir Gawain, now I feel ye have done; now my lord Sir Gawain, I must do my part, for many great and grievous strokes I have endured you this day with great pain.'

Then Sir Launcelot doubled his strokes and gave Sir Gawain such a buffet on the helmet that he fell down on his side, and Sir Launcelot withdrew him from him.

braid: attack.

500

'Why withdrawest thou thee?' said Sir Gawain. 'Now turn again, false traitor knight, and slay me, for and thou leave me thus, when I am whole I shall do battle with thee again.'

'I shall endure you, sir, by God's grace, but wit thou well, Sir Gawain, I will never smite a felled knight.'

And so Sir Launcelot went into the city; and Sir Gawain was borne into King Arthur's pavilion, and leeches were brought to him, and searched and salved with soft ointments.

And then Sir Launcelot said, 'Now have good day, my lord the king, for wit you well ye win no worship at these walls; and if I would my knights outbring, there should many a man die. Therefore, my lord Arthur, remember you of old kindness; and however I fare, Jesu be your guide in all places.'

CHAPTER 22: *Of the sorrow that King Arthur made for the war, and of another battle where also Sir Gawain had the worse*

'Alas,' said the king, 'that ever this unhappy war was begun; for ever Sir Launcelot forbeareth me in all places, and in likewise my kin, and that is seen well this day by my nephew Sir Gawain.'

Then King Arthur fell sick for sorrow of Sir Gawain, that he was so sore hurt, and because of the war betwixt him and Sir Launcelot. So then they on King Arthur's part kept the siege with little war withoutforth; and they withinforth kept their walls, and defended them when need was.

Thus Sir Gawain lay sick three weeks in his tents, with all manner of leechcraft that might be had. And as soon as Sir Gawain might go and ride, he armed him at all points, and start upon a courser, and gat a spear in his hand, and so he came riding afore the chief gate of Benwick and there he cried on height, 'Where art thou, Sir Launcelot? Come forth, thou false traitor knight and recreant, for I am here, Sir Gawain, will prove this that I say on thee.'

All this language Sir Launcelot heard, and then he said thus:

'Sir Gawain, me repents of your foul saying, that ye will not cease of your language; for you wot well, Sir Gawain, I know your might and all that ye may do; and well ye wot, Sir Gawain, ye may not greatly hurt me.'

'Come down, traitor knight,' said he, 'and make it good the contrary with thy hands, for it mishapped me the last battle to be hurt of thy hands; therefore wit thou well I am come this day to make amends, for I ween this day to lay thee as low as thou laidest me.'

'Jesu defend me,' said Sir Launcelot, 'that ever I be so far in your danger as ye have been in mine, for then my days were done. But Sir Gawain,' said Sir Launcelot, 'ye shall not think that I tarry long, but sithen that ye so unknightly call me of treason, ye shall have both your hands full of me.'

And then Sir Launcelot armed him at all points, and mounted upon his horse, and gat a great spear in his hand, and rode out at the gate. And both the hosts were assembled, of them without and of them within, and stood in array full manly. And both parties were charged to hold them still, to see and behold the battle of these two noble knights.

And then they laid their spears in their rests, and they came together as thunder, and Sir Gawain brake his spear upon Sir Launcelot in a hundred pieces unto his hand; and Sir Launcelot smote him with a greater might, that Sir Gawain's horse's feet raised, and so the horse and he fell to the earth. Then Sir Gawain deliverly avoided his horse, and put his shield afore him, and eagerly drew his sword, and bad Sir Launcelot: 'Alight, traitor knight, for if this mare's son hath failed me wit thou well a king's son and a queen's son shall not fail thee.'

Then Sir Launcelot avoided his horse, and dressed his shield afore him, and drew his sword; and so stood they together and gave many sad strokes, that all men on both parties had thereof passing great wonder.

deliverly: neatly.

But when Sir Launcelot felt Sir Gawain's might so marvellously increase, he then withheld his courage and his wind, and kept himself wonder covert of his might; and under his shield he traced and traversed here and there, to break Sir Gawain's strokes and his courage; and Sir Gawain enforced himself with all his might and power to destroy Sir Launcelot; for as the French book saith, ever as Sir Gawain's might increased, right so increased his wind and his evil will. Thus Sir Gawain did great pain unto Sir Launcelot three hours, that he had right great pain for to defend him.

And when the three hours were passed, that Sir Launcelot felt that Sir Gawain was comen to his own proper strength, then Sir Launcelot said unto Sir Gawain, 'Now have I proved you twice, that ye are a full dangerous knight, and a wonderful man of your might; and many wonderful deeds have ye done in your days, for by your might increasing you have deceived many a full noble and valiant knight; and, now I feel that ye have done your mighty deeds, now wit you well I must do my deeds.'

And then Sir Launcelot stood near Sir Gawain, and then Sir Launcelot doubled his strokes; and Sir Gawain defended him mightily, but nevertheless Sir Launcelot smote such a stroke upon Sir Gawain's helm, and upon the old wound, that Sir Gawain sinked down upon his one side in a swoon.

And anon as he did awake he waved and foined at Sir Launcelot as he lay, and said, 'Traitor knight, wit thou well I am not yet slain, come thou near me and perform this battle unto the uttermost.'

'I will no more do than I have done,' said Sir Launcelot, 'for when I see you on foot I will do battle upon you all the while I see you stand on your feet; but for to smite a wounded man that may not stand, God defend me from such a shame.'

And then he turned him and went his way toward the city, and Sir Gawain evermore calling him traitor knight, and said, 'Wit thou well Sir Launcelot, when I am whole I shall do battle with thee again, for I shall never leave thee till that one of us be slain.'

Thus as this siege endured, and as Sir Gawain lay sick near a month, and when he was well recovered and ready within three days to do battle again with Sir Launcelot, right so came tidings unto Arthur from England that made King Arthur and all his host to remove.

Here followeth the xxi book

Book XXI

CHAPTER 1: *How Sir Mordred presumed and took on him to be king of England, and would have married the queen, his father's wife*

As Sir Mordred was ruler of all England, he did do make letters as though that they came from beyond the sea, and the letters specified that King Arthur was slain in battle with Sir Launcelot. Wherefore Sir Mordred made a parliament, and called the lords together, and there he made them to choose him king; and so was he crowned at Canterbury, and held a feast there fifteen days; and afterward he drew him unto Winchester, and there he took the queen Guenever, and said plainly that he would wed her which was his uncle's wife and his father's wife. And so he made ready for the feast, and a day prefixed that they should be wedded; wherefore Queen Guenever was passing heavy. But she durst not discover her heart, but spake fair, and agreed to Sir Mordred's will.

Then she desired of Sir Mordred for to go to London, to buy all manner of things that longed unto the wedding. And because of her fair speech Sir Mordred trusted her well enough, and gave her leave to go. And so when she came to London she took the Tower of London, and suddenly in all haste possible she stuffed it with all manner of victual, and well garnished it with men, and so kept it.

Then when Sir Mordred wist and understood how he was beguiled, he was passing wroth out of measure. And a short tale for to make, he went and laid a mighty siege about the Tower of London, and made many great assaults thereat, and threw many great engines unto them, and shot great guns. But all might not prevail Sir Mordred, for Queen Guenever would never for fair speech nor for foul, would never trust to come in his hands again.

Then came the Bishop of Canterbury, the which was a noble clerk and an holy man, and thus he said to Sir Mordred: 'Sir, what will do? Will ye first displease God and sithen shame yourself, and all knighthood? Is not King Arthur your uncle, no farther but your mother's brother, and on her himself King Arthur begat you, upon his own sister, therefore how may you wed your father's wife? Sir,' said the noble clerk, 'leave this opinion or I shall curse you with book and bell and candle.'

'Do thou thy worst,' said Sir Mordred, 'wit thou well I shall defy thee.'

'Sir,' said the Bishop, 'and wit you well I shall not fear me to do that me ought to do. Also where ye noise where my lord Arthur is slain, and that is not so, and therefore ye will make a foul work in this land.'

'Peace, thou false priest,' said Sir Mordred, 'for and thou chafe me any more I shall make strike off thy head.'

So the Bishop departed and did the cursing in the most orgulest wise that might be done. And then Sir Mordred sought the Bishop of Canterbury, for to have slain him. Then the Bishop fled, and took part of his goods with him, and went nigh unto Glastonbury; and there he was as priest hermit in a chapel, and lived in poverty and in holy prayers, for well he understood that mischievous war was at hand.

Then Sir Mordred sought on Queen Guenever by letters and sondes, and by fair means and foul means, for to have her to come out of the Tower of London; but all this availed not, for she answered him shortly, openly and privily, that she had lever slay herself than to be married with him.

Then came word to Sir Mordred that King Arthur had araised the siege for Sir Launcelot,[1] and he was coming homeward with a great host, to be avenged upon Sir Mordred; wherefore Sir Mordred made write writs to all the barony of this land, and much people drew to him. For then was the
sondes: messengers.

506

common voice among them that with Arthur was none other life but war and strife, and with Sir Mordred was great joy and bliss. Thus was Sir Arthur depraved, and evil said of. And many there were that King Arthur had made up of nought, and given them lands, might not then say him a good word.

Lo ye all Englishmen, see ye not what a mischief here was? For he that was the most king and knight of the world, and most loved the fellowship of noble knights, and by him they were all upholden, now might not these Englishmen hold them content with him. Lo thus was the old custom and usage of this land; and also men say that we of this land have not yet lost ne forgotten that custom and usage. Alas, this is a great default of us Englishmen, for there may nothing please us no term.

And so fared the people at that time, they were better pleased with Sir Mordred than they were with King Arthur; and much people drew unto Sir Mordred, and said they would abide with him for better and for worse. And so Sir Mordred drew with a great host to Dover, for there he heard say that Sir Arthur would arrive, and so he thought to beat his own father from his lands; and the most part of all England held with Sir Mordred, the people were so new fangle.

CHAPTER 2 : *How after that King Arthur had tidings, he returned and came to Dover, where Sir Mordred met him to let his landing; and of the death of Sir Gawain*

And so as Sir Mordred was at Dover with his host, there came King Arthur with a great navy of ships, and galleys, and carracks. And there was Sir Mordred ready awaiting upon his landage, to let his own father to land up the land that he was king over.

Then there was launching of great boats and small, and full of noble men of arms; and there was much slaughter of gentle knights, and many a full bold baron was laid full low, on both parties.

landage: landing.

But King Arthur was so courageous that there might no
manner of knights let him to land, and his knights fiercely
followed him; and so they landed maugre Sir Mordred's and
all his power, and put Sir Mordred aback, that he fled and all
his people.

So when this battle was done, King Arthur let bury his
people that were dead. And then was noble Sir Gawain found
in a great boat, lying more than half dead. When Sir Arthur
wist that Sir Gawain was laid so low, he went unto him; and
there the king made sorrow out of measure, and took Sir
Gawain in his arms, and thrice he there swooned.

And then when he awaked, he said, 'Alas, Sir Gawain, my
sister's son, here now thou liest, the man in the world that
I loved most; and now is my joy gone, for now, my nephew
Sir Gawain, I will discover me unto your person: in Sir Launcelot and you I most had my joy, and mine affiance, and now
have I lost my joy of you both; wherefore all mine earthly
joy is gone from me.'

'Mine uncle King Arthur,' said Sir Gawain, 'wit you well
my death day is come, and all is through mine own hastiness
and wilfulness; for I am smitten upon the old wound the
which Sir Launcelot gave me, on the which I feel well I must
die; and had Sir Launcelot been with you as he was, this unhappy war had never begun; and of all this am I causer, for
Sir Launcelot and his blood, through their prowess, held all
your cankered enemies in subjection and danger. And now,'
said Sir Gawain, 'ye shall miss Sir Launcelot. But alas, I
would not accord with him, and therefore,' said Sir Gawain,
'I pray you, fair uncle, that I may have paper, pen and ink,
that I may write to Sir Launcelot a cedle with mine own
hands.'

And then when paper and ink was brought, then Gawain
was set up weakly by King Arthur, for he was shriven a
little tofore; and then he wrote thus, as the French book
maketh mention:

'Unto Sir Launcelot, flower of all noble knights that ever
affiance: trust. *cedle*: letter.

I heard of or saw by my days, I, Sir Gawain, King Lot's son of Orkney, sister's son unto the noble King Arthur, send thee greeting, and let thee have knowledge that the tenth day of May I was smitten upon the old wound that thou gavest me afore the city of Benwick, and through the same wound that thou gavest me I am come to my death day. And I will that all the world wit, that I, Sir Gawain, knight of the Table Round, sought my death, and not through thy deserving, but it was mine own seeking; wherefore I beseech thee, Sir Launcelot, to return again unto this realm, and see my tomb, and pray some prayer more or less for my soul. And this same day that I wrote this cedle, I was hurt to the death in the same wound, the which I had of thy hand, Sir Launcelot; for of a more nobler man might I not be slain.

'Also Sir Launcelot, for all the love that ever was betwixt us, make no tarrying, but come over the sea in all haste, that thou mayst with thy noble knights rescue that noble king that made thee knight, that is my lord Arthur, for he is full straitly bestad with a false traitor, that is my half-brother, Sir Mordred; and he hath let crown him king, and would have wedded my lady Queen Guenever, and so had he done had she not put herself in the Tower of London. And so the tenth day of May last past, my lord Arthur and we all landed upon them at Dover; and there we put that false traitor, Sir Mordred, to flight, and there it misfortuned me to be stricken upon thy stroke. And at the date of this letter was written, but two hours and a half afore my death, written with mine own hand, and so subscribed with part of my heart's blood. And I require thee, most famous knight of the world, that thou wilt see my tomb.'

And then Sir Gawain wept, and King Arthur wept; and then they swooned both. And when they awaked both, the king made Sir Gawain to receive his Saviour. And then Sir Gawain prayed the king for to send for Sir Launcelot, and to cherish him above all other knights.

And so at the hour of noon Sir Gawain yielded up the spirit; and then the king let inter him in a chapel within

Dover Castle; and there yet all men may see the skull of him, and the same wound is seen that Sir Launcelot gave him in battle.

Then was it told the king that Sir Mordred had pitched a new field upon Barham Down. And upon the morn the king rode thither to him, and there was a great battle betwixt them, and much people was slain on both parties; but at the last Sir Arthur's party stood best, and Sir Mordred and his party fled unto Canterbury.

CHAPTER 3: *How after, Sir Gawain's ghost appeared to King Arthur, and warned him that he should not fight that day*

And then the king let search all the towns for his knights that were slain, and interred them; and salved them with soft salves that so sore were wounded.

Then much people drew unto King Arthur. And then they said that Sir Mordred warred upon King Arthur with wrong. And then King Arthur drew him with his host down by the seaside westward toward Salisbury; and there was a day assigned betwixt King Arthur and Sir Mordred, that they should meet upon a down beside Salisbury, and not far from the seaside; and this day was assigned on a Monday after Trinity Sunday, whereof King Arthur was passing glad, that he might be avenged upon Sir Mordred.

Then Sir Mordred araised much people about London, for they of Kent, Sussex and Surrey, Essex, and of Suffolk, and of Norfolk, held the most part with Sir Mordred; and many a full noble knight drew unto Sir Mordred and to the king; but they loved Sir Launcelot drew unto Sir Mordred.

So upon Trinity Sunday at night, King Arthur dreamed a wonderful dream, and that was this: that him seemed he sat upon a chaflet in a chair, and the chair was fast to a wheel, and thereupon sat King Arthur in the richest cloth of

chaflet: platform.

gold that might be made; and the king thought there was under him, far from him, an hideous deep black water, and therein were all manner of serpents, and worms, and wild beasts, foul and horrible; and suddenly the king thought the wheel turned up-so-down, and he fell among the serpents, and every beast took him by a limb; and then the king cried as he lay in his bed and slept, 'Help.'

And then knights, squires, and yeomen, awaked the king; and then he was so amazed that he wist not where he was; and then he fell on slumbering again, not sleeping nor thoroughly waking.

So the king seemed verily that there came Sir Gawain unto him with a number of fair ladies with him. And when King Arthur saw him, then he said, 'Welcome my sister's son; I weened thou hadst been dead, and now I see thee alive, much am I beholding unto Almighty Jesu. O fair nephew and my sister's son, what be these ladies that hither be come with you?'

'Sir,' said Sir Gawain, 'all these be ladies for whom I have foughten when I was man living, and all these are those that I did battle for in righteous quarrel; and God hath given them that grace at their great prayer, because I did battle for them, that they should bring me hither unto you : thus much hath God given me leave, for to warn you of your death; for and ye fight as tomorn with Sir Mordred, as ye both have assigned, doubt ye not ye must be slain, and the most part of your people on both parties. And for the great grace and goodness that Almighty Jesu hath unto you, and for pity of you, and many more other good men there shall be slain, God hath sent me to you of his special grace, to give you warning that in no wise ye do battle as tomorn, but that ye take a treaty for a month day; and proffer you largely, so as tomorn to be put in a delay. For within a month shall come Sir Launcelot with all his noble knights, and rescue you worshipfully, and slay Sir Mordred, and all that ever will hold with him.'

Then Sir Gawain and all the ladies vanished.[1] And anon

the king called upon his knights, squires, and yeomen, and charged them wightly to fetch his noble lords and wise bishops unto him. And when they were come, the king told them his avision, what Sir Gawain had told him, and warned him that if he fought on the morn he should be slain.

Then the king commanded Sir Lucan the Butler, and his brother Sir Bedevere, with two bishops with them, and charged them in any wise, and they might: 'Take a treaty for a month day with Sir Mordred, and spare not, proffer him lands and goods as much as ye think best.'

So then they departed, and came to Sir Mordred, where he had a grim host of an hundred thousand men. And there they entreated Sir Mordred long time; and at the last Sir Mordred was agreed for to have Cornwall and Kent, by Arthur's days; after, all England, after the days of King Arthur.

CHAPTER 4: *How by misadventure of an adder the battle began, where Mordred was slain, and Arthur hurt to the death*

Then were they condescended that King Arthur and Sir Mordred should meet betwixt both their hosts, and every each of them should bring fourteen persons; and they came with this word unto Arthur.

Then said he, 'I am glad that this is done': and so he went into the field.

And when Arthur should depart, he warned all his host that and they see any sword drawn, 'look ye come on fiercely, and slay that traitor, Sir Mordred, for I in no wise trust him.'

In likewise Sir Mordred warned his host that: 'And ye see any sword drawn, look that ye come on fiercely, and so slay all that ever before you standeth; for in no wise I will not trust for this treaty, for I know well my father will be avenged on me.'

And so they met as their pointment was, and so they were agreed and accorded thoroughly; and wine was fetched, and they drank.

Right soon came an adder out of a little heath bush, and it stung a knight on the foot. And when the knight felt him stungen, he looked down and saw the adder, and then he drew his sword to slay the adder, and thought of none other harm. And when the host on both parties saw that sword drawn, then they blew beams, trumpets, and horns, and shouted grimly. And so both hosts dressed them together.

And King Arthur took his horse, and said, 'Alas this unhappy day!' and so rode to his party. And Sir Mordred in likewise. And never was there seen a more dolefuller battle in no Christian land; for there was but rushing and riding, foining and striking, and many a grim word was there spoken either to other, and many a deadly stroke. But ever King Arthur rode throughout the battle of Sir Mordred many times, and did full nobly as a noble king should, and at all times he fainted never; and Sir Mordred that day put him in devoir, and in great peril. And thus they fought all the long day, and never stinted till the noble knights were laid to the cold earth; and ever they fought still till it was near night, and by that time was there an hundred thousand laid dead upon the down. Then was Arthur wood wroth out of measure, when he saw his people so slain from him.

Then the king looked about him, and then was he ware, of all his host and of all his good knights, were left no more alive but two knights; that one was Sir Lucan the Butler, and his brother Sir Bedevere, and they were full sore wounded.

'Jesu mercy,' said the king, 'where are all my noble knights becomen? Alas that ever I should see this doleful day, for now,' said Arthur, 'I am come to mine end. But would to God that I wist where were that traitor Sir Mordred, that hath caused all this mischief.'

Then was King Arthur ware where Sir Mordred leaned upon his sword among a great heap of dead men.

beams: bugles.

'Now give me my spear,' said Arthur unto Sir Lucan, 'for yonder I have espied the traitor that all this woe hath wrought.'

'Sir, let him be,' said Sir Lucan, 'for he is unhappy; and if ye pass this unhappy day ye shall be right well revenged upon him. Good lord, remember ye of your night's dream, and what the spirit of Sir Gawain told you this night, yet God of his great goodness hath preserved you hitherto. Therefore, for God's sake, my lord, leave off by this, for blessed be God ye have won the field, for here we be three alive, and with Sir Mordred is none alive; and if ye leave off now this wicked day of destiny is past.'

'Tide me death, betide me life,' saith the king, 'now I see him yonder alone he shall never escape mine hands, for at a better avail shall I never have him.'

'God speed you well,' said Sir Bedevere.

Then the king gat his spear in both his hands, and ran toward Sir Mordred, crying, 'Traitor, now is thy death day come.'

And when Sir Mordred heard Sir Arthur, he ran until him with his sword drawn in his hand. And there King Arthur smote Sir Mordred under the shield, with a foin of his spear, throughout the body, more than a fathom. And when Sir Mordred felt that he had his death's wound he thrust himself with the might that he had up to the bur of King Arthur's spear. And right so he smote his father Arthur, with his sword holden in both his hands, on the side of the head, that the sword pierced the helmet and the brain pan, and therewithal Sir Mordred fell stark dead to the earth; and the noble Arthur fell in a swoon to the earth and there he swooned ofttimes.

And Sir Lucan the Butler and Sir Bedevere ofttimes heave him up. And so weakly they led him betwixt them both, to a little chapel not far from the seaside. And when the king was there he thought him well eased. Then heard they people cry in the field.

bur : broad ring on a spear to protect the hand.

514

'Now go thou, Sir Lucan,' said the king, 'and do me to wit what betokens that noise in the field.'

So Sir Lucan departed, for he was grievously wounded in many places. And so as he yede, he saw and hearkened by the moonlight, how that pillers and robbers were comen into the field, to pill and to rob many a full noble knight of brooches, and beads, of many a good ring, and of many a rich jewel; and who that were not dead all out, there they slew them for their harness and their riches. When Sir Lucan understood this work, he came to the king as soon as he might, and told him all what he had heard and seen.

'Therefore by my rede,' said Sir Lucan, 'it is best that we bring you to some town.'

'I would it were so,' said the king.

CHAPTER 5: *How King Arthur commanded to cast his sword Excalibur into the water, and how he was delivered to ladies in a barge*

'But I may not stand, mine head works so. Ah Sir Launcelot,' said King Arthur, 'this day have I sore missed thee: alas, that ever I was against thee, for now have I my death, where-of Sir Gawain me warned in my dream.'

Then Sir Lucan took up the king the one part, and Sir Bedevere the other part, and in the lifting the king swooned; and Sir Lucan fell in a swoon with the lift, that the part of his guts fell out of his body, and therewith the noble knight's heart brast. And when the king awoke, he beheld Sir Lucan, how he lay foaming at the mouth, and part of his guts lay at his feet.

'Alas,' said the king, 'this is to me a full heavy sight, to see this noble duke so die for my sake, for he would have holpen me, that had more need of help than I. Alas, he would not complain him, his heart was so set to help me: now Jesu have mercy upon his soul!'

Then Sir Bedevere wept for the death of his brother.

'Leave this mourning and weeping,' said the king, 'for all this will not avail me, for wit thou well and I might live myself, the death of Sir Lucan would grieve me evermore; but my time hieth fast,' said the king. 'Therefore,' said Arthur unto Sir Bedevere, 'take thou Excalibur, my good sword, and go with it to yonder water side, and when thou comest there I charge thee throw my sword in that water, and come again and tell me what thou there seest.'

'My lord,' said Bedevere, 'your commandment shall be done, and lightly bring you word again.'

So Sir Bedevere departed, and by the way he beheld that noble sword, that the pommel and the haft was all of precious stones; and then he said to himself, 'If I throw this rich sword in the water, thereof shall never come good, but harm and loss.' And then Sir Bedevere hid Excalibur under a tree.

And so, as soon as he might, he came again unto the king, and said he had been at the water, and had thrown the sword in the water.

'What saw thou there?' said the king.

'Sir,' he said, 'I saw nothing but waves and winds.'

'That is untruly said of thee,' said the king, 'therefore go thou lightly again, and do my commandment; as thou art to me leve and dear, spare not, but throw it in.'

Then Sir Bedevere returned again, and took the sword in his hand; and then him thought sin and shame to throw away that noble sword, and so eft he hid the sword, and returned again, and told to the king that he had been at the water and done his commandment.

'What saw thou there?' said the king.

'Sir,' he said, 'I saw nothing but the waters wap and waves wan.'

'Ah, traitor untrue,' said King Arthur, 'now hast thou betrayed me twice. Who would have weened that thou that hast been to me so leve and dear, and thou art named a noble knight, and would betray me for the riches of the sword? But now go again lightly, for thy long tarrying putteth me in

wap: lap.   wan: grow dark.

516

great jeopardy of my life, for I have taken cold. And but if thou do now as I bid thee, if ever I may see thee, I shall slay thee mine own hands; for thou wouldst for my rich sword see me dead.'

Then Sir Bedevere departed, and went to the sword, and lightly took it up, and went to the water side; and there he bound the girdle about the hilts, and then he threw the sword as far into the water as he might; and there came an arm and an hand above the water and met it, and caught it, and so shook it thrice and brandished, and then vanished away the hand with the sword in the water. So Sir Bedevere came again to the king, and told him what he saw.

'Alas,' said the king, 'help me hence, for I dread me I have tarried over long.'

Then Sir Bedevere took the king upon his back, and so went with him to that water side. And when they were at the water side, even fast by the bank hoved a little barge with many fair ladies in it, and among them all was a queen, and all they had black hoods, and all they wept and shrieked when they saw King Arthur.

'Now put me into the barge,' said the king.

And so he did softly; and there received him three queens with great mourning; and so they set them down, and in one of their laps King Arthur laid his head.

And then that queen said, 'Ah, dear brother, why have ye tarried so long from me? Alas, this wound on your head hath caught over-much cold.'

And so then they rowed from the land, and Sir Bedevere beheld all those ladies go from him.

Then Sir Bedevere cried, 'Ah my lord Arthur, what shall become of me, now ye go from me and leave me here alone among mine enemies?'

'Comfort thyself,' said the king, 'and do as well as thou mayest, for in me is no trust for to trust in; for I will into the vale of Avilion to heal me of my grievous wound: and if thou hear never more of me, pray for my soul.'

But ever the queens and ladies wept and shrieked, that it

was pity to hear. And as soon as Sir Bedevere had lost the sight of the barge, he wept and wailed, and so took the forest; and so he went all that night, and in the morning he was ware betwixt two holts hoar, of a chapel and an hermitage.

CHAPTER 6: *How Sir Bedevere found him on the morn dead in an hermitage, and how he abode there with the hermit*

Then was Sir Bedevere glad, and thither he went; and when he came into the chapel, he saw where lay an hermit grovelling on all four, there fast by a tomb was new graven. When the hermit saw Sir Bedevere he knew him well, for he was but little tofore Bishop of Canterbury, that Sir Mordred flemed.

'Sir,' said Bedevere, 'what man is there interred that ye pray so fast for?'

'Fair son,' said the hermit, 'I wot not verily, but by deeming. But this night, at midnight, here came a number of ladies, and brought hither a dead corpse, and prayed me to bury him; and here they offered an hundred tapers, and they gave me an hundred bezants.'

'Alas,' said Sir Bedevere, 'that was my lord King Arthur, that here lieth buried in this chapel.'

Then Sir Bedevere swooned; and when he awoke he prayed the hermit he might abide with him still there, to live with fasting and prayers. 'For from hence will I never go,' said Sir Bedevere, 'by my will, but all the days of my life here to pray for my lord Arthur.'

'Ye are welcome to me,' said the hermit, 'for I know you better than ye ween that I do. Ye are the bold Bedevere, and the full noble duke, Sir Lucan the Butler, was your brother.'

Then Sir Bedevere told the hermit all as ye have heard tofore. So there bode Sir Bedevere with the hermit that was tofore Bishop of Canterbury, and there Sir Bedevere put upon him poor clothes, and served the hermit full lowly in fasting and in prayers.

Thus of Arthur I find never more written in books that be authorised, nor more of the very certainty of his death heard I never read, but thus was he led away in a ship wherein were three queens; that one was King Arthur's sister, Queen Morgan le Fay; the other was the Queen of Northgales; the third was the Queen of the Waste Lands. Also there was Nimue, the chief lady of the lake, that had wedded Pelleas the good knight; and this lady had done much for King Arthur, for she would never suffer Sir Pelleas to be in no place where he should be in danger of his life; and so he lived to the uttermost of his days with her in great rest. More of the death of King Arthur could I never find, but that ladies brought him to his burials; and such one was buried there, that the hermit bare witness that sometime was Bishop of Canterbury, but yet the hermit knew not in certain that he was verily the body of King Arthur; for this tale Sir Bedevere, knight of the Table Round, made it to be written.

CHAPTER 7: *Of the opinion of some men of the death of King Arthur; and how Queen Guenever made her a nun in Almesbury*

Yet some men say in many parts of England that King Arthur is not dead, but had by the will of Our Lord Jesu into another place; and men say that he shall come again, and he shall win the holy cross. I will not say that it shall be so, but rather I will say, here in this world he changed his life. But many men say that there is written upon his tomb this verse: HIC IACET ARTHURUS, REX QUONDAM REXQUE FUTURUS.

Thus leave I here Sir Bedevere with the hermit, that dwelled that time in a chapel beside Glastonbury, and there was his hermitage. And so they lived in their prayers, and fastings, and great abstinence.

And when Queen Guenever understood that King Arthur was slain, and all the noble knights, Sir Mordred and all the remnant, then the queen stole away, and five ladies with her, and so she went to Almesbury; and there she let make herself a nun, and ware white clothes and black, and great penance she took, as ever did sinful lady in this land, and never creature could make her merry; but lived in fasting, prayers, and alms-deeds, that all manner of people marvelled how virtuously she was changed.

Now leave we Queen Guenever in Almesbury, a nun in white clothes and black, and there she was abbess and ruler as reason would; and turn we from her, and speak we of Sir Launcelot du Lake.

CHAPTER 8: *How when Sir Launcelot heard of the death of King Arthur, and of Sir Gawain, and other matters, [he] came into England*

And when he heard in his country that Sir Mordred was crowned king in England, and made war against King Arthur, his own father, and would let him to land in his own land, also it was told Sir Launcelot how that Sir Mordred had laid siege about the Tower of London, because the queen would not wed him, then was Sir Launcelot wroth out of measure, and said to his kinsmen,

'Alas, that double traitor Sir Mordred, now me repenteth that ever he escaped my hands, for much shame hath he done unto my lord Arthur; for all I feel by the doleful letter that my lord Sir Gawain sent me, on whose soul Jesu have mercy, that my lord Arthur is full hard bestad. Alas,' said Sir Launcelot, 'that ever I should live to hear that most noble king that made me knight thus to be overset with his subject in his own realm. And this doleful letter that my lord, Sir Gawain, hath sent me afore his death, praying me to see his tomb, wit you well his doleful words shall never go from mine heart, for he was a full noble knight as ever was born;

and in an unhappy hour was I born that ever I should have that unhap to slay first Sir Gawain, Sir Gaheris the good knight, and mine own friend Sir Gareth, that full noble knight. Alas, I may say I am unhappy,' said Sir Launcelot, 'that ever I should do thus unhappily, and, alas, yet might I never have hap to slay that traitor, Sir Mordred.'

'Leave your complaints,' said Sir Bors, 'and first revenge you of the death of Sir Gawain; and it will be well done that ye see Sir Gawain's tomb, and secondly that ye revenge my lord Arthur, and my lady, Queen Guenever.'

'I thank you,' said Sir Launcelot, 'for ever ye will my worship.'

Then they made them ready in all the haste that might be, with ships and galleys, with Sir Launcelot and his host to pass into England. And so he passed over the sea till he came to Dover, and there he landed with seven kings, and the number was hideous to behold.

Then Sir Launcelot spered of men of Dover where was King Arthur become. Then the people told him how that he was slain, and Sir Mordred and an hundred thousand died on a day; and how Sir Mordred gave King Arthur there the first battle at his landing, and there was good Sir Gawain slain; and on the morn Sir Mordred fought with the king upon Barham Down, and there the king put Sir Mordred to the worse.

'Alas,' said Sir Launcelot, 'this is the heaviest tidings that ever came to me. Now, fair sirs,' said Sir Launcelot, 'show me the tomb of Sir Gawain.'

And then certain people of the town brought him into the Castle of Dover, and showed him the tomb. Then Sir Launcelot kneeled down and wept, and prayed heartily for his soul. And that night he made a dole, and all they that would come had as much flesh, fish, wine and ale, and every man and woman had twelve pence, come who would. Thus with his own hand dealt he this money, in a mourning gown; and ever he wept, and prayed them to pray for the soul of Sir Gawain. And on the morn all the priests and clerks that might be gotten in the country were there, and sang mass of requiem; and there offered first Sir Launcelot, and he offered an hundred pound; and then the seven kings offered forty pound apiece; and also there was a thousand knights, and each of them offered a pound; and the offering dured from morn till night, and Sir Launcelot lay two nights on his tomb in prayers and weeping. Then on the third day Sir Launcelot called the kings, dukes, earls, barons, and knights, and said thus:

'My fair lords, I thank you all of your coming into this country with me, but we came too late, and that shall repent me while I live, but against death may no man rebel. But sithen it is so,' said Sir Launcelot, 'I will myself ride and seek my lady, Queen Guenever, for as I hear say she hath had great pain and much disease; and I heard say that she is fled into the west. Therefore ye all shall abide me here, and but if I come again within fifteen days, then take your ships and your fellowship, and depart into your country, for I will do as I say to you.'

CHAPTER 9: *How Sir Launcelot departed to seek the queen Guenever, and how he found her at Almesbury*

Then came Sir Bors de Ganis, and said, 'My lord Sir Launcelot, what think ye for to do, now to ride in this realm? Wit ye well ye shall find few friends.'

'Be as be may,' said Sir Launcelot, 'keep you still here, for I will forth on my journey, and no man nor child shall go with me.'

So it was no boot to strive, but he departed and rode westerly, and there he sought a seven or eight days; and at the last he came to a nunnery, and then was Queen Guenever ware of Sir Launcelot as he walked in the cloister. And when she saw him there she swooned thrice, that all the ladies and gentlewomen had work enough to hold the queen up.

So when she might speak, she called ladies and gentlewomen to her, and said, 'Ye marvel, fair ladies, why I make this fare. Truly,' she said, 'it is for the sight of yonder knight that yonder standeth; wherefore I pray you all call him to me.'

When Sir Launcelot was brought to her, then she said to all the ladies, 'Through this man and me hath all this war been wrought, and the death of the most noblest knights of the world; for through our love that we have loved together is my most noble lord slain. Therefore, Sir Launcelot, wit thou well I am set in such a plight to get my soul health; and yet I trust through God's grace that after my death to have a sight of the blessed face of Christ, and at doomsday to sit on His right side, for as sinful as ever I was are saints in heaven. Therefore, Sir Launcelot, I require thee and beseech thee heartily, for all the love that ever was betwixt us, that thou never see me more in the visage; and I command thee, on God's behalf, that thou forsake my company, and to thy kingdom thou turn again, and keep well thy realm from war and wrack; for as well as I have loved thee, mine heart will not serve me to see thee, for through thee and me is the flower of kings and knights destroyed; therefore, Sir Launcelot, go to thy realm, and there take thee a wife, and live with her with joy and bliss; and I pray thee heartily, pray for me to Our Lord that I may amend my misliving.'

'Now, sweet madam,' said Sir Launcelot, 'would ye that I should turn again unto my country, and there to wed a lady? Nay, madam, wit you well that shall I never do, for I shall never be so false to you of that I have promised; but the same destiny that ye have taken you to, I will take me unto, for to please Jesu, and ever for you I cast me specially to pray.'

'If thou wilt do so,' said the queen, 'hold thy promise, but I may never believe but that thou wilt turn to the world again.'

'Well, madam,' said he, 'ye say as pleaseth you, yet wist you me never false of my promise, and God defend but I should forsake the world as ye have done. For in the quest of the Sangrail I had forsaken the vanities of the world had not your lord[1] been. And if I had done so at that time, with my heart, will, and thought, I had passed all the knights that were in the Sangrail except Sir Galahad, my son. And therefore, lady, sithen ye have taken you to perfection, I must needs take me to perfection, of right. For I take record of God, in you I have had mine earthly joy; and if I had founden you now so disposed, I had cast me to have had you into mine own realm.

CHAPTER 10: *How Sir Launcelot came to the hermitage where the Archbishop of Canterbury was, and how he took the habit on him.*

'But sithen I find you thus disposed, I ensure you faithfully, I will ever take me to penance, and pray while my life lasteth, if that I may find any hermit, either gray or white, that will receive me. Wherefore, madam, I pray you kiss me and never no more.'

'Nay,' said the queen, 'that shall I never do, but abstain you from such works.' And they departed. But there was never so hard an hearted man but he would have wept to see the dolour that they made; for there was lamentation as they had been stungen with spears; and many times they swooned, and the ladies bare the queen to her chamber. And Sir Launcelot awoke, and went and took his horse, and rode all that day and all night in a forest, weeping.

And at the last he was ware of an hermitage and a chapel stood betwixt two cliffs; and then he heard a little bell ring to mass, and thither he rode and alit, and tied his horse to the gate, and heard mass. And he that sang mass was the Bishop of Canterbury.

Both the Bishop and Sir Bedevere knew Sir Launcelot, and they spake together after mass. But when Sir Bedevere had told his tale all whole, Sir Launcelot's heart almost brast for sorrow, and Sir Launcelot threw his arms abroad, and said, 'Alas, who may trust this world.'

And then he kneeled down on his knee, and prayed the

Bishop to shrive him and assoil him. And then he besought the Bishop that he might be his brother.

Then the Bishop said, 'I will gladly,' and there he put an habit upon Sir Launcelot, and there he served God day and night with prayers and fastings.

Thus the great host abode at Dover. And then Sir Lionel took fifteen lords with him, and rode to London to seek Sir Launcelot; and there Sir Lionel was slain and many of his lords. Then Sir Bors de Ganis made the great host for to go home again; and Sir Bors, Sir Ector de Maris, Sir Blamor, Sir Bleoberis, with more other of Sir Launcelot's kin, took on them to ride all England overthwart and endlong, to seek Sir Launcelot. So Sir Bors by fortune rode so long till he came to the same chapel where Sir Launcelot was; and so Sir Bors heard a little bell knell, that rang to mass; and there he alit and heard mass. And when mass was done, the Bishop, Sir Launcelot, and Sir Bedevere, came to Sir Bors. And when Sir Bors saw Sir Launcelot in that manner clothing, then he prayed the Bishop that he might be in the same suit. And so there was an habit put upon him, and there he lived in prayers and fasting.

And within half a year, there was come Sir Galihud, Sir Galihodin, Sir Blamor, Sir Bleoberis, Sir Villiars, Sir Clarrus, and Sir Gahalantine. So all these seven noble knights there abode still. And when they saw Sir Launcelot had taken him to such perfection, they had no lust to depart, but took such an habit as he had. Thus they endured in great penance six year; and then Sir Launcelot took the habit of priesthood of the Bishop, and a twelvemonth he sang mass. And there was none of these other knights but they read in books, and holp for to sing mass, and rang bells, and did lowly all manner of service. And so their horses went where they would, for they took no regard of no worldly riches. For when they saw Sir Launcelot endure such penance, in prayers and fastings, they took no force what pain they endured, for to see the noblest knight of the world take such abstinence that he waxed full lean.

And thus upon a night, there came a vision to Sir Launcelot, and charged him, in remission of his sins, to haste him unto Almesbury: 'And by then thou come there, thou shalt find Queen Guenever dead. And therefore take thy fellows with thee, and purvey them of an horse bier, and fetch thou the corpse of her, and bury her by her husband, the noble King Arthur.' So this avision came to Sir Launcelot thrice in one night.

CHAPTER 11: *How Sir Launcelot went with his seven fellows to Almesbury, and found there Queen Guenever dead, whom they brought to Glastonbury*

Then Sir Launcelot rose up or day, and told the hermit.

'It were well done,' said the hermit, 'that ye made you ready, and that ye disobey not the avision.'

Then Sir Launcelot took his seven fellows with him, and on foot they yede from Glastonbury to Almesbury, the which is little more than thirty mile. And thither they came within two days, for they were weak and feeble to go. And when Sir Launcelot was come to Almesbury within the nunnery, Queen Guenever died but half an hour afore.

And the ladies told Sir Launcelot that Queen Guenever told them all or she passed, that Sir Launcelot had been priest near a twelvemonth, "And hither he cometh as fast as he may to fetch my corpse; and beside my lord, King Arthur, he shall bury me." Wherefore the queen said in hearing of them all, "I beseech Almighty God that I may never have power to see Sir Launcelot with my worldly eyen". 'And thus,' said all the ladies, 'was ever her prayer these two days, till she was dead.'

Then Sir Launcelot saw her visage, but he wept not greatly, but sighed. And so he did all the observance of the service himself, both the dirge, and on the morn he sang mass. And there was ordained an horse bier; and so with an hundred torches ever burning about the corpse of the queen, and ever

Sir Launcelot with his seven[1] fellows went about the horse bier, singing and reading many an holy orison, and frankincense upon the corpse incensed. Thus Sir Launcelot and his seven fellows went on foot from Almesbury unto Glastonbury.

And when they were come to the chapel and the hermitage, there she had a dirge, with great devotion. And on the morn the hermit that sometime was Bishop of Canterbury sang the mass of requiem with great devotion. And Sir Launcelot was the first that offered, and then all his eight fellows. And then she was wrapped in cered cloth of Rennes, from the top to the toe, in thirtyfold; and after she was put in a web of lead, and then in a coffin of marble. And when she was put in the earth Sir Launcelot swooned, and lay long still, while the hermit came and awaked him, and said, 'Ye be to blame, for ye displease God with such manner of sorrow making.'

'Truly,' said Sir Launcelot, 'I trust I do not displease God, for He knoweth mine intent. For my sorrow was not, nor is not, for any rejoicing of sin, but my sorrow may never have end. For when I remember of her beauty, and of her noblesse, that was both with her king and with her, so when I saw his corpse and her corpse so lie together, truly mine heart would not serve to sustain my careful body. Also when I remember me how by my default, mine orgule and my pride, that they were both laid full low, that were peerless that ever was living of Christian people, wit you well,' said Sir Launcelot, 'this remembered, of their kindness and mine unkindness, sank so to mine heart, that I might not sustain myself.' So the French book maketh mention.

CHAPTER 12: *How Sir Launcelot began to sicken, and after died, whose body was borne to Joyous Gard for to be buried*

Then Sir Launcelot never after ate but little meat, nor drank, till he was dead. For then he sickened more and more, and dried, and dwined away. For the Bishop nor none of his fellows might not make him to eat, and little he drank, that he was waxen by a cubit shorter than he was, that the people could not know him. For evermore, day and night, he prayed, but sometime he slumbered a broken sleep; ever he was lying grovelling on the tomb of King Arthur and Queen Guenever. And there was no comfort that the Bishop, nor Sir Bors, nor none of his fellows, could make him, it availed not.

So within six weeks after, Sir Launcelot fell sick, and lay in his bed; and then he sent for the Bishop that there was hermit, and all his true fellows. Then Sir Launcelot said with dreary steven, 'Sir Bishop, I pray you give to me all my rites that longeth to a Christian man.'

'It shall not need you,' said the hermit and all his fellows, 'it is but heaviness of your blood, ye shall be well mended by the grace of God tomorn.'

'My fair lords,' said Sir Launcelot, 'wit you well my careful body will into the earth, I have warning more than now I will say; therefore give me my rites.'

So when he was houselled and eneled, and had all that a Christian man ought to have, he prayed the Bishop that his fellows might bear his body to Joyous Gard. Some men say it was Alnwick, and some men say it was Bamborough.

'Howbeit,' said Sir Launcelot, 'me repenteth sore, but I made mine avow sometime, that in Joyous Gard I would be buried. And because of breaking of mine avow, I pray you all, lead me thither.'

Then there was weeping and wringing of hands among his fellows. So at a season of the night they all went to their

dwined: wasted.   *steven*: voice.   *eneled*: anointed.

beds, for they all lay in one chamber. And so after midnight, against day, the Bishop that was hermit, as he lay in his bed asleep, he fell upon a great laughter. And therewithal the fellowship awoke, and come to the Bishop, and asked him what he ailed.

'Ah Jesu mercy,' said the Bishop, 'why did ye awake me? I was never in all my life so merry and so well at ease.'

'Wherefore?' said Sir Bors.

'Truly,' said the Bishop, 'here was Sir Launcelot with me with more angels than ever I saw men in one day. And I saw the angels heave up Sir Launcelot unto heaven, and the gates of heaven opened against him.'

'It is but dretching of swevens,' said Sir Bors, 'for I doubt not Sir Launcelot aileth nothing but good.'

'It may well be,' said the Bishop; 'go ye to his bed, and then shall ye prove the sooth.'

So when Sir Bors and his fellows came to his bed they found him stark dead, and he lay as he had smiled, and the sweetest savour about him that ever they felt. Then was there weeping and wringing of hands, and the greatest dole they made that ever made men.

And on the morn the Bishop did his mass of requiem; and after, the Bishop and all the nine knights put Sir Launcelot in the same horse bier that Queen Guenever was laid in tofore that she was buried. And so the Bishop and they all together went with the body of Sir Launcelot daily, till they came to Joyous Gard; and ever they had an hundred torches burning about him. And so within fifteen days they came to Joyous Gard.

And there they laid his corpse in the body of the choir, and sang and read many psalters and prayers over him and about him. And ever his visage was laid open and naked, that all folks might behold him. For such was the custom in those days, that all men of worship should so lie with open visage till that they were buried.

And right thus as they were at their service, there came

dretching: disturbance.

Sir Ector de Maris, that had seven year sought all England, Scotland, and Wales, seeking his brother, Sir Launcelot.

CHAPTER 13 : *How Sir Ector found Sir Launcelot his brother dead, and how Constantine reigned next after Arthur; and of the end of this book*

And when Sir Ector heard such noise and light in the choir of Joyous Gard, he alit and put his horse from him, and came into the choir, and there he saw men sing, weep, and all they knew Sir Ector, but he knew not them.

Then went Sir Bors unto Sir Ector, and told him how there lay his brother, Sir Launcelot, dead; and then Sir Ector threw his shield, sword, and helm from him. And when he beheld Sir Launcelot's visage, he fell down in a swoon. And when he waked it were hard any tongue to tell the doleful complaints that he made for his brother.

'Ah Launcelot,' he said, 'thou were head of all Christian knights, and now I dare say,' said Sir Ector, 'thou Sir Launcelot, there thou liest, that thou were never matched of earthly knight's hand. And thou were the couteoust knight that ever bare shield. And thou were the truest friend to thy lover that ever bestrad horse. And thou were the truest lover of a sinful man that ever loved woman. And thou were the kindest man that ever struck with sword. And thou were the goodliest person that ever came among press of knights. And thou was the meekest man and the gentlest that ever ate in hall among ladies. And thou were the sternest knight to thy mortal foe that ever put spear in the rest.'

Then there was weeping and dolour out of measure. Thus they kept Sir Launcelot's corpse loft fifteen days, and then they buried it with great devotion.

And then at leisure they went all with the Bishop of Canterbury to his hermitage, and there they were together more than a month.

Then Sir Constantine, that was Sir Cador's son of Cornwall, was chosen king of England. And he was a full noble knight, and worshipfully he ruled this realm. And then this King Constantine sent for the Bishop of Canterbury, for he heard say where he was. And so he was restored unto his bishopric, and left that hermitage. And Sir Bedevere was there ever still hermit to his life's end.

Then Sir Bors de Ganis, Sir Ector de Maris, Sir Gahalantine, Sir Galihud, Sir Galihodin, Sir Blamore, Sir Bleoberis, Sir Villiars le Valiant, Sir Clarrus of Cleremont, all these knights drew them to their countries. Howbeit King Constantine would have had them with him, but they would not abide in this realm. And there they all lived in their countries as holy men.

And some English books maken mention that they went never out of England after the death of Sir Launcelot, but that was but favour of makers. For the French book maketh mention, and is authorised, that Sir Bors, Sir Ector, Sir Blamor, and Sir Bleoberis, went into the Holy Land thereas Jesu Christ was quick and dead, and anon as they had stablished their lands. For the book saith, so Sir Launcelot commanded them for to do, or ever he passed out of this world. And these four knights did many battles upon the miscreants or Turks. And there they died upon a Good Friday for God's sake.

Here is the end of the whole book of King Arthur, and of his noble knights of the Round Table, that when they were whole together there was ever an hundred and forty. And here is the end of the death of Arthur. I pray you all, gentlemen and gentlewomen that readeth this book of Arthur and his knights from the beginning to the ending, pray for me while I am alive, that God send me good deliverance, and when I am dead, I pray you all pray for my soul. For this book was ended the ninth year of the reign of King Edward the Fourth, by Sir Thomas Malory, knight, as Jesu help him for His great might, as he is the servant of Jesu both day and night.

favour of makers: partiality of authors.

[1]*Thus endeth this noble and joyous book entitled Le Morte Darthur. Notwithstanding it treateth of the birth, life, and acts of the said King Arthur, of his noble knights of the Round Table, their marvellous enquests and adventures, the achieving of the Sangrail, and in the end the dolorous death and departing out of this world of them all. Which book was reduced into English by Sir Thomas Malory, knight, as afore is said, and by me divided into twenty-one books, chaptered and imprinted, and finished in the abbey Westminster the last day of July the year of Our Lord MCCCCLXXXV*

Caxton me fieri fecit.

NOTES TO VOLUME II

BOOK X

ch. 5 1. *took off their helms*: repeated from the previous sentence. W: 'took their horses'.

ch. 18 1. *he*: not in C.

ch. 19 1. C: 'repented'.

ch. 22 1. C: 'man man'.

ch. 24 1. C: 'their being'. Cf. Vinaver, p. 1493, n. 611. 38.

ch. 30 1. C: 'your lives'.

ch. 36 1. C. omits the fact that the damosel has told Morgan le Fay of what she has seen. W. reads: 'and all this saw a damosel, and went to Morgan le Fay and told her how she saw the best knight joust . . .'

ch. 46 1. W: *Elyce, his sonne*, i.e. son of the duke. C., mistaking *Elyce his* for the genitive, has added a new character.

ch. 52 1. The idea that Tristram was the founder of the art of venery is found elsewhere, in an English version of the Tristan romance, and in some late medieval treatises on hunting.

ch. 58 1. *as they might*. The emendation *as* for the *and* found in both C. and W. is suggested by Vinaver, p. 1513, n. 700. 4–5.

ch. 71 1. C: 'said Sir Palomides'; W: 'Sir Palomides.'

ch. 87 1. C: 'Launcelot'; W: 'Palomides'.

BOOK XI

ch. 5 1. C: *owne*; W: *one*.

BOOK XII

ch. 6 1. *beclosed in iron*: probably a misprint. W: *beclosed envy-rowne* ('about').

ch. 9 1. C: *venetreted*.

BOOK XIII

ch. 10 1. *Mondrames*, treated here as a separate character, is a misreading of *Mordrains*, baptismal name of King Evelake. See Vinaver, p. 1549, n. 880. 23–4.

ch. 14 1. C: *thy*; W: *the*.

BOOK XIV

ch. 5 1. *inly* may be an error for 'inky' or 'inkly'. Vinaver (p. 1555, n. 911. 31) suggests an etymology from *Inde* ('dark blue')+ly.

ch. 7 1. C.'s omission of *that* (present in W.) has obscured the sense.

BOOK XV

ch. 2 1. C: *loetryd.*

BOOK XVI

ch. 2 1. *he had.* Both C. and W. have *the hede.* The emendation is suggested by Vinaver, p. 1562, n. 942. 32.

2. *himself, Sir Ector.* Both C. and W. have *and* between *himself* and *Sir*, and *they* later in the sentence. Thus Launcelot is made the subject of the verb *trowed*, which in the context clearly refers more appropriately to Ector's vision. For the emendation, see Vinaver, p. 1562, n. 942. 33–4.

ch. 8 1. *the one,* not in C.

ch. 12 1. *not,* omitted in C. but found in W., is essential for the sense of the passage: 'Nevertheless he had made up his mind that he had rather they had all lost their souls than he his.'

BOOK XVII

ch. 3 1. C: 'ship that'.

ch. 16 1. C: *sone*; W: *synne.*

ch. 22 1. W. has the correct reading 'Joseph, son of Joseph of Arimathea.' It is easy to see how the omission occurred in C.

BOOK XVIII

ch. 4 1. *Winchester* (W.). C's 'Westminster' conflicts with the later reference in ch. 6.

2. Even with the use of punctuation it is difficult to make sense of C. here. W. has the more coherent reading: 'that ye go unto Sir Bors and pray him for to battle for you for Sir Launcelot's sake'.

ch. 7 1. *king* (W.); C: 'queen'.

ch. 11 1. C: *wot not.*

ch. 14 1. W: 'and departed before Sir Gawain'.

ch. 15 1. C: *stryked*; W: *shryked.*

ch. 21 1. *for the string* may mean 'in tracking down the quarry'. Early on the morning of the day appointed for a hunt, the huntsman would take a limer, or scenting hound, held on a leash, to trace the quarry to its lair.

bait is used here to mean the act of setting dogs to worry other animals.

BOOK XIX

ch. 2 1. C: 'in their presence'.

ch. 9 1. *Lesses les aler*: 'Let them go': a signal to spur the horses.

ch. 13 1. C: *ouer hyp*; W: *overlepe.*

BOOK XX

ch. 5 1. C: *wan;* W: *than.*

ch. 7 1. *men*: probably a mistaken contraction. W. has *menour* ('behaviour'). See Vinaver, p. cix.

ch. 11 1. C: *and than all;* W: *than me and all.*

BOOK XXI

ch. 1 1. W. has the better reading: 'from Sir Launcelot'.

ch. 3 1. C: *vaynquysshed.*

ch. 9 1. W: 'love'.

ch. 11 1. C, W: 'eight'.

ch. 13 1. Caxton's own colophon. The colophon above (found also in W.) implies that the title 'the death of Arthur' applies only to the last section of the work.

GLOSSARY OF PROPER NOUNS

The following list contains only the major proper nouns and those likely to cause difficulty.

Accolon of Gaul, lover and champion of Morgan le Fay.
Agloval, brother of Percival.
Agravain, son of King Lot of Orkney.
Agwisance, King of Ireland, father of Isoud.
Alice la Beale Pilgrim, wife of Alisander le Orphelin.
Alisander le Orphelin, son of Boudwin and nephew of King Mark.
Almain, Germany.
Andred, cousin and enemy of Tristram.
Anglides, wife of Boudwin and mother of Alisander le Orphelin.
Aries, the cow-herd whose wife was mother of Tor.
Astlabor, father of Palomides.
Avelion, territory of the Lady Lile.
Avilion, isle of, home of Gringamore.
    vale of, valley to which the queens carry the dying Arthur.
Bagdemagus, King of Gore, cousin of King Uriens.
Balan, brother of Balin.
Balin le Savage, 'the Knight with the Two Swords'.
Ban, King of Benwick, father of Launcelot de Lake.
Baudwin of Britain, appointed as viceroy during Arthur's Roman campaign; later a hermit.
Beaumains, nickname given by Kay to Gareth.
Bedevere, brother of Lucan.
Bellengerus le Beuse, son of Alisander le Orphelin.
Benwick, realm and city of King Ban.
Bernard, father of Elaine, maiden of Astolat.
Berrant le Apres, 'the King with the Hundred Knights'.
Blamor de Ganis, brother of Bleoberis.
Bleise, Merlin's master, chronicler of Arthur's reign.
Bleoberis de Ganis, brother of Blamor.
Borre, son of Arthur and Lionors.
Bors de Ganis, son of King Bors of Gaul.
Boudwin, brother of King Mark; father of Alisander le Orphelin.
Bragwaine, servant of Isoud.
Brandegoris, King of Strangore.
Brandiles, one of the knights delivered from Turquin by Launcelot.

Brastias, knight of the Duke of Tintagel, afterwards of Arthur; hermit in the Forest of Windsor who offers hospitality to Launcelot.

Breunis Saunce Pité, enemy of Arthur's knights, identical with the Brown Knight Without Pity.

Breunor, knight of the Castle Pluere (Book VIII, ch. 24).

Breunor le Noire, called 'La Cote Male Taile' by Kay.

Brian of the Isles, sworn brother of Meliot of Logris (Book III, ch. 13); probably distinct from *Brian de les Isles*, lord of the Castle of Pendragon and enemy of Arthur.

Cador of Cornwall, leader in Arthur's army, father of Constantine.

Camelerd, realm of King Leodegrance.

Camelot, Arthur's residence, identified with Winchester.

Carados, King of Scotland.

Carados of the Dolorous Tower, brother of Turquin.

Carbonek, city and castle of the Grail.

Clariance de la Forest Savage, knight defeated by King Lot in the war against the eleven kings.

Clarivaus, King of Northumberland.

Clarrus of Cleremont, supporter of Launcelot.

Claudas, king, enemy of Ban and Bors.

Clegis, leader in Arthur's army.

Colgrevaunce of Gore, knight who fights against the eleven kings; slain by Lionel.

Constantine, son of Cador; king after Arthur.

Cradelment, King of North Wales.

Dagonet, Arthur's fool.

Damas, knight who imprisons Arthur (Book IV).

Dinadan, companion of Tristram.

Dinas, seneschal of King Mark.

Dodinas le Savage, knight of Arthur's court.

Dornard, son of Pellinor.

Ector, foster father of Arthur.

Ector de Maris, brother of Launcelot.

Elaine, wife of King Nentres.

Elaine, daughter of King Pellinor and the Lady of the Rule.

Elaine, wife of King Ban.

Elaine, daughter of King Pelles; mother of Galahad.

Elaine le Blank, the maiden of Astolat, daughter of Bernard.

Eliazar, son of King Pelles.

Elizabeth, wife of Meliodas and mother of Tristram.

Epinogrus, son of the King of Northumberland.

Ettard, unfaithful lover of Pelleas.

GLOSSARY OF PROPER NOUNS

Eustace, Duke of Canbenet, one of the eleven kings who oppose Arthur.

Evelake, pagan king, receives the baptismal name of *Mordrains*; cured by Galahad.

Excalibur, Arthur's sword.

Florence, son of Gawain.

Gahalatine, supporter of Launcelot.

Gaheris, son of King Lot; brother of Gawain.

Galagars, chosen by Pellinor to be a knight of the Round Table.

Galahad, son of Launcelot and Elaine.

Galahad, baptismal name of Launcelot.

Galahaut the Haut Prince, lord of Surluse.

Gales, Wales.

Galihodin, king 'within the country of Surluse'.

Galihud, one of the knights delivered from Turquin by Launcelot; takes part in the quest for Tristram.

Galleron of Galway, knight of the Round Table, one of the twelve who join Agravain.

Gareth, son of King Lot; called Beaumains by Kay.

Gawain, son of King Lot; nephew of Arthur.

Gingalin, son of Gawain.

Gore, realm of King Uriens.

Gouvernail, attendant of Tristram.

Griflet le Fise de Dieu, knight of Arthur's court, chosen by Pellinor to be a knight of the Round Table.

Gringamore, brother of Lyonesse.

Grummor Grummorson, Scottish knight (Caxton's conflation of two characters).

Guenever, daughter of Leodegrance and wife of Arthur.

Harry le Fise Lake, one of the three knights of the Round Table who fight Breunis Saunce Pité.

Harsouse le Berbeus, defeated by Alisander le Orphelin.

Hebes le Renoumes, knight of Launcelot's kin; squire to Tristram.

Helin le Blank, son of Sir Bors.

Herlews le Berbeus, slain by Garlon (Book II, ch. 12).

Hermance, King of the Red City.

Hervis de Revel, chosen by Pellinor to be a knight of the Round Table.

Hontzlake of Wentland, knight slain by Pellinor.

Howel, King of Brittany, father of Isoud la Blanche Mains; possibly identical with Howell, Duke of Brittany, whose wife is murdered by a giant (Book V, ch. 5).

Idres, King of Cornwall.

GLOSSARY OF PROPER NOUNS

Idrus, son of Uwain.

Igraine, mother of Arthur.

Ironside, name of the Red Knight of the Red Launds.

Isoud, La Beale, daughter of King Agwisance of Ireland; wife of King Mark of Cornwall.

Isoud la Blanche Mains, daughter of King Howel of Brittany; married to Tristram.

Kay, the Seneschal, son of Ector and foster brother of Arthur.

Kehydius, son of King Howel of Brittany; falls in love with La Beale Isoud.

King with the Hundred Knights, The, see Berrant.

La Cote Male Taile, 'The Ill-Tailored Coat' – nickname given to Breunor by Kay.

Lamorak de Gales, son of Pellinor.

Lanceor, son of the King of Ireland.

Launcelot de Lake, son of King Ban of Benwick.

Lavaine, son of Bernard of Astolat.

Leodegrance, King of Camelerd, father of Guenever.

Lile, Lady, of Avelion, enemy of Balin.

Lionel, nephew of Launcelot.

Liones, territory of Tristram.

Lionors, daughter of Sanam and mother of Borre.

Listinoise, kingdom of Pellam and Pellinor.

Logris, a kingdom of Great Britain ruled by Arthur.

Lot, King of Lothian and Orkney.

Lovel, son of Gawain.

Lucan the Butler, knight of Arthur's court, son of Corneus.

Lynet, sister of Lyonesse.

Lyonesse, sister of Lynet; rescued by Gareth.

Margawse, wife of King Lot.

Marhaus, brother of the Queen of Ireland; slain by Tristram.

Mark, King of Cornwall, uncle of Tristram.

Meliagaunt, son of Bagdemagus.

Meliodas, King of Liones, father of Tristram.

Meliot de Logris, cousin of Nimue (Book III); wounded by Gilbert the Bastard and healed by Launcelot (Book VI); joins Agravain's plot against Launcelot (Book XX).

Merlin, magician and soothsayer.

Mondrames, a misreading of *Mordrains*, q.v., treated as a separate character (Book XIII, ch. 10).

Mordrains, see *Evelake*.

Morgan le Fay, wife of Uriens; sister of Arthur.

Nacien, an ancestor of Launcelot.

Nacien, hermit, a descendant of Joseph of Arimathea.

Nentres, King of Garlot.

Nimue, called 'the chief Lady of the Lake'; caused the death of Merlin; married Pelleas.

Ontzlake, brother of Damas.

Ozanna le Cure Hardy, knight of Arthur's court.

Palomides, the Saracen, son of Astlabor and brother of Safer.

Pellam, of Listinoise, father of Pelles; 'the Maimed King', injured by Balin with a magic spear (Book II, ch. 15) and later healed by Galahad (his great-grandson).

Pelleas, lover of the Lady Ettard; accompanied Guenever on her Maying expedition; married Nimue.

Pelles, son of Pellam and father of Elaine, mother of Galahad; also called 'the Maimed King'; wounded as a result of drawing the mysterious sword (Book XVII, ch. 5).

Pellinor, of Listinoise, father of Lamorak.

Percival de Gales, one of the three Grail knights.

Perimones, name of the Red Knight.

Persant of Inde, name of the Blue Knight.

Pertelope, name of the Green Knight.

Priamus, son of a pagan prince who rebelled against Rome; brother of Dinas.

Rience, King of North Wales.

Sadok, friend of Alisander and Tristram.

Safer, brother of Palomides.

Sagramore le Desirous, knight of Arthur's court.

Sangrail, the Holy Grail.

Segwarides, enemy of Tristram.

Selises of the Dolorous Tower, nephew of the King with the Hundred Knights.

Strangore, kingdom of Brandegoris.

Surluse, realm of Galahaut the Haut Prince.

Tor le Fise de Vayshoure; le Fise Aries, son of Pellinor and Aries' wife.

Tristram de Liones, son of Meliodas; nephew of King Mark.

Turquin, enemy of Arthur's knights.

Ulfius, knight of Uther Pendragon.

Uriens, King of Gore.

Urré of the Mount, Hungarian knight; comes to Arthur's court to be healed.

Uther Pendragon, father of Arthur.

Uwain le Blanchemains; les Avoutres, son of King Uriens. (Treated as two separate characters, Book X, ch. 11.)

Waste Lands, Queen of the, aunt of Percival; one of the queens who bear away the dying Arthur.

GLOSSARY

abode	v. pret.	withstood
abought	v. pret.	paid for
abrayed	v. pret.	started up
accord	n.	reconciliation
adoubted	p. p.	afraid
affiance	n.	trust
afterdeal	n.	disadvantage
against	prep.	in the presence of
aknown	ppl. adj.	aware
allow	v.	to commend
almeries	n. pl.	libraries
alther	adj. gen. pl.	of all
and	conj.	if
apayed	ppl. adj	pleased
apel	v.	to impeach, accuse
appeach	v.	to accuse
appertices	n. pl.	feats
aretted	p. p.	reckoned
arson	n.	saddle bow
assoil	v.	to absolve
astonied	p. p.	stunned
attaint	ppl. adj.	exhausted
avail	n.	advantage
avaled	v. pret.	lowered
aventred	v. pret.	set (spear) in position for a charge
avoid	v.	to leave, send away
avow	v.	to admit, promise
awke	adj.	back-handed
awroke	p. p.	avenged
bachelor	n.	young knight
bain	n.	bath
bated	v. pret.	abated
battle	n.	battalion
bawdy	adj.	dirty
beams	n. pl.	bugles
bee	n.	ring, bracelet
be	v. pres. pl.	are
behest	n.	promise
behight	v. pret.	see *behote*

behote	v.	to promise
behove	v.	to be necessary
benome	p. p.	taken away
beseem	v.	to befit, appear
beseen	adj.	looking, having an appearance
beskift	v.	to thrust off
bestad	p. p.	biset
bestial	n.	cattle
betake	v.	to entrust
betaught	v. pret.	commended
bevered	v. pret.	trembled
bewared	p. p.	bestowed
bezant	n.	gold coin
blee	n.	complexion
bless	v. reflex.	to cross oneself
bobaunce	n.	boasting
boistous	adj.	unsophisticated, rough
boot	n.	remedy
borow	n.	pledge
	v.	to rescue, ransom
bounty	n.	goodness, favour
bourd	v.	to jest
braid	n.	attack
brain-pan	n.	skull
brast	v. pret. and p. p.	burst
brim	adj.	fierce
broached	v. pret.	pierced
brose	n.	a kind of broth
bruise	v.	to shatter, hurt
bur	n.	broad ring on a spear to protect the hand
burgh	n.	town
bushment	n.	ambush
by	prep.	about
caitiff	n. as adj.	miserable, wretched
cantel	n.	piece
cast	v.	to intend, imagine
cedle	n.	letter
cere	n.	wax
chaflet	n.	platform
champaign	n.	plain, field
charge	n. and v.	command
cheer	n.	entertainment, appearance
clean	adj.	excellent, pure

clean	adv.	completely
cleped	v. pret.	called
cleyght	v. pret.	seized
clip	v.	to embrace
cog	n.	broadly built ship
coif	n.	close fitting cap
complished	p. p.	filled
conceit	n.	judgement
conversant	adj.	living
cording	n.	agreement
cost	n.	side
costed	v. pret.	followed
couch	v.	to lower spear for attack
courage	n.	desire
courtelage	n.	court-yard
covin	n.	conspiracy
cream	n.	chrism
credence	n.	message
cunning	n.	ability
daffish	adj.	stupid
damage	n.	grief, injury
damosel	n.	maiden
danger	n.	power
dawe	v.	to revive
deal	n.	part
debonair	adj.	gracious
deem	v.	to judge
defend	v.	to forbid
defendant	n.	defence
defile	v.	to afflict, put to shame
delibered	p. p.	considered
deliverly	adv.	neatly
dere	v.	to harm
descrive	v.	to interpret
device	n.	arrangement, conversation
devise	v.	to think about
devoided	v. pret.	dismounted
devoir	n.	endeavour
dight	v. pret. and p. p.	furnished, prepared
dindled	v. pret.	trembled
dint	n.	blow
diseased	adj.	weary
disperpled	p. p.	dispersed
dispoil	v.	to undress

GLOSSARY

dissever	v.	to distinguish
distained	p. p.	dishonoured
dole	n.	lamentation, sorrow
domineth	v. pres. 3 sg.	holds sway
doubt	n.	fearful thing
	v.	to fear
drenched	p. p.	drowned
dress	v.	to set in position, prepare, step forward
dretch	v.	to harass, disturb
dromond	n.	large ship
duress	n.	affliction
dwell	v.	to delay
dwined	v. pret.	wasted
eagerness	n.	violence
eft	adv.	again
ell	n.	a measure of length : 45 inches
eme	n.	uncle
enchafe	v.	to make warm
endlong	adv. and prep.	along
eneled	p. p.	anointed
enewed	ppl. adj.	coloured
engine	n.	evil device
enow	adj.	enough
enprise	v.	to undertake
entreat	v.	to negotiate
erst	adv.	before
estures	n. pl.	rooms
eure	n.	fortune
evenlong	adv. and prep.	along
fain	adv.	gladly
	adj.	glad
faiter	n.	imposter
fare	v.	to act, behave
fault	v.	to lack
feute	n.	track
fewter	n.	rest for spear
	v.	to fix a spear in its rest
fiance	n.	promise
flacket	n.	flask
flemed	v. pret. and p. p.	put to flight

GLOSSARY

foin	n.	thrust
force	n.	strength, might
no force		that does not matter
fordeal	n.	advantage
fordo	v.	to render powerless
forfend	v.	to forbid
forfoughten	ppl. adj.	weary with fighting
forthink	v. reflex and impers.	to regret
gad	n.	rod
gainest	adj. superl.	quickest
gar	v.	to cause
gat	v. pret.	got, begot
gisarme	n.	battle-axe
glasting, *glatisant*	adj.	barking
graithed	v. pret.	prepared
grame	n.	harm
gramercy		many thanks
greces	n. pl.	stairs
gree	n.	victory
guardrobe	n.	wardrobe
guise	n.	custom
gules	adj.	(heraldic) red
habergeon	n.	coat of mail
halp	v. pret.	helped
halse	v.	to embrace
handsel	n.	gift
hete	n.	reproach
hie	v. reflex.	to hasten
hight	v. pres. and pret.	to be called
hill	v.	to cover
holden	p. p.	held
holpen	p. p.	helped
hough	n.	back part of the knee joint
houselled	p. p.	given the sacrament
hove	v.	to remain, wait
intermit	v.	to concern oneself
item	adv.	likewise, also
iwis	adv.	indeed
jesseraunte	n.	coat of armour

keep	v.	to care, guard
kemp	n.	warrior
kind	n.	nature
kindly	adj.	natural
large	adj.	generous
laund	n.	glade
layne	v.	to conceal
lazar-cote	n.	hut for lepers
lears	n. pl.	cheeks
leech	n.	physician
let	v.	to cease, prevent
leve	v.	to believe
leve	adj.	pleasing, dear
lever	adv. comp.	more gladly, rather
lewd	adj.	ignorant, boorish
licours	adj.	lecherous
lightly	adv.	quickly, easily
like	adv.	equally
limb-meal	adv.	limb from limb
list	v.	to wish
lith	n.	joint
long	v.	to belong
loth	adj.	unwilling, hateful
loos	n.	renown
lotless	adj.	without harm
lune	n.	leash for a hawk
lusk	n.	idle lout
lust	n.	wish
lygement	n.	alleviation
maims	n. pl	wounds
mainten	n.	manner of life
makeless	adj.	matchless
maugre	n.	ill-will
	prep.	in spite of
measure	n.	moderation
medley	n.	conflict
meet	adj.	suitable, useful
mesel	n.	sickness
mette	v. pret.	dreamed
meyne	n.	retinue
mickle	adv. and adj.	much
minever	n.	fur trimming
mishaply	adv.	by misfortune

mister	n.	need
morte	n.	death
mote	n.	note on a horn or trumpet
	v. pres. 3 sg.	might
mountenance	n.	amount, space
ne	adv. and conj.	not, nor
nesh	adj.	soft
nis	v. pres. 3 sg.	is not
nobley	n.	pomp
noforthan	adv.	nevertheless
	conj.	although
noyous	adj.	troublesome
oftsides	adv.	often
or	conj. and prep.	before
ordain	v.	to arrange, appoint, command
ordinance	n.	command
orgulity	n.	pride
orgulous	adj.	proud
other	conj.	either, or
ouch	n.	clasp
ought	v. pret.	owed, possessed
outcept	v.	to except
out-take	v.	to except
overthwart(ly)	adv.	crosswise
paltock	n.	doublet
parage	n.	lineage
paramour(s)	adv.	as a lover
pareil	adj.	equal
passing	adv.	exceedingly
paynim	n.	pagan
paytrels	n. pl.	breast armour for a horse
pensel	n.	small pennon
perclose	n.	enclosure
perdy	adv.	indeed
peron	n.	large block of stone
pick	v. reflex.	to go away secretly
piller	n.	plunderer
plain	adj.	open, regular
plenour	adv.	with the full number
plumb	n.	block
point	v.	to lace
pounte	n.	bridge
press	n.	crowd

pretend	v.	to pertain
prize	n.	capture
puissance	n.	power
purfle	n.	trimming
purfled	p. p.	trimmed
pursuivant	n.	herald
purvey	v.	to provide
	reflex.	to prepare oneself
quarrel	n.	short arrow
quest	n.	judgement
quit	adj.	free
	v.	to repay, avenge
	reflex.	to acquit oneself
range	n.	line of battle
rase	v.	to tear, slash
rash	v.	to dash, slash, drag violently
rasure	n.	destruction
raught	v. pret.	reached
raundon	n.	force
rechate	n.	calling back the hounds
reck	v.	to care
recreant	adj.	surrendering, cowardly
rede	n.	advice
	v.	to advise
reney	v.	to deny
retray	v. reflex.	to draw back
rivage	n.	shore
roted	p. p.	practised
rush	v. trans.	to drag, smash
sacring	n.	consecration
sadly	adv.	soundly
sale	n.	hall
samite	n.	a rich silk material, often inter-woven with gold or silver threads
sarpe	n.	chain
scathe	n. and v.	harm
scomfit	v.	to defeat
selar	n.	canopy
semblable	adj.	comparable
sendal	n.	fine cloth
seneschal	n.	steward
senship	n.	censure

sewer	n.	serving-man
shaftmon	n.	hand breadth
shaw	n.	thicket
shend	v.	to disgrace
	[p. p. shent.]	
shenship	n.	disgrace
shower	n.	misfortune
shrewd	adj.	mischievous, wicked
sib	adj.	related
siege	n.	seat
siker	adj.	sure
sikerness	n.	assurance
sith, sithen	adv.	then
	conj.	since
skift	n.	fate
	adj.	rid
	v.	to manage
slade	n.	valley
slake	n.	ravine
	v.	to abate
sodden	p. p.	boiled
sond	n.	messenger
sooth	adj.	true
	n.	truth
speed	v.	to succeed
	[p. p. sped]	
spere	v.	to ask
sperhawk	n.	sparrow-hawk
sprent	v. pret.	sprinkled
stale	n.	position
stalled	p. p.	put, installed
stead	n.	place
steven	n.	occasion, assignation, voice
stigh	n.	path
stint	v.	to cease, put an end to
stonied	p. p.	see astonied
stour	n.	battle
strait	adj.	narrow, confined
straitly	adv.	severely
strake	n.	signal with hunting horn
	v.	to sound a note on a horn
strong	adj.	severe
sue	v.	to follow
surcingle	n.	girth for a horse
swallow	n.	whirlpool

swapped	v. pret.	struck
sweven	n.	dream
swough	n.	swoop
tailles	n. pl.	taxes
take	v.	to give
tale	n.	reckoning
tame	v.	to pierce
tatch	n.	quality, habit
tene	n.	grief
thilk	demons. adj.	that
thrang	v. pret.	thrust
thrulled	v. pret.	pierced
till	prep.	to
tofore	adv., conj. and prep.	before
trace	v.	to go, pass, pursue
trains	n. pl.	enticements
trapper	n.	trapping
traverse	adv.	crossways
tray	n.	sorrow
trist	n.	hunting station
trow	v.	to think, believe
truss	v.	to bundle, equip
ubblye	n.	oblation
umbecast	v. pret.	cast around
umberere	n.	visor
umbre	n.	shadow
unadvised	adv.	rashly
undern	n.	about 9.0 a.m. or later
unnethe(s)	adv.	scarcely
up	prep.	on
utas	n.	octave; eighth day after festival
ventail	n.	vent
wag	v.	to shake, totter
wage	v.	to pay
wait	n.	watchman
	v.	to watch, be careful
wallop	v.	to gallop
wan	v.	to grow dark
wanhope	n.	despair
wap	v.	to lap
warison	n.	reward

warn	v.	to prevent
ween	v.	to think
whether	pron.	which of two, whichever
wide-where	adv.	far and wide
wield	v.	to possess, control
wight	adj.	stalwart
wist	v. pret.	see *wit* v. (1)
wit	v. (1)	to know
	v. (2)	to blame
wite	n.	blame
wittily	adj.	cleverly
witting	n.	knowledge
witty	adj.	wise
wood	adv.	madly, fiercely
	adj.	mad
woodness	n.	madness
worship	n.	worth, honour
	v.	to honour
wot	v. pres.	see *wit* v. (1)
wrack	n.	strife
wrast	v. pret.	wrenched
wrath	v.	to anger
wroken	p. p.	see *awroke*
wrothe	v. pret.	twisted
yard	n.	branch
yede, yode	v. pret.	went

THE PENGUIN ENGLISH LIBRARY

Some Recent and Forthcoming Volumes

LADY SUSAN / THE WATSONS / SANDITON
Jane Austen   *Edited by Margaret Drabble*

LIFE OF CHARLOTTE BRONTË
Elizabeth Gaskell   *Edited by Alan Shelston*

ENGLISH MYSTERY PLAYS
Edited by Peter Happé

OLD MORTALITY
Sir Walter Scott   *Edited by Angus Calder*

FOUR JACOBEAN CITY COMEDIES
Edited by Gāmini Salgādo

DICKENS
Selected Short Fiction

THE NARRATIVE OF ARTHUR GORDON PYM OF NANTUCKET
Edgar Allen Poe   *Edited by Harold Beaver*